SWORDS
IN THE
EAST

P.F. CHISHOLM

Comprising

A CHORUS OF INNOCENTS
A CLASH OF SPHERES

HEAD
ZEUS

This omnibus edition first published in the UK in 2018 by Head of Zeus Ltd
This paperback edition published in the UK in 2019 by Head of Zeus Ltd

9 7 5 3 1 2 4 6 8

A CIP catalogue record for this book is available
from the British Library.

ISBN (PB): 9781786696151
ISBN (E): 9781786696182

Printed and bound in Great Britain by
CPI Group Ltd (UK), Croydon CR0 4YY

Head of Zeus Ltd
First Floor East
5–8 Hardwick Street
London EC1R 4RG
WWW.HEADOFZEUS.COM

Pol \Don **Blackpool**Council

24/7/23
1 1 JUN 2024

Please return/renew this item
by the last date shown.
Books may also be renewed by
phone or the Internet.
Tel: 01253 478070
www.blackpool.gov.uk

CONTENTS

A CHORUS
OF INNOCENTS

To Jane Conway-Gordon, with many thanks

PROLOGUE

It was a small chapel, stone built and once dedicated to some Papist saint. Since then it had been whitewashed, had its superstitious coloured windows broken with stones and the head knocked off the saint, although her cow was left in peace. The old altar had been broken up as the reign of the King's scandalous mother came to its riotous end, the relics hidden in it levered out and thrown on a bonfire to burn as superstitious trash. By the early 1570s there was a respectably plain altar table, well away from the eastern end so as not to be idolatrous and a very well-made plain and solid high pulpit for preaching. Mostly by visiting preachers, though, because who would choose to live in the village so close to the Border with England and the bastard English raiders?

Once upon a time, memorably, the Reverend Gilpin had come there after the mermaid Queen was safely locked up in England. This was very unusual. The Reverend's summer journeys kept him on the southern side of the Faery Wall, among the God-cursed English, but a laird had heard him there and invited him to come and preach and paid his expenses forebye, and everyone for miles about had gone to listen. They still tutted about it.

They had heard some very strange things from the pulpit that day. For a start, Gilpin didn't read the Bible texts they knew and liked, the good ones about smiting the Philistines or the book of Joshua or an eye for an eye and a tooth for a tooth, which was good sense they wholeheartedly agreed with. Nor did he talk about the wickedness of starched ruffs, or vestments, even.

He read them some unfamiliar parts of the Gospels: nothing useful about Jesus bringing a sword, no. Strange unaccustomed things he read them about making peace with your brother before you laid your sacrifice on the altar and some outrageous stuff about loving your enemy.

The men and women shifted their feet where they stood and looked at each other sidelong. Did Christ really say that? Really? Loving your enemy? Was the English Reverend sure? It sounded…well, it sounded Papistical.

Love everybody? What? The English, too? Jesus never said that, did he?

And the Reverend had smiled with a twinkle in his small grey eyes and closed the Bible with a snap, then leaned his arms familiarly on the rail of the pulpit as if he was leaning on a fence.

"Did you ever in all your lives hear anything so mad?" he asked in reasonable Scotch and they all laughed with relief.

He must have been reading one of those wicked Papistical Bibles the Jesuits spread about, that must be it. Jesus couldn't have said that about enemies. What you did with enemies was you hunted them down and killed them and all their kin, which made far better sense. Honestly, the idea!

But as the Reverend had spoken on, they felt uneasy again. It seemed Jesus had said those mad things. He had actually said, right out, that they must love each other, not just their own surnames—which was just about doable, mostly—but everybody. Even the English.

It seemed Jesus had said the thing about enemies too; he really had. There it was, in the Bible, which was as true and good as gold, golden words from God, incorruptible, like blasts of the trumpet against the ungodly. The foolish Papists had hidden the glorious words of Jesus in Latin black as pitch so only priests could know them; now the words were Englished and turned to Scotch as well, so anybody could read them, yes, even women.

So what were they to think? What should they think—that Jesus was mad? Crazy?

Everyone had goggled at such…surely it was blasphemy?

A stout woman spoke up from the back of the church where she was standing with the other women. "That's blasphemy!" she shouted. "You can't say Our Lord was mad…"

The English Reverend's long finger stabbed the air as he pointed at her.

4

"That's right, goodwife!" he bellowed. "You are the truest Christian here! It's blasphemy to say or even to think that Jesus Christ was mad because he was the Son of God!"

He was standing up straight now, leaning over the rail. "And if he was the Son of God, then how dare we listen to his words in the Bible and not follow his orders? How dare we hate our enemies? How dare we feud and kill and raid and burn? For if we do, shall we not burn in Hell?"

And from there the sermon had turned both familiar and frightening. Familiar in the loud words and gestures, but frightening in the meaning. For the Reverend was not inveighing against the Papists nor the French nor the courtiers. He was preaching against themselves. Against any of them who went up against an enemy to fight him, steal his cows and sheep and burn his steadings—which meant pretty much every man there of fighting age. He bellowed against those who cooked and brewed ale for the fighting men or quilted their jacks in the old surname patterns—which meant every woman and girl there.

He told them that they were wrong and damned, that keeping a boychild's right hand covered with a cloth at baptism so it was unblessed and could kill without sin was a wicked Papist superstition. That the whole of them, body and soul, was blessed in baptism, so that they could rise up, soul and body both, at the Judgement Day—which might be very soon.

Yet because they had not obeyed their true headman, Jesus Christ, then they would be damned just as infallibly as the Papists or the wicked Anabaptists.

Many of the men were scowling and putting their hands on their knives or swords. The women were gasping with outrage while the children stared in astonishment at the small man's daring. What was an Anabaptist? Did it have a tail?

He quieted for a while, playing them like a violin. It was all right. Jesus was a just and kindly headman, unlike many of the lairds hereabouts (that got a small titter). They could make things right anytime they wanted: All they had to do was love their enemies, make peace with those they were at feud with, and…

"Die?" sneered the laird at the front, who had his arms folded across his barrel chest and his henchmen in a tight knot around him. As he was the one who had paid for the Reverend to preach he was understandably angry. "That's what will happen if we make peace with the bastard English. We'll die and our families with us!"

"You will not die," said the Reverend Gilpin, pointing at the laird. "You will receive eternal life."

The headman spat on the stones. "I didna pay your expenses for ye to preach this shite," said the headman. "Get on wi' yer job and curse the ungodly, man!"

"I am," said Gilpin, seeming blithely unaware that every man there was on the point of drawing steel. Or perhaps he believed God would protect him. Or perhaps he didn't care. "If you fail to do what our Lord Jesus ordered—love God and love each other—*you* are the ungodly! You and the English both. All of you, both sides of the Border, are the ungodly."

The laird drew his sword and shouldered to the front. "I paid ye!" he bellowed. "Now do whit I paid ye to do!"

A purse full of money flew through the air and bounced off the headman's doublet with a thump.

"I don't need yer money," said Gilpin. "Thanks to God and mine own weakness, I am a wealthy man. Ye've got a free sermon here. Now will ye listen to the Word of God, or not?"

There was a moment of total silence. Then the woman who had spoken before (against all scripture) started laughing.

"Och," she shouted, "he's a brave man at least, not an arselicker like the last one. You let him preach, Jock o' the Coates."

"So," said Gilpin after a pause, with a friendly smile to all of them as some hands relaxed from the hilts of their weapons, "we have a problem. If the Lord Jesus wisnae a madman, then ye all are mad for ignoring his orders."

There was a growl from some of the men and more laughter from the women, sniggers from the children. You had to say this: It was a more exciting sermon than the last preacher who had had a lot to say about the wickedness of vestments, whatever they were.

6

Over the next hour the Reverend Gilpin proved that Jesus had actually said they should love their enemies and that He had actually done that very thing when the Romans had nailed Him to a cross, which must have hurt. And then, to show them all what they were dealing with, hadn't He risen from the dead, come back to life, not like a ghost or the curs'd knight in the ballad, but as a living, breathing man who ate grilled fish and drank with his friends?

There was no possible question that He had said it and meant it and done it.

Now they had to forgive their enemies, too, and live in peace with them. That was all there was to it. And once they set their minds to it, they would find it easier than they expected; for wouldn't the Lord Jesus be right there at their side, helping them all the way?

By the end of the sermon some of the more impressionable had been weeping. One of the Burn grandsons was staring transfixed into space, as if he could see something marvellous there instead of just a smashed Papist window.

Gilpin left them all with the blessing, the full blessing from the evening service: "The Lord bless you and keep you. The Lord make His face to shine upon you and be gracious unto you. The Lord lift up his countenance upon you and give you peace."

Then he went calmly to his horse that was tethered outside and, with his servant behind him, mounted up and trotted slowly away so the laird could catch him if he wanted.

It was so memorable a sermon that the laird sent a message to an Edinburgh minister, in case Jesus really had said that about enemies.

He had, apparently. He really had, though according to the Edinburgh minister, that didn't count for Papists and a number of other people—including, of course, the English.

So that was all right then.

Strangely, the laird invited Reverend Gilpin again and, even more strangely, he came, riding a solid ordinary hobby with his silent deacon behind him on a long-legged mare.

However as he came to unlock the wooden chapel door, he found a gauntlet nailed to it with a badly penned paper that said whoever took it down would be the Burns' blood-enemy for life.

Gilpin looked at it for a moment and then ripped it down. He carried the gauntlet into the church with him where he explained to the assembled people why feud was wrong, challenges to single combat were wrong, and the headman who had challenged him was not only wrong but stupid. He was risking not only a lightning bolt, not only the wrath of God, but also an eternity in Hell, which was no laughing matter.

Foolishly, the headman wouldn't leave it be. He sent to Gilpin to ask where he proposed to meet and what his weapon would be. Gilpin replied that it would be at the tower of his Lord with the sword and shield of God.

The headman arrived at the chapel the next day with his sword and buckler and a crowd of his surname who came to see him beat up the preacher who had defied him, or to laugh at him when he didn't arrive.

They found Gilpin standing there in his plain cassock, holding a large Bible.

"Och," Jock o' the Coates said disgustedly. That wasn't fair. The book looked heavy enough to do some damage if he threw it, but what if he made a lightning bolt come out of it?

"Well?" said Gilpin, coming forward with the Bible open and his thumb set in one of the end chapters. "Will you draw and strike, Jock Burn?"

"Ye're not...ye're not armed," growled Jock, horribly suspecting some of his grandsons and nephews were laughing at him inside, which indeed they were.

"I am armed," said the mad preacher. "I am armed with the sword of God's Truth and the shield of God's Word. Will ye not strike? Perhaps yer sword will not wither like a twig in the fire nor your whole surname go to dust and ashes with you left alone until your enemies catch ye. For those who live by the sword shall die by it."

Jock Burn backed off, paling. No more was ever said about the challenge and the gauntlet.

That was the Reverend Gilpin. He helped broker the deal between the Dodds and the Elliots in the late 1570s, which calmed upper Tynedale no end, and saw to it that the worst offenders left the area. He kept coming every summer, at first with his quiet young manservant and then, after the man died of a fever, he came on his own, sadder, gentler now. He preached at several Warden Days, on the invitation of Sir John Forster, the English Middle March Warden. He carried no more than an eating knife and a Bible, he slept wherever he could find shelter, and he ate whatever the poor people he lodged with could give him. He preached from his Bible whenever anyone asked him to and always on Sundays.

Nobody had ever seen or heard of such a strong minister, such a mad churchman, who had said publicly that he gave not a feather for vestments and as for the Papists—well, hadn't he been a Papist himself once, before he read the Bible and understood God's Word better? And surely most of them were good men misguided, with only a few actively serving the Evil One.

What was more he never laid a hand on girl or boy, though he had no wife either. Many were the snares and traps set for him by cunning mothers with girls who would have liked to be mistress of his rumoured large and comfortable living in the south. When a gentlewoman twitted him on his wifeless state across her dinner table, with her daughters on either side of him, he smiled and toasted her and her daughters.

"You see," he told her, "I swore before the altar of God to keep chastity and although I was certainly a sinner when I was young and hot-blooded, now I am old and tired and no use whatever to a woman." He smiled and bowed to both the girls who blushed. The mother found herself wondering about his deacon who had died of the fever but she said nothing and nor did he. All the girls who had hopes of his rumoured magnificent house at Houghton le Spring were sadly disappointed.

He only came to the Borders in summer. For the rest of the year he kept a school at Houghton le Spring, boarded likely boys at his own expense, and paid for some of them to go to Oxford where he himself had studied Divinity and sung the Masses with the rest of the young men before Henry VIII's divorce.

Slowly, little by little, some of the men of the surnames came to like him, the women too, despite his obstinate refusal to wed any of them. The children had loved him from the start and the lads ran to meet him when they saw his solitary silhouette with his soft flat churchman's cap and warm cloak over a ridge along the road from Berwick.

Then in 1583 sad word came. He had been trampled by an escaped ox in Houghton market, lay wounded for a month and died of lungfever on the fourth of March. Both sides of the Border were stricken at the news and Jock o' the Coates Burn and some of the headmen from south of the Border as well went to pay their respects in the south at Houghton le Spring, and with them they brought some of the boys Gilpin had taught, the bigger ones, to sing for him at his funeral. Jock died a few months later, leaving his grown son Ralph as headman and the grandsons grown as well—a lucky life Jock never admitted he attributed to not cutting Gilpin's head off when they had met at the chapel in the early 1570s.

And the seeds that Gilpin had sown, dangerous and revolutionary seeds that they were, lay in the soil of the people's minds, and here and there they set down their roots.

The men had been riding for two days, and were now into the broad fat lands of the East March of Scotland where the Humes held sway. They had instructions but those had been vague on the important point of position.

"Och, we'll never find him," complained the younger one. "A' the villages look the same."

The older one shook his head. "We ainly need his kirk," he said.

"Ay, one kirk in hundreds."

It was surprising and the older one thought a little shocking that there were so many kirks, and not all of them burnt or in ruins like in the Low Countries. Some old Catholic churches had been torn down and a new one put up, but more often they were just altered with the heads of the saints knocked off and the paintings whitewashed. Not every village had a kirk, by a long way, but a lot did.

They came over the top of a shallow hill and saw another little scatter of cottages and the kirk on the next hill, with a nice tower on it to keep an eye out for raids. It was October, so only a few women were out in the gardens, mostly tidying up for winter or planting winter cabbages. The surviving cattle and sheep were scattered over the infield and most of the pigs had gone to make sausages now so there wasn't a lot of noise. There was ploughing going on nearby, with the village plow and its oxen struggling through some new Earth that might grow some wheat next year, while the children followed it gathering up the stones. The harvest had been poor thanks to the bad weather in July, and no doubt the people were hoping to grow a bit more on the new field next year.

The two of them didn't need to talk much. They knew what they were about, had done it before, and so they decided to make for the church alehouse. That was a small thatched building next to the church in the old way and the church was one of those that had been altered, not demolished.

It was cold and damp and the men were out of their own country. They rode into the village, tethered their horses by the duck pond and walked up to the alehouse. They weren't very many miles north of Berwick itself and hoped to get to the city that night and find lodgings there. They didn't expect to find any in this village, any more than they had in the last two or three.

The village alehouse was no longer run by the church. A young man stood behind the bar and the usual people were there, despite it being afternoon. Two men sat in the corner playing dice, a third was hunched over his quart by the fire, a fourth was asleep. The fifth and sixth were standing by the bar, arguing over whether a billy goat could beat a ram in a fight, if you could get them to fight and how would you do that anyway. The seventh was a travelling barber surgeon, obvious from his pack, sitting in the corner, reading a book. As they came in, he stood up and stretched his back, put his book carefully in his large pack, and said in a London voice, "I'll pay you now, shall I, Tim?"

"Nae need, Mr Anricks, ye paid for more than your tab when ye drew my tooth for me."

"Are you sure? You paid me for it at the time."

"Ay, but I never lost a tooth before so nice and easy. I'll be telling ma dad about ye, that's sure, he's got a bad tooth too."

"Well thank you, I appreciate it. I'm for Edinburgh now and after I think I'll head west and see if there are any bad teeth in Dumfriesshire or even Carlisle."

"Bound to be, Mr Anricks. Me dad'll be waiting for when ye come back."

"Now mind what I tell you, the invisible worms that eat your teeth, they love sugar and honey and so if you scrub your teeth with a cloth and salt, that'll keep them away."

"Ay, and I'll keep the charm ye sold me too, that's even better."

"Hm. Good day to you."

"Clem!" bellowed Tim. "Bring Mr Anricks' pony round for him."

A boy leapt out from under the counter and pelted out the door and the tooth-drawer followed him out, moving a little stiffly, as if his back hurt.

"Ehm…" said the older traveller, "good day to you." Everybody turned and looked. "That'll be two quarts, please."

This was an event. Two strangers coming into the alehouse. A smaller boy was staring from where he'd been whittling under the counter. The older man hated the feeling of being conspicuous, but you couldn't help it.

The quarts were drawn from the only barrel and the younger man paid, twice as much as usual on account of them being foreigners of course. That was all right, they had plenty of money.

After both had taken a drink, the older one said, "What's the name of this village?"

Several people answered and it seemed you could choose between Lesser Wendron or Minor or the old one of Wendron St Cuthberts.

"Ah. St Cuthberts," said the older man wisely, "would the minister here be a Mr Burn? A Mr James Burn?"

"Why?" asked the man at the bar, with narrow suspicious eyes.

"Well," said the older one, not looking at the younger one, "we're from a printer in Edinburgh to see about the printing of his sermons and selling them too."

This was what he had been told to say by his principal and he was happy to see it worked like a charm. The man might well have been suspicious, after all, and it would be so much easier if they could get him alone.

"Yes," said the barman, "that'd be the pastor." He wasn't at the alehouse which was a little odd for a pastor. What was more, he was at the manse and teaching the children.

The younger man choked on his beer. "Teaching?" he asked. "Why?"

This touched off a dispute. The dice players looked around and said it was all this new-fangled religion, the arguers agreed and sniggered about it, the barman said it was all very well learning your letters but then what could you do with it, the sleeper said nothing because he stayed asleep, and the man who was hunched over his quart straightened up and told them all that they were fools because the truth was in the Bible and the children would be able to read it for themselves, whereas they couldn't. One of the dice players snorted and said that was all very well and the truth might be in the Bible at that, but what was the use of it?

The older man cut through the talk and asked where the manse might be, and learned it was right behind the alehouse from the days when the alehouse was the church's and ran church ales.

Both men finished their ales, parried a couple of questions about where they came from. No need to send the boy with them, they could find the manse themselves from the sound of it.

They went out the door and round the back of the place and there, sure enough, was the manse, a handsome building of stone like the church, though perhaps older. It looked like part of it had once been something else, maybe a little house for monks or something.

The door flung open and twelve boys came pouring out, shouting and pummeling each other, two of them fell wrestling at the feet of the men. They stepped around the boys and spoke to the man standing at the door, smiling at them.

He bowed slightly and led them inside. The boys all scattered to their homes except for three who had planned a fishing expedition at the stream. A woman arrived in a hurry, and went in smiling. There was a quiet sound of talking, a woman's voice, a man's voice.

A pause. Then a sudden grunt, like a pig being stuck with a lance, a thump, then a sound like a cabbage being cut. Then the sound of a stifled scream, thumping and bumping and some muffled groans, going on for a while.

The two men walked out of the house, grinning and rearranging their hose and round the duck pond to where their horses were tethered. Unhurriedly they untied them, mounted and trotted away to the little copse nearby where they had some remounts and a boy guarding them.

Then they changed horses and went to a canter out of the copse and round by the little lanes that threaded across the countryside, although they could have crossed the ploughed fields in a straight line. As it happened they went north first on an errand and to throw anyone off the trail, and then they went south and west. The boy took the West March-branded horses straight south to a horse-trader.

FRIDAY MORNING 13TH OCTOBER 1592

Lady Widdrington looked at the farmer in front of her and waited for him to stop lying. The horses in question were nice beasts and she knew they were not local. The question was, where had they come from and had they been reived.

"Mr Tully," she said, "I've never seen the brands before. Where are they from?"

"They're Middle March horses, your ladyship," he said promptly. "Bought from my brother-in-law in Jedburgh."

She sighed. "Those aren't Jedburgh brands."

His face flinched a little and she read it easily. She was a woman; she wasn't supposed to know about brands. It had taken Elizabeth two years to know all the main brands and variations hereabouts, but she knew them now. In fact she wasn't completely sure she didn't know these particular brands, only she couldn't bring to mind which surname they belonged to, which was odd. They niggled her. Probably they came from the West March, Armstrong, Nixon, Graham? But they certainly weren't from Jedburgh and they were good horses. Not as good as Robin Carey's beautiful tournament charger Thunder, which he had sort of sold to the King of Scots that summer, but...

She sighed and pressed her lips together. That familiar ache in her chest had started up again. It had been three and a half months since she saw him riding Thunder, tipping his hat to her seriously as he rode past. Less time since she saw him at the Scottish Court where…

Mr Tully saw her face lengthen and become stern. It was a handsome face, rather than pretty, the long nose and chin would probably draw together eventually but hadn't yet. He drew a couple of wrong conclusions and decided she must be a witch.

"A' right," he said sadly, "they're no' from Jedburgh."

"I know that," agreed Elizabeth.

"Fact is, I dinna ken where they're from. So now…"

Elizabeth folded her gloved hands on the reins and leaned back slightly. Her horse tipped a hoof and gave a resigned snort.

"They were running loose in the woods."

She looked around her at the plump farms and copses. There weren't a lot of woods anywhere near.

"Which woods?"

"Aah…in Scotland."

She could have asked what he was doing north of the Border, but she didn't. She nodded invitingly.

"Ay, I'd been north of Berwick getting…ah…getting supplies and up to Edinburgh forebye for I couldna find what I was looking for and I got lost in the wood meself and so I found 'em."

She waited patiently for him to start telling the truth. "They had nae tack on them or nae ither signs and they were sad and sorry for themselves, so they were, and when I found them they were hungry too…"

Likely since these weren't tough little hobbies who could live on a couple of blades of grass a day, but taller bigger horses who would need more food.

"And one of them had thrown a shoe and the other was lame too, and so I brung them south with me to help and comfort them and that one's called Blackie…"

"That's the grey?"

"Ay and that one's called Pinky."

"The chestnut?"

"Ay," Tully looked at her cautiously. "It's a joke, ye ken, missus. Ah niver name my animals for their right colours."

Elizabeth nodded. Why else would the man be riding a beast as black as pitch and known to all as Milky?

One of the Widdrington cousins who was riding with her and waiting a little way off, chuckled softly.

Elizabeth moved her own horse, a very dull dark chestnut called Mouse for good and sufficient reasons, to a nearby stone wall. She unhooked her knee from the sidesaddle and stepped down to the wall, then picked up her skirts and climbed down the other side to go into the paddock with the horses. There were other animals dotted around the pasture, which was looking bare and brown. Among them were two billy kids, nearly grown and making themselves useful by calming the horses while awaiting their inevitable fate.

She went among the horses and patted them, felt their legs, lifted their feet—yes, they had been shod a while ago, though Tully hadn't re-shod them yet because that was expensive. She checked their teeth as well. Blackie, the grey, snickered with his lips and pushed his nose into her chest, looking for carrots, no doubt. She patted his neck and found Pinky on her other side also wanting attention.

"These are quite young and good horses," she said.

"Ay, ladyship," said Tully, looking at her sadly. "But I didna reive 'em."

"No," she agreed to his great surprise, "I don't think you did but you'll have to wait until I write to the Scotch Warden and ask about them." Tully sighed. "I'll try and get you a finder's fee for them if I can," she added since he had told her some of the truth eventually, and what he had been doing in Scotland was probably just smuggling and nothing worse.

"Or," she said thoughtfully, "I could take them off your hands now and give you something for them and then keep the fee if we find the owner."

Tully scratched the back of his head and looked at the sky scattered with clouds, though it was not raining yet. He was not a wealthy man and although there was horse feed available now, it would get short before spring because the harvest had been bad. The horses were geldings and she could put them to use, whereas he couldn't. On the other hand, the Borderers all loved horses, which she did herself, of course, and were ridiculously sentimental about them, too, when they could be.

Slowly Tully nodded. If the horses did turn out to have been reived in some way, the Widdrington surname would be better able to deal with that than Tully, who had come to the area from further south and only had two sons and a daughter.

"Ay," he said. "Ay, that's fair, my lady. I dinna need them, only they was there, ye ken."

"Of course." She smiled at him. "I can give you twenty shillings each or take it off your rent."

Tully nodded. It was less than the beasts were worth but not much less. It more or less split the difference between that and the risk that they would be trouble.

She came back across the field and climbed the stile, drew off her glove and spat in her palm to clap her hand to Tully's and shake on it.

"There's ma hand, there's ma heart," he said. "Ye can take 'em now if ye like. I trust ye."

"Do you want money or credit?"

"Oh money, missus."

She checked her purse which only had a couple of shillings in it.

"I'll send the reeve to you tomorrow."

Half an hour later she was riding back to Widdrington with the horses on rope halters and feeling quite pleased with the deal. They were nice horses with nothing obviously wrong with them, and she always needed horses for the eternal problem of dispatches. Sir Henry would probably tell her she should have paid less and he would probably find something else to complain about, but he knew they needed horses.

She took the horses up to a gallop along a little ridge of the road, feeling happy as she always did when she was riding. Sir Henry was in Berwick on Tweed doing his duty as a Deputy Warden. He would turn up to harass her at some stage but probably not yet because October was peak raiding season and he would be dealing with raiders from the Middle March or, indeed, doing a bit of raiding himself.

She came onto the Great North Road which actually passed through the village of Widdrington and cantered until she came to the stone tower and barnekin of her castle. Some of the women tidying gardens, or sitting on their doorsteps knitting or spinning, waved to her as she went by with her colour high and her hat pinned firmly to her cap so it didn't come off. She found Mr Heron, the reeve, up to his knees in a collapsed drainage ditch and asked if he would take forty shillings to Tully the next day. Heron smiled at her, came and examined the two new horses and said he thought they were worth forty shillings each, unless they had some kind of horse disease, of course. "I think they're healthy enough," Elizabeth said, "but we'll see."

The boy on the gate opened to her and came to take her horses as she clattered into the yard. Two more boys were hard at work on the dung heap in the corner but they stopped to come and stare at the new horses.

"They're nice," said one of them, "not hobbies, though."

She dismounted to the stone by herself and passed Mouse to the biggest boy to whisp down and feed. One of the empty stalls had a very tired hobby in it, snoozing on his feet. She knew him but couldn't remember his name so she assumed it was a messenger's. "Yes," she said, "that's Blackie and that's Pinky."

The youngest lad snickered and the middle boy elbowed him and told him whose they were. She let their curiosity fester and was about to go and check the new horse in the stable when a girl came running out of the manor house by the tower.

"Missus," she shouted. "Ladyship, you've got to come quick."

It was a Trevannion cousin, sent to her to learn huswifery, a scatterbrained good-hearted creature with brown hair and eyes, who was being assiduously stalked by several unsuitable men.

"What is it, Mary?" she asked, expecting some tale about a spider.

"It's Mrs Burn, missus, she's been crying and crying and I can't get her to stop..." Mary's eyes were full of tears. "I don't know why either and I'm frightened for the babby..."

Elizabeth had already changed course and headed for the manor, the back way through the stableyard, into the kitchenyard, through the kitchen—where she saw that the last pig carcass for winter had been delivered and was awaiting her attention in the wet larder—into the hall and through into the parlour, which had been built by Sir Henry's father soon after he had taken over the little chantry down the road. The chantry had provided the handsome stones and was now almost gone.

There sat Poppy Burn, otherwise Proserpina, one of the few women with whom Elizabeth could have a good conversation, and she was in a terrible state. Around seven months pregnant, in a blue velvet English gown that had some mysterious dark stains on it, hunched over like a little old woman and tears dripping steadily out of her eyes into a sodden wad of linen. She lifted her head slightly, saw Elizabeth, and tried to rise to curtsey to her but couldn't get up.

Elizabeth went to her and put her arms around her as tight as she could and said things like "there there" and "now now" and signalled Mary closer with her eyes. There was a distinct metallic smell around Poppy.

"Fetch in some wine, mull it, and put in a tot of aqua vitae from the barrel in my still room," she instructed Mary. "Where's Young Henry?"

"He's out checking drainage ditches."

Probably findable then, but he wouldn't want to be bothered. "Fine. Go and get the wine."

Mary came clattering back grasping a tankard full of hot wine and Elizabeth put it in Poppy's cold white fingers.

"You're freezing, and wet through," she said as she felt the heavy velvet of the gown. "What happened, Poppy? What happened?"

"It...it..." The woman started hiccupping and stared into space, as if seeing something terrible, her fingers gripping the hanky and the tankard until Elizabeth wondered if the handle would come off.

"Has something bad happened to James?" Elizabeth asked carefully, it was the only thing she could think of that could cause this. Poppy was not an hysterical person, though she was young and perhaps idealistic for the Borders.

Poppy nodded once and tears started to flow again.

"My dear, we must get you out of your wet clothes and into bed. I'm worried about your baby."

She looked down in surprise at the mound of her stomach and then crossed her arms over it and started to wail. It was a terrifying sound that made Elizabeth's hair stand on end.

Right, she said to herself, this is obviously worse than just James being dead. She sent Mary upstairs to get the smallest bedroom cleared of her sewing things and the bed made, and sent a boy out to find Young Henry and bid him come in at once with some men. Then she untangled herself from Poppy and went to the dairy to tell Jane and Fiona to come and help. When the two girls came with her, she told them to keep their mouths shut.

Jane and Fiona formed a bridge with their strong white arms smelling of cheese and milk. Elizabeth sat Poppy on their arms and they carried her up to bed that way, with Poppy still hunched and still weeping.

"Milk Dandelion—she still has good milk—and bring the milk straight to me," said Elizabeth to Fiona. "And, Jane, bring me up a bowl of hot water and some clean cloths." She settled Poppy on the bed and unbuttoned the doublet front of the English gown and the let-out petticoat and shift under it. The petticoat, too, had brown stains on it which Elizabeth sniffed and confirmed her suspicions.

"Poppy, my dear, are you miscarrying?" Elizabeth asked. Poppy shook her head and hunched over tighter. "Then is the blood someone else's? James'?"

No answer and no sense. What in God's name had happened to the woman to cause this? Elizabeth had to check to see if she was in fact miscarrying, because in that case she needed to call Mrs Stirling immediately. Luckily she lived in the village, though she might be out with a patient anywhere around the country from here to Alnwick.

When Jane came hurrying back with a big bowl of hot water, cloths, and—praise God—one of Elizabeth's shifts under her arm, Elizabeth thanked her and sent her out. Then she stripped off the rest of Poppy's clothes and found what had turned her from a bright-faced happy person into sobbing human wreckage.

She could see bruises and grazes all round the tops of Poppy's legs and lower down as well, grazes and blood on Poppy's privates, too. She stopped for a moment to take a breath and calm herself because Poppy had clearly been raped. She put her ear to the big belly and thought she heard a heartbeat, thought she felt movement but she wasn't a midwife and she wasn't sure. She put her head round the door and told the waiting Jane to run for Mrs Stirling at once. The dairymaid's eyes met hers with understanding and then Jane turned and fairly sprinted down the stairs. Jane didn't say much, and wasn't pretty with her square young face and broad figure, but there was something steady about her that Elizabeth liked.

She looked out the window and saw Jane running at a good clip out of the gate and into the village with her skirts bundled up into her belt and her boots occasionally striking sparks from the cobbles. Elizabeth's hat was still on her head and she had her velvet gown on, but Poppy needed to get warm as quickly as possible, so she turned back to her and started washing her gently with the hot water and cloths. Poppy let her do it, passively, only tears leaked out from under her shut eyelids. When that was done Elizabeth put her own smock over the woman's head, chafed her freezing hands and feet, and went and got some socks from the linen cupboard. She had to pause again as she did it: What kind of man did that to a pregnant woman? And what had happened to James? It was clear he was dead, probably killed. Had there been a raid?

Poppy was still sitting on the side of the bed and so Elizabeth gently lifted up her legs, put the socks on her feet, and got her under the coverlets at last. She got the brandywine into her, which was the best thing to stop a miscarriage and seemed to relax Poppy a little.

Just as the last of the wine went down, Fiona came back with a bowl of Dandelion's best creamy milk, still hot from the cow. Elizabeth left her with Poppy, went to her stillroom, and found the precious bottle of laudanum and put a few drops in the milk, then spooned it into Poppy while Fiona stared unselfconsciously at her. Elizabeth sent Fiona to finish up in the dairy, and in particular, wash and salt the butter. It was aggravating that the time of year when cows gave the most milk was in summer when it was too warm to keep butter very long, whereas in autumn and winter, the milk was much less in quantity and creaminess. The butter made now was paler than summer butter, but if the weather didn't get warm it might keep to be used for Christmas.

The pig wouldn't wait forever, either, but it could wait a while. Elizabeth went and got her work from her bedroom and took off her hat and gown while she was at it, put on an apron at last, and went back to Poppy.

Poppy was sitting bolt upright again, twisting her hands together and making little moaning sounds. It would take a while for the laudanum to work.

"Well, I think this gown is wet through," Elizabeth burbled at random as she picked up the heavy weight. "I'll hang it up and brush it once it's dry. The colour's good, though, it didn't...er... get on your clothes so we'll see if we can rescue it."

She put a broomhandle through the arms and hung the gown up on the wall to dry, bundled Poppy's shift and petticoats for the laundrywoman to have when they next did a wash, and put them in the bag. Then she sat down and started stitching a new shirt for Young Henry, who got through them faster than anyone she had ever heard of. She continued burbling about the cows and how she would keep Dandelion's calf even though it was male because Dandelion's milk was so good, and the old bull was getting on a bit, and Dandelion's son might make a good replacement.

By that time, the sound of boots on the stairs told her that Jane had found and brought Mrs Stirling. There was a knock on the door and Elizabeth answered it to find a flushed and triumphant Jane and the small grey-haired midwife.

"I woke her up, missus," said Jane, not breathing too hard.

"I'm very sorry, Mrs Stirling," said Elizabeth politely, "but I think this is an emergency."

"Ay," said the midwife. "Ah heard fra Jane."

"Jane, will you wait in the house? Fiona's finishing up for you. And thank you for running so fast."

"I like running," Jane said. "Is Mrs Burn better?"

"I hope she will be."

Jane nodded and plumped herself down on a bench in the corridor.

The midwife had already gone to Poppy and held her hand to feel the pulses. "Now, hinny, ye're to be a brave big girl. Is there pains?" Poppy shook her head. "Did ye feel a great movement or turn at any time?" Poppy started leaking tears again.

"When he…when he…"

"Ay, when he was on ye, the filthy bastard. Were there pains after, coming in waves, like this? Like ghost-pains but stronger?" Mrs Stirling held up a fist and clenched and unclenched it. Poppy shook her head. "Now my dear, I need to have a feel of ye, inside, ye follow? Will ye let me?"

Poppy nodded. "I thought…the babe was killed for sure." She was whispering but at least making sense.

"Well, mebbe not."

Mrs Stirling was gentle as she slipped her strong wiry hands under the covers and felt Poppy. She smiled. "Well, ye're still closed up tight there and the babe isna head down yet, so that's a mercy. How did ye get here?"

"I…I rode. I got on Prince and rode to the Great North Road and rode south and…"

"Did you find lodgings in Berwick?"

Poppy shook her head. "I just rode round the walls because it was night and kept on because…because…I wanted to find you."

Mrs Stirling and Elizabeth exchanged looks. "Wis there naebody nearer ye could ha' gone to?" asked the midwife.

"I wanted Lady Widdrington," said Poppy, as if this was obvious. "They killed Jamie and they…and they…"

Mrs Stirling held her hands for her.

"…and I want them hanged for it."

"Them?"

"Two men, not from round here, strangers. They came when I was at the river with the laundry and I came back because I thought they were the men from the Edinburgh printers about James' book of sermons, and they were talking awhile. I went to get some wafers and wine and while I was away…they killed Jamie. They stabbed him and he tried to fight so they cut half his head off."

"God above," said Mrs Stirling, shaking her head. "God a'mighty."

"Then they…did this. Then they went. And then I thought, if I can find Lady Widdrington right away, she'll help me find them again and hang them. So I tacked up Jamie's hobby, Prince, and I rode."

"When was this?"

"Yesterday. I don't know when."

Mrs Stirling had brought out her ear trumpet and put the large end on Poppy's belly, moving it around with her ear pressed to the other end. She paused and a large smile briefly lit her face.

"Well now, that's a lovely heartbeat," she said. "Would ye like to listen?"

Elizabeth would, very much, but hadn't liked to ask. She put her ear to the narrow part of the ear trumpet and heard Poppy's own heartbeat and then the lighter quicker beat from the babe. Her face lit up too. "Oh yes," she said, "That's a good strong beat."

"It didn't get killed by the…by them?" asked Poppy.

Mrs Stirling took her hands and sat down next to her on the bed. "Listen, child," she said, "it's a terrible thing that happened and ye'll want yer vengeance, I understand that. But you must try not to mither over it nor yer man's death. Ye must be calm as ye can until the babe is born and then while it's a little babby too. Take your vengeance late and cold."

Poppy nodded. "The Good Book says, 'Vengeance is mine, saith the Lord, I will repay.'"

"It does," allowed Mrs Stirling, "though sometimes the Lord needs a little bit o' prodding. Now go to sleep and think of the babby."

Poppy lay down obediently and closed her eyes. Elizabeth led Mrs Stirling out of the room and took her downstairs to the parlour for wafers and wine and advice.

"She should be no worse for it than bruises and a sore quim for a few days, if she hasnae bin poxed," said Mrs Stirling consideringly. "As to her body, with luck. As to her mind, who can say? There was a girl raped in a raid that never spoke again nor made any sense. Another girl who was treated the same in another raid by the same man, as it happens, was well enough in a month, though a mite jumpy and couldna abide the tolling of a bell."

"Does it happen often?"

"Not often. But it happens. Especially when the raiders are far out of their ain country and they've caught a girl who's not from a riding surname and think they willna be known."

"I've never heard of it…"

"Ay, well, they dinna tell anyone but the midwife when they come to me for tansy tea and if they're a married woman, especially, for they'll be afeared their husbands will think they were willing, especially if they kindle."

Mrs Stirling polished off her wine and Elizabeth paid her.

"Don't leave her alone," advised the midwife as Elizabeth saw her out the door. "She was alone when it happened, keep her company. I'll call back in a day or two."

Elizabeth nodded at this and went into the dairy first to see that the place was clean and tidy to keep the faeries happy. It was, so she told Fiona and Jane they could go home. She found young Mary sitting eating hazelnuts in the hall and told her to come with her and went back upstairs to Poppy who was lying rigid with her eyes open. She relaxed as they came in.

Mary she sent to get her crewelwork and sat down by Poppy.

"Will you be able to sleep with Mary here?" she asked. "I must make a start on salting the pig for winter."

Poppy was weeping again and her poor eyes were already red and swollen.

"Read to me," she whispered. "Please."

"What shall I read?"

"Anything."

Elizabeth went back to the bedroom and looked at her precious store of books, kept in a box under the bed where

Sir Henry couldn't see them. He didn't see the point of women reading and had burned some of her books once. She chose a couple—one a book of sermons of staggering dullness that she used to get herself to sleep sometimes and the other a Tyndale Bible.

She read the Gospel of Matthew about the Nativity and a couple of Psalms and then decided that beautiful though the language was, what Poppy needed was dullness. She chose the dullest sermon in a very dull book and started reading about how one should never wear velvet or any colour other than black, brown, grey, or white because of worldliness and the sins of the flesh.

Poppy shut her eyes and seemed to doze off at last and Elizabeth left Mary to sit in the same chair and read the same book if necessary.

She went downstairs, ready to make a start on the pig and found Young Henry and four other Widdringtons tramping their boots into the hall.

"What's happened?" asked Young Henry, looming over her as he always did now. When first she had known him, he was a boy and much shorter than her. She hardly noticed his spots anymore but there was a particularly fine one on the end of his nose—a beacon of red and white. She found it mesmerising.

She told him to come with her into the wet larder where she took her sleeves off and put on her wet larder apron to make a start on the pig—opening it up and taking out the innards. She called the boys in from the stables and set them to fetching buckets of water from the well and then to the really unpleasant job of cleaning the intestines, to ready them to make sausages, while she dealt with the pluck and got it ready to make a haggis. It was a nice pig, quite fat and had come from the post inn where they got a lot of leftovers. She believed the pig had been called Bucket, like its predecessors, for obvious reasons.

Young Henry stood in her wet larder in his third best suit and his buff jerkin, which he was wearing because it was a bit proof against water and didn't get as heavy as a jack when it was wet. His boots were in a terrible state because inspecting drainage ditches often meant you had to get muddy. The four Widdrington cousins were no better and had wisely decided to come in no further than the kitchen where they were getting some ale from the cook.

"Just like that?" asked Henry. "They just rode in, found out his name and killed him?"

"And raped his wife."

Young Henry shook his head. "Have you told Father?"

"I've told you," she said. "You can decide whether to tell him or not when you go through Berwick, though I don't think he'll care because it's Scotch East March business, not his."

Young Henry nodded at that and Elizabeth finished putting bits of pig in various bowls and cleaned her knives carefully before giving them to the smallest boy for further cleaning and sharpening. The first stage was over and the carcass clean inside, with a bit of washing by the middle-sized boy, and the next stage of cutting up and salting could wait several days, unlike the innards. The liver was nice and big; she thought she might make a liversausage out of it. The other two were gasping and complaining in the kitchenyard at the disgusting job she had put them to.

What she really wanted to do was go north to Wendron and take a look at the house where it had happened and see the corpse if it was still there. Had anyone found it yet, done anything about it? What had happened afterwards, after Poppy left? She particularly wanted to know if Tully's two found horses had anything to do with it.

The problem was Sir Henry. He thought women should stay at home and do as they were told, not ride about the countryside. Ever since she had been to Carlisle and back in the summer and with what had happened there and in Dumfries, he was even worse than before.

On the other hand, he was in Berwick at the moment, concerned with governing the East March with Robert Carey's pompous elder brother, John. He'd find out about it, of course, but if she could find a good enough excuse...

She shrugged as she washed her hands in the bucket of cold water and took off her wet canvas larder apron, hung it up on its hook, and put on another clean linen one. He would probably beat her again, and if she didn't go to Wendron, he would find another reason to beat her. There was no point trying to please him because he could not be pleased with her.

Young Henry was still there, looking shrewdly at her. "It's only about forty miles across country," he said, "but I don't think you should go."

She said nothing to this. He was right, of course, but she had a terrible itch to see for herself.

She went upstairs to check on Poppy and found her awake again but not crying. The rest of the milk with laudanum in it was cold now and Poppy wouldn't take it.

"I've been thinking," she said. "I shouldn't have come here, should I?"

"No," agreed Elizabeth, "with the babe and all, it would have been better if you'd sent for me. Not ridden for a day and a night on Prince."

"I couldn't think," Poppy said. "All I could think of was getting to you and telling you."

Poppy had her fists clenched but was at least making sense now. She had no family nearer than Carlisle and her mother and father were dead; there was only an uninterested uncle who had something to do with mines in the lakes and not of a riding surname. Nobody could actually say Poppy's maiden name either, it was so foreign, though she herself had been born in Keswick.

James Burn came of the Burns, all right, but had shocked the family by going to university as a servitor and gaining a degree in Divinity and then coming back to the East March to be a minister of the kirk. Elizabeth had made the match at Christmas two years ago and had been there when they had married the following March. She had also prodded a powerful friend of hers into preferring Jamie to St Cuthberts with some sweeteners to the Elders to ensure his election.

"Well," said Poppy, "I've come here and I'll not leave for a while."

"I don't think you should ride anywhere until after you're churched, at the earliest," Elizabeth agreed with her. "In fact, you should be sleeping now." She picked up the milk and prepared to spoon it into Poppy.

Poppy shook her head. "Ye have to go to Wendron for me," she said. "Ye have to. Please? Who's the living going to go to now that Jamie's dead? There's things I need like my other kirtle, there's his will, and who else can I trust? And make sure he's buried right. Make sure..." She stopped, clenched her fists and took a deep breath. "Otherwise he'll walk for sure."

Elizabeth wanted to get away from that kind of thinking. "Ah," she said. "What did the men talk about with the minister before they killed him?"

"I don't know. They were talking quietly, Jamie sent me out to get the wine and the wafers and when I came back he was... he was..."

"Can you remember anything, anything at all about what they said?"

"It was just talk. Oh, the older one said something about scripture. He was quoting some scripture."

"Which verse?" Poppy just shrugged. "No threats, nothing?"

Poppy looked proud. "My man wis a man of peace, he was a man that turned away from war and reiving and toward the Gospels. But he knew how to fight, so if they'd given him any warning at all, or a threat, it wouldn't have been so easy for them. And he knew them. He recognised the younger one as I went out. He shook their hands and he was asking them about the Low Countries and were they back for good now?"

"All right, Poppy, I'll go to Wendron for you. It'll take a few days and I want you to stay right here and not go anywhere. You can borrow my English gown if you want to walk about, but I wouldn't even go out the door. Give the babby a chance to rest. He's had a couple of shocks."

"You don't mind all that riding?"

"Not in the least."

Elizabeth started feeding Poppy the milk and halfway through she suddenly bent over and cried again.

"Och Jamie," she sobbed. "You'll never have curds and whey to your breakfast again."

Friday Afternoon 13th October 1592

Two hours later Elizabeth was in her green riding habit with her best black velvet gown trimmed with coney in honour of the funeral, a cloak over her shoulders and her low-crowned hat on her head, in a style that had been fashionable in London four years before. She was cantering north along the Great North Road that passed through Widdrington and had done for hundreds of years, the second-to-last post inn before Berwick. Young Henry rode beside her and the Widdrington cousins were two in front and two behind, very happy to have escaped from the eternal autumn job of clearing ditches and checking waterways. Young Henry was happy as well because he liked his stepmother and it always made him feel better about his father when he saw her like this, cheeks flushed, eyes sparkling, swinging along with the rhythm of the horse. She was riding a half-hobby called Rat, because he looked like one with his pointed nose, and had her jennet, Mouse, behind her for a remount.

They would break their journey at Bamburgh on the coast, and from there it was only fifteen miles to Berwick. They would take fresh horses from the stables in Berwick that Young Henry's father maintained, go into Scotland there in daylight, and into the Merse, and so to the quiet village full of raspberry canes that Jamie Burn had been living in.

They wouldn't be visiting the Burns in East Teviotdale, which was his family and a dangerous riding surname, with a Jock Burn in every generation. Jamie was the second son of Ralph o' the Coate.

The management of Sir Henry had taken half an hour to think about. In the end, Elizabeth had prayed about it to God and left it to Him. If God wanted her to go to Wendron, Sir Henry would agree and if He didn't want her to go to Wendron, she'd catch the Berwick market because she needed more salt, since the salt in the wet larder was poor stuff, and go home again.

As usual she was thinking about Sir Robert Carey while she rode because Sir Robert was always where her thoughts went when they weren't occupied by something else. His behaviour in Scotland in the summer had been disgraceful and then he had been ordered south by his father at the end of August. Since then she hadn't heard a word about him; she wouldn't hear from him because Sir Henry had forced her to write that letter to him, ending their friendship. She didn't know for certain if her verbal message had got through but she thought it had.

Sir Henry had overreached himself at Court in his attempt to kill Carey. The Scottish king liked Carey and had said some things privately to Sir Henry that he hadn't seen fit to tell his wife but which seemed to give him pause sometimes. There had only been one really bad beating since then. He always kept away from her face because he didn't want the rumours to start going round as they had with his first wife, but now he didn't use his belt so much. It was something.

Carey would love to have an excuse to kill him but wouldn't get it. Sir Henry was not a young man to be inveigled into a duel; if Sir Robert challenged him, he'd use a champion. And probably cheat. Nobody stayed headman of an English riding surname like the Widdringtons without being canny and clever and hard to kill. However Sir Henry had gout which didn't usually kill you but was very painful when he had an attack. She tried to think of him charitably as a creature in pain who wanted to lash out, rather than a man who enjoyed hurting her and humiliating her, but it was hard.

They clattered through the gate at Bamburgh just before it shut at dusk and up to the keep where Sir John Forster's unfortunate son, also called John, held sway. He was drunk as he usually was and explained the rotten state of the rushes and the filth of the solar as the consequence of there being no woman there. Elizabeth had seen worse, though not much worse, and accepted Johnny Forster's offer of the main bedroom which at least had a four-poster, though no clean sheets. Or blankets. In the end she rolled out the truckle bed and slept fully clothed on that because it seemed to have fewer fleas and much less dog hair. Johnny Forster was no threat to her virtue, not as drunk as he was, and with Young Henry endearingly sleeping on a pallet across the doorway with his knife in his hand.

She was up before dawn and saw no reason to awaken the marshal of the castle who had passed out in the hall while explaining how heavy his responsibilities were to his two lovely hunting dogs, both of whom listened carefully and were as sympathetic as they could be. From the state of the blankets in the four-poster they normally slept there with him when he went to bed. Not one of the servants in the place had changed the bedclothes since last Christmas at the latest.

She shook her head at it. Men were very strange creatures. Surely even if you were drunk it was uncomfortable to sleep in a dirty bed full of dog hair and an old bit of mince pie turned to rock?

SATURDAY 14TH OCTOBER 1592

They were out of a postern gate, opened by a heavy-eyed Forster cousin, and back on the Great North Road before the gate usually opened. The fifteen miles to Berwick were gone in a flash because the road was very good here, where the town council of Berwick maintained it, with hardly any potholes.

At the Widdrington house in Berwick they found that Sir Henry wasn't there. The steward explained to Elizabeth that Sir Henry had gone north of the Border two days before and was suppposed to be meeting the opposite Warden and somebody from the Scottish Court, in a secret matter. Yes, John Carey was in town and they could see him tomorrow but not today because he was busy, which she suspected meant he was hungover. That suited her perfectly and meant she got out of hearing John's perennial complaints about the town council and mayor of Berwick, as well as not having to deal with her husband. She,

Young Henry, and the four Widdringtons stayed only long enough for breakfast, with Sir Henry's steward tutting because she expected bread and ale for six.

They were out the northward gate against the flow of people, crossing the Tweed on the narrow rickety Scotch bridge into the Merse, with Elizabeth now on Mouse with Rat behind. Everyone else had got hobbies from the stables. The hobbies needed a lot of persuasion to set foot on the bridge which was in a bad condition. This was one of the major connections between Scotland and England; couriers passed both ways across it every week—it was like Bamburgh. What was the point of not keeping it in good condition?

She shook her head again as her horse stepped off the end of the bridge and both of them breathed easier. No doubt the King of Scotland thought it was better to have a bridge that would not stand an army crossing it.

Wendron wasn't very far from the road to Edinburgh, the continuation of the Great North Road which was well-used by travellers and merchants, not to mention the ceaseless hurry of post messengers riding to and from London and Edinburgh. There was at least one bag of dispatches a week and sometimes one a day if Scottish politics suddenly got interesting. The raid on Falkland in the summer had produced staggering quantities of paperwork.

As they rode into the village they found two boys sitting in a tree by the side of the road and one ran off purposefully as they passed. Young Henry nodded approvingly. The church alehouse was full and the manse had a man standing by the door with a reasonably good jack on his back and a billhook in his fist. Young Henry dismounted and went forward to speak to the man who pointed at the alehouse.

Eyes watched as they left their horses tethered near the alehouse, leaving two of the lads outside to keep an eye on them, and went into the smoky commonroom. The laird of the area had died of a flux a year before, and his wife had died in childbirth ten years before, so the land was in wardship to the Crown and theoretically being administered by Lord Spynie on behalf of the ten-year-old boy who was the only heir and now his ward.

His grandmother sat in the best chair in the house, the Dowager Lady Hume of Norland, a tall hat on her head and a ruff at her neck, her fine dark grey wool kirtle under a magnificent gown lined with sable from Muscovy.

Elizabeth hadn't met her before. She thought she had been a great beauty fifty years before and her face still had the bones of it, but the flesh was gone the way flesh goes and she had two grim lines on either side of her mouth.

Young Henry did a tolerable bow and Elizabeth swept a curtsey to her. She felt dowdy in her small hat and old green riding habit, but on the other hand, perhaps that was all to the good. At least she had her furred velvet gown.

Grey eyes narrowed as the lady took in the whole of them.

"Whit's the interest of the Widdringtons in this outrage?" she demanded. "Our minister's been foully murthered and his wife is aye missing. Well?"

"My lady," said Elizabeth, "Mrs Burn is at Widdrington and as far as we can tell both she and the baby are well."

The creased face relaxed a tiny bit. "How did she get sae far south?"

"She rode, ma'am. She was in a terrible state and all she could think of was to get to me. I have no idea why. She rode Mr Burn's hobby south all night and came to us yesterday afternoon."

"Is she hurt?"

How could you answer that? "She is getting better and I've had the midwife to her and she says the babe is well."

The eyes narrowed again. "Why did ye come all this way?"

"I wanted to fetch clothes for Mrs Burn as I feel she'll be better to stay at Widdrington until she's churched and I wanted to find out the truth of what happened to Mr Burn if I could. And of course, Mrs Burn asked me to see to it that her husband is properly buried."

It was an honest answer and there came a single proud nod. She didn't mean to, but her eyes locked on Lady Hume's. Lady Hume could choose to send her away once she had the clothes, but she hoped…She really hoped she wouldn't. She had liked Jamie Burn; he was a good man, perhaps a little hot-tempered, perhaps a little intolerant, but he had started a school for the children of the village and his sermons were only an hour long. She had come to Wendron to stay several times when Young Henry was in Berwick, and it had touched her heart to see how he smiled and let his wife speak and would find excuses to touch her hand or her shoulder and how Poppy would find excuses to do the same.

Touched her heart with envy, true, but it was good to see that a marriage could be…kindly.

"Ay, the truth," said Lady Hume, the two lines by the corners of her mouth lengthening and deepening. "The truth is, we dinna ken. He was stabbed and had his brainpan laid open in his ain parlour, we dinna ken who by, except there were two strangers in the village. D'ye know aught of them?"

"Nothing except that two horses with West March brands were found by a man called Tully. He says they were wandering in the forest not ten miles south."

"Hm," said Lady Hume, tilting her head on its long neck. "Come with me."

The manse was a scene of frantic activity as women scrubbed the walls by the plate cupboard and swept the rushes into the yard.

"Where's the corpse?"

"In his church, in the crypt."

"May I see it, to pay my respects? I'm sorry for his death for he was a good man."

"Ay," said Lady Hume, "he was."

She led the way to the church, where there were black candles lit, and down the narrow steps into the ancient vaulted crypt. Among the Papist statues lying as if it was a strange stone dormitory, was the bier with James Burn's body.

His head was actually in two bits, sliced through his face, held together awkwardly by a linen bandage. There wasn't much blood. The corpse lay as it had fallen, twisted to the right, though he had been laid out and cleaned and wrapped in his shroud ready for burial.

"Ye canna see the stab wound. It's in his back, the cowards. Stabbed in the back first, then that done by a good sword."

Elizabeth took a look at the hands. They were big hands and the knuckles of his right were grazed.

"He tried to fight, I think."

"Ay," sniffed the Dowager Lady, "of course."

"When is the funeral?"

"Tomorrow or the day after. Nae reason to wait about, some of the Burns are here already. His wife willna be coming, I think?"

"No," said Elizabeth. "It's a miracle she didn't miscarry the wean as it is. I can be her proxy if you like, ma'am."

"Yes, that would be fitting, Lady Widdrington."

Young Henry had come down the steps behind them and was standing, head bowed by the body.

"Ye willna be praying for his soul," said Lady Hume flintily.

Young Henry lifted his head in surprise. "No," he said, "for his family and his wife. He's already gone to Judgement."

Lady Hume nodded once. Elizabeth felt sad that you couldn't pray for souls the way you could in the old days that her nurse had told her about. What harm did it do? But only Papists did that nowadays and she wasn't a Papist so she kept quiet about it. Silently she asked God to have mercy on Jamie and keep him safe until Judgement Day.

"God rest him and keep him," she said. "He was a good man and a good husband."

Lady Hume sniffed eloquently. "A pity his wife betrayed him, then."

"What?"

"Ay well, why else would she ride all that way? You mark my words, Lady Widdrington, the girl brought in the strangers to kill him and then rode off wi' them and she's told ye a fine tale to draw your sympathies but."

Elizabeth felt her colour and temper rise at the idea that Poppy could have betrayed her husband like that, but she said nothing for a while. Lady Hume was a powerful woman and no doubt would be even more convinced of Poppy's guilt if she knew of the rape.

"I doubt it," she said finally with a glint of humour. "I really doubt it, Lady Hume." She shook her head at the idea.

"Well then, explain the death of Mr Burn."

"I can't. He was a good pastor."

"Ay, he was, a good pastor and a good dominie but a fire-eater he was not. His sermons were respectable and his life exemplary. He may have come from a riding surname but he himself was no reiver."

Elizabeth nodded. "You're right, Lady Hume. He never showed any signs of being a reiver." Lady Hume gave Elizabeth a long and considering look which Elizabeth returned blandly and then curtseyed low to her again.

They went in silence up the steps from the crypt and straight into the alehouse which was full. Elizabeth went into a corner, called for double beer for Young Henry and his cousins and mild for herself and settled down on the bench to watch what happened. The presence of Lady Hume made the church alehouse respectable. She wondered whether the lady had simply taken up residence in the manse for the duration. Elizabeth also wondered where she herself would sleep. At least she had an official position here for the funeral, so she supposed Lady Hume might do something about it eventually.

Jamie Burn had come from a riding surname of the Middle March and was a son of the headman. The Burns were coming in all day to the funeral, feeling the need to make a point of it, and she hoped that Lady Hume had brought supplies with her to help with that. She watched the man she thought was Jamie's father by the bar as he drank and stared into space and stared into space and drank. She wasn't sure what had happened between him and his son when Jamie decided to go to university. Had that been with his father's consent or had there been a quarrel?

After a moment she got up, left her pewter mug of mild ale on the table next to Young Henry, and went over to the man.

"Mr Burn?" she asked.

"Ay. Ay missus."

"Are you Minister Burn's father?"

"Nay missus, his uncle, Jock. His dad's Ralph o' the Coates."

"May I speak with you?"

"Ay, why not?"

"I was very, very sorry to hear of Jamie Burn's death, Mr Burn," she began inadequately.

"Ye were. Why?"

"He was a good man and a good pastor. There aren't enough of those about that we can afford to waste them."

Strangely there was a brief moment when the man in front of her seemed about to laugh, but she thought she had mistaken it. "Ay," came the answer, "I backed him agin his father when he wanted to dae it."

"You did?"

"I backed him, ay. His big brother Geordie thought it was hilarious, him studying Divinity at St Andrews as a servitor, and his dad wanted him to stay with the family. There was a lot of argufying."

"I wondered if his father was against it."

"Ay. Agin it. Ye could say that."

"Will he be coming to the funeral?"

Jock Burn's face shut tight. "Ay well. I dinna ken. He might."

"The rest of the surname seem to be coming in."

"Ay," said Jock Burn, "we need to make a bit of a show."

"Why?"

He paused, thinking. "Somebody came up to a Burn, stabbed him, and part took his heid off wi' an axe. We're coming in so no one thinks we're afeared."

"Good Lord, Mr Burn, I don't think anyone could possibly think that."

"Hm. And I think kindly on ye, that the Widdringtons are showing support."

"I liked the minister, Mr Burn. He was a good man."

"Ay."

She went back to Young Henry who was looking wistfully at a game of shove ha'penny that was starting up in the corner.

"What do you think about it?" she asked as she sat down with him again and finished her mild ale. Young Henry flushed and hid his nose in his beer.

"About Jamie?"

"Yes."

"Well, I liked him too. I wish he wisnae dead. That's about the size of it."

"Hm. What do you think about how he was killed with an axe?"

"It wisnae an axe; it was a broadsword."

"How do you know?"

"Well an axe mashes up more of the flesh and that was a sharp edge that took him, right down through his skull at an angle, left to right. That's not an easy blow forbye, it was an expert with a good sword."

"And stabbed from behind. Before or after?"

Young Henry didn't need to think. "Before. If ye get his kidneys or his heart, it's all over. He probably didn't even shout."

She thought about this and nodded.

"Ay," Young Henry said judiciously. "So one man kept him talking and the other went round, drew his poignard, and struck from behind."

"They didn't want him to know."

"No, well, he's a Burn. They're a' good fighters."

"Even the one who got away and into the church."

A fractional pause. "Ay."

Elizabeth smiled brightly at Young Henry and left it. He went off to join the shouting crowd round the shove ha'penny board and started betting on it. Even without the murder, she was beginning to feel very interested in Jamie Burn and his history. What had he done before he went to St Andrews, and why had he decided to become a minister in the first place?

It was a nuisance that Poppy Burn was at Widdrington and not here, thought Elizabeth. Blast the woman for taking it into her head to ride away. It gave a perfect opportunity for all the clacking nasty tongues to work.

Looking at the problem from a man's point of view, Elizabeth had to admit that the killers would have had an easy job of it if they had had Poppy's help—and it was very difficult to show she hadn't helped them. Elizabeth was sure she hadn't, but who could be certain of anything like that? The bruises and the state of her showed it had been rape, but a man might say she was willing to start with, and then changed her mind and it wasn't his fault if he couldn't stop.

Elizabeth shook her head and frowned. Lady Hume had been welcoming the headmen of the surnames coming in to the funeral, who certainly were an impressive bunch of killers and robbers. Now she was gathering herself up to go, and so Elizabeth went over to her and asked where she would advise Elizabeth to find lodging?

"Are ye afeared of ghosts?" asked Lady Hume.

"I've never seen one," Elizabeth answered steadily.

"Well I'm staying at the manse since it's a ten-mile ride back to my Lord Hughie. You're welcome to join me, Lady Widdrington, and your stepson as well, though your men will have to find space in the alehouse."

"Thank you, Lady Hume." Elizabeth was relieved at solving the problem so easily. She went back to Young Henry with the news and discovered that he'd rather find a space at the alehouse than the manse. Not that he was afeared of ghosts, oh no, but he felt he should stay with his cousins since there were a number of reivers come into the village and while none of his men had feuds with anyone likely to come that he knew of, it would be well if no feuds started up, especially with the Burns, who were dangerous that way.

With the village full of reivers, she decided to bring the hobbies and Mouse and Rat into the manse with her. Lady Hume was agreeable and so Elizabeth went back to Young Henry who thought it was an excellent idea and sent the youngest Widdrington cousin with her to lead the horses.

They went round the back to the stableyard where the hobbies shared two loose-boxes and Mouse and Rat shared another since they were friends. There wasn't much horse feed there but all the horses got enough to tide them over.

The manse was a small stone-built house, the chantry of St Cuthberts somewhat altered by the previous incumbent. Poppy had been proud of that—living in a stone house with a slate roof was better than one of wattle and daub and thatch, though she admitted that it was a lot colder and harder to heat. There was a large handsome entrance hall, decorated with Papistical carvings nobody understood anymore—who was the woman with a towel in her hand and why did a stag have a cross between its antlers?

The small parlour was still damp and had no rushes on the tiled floor. Lady Hume led Elizabeth to it and opened the door.

"Ye may as well satisfy yer curiosity," she said.

"Thank you, Lady Hume," said Elizabeth and went in to look. That the plate cupboard was open and bare of plate was the first thing she saw, gone were the three silver goblets and a handsome bowl with dancing cherubs on it that she had seen when she stayed with Poppy. The benches along the wall were a little at angles, probably moved by the village women when they cleaned out the rushes. There must have been a lot of brains to clean up, very unpleasant and fatty.

The gore was gone but she could trace where it had been from the scrubbing and wet walls. It was mainly around the plate cupboard, though not on the cupboard itself. She shut her eyes and tried to imagine James going to get the plate, probably the three goblets, and then one man coming up behind him with a knife, the other man sweeping his sword out and finishing the job when it went a little wrong.

Who had held Poppy still? Or no, she had been fetching wafers and wine. And who had taken the plate which belonged to Poppy?

"Hm," she said aloud, "where are Poppy's silver goblets and bowl?"

Lady Hume shrugged. "Nae doubt but they took them. Why not?"

Reivers would know someone who could melt it down for the silver, probably Richie Graham of Brackenhill who made a very good thing out of buying plates off reivers for not very much and then minting it up himself into the debauched Scottish shillings to trade over the Border. The plate had been taken by way of a bonus; it was far too little to be worth the raid by itself.

Still, the fact Jamie had opened the plate cupboard was very interesting, since it showed that the men were indeed known to Jamie, were in fact honoured guests. You wouldn't give them wine in silver goblets if they were just messengers or strangers unless there was something else about them that made them important.

"Hm," she said, pleased with herself for thinking that one out, and looked around for more interesting details. Robin Carey had told her something about that once, that truth was like gold and essentially indestructible although you could bury it. But there would be traces.

What would he do, faced with such a puzzle? Well for a start he would be in the saddle looking for the tracks and prints that would show which way the killers had gone, probably with Sergeant Dodd alongside. She couldn't do that, and in any case, any hoofprints would be indistinguishable from all the people coming into the village. Robin would also be charming the Dowager Lady Hume like a bird out of a tree.

Before she could get lost in thinking about him, she turned and came out of the parlour, shutting the door firmly behind her.

"I suppose Mrs Burn's larder has been pillaged?" she said to the lady, who sniffed.

"Since she no longer has any claim to it, I have taken it over." She gave Elizabeth a bold look. Elizabeth knew well that the living was not in her gift but in fact in the gift of the man who held the Lord Hughie's wardship, which alas, currently was Lord Spynie, the King's minion. Elizabeth also knew that it could be hard to make ends meet even if you were a lady, here in the north where the living was difficult, certainly if you were trying to hold the lands together for a son and heir aged ten.

It had taken a great deal of conniving and letter-writing for her to get the living for Jamie a couple of years ago when Chancellor Maitland held the wardship, and it was annoying that the effort had all gone to waste. How inconsiderate of Jamie to die like that! she caught herself thinking.

"Ah," said Elizabeth with a smile, "I wondered if there's anything there I could make a supper out of."

"I'm afraid I don't know," was the withering response, from someone who had probably always had a cook and was therefore helpless.

Elizabeth forayed into the kitchen, where the fire hadn't been lit and where there were no servants at all, and found a hacked loaf of bread and the end of a ham hock and some crumbs of cheese. In a crock in the wet larder behind she found some soused herring, and in a bag in the scullery she found some carrots and parsnips, a little withered but perfectly edible. She took a look at the modern brick range and found it was stone cold, which was a pity because her stomach was aching with hunger.

She peered out of the wet larder door into the little stableyard and found two boys there, arguing over whether they should knock and ask for some pennies for a job or two, and pounced. One, she sent to the alehouse to fetch some hot coals. The other she sent to the woodshed for kindling and logs, and then to the well to fetch water.

Half an hour later she was boiling the parsnips in a saucepan on a sharp fire at the small end of the range and heating the soused herring in the warmer.

She found the plates for the Burns' dinner sitting in cold scummy water and gone mouldy, so she trimmed some bread trenchers from the stale loaf and even found a wooden platter and two serving spoons. The pantry had a crock of butter, which was wonderful news, and even a big crock of oatmeal for the morrow, which she immediately mixed up with some water, butter, and salt ready to go in the warmer overnight when the herrings came out.

Best of all, in a carefully hidden crock amongst the dirty pans, she found Poppy's little honey oatcakes which weren't even stale.

Lady Hume seemed astonished when Elizabeth called her to a late dinner at the table in the parlour, but she took the place at the head of the table when Elizabeth invited her. Over the food she folded her hands and said grace.

"Lord and father, we thank thee for this food which thou hast vouchsafed to us here in this house of sorrow…" There was quite

44

a lot more of that until Elizabeth's stomach gave a heroic growl at which Lady Hume said amen halfway through a sentence. They didn't speak for a while after that except to say things like "pass the salt" and "would you help me to some more neeps?"

The soused herrings were very good, well soaked to clear them of salt and then cooked in a mixture of stock and vinegar until they melted like butter in the mouth. Elizabeth's neeps were less good, as they could have done with a little more time in the water, but the butter made up for that.

Lady Hume had a good stomach to her meat despite her frail looks and her eyes lit up when she saw Poppy's honey oatcakes.

"Ay," she said, a little strictly, "I'll have just the one of those."

Elizabeth felt pleasantly full if a little guilty at eating Poppy's food. Only it wasn't her food, anymore, was it? Surely Lord Spynie would give her a month or two to get her bearings after the will was read? It wasn't a rich living, nor yet a multiple, surely nobody would want it too quickly.

Of course, if they did, that could be a motive for murder by itself.

Lady Hume ate four of the oatcakes and then declared herself full. Elizabeth gave the bread trenchers to the boys who had done errands for her and an oatcake each, plus a penny each from her private funds. The lads ran off with the news, very happy to be gulping down the soaked bread, and Elizabeth suspected that every boy in the village would turn up in the morning. That suited her because she suspected there would be things she could find for them to do.

"I can fetch the coals from the kitchen range and get a fire going here in the parlour," she said as it finally got too dark for her to see. "Or perhaps we could move to the kitchen where it's already quite warm." It was going to be extremely cold in the bedroom.

After only a moment's hesitation, Lady Hume approved the move to the kitchen where Elizabeth sat her in the only chair there and brought a stool in from the pantry for herself. She had also found some aqua vitae in a small bottle, or uisgebeath as the Scots called it, and Lady Hume accepted a small cupful.

Like many elderly people, Lady Hume didn't know when she was cold and hungry. Now she was fed and warm she began slowly to thaw.

"Yes, I was married for twenty years until my lord died of gout," she told Elizabeth. "And my son died of a quartan fever a few years ago. I never thought he would, which was my black sin and God's just judgement upon me. I thought he might die in a raid, never of sickness."

Elizabeth made a sympathetic noise. She learned many things about the son but the main one was that he had left her a grandson called Hughie who was the light of Lady Hume's life and the apple of her eye. And she would sooner die than let him go to the household of the Lord Spynie to learn knighthood.

"Ah," said Elizabeth, "is he a good-looking child?"

"Ay," said Lady Hume, sourly, "fair as the month of May and blue eyes and blond hair. Lord Spynie saw him last year and since then has been badgering me to let him come to Court, saying it will be the making of him and I'll have a dower house and a better jointure and such things." The firm jaw clenched. "But I willna." The eyes narrowed. "He's wasting the land, too. He's already cut down two woods and sold the timber and nobody's seen to the drainage ditches since my son died."

"Does Chancellor Maitland know this?"

Lady Hume shrugged. "Disnae know, disnae care."

"How did the wardship change hands? Was it when my Lord Maitland was in trouble with the King a couple of years ago?"

"Ay. That's when. How d'ye know?"

"I took in Maitland's son for a year when he was frightened for the boy. He's an old friend of mine."

"Ay?"

That had been an odd year. Carey had been in France and she had been praying for his safety every night. Maitland's son had been running about the place, full of delight at getting away from his tutor and riding for England in the middle of the night with his father. The political weather had changed again in Scotland a year later and he'd left her without a backward look, feeling even sadder that she had no children and wasn't likely to have any.

46

Sir Henry, surprisingly, had been very pleased to take in Maitland's son and had taught him to use a longbow. She had seen a glimpse of her husband then that had made her confused: He had been a little bit kind to the boy, why couldn't he be kind to her?

Kindness. It was such an important thing, she thought, once more seeing Robin with his horse Thunder and how he had gentled the animal, how he had even dealt gently with Young Hutchin Graham, despite the fact that the boy betrayed him. You could say that the entirety of the Gospels was a plea for kindness. Not the Epistles, though, nor yet the Apocalypse.

Lady Hume had been speaking. "I'm sorry, my Lady?"

"I asked, would ye be willing to try and get the wardship shifted to the Chancellor again? I'd make it worth your while."

Elizabeth paused, thought about this. "I'm not sure, my Lady. I could tell you all sorts of lies about how I'm certain I could, but you wouldn't believe me." There was a tiny grunt and a little flash of a smile. "I'll think about it. Chancellor Maitland is quite old now and doesn't want to deal with wardships anymore." Also Chancellor Maitland had made enough money out of wardships and other perks to build a large and handsome fortress for himself at Thirlstane. Quite good for a man who had been arraigned for treason on account of fighting for Mary Queen of Scots many years before.

"I can hold out for a while but no' for long," said the Lady. "Spynie's already sent Hughie a lovely chestnut horse and a boy's back and breast for martial exercises."

The sarcasm in the Lady's voice could have withered a stand of pine trees.

"Can I ask you if you knew the Burns?"

"The riding surname?" Her voice was wary.

"No, just the minister and Mrs Burn."

"Ay, I'd come to dinner a few times and fed them as well. Minister Burn was a good sound man as to religion but his wife was a silly little fool."

"Really?" Elizabeth said, trying not to sound offended on Poppy's behalf.

"I'll say nothing against her kitchen skills, she understood them. In fact, she didn't have a cook. The last one had left and she was doing his job."

"Oh?"

"Only temporarily of course."

"Of course."

"And it kept her away from the books which was all to the good. What business does a woman have with reading, answer me that?"

"Er…she can read the Gospels for herself."

"Well the Gospels…yes. But not wicked books full of lies and phantasies like that shocking thing the Morte d'Arthur."

"Hmm." Elizabeth enjoyed chivalrous romance, though she always found it very funny that there were only three possible women: the young and beautiful maiden, the lady of the house, the wicked crone. "I'm wondering did anyone else see the strangers before they did the murder?"

"Och, aye," said Lady Hume. "They had quarts of beer at the alehouse and asked the way to the manse."

"And how was the murder discovered? With Poppy ridden off in a panic?"

"Hmf. In a panic. Ay. He wisnae found until yesterday morning, when the boys came to the school and found him on the floor and blood and brain all over the place."

"What about the servants? Surely they saw the body?"

"Ay. Well, they were trying to save money. They only had a woman coming in to help Poppy and the rest of the men were working on the estate."

"How about the tithes. Were they paid?" Elizabeth knew how bitterly arguments over tithes could work in a village.

"Ay they were, though usually in kind, ye follow, naebody has much money here."

"So Poppy and Jamie Burn would be alone in the evening?"

"Ay. They invited me to dinner a few times and ithers of their friends but they were allus pawing at each other, kissing and cuddling and the like. Disgusting, it was."

"And James Burn's body lay where it fell until the next morning?"

"Ay. Shocking."

"Could I talk to the schoolboys who made the discovery?"

Lady Hume shrugged. "If ye want, though they'll likely tell ye a pack of lies."

Elizabeth smiled at that. According to Robin, lies were often more informative than the truth.

"What did the boys do?"

"They ran for the nearest dad and told him and he ran in from the field and saw and sent one of them off on a pony to tell me."

"So they didn't hit anyone else for his plate cupboard?"

Lady Hume shook her head. It was now getting too dark to see, despite the glow from the brick range with its door open. "I came out as soon as I could. I saw the body with half the head nearby and the blood and I tried to find Mrs Burn but I couldna and so I went and found Jock Crosby, who was there cutting back the hazels, and Sim Routledge to take the corpse into the crypt of the church. Then I turned out the women to clear the blood from everywhere. There was something not quite right about that."

Elizabeth could imagine it and how the women must have disliked being called from their own work to deal with such horror. "I was still looking for Mrs Burn but then I saw that Prince was missing from the stable and that was when I knew she betrayed her husband."

Elizabeth got up to light a taper which made the wrinkled planes of Lady Hume's face even stronger. "That's what you learn from that kind of nonsense in books, you mark my words," she added.

"Goodness," said Elizabeth, working hard not to sound sarcastic. "And why did she do it? After all she now has nothing since the living was settled on the minister and she doesn't have much for a jointure and the babe on the way. I'm not certain she has anything at jointure. At least I have five hundred pounds a year when Sir Henry dies." When I'm old and grey at forty and

Robin will have gone off and married money by then as he ought to do and as every one of his friends, including me, has advised him to do.

"She was in love with one of the strangers," said Lady Hume with a straight face.

"Really? How do you know?"

Lady Hume's face tilted up slightly. "It's the only explanation for why she did it, is it no'?"

"Lady Hume, this is fascinating. If you know she was in love with one of the strangers, then you know his name and where he might be found."

"I do not."

"I think you do," said Elizabeth, thoroughly annoyed with the old lady now. "I think you know a great deal more about this killing than you say. Either that or you are allowing romantic phantasy to run away with you."

"I?"

"Yes, Lady Hume. If you have a reason for thinking that Mrs Burn knew the strangers, then say what it is—it may help us to find them. If your only reason is that you dislike Mrs Burn, then, with respect ma'am, that is not enough." Though it might be enough for a Scottish jury of men.

Lady Hume glared at Elizabeth and then rose with final dignity. "Good night, Lady Widdrington, I am going tae my bed. Thank ye for the supper."

Elizabeth rose and curtseyed to her and watched her as she went out and to the hall where the smart stair used each of the walls in turn as support. So much for charming her like a bird out of a tree, Elizabeth thought, that's put her against me and Poppy as well.

Although it was cold in the rest of the house and still quite warm in the kitchen, Elizabeth felt too restless to sit there and too wide awake to go to bed yet. She slid the crock of mixed porridge into the warmer, ready for the morning, and put the curfew over the coals. She picked up the taper and went back to the parlour with its odd-looking tiles bare of rushes. It was still damp in places. She tried again to imagine what had happened...

The strangers come to the manse and Jamie invites them in. He goes to unlock the plate cupboard and while his back is turned, they kill him. Poppy says she was out of the room because she went to fetch the wine and wafers, so she might have come in later, perhaps after she heard the body slump to the floor. She is raped. Then the two of them leave, mount up and ride away. Later two good horses turn up south in Tully's keeping with West March brands on them, so the men must have come from the Debateable Land or possibly Carlisle. If the horses are theirs.

And then nothing happens. Poppy is riding desperately south on Prince; they have no live-in servants, no children, no relatives. A very peculiar household, in fact. Poppy had told Elizabeth how lonely she sometimes was in the evenings when Jamie was riding around his large parish, and Elizabeth had advised that she should certainly bring in a woman to keep her company. She said she did, one of the boys' mothers usually.

Had she perhaps found a friend, someone who could comfort her ? It wouldn't be easy in a place where everyone knew everyone else and their business, but Elizabeth supposed it could be done. She had never tried it but it was possible.

So her lover comes with a friend of his and cuts off Jamie's head. One of them rapes her, they leave, and Poppy rides about forty miles to her friend Elizabeth in England, without even a cloak against the wet. Why?

She had made soused herring for their supper and taken trouble over it. Why would you do that if your husband was about to be killed and you knew it?

There was another room downstairs—James' large study—which Elizabeth hadn't looked in yet. She went to it, carrying the taper, and found the door locked. She checked for a key but there wasn't one. Infuriated, she pushed it hard and then put the taper on the table and went out the kitchen door and round the house to see if there was another way in. That part of the manse joined onto the church alehouse in the higgledy-piggledy way of old church architecture. If there was another door into the study, it was through the alehouse and at nearly midnight, it was locked and there was no one in the place to let her in. The village was as quiet and dead as a doornail.

She went back into the house through the kitchen and as she passed into the hall and went toward the stairs to go to bed, someone hit her with a piece of wood.

It cracked across the side of her skull and made stars cartwheel round the place, she went sideways and almost down and glimpsed white linen, thought briefly about ghosts, then grappled the very solid though small attacker. She was used to being hit; she wasn't as shocked by it as someone who wasn't. She twisted the arm up the back and managed to take the bit of wood away, although it had broken when it connected with her. The taper was still alight on the table and then she realised that it was an old face and white straggly hair plaited for sleep.

"Lady Hume?" she asked in astonishment.

"Ye'll no' get me again, ye wilna, ye bastard...Lady Widdrington?"

"Jesu, ma'am, why did you hit me?"

"I didna."

"What?"

"I hit a reiver that was sneaking in the house. What are ye doing here?"

"You hit me with a piece of firewood and..." She felt her ear which had taken some of the blow though her cap had protected it a little. "...crushed my ear." She shook her head to try and clear it. "What were you thinking, ma'am?"

"It was a reiver."

"No," said Elizabeth, "it was me. I was coming upstairs to go to bed. Are you quite well, ma'am?"

"Oh." Lady Hume's eyes had cleared. "Perhaps I was dreaming."

"Yes." She let go of the old woman's arm and picked up the bit of firewood that had broken. "If I come to bed upstairs, will you knife me?"

"I don't know what you're talking about."

Elizabeth rubbed her ear and blinked at Lady Hume. "Do you remember me?" she asked, "Lady Widdrington? Mrs Burn's friend?"

"Of course I do. Now the reiver's gone, will ye come ben to bed?"

Elizabeth was too tired and still muzzy from the blow to work out what was going on. She picked up the taper, gestured for Lady Hume to go in front of her and followed, feeling a headache on its way.

There were four bedrooms upstairs and Lady Hume gestured to one where there were rushes on the floor and hangings on the wall to try to do something about the perennial chill from the stone. Really, thought Elizabeth abstractedly, you needed to put in paneling to get it to warm up a little. Sir Henry had required careful manouevring to get paneling installed in the main bedroom at Widdrington castle, but it had been worth it.

There was a four-poster bed and a truckle under it as well, a jordan, and a couple of clothes chests and a table covered with clutter that Elizabeth couldn't identify in the darkness. Lady Hume went and used the jordan and then sat on the bed and watched her every move like a little bird while Elizabeth got ready for bed.

Despite the freezing cold, she took her gown and riding habit off because she wasn't prepared to go to bed fully clothed for a second night running. She draped them on a clothes chest because Lady Hume's clothes were on all the available hooks, dropped her petticoats, bumroll, and stays and left her stockings on because they were warm knitted ones. She shivered in her shift and started to pull the truckle bed out.

"Get in wi' me," ordered Lady Hume. "There's a hole in the truckle's mattress and it's aye cold."

There was indeed a hole in the truckle's mattress, and it was indeed cold. But Elizabeth hesitated. She didn't mind sharing a bed, what she minded was being hit on the head with firewood by an old lady.

"Get in," said Lady Hume. "That reiver's gone and he's hurt my wrist forebye." She held out her wrist and Elizabeth saw that she had grabbed it tighter than she thought and there would be bruises in the morning. Well, she'd been stunned. "I'll see to him if he comes back, hinny. Ye're safe wi' me."

Jesu, thought Elizabeth, I'm too tired and muzzy-headed for this. So she smiled and climbed in next to Lady Hume, who immediately curled onto her side.

"Now curl into mah back to keep me warm there," said the old lady. "Dinna kick, dinna wriggle, dinna talk, and we'll hae a story to help ye sleep. Would ye like a story?"

"Ah..."

"Ay, I'll tell ye of when I wis a girl and it wis all different, eh?"

Lying curled into the old lady's back with her ear throbbing and her headache setting in properly, Elizabeth thought that the last thing she needed was a story. She got one anyway.

Once upon a time, and a very good time it was, there was a little girl called Agnes, which means lamb in the Latin, and she had three brothers called Ralph and Jock and Hughie, ay, Hughie like you, and they played nicely though sometimes Jock and Hughie were rough. Jock and Hughie were boys so they would practise with swords and spears and Agnes had to learn to be a wife so she had to learn huswifery and a little cooking, which she didn't like, and needlework, which she loved. She had a beautiful piece of silk that she was embroidering for an altar front, for it was before the change and churches were pretty places, all fu' wi' pictures ye could make up stories wi'. And they were as happy as could be in their tower and farm with all their surname around them and so they were as happy as birds in a tree, as happy as conies in a meadow. Then Agnes went away to her aunt at the big castle to learn huswifery better and that was sad for then they weren't together anymore and the boys were riders like their father and uncles before them.

And then war came and Agnes rode away with her aunt from Bad King Henry's men, she rode and rode, all day and night she rode for there was no telling which way to go, and all you could see was the smoke by day and the fire by night and she didna know what had happened to Ralph and Jock and Hughie nor any of her family, for Bad King Henry's men were burning and killing all the way up the Merse to Edinburgh, the Rough Wooing they called it, for it was to get the little Queen to marry the little Prince Edward.

And one day Agnes was in a wood and she had been riding and riding with her aunt's people and the men around her frightened, and she fell asleep for she was very tired and when she woke up she was all alone. That was frightening for she didna ken which way to go, didna ken even which way was north nor she had no horse neither for her palfrey had wandered off. She wandered for a while and so she came on a pavilion and in the pavilion was a sleeping knight wearing white samite and gold. She went away from there and found a man shooting arrows at a target in a red coat. She went away from there to a cave and the King of Elfland came to her. He was in disguise, of course, as an English archer and he treated her gently enough and he was kind to her and he gave her a beautiful collar of gold with emeralds and sapphires in it and showed her the way back to her aunt and...

At that point Lady Hume started snoring, leaving Elizabeth wondering just how gently the King of Elfland in disguise as an English archer had treated her in fact. It took her a while to go to sleep, with not being accustomed to sleeping with anyone else since she usually took the truckle bed when Sir Henry was home so she wouldn't accidentally bump him in the night and hurt his gouty leg.

Sunday Morning 15th October 1592

Elizabeth woke before dawn as she usually did, lay for a while listening to Lady Hume's snores and wondering why she had no woman with her. You'd expect at least one to help her with dressing and undressing and to do necessary things like emptying the jordan. It seemed the Lady Hume had come from whatever she was doing, straight to Wendron without even stopping to change her clothes. That was odd as well.

She got up into the freezing dawn, used the pot and wiped her face with a napkin from the cupboard, then she dressed herself in her old riding habit again and put on her riding boots before kneeling to pray as she always did.

It always took a lot of effort now to bring her mind to God. It was as if her mind was a tent and outside it was Sir Robert Carey, in a sportive mood, poking his head between the tent's walls and smiling at her with that wonderful smile of his, that curled up on either side and had a little bit of danger in it for salt.

She sighed and brought her mind back to the Lord's Prayer again. Forgive us our trespasses as we forgive those who trespass against us. She always tried to forgive Sir Henry for the way he treated her since he had a right to do it as he'd told her many times...But he did it without justice, that's what made her angry. She tried to smooth out the anger, pat it down, but there it was living inside her and making her feel contempt for her husband. She knew that was wrong. She may not love him, and indeed she didn't, but she should respect him as her lord. She could respect Robin, despite his love of finery, which kept beggaring him, and despite his tendency to come up with crazy dangerous schemes that could get him killed in dozens of different ways...The way he kept finding excuses to come north to see her, for instance, despite the fact that Sir Henry hated his guts even before he had any idea that Elizabeth had lost her heart to the man. That crazy wager of his a few years ago, when Carey had seemingly bet everyone at Court that he could walk to Berwick from London in ten days and had done it with a day to spare by running some of the way where the road was good—he did that so he could come upon her unexpectedly while she was dealing with the very stinkiest part of the flax harvest and...For a moment she thought about how near an escape that had been for her virtue. The lord he had riding behind him to make sure he didn't get on a horse had kept tactfully back at a distance. And she had been so surprised and pleased and flattered at how Robin had come to her, she had let him kiss her and been utterly overwhelmed by the...the happiness of being kissed. The utter pure joy of it.

She sighed again. And lead us not into temptation but deliver us from evil. That was the line from the Lord's Prayer she always had trouble with, and for good reason. Robin Carey was temptation personified. Robin Carey was every married old man's fear. She wanted to be tempted by him.

She finished her prayers while Lady Hume still snored and went out into the dawn to see what needed doing. It was Sunday but there was no minister to give the church service so she supposed that would go by the board. For instance, would the Burns want some kind of funeral feast? If they did she had no idea how she could provide it without a trip to Berwick to get supplies and more money than she'd brought for the journey.

Jock Burn was there, practising a veney with a young lad who was enthusiastic but rotten at swordplay. He stopped and had a drink when he saw her and pulled his cap off a bit.

"Good day, Mr Burn," she said, as always promoting him above his proper rank which was goodman. Robin had taught her that as a quick and cheap way of flattering people.

"Ay missus," he said, "m' lady."

"I was wondering about the funeral meats," she said without preamble. "Would your family be wanting to go to Berwick...?"

"Ay," he said, with a broad smile, "we thocht of that last night and my little brother Jemmy and his son Archie and some of our cousins went out the night to...ah...to find some sheep."

She glared at him in annoyance. "From our ain herds," added Jock, "our ain herds and...And our friends' herds..."

"I hope," she said freezingly, "that you weren't planning a raid into the East March of England."

"Nay, nay," he said hurriedly, "ainly the Middle March...ah. Where our friends live, ye follow?"

"Well, I hope, if your friends miss any beasts, that you'll pay for them."

"Och aye, we will, missus. Sir John Forster'll see us right."

"Hmf." She didn't doubt that the deeply corrupt and ancient Middle March Warden would want paying; she was thinking of the families that owned the herds.

She thought about that and although it was probably too late, she went over to the alehouse and found Young Henry out in the front on the village green with the targets, practising archery.

"We should send a message to John Carey and Sir John Forster, the Burns are out looking for funeral meats."

Henry looked annoyed. "I should have thought of that," he said. "I haven't got a man to send but I'll find a boy."

"So should I," Elizabeth agreed. "I think Forster in the Middle March is more urgent."

Young Henry nodded, handed his bow to a cousin and went into the alehouse. Elizabeth went to enquire among the women about beer and found they only brewed for themselves and their families and none of them could supply anything like enough for a funeral. She went back to the manse and up the stairs and found Lady Hume sitting on the bed, ordering a village girl around.

"Child, I want ye to fetch me water in that bowl and while ye're at it, take the jordan and swill it out and come back quick for to bring me my breakfast."

"I'll bring that," said Elizabeth pleasantly. "I need to talk to you, my lady."

"Och aye, and who're ye?"

"Lady Elizabeth Widdrington, ma'am. We met yesterday and shared a bed last night."

"Oh."

"I'm not sure about beer but there's some hot porridge in the warmer."

"Ay," said the old lady with dignity, "that's a' I ever have is porridge or toast if the bread's old."

Porridge it was, with the last heel of the loaf, and the crock of butter and some mild ale that Elizabeth had begged from the girl's mother who was cleaning downstairs. The hot coals in the brick range had been hot enough to bring the fire back and there was quite a sharp fire in there now, enough to fry bacon if there had been bacon to fry.

By the time Lady Hume had eaten her breakfast with Elizabeth keeping her company, they had agreed that the funeral could not be held without baked meats nor beer and that Elizabeth would take one of the cousins and go to Berwick in search of beer—which was plentiful there, thank the Lord. That meant the funeral would be tomorrow. Lady Hume recommended a brewer called Atchison in Berwick, whom Elizabeth had never heard of. As for money, she went to Jock Burn who was now playing a veney with another black-haired, grey-eyed man who looked remarkably like himself and doing rather better, while a nice-looking young man watched carefully.

"Ay," said Jock. "Ah wis wondering about beer and I'd think kindly of ye if ye'd see to it, my lady." He reached in his purse and brought out two English pounds and some Scotch shillings which made Elizabeth frown because she knew so much money could only have come from blackrent.

There were still some Burns coming in and Robsons and Pringles as well, so she estimated she'd need a cartload of beer at least. She found a Widdrington cousin by the name of Humphrey Fenwick and he agreed to come with her to Berwick. She saddled and bridled Rat herself and mounted up.

"Will ye fetch marchpane fra Berwick too?" said Lady Hume, coming out into the stableyard. "And I've found her store of raisins o'the sun and dried plums fra last year and I'll make a cake wi' them but I've nae marchpane for a cover."

Elizabeth nodded. "I'll try, ma'am," she said. "I'll go to Sixsmith and see if he's got some."

"Ay, he's good. Or Johnstone?"

Elizabeth said nothing. There was no confectioner in Berwick called Johnstone, although she thought there had been one long ago. She walked her horse out of the yard and joined up with Humphrey, waved to Jock who waved back, and put her heels in.

SATURDAY 14TH TO SUNDAY

15TH OCTOBER 1592

The bell had rung at two in the morning and they had gone out half an hour later with the trod. Dodd carried the lance with the burning turf on it and Red Sandy behind him with the other men, including three of the Southerners who could ride well enough. It wasn't raining for a wonder and they had caught up with the running herds on the edge of the Bewcastle waste and had a running fight of it all the way to Kershopefoot where the Elliots and English Armstrongs had broken for Liddesdale, leaving most of their booty.

So all in all it was quite a successful night with some nice kine and sheep to choose Warden fees from and nobody had taken any hurt except for Bangtail who had managed to twist his ankle somehow and the Courtier was getting much better at letting his hobby choose his own pace and just going with it. The Earl of Essex's men were still stiff-backed, though, and seemed to get very tired as the night went on. Carey was happy as they sorted out the herd on the hills and took them back to their owners—for a wonder, most of the beasts were branded and identifiable —but as they came back toward Carlisle he seemed to lose his bounce again and become morose. Now Dodd wouldn't have been surprised at, say, Ill-Willit Daniel Nixon being in a bad temper, but, really, the Courtier should have been happy at the way the night had gone.

He had bags under his eyes as well and now he thought about it, Carey had been in a bad mood for over a week. Was he missing London and the South? Was he missing his lady-love Elizabeth Widdrington? Was he missing pretty doublets and hose? What the devil was wrong with him?

As they returned the last of the sheep to some Carletons and took their fees on to Carlisle, Dodd dropped the last bits of turf off his lance and hurried his horse up to Carey's. The man was swinging along and didn't look sick. He had the loose-backed look of a proper reiver. If it wasn't for the plain anonymous stitching on his jack and his fancy chased and half-gilded morion helmet, you couldn't tell the difference, really, especially as his goatee beard was getting a bit overgrown.

Being late in the year, the Sun was only just up, and in fact it was a nice day. You couldn't complain at the weather; the Moon had been at half but the skies had been clear and they'd had plenty of light...

Maybe it was Carey's creditors again? He'd managed to pay the men for September with what he'd brought with them from the South, and as far as Dodd knew, his tab wasn't too heroic at Bessie's. Had he been gambling at cards? But Carey was the best player in Carlisle; if he had, he'd likely be happy. Was he bored?

Was it some problem with his ugly Scottish servant Hughie Tyndale or that skinny boy John Tovey he had acquired as a clerk? Or with Philadelphia, his sister, who was tired of the north and talking about going south again to serve the Queen at Court once more. The Queen had sent her a letter, what had been in it?

So when they clattered through the town and up to the castle yard, Dodd stuck by Carey. They penned their fees in the enclosure for the purpose and then there was what looked like a great confusion of men dismounting and leading horses into their stalls and untacking them and rubbing them down. It wasn't, it was highly organised because Carey had ended the habit the men had of leaving their horses to the care of the boys. Each man took care of his own horse and there were nosebags and buckets of water there in the yard ready, on Carey's insistence that your hobby was in fact more important than you were, and harder to replace, and you had better see him or her fed, watered, untacked, wiped down and comfortable before you went to breakfast, or he would want to know why. The southerners had moaned about it for a bit but they got no sympathy and Dodd had given one of them a kicking to make the point. The habit had spread to all the men of the Castle guard because the hobbies went better and didn't go lame so often.

Oddly enough, Carey did exactly the same as the men though of course he could have used one of the boys running about with feedbuckets. Dodd stood in the next stall with a whisp of hay, rubbing down his horse, a big lad called Patch, while Carey did the same thing with his usual hobby whom he had named Sorrel.

The movements were the same, but there was something still very wrong with Carey. Dodd realised what it was when he found himself whistling "The Three Witches" between his teeth and realised that Carey wasn't singing, humming, or whistling anything, not even one of those irritating Court tunes he liked so well.

Dodd was shocked enough to stop rubbing Patch's big black and white whithers and peer over his horse at the Courtier. Carey had given Sorrel a swift wipe-down while he munched, was just now checking the hooves as he always did and after a stern look around the stall, picked his helmet off the manger and walked out into the yard again. Dodd finished up quickly and followed him.

Carey stood for a while, watching what was going on in the stableyard. Young Hutchin Graham was now in charge of the boys, by dint of fighting and beating the boy who had been doing it before, and his soprano yell rang out at once when a hobby took a bite at the one next to him.

"Ye're soft, ye are," sneered Hutchin to the small lad there. "D'ye no' ken Twice and Blackie are at feud, eh? Go on, take Twice down th'ither end o' the yard."

Andy Nixon looked abashed as well and went with his horse.

Carey nodded once and continued across the yard and down the passageway to Bessie's, where the breakfasts would be hot and waiting—bacon, sausage, black pudding, onions, sippets, eggs. Bessie could hear the bell as well as anyone in Carlisle and knew to get ready for when they came back.

Dodd followed him, trying to look as if he was just going the same way into Bessie's very loud commonroom, which was already full of men filling their stomachs. Dodd got himself a trencher, served himself from the dishes laid out on the tables, and sat opposite Carey where he could keep an eye on him without being too obvious about it.

Now that was odd. Carey had taken black pudding, onions, and eggs, but no sausages and no bacon. And it was Bessie's bacon, which was more in the nature of fried collops and smoked in the large chimney. There were half a dozen flanks and haunches hanging there now, getting ready for Christmas.

Dodd put his head down and started to eat into his pile of food because his belly was cleaving to his backbone and he was starved.

Once he'd taken the edge off his hunger with a few sausages—not so good these, from the butcher and not of Bessie's making; she probably hadn't done her sausages yet—and three large slices of bacon and the fried sippets of bread he liked so well, he took a glance at Carey's trencher and saw that the eggs and onions had gone but the black pudding was still there. Why? What was wrong with it? He tried some and it was fine. And no lovely golden crispy chunks of stale bread fried in the bacon fat for sippets either; what was wrong with the Courtier? The three Southerners were sitting at the next table with the other ones that couldn't ride properly yet and Dodd could hear them boasting about what they had done while they powered through their breakfasts.

However Carey was on his second quart of beer and sitting back. While Dodd watched, he beckoned one of the potboys, said something quiet to him. The boy came back with a small horn cup of something Dodd would swear was aqua vitae and Carey knocked it back with an odd swilling motion then drank more beer.

Dodd cleared his plate and leaned back himself to drink beer and keep an eye on Carey. Everybody else was in a good mood, shouting at each other, paying bets they had made on how many sheep there would be or similar, twitting Bangtail for twisting his ankle when he was running after a calf that had gone up the side of a hill. Not Carey. Carey was staring into space and pulling a sour expression with his mouth sideways.

Dodd was on the point of asking the man what was wrong, when he scowled and stood up, stalked out of Bessie's and away up through the orchard to the castle. Dodd thought of going after him, but then decided to finish up Carey's black pudding for him.

"What's up wi' the Courtier?" asked his brother, Red Sandy, who had taken seconds of the sausages since no one else was finishing them. "He's gey grumpy."

"Ay," said Sim's Will Croser, who usually said very little. "He damned my eyes when we was fighting the Armstrongs and I knocked him accidentally and then he said nathing all the way home."

"He's been like it for a week," said Bessie's Andrew Storey, "like me mam sometimes, says nothing and then shouts at ye for nothing."

"Ten days," put in Bangtail, "after ye came back from the Southland, Sergeant."

Dodd nodded. "Ah dinna ken but ye're right," he said. "He wisnae so quiet on the road back fra London and Oxford town. He was in a good mood."

Dodd had been in a good mood himself. Carey, Dodd, and the two new servants had arrived in the late afternoon, down the road from Newcastle with a couple of extra lads on horseback with the dispatches to help out if someone thought it worthwhile to take the Grahams up on their offer of ten pounds for Carey's head. It wasn't worth taking more, despite the Borders being in a tickle state, what with the Earl of Bothwell still hanging around and the Maxwells and Johnstones at each other's throats again. If you needed more, what you needed was an army and it was better to be inconspicuous. Carey kept his flashy morion in his saddle bag, wrapped up, and just wore an old-fashioned velvet hat.

The Earl of Essex's quondam soldiers were on the way but they were walking and would take longer. Eight had already gone to John Carey in Berwick and the remaining eight could shape up or die in Carlisle. And little Kat Leman had been left with Lord Hunsdon's household after Dodd had had a serious word with her to explain what it was like in the North and how hard it was for small maids. She had looked at him grimly, with her little face set.

"I want to stay with you," she insisted. "Could I come and be your maidservant in your tower in Gilling?"

"Gilsland," Dodd had corrected her automatically, and he'd thought about it. There were a few girls around the place, relatives of Janet's, so it wasn't half as impossible as Carlisle castle.

"Mebbe," he'd admitted, "that's possible. But ye're still too young for huswifery and my wife can be rough with the girls." Kat had nodded. "In a year or two, perhaps, when ye've grown a bit. All right, Kat? Stay wi' my Lord Hunsdon's household, he'll see ye right and then in a few years when ye're grown a bit, ye can write tae me."

Her face had screwed up at that. "I don't know how," she said. "That's priests' work."

"Ye can learn," Dodd told her. "And be a good girl for the Steward's wife."

Kat nodded, her face very serious. "I like my Lord Hunsdon," she said decidedly, "even though he shouts. He told Mrs Leigham to get me some new duds and these are wool and nice and warm." She looked proudly at her cut down old blue kirtle and the different coloured sleeves. "I'll do what you say, Sergeant Dodd, and I'll see you in a few years."

He had left her with a slight feeling of uneasiness. Why was she so determined to come to Carlisle with him? Perhaps a few years in Hunsdon's enormous household would convince her to stay in the South. He hoped so. By the time they got to Newcastle he had put her to the back of his mind.

The Courtier seemed to be in funds again, which was all to the good. He had apparently played primero with the merchants of Oxford on their last night, and begged all of them, although Dodd knew better than to think that the money would last. He had already spent a horrible amount on secondhand doublets for Essex's deserters to replace their tattered and impractical tangerine and white.

Carey hadn't sent anyone ahead and so the first the garrison knew about their arrival was when they clopped through the gate of the city and two of Lowther's bad bargains had called out to them. A boy was sent running up to the castle to tell Lady Scrope and they had carried on up English Street and past Bessie's, up the covered passage, and into the castleyard itself. Dodd had felt very self-conscious in his fancy wool suit, which wasn't as fancy as the previous wool suit he had lost, but fancy enough since it wasn't homespun like everybody else's. Hardly anyone in Carlisle had anything like it. Thomas the Merchant Hetherington wore black brocade and the headmen of the big surnames would have their finery from Edinburgh, maybe a few of the merchants or the mayor would have something like it.

"Where's ma brother, and whit have ye done wi' him?" demanded Red Sandy with a fake scowl. He'd come hurrying into the yard almost before Dodd had dismounted and there was the usual commotion and fuss with the horses.

"Ah killt him and left him in a ditch," said Dodd dryly, because he did feel a completely different man from the one who had ridden South some weeks before.

"I know that's a lie, ye musta poisoned him," said Sandy and clapped Dodd on the back. "Who did ye kill for the clothes, brother? Ye look like the mayor."

"I'm no' as broad as him, and the man give me the clothes nice as ye like and I didna even ask him," Dodd said, which was true because his fine new duds had been Hunsdon's under-steward's and the man had been perfectly willing to give them up in exchange for a new suit from Hunsdon. That made the other men laugh, though, as they crowded round him and they were all asking the usual questions about London such as: Was it as big as they said? And did Londoners have tails like Frenchmen? Dodd allowed as how London was far bigger than it had any business to be and no, as far as he could tell, Londoners didn't have tails like Frenchmen, though their hose were so fat they might. Certainly the women didn't.

"Ay, I told you," said Bangtail knowingly.

Carey's sister had come running from the sausage-making and he'd embraced her and swung her round as he always did. Scrope wasn't there; he'd gone hunting and Philadelphia was furious with him for some reason, possibly connected to Madam Hetherington's bawdy house.

Bessie's Andrew was the one who told Dodd about the mysterious package that had arrived by way of the carter from York a few days before. They went in a body to Dodd's cubbyhole next to the door of the barracks and found it sitting on the bed—which someone, probably Janet, had seen to having the sheets changed. There it sat with the label on it in Dodd's handwriting which only Sim's Will had been able to read. Red Sandy had been too young to go to the Reverend Gilpin and then there had been the feud with the Elliots so he never got the chance to learn to read.

Dodd looked at the package and remembered sending it and felt utterly estranged from the man who had done that, and he almost couldn't think what was in it—his homespun doublet and breeches, to be sure, dyed dark red with madder by Janet, the breeches made of wool from a black sheep so they didn't need dyeing and wouldn't run in the wet either. And the hat.

He batted the men back from the package and started undoing the painstaking hessian wrappings and lifted the wicker lid to find his doublet there. He unpacked his clothes from round the hat and then unwrapped the linen folds from around it and held it up.

"This is for Janet," he said, thinking how Barnabus had told him she'd forgive him anything when she had a hat like that and wondering if it was true. Not that he planned to tell her some of the things that had happened in London, but still.

There was a silence from the men. They may never have been south of Carlisle in their lives but you could see the London fashion almost glowing in that hat: dark green, high crowned, and with a long pheasant's feather in it. It looked as out of place there as Carey; more so because at his roots, Carey was in fact a Berwick man. That hat was all London.

"Och," said Bangtail, "what did ye pay for it?"

"Ye ken the infield at Gilsland?"

"Ay."

"More than ye'd pay for that."

"Twenty shillings?"

"Twenty-five shillings."

More silence. Come to think of it, he wasn't quite sure why he had done it now, especially as he had lost the rest of the bribe shortly after. But the Queen had made that up to him and more. He wasn't going to mention that, though, until he had talked to Janet about it.

"Er...where did ye rob sae much cash from?" Red Sandy asked tactfully.

"I didna," said Dodd. "It was a bribe, fair and square."

The men looked at each other. "A bribe?" squeaked Bessie's Andrew. "Who did ye have to kill for it?"

"I didna. It was what they call a sweetener. There's sae much money in London, it just flows around. The serving maids have velvet ribbons to their sleeves and golden pins to their hair. The serving men wear brocade some of them, secondhand, but rich as Thomas the Merchant's. Ye have no idea...There's a street called Cheapside where they have shops with great plates and goblets and bowls of gold and siller in the windows and nought but a couple of bullyboys and some bars to keep them."

The men were exchanging looks again.

"The Bridge...the Bridge has got shops full of silks and velvets...The armourers, oh, the armourers..." Dodd felt overwhelmed at the task of telling them what he had seen in the South. "They have armourers that sell nought but swords and some that sell guns and ay, they cost a lot but..."

"Where's London exactly?" asked Bangtail, with the slitty-eyed look of a Graham with a plan.

"Hundreds of miles south. Three hundred at least." Dodd smiled at him. "D'ye think I didna think what you're thinking now, how could I raid it?"

Bangtail nodded and so did Red Sandy. "It's a long way," said Bessie's Andrew, "and wi' the cattle to drive..."

"Cattle, sheep, all out in the fields with naebody bar a boy to keep them," Dodd amplified. "Ah've thought and thought and I canna think how to bring the loot back. Go there, ay, get it—ay, though they've Trained Bands in London. But bring it back—that's yer problem."

More silence as seven highly honed reivers' brains considered the problem of bringing your loot all the way from London with the hot trod after you.

"Anyway, I bought it and I'm fer Gilsland tomorrow to give it to Janet..."

"Nae need, brother, she's in town."

***

Dodd had waited right there by the hat while someone went to fetch Janet, his heart suddenly beating hard and fast. He heard her voice in the doorway.

"What are ye doing, Bangtail? I've no need to check the bed, I changed it last week and I'll thank ye…"

Red Sandy ceremonially opened the little door and Dodd stood up and there she was, in her second-best homespun kirtle, coloured dark green with moss and nothing like the London fashions, and her shift open at the top and her cap and old hat over her blazing red Armstrong hair. She paused as if she didn't know him.

"Henry Dodd, is that you?" she asked, looking him up and down as if they were at a harvest dinner and he was asking would she like to dance.

"Ay, wife, it's me."

"Well, look at ye," she said with a slow smile. "Look at ye," and she gave him a nice curtsey. Not to be outdone he did a bow which was getting better, he knew, and then he stepped one step across the narrow floor and grabbed her and held her.

"Och Janet," he heard himself say. "Ah missed ye," which was true, he had, worse than he would ever have believed he could miss his woman. She had been there in his imagination but now that he was holding her tight, he knew the difference.

"Well, Henry…" she started and he stopped her mouth with his and Bangtail ceremoniously shut the door on them and Red Sandy sat down next to it to make sure nobody barged in on them.

They were lying in a breathless heap on the bed when Janet said, "What's that?" and pointed at the linen-wrapped item they had somehow moved to the floor and then somebody had put a pair of breeches over the top of. Dodd retrieved his breeches and put them on again, while Janet had less to do, she only needed to do her stays up at the top again and rearrange her petticoats.

Suddenly Dodd felt worried and embarrassed at his extravagance. Surely she would prefer the money to the hat, to buy a field with, but then he remembered he had got most of his bribe back, less the forged coins, and it was still a substantial sum as you reckoned things in the North. But still. Would she like it? Maybe he could sell it to Lady Scrope if she didn't, though the colour was wrong for my lady.

Janet was up off the bed and picking it up. She looked narrow-eyed at Dodd and when he nodded gravely, she started unwinding the linen. Before she'd finished unwrapping it he had decided she wouldn't like it and would call him a fool and his mouth turned down.

The glory of London fashion glowed in the tiny room, smaller in fact than the inside of the four-poster bed Dodd had slept in down in London. In silence Janet put it carefully on the bed and folded up the linen wrapping, then she lifted it up and held it out at arm's length.

"For me?" she asked, in a thunderstruck voice. "From…you, Henry?"

"Ay, ah'm sorry, it cost a lot but I looked at it down in London and I thought, that'll look fine on Janet to go to church, that green on your red hair, that'll look finer than all the fine ladies down in London and their powders and paints and their gowns, and so I bought it." That wasn't exactly what had happened, but it was indeed how he had thought. "Barnabus helped," he added, lamely, though the man was dead and couldn't call him out, "I didn't want to at first because of the cost of it and then…"

He couldn't speak anymore and he saw something glittering in her eyes before they reeled backwards onto the bed again and the hat was nearly crushed.

Outside Red Sandy tipped his head at the closed door. "Is Sergeant Dodd no' finished yet?" Bessie's Andrew was saying. "Ah wanted tae ask him about Blackie…"

"Ye've no style at all," said Red Sandy. "Get oot of it, the man's back fra London and discussing matters wi' his wife and ye want tae bother him about a hobby?"

Bessie's Andrew looked bewildered for a moment and then looked sly. "Och," he said, "Is he no' finished yet?"

Both of them listened. "No," said Red Sandy, raising his voice slightly. "Ah think he's still busy."

Bessie's Andrew was standing there like a lummock with his mouth slightly open.

"Oot!" said Red Sandy and he went, while Red Sandy went back to his whittling on a bit of firewood.

After the hat had been rescued and dusted off, Dodd watched while Janet tried it on in front of the piece of mirror she had found. She wasn't a woman who liked fripperies and yet there she was, tilting it one way and then the other to see which looked better.

"Ye like it?" Dodd was surprised. What Barnabus had said looked like it was true. "Even though it cost twenty-five shillings?"

She shook her head and grinned. "Well," she said, "I'd like it more if ye'd reived it o' course, but I like it fine as it is. What else did ye get down South? A pot o' gold?"

Was now the time to tell her or should he keep it quiet still? It was a serious business and changed everything and nothing.

"Ay, I did. In a way."

She sat down next to him on the bed. "Och, what?"

He thought he should tell her the story of how he came by it and then he thought it would be simpler to tell her after, and so he reached in his smart wool doublet front and pulled out a leather packet, opened it, and took out the legal document. Gilsland had come to him from her after Will the Tod, her father, had acquired the leasehold in a mysterious way from the Carletons. Come to him—but he was a tenant-at-will, who owed rent. Or he had been.

"What's this?" Janet asked. "I can read the letters but not the words."

She was an amazing woman, he thought, learning to read and all. "Nay, nor can I. It's in Latin. See that word there, it's 'dedo' which means 'I give'."

"And who gives what?" she was frowning now.

"Gilsland. That paper there is the deed to Gilsland. I...we own it now, freehold. There's ma name in Latin, see, Henricius Doddus."

It suddenly struck him that he could even vote in an election for parliament now, or better still sell his vote to the highest bidder. Janet was staring at him, open-mouthed.

"We already own Gilsland..."

"Ay, but no' legally. We're tenants, we should pay rent." She paused and then nodded slowly. "Tae the Earl of Cumberland, ay?"

"Ay. I think ma dad paid him something in the seventies."

"Now we don't owe rent. We own it. We own it. We could sell it, we could...mortgage it, we can pass it to our children. The Courtier tellt me it doesnae matter so much now but when the old Queen dies and James of Scotland comes in, it could matter a lot that we own it."

She looked down at it and spotted the signatures. The Earl of Cumberland's scrawl was there and next to it the graceful sweeping tropes of the Queen's signature.

"The Queen gave you this, Henry?"

"Ay," he said, thinking of the Queen's red hair and snapping black eyes and how he hadn't known who she was. "I met her twice and the second time she give me that."

"But why, Henry? Why would she do that? You haven't got the money..."

"Och no, I saved her life..." he explained. "It's a wee bit complicated but there was a petard under her coach and I pit the fuse out."

She took a sudden breath. "You put the fuse out?"

"Ay, it was lit and a' and I cut the coal off the match with ma iron cap and emptied the chamber o' powder and so it was all right."

Suddenly her arms were round him so tight he could hardly breathe. "Jesu, Henry!"

"Ay, what of it, Janet?"

"You could have been blown to pieces."

"Ay, but I wasn't. And she gi' me that."

He didn't understand why she had tears in her eyes for something in the past that hadn't happened anyway, but he liked it when she held him too tight so he let her.

"Och dinna fret Janet, it coulda happened any time, oot on the Border or in a tower or something, and me nae better for it after than a bit of a Warden's fee."

She laughed then and folded the paper up again and put it in the leather pouch and gave it back to him with her colour high in her cheeks.

"We'll keep that safe and tell nae one."

"Ay, I think so too. Though the Courtier says it has to be entered in the rolls and he'll see tae it."

They looked at each other for a while. "Ye went down South my ain Henry Dodd, Land Sergeant of Gilsland, but what have ye come back as," said Janet slowly. "Is it a lord, mebbe, wi' all the fancy foreign people ye know."

"Sir Henry Dodd," said Dodd and laughed at the sound of it. Janet didn't laugh, though.

"Could be ye'll end as that, ay."

"Och come on, Janet, the sea will a' run dry and the land turn tae haggis before that'll come aboot."

She was doing something to him that he liked while she was busy with her other hand, unlacing her bodice. Now her kirtle came off with a heave and she had to leave off while she undid the strings of her petticoats and then again with her stays and her shift under that and there she was in all her pale, freckled glory with her cap off and the London hat perched sideways again on her red curls. Dodd took in a deep breath at the sight. He'd imagined it often enough down in London but this was much better because he could smell that smell of warm woman and he could cup her breasts and take a taste and listen to the fast beating of her heart and start counting her freckles again. He never counted more than twenty of them because he always got distracted. Dodd was tired but not too tired and for a miracle the hat survived the next ten minutes as well, making it a three-times lucky hat, only slightly dented from the pillow.

Outside Red Sandy shook his head and grinned and wished he'd had a bet about it with Bangtail. That was a wonder and all, the way miserable Henry was still as smitten with Janet as he had been as a young man and she was working for her dowry in the castle. It was hard to know why there wasn't a whole string of sons and daughters considering they'd been married nearly ten years.

SUNDAY 15TH OCTOBER 1592

Elizabeth drove a hard bargain with the brewsters of Berwick and with Mr Sixsmith the confectioner as well, and came back to Wendron with not one but two wagons of beer, albeit the second wagon was mainly mild, and a couple of pounds of marchpane.

She came back as the dusk came down on the Merse and found Lady Hume tired but triumphant with two large cakes cast in barrel hoops and proving in the kitchen of the manse, waiting to be baked. The village baker had agreed to fire his oven twice that night so long as someone else paid for the wood, which the Robsons had agreed to do after some discussion with Jock Burn and so the faggots were being fed into the oven and the flames leaping high.

The two beer wagons were greeted with cheers and cheeky orders for gallons of the double beer, and so Elizabeth instructed the drivers to bring them both into the stableyard of the manse where they only just fitted. She set all four of the Widdrington cousins to guard the beer in watches during the night.

There was one fine bullock already butchered and being colloped by the cooking fires of the Burns and several sheep on the way to the same fate. She glowered at Jock Burn who told her they had been bought and paid for from some Routledges, which was obviously a lie. Nobody ever paid the Routledges.

She found another elderly woman in the house with Lady Hume who turned out to be her tiring woman, a stout person called Kat Ridley, who beamed at Elizabeth as she came into the kitchen of the manse.

"Will ye like to see the funeral cakes go in, my lady?" she asked and Elizabeth, tired from the ride back from Berwick and from the long arguments she'd had with the four main brewsters of Berwick, suppressed a sigh and agreed she would.

They smelled good with the winey smell of dough and she helped Kat carry them over on their slates to the baker who opened his oven ceremoniously and slid them in on his long spade, to sit side by side.

"She ay had a good time wi' the kneading and the pulling," said Kat confidentially to Elizabeth as Lady Hume watched the cakes going in with an odd expression on her face.

"Good," said Elizabeth, wondering why Lady Hume was being spoken of as if she was a child. Lady Hume didn't seem to notice.

"She'll sleep well the night. Did ye have any trouble wi' her last night? She tellt me ye shared."

"Ah…well she hit me with a piece of firewood."

"Ay, she does that. She's very afeared o' reivers, poor soul."

"And she told me a story about the King of Elfland in disguise as an English archer."

"Ay. Ye ken, she's well enough i' the day, but nights trouble her sorely. I was afeared maself when I found she'd gone from Norwood yesterday morning and not told a soul where."

"I see."

"I thocht she'd gone over to Hume castle and sent a boy over there and then when he came back wi'out news of her, well, I was mithered all day, I dinna mind telling you."

"Of course."

"But then I heard that the minister was killt and o' course I knew where she was then and come over as fast as I could this morning. I dinna ken how she knew the minister was dead…"

"Didn't a boy come out to her?"

"Nay, I dinna think so. But o' course when she knew, she had tae come."

"Why?"

"She's a Burn herself, Ralph o' the Coates' auntie, I think. It's family."

"Ah. Is that why she doesn't like Poppy Burn?"

There was a kind of twitch of Kat's broad face there. "Ay, in a way," she allowed and then closed her mouth firmly.

Shaking her head, Elizabeth saw the oven door closed up properly with bits of dough which would fall off when the cakes were likely to be baked and agreed that the baking of the funeral cakes was thirsty work and worthy of some of the beer. She brought a firkin of the mild over herself rather than allowing anybody near the beer and causing a riot.

She tried some and found it was well enough but would be sour in a couple of days, which explained the excellent price she had got it for. Never mind. If there was anything left of the beer by evening tomorrow, she would be extremely surprised.

They sat in silence for a while around the kitchen range with the door part open, the three of them, Lady Hume who was nodding off, Kat Ridley who was knitting a sock on four needles, and Elizabeth who was tired herself but couldn't go to sleep. In all the hurry and business of getting the funeral beer, she had forgotten the oddity of the killing and now it had come back to her redoubled. Also she was in no haste to go to bed since she would no doubt be sharing with Kat as well as Lady Hume.

"I'm puzzled," she said slowly at last, on the grounds that asking was probably the simplest way of going about it, "how did Lady Hume know that the minister was dead before anyone else did?"

"Ay," said Kat Ridley, "it's a wonder. Ah wisna there; I was taking the linen down to Goody Robson before dawn and there was a big load of it. Last time we can dry anything outside this year, I shouldn't wonder…"

Elizabeth nodded. She'd taken a cartload of linen to her washerwoman two days before Poppy arrived, shirts and shifts and caps and underbreeks, quite apart from all the sheets to the good beds and pillowcases and cloths for the dairy and the wet larder. She thought of Poppy's bloodstained shift and petticoat in the linen bag and wondered when they'd be able to launder it. She'd put it in some cold water as soon as she got home to start taking the set stains out of it.

"I left her at the needlework in the solar with a candle till the Sun rose and she was happy enough for she allus is when she's making something with her needle. Ye should see what she makes, all bright colours and strange figures, and she never uses a pattern. It's some hangings for Young Hughie's bed and she only has one more curtain to make. She has stories on them, she's a wonder for the stories."

"Yes, she told me a story last night after she hit me with the firewood."

"Yes. She gets confused at night. Not in daylight, but when the light goes she often thinks she's a girl again and lost in the woods with the English army after her."

"How old is young Lord Hughie?"

"He's ten. He's a quiet boy, very well-looking. He likes reading ye ken and the minister was tutoring him twice a week for Latin too. He's clever. He said he wishes he wasn't a lord and it was the old days so he could go to university at St Andrews like the minister."

Lord, how did that happen with Hume blood? Elizabeth wondered. "And his parents are dead?"

"Ay, poor wean. He never knew his mother, for she died to give him light, and his dad died of a quartan ague about three years ago so that was hard for him. There's an uncle at Court, but the land goes to Hughie first. The wardship is with Lord Spynie now, who thinks the world of him, he says, but her ladyship willna let the boy go to Court, not even to his uncle."

Elizabeth nodded tactfully at this. "He's far too young," she said. "I wouldn't send him myself."

"The minister liked the boy and the boy liked him. I think he may come to the funeral tomorrow if Cousin William allows it."

"Cousin William?"

"A byblow of Lord Hume of Wendron, he acts as steward and he's good at it."

"So you left her at her needlework in the early morning to take the washing down to the washerwomen…?"

"Ay and I left it wi' them and came back after they'd started in on boiling it, down by the river, ye ken, where the water's clear, and there she was, gone. Naebody had seen her go for they were all busy except she'd taken the boy's horse."

"What did the groom say?"

Kat looked a little uncomfortable. "Well he's no' too strong i'the head is Jimmy and he just said her ladyship had come tae him before the Sun was up, must have been as soon as I went, and he'd saddled the horse as she bade him and helped her to the saddle and then she was off. She's a good rider. She still goes hunting sometimes with Lord Hughie and Cousin William."

"Without a woman to see to her?"

Kat shrugged. "Well there's only young Fran and Cissy and the girls in the dairy, and none o' them can ride better than a sack o'meal so I see why she didna take one, and she allus forgets what happens at night."

For a moment Elizabeth had a strange thought of Lady Hume being the murderer and then dismissed it. How could she have handled a sword like that, to cut the man's head in two? It would explain the plate cupboard, though.

Elizabeth shook her head. Lady Hume could not have wielded a sword like that; Elizabeth couldn't herself. She was strong enough, perhaps, but it was a matter of skill that took years to grow.

Robin Carey of course, could have…She thought of him once, in the garden at Court in the Armada year, in his fine blackworked shirt and breeches and boots, showing off to her his skills with a sword, playing a veney with George Clifford, the Earl of Cumberland, and then playing tricks with his rapier like lunging through a thrown apple and slicing a hanging bread roll. Putting his head back and laughing with delight at her admiration and…

"When did she ride off to Wendron?" she asked, automatically crushing the memory because the pleasure it gave her hurt so much.

"The morning after the minister died," said Kat.

The man's body was lying unburied in his own parlour and his wife had fled. Who had come to Lady Hume to tell her?

"Was there anyone new at the castle, anyone you didn't know?"

Kat shook her head. "Only of course I dinna ken who may have come after I left with the wagon."

A piece of wood in the fire broke and settled with a shower of sparks and Lady Hume suddenly woke up. "Oh," she said, looking hard at Elizabeth, "who are ye?"

"Lady Elizabeth Widdrington, ma'am. Would you like to get to bed now?"

"I'll get yer spiced wine, m'lady, will ye go up wi' her ladyship?"

"Oh Kat, there you are, I wis having the dream again."

"Ay, but it's only a dream. Only a dream, my lady."

"Ay but..." The old lady looked about the kitchen at the shadows. "Who's outed the light, then?"

"Ay, the Sun's gone down a while now. We'll get ye to bed..."

"I'll make the spiced wine," said Elizabeth quietly. "You take her ladyship to bed. I don't want to get hit on the head again."

"I've brung it in ma work bag down there, in a flask, it's a syrop wine water, all ye need to do is mix it wi' the red wine and the aqua vitae, half and half."

"I'll manage. Do you have any?"

"I'll share with her ladyship."

Lady Hume went upstairs to bed with Kat, holding her arm and asking querulously where the light had gone, while Elizabeth bustled about the kitchen, cleaned a goblet she found on the table and used a chafing dish to warm the spice syrup on the hottest part of the range.

There was a man standing by the entrance, looking at her oddly. For just a second she wondered about ghosts and then she realised it was only one of the Burn cousins. She hadn't seen him before.

"Good evening," she said to him forbiddingly, "can I help you?"

"Jock tellt me to come and see if ye needed anything. He's right happy about the beer."

"So am I. Please thank Mr Burn and tell him I think we're well enough now."

"I'll be guarding the door in case anyone thinks of trying it on, missus. And the beer of course."

"Hm, yes. I already have two cousins of mine supposed to be guarding that."

For a second he looked nonplussed. Elizabeth took the spice syrup off the heat, wiped her hands in her apron, and walked out the door ahead of the man.

"Who are you?"

"I'm Archie Burn," he said, with a knowing grin, pulling his cap off, "yer servant, ma'am."

"Come with me, Archie." She walked round to the back of the stableyard where there was a gate, and found nobody there. Nearby round a corner, however, she saw a little campfire and a couple of figures who seemed to be drunk. At least one of them was singing tunelessly.

She shut her eyes and struggled for a second. She was tired, her ear was sore from last night, she had spent the entire day going to and coming from Berwick to get the beer, and now, in a village full of reivers who were no doubt at that moment advancing from all sides on the beer, the men she had asked to guard the gate were drunk and blatantly not guarding it.

Her temper snapped. She could almost hear it. She marched over to the campfire where one man was lying down and the other man was sitting giggling over some incomprehensible drunken story and she kicked him in the bollocks as hard as she could. She then turned on the other one who was trying to get to his feet and kicked him in the face so he went over again.

She lit a torch at the fire and then she went to the two precious wagons and found that the barrel she had tapped for herself and the other women had mysteriously gone missing and she thought she heard a suspicious noise as if someone was scurrying away as fast as they could from the other wagon. "Young Henry Widdrington," she bellowed, "get out here."

She checked all the others and found none tapped and none of the ropes loose, went back to the other wagon to find at least one other barrel loose and a third with the ropes cut.

The one she'd kicked in the face was on his feet, wambling toward her with a knife in his fist while the other one was still lying on his side nursing his cods. Which only went to prove, she thought, where men kept their brains.

Archie Burn was grinning by the gate and drew his sword as she was looking at him and the firelight went up and down the blade and made the waterings in the metal beautiful. However she was too annoyed to let him deal with Hector Widdrington, who was coming toward her with blood going down his face and a knife.

She unknotted her apron and flapped it in the air in front of him so he flinched and paused and swayed. Then she put it over his head and punched him several times somewhere so he went down again tangled up in her apron and dropped the knife since he was drunk. She picked it up and waited for him to fight free of the apron and let him see she had it. He paused and then looked around at Archie Burn and Jock Burn and Daniel Widdrington and Young Henry Widdrington, who had all come to the sound of fighting. Jock was laughing so much he had to hold onto the gate of a stall with tears of laughter rolling down his face.

"Get them out of here," she snarled. "I never want to see either one of the useless lunks again, that means you, Hector, and you, Sim, as well."

Sim still had hold of his cods but was on his feet. Then he was sick down his jerkin, which made Jock hoot even more and even Young Henry crack a smile.

"Out!" she shrieked and pulled her now dirty apron off Hector as he struggled to his feet and kicked him in the arse so he landed on his face in some manure from the carthorses. Sim broke into an unsteady run out of the gate, followed a moment later by Hector. She went after them at a fast walk and closed it with a loud slam and barred it.

Archie and Young Henry put their swords away and tried to stop grinning. Jock was starting to calm down again with "ahoo" noises. There was the ugly sound of him blowing his nose onto the ground for want of any such thing as a handkerchief.

"I did not spend the whole day getting beer for the funeral to have it drunk by Hector and Sim Widdrington," she said icily to Young Henry. He looked contrite, as well he should since it was his fault he had put the two of them on to guard.

"Ay, my lady," said Young Henry, "I'll see it's safe."

She turned on Jock Burn. "And you can find the barrel that's gone missing," she said to him.

"Och, we haven't got it…" he started.

"It's yer ain beer," she shouted at him. "I bought it with your money for your nephew's funeral, who's lying in the crypt with half his head off. He's no kin of mine, I don't care if his funeral has nathing to drink but I thought that at least ye might."

She folded her arms and stared him down. "Ay, missus," he said, "ay. We'll find it, though it'll likely be empty."

They agreed on three watches of four men each, mixed Burns and Widdringtons so they could keep an eye on each other as well as the beer. Elizabeth waited until the watches were set and the barrels tied down again and then stalked back into the house where she found Kat just finishing with the spiced wine. She was carefully filling three silver goblets with the mixture.

"The men were at the booze, nae doot," said Kat. "Is there any left?"

"Ay there is," said Elizabeth, "we only lost a barrel."

"That's a mercy," said Kat. She emptied the chafing dish of coals into the main part of the range and piled them up and put the curfew on. Then she took the stems of the two goblets while Elizabeth took the stem of the third goblet and followed her upstairs into the main bedroom where Lady Hume was tucked up in bed in her shift already and her clothes hung on one of the hooks on the wall. She looked fragile and little as she sat up and took the goblet, warming her knotted hands on it and sipping the hot wine-water. Kat sat beside her and took several sips before putting down the goblet.

"So the King of Elfland came to ye, did he?" she said encouragingly.

The little bird nodded and took a bigger sip. "Ay, he did. He was disguised as an English archer, so first I was affeared of him for they were bad men, all of them. He was disguised with brown hair and blue eyes and he was a big strong man with a big chest and big strong arms and he said, 'Dinna be afraid, I'll not hurt you.'"

And he showed her his big bow, as big as himself it was, and she had a try at pulling it but she couldna budge it o' course, for it was a magic bow and the King of Elfland was the only man i'the world that could string it. Then he strung it and he said to her, "Will ye come to my kingdom with me?" And she was all dirty with running through the woods so she said, "I'm ashamed to come to your kingdom," and he took out his pack and gave her a beautiful collar, a necklace of gold with emeralds and sapphires, fit for the Queen of Elfland herself and so she put that on and didna feel so bad. And then he pit her on his horse and he rode behind her through the terrible dark woods where terrible dark deeds were being done and he took her to Elfland where there are great round houses with pillars of gold and garnets and lapis lazuli and tourmaline and cat's-eye, like in the story of Tam Lin. And there he took out his other stringed instrument for he was a harper as well, and he played to her all night long, beautiful music he played to her...

The little bird had snuggled down under the covers with her head on the pillow and her hand under her cheek and she slept. Elizabeth and Kat's eyes met and then Kat stood up and started undoing her kirtle.

They peacefully helped each other to undress, which speeded the process considerably.

"I'll drink my wine now," said Kat. "It's got a spot of laudanum in it to help her rest but she willna drink it if I dinna keep her company." And she drank down the lukewarm spiced wine, got into bed next to Lady Hume and went to sleep.

Elizabeth left hers on the table and went downstairs again with the taper. She didn't have keys to the place, but she pushed the kitchen table against the back door and barred the main door from the inside. Then she went wearily upstairs again, thought about taking off and washing her stockings which were beginning to smell but didn't have the energy for heating the water to start with and picked up the goblet of spiced wine-water to drink.

And stopped dead. She lifted the goblet up and looked at it carefully. Yes. It was Poppy's. So were the other two.

She lifted the quilt and checked in the bed, then looked under it and saw a nicely washed and scoured jordan, blessings upon you, Kat, and next to it the beautiful silver bowl that Poppy had from her mother and was most of her dowry.

So the plate cupboard hadn't been raided by the murderers. On the other hand, that meant it should have been closed and locked and if anyone wanted the contents they would have had to break it open. So the plate cupboard had been opened by

Jamie and then even after he was killed, the murderers hadn't bothered with the plate.

She looked at the goblets again—they were nicely made with roses and lilies chased around them, probably from an Edinburgh silversmith. Perhaps Lady Hume had found them in the plate cupboard and put them upstairs for safekeeping and then forgotten about it. She drank only half of the wine-water because she didn't like the thick-headedness you got from laudanum, climbed into bed on the other side of Lady Hume and fell asleep with Hector and Sim Widdrington and the goblets whirling round her head.

MONDAY 16TH OCTOBER 1592

Around eight in the morning the tooth-drawer came back into the village on his little pony from Edinburgh where he was starting to get a good reputation although he had only been there a day this time. He tethered his pony in the yard and went into the commonroom of the alehouse, finding it a great deal more full with people than he had ever known.

"So it's true," he said to Tim, "Minister Burn was killed. I came back when I heard."

"Mr Anricks, I'm glad to see ye. Were there no teeth to be drawn in Edinburgh?"

"Hundreds, possibly thousands, but there are also barber surgeons there who don't like competition. What happened here?"

"Well, ye wouldna credit it, but the minister was killt stone dead wi' his head chopped off not an hour after ye left..."

Mr Anricks was a good listener and sat seriously while everyone vied to give him the story which everyone else had heard. There had been two strangers in the village, that was certain, or perhaps there were three, oh no, that included him and you're no stranger, Mr Anricks. The minister had his brainpan sliced for him probably in the afternoon but no one was sure because his wife had disappeared, though the word was she had ridden all the way to Widdrington and was there now. He had been found in the morning by Lady Hume who had come avisiting and been taken into the crypt and wrapped in his shroud and the house cleaned up a bit by some of the village women and then Lady Widdrington had arrived too. And the Burns were coming in, so they knew, and some of the Pringles and Routledges...

He listened, he nodded and he agreed with the storyteller. Whatever the story, no matter how wild the story—there were several who were convinced it was his wife that did the job or helped in it somehow—he agreed with the storyteller.

The strangers were the favourites, though, especially as there were two horses apparently found in the South with West March brands on them, just left to take their own way home.

***

"My lady, could we sing for the minister's funeral?"

Lady Widdrington looked around and down and found a boy standing there, twisting his cap in his hands, with two others behind him. The boy talking to her had red hair and freckles. All three of them had red-rimmed eyes and blotchy faces.

"What?"

"Only we're the boys from his school," said the boy. "He was teachin' us oor letters and numbers, like the Reverend Gilpin did him, and now he's deid and we willna learn them at a' nor be ministers like him and...and..."

"We wantae sing for him," said another boy. "We wantae make a song tae the Lord..."

"And warn 'em in heaven, there's a Burn on his way..."

"...ay, and so everyone can see what we wis learnin' and that we learnt it gude."

"Will ye let us, yer ladyship?"

The red-haired lad had tears rolling down his face and the brown-haired boy behind him had his face screwed up. The black-haired boy was gripping his fists together until the knuckles showed white.

"How many of you are there?" she asked.

"There's twelve on us, ladyship, like the Apostles," said the black-haired boy.

"But we're the eldest so we came to ye."

"What are your names?"

The red-headed lad ducked his head. "I'm Cuddy Trotter, he's Andy Hume, and that's Piers Dixon."

"Come with me."

She led the way into the parlour of the manse and the boys looked sideways at each other and the black-haired boy who was a Hume said, "Can we no' go intae his study, ma'am? That's where he taught us."

"I'm sorry, boys, the study is locked and I haven't the key."

They looked at each other, looked down. Piers Dixon started to speak, "Ay, but..."

"Och," said Cuddy Trotter.

"Where's his lady, ma'am?" asked Andy Hume.

"Mrs Burn is at Widdrington in the English East March and I hope she's staying in bed and resting so she doesn't have her babe too soon."

All three of them nodded solemnly. "Ay," said Cuddy, "the minister was right proud o' that..."

"Do you have a key, or know where the key is? For otherwise I shall have to ask some of the men to break the door because I need to know if the minister left a will."

"Ay, he did, ma'am," said Piers. "He made it last month and he got Cousin William and Tim at the alehouse to witness it forebye, so it's as legal as can be."

"Oh, did he?"

There was a certain amount of elbowing and looks exchanged.

"Do you know of a key?"

"In a manner of speaking," said Cuddy. "Here, I'll show ye."

He went across the hall to the door of the study and he took his knife out. Then he jiggled it in the lock until the old-fashioned levers moved and the door opened.

Lady Widdrington went first into the study and found it neatly arranged as a schoolroom with three benches and a teacher's lectern pushed to one side, a clerk's desk at the other side, a chair with arms, and a whole wall of books. There was a pile of papers on the clerk's desk, an inkpot, and several pens. The window was locked shut. She sat at the clerk's desk, opened the drawer and there was Jamie Burn's last will and testament staring up at her. She picked it up, folded it in three and put it in the inner pocket of her kirtle.

"Did the minister always lock his study when he went out of it?" she asked.

Andy nodded vigorously. "Always, even if he went out to the jakes."

"Did he know how easy it was to pick the lock?"

"Ehmm...he might of," offered Piers.

"What do you mean?"

"Well, we used tae steal books, ye see, fra his bookshelf. We'd allus bring 'em back 'cos he said they were too hard for us tae read..."

"...which they weren't..."

"...and Andy said it was all a joke 'cos the books changed, the ones we could reach..."

"I've brung the one back I wis reading," said Cuddy dolefully. "It's in Scots about a' Greek gods and that."

He brought a worn copy of an Ovid from under his shirt, wiped it off ineffectually with his sleeve and then went solemnly to the shelf and put it back.

"Ay, he said he wis a minister and couldnae let us read pagans like Ovid..."

"Or Loo-creesh-us..."

"But there they wis on the shelf and he never noticed even if we took a big thick book..."

"...and he'd ask us aboot 'em and laugh when Piers knew the answers..."

"Ay, ye're soft, ye are..."

"He wanted us tae steal 'em..."

"So long as we brung 'em back."

"I didn't once, because I liked it, it was *Holinshed's Chronicles* and it was so exciting…"

"And he said some wicked puck had gone and ta'en it and we'd best tell the fairies tae bring it back cos he needed it for a sermon…"

"And when we did we found there was a book aboot Scots history and so we took that…"

"So he wanted us to steal 'em, didn't he, ma'am?" finished Andy. "Didn't he?"

Elizabeth was trying not to laugh. How did you get the sons of reivers to read books? Well, you told them they couldn't have them and let nature take its course.

"I think so."

"Told you!"

"Ay, Cuddy, all yer worriting for naething…"

"Did he never beat you?"

"Beat us?" Cuddy looked bewildered. "Why would he?"

"He beat my brother Sim for pissing on a Bible for a bet," said Piers Dixon. "But nae more'n that."

"Ay, he were right to do that. It weren't Papist superstition either, it were wickedness because a Bible's expensive and it wouldnae burst into flames if ye pissed on it, which was a lot of super-steeshious nonsense and Sim should be ashamed of hisself," explained Andy seriously.

"It made my dad laugh," said Piers. "He didn't laugh so loud when he had to pay for a new Bible, he were furious, said ye could still use the old one when once ye'd got it dried out—and the minister wouldn't have it."

"Ay," said Andy, "and Sim got another leathering fra his dad for that."

"Ay," said Piers, "so did I."

"Why?"

"Cos I didnae stop him, o' course."

"So can we sing for him?" Cuddy asked. "We know lots of psalms, we allus sang 'em first and we did reading from them too."

"Can you show me?"

The boys looked at each other. "Just us?"

"Well, can you get the others together?"

They looked at each other again. "Ay, we can. Gi' us a while, missus, we'll run and fetch 'em."

She waited in the study and only half an hour later, eleven breathless boys, ranging in age from eleven down to seven formed up in front of her by the benches.

"We havenae Lord Hughie because he's at Norwood so we're eleven."

"Like the Apostles."

"Ay, after the Crucifixion, when Judas'd done 'imself in, the coward…"

"Will we sing for ye now, missus."

"Who'll gi' the note, wi'out the minister?" asked Piers Dixon in a panic.

"I will," said Andy Hume firmly. "I'm no' as good as him, but it'll have to do."

There was a while of whispering while they thrashed out which ones they would sing and then Andy Hume hummed three notes and they began.

One boy there was clearly tone deaf and droned away, the rest had clear, true voices improved by training. Elizabeth was almost more impressed that the boy who couldn't sing had been allowed to go on singing with them, than she was by the others.

They sang of the rivers of Babylon and they sang the "Lord is my shepherd" and by the end of it, Elizabeth's eyes had filled and overflowed.

The boys stood and fidgeted and elbowed each other. "Are ye a'right, missus?" asked Cuddy, very concerned.

"Ladyship…" hissed Andy.

"Missus ladyship, are ye hurting?"

Elizabeth blew her nose. "That was beautiful, boys," she said inadequately, "and I'm sad about the minister too, so…"

"Mebbe we shouldna sing if it makes people sadder," said Cuddy anxiously.

"You should," Elizabeth told him, "it helps the sadness to come out, like draining a sore. And why shouldn't we be weeping at Jamie Burn's funeral? He was a good man and we'll miss him."

"Ay," said Andy, "that's the right of it! D'ye ken who it was did it, ladyship?"

"No," she admitted, "do you?"

"It were the strangers, the two men naebody knew," said Cuddy. "I wish I'd known what they were at when I seen 'em. I'd mind 'em and I'd kill 'em too."

"Ay," said Andy Hume, "ay, we a' will if ye can just find who they were. We'll ride oot wi' our families and kill 'em stone deid, so we will."

There were soprano growls and promises of vengeance from every one of the boys and the second-youngest started crying again.

"Dinna greet," said Andy roughly, "ye'll stuff yer nose up and willna be able to sing."

"I only know ma letters, I dinna ken the putting together o' them..." choked the boy, "how'll I learn that?"

"Och, shut it," said Piers, punching him lightly. "It's no' sae hard, once ye know the letters, I'll tell ye."

"Ay, or me," said Andy Hume, "it's whit the minister would'a wanted."

Elizabeth asked each boy what he had seen on the day before yesterday. They had had a usual school day, with the two eldest beginning some Latin grammar and the rest learning to read and write. Yes, they had begun with psalms, they always did, and they ended with a prayer. And then the two strangers had come.

The boys could not agree about the strangers. They were dark-haired, they were light-haired, they were wide, they were short, they were tall, they had the look of Grahams or Armstrongs or Maxwells or Johnstones or Fenwicks...No, they weren't wearing jacks, just ordinary homespun, dyed brown and blue like anybody's father might wear. No, they didn't have spears or dags or nothing, only both had swords, of course. No, not one boy could tell what the swords had been like. One was older, one was younger, that was all they could say. They spoke Scots, like anyone else. No, neither of them had a finger missing or anything useful like that. They were just men. They'd said they were printers from Edinburgh.

"Did they have inky hands?"

"Eh?"

"Were their hands stained? I never knew a printer that didn't have his hands black with ink."

The boys thought, argued a bit and agreed. No, the strangers' hands had been normal, no ink.

Had the minister known them? Cuddy and Andy wrinkled their brows at that. Piers thought carefully. "I think he did," he said, "or he knew of them. He bowed a little to them and invited them into the house. We were going fishing so we went off with oor fishing rods and a basket and he didn't say, good luck boys, but we didn't notice, we just went. Down to the stream, missus, where it hooks round and ye can get salmon sometimes."

"Yeah," said Cuddy, "but we couldna fish there that day, for Mrs Burn was there with Sissy and Mary and me mam to do the linen and the sheets and so we had to go off to the ither place that isn't sae good and none of us catched anything."

"Oh. And did you tell Mrs Burn anything?"

"Ay missus, we told her there were two printers from Edinburgh come to see her husband and she told me mam to take over for a little and finish wringing them out and dry them on the bushes ready for the next day and she went off to see them."

"Oh really. How did she look? Was she frightened?"

Both Cuddy and Andy were scowling. "Not frightened, but she looked excited. Ye ken? As if something good was happening? She hurried up away from the stream to the manse and she was straightening her cap while she went."

"Hm. So do you think she knew who the men were?"

"Nay, ladyship, but I think she knew about them, if ye follow. It wasnae the surprise to her, two strangers in the village."

Elizabeth nodded and wished again that Poppy Burn had stayed in the village and sent for her instead, so that she could ask her about this.

"All right. So what happened after that?"

"After, missus?"

It had been a day like any other. They had gone home with long faces and no fish for the table, and Cuddy's mam had left the linen on the bushes overnight for she didn't think there'd be too bad a dew and the weather looked set fair and come home and done their usual nighttime porridge with some bits of carrot in it, Cuddy hated that, and Cuddy had milked the goats though there wasn't a lot there and then his mam had told him a story and he'd gone to sleep. His dad? Oh his dad was out guarding the Hume flocks and their own animals. "It's the raiding season, missus, ye ken?" She did, though not being born to it as these children were, it wasn't part of her normal assumptions. But all over the Border, most of the men were out in the pasture guarding the animals that were too far away to bring in or that they didn't have enough fodder for.

At some time in the afternoon, Poppy Burn had saddled and bridled her husband's hobby and ridden off on him on the Great North Road, heading south, and had been rained on.

"What about the next day?"

"Ay, well, me mam was in a bad mood for it rained in the night when she said it wouldn't, and so she couldna bring in the linen and she went to speak to Mrs Burn about it early and that's when my Lady Hume tellt her the minister was dead and his wife had run away."

That flatly contradicted what Lady Hume had said about the boys discovering the body.

She couldn't get any kind of story from the youngest, a thin lad of about seven, called Jimmy Tait. He simply cried steadily until the snot was dribbling down his face and Elizabeth gave him her handkerchief because she couldn't stand it. He balled it up and continued to cry and so she left it for the moment.

She sent them all off home to clean their faces and in two cases to put some shoes or clogs on and told them to be back when the bell started tolling. She had asked a minister to come from Berwick but he had refused on the grounds that it was the Scotch kirk and they were all heathens anyway. And all the pastors she knew in Scotland were in Edinburgh, which was too far away.

The smells of spit-roasting meat were crossing the village green which was thickly camped upon. Elizabeth went out through the main door and crossed the little yard there to look out across the green. Her precious wagonloads of beer were still secure in the stableyard and she nodded at the large cousin Daniel Widdrington who was guarding the gate. He touched his cap to her respectfully and she knew that the story of her beating of Sim and Ekie had already started growing. She was annoyed with herself for losing her temper, but there again, what else was she supposed to do? Allow the beer to be pillaged? She didn't think so.

Lady Hume's two large funeral cakes were being borne back from the baker's, half the lads from the school were following the two big lads carrying each cake. Lady Hume herself was standing there with an apron over her velvet kirtle and she was rubbing her hands in glee. "Och," she said, "we willna bake the marchpane but still it'll be fine, Lady Widdrington. Look, not a bit of it burnt."

Elizabeth investigated the cakes with her knife, they were far too big to turn over and knock on the bottom as she would do with a loaf. They seemed well-cooked—a bread dough with some butter and spices in it and then all the raisins and currants and candied fruit from Poppy's store cupboard to make it sweet.

She went into the kitchen and found that Lady Hume and Kat had been very busy about the marchpane and had even managed to find some red and yellow sanders for colouring. They'd also opened two pots of Poppy's raspberry and blackberry jam and they had formed the coloured marchpane into two astonishing flat designs in the old-fashioned way, all curls and curves that looked like dragons. Kat set about painting some of the heated jam onto the tops of the cakes.

With a palette knife and a bit of wood, Lady Hume gathered up the first of the marchpane lids and popped it on the top, then she did it again, her old fingers light and delicate on the fragile creations, so that the two cakes looked like the illustrations from an old book.

"Why, that looks wonderful, my lady," said Elizabeth.

"Ay, I can allus do marchpane."

She used some of the jam to fill up some openings into the swirls and the cakes needed to rest then. They were a very creditable effort despite the lack of time to bake the paste because that took some careful management of the fire and most of the day.

Elizabeth went back into the minister's study. She was looking for something but not at all sure what it was. He always locked the door though he knew the lock could be picked by the boys, and therefore presumably anyone. What was the point of that? She had checked through the other papers on his desk and found only notes for the next Sunday's sermon. Everything was neat and tidy, nothing out of place. On the shelves was a neat pile of sermons that he had given, beautifully written out in his best italic. That was a little surprising, for he had given those. But they were good sermons: well-founded in Scripture, well-thought through and each with a pithy moral at the end. On that shelf there were a number of books on teaching, some in Latin, including Ascham's original, *The Schoolmaster*, well worn and in English. He was the one who had recommended not beating the boys too much since they seemed to learn better for it. She weighed the book in her hand absentmindedly and then put it in her petticoat pocket to read later. James wouldn't mind if she borrowed it now. Then she went and sat in Jamie's chair, looked about her.

It was annoying because the whole thing refused to hang together. If she was honest with herself, she had pictured herself as like Robin, using her brain to pick through all the tiny fragments of truth in front of her and gradually build up the shape of the whole truth. And that would give her the murderers, she was sure of it. But here she was and she had nothing but odd fragments that might or might not have been truth and no shape whatever.

Her husband would have laughed at her and possibly pinched her somewhere for being presumptuous. As far as he was concerned, she was a woman and women naturally have less sense than men and she should leave such things to the men and get back to her business of running his estate and saving him the cost of a steward. The pinches he gave annoyed her more than his slaps and punches because they were so mean and underhand. And often unexpected still.

She sighed. There was Robin Carey in her imagination, wearing the astonishing clothes he had proudly worn at Court, not the one with the lilies, but the tawny doublet and the black trunk hose with the embroidered and pearl-encrusted black cape off one shoulder, the one that had been pawned the longest because it was worth a blinding amount of money. He had worn the clothes for the portrait he had painted to celebrate his knighthood. Elizabeth didn't think it was a good likeness. He was wearing the massive rope of pearls the Queen had given him across his body—though in fact the pearl rope was half the length it had been because he had sold a lot of them and pawned the rest. It was shrewd of the Queen to give them to him and not money, seeing how helpless he was with the stuff.

He was bowing and smiling at her, as he had in fact. He was the very picture of a confident courtier and a very different creature from the battered man she had said good-bye to at the Scottish Court in summer. She had given him back his ring and their eyes had met and...

Their eyes had met. Their bodies had known their business and kept a distance, but their eyes...

She suddenly put her face in her hands and tried not to sob. There were tears coming from her eyes and trying to push them back did no good at all, it was stupid to cry like this and besides she wasn't one of those delicate Court maidens who could weep a couple of crystal tears and not become a sniffling stuffed-up lump. She was Lady Widdrington and had to make sure the minister's funeral, such as it was, went in a reasonably respectful fashion and...

I want him, she almost wailed, I want him to come to me and put his arms around me and tell me it's all right and he'll take care of it and that he loves me. The constant pain in her heart, deeply buried and numbed though it usually was, sharpened and strengthened. I want him now and I want to ride off with him and stay with him and have his babes and nurse him when he's ill or wounded and laugh with him and eat with him and be with him and…

And I can't have that, said the sensible part of her. I can't have it until Sir Henry is dead and buried and maybe not then, if Robin has any sense and marries money like he should. So I should get used to it and not fret after nonsense.

There was a little paw patting her shoulder. She looked and it was the skinny little boy, Jimmy Tait.

"Och," he said, "I'm sad, too, missus, it's awful sad about the minister. Dinna greet though."

How does he know…? Ah yes, he thinks I'm crying for Jamie Burn. Well, in a way I am, for Poppy's lost a good husband and there aren't enough good men around. She coughed and tried to smile at the boy though it was watery.

"Now Jimmy," she said, "what is it?"

"I come to tell ye I canna sing for the minister's funeral." His face was shut down like a little old man's, no more tears, only a sort of despair.

"Why's that?"

"Me dad don't like it?"

"Really?"

"Ay, he says I shouldnae have been going to the school in the first place and I'm tae stop home and help wi' the goats and turn over the muckheap."

"I'm sorry to hear that, Jimmy. Can I come and speak with him about it?"

"Why? Me mam tried to change his mind and he's knocked her down, he disnae like the minister."

"I'll come anyway. I think Sir Henry Widdrington would have something to say about it if he knocked me down." And he would. Sir Henry Widdrington was the headman of the Widdrington surname and his wife was his property. The only person who could hit her was himself, which she supposed was something.

She had her hobnail boots on which was just as well because the Taits lived in a tiny little wattle-and-daub cottage, half dug into the damp Earth and only three rooms—one for the animals, one for living in, and up a ladder under the roof for sleeping. Compared to some of the turf bothies the people put up after their homes had been burned down again, it was luxurious but only compared with them.

The woman was stirring porridge at the fire in the middle of the living room and had a red wheal down the side of her face. She curtseyed anxiously to Lady Widdrington at the door and showed her to the only chair in the place.

"I wonder if I might speak with Goodman Tait?" Elizabeth asked politely.

"Lily, go fetch yer dad," said her mother. "He's fixing the infield fencing."

A girl in a homespun kirtle and dirty short shirt ran off barefoot without a word. Elizabeth thought about sitting on the rickety chair but decided against it in case she broke it. Also it was no doubt the goodman's chair and she didn't want to offend him.

Tait arrived with a brow of thunder and an older boy trotting behind him. He had a dense black beard and black hair and a truculent expression.

"Ay missus," he said suspiciously.

"It's Lady Widdrington."

"Ay. What of it?"

She looked at him carefully for a moment and abandoned what she had planned to say. She looked down at the boy, Jimmy, who was staring at the ground fixedly.

"I understand you didn't like the minister. May I ask why?"

"He was a two-faced bastard."

"Really?"

"Ay. All the time psalms and prayer wi' the boys, and under it he were a bastard, a reiver like any one of us, though he was always preaching against feuding."

"He was?"

"Ay. Ah'm no' a man that goes runnin' to God every time I have troubles, but I draw the line somewhere. I remember the mermaid queen and her connivin' ways and I remember the fighting to stop them and the French, and I'll no' have a son o' mine warbling psalms and what have ye at his funeral. I'm glad he's deid and I hope he rots in hell like all the other Papists."

"Goodman Tait, this is a very serious matter. Did you think the minister was a Papist?"

Jock Tait's face became cunning. "I caught him at it, didn't I? Him wi' his book and his Latin writing. He didnae hide it, only smiled but it wisnae English, for I learned a little off…off of a friend I had once that went tae the Reverend Gilpin. I know the difference." Odd the way he had gulped when he mentioned the friend who could read.

"Was there anything else?"

"Ay, and that slimy tooth-drawer. Everyone thinks he's so great, but he's a London man and what would a London man want wi' us? We canna pay him what London folks can pay. I think he's a Papist, for sure."

"Tooth-drawer?"

"Mr Anricks drew my tooth for me when it was rotten," said the woman. "He gave me a cloth to sniff and when I went to sleep he did it so quickly it almost didna hurt."

Tait snorted. "Ye see? I paid him and I saw him going off to the manse after, in the dusk, like a Jesuit. Maybe he's a Jesuit? In he went and he stayed an hour or two and then he wis out again and on the road south. I saw it wi' my ain eyes."

"I see."

"So I say good riddance tae him and his letters, I'll not have my sons' brains rotted wi' Jesuit teaching."

"Did you kill the minister, Goodman?"

Tait drew himself up and his fists bunched. "I didna," he said, "though I'm glad he's dead. I wis off wi' my brothers and Jock Burn to see to the horses over by Berwick and I'll get every one o' them to swear for me. So now."

Elizabeth nodded. "Is there anyone else in the village who thinks like you—that has the same opinion of the minister?"

"Ay and he wis a reiver once, a good one, when he was young. I knew him then too. And ay, there are some that know him for what he was."

"Who?"

"Why d'ye want tae know?"

Elizabeth thought fast. "If he was a Papist spy then I should tell my husband Sir Henry Widdrington about it, for he's the Deputy Warden of the East March of England. It could be important."

The jaw and fists unclenched slightly. "Oh ay? Ye dinna disbelieve me?"

"Goodman, I don't know. I don't want to tell my husband a pack of lies and yet if there are Papists hanging around here and Jesuits, he needs to know."

That was true as far as it went, although Sir Henry was as likely to take bribes off the Jesuits as arrest them. But she wanted to know. She didn't think Jamie Burn had really been a Catholic; he seemed far too sincere for that, but if others thought he was a Papist that could account for his murder.

There were two others in the village who apparently weren't fooled by Jamie Burn and Elizabeth got their names. Then she tried another tack.

"Goodman, do you think it's wise for young Jimmy to miss the funeral?"

"Eh?"

"Well, you don't want any of the Papists to realise you've spotted them, do you?"

"What're ye saying, missus…ladyship?"

"Just that it'll make Jimmy stand out a bit, won't it? If he misses the minister's funeral and him being needed to sing?"

There was a slight softening now. "Ay," said his father, "he sings well, does Jimmy."

"It's not as if any Jesuits or Papists could get at him at the funeral. I'll be there and Lady Hume and the young Lord Hume and Jock Burn and all the Burns. But someone might notice he's not there and ask why."

Very slowly Tait nodded. "Ay, ladyship, ye're right. But he disnae have any shoes tae wear for it."

"Does he have a jerkin?"

"He's got mine if he wants?" said the other lad, "and my clogs."

"That'll do."

Jimmy trotted after her proudly, nearly drowned in his elder brother's jerkin and tripping every second step in his clogs.

"I'll hae a pair of clogs when me dad finishes them. He's only whittled the one so far, because I grew out of my baby pair."

"That's good," she said, absentmindedly.

"Ay, and I like me bare feet better, though it's cold in winter. My clogs pinched something terrible and I like to feel the Earth with my toes."

"Hm."

"D'ye think the minister's ghost'll walk, missus? With him being murdered and his murderers not hanged yet?"

"I haven't seen him, Jimmy, and I've slept two nights in the house where it happened."

Jimmy's mouth opened in an 'o' of astonishment and he stopped.

"In the manse?"

"Yes, Jimmy, with Lady Hume and her woman. Where else did you think I was going to sleep?"

"I didna think ye slept."

Elizabeth smiled. "I do."

"Och. So ye havenae seen anything?"

"Nothing at all."

He nodded. "Ye don't think his ghost'll come after his murderers and their helpers, do ye?"

"I don't."

He nodded again. "That's good is that."

"And anyway, they say that his soul's already gone to God."

"Ay, but if he were a Papist then he's gone to hell. Or he knows that's where he's going and he doesnae want to go and so his ghost's walking."

Elizabeth couldn't really think what to say. "I think the funeral will stop any of that nonsense," she said eventually, "and perhaps your singing will help him go to Heaven."

"Nay, lady," said the boy gently, "everybody goes to hell, really, only some o' the pastors don't. I was happy the minister might go to heaven, but if he was a Papist there's no chance."

"Will you go to hell then?"

"Ay, o' course," he said. "The minister said not but mebbe he's a Papist. Was. But all the Borderers go to hell; it's warmer there and better company."

She had nothing to say to that.

***

It was the baker who told her something about Jamie Burn, one of the two names Tait gave. He was only a part-time baker, firing up his rock and clay oven in his yard about twice a week for those who wanted bread rather than oat bannocks, quite daring and modern. Otherwise he was a farmer like all of them and he had his vegetable garden as well and even a couple of apple trees that were only thirty years old that his father had planted after the fighting. His father was an enterprising man and had laboured to build the oven, but then died of a flux the year before.

"Ay," said Clemmie Pringle, "that's why I know it, from being up in the middle of the night to fire the oven. I'd see things, men going to and from the manse, well huddled up under their cloaks and sometimes men who went into the manse and didn't come out for a couple of days but ye wouldna ken they were there."

They had been careful but of course that had encouraged nosiness and like all villages everyone was starved for news and delighted to chew over the comings and goings at the manse.

"That barber surgeon, Mr Anricks, I seen him go in any number of times coming to and from Edinburgh and London I shouldn't wonder."

"What do you think it's all about?"

"Papists, of course!" And Clemmie crossed himself against the thought.

"There aren't any here, surely?"

"Ay, well, how would ye know seeing how they have to be secret here where the Humes are for the new religion. It's not like the West March where the Maxwell keeps Jesuits in his household and pops a fig to the king except when he comes on a justice raid."

"And you, Mr Pringle, are you a Papist?"

Clemmie crossed himself again and shuddered. "Nay, I'm a' for the Protestants. Who wants priests coming here telling us what to do and praying in Latin where ye dinna ken what they're saying at all? If I could read, I could even read the Bible because it's in Scots."

It would soon be time to wait by the grave for Jamie Burn's corpse; there were three men digging the grave in the old churchyard now, though given the amount of argument over it, it was just as well that the ground was soft from the wet.

Elizabeth wondered what had happened to the linen and after getting directions from Clemmie, she went down there and found the bushes still festooned with it and most of it dry by now. Well Poppy would need her linen so she found two of the women of the village and convinced them to come and help her fold it up and bring it into the manse.

**

Afterwards, she had to hurry to the church where Jock Burn and three others of the family had a litter and put onto it Jamie's body, wrapped in its shroud. They walked over to the churchyard with it, a good procession of all the people in the village, all the children too, down to the babies in their swaddling clothes raging at the world. Even Clemmie Pringle the baker was there and Jock Tait and the Taits, narrow-eyed and sour-faced, but there. Elizabeth wished Poppy could have seen it.

There were two new people as well who stood next to the Dowager Lady and Kat. One was a ten-year-old boy of outlandish, almost elven beauty, fair hair, and blue eyes. The other was a broad middle-aged man, with brown hair and grey eyes, and a solid look around his mouth with broad sturdy arms and shoulders. They must be Cousin William and Lord Hughie, she thought.

It was Jock who said a few words at the graveside. "Ay well," he said, "ye ken this is my nephew, Jamie Burn. Some of ye ken what he was, when he rode wi' me and his brothers and his cousins and he was a good brave man, though he was young. And then he changed. He went tae the university as a servitor, and he took his degree in Divinity, something no other Burn has done nor will do, quite likely. And then he came back here to be your minister and I hear he did as good a job o' being a minister as he did when he wis reiving Fenwick cattle." There was a subdued snicker from the Burns—clearly a story there. "And somebody came to him two days gone and twinned his body and his head, took his head right off wi' a sword and we dinna ken who it was or we'd do something about it, ay, we would." He paused there and everyone was silent, even the squalling baby. "So...eh...we hereby commit his body to the Earth, dust to dust, ashes to ashes. He's deid and God's got him and there's the end on it."

They took the corpse off the litter and put it in its grave and Jock sprinkled the first spadeful of Earth. The others put more Earth on top.

Elizabeth wished she could have said something about Jamie, about him being a good husband and a good dominie and schoolmaster, about him being a good man whatever he had done in the past. But women didn't speak at church. So she nodded at the boys of the school and they lined up by the grave, pushing and shoving a little. Lord Hughie gravely left his grandam's side and went and stood with the school, who made room for him among the altos. Jimmy Tait was shining and serious in the front.

They sang about the rivers of Babylon, in parts, with Jimmy's voice soaring up the register like a lark and the voices of the other boys turning and twisting in the patterns of the psalms. Then Jimmy started "The Lord's my shepherd" all by himself, only a little sharp from nerves, and the others came in until they were in the House of the Lord together and you could see it in their minds, almost, a good strong defensible bastle with a wall.

Elizabeth had already heard them sing it once so she could look about her and see that rough reivers and Jock himself were crying great tears down their faces, but that Lady Hume had her mouth shut like a trap and a frown of disapproval on her face; others in the village, like Clemmie Pringle and Jock Tait, they were open-mouthed with astonishment at what the boys were doing. At the end of it, Lord Hughie went back to his grandam, who ignored him.

And then as the grave mound was finished and patted smooth with the spades and shovels, Jock Burn hurried back to where the smell of mutton and beef was clear as a bell.

She had arranged with Young Henry to bring the beer out after the body was in the ground, for fear of cunning reivers and also in case anyone disapproved of ale-drinking before the burial, which smacked of Papistry and waking the dead.

They had two trestle tables set up on the green to take the barrels and Jock Burn called Elizabeth over to take the first mug of the mild, seeing as how she'd been defending it all night and her with only an apron to help.

She smiled and laughed, and Sim and Ekie Widdrington were there, with a different set of bruises on their faces, possibly from Young Henry, to apologise for conniving at the theft of one of the barrels and drinking some of it theirselves. Elizabeth listened graciously and said all was well that ended well.

She saw a man standing in the corner by the barrel, drinking from a horn cup of his own and wondered who it was for his black wool doublet and hose were London tailoring, if she was any judge, though from a long time ago. Well she could ask him, so she went over to him and said, "Good day to you, sir, though it's a sad occasion."

He took his old low-crowned hat off to her and made a neat bow. The man was balding though not very old, balding in the ugliest way possible: up the sides and from a bald patch in the centre so there was a moat of baldness around a lone patch of hair on his forehead. It was dull sandy coloured hair; he was not a big man though he had big knuckled hands and a small potbelly and altogether, although he wasn't positively ugly, you would never look at him twice.

"Yes, it is, my lady," he said. "A great loss."

"And who are you? Are you one of Jamie's university friends?"

"Not quite, ma'am. My name is Simon Anricks, I'm a tooth-puller, a barber surgeon."

Ah, the putative Jesuit. His voice was London with a tinge of

West Country in it and clearly educated. Very different from the old tooth-drawer they had had before the Armada that Sir John Forster had arrested and found in fact to be a Papist spy. Was that why Tait was so suspicious? Was he mixing them up?

"Is business good?"

The man smiled. "Good enough. There are plentiful broken teeth from fights and of course scurvy-rotted teeth as well, though I find fewer of the worm-rotted teeth here than I do in Bristol or London."

"Worm-rotted?"

"Why yes, ma'am. There's a school of thought that says the holes in the teeth we find in courtiers and merchants' wives are chewed by tiny worms that live in the stomach and come up into the mouth at night."

"Good God!"

"It's hard to know what else would make holes so I admit that as a working hypothesis. I have a suspicion that they are attracted by sugar, for in days of old, before we brought sugar from Araby, it's said there were far fewer of them, though more of the flat worn-down teeth."

"What about people who can't afford sugar?"

"Exactly ma'am. I find very few of the holes indeed among the poor and the peasants, and when I do, a little questioning often finds that they have a taste for sugar plums or honey or orangeadoes. Here, in the north, of course such refinements are almost unknown and indeed there are even fewer of the wormholes."

"Have you ever seen a...a toothworm?" asked Elizabeth, fascinated against her will.

"I have made some efforts to find them, sitting up till past midnight in the dark with a patient and then opening the mouth very gently with a candle—alas, I have never seen the worms themselves except of course in the stool where they are so common as to be unsuspicious. They must be a special variety of the normal worms of the stomach. Perhaps, as some say, they are invisible—but I do not think so, only very hard to see and perhaps very shy of light."

"Why can't they be invisible?"

"Because then we could not hope to see them, and so I prefer to believe the optimistic view."

Well that certainly sounded a bit Jesuitical, but it could just be that he had read a lot of books. How on earth did you find out if someone was a Jesuit without actually asking them outright?

"Perhaps I should eat fewer of the sugar plums I like myself."

"Indeed, my lady. I would recommend it. I would also recommend scrubbing your teeth every night with a good rough toothcloth dipped in salt."

"I've always done that. Doesn't everyone?"

"Well they should."

"Did Jamie Burn have bad teeth then?" She knew he didn't. His teeth were white and even and like a horse's.

The man laughed a little and Elizabeth tried hard not to suspect he was laughing at her clumsy attempts to cross-examine him.

"He had one tooth he had broken years before which needed drawing and I drew for him. And then we got talking over brandywine and ended by being friends. He needed to talk to someone who read the kind of books he did. I was able to lend him my favourite book by Thomas Digges, about the heavens and crystal spheres, and we had many good discussions about it and others like Lucretius' *De Rerum Naturae* and of course some of the Hermetic books."

"What are they?"

"They are books written by Hermes Trismegistus which deal with…er…well with astrology, among other things."

Elizabeth felt a thrill of suspicion go through her and then damped it down. Astrology was perfectly unexceptionable and didn't the Queen have Dr Dee, her own personal astrologer to cast her horoscope for her? In fact an astrologer was much more respectable than a Papist.

"As Dr Dee does?"

"Yes, indeed, although the good doctor is now more interested in angel magic, which I believe is leading him astray."

"Astray from what?"

"Why, my lady, from the far more interesting question of what are the crystal spheres made of and is it true, as Copernicus writes, that the Earth goes around the Sun and not the other way about?"

"What?"

Mr Anricks smiled diffidently. "I know, ma'am, it sounds quite insane and so I thought it when I first came across the idea, oh, years ago now. But if you read the account of it in Thomas Digges and think about it, well, it seems less mad the more you think about it, that's all I can say."

Elizabeth blinked at him. The idea made her feel very queasy, as if the Earth underfoot were not quite as solid as it seemed.

"Well, everyone knows the Earth is round," she began slowly, "but surely it's at the centre of the universe? How can it not be? And wouldn't we feel it if the Earth were…were moving around the Sun?"

"Perhaps not, if the movement was very smooth. The Earth is enormous, of course, that was measured by Eratosthenes of Cyrene before Christ was born."

"How did he do that?"

"He was very clever: he measured the exact curve of a row of posts of exactly the same length placed beside the Nile at intervals and from that worked out the curve of the Earth by the Art Geometrica. Some twenty-five thousand miles around."

"Good…heavens."

"Quite. If Columbus had heard of Eratosthenes, he would probably never have set out."

There were so many questions she wanted to ask him. Are you a Papist? Are you a Jesuit? What was it you really talked about with Jamie? Not for the first time, she wished Poppy was there where she should have been instead of nearly forty miles away in England.

They were tapping the third barrel of beer over by the trestle tables and the spit-roasted mutton and beef was being consumed by hungry men who were standing around shouting at each other. Behind her she could hear an argument that was not, for a wonder, about whether a shod horse went better than an unshod one. It was a new one and equally fatuous: Which would win in a fight, a billy goat or a ram? It seemed plans were afoot to find out.

The boys were being congratulated on their singing and munching hunks of mutton themselves, while their parents did the same. Little Jimmy Tait was swaying already with the mild ale he'd drunk. It was mid-afternoon and the party would go on into the night. Now if Robin were here he would be wandering around asking Jock Burn how his horses were and telling stories and he would stand over there, by the untapped barrels and laugh and accept a bet on the idiotic ram versus goat question.

He wasn't here. He was far away in the West March and probably thinking of any number of things, none of which were her. Probably he had forgotten all about her as indeed he should. Perhaps his father had found him an heiress to marry and rescue his fortunes. Perhaps he had found another woman to be his ladylove—or at least to bed since the Italian woman who had been all over him in Scotland was now rumoured to be the Earl of Essex's mistress.

She had eaten a trencher of roast mutton and some bread. She had to stay until the cakes were brought out but then she thought she would retire from the fray and try and get an early night. But no, she would have to wait until Lady Hume and Kat went to bed.

Could she start for home now? No. The earliest she could do that was tomorrow when she planned to be up early—though she would have to make allowances for Young Henry's hangover and the hangovers of the cousins. Probably not tomorrow then, or only late tomorrow, she could stay the night at Sir Henry's house in Berwick and hope he hadn't finished whatever he was up to in Scotland so she wouldn't have to deal with him. Then a long run down to Widdrington. If she could take remounts she might be able to do it in one day. It was an awkward distance, about forty miles as the crow flies.

Absentmindedly she drank a bit more of the mild ale she preferred. Two men were taking their doublets and shirts off—why? Ah yes, a ring was forming of cheering men and some of the women, with the boys at the front. Two of the lads were also taking off their jerkins. Cumbrian wrestling. It wasn't really the season for it, but no doubt there was a bet involved, or more likely several.

There was Mr Anricks again, eating some beef and mutton—most of the beef had gone to the senior men of the Burn clan who had large appetites. He was back near her again.

"Lady Widdrington," he said, "I wonder if I could trouble you to let me into the manse? I lent Jamie a couple of books I'd like to get back."

Interesting. She smiled brightly. "Of course," she said, "I'll come with you. I'm not really interested in who can throw someone else into the mud."

The boys were already at it, gripping each other round the middle and trying to get their legs round between the other's legs and then trying to lift and drop, red in the face and shouting insults. One went over on his back, squirmed and turned so the other one was down on his back. There was ironic cheering and clapping.

She walked with the barber surgeon across to the manse and found that it was indeed locked—wise with the number of reivers in the village but who had the key? She went back to the party and found Lady Hume chatting away to Young Henry about how funerals had been in her youth.

"I have a headache," she said, which was actually true she realised. "I'd like to lie down. Do you have the key to the manse?"

"No," said Lady Hume, "I'm sure I gave it to Kat…"

It took a little longer to find Kat who was in a circle of village women singing a long song about spinning while the younger girls danced something energetic. "Oh yes," she said, "I thought it better to lock the place and Lady Hume usually gives keys to me, now where did I put it…?"

The key ring was a large one and must have been taken from Jamie Burn's body. Elizabeth took it and went over to the manse where she found the tooth-drawer waiting patiently by the wall. She found the key to the kitchen door and they went in, through to the entrance hall, and then into the open study which was exactly the same as it had been.

Mr Anricks looked about him and sighed. "I enjoyed my conversations with the minister," he said. "We disagreed about religion and never found it a hindrance. He was very strong for the new religion, for Calvinism, which I find...too logical. But we never quarreled over it. Or we did but not personally; we argued about it and ended as good friends as we had started."

He looked about him at the wall of books and checked some of them, smiled ruefully. "I'm sorry, my lady, but he's double rowed them." It was true: the shelves were deep and there was a row of books behind the ones you could see. "This could take some time."

She smiled, took a spill from the desk and went to get a light from the fire in the kitchen. She lit Jamie's thrifty mutton fat rushdip and sat down in Jamie's chair. "That's all right, Mr Anricks. I'll read some of his sermons—they're excellent."

"Yes, there was an Edinburgh printer interested in them—to publish them, I mean. I advised him to try it, send out some copies of his sermons to printers and see what happened—there are plenty of books of sermons but few that are as pithy as his. I believe none of them are more than an hour long, which is something of a miracle for a Calvinist pastor. If he made any money at it, he could have used it to help poor boys like himself go to university at St Andrews, which he thought was an excellent idea. It might also have got him preferment to another living in addition to this one which would have made his wife's life a little easier with more money, only like the Reverend Gilpin, he didn't approve of having more than one."

Mr Anricks found a set of steps, took the other rushdip and started methodically at the far left top corner of the wall. Elizabeth took one of the italic sheets and found she was distracted by all the books. So many books. Who would have them now? Perhaps the next pastor who got the living, although it was likely he would have other parishes and would probably never come to Wendron. And the boys would forget how to read and become farmers as their fathers had been before.

It was all such a waste. She started to read the top sermon, just to have something to do as she had left her workbag in Widdrington and so couldn't get on with the new shirt for Young Henry. She could hear Jamie's voice as he gave it, the Scots even and musical but the voice deep enough to hold attention. It was about giving praise to God: how it was necessary and comfortable for the spirit to praise God, not because God needed flattery, no, but because it made us feel better. We should praise God always, both when we liked our life and when we hated it. She found herself held and warmed by it, as if he was preaching to her personally.

"Ma'am," came a diffident voice.

"Yes Mr Anricks?"

"Do you know if the minister kept his books anywhere else? I've found one that I lent him but there's another I can't find."

"No, I don't. But we can look."

They did, in the three spare bedrooms, dark and cold and two of them unfurnished, one with just a small bed with a half-tester and a truckle for the servant. Anricks smiled at it.

"I used to stay there when I came to visit. It was very comfortable. Much better than a bench at the alehouse."

"So did I, Mr Anricks, when I came to visit my friend Poppy. I'll see if I can convince Lady Hume to let you stay in it tonight—I doubt you'll get any sleep at all at the alehouse."

"Well," said Anricks, "I've slept in worse places, but yes, that would be very kind of you."

"I can't promise anything until I've spoken to Lady Hume," she warned and he ducked his head.

At the end of it he looked baffled. "I can't imagine he sold it, maybe he lent it to someone else. It's a pity, it was an old friend of mine."

"The book?"

"Yes. Ah well. Never mind, the Almighty giveth and He taketh away, blessed is the name of the Lord."

He smiled at her and she smiled back, somehow liking him despite being near convinced he was in fact a Jesuit. So they had disputed on religion in a civilized way? Jamie was strong for the new religion as she was herself, which meant Anricks must be a Catholic, surely?

She kept her promise and spoke to Lady Hume who was sitting on a barrel clapping to the music from a fiddle and a couple of shawms while the couples swung each other round and jigged. From the look of her she'd had plenty of beer and some aqua vitae from Kat's flask.

Everyone was red-faced and shouting. The cakes had come out and were sitting on the table for the bread, their elaborate marchpane covers shining in the torchlight. Lady Hume took a sharp knife and sliced it all up deftly and everyone got a bit, with the little children getting quite a lot of the marchpane. Mr Anricks nibbled a bit of the cake and smiled when Elizabeth accused him of keeping an eye on who winced when they ate the marchpane as they would be customers for his pliers.

"Have you tried luring the toothworms out with some marchpane?" she asked, and he smiled and admitted that he hadn't but it was a good idea. She introduced him to Lady Hume who looked him up and down and asked him point blank if he was a Papist spy like the last tooth-drawer in these parts.

"No, my lady," he answered, "I'm not, but I don't expect you to believe me. Everyone hates tooth-drawers."

"Nor a Jesuit?"

He smiled and shook his head. "I'm not nearly intelligent enough."

"I willna have ye bothering God in Latin."

"I never speak to God in Latin, my lady."

As there were three women in the main bedroom to keep propriety and the spare bedroom was at the other end of the landing, Lady Hume graciously gave her permission for him to stay the night there, only a little spoiled by hiccups. Cousin William and Lord Hughie came by then, to pay their respects before they rode home. Lady Hume hugged the young lord tight for a moment, unexplained tears making her eyes glitter. The boy took it well, though you could see he was relieved to be away when he mounted up with a steed-leap that nearly took him over the horse's back and down on the other side. He laughed at that, patted the horse for staying still for him and followed after Cousin William.

In the end it was quite easy to get Lady Hume to bed as she drank another cup of aqua vitae and passed out. Young Henry carried her up to bed and Kat and Elizabeth got her undressed down to her shift and put her into bed in the middle. Elizabeth wasn't looking forward to it and envied Mr Anricks his solitary state although it would be cold without a fire. Kat was too much the worse for wear to do more than get undressed herself, take her dose of medicine and fall asleep. The snoring started, Kat's was deep and rhythmical while Lady Hume made a succession of irregular little grunts and mews that was somehow more annoying.

Elizabeth heard Mr Anricks come back with his pack and go into his room. Outside the noise was starting to die down as people passed out or went home if they lived in the village. It had been a good send off for the minister. Tomorrow the village would start to empty of Burns and Taits and Pringles from the raiding families and turn back into the sleepy place it had been before.

MONDAY 16TH OCTOBER 1592

Carey was standing in the little kennelyard looking at the hounds with Scrope. He seemed distracted by something and he looked very tired, with bags under his eyes and he had clearly had brandy for breakfast. Dodd came into the yard in search of him and found him wearily agreeing with Scrope that the hounds needed a good run. Scrope wandered off to look at the latest four-month-old pups with the master of hounds.

A half-grown yellow lymer pup came trotting out of one of the sheds with a stick held proudly in his mouth. He brought it right over to the Courtier and dropped it at his feet in an unmistakable hint. Carey picked it up and threw it over to the other side of the yard, the pup galloped happily off to get it and then found a bit of cow bone that interested him more and forgot the stick. Carey went over to get the stick himself and this time when he threw it, the pup brought it back to Dodd, laying it at his feet with great pride.

Carey smiled at something that would have had him laughing a few weeks before and bent down to ruffle the pup's ears. At that exact moment, the pup jumped up to lick Carey in the face and the pup's nose collided with Carey's chin.

"Aargh, Jesus," shouted Carey, and bent over with his hand to his jaw. "Jesus, you stupid dog."

The dog tried to lick his face again and Carey fended him off. "No, get down, goddamn it!" he roared, and the pup plopped down on his back, peering anxiously at Carey.

The pup's nose hadn't hit him that hard and Dodd wondered what the hell was ailing the Courtier that he made such a fuss about it. The Courtier seemed a little sorry for his ill-temper and he squatted to pat the pup and check his paws. Another determined lick from the dog, still aimed at the lower part of Carey's face and Dodd suddenly understood.

"Sir, have ye a toothache?"

Carey half-looked up at him and nodded.

"It's my back tooth, been giving me trouble for years and now it's bloody killing me."

It was, too. Carey was looking distinctly unhealthy and, come to think of it, his right jawline was swollen. He picked up the stick, threw it again and this time the pup galloped back with it and tripped over his large paws and rolled. Then he lay on his back and let Carey rub his tum, wriggling with ecstasy at it. Carey had his other hand cupped round his face and was still preoccupied.

"Ay, I see, will ye not get it drawn?"

"I suppose I'll have to but there isn't a tooth-drawer in Carlisle at the moment. I asked Mr Lugg but he says he doesn't do teeth, says they're too fiddly and nobody is ever satisfied."

"I heard tell there's a new man who's good over in Scotland the day; will I try and see if I can get him here?"

"If you can, Sergeant."

Dodd nodded. Teeth could be the very devil. He'd never had toothache himself, apart from when he was a wean and his new teeth were growing, oh and when his wisdom teeth were coming in when he was twenty, but he knew people who had. Apart from getting loose in spring and worn down when you were old, if they went seriously rotten they could actually kill you if your face swelled up and the sickness went into your blood. Since Carey was the only thing between Sir Richard Lowther and the West March, apart from the ineffectual Lord Scrope, Dodd wanted him alive and healthy and he sighed at the thought of tracking down a good tooth-drawer, or a tooth-drawer of any kind on the Marches.

They went out to the Eden meadows with all the lymer pups from Buttercup's litter that she had on Carey's bed in the summer, to see how they shaped. The yellow one with the big head was clearly not very bright but he was the friendliest and most willing dog Dodd or Carey had ever seen, and Carey had already decided to have him as his own in exchange for providing his bed for Buttercup's lying-in.

"I'll call him Jack," he said, as they came back a couple of hours later with the five dogs milling around them on leashes. "I don't suppose he'll be much use as a lymer but he's a nice dog."

"Why Jack?"

"Oh my first two dogs were called King and Queenie, but he isn't really a Knave, so I'll call him after the Jack in the All Fours game. It's appropriate."

"Ay," said Dodd. Thinking about it, it was too. Nobody would play cards with the Courtier in the West March now for more than penny stakes.

They let the dogs go off the leashes in the kennelyard and Sandy and Eric, the two dogboys, came out with buckets of bones and guts for them from the butcher's shambles and stale bread from the castle bakery and there was much snarling and gulping until all of it was finished in about ten seconds. The dogboys had brushes and they started the endless job of grooming the hairy dogs until they shone.

Dodd and Carey retired to Bessie's for a bite of lunch. Carey ate the pottage, a thick soupy mixture of pot-herbs, meat, and beans, but only when it was half-cold. He shook his head at the steak and kidney pie.

"I'm like a bloody Papist monk," he said, "no women, soup every meal, wake up at two every morning." He lifted a finger to the potboy and got a cup of brandy. He swilled the brandy round his mouth before swallowing it.

"Hmm," said Dodd, deep in the pie and chewing on the bread he dipped in it. He was considering passing on a prime piece of information he'd heard from Janet that morning before she went back to Gilsland. The trouble was it was vague and Dodd knew Carey always wanted specifics before he would take action. On the other hand he clearly needed something to take his mind off his tooth for the moment.

"I heard tell," he said as he reached for the bag pudding full of plums as his second cover, "that Jock Elliot and Wee Colin have bought theirselves new doublets."

"Oh yes," grunted Carey, ordering more brandy. "So what?"

There was an expensive hard sauce to go with the plum pudding, of sherry sack, butter and sugar, which even Dodd had to admit was delicious. He offered some to Carey who held up his hand palm out and shook his head.

"It'd kill me," he said.

"Well, Jock Elliot and Wee Colin Elliot arenae the ones for fashion. And they may have kin and kine and towers, but they havenae money no more than I do. And I heard that Jock's been seen walking oot in Jedburgh in a tawny velvet doublet that's Edinburgh work and Wee Colin has one the same but in black currant colour."

"Cramoisie," corrected Carey, who knew about fashionable colour names. "So?"

It was obvious but Dodd made allowances for the tooth.

"They've made some siller, that's all. Somebody's paid them a lot of money, on top o' what they normally get from black-renting and kidnapping."

"So they've had some successful raids. What are you suggesting?"

"A Warden Rode on 'em," said Dodd, "find out what they got paid for." He didn't think Carey would really go for it, but it was worth a try.

"Nothing to do with the feud the Dodds have with the Elliots, is it?"

"Och no, that's composed now," lied Dodd. "It was a' arranged back in 1581 wi' the Reverend Gilpin's help and your father presiding." Well, that bit was true, but as for the feud being composed…The Elliots had killed Dodd's father, caused the death of his mother, and the deaths of two of his brothers and a sister. The fact that he had got lucky when he led the remnants of the Dodd surname in the final battle so the bastards had had to come to negotiate was neither here nor there. He still wanted to wipe the Elliots out. Of course they thought the same of him, and that was why he'd had to leave upper Tynedale and come to Carlisle Castle when he was twenty-one, it was part of the deal. Which had held so far, but not for want of his thinking how to break it to his advantage.

And weren't the Johnstones and the Maxwells at it hammer and tongs again in the Scots West March?

"I'm not running a Warden Rode so you can have at the Elliots again," growled Carey at him. "Besides, it's Scrope you'd have to convince of that, not me. He's the bloody Warden."

"Is he no' thinking of going back to his ain lands and his lady wife down to London to serve the Queen?"

"Well he is, but how the devil did you know that?"

Dodd didn't feel it necessary to explain that the men of the guard had been talking about little else since they came back and the bets on it had gone to stupid levels. At least Dodd's investment looked safe.

"When's he leaving?"

"You know Scrope, dithers over everything. Also Richard Lowther would likely be acting Warden in his place, not me."

"Ay? What'll happen to you?"

"Well, that depends on the Queen. If she confirms me as Deputy Warden then there isn't a lot he can do about it, though it would make my life infernally difficult. If she doesn't…" Carey shrugged a shoulder and scowled. "Maybe I'll take up the King of Navarre's offer. I'm not going back to London."

"Och," Dodd was stricken. All that work, going down to the horrible alleys and dangerous women of London, all gone to waste and he'd have to start buttering up Lowther again. "Why not ye as acting Warden?"

Carey's face was as grim as a crow at an execution. "Not senior enough, apparently," he muttered, knocking back his third cup of brandy.

Seemingly there had been arguments and words exchanged between Scrope and his brother-in-law and Dodd now understood why Philadelphia was contemplating going to serve the Queen again. He sighed heavily.

"That's bad news, is that," he said as he finished the bag pudding and sauce and leaned back with his belly comfortably tight. "I didna ken."

A half smile briefly crossed Carey's face. "Well, I'm glad you're on my side, Sergeant, but I may be out on my ear in a few weeks."

"Ay," said Dodd mournfully. "Well, I'll get a nap before we go out on patrol the night."

Carey nodded but stayed sitting in Bessie's commonroom while Dodd set off back up to the castle. A fourth cup of brandy arrived to keep him company.

TUESDAY, BEFORE DAWN, 17TH OCTOBER 1592

Elizabeth woke in the dark and wondered why. She was awake and alert, as if someone had called her name. Had they? She had been dreaming of Robin again, but that was normal, the part of her that dreamt was carrying on with its ridiculous notion that she could ever marry him, just as if reality and Sir Henry did not exist. She hated the awakenings from those dreams because they made her feel so sad.

But that wasn't what had awakened her. What had?

She lay on her side with Lady Hume fitted into her back and Kat Ridley lying on her back and giving a slow rolling grunt. That hadn't awoken her either; she was too awake.

She listened in the dark, probably about two hours after midnight, the darkest part of the night. There was a Moon but it was clouded over. What was it?

Absolute silence pressed in on her. No sound at all, not even the barn owls and the occasional bark from a fox, protests of dreaming sheep, sometimes a snort from a horse. Nothing except loud snoring from drunks outside.

Well, that was it, of course. Why was everything else so silent?

She sat up and decided against lighting a taper from the watch candle. She didn't have a dressing gown against the cold and it was very cold, perhaps not freezing yet but near it.

She found her riding kirtle by touch, missed out the petticoats and bumroll and pulled it on over her head, found her hobnailed boots by the bed and put them on as well.

There was a clink of metal on metal, and a couple of dull thuds, very near the house. Was someone trying to steal the horses? Goddamn it, if Jock Burn thought he could do that, he could think again.

Mind you, if it was Jock Burn then he was a better actor than she gave him credit for. He had been laughing and rolling drunk the last time she saw him and she had seen him pass out contentedly in a pile of hay.

She paused in the passageway to look out the window. Were there more horses in the stableyard than there should have been? It was hard to tell with the two wagons there and the empty barrels waiting to be loaded and taken back to Berwick. Even with her nightsight well in, it was very dark.

Her heart was beating hard and yet she wasn't sure. She didn't dare give the alarm for nothing because the village was full of drunken reivers who would likely wake and then fall to fighting each other if there was nobody else to fight.

She went down the stairs as quietly as she could, then stopped in the hall. She had barred the door herself so why was there a draught from the open window...?

She took breath to give the alarm and found a hard hand wrap itself round her mouth and pull her backwards off her feet. She fought then, fought for breath and to make a sound, was cuffed a couple of times across the ears and then when she managed a small yelp, punched hard in the side of the head with a dagger hilt so the world was turned into a whirligig and she couldn't see at all, couldn't hear anything except voices far away, hissing at each other. Somebody laughed, a thick sound that terrified her.

They laid her down and pawed at her skirts, kicking her legs apart, she closed them with enormous effort, they were kicked apart again and she was kicked in the privates as well. It hurt. Argument again, they were doing what? Tossing a coin? There was another harsh laugh and then a strange noise...A hissing noise like a snake or a burning slow match.

It was a burning slow match. Someone was coming into the minister's study in his shirt and breeches, but with a thing that had a small red light that lit up his mouth and jaw, which were set firm. She part-sat up, shook her head slowly against the dripping stuff going into her eyes, tried to make it out.

"It's true," said the man with the gun coldly, "that I can only shoot one of you and the other can likely kill me. So which one will it be, gentlemen? Which of you shall I shoot?"

At last Elizabeth knew who it was for the London vowels and West Country sounds, it was the barber surgeon, Mr Anricks. He was standing in the doorway, oddly hunched, a dag rested on his left wrist, gripped by his right hand and the slow match hissing in the lock.

The two muffled-up men were backing away from her and Anricks came forward slowly. Suddenly the two made a break for the window, one leapt through, the other followed and the gun bellowed in the confined space.

Anricks was following up, grasping the dag by the muzzle and wielding the heavy ball on the grip like a club but by that time both were through the window and he missed again. The ball connected with the window frame and left a dent. Next moment there was the sound of two horses with muffled unshod hooves and muffled tack riding off into the night. And the moment after that the shouting starting as Jock Burn and the Taits and Pringles came to and started looking for people to fight.

Elizabeth found the world went away and came back again and she was surrounded by anxious faces in the light of several candles as Kat Ridley mopped the side of her head with a cloth. There was shouting outside, Young Henry's voice, bellowing with anger, then hooves galloping... *You won't find them that way*, she thought muzzily, *they're too clever for that*.

Mr Anricks was there, too, decently dressed now in his black wool suit and his hat on.

"I heard Lady Widdrington go down the stairs," he was saying. "I had been woken by something and so I loaded my dag and lit the match off the watch candle, came down with it and by the Almighty's help was able to chase them away."

Elizabeth tried to get up and deal with events and found her limbs go to water and her head whirling when she started to sit up. Behind the crowd, Lady Hume was in her shift and the fur coverlet, watching everything beadily.

She tried again and found it worse, her body refusing to obey her and her head pounding away like a rock-crushing hammer at Keswick.

She was frightened she might die, as you did sometimes from being hit on the head. She beckoned Anricks closer while an argument broke out between Kat Ridley and two of the village women as to how to get her back to bed. "They were Jamie Burn's murderers," she whispered when he squatted down to her.

"How do you know, ma'am?"

Suddenly she realised she couldn't say it was because one or both of them had raped Poppy and had been about to rape her as well. She simply couldn't.

"I..." she started and found she had nothing more to say. His pale brown eyes narrowed shrewdly at her expression. He had seen how she lay, where the men were. And then a miracle happened, he understood.

"Was Mrs Burn also…?" he asked very softly, while making a small gesture at her legs. She nodded and wished she hadn't for the movement made her head hurt and unloosed the bandage so that blood started leaking again into her hair.

"Only…he did it. He did it to her. You came in time for me."

His mouth twisted a little. "I see," he said softly. There was a sudden sense of boiling fury within him and yet none of it was visible on the outside. "I'm glad I was here."

Her tongue wasn't working properly. "I am, too," she managed finally as the cloth on her head fell off. "Ach," she said, and put her hand to the wound there. He brought the candle closer and tutted.

With Kat's help she staggered to her feet, knees feeling like they were made of hanks of wool and bending all the time, was supported into the kitchen and sat on the chair. Mr Anricks was the nearest approach to a medical man there and he brought up all three of the candles so it felt hot. Gently he parted her hair. She hadn't her cap and her hair was plaited for sleep so it could have been worse but it seemed there was a nasty cut where the man had punched her and as head wounds will, it was bleeding again.

Later Elizabeth only remembered little flashes because most of it was the pain in her head and the nuisance of the blood and keeping a cloth wrapped around her neck so it wouldn't mark her kirtle. Lady Hume came trotting in with a pair of sewing shears and a small bottle of aqua vitae and Kat Ridley produced more linen cloths and a bowl of cold water.

Mr Anricks had gentle fingers: he sheared some of the hair short on that side of her head and used the cold water on the cut and then put brandy on it so Elizabeth had to bite her lip to stop herself from yelling. By that time it was dawn and the men were back from their ridiculous chasing across the countryside after two clever men who had crept in among a large number of snoring reivers to raid the manse itself.

Jock Burn was loud in his fury at it, louder because of his hangover. Just as Anricks was wrapping more linen bandages round her head Young Henry came stamping into the kitchen, grabbed her and hugged her.

"Are you all right, mam, did you get shot?"

She hugged him back, feeling the little boy inside the large-shouldered large young man and loving him as she had since she first met him, when he was ten and desperately trying to be brave about his mother. "I'm all right, Harry, truly I am. Just a little bump on the head…"

"Mr Widdrington, one of them hit her on the side of the head and also kicked her a number of times in the legs," said Anricks. "She must go back to bed."

"It was you fired the dag at them, sir?"

"Yes, though I think I missed. At least there's no blood from anyone except Lady Widdrington."

"No matter, sir, no matter. Thank you. Thank you very much." Young Henry was shaking Anricks' hand, pumping it up and down.

"Lady Widdrington must go back to bed," said Anricks very loud and distinctly as to one wandering in his wits, "She has been struck on the head and kicked while on the ground."

"I'm sure I can ride…" Elizabeth started though she wondered how she would get back to Widdrington with her legs like hanks of wool.

"I'm sure she can't," said Anricks.

Young Henry then picked up Elizabeth easily in his arms and carried her up the stairs with no more ado than he had Lady Hume the night before, although she was twice the old lady's size. *When did he get so strong?* she wondered muzzily. *I knew he was large but I didn't know he could lift me.*

Young Henry put her into the bed and she lay back on the pillows and felt deeply grateful she hadn't had to get up the stairs.

"Thank you, Harry," she said, and found he was hugging her again.

"We'll catch them," he said into her neck. "We'll catch them, mam, and kill them. They'll be sorry they tangled wi' the Widdringtons."

"Listen Harry, I think they were the men that killed Jamie Burn."

"Ay," said Young Henry, "I'm thinking the same. But where ha' they gone?"

"I'm more interested in why they came back. They'd got clean away and nobody any the wiser, why the devil did they come back? What for?"

Young Henry was feeling the large spot on the end of his nose that Elizabeth privately thought of as his thinking spot. "Hm, yes, why?"

She was suddenly dizzy again and found it hard to speak. She wanted to tell them that there must be something in the house they wanted and it was possible the tooth-drawer, Mr Anricks, wanted it too although he had saved her. She slowly got her tongue and lips to say all that.

"We'll go out with lymers today and try to find them," Young Henry explained because he wasn't listening properly. "William Hume is lending me a couple of his hunting dogs, he's furious as well."

Young Henry's voice faded as he told Elizabeth what good dogs they were and how Cousin William was also bringing along his forester who was an excellent tracker. She was suddenly exhausted and sleepy. She laid her sore head back on the pillow and let the world disappear again.

***

She woke to the sound of rain and the certain knowledge that she had forgotten something important. She was only in her shift again, her velvet gown hung up and her kirtle likewise. She lay there feeling the old fur coverlet over the bed, it was deer fur and well-cured so it was soft and supple and hardly shed at all. Perhaps it was noon though she didn't feel hungry.

What had Jamie Burn been mixed up in and where did Simon Anricks come in all this? Two strangers had come into the village and killed the minister, then ridden away again after raping Poppy. Two strangers had come into the village again the night before to find something they presumably hadn't got the first time, knocked her down and ridden away again, and given the searchers the slip as well. Simon Anricks had missed at point-blank range but then you often did with a dag; they were hopelessly inaccurate. Was he a Jesuit? To be sure he had carte blanche now that he was inside the manse. If he wanted to find something he didn't need to be elaborate about it. So was there something in the house that two parties wanted, was that it? And what was it? Why was it important? Was it a book? Why would a book be important? Was it a seditious book, perhaps something printed by the Catholics at Rheims to lead folk astray?

She pressed her lips together and scowled. If it was seditious then why would a Jesuit want it? Surely it would be better to leave it where it was and deny all knowledge?

She started to doze off again and there was Robin again, half in her dreams and half out of them, telling her about the different kinds of coding Sir Francis Walsingham had taught him when he was a very good-looking young man and in Scotland with him. He had told her about them in the North, in fact, before she even knew she loved him, way back in 1585, when he had been staying at Sir Henry's house in Berwick, waiting to find out if the Scotch king would let him into the realm with the impossible dangerous message about the Queen of Scots. The one that said that Her Majesty of England had somehow, unaccountably and accidentally and due to her wicked courtiers and in particular one Mr Davison, sent the King of Scotland's sovereign and mother to the block.

Scotland had been a tinderbox and most of the surnames had been united for once in their fury: so what if they had tried to kill the Queen twenty years before? She was their Queen and theirs to kill. How *dare* the Queen of England lop her head off on the specious grounds of treason when she was a sovereign queen and certainly not Elizabeth I's subject? It was outrageous. The Maxwell had sworn to kill Carey for carrying the message, as had Buccleuch and Ferniehurst and most of the headmen of the Marches.

She still remembered the first time she had seen him, wearing a forest-green hunting suit, rings on his fingers, his hat on his head, sweeping it off in a Court bow to her when her husband, of all people, introduced them. She had curtseyed wondering why her heart was suddenly thumping inside her stays and why her knees were knocking. Her body had known him before she did, she thought.

It had taken months for the careful messages to go to and fro to Edinburgh and back, and all that time, Elizabeth had found plain Mr Robert Carey, as he was then, a terrible distraction and worry to her. He had gone hunting a couple of times but stopped when he was chased back to Berwick by a large group of men who had also shot arrows at him. Apparently he had put his head down beside the horse's neck in the true Border style he'd learned when he was a boy in Berwick and galloped into Sir Henry's stableyard with an arrow actually through his smart London hat. He had laughed uproariously at it and worn the hat with a hole in it until he bought a newer higher-crowned one a couple of years later.

"The easiest method for coding for someone who isn't able to figure and calculate the numbers is to make your code another book and refer to the page and line and letter. If you use the Bible, which you shouldn't because it's the first book anyone checks, then page 1, line 1a, word 3 is 'beginning.'"

"1a?"

"That's another reason for not using the Bible because there are often two columns on a page and you have to call them a and b—gives the game away at once."

That had been after a fashionably late dinner in Berwick with two covers of food and a large salmon for the cheapness, as it was a fish day. They had been discussing other ways of getting messages to people. It was not relevant since the point of Mr Carey was that someone had to carry the message and apologise on his knees to the Scottish King, and Robin had volunteered for the dangerous job as he tended to do for any dangerous job that happened to be lying around and looked interesting.

Carey had sung the praises of Mr Phelippes who was Walsingham's chief code breaker. Mr Phelippes had once taken a despatch that had just come in, looked at it and immediately held it to the candle to find the invisible writing on it in orange juice. He had also broken the codes painstakingly used by the Queen of Scots in her imprisonment so as to catch her red-handed plotting against Queen Elizabeth. After the meal, Carey had sung for them from memory several of the Italian madrigals that were so fashionable at Court and taught them a complicated round that Young Henry could manage and Elizabeth could sing as well, while Sir Henry drank sack and watched them.

It had been a delightful evening, a pleasant interlude and afterwards she had realised that she loved the man because she dreamed a lewd dream of him and woke flushed and excited in the cold early morning with Sir Henry snoring beside her. In the dregs of the dream, Robin had kissed her gently and then faded as she realised they were both mother-naked.

Eight years gone. Eight years. Jesu.

She sat up carefully and rubbed her face, carefully felt the side of her head that still had bandages on it. It hurt but not too badly and her legs and crotch hurt, too, but she was used to bruises. She really wanted to get back to Poppy and find out what was going on there but she felt she couldn't leave while the killers of Jamie were at large and coming into the manse. What if they came when Poppy was there or tracked her down to Widdrington?

She found a mug of ale put beside the bed, sniffed it and found it had laudanum in it, which she didn't like. She got up and reached under the bed for the jordan and her hand brushed homespun wool and a bony leg. She pulled back with a cry and backed off, found a rushlight holder and grabbed it as the nearest thing to a weapon.

There was a squawk from under the bed as well and a head poked out from under, a thin little face with swollen red eyes.

"Jimmy Tait!" she snapped. "What the devil are you doing under my bed?"

"I'm sorry, missus, I'm sorry..." sniffled Jimmy, "I wanted to get awa' from the minister's ghost and ye said ye hadn't seen him and I thocht ye might be safer..."

She put the rushlight holder down and clasped her hand over her heart which was drumming like a maying drum.

"Jesu," she said, sitting down on the bed and fighting a wall of dizziness that came out of nowhere, "when did you get in there?"

"Och, last night, I crep' up the stairs last night."

"When?"

There was panic on the bony face. "I didna do naught, missus, I didna, I only crep' up the stairs while ye were busy in the kitchen…"

"While Mr Anricks was treating my head?"

"Ay."

"And what were you doing here last night anyway? Why weren't you at home in bed?"

For an answer the child started a steady ugly snivelling, with a great deal of snot.

The dizziness had passed again and Elizabeth advanced on the boy where he sat like a little frog by the bed with his face in his hands. She picked him up, feeling his cold hands and feet which were bare of his brother's clogs again. He weighed hardly anything, nothing like the sturdy lads that Young Henry and Roger had been when they were a similar age.

God knew what kind of passengers he had in his clothes, but there was no help for it; she had to know what was wrong with him. She wrapped the deer hide round the boy and gave him her ale with the laudanum in it.

"Are you hungry, Jimmy?" she asked and he nodded. "Can ye bide there a while and I'll get you something to eat." He nodded again but the tears kept coming.

She pulled her velvet gown on again over her shift and went down in her bare feet as she had no slippers. The house seemed empty, no sign of Kat or Lady Hume either. Perhaps they had gone back to the castle. Looking out the windows the village had gone back to its sleepy emptiness with most of the men busy with plowing or up in the hills with the stock, some of the women working in their gardens or in their houses.

In the kitchen she found the remains of the calf—really fit only for soup—and about half a roast sheep. She cut some collops off, found the range fire had been allowed to go out, and went back upstairs with a trencher of wood and a stale pennyloaf.

She had to go back for seconds about ten minutes later as Jimmy wolfed his way steadily through the food and drank the ale. Elizabeth had found a half barrel of mild ale that hadn't gone off yet and tapped it for herself.

At last Jimmy stopped chewing and gulping and burped.

"Thank 'ee missus," he said. "Ah'll be going now…"

"There's no hurry, Jimmy," she said, "unless your father's waiting for you?" A firm shake of the head. "Well then, bide here and keep me company."

She got back in the bed with her gown on, and pulled the sheets and blankets round her.

"I've decided to go back to Berwick tomorrow not today," she explained to Jimmy. "My head's still sore and I keep feeling dizzy. So I'm staying in bed today but it's lonely." It wasn't; she liked being on her own and she could have gone down and borrowed a book as well and risked being found reading it.

"Will I sing to ye, missus? Me mam likes it."

"Yes please, Jimmy. Can you sing me a ballad?"

He could. He opened his mouth unselfconsciously and sang her all of Tam Lin with both the tunes—quite an achievement for a lad of his age—and then a couple of the psalms. His voice was high, sweet and as true as a bell, silver to Robin's bronze, now she thought of it. Robin too had a marvellous voice but she thought this boy's voice was better. It was so pure she felt a thrill down her back at it, that something as clean and clear could exist in the fallen world.

"My dear," she said, "that's wonderful. You have a gift from God there."

He ducked his head awkwardly. "Thank 'ee missus."

"I expect the minister liked it too?"

"Ay," piped the boy. "He said the same, a gift from God too. His eyes were watering, I remember."

They may well have done, Elizabeth thought, at finding something so beautiful and fragile in the ugly mud and blood of the Borders.

"Are ye truly no' afeared of the minister's ghost?"

"No," she said, "I'm not. He was a good man in his life, wasn't he?"

"Ay, missus, he was. He gave me food sometimes like you, he gave me a bun once and he taught me to read singing as well as letters, said my voice might get me into Carlisle Cathedral choir if I worked hard."

"Now did he?"

"Ay missus, he did. He wanted me to grow a little and then he said he might take me there hisself if my father was agreeable and 'prentice me to the choir. Is it true they do that, missus? That ye can get your living by singing?"

"Yes, it is. What a splendid idea!" Elizabeth's mind was instantly onto the possible solution to Jimmy Tait. Could she take him to Carlisle herself and perhaps meet Robin...? No, she couldn't. It was a lovely idea but Sir Henry would instantly see through it and give her another beating. That no longer worried her the way it had, though she was afraid of it, of course. But in fact to do something like that would be dishonourable. And what would be the point of her torturing herself by getting nearer to Robin when she couldn't have him?

She sighed. In any case, she could surely find someone to take the lad to Carlisle, Young Henry for example. There was no need to go herself.

Suddenly the child had jacknifed over and was crying again. "That's why...that's why..." he was saying, "...that's why I'm so sad, missus...He...he..."

She stroked his nitty hair and let him cry.

"Listen to me, Jimmy, the minister was a good man, wasn't he? Would he ever have done you any harm while he was alive?" She waited until she got a watery shake of the head. "Well then, why do you think he would harm you when he was dead, even if he hadn't already gone to Judgement?"

For answer she got more tears and finally she understood something.

"Did you do something you think might make him angry?" she asked. "Did you, Jimmy?"

His thin face had snot teeming down it as well as tears and dirt but she saw the tiny nod.

"What was it?"

The voice was almost too small to hear. She thought it was something about horses.

"Whose horses did you guard?"

"Them!" cried Jimmy, "The murderers. Ah wis set to it by my father, and I didna think any harm to it, he said they wis just coming to ask the minister nicely for something and I stayed by the horses in the wood and after a bit they come back and they gave me a Scotch shilling for the work and rode off and I didna ken till the next day what they'd done. I didna ken."

"Did you know the men? Had you ever seen them before?"

"Nay missus, they wis strangers, naebody fra the village nor the castle. I never seen 'em in my life and they wis muffled up too."

"How did they sound? Were they Scots?"

"I dinna ken. They didna say much. Mebbe not."

"What did they look like?"

"Och they wis big and the older one had some grey in his beard and the younger one smiled at me and that's all I can tell ye, missus. I often look after strangers' horses for me dad."

"Do you now?"

"Ay. Or pack ponies."

Smuggling probably, thought Elizabeth.

"Do you think you might know them again if you saw them?"

"Ay missus, I think so." He started crying again, "If I hadnae looked after their horses…Och, the minister wad still be here and we'd be learning us oor lessons and…"

"Now Jimmy, I want you to stop thinking that way." Elizabeth paused. "You didn't know when you looked after their horses that they were going to kill the minister, did you?"

"No, missus. Ah thocht it was just business, ye ken."

"Quite so. You couldn't have known that they were going to do anything of the sort and even if you had known, what could you have done about it?"

"I could ha' shouted, or run ahead and warned him? He

didna wear a sword but I heard tell fra my dad he was a bonny fighter once the day."

"Of course you could, if you'd known. If you'd known you'd have done that, wouldn't you?"

"O' course I would and got my friends to come and they'd have all come running and we could have stood between the minister and the murderers and…"

"And probably Jimmy, they'd have knocked you aside and done it anyway. You'd have done that if you'd known what they were about but you didn't know. So it isn't your fault at all. It's the fault of the men that did the killing."

"Mebbe I could have guessed?"

"How? How could you have guessed? Did they say anything like, now we're going to kill Minister Burn by chopping his head in two?"

"No. They wis arguing about somebody called Bessie and whether her steak and kidney pie or her chicken pie was the best."

"There you are. How could you have guessed from that?" Though it was interesting and backed up the idea they had come from the West March.

He was staring at the rucked up deerskin. "No, I couldn't."

"Ye could not."

"But mebbe his ghost will come after me anyway."

Elizabeth paused a moment to think and took a deep breath. What she was saying was probably heresy, but she needed to stop the child crying. He was a witness, she needed him able to think and speak. "If there are ghosts then they're the spirit of the dead person, aren't they?"

He clutched the deerskin round himself tighter and nodded. He had deep circles round his eyes as well, poor lad.

"And do you know what a spirit is?" He shook his head. "A spirit is the soul of the person, the deepest part, the part that goes to God. Yes?" A small nod. "Now is your soul better or worse than the rest of you?"

"It's better, I think, missus."

"I think so, too. So even if the minister had been a bad man and full of sin, his soul would be the best part of him. But he was a good man with no more sin than most of us so his soul will be better still, yes?" Another tiny nod. "So his soul would never hurt you, Jimmy, nor even frighten you. He's gone to God anyway."

"I dreamed of him."

Elizabeth tried not to sigh. "What did you dream?"

"I don't know. I just saw him in my dream and tried to run away."

"Did he say anything to you?"

"I couldn't hear it so I ran. And then I got stuck in a bog in the middle of the study."

"Well Jimmy, perhaps he was trying to tell you it was all right and he wasn't angry? Did you think of that?" A tiny shake of the head. "Perhaps if he comes back he'll just say, 'Jimmy, I loved yer singing at my funeral. Thanks lad.' Do you think?"

At last a tiny smile. "Mebbe."

"Can you think of anything else they said, no matter how little? Can ye tell me from the start, what happened."

"Well I wis milking the goats because I was late home from the minister and they were making a noise and carrying on and I was milking them and my dad sent Young Jock to me to say he had a job for me and Young Jock would finish the goats. So I run to my dad and he says I'm to go to the steward's copse and I'd find some horses there and I'm tae look after them till their owners come, which was two business friends of his and I done it before and so I…"

"Why were you late home?"

"Och, me and Archie were watching some slugs to see if they turn into birds but they didna and so we stamped on them. So I went to the copse and there were four nice horses there, wi' different brands on 'em, two one brand, two the other. I gave 'em some horse nuts my dad sent with me and gave 'em all a rub down and then I waited wi' them. And then the men come back and one was older, I remember that, didn't know them, I'd never seen 'em before in my life…"

"Would ye know them if you saw them again?"

Jimmy nodded slowly, his black circled eyes enormous. "Ay,"

he said, "that'd help the minister to rest, wouldn't it? If he saw the murderers hang?"

"I'm certain it would," said Elizabeth, still heretical.

"So they wis arguing about Bessie and which pie wis better and one was laughing and saying the little wifey wad remember him too and the other one..."

"Which was that? Who said that about Mrs Burn?"

"The younger one, with black hair, and the older one said, ay, ye were lucky again."

"Again!"

"Ay, and then they said they'd be going and the younger one giv me a Scotch shilling..."

"Did you keep it?"

"No, I gave it to me dad and he said it was forged but he might get someone to take it."

"And the men went away?"

"Ay, and I took the Graham horses all the way South to where they told me. Nice horses they were too, though one had thrown a shoe."

"The men asked you to do that?"

"Ay, the older one, he said, the shilling is for you to take the horses down to the Border and not tell anyone, so I took 'em nearly all the way and give 'em to a horse trader named Tully."

"One was grey and one was chestnut?"

"Ay missus, how did ye know?"

"I know those horses. They'd been ridden hard too?"

"Ay, and the hobbies wis fresh. So I took them all that way and come back and I got me bread and milk for the evening late and went to sleep with Young Jock and in the morning..." Jimmy shook his head and tears started leaking again. "In the morning Andy Hume came running to tell us the minister was killt and... and I didn't know what to do or nothing, missus, it was terrible, worse than when the Widdringtons raided the infield and took our four mares and a gelding. Andy said, they've killt him, they took the top of his heid off."

"How did you know it was the strangers?"

"We saw them go in, didn't we? We saw them and never tried

to stop them. I saw them too, when I come out of school and they went in and they was talking when they went."

"How did the minister seem? Was he laughing, pleased to see them?"

"Not exactly, more serious and stern but he knew 'em."

"What did they say?"

"The minister said, 'I'm not going out again. Spiny can wait.'"

"'I'm not going out again.' Are you sure he said that?"

"Ay, 'I'm no' ganging out again, Spiny can wait.' Then they was in the house and I didna think nothing of it."

She took him through the tale again and it came out pretty much the same and there was the name she knew, or might know.

"Is there any reiver around here called Spiny?"

Jimmy frowned and thought. "Not that I know of, missus. I did wonder but it might be someone fra foreign parts like the West March or England."

"Or Edinburgh?"

"Maybe."

That name made it something different from a Border matter, that made it a Court matter. The Earl of Spynie was King James' current favourite and a bad man to cross for all his youth, although he was starting to lose his beauty already, and with it, his hold over the king. She had known him when he was plain Alexander Lindsay, laird of Crawford too, and hadn't liked him then for all his pretty ways and charming smiles.

What had Jamie Burn done for Lord Spynie? Or to Lord Spynie? If Spynie had had Jamie killed, it accounted for the way of it and for the fact that the men had had money to spend on horses and hadn't been interested in the contents of the plate cupboard.

And Jock Tait had known the men, had he? He might not have known what they planned, but he knew them. Jimmy was useless as a witness but Jock Tait was ideal, an adult male who hated the minister.

The problem was how to get hold of him and find out the names from him. Oh, and persuade him to be a witness.

MONDAY 16TH OCTOBER 1592

Dodd was irritable. He had been looking for a tooth-drawer all morning, had found it was true that Mr Lugg didn't do teeth, had heard tell of a tooth-drawer in Scotland but the man was called Johnstone and he didn't like to risk it. He had heard from two sources, the undertaker and Thomas the Merchant, that there was someone lately over on the East March and one said the man's name was Ricker and the other that he was called Henry. It wasn't enough to go on, but the swelling on the Courtier's jaw was getting worse. He had wrapped a scarf round his face against the cold and he was looking distinctly peaky. And he was drunk as well.

The only thing Dodd could think of was to go and find Lady Widdrington. She seemed to have a good grasp of the East March, her husband was the Deputy Warden, and the tooth-drawer probably had needed to bribe him anyway.

He asked permission from Carey to ride to the East March on the grounds his wife wanted something from Berwick, and Carey had given it without much attention. He was at Bessie's playing cards on his own; he called it a fancy Italian name, and it was clearly his way of distracting himself. Dodd took his favourite horse, Whitesock, legally bought and his this time, with the Queen's brand now cancelled by another one, half-healed. He had a warrant from Scrope, who was happy to give Dodd some despatches as well so he could ride post.

He liked riding post. You could do a hundred miles in a day with luck, probably less going across the Border, and he'd have to be careful in some places, but he could be in Widdrington at the end of a long day and he planned to be. Also the Courtier's sarcastic temper was getting on his nerves and he wanted to be away from it.

Widdrington was quiet and peaceful in the evening when he clattered in on the last post-house's horse, which was blowing and making a fuss. He'd never been there before and eyed it carefully despite the dusk, in case Carey could get over his stupid scruples and they needed to make a rough wedding party.

There was the castle, not on a hill—the whole village was flat and the sea nearby, the road the most important part of it. It was rich, you could see, a village supplying grain and horse feed and food to Berwick.

The castle wasn't large, not much more than a sturdy manor house with a much older tower and a wall around it for the villagers to bring their stock into when raiders came. He came to the gate, showed his warrant and went on into the main yard to find a pretty young woman who was heavily pregnant and an elderly man receiving him with a couple of the broad young Widdringtons hanging around as well to see he behaved himself. He smiled at them, liked it that they bothered.

"Ma name's Sergeant Dodd. I've come tae see Lady Widdrington. Is she about?"

"Lady Widdrington isn't here, sir," said the man. "She's north of the Border in Wendron."

"Can I help you, sir?" asked the woman. "My name is Mrs Burn. I'm a friend of Lady Widdrington's."

"Ach," said Dodd, very annoyed. He had dismounted and the horse was pulling toward the stables after his fodder. Dodd had ridden hard for the last ten miles to be into Widdrington before dusk. He took the horse into the stables, was shown the feedbins and set up the horse with a nosebag and a bucket and started whisping him down with brisk strong strokes. "Where's Wendron then?"

"It's about forty miles from here, sir," said Mrs Burn who had followed him. The steward had gone off somewhere else. "Would you like to stay here this night and start in the morning?"

Dodd thought about it. He could have kept going, though he'd need a different horse, but it was full dark now and the Moon not much use. He had to admit he was a bit tired after cantering and galloping for most of the day, and hungry as well since he'd eaten his bread and cheese in Haltwhistle on the Giant's Wall.

"Ay," he said, "that's kind o' ye, missus. I could do wi' a bite to eat as well."

"I think there's a pie and the cook's made a pottage and a stew, or there's bread and cheese and some apples too."

That sounded more like it. "Thank 'ee kindly, missus, I appreciate it."

"Oh, Sergeant Dodd, I've heard about you from Lady Widdrington. I'm very pleased to meet you at last and you can keep me company at dinner."

He wasn't sure about that since he was no kind of gentleman and would have preferred the despatch rider's room at the inn and beer in the commonroom, but he supposed it would be rude to refuse.

He found Roger Widdrington, the younger son of Sir Henry, was also in the dining parlour, making himself pleasant, which was interesting. Dodd knew about his part in the disaster in Dumfries that summer. Mrs Burn sat beside him with a girl—who was clearly there to learn huswifery, and Mr Heron, the reeve, as well, so it was quite a supper party.

Roger Widdrington said grace and the great pie was on the table with some soused hog's cheese and the pottage and stew, so Dodd helped himself to the venison and rabbit pie and the pottage as well.

He asked eventually about the tooth-drawer, though he said it was Scrope who needed a tooth out, since he was in Widdrington, after all. Mrs Burn's face, which was rather sad in repose, lit up.

"Oh yes, Sergeant Dodd, there's a new man in the area. In fact he was planning to go over to the West March soon."

"Ay? Do ye ken where he might be?"

"Yes. Minister Burn and I know him quite well. He's not like the usual run of barber surgeons. He's interested in reading and books and he's supposed to be very good at drawing teeth too. He's called Mr Simon Anricks and he's all the way from London."

"Fancy that," said Dodd, reaching for more hog's cheese since it was very good. He took some more bread too, since that was manchet. You had to admit that lords and ladies saw themselves well for food. "Is he a spy? The last tooth-drawer but one in the Middle March got caught with a mirror with letters fra the Pope behind it."

Mrs Burn laughed. "I don't know. Perhaps he is, you'll have to ask him. Now I think about it, he's probably in Wendron now with Lady Widdrington because...because..."

And just like that she turned to crying. Dodd sat back in astonishment and watched.

"Her husband was killed a week ago," Roger Widdrington explained quietly. He didn't do much about it, just let the woman greet into a handkerchief. "Two men walked into his house and cut his head off."

"Och, that's bad," said Dodd, sympathetically. "It wasna even on a raid? I'm sorry for yer trouble, missus."

She nodded at him as she tried to get a hold of herself.

"We'd like to find out who the men are, obviously," said Widdrington pompously. "I'm waiting for another despatch from my elder brother who is with Lady Widdrington."

Dodd nodded. It was cheeky, that's what it was. And it would be difficult to find them too, because they could just ride away and nobody any the wiser. Or at any rate, nobody any the wiser who would tell on them.

"Mrs Burn was there at the time too," said Widdrington, "that's why she's so distressed."

"Ay?" said Dodd. "That's shocking." He supposed she couldn't be expected to do anything about it since she was clearly not a Border woman. Her accent was a little strange, something like Scottish, something like English from the West March, something guttural. The woman got awkwardly to her feet and curtseyed to Widdrington, left the room still crying, followed anxiously by the girl.

Dodd, Widdrington and the steward ate most of what was left of the hog's cheese and the pottage, though the pie was a giant and they left three quarters of it for the morning. They talked about drainage ditches and they talked about hobbies and who was raiding whom in the Middle March and the West March. Dodd brought them up to date with the Maxwells and the Johnstones, who were only raiding sheep and cattle at the moment, feints to see where the weaknesses were.

At last Dodd was shown to a little room next to the stables that was full of the comforting scent of horses and a bed with a tester as well, and so he got to undress, which he wouldn't at the inn.

TUESDAY 17TH OCTOBER 1592

He was up as early as he could manage the next morning, two hours before dawn, feeling cold and miserable as usual. When he went to the kitchen in the hope of pillaging some more of the pie, he found it unlocked and a candle lit and Mrs Burn sitting there alone, waiting for him, while the kitchen boy snored on his pallet with his blankets round his ears.

"Sergeant Dodd," she said, "I'm so sorry I had to leave the dinner table last night, but it comes on me sometimes and I can't stop crying. I loved Jamie Burn, no matter what he was before and it...I can't help it."

Poor woman, Dodd thought, that's worse is that, if you loved your husband as well. His mam had loved his dad and she'd gone from being a big plump happy woman to a sad skinny one in a matter of months after he'd been killed. What would he feel if Janet was dead, now?

It was the first time he'd thought of it, strangely, and just the thought made his stomach squinch up under his ribs and his bowels go to water. Jesu, he thought, I'd be a lost man. He shook his head and deliberately crushed the thought. Janet would have to outlive him, that was all.

"Ay," he said inadequately, "Eh...Ah wis wondering if there's any pie...?"

She smiled at him. "It's a good one, isn't it? I've got some breakfast and lunch here, ready packed, and I'm hoping you'll do me a favour for it."

"Ay missus," he said cautiously, sitting down facing her.

"It's all right," she said, "I won't ask you to kill my husband's murderers for me, unless you happen to come upon them and have a rope ready…"

He smiled. "Ay missus, I can promise that…"

"I just want to send a letter to Mr Anricks. He was such a good friend to Jamie, I want him to know that I think Jamie left him something in his will and a few other things."

She had a letter from her bodice, quite a thick packet. Dodd hesitated and then took it. He'd already given the despatches from Scrope to Roger Widdrington who would pass them to his father; he might as well take this.

He put it inside his doublet, inside his buff leather jerkin that he wore because it wasn't exactly business and you went quicker if you didn't wear a jack.

"If you could give that to Mr Anricks personally," she said, "I'd be very grateful."

Maybe she was having an affair with the tooth-drawer, Dodd speculated. She was a pretty woman or she would be if she didn't have such black circles round her eyes.

"Ay missus," he said. She smiled at him then and gave him two neatly wrapped packages which he carried into the stableyard where he found a sleepy young boy holding a nice-looking hobby for him, already tacked up.

He was off a couple of minutes later, taking the hobby at a brisk walk and then to a trot for half a mile before he put his heels in and went to a canter.

TUESDAY 17TH OCTOBER 1592

The boy went to sleep eventually and Elizabeth dressed and left him there to go to see his mother. The father wasn't there and she had bruises on her wrist and the bruise on her face was the shape of a hand. At least it was an open one.

Not thinking about Sir Henry with great difficulty, Elizabeth sat down on the stool the woman offered her.

"Now, Mrs Tait," she said, "your lad Jimmy has a beautiful voice, hasn't he?"

The woman smiled and her face changed from its watchful shut-in look.

"Ay," she said, "The minister heard him once when he was scaring crows and singing the Twa Corbies to frighten them and then nothing would do but that he'd go tae the school and learn his letters and sing for the minister. My man didna like it at first, but after a while he said it was fair enough since he got bread and cheese at the school to his dinner and so he didn't need so much as Young Jock and Lily and the babby."

There was no babby visible. The woman coloured and paled. "He died, the babby. In the spring. Eh...he fell over and...hit his head and that was the end of him."

I don't think so, thought Elizabeth, but didn't say, *I think he annoyed his dad and got hit too hard*.

The woman wasn't looking at her. "Young Jock's the apple of his eye mind, but..." She shrugged and looked away and gave her sore bruised wrist a rub. Well, to business. It looked like Elizabeth was following in Jamie Burn's footsteps but no matter. There were worse ones she could choose.

"I think your young Jimmy could go to the cathedral in Carlisle and be a singer at the services there. How old is he?"

"About seven, I think. He came before the Armada, any road."

"Well he's young, but that's no hindrance. Did the minister speak of this with you?"

"He talked to Jock about sending Jimmy to Carlisle," said the woman, "And Jock wanted money for the boy."

"Really?"

"To...to replace him as a crow scarer, ye ken. And his labour in the fields when he got big. And..."

"What did the minister say to that?"

"He said he'd think about it and we left it at that."

"When did he talk to you about it?"

"About a month ago, when we were sowing the winter wheat."

Elizabeth drew a deep breath and let it out again. "What did Mr Tait need the money for?"

"He wants a new helmet, he said."

"How much?"

"Ten pounds."

It was outrageous. Fifty shillings for the boy would have been the going rate, but ten pounds? Tait was clearly a canny father with a good grasp of bargaining.

"I see."

"And the minister got him down fra twenty. I dinna think the minister had ten pounds but maybe he saw a way to get it, ye ken," said the woman in a whisper.

"Oh? What way was that?"

The whisper was so tiny, so soft, Elizabeth couldn't quite make it out. "What?"

"The old way," she said, a little louder. "The way the minister's brother Geordie would get it, or any one o' Ralph o' the Coates' boys. The way Jock would hisself. Reiving or killing. Insight."

"Ah," said Elizabeth. After a moment she rose to go. "Thank you, Mrs Tait, that's very helpful. I'll think about the money."

She didn't have ten pounds herself; it was an enormous sum, although a reasonably respectable suit would cost you ten times that. But you'd get the suit on credit and pay for it over six months or a year. She felt quite dizzy again as she walked up the hill from the Taits' farm and had to stop for a moment at some stones from a peel tower destroyed in the Rough Wooing.

There wasn't a lot of reiving now in the Scots East March, or the English East March, most of the trouble happened in the West or Middle March. The Humes held sway in Scotland and dealt with troublemakers their way, the Widdringtons and the Fenwicks were strong enough to deal with troublemakers in England. Blackrent was another matter. Occasionally you'd get a big invasion, forty or eighty men from the Middle March might come riding into a valley at night and take all the stock and insight that wasn't locked inside a wall, and ride off again. Then there'd be the usual arguments over it at the next

Warden's Day and eventually it would all be composed, but nobody would get back all they had lost or expect to.

Murders happened, too, mainly for not paying blackrent or for revenge. And yet when you thought about it, what had been the reason for Jamie Burn to get his head taken off? A pastor didn't pay blackrent, and revenge…

Elizabeth's eyes narrowed as she stared at some large stones leaned on even older ones. Revenge might well be a reason, especially given the way the minister had been spoken of. Perhaps it was for something he did when he was younger.

She realised that one of the rocks in the grey light was not a rock, but a straight back wrapped in a wolf fur. It was too small to be a man so after she stepped back she stepped forward again. Who was it? It turned a little face under a shock of white hair and a linen cap a little sideways, with a fine Edinburgh hat on top of that.

"Ma'am, Lady Hume?" she asked, in astonishment, "what are you doing here?"

"Well I like it here, my dear. Do ye not know it's a faerie fort? At night the stones all float together and build themselves up again and then ye can dance and sing with the lairds and the ladies too, dance yer heart out and then in the morning it's grey and fifty years ha' passed ower yer head and ye're an old woman and al' the lairds and ladies are deid and gone and passed."

Elizabeth looked about for Kat Ridley and saw her, sitting on another moth-eaten old wolfskin, some way back, watching carefully. A little further off was a lad with two ponies, a palfrey and a jennet, nice animals both of them.

Lady Hume seemed to be waiting for something as the late afternoon squelched away, sitting patiently and bolt upright, her head a little tilted on her ruff. Elizabeth moved round to where Kat Ridley sat, knitting away at a pair of socks.

"Er…"

"She's waiting for the fairy fort to build itself—she does it when she's like this. She willna have nathing but to come here and wait till night for the fair fort and she usually dozes off and then she'll go hame quite happily. Cousin William's no' far away, he bides out o' sight for she doesnae like a man too near when she's awa' wi' the fairies like she is the day."

"Ah. Do you know whose tower this was?"

"Ay, it were the Taits', pulled down by Wharton, and his grandfather hanged by the gateposts."

"You mean Jock Tait, in the village, his grandfather?"

"Ay, who else would I mean, there's nae ithers round here. There may be some distant cousins in Upper Tynedale, but this was their easternmost tower and a fine place it was."

Elizabeth was starting to understand.

"The grandfather?" she asked.

"Nay, the eldest son," said Kat Ridley, "Hanged next tae his father to learn 'em for being reivers and Scotch forbye. By Lord Wharton in 1544."

Elizabeth nodded.

"It wisnae a bad match for a Burn girl, mind, and she wis the pick o'the Border then, a little delicate girl with white blonde hair, so I hear, but then after it was all over and we were picking up the pieces and building turf bothies, she was seen by one of the younger sons of the Laird Hume of Norwood and it wisnae a good match for him but it wisnae so bad the old Laird forbade it for a younger son so they married. Then when the elder brother died of a fever, she became Lady Hume."

Elizabeth moved back and sat next to Lady Hume, erect and still as the twilight came down.

"It's aye hard," said the old lady, "I allus doze off and I wake and the music's still ringing in my heid, Chevy Chase, and my feet are tapping and a foul spell's come upon me for I'm an old woman again."

Elizabeth could think of nothing to say to that. She started to hum Chevy Chase, though, the repetitive song so you could hear the verses. Lady Hume smiled and nodded at her.

"Ay, ye're right, it's like that. And who're ye, girl?"

"Lady Widdrington?"

"Och, ye've got an ill man to wed there, if it's the Henry I knew. He liked breaking the wings of birds when I saw him when he wis a child, but he's terrible afeared of heights."

"I didn't know that."

"He allus kept it secret. And the puir minister. He shouldnae have gone back to the reiving, should he?"

"Did he?"

A sharp elbow went into Elizabeth's ribs. "Och, ye know he did, he was out last month in the Middle March. Couldnae keep hisself from it, could he? Once a reiver, allus a reiver, I say."

Elizabeth nodded. "You're right. But he must have reived the wrong cattle."

Lady Hume giggled at that. "In a manner o' speakin', aye, that's why they killt him so gentle. Not hanging so he danced for half an hour like my Archie, but off wi' his brainpan."

"Do you know who did it, Lady Hume?"

She just frowned. And then she stopped and sighed and turned her head as the stars came out in a couple of gaps in the clouds. "Ay, d'ye hear the music? Ay?" She sat rapt, her eyes shut, her head nodding slightly to the beat of the silent music. After a while she drew in a deep breath and sighed it out again.

She dropped off to sleep then, curled over and down like a small animal, laid her head in Elizabeth's lap and went to sleep with a smile on her face.

Elizabeth sat and thought. Killed him so gentle: compared with many a Border killing or indeed a judicial death with no drop and a long choking death on the end of a rope, it was a gentle death. Paradoxically because it was hard to think of anything much more brutal than a knife under the ribs followed by a long sharpened metal bar coming around and cutting half your head off, but yes, it had been a quick death and a clean one. Almost a kind one, as such things were reckoned on the Borders.

That was interesting. It was also interesting that Lady Hume had been the first to know, seeing she was a Burn and some kind of aunt to Jamie Burn. Somebody must have told her, or she was a witch or the faery folk had told her.

You could but ask. Elizabeth stroked the old head in her lap, pushed the white hair back and straightened the cap and took off the hat which was getting slightly crushed. It was a respectable hat.

"Lady Hume," she asked softly. "Lady Hume, who was it told you Jamie was dead?"

She asked a few more times and was about to give up when Lady Hume moved her head and answered with her eyes tight shut.

"They did, ma'am, the two men that killed him. They rode over and told me all about it and I was sick and sorry for it, that I was, but I knew Jamie had been out the month before and I knew what he was at and…that's why they tellt me. It was a way too high for him and me, I know it now. And they rade away intae the night and I went to horse meself the next morning for it wouldna be right for the minister to be unburied, no matter what."

"What was it? What had he done?"

"Ay, it was terrible, how he was, part of his head had rolled a way but I brought it back tae his body."

Her eyes were still shut, was she awake? "He's dancing with me now, ye know, he's dancing and laughing and his head's back together again, dancing along of all the ither people, like my Archie Tait and the people in the wood and the archers and the English archer and a' the puir folk we couldna feed for the English had burned their fields and their goods and they had nothing and they starved and died. They're all dancing with me here now."

"Who were the men? Can you tell me that at least?"

"Och, I don't know, I couldna tell ye any more, it's hard to tell all o' them now. Not Geordie, that's sure."

"But…"

"And they're bringing in the boar's head now and we're singing for it," said Lady Hume, eyes tight shut, the night making it hard even to see her face, and she started humming a version of the Boar's Head Carol.

Elizabeth sat with her until her arm was cramped and her bum had gone numb from sitting on the rock. Kat Ridley came with a blanket and behind her the broad silent man who nodded and said "ma'am" to Elizabeth, and then took the old lady in his large strong arms. Kat held her while he mounted his horse and then handed her up to him with her hat and he rode off northwards to the castle.

Elizabeth looked impatiently at Kat Ridley. "Do you know who came to her to tell her Jamie Burn was dead? Do you know their names?"

"Nay, ma'am, I told ye, I took the washing down to the washerwoman and I didna…"

"They came at night."

That gave Kat Ridley pause. She put her head on one side. "No," she said, though Elizabeth thought she was lying, "I must have been asleep."

"Were you?"

"Ay."

"And do you know what the minister was at a month ago?"

An almost invisible shake of the head. "Nay, ma'am, he wouldna tell me, ainly herself."

Elizabeth sighed and said good-bye to the woman who was only doing what she was told, trudged on through the night to the manse where she found Young Henry and all four of the cousins anxiously waiting for her and found herself being scolded by him for wandering around the village on her own.

"Don't be daft, Young Henry," she laughed. "I'll come to no harm…"

"Ma'am, a man punched ye in the heid and knocked you out a day or two ago, how do ye know they're not still here?"

"Well he…"

"They might still be after whatever it was they was looking for and…they might see ye and think it's a great time to find out where it is, or kidnap you and make us give it them, whatever it is."

"Oh." Now she thought of it, she had been careless. "I'm sorry, Henry, you're right. I started in daylight and went down to see the Taits and then came back and met Lady Hume at the old burnt peel tower and got overtaken by dusk. I never thought of that."

Now she had thought of it, it gave her a bad feeling in her stomach, an anxious unhappy feeling. Henry made a few more pompous speeches about being more careful and she waited him out because he was right. She wasn't at Widdrington now, where the only real danger to her was Sir Henry.

"You're quite right," she said. "I'll start for home tomorrow."

Well that was no good, either, apparently. Was she quite sure she was all right, had she felt dizzy…? She had, but she certainly didn't want to tell him. "I'll decide in the morning," she said after she had listened patiently to about enough of it. "I'm for my bed."

She went upstairs to the big bed with its tester and curtains and found herself the only occupant, not even a girl sleeping on the truckle. Henry and the cousins were sleeping downstairs and where, she wondered, was Anricks?

Before she got undressed, she took a look in his room with the old bed in it and saw his pack still there, half open and with his instrument case taken out so presumably he was treating someone.

She thought about it, and went downstairs again. A little later she had young Cuddy Trotter's mam coming pink-faced and flustered up the stairs to sleep in her bedroom with her and keep the proprieties. Henry had the grace to be embarrassed about that, he'd forgotten about the barber surgeon.

When Anricks came back, with blood still under his nails, Henry asked him belligerently if he still wanted to sleep upstairs.

"It's perfectly all right, Mr Widdrington," said Elizabeth to her stepson. "I have Mrs Trotter to sleep with me."

Henry scowled at Anricks as if it was his fault everyone thought he might be a Jesuit.

Anricks took his instrument case into the scullery and used a bucket of water there to wash his instruments, which were fine ones of steel and looked fragile for the heavy work of pulling teeth.

"Mr Widdrington, would you like to inspect my mirror and my tools?" asked Anricks with a perfectly straight face. "I assure you I'm not any kind of Jesuit or Papist."

"So you say, sir," said Henry who was clearly still upset about something, although Elizabeth had no idea what.

Anricks brought the pack over and the instruments and plopped them down in front of him. "There you are, sir," he said. "Will you be wanting to search me personally?"

"Er...no."

Henry made a half-hearted search of the pack which contained shirts, hose, breeks, bandages, a packet of mouldy lamb pasties that had to go out into the yard and onto the dung heap, several small books including Ascham's *The Schoolmaster*, and a great deal of writing paper thickly scrawled.

"What's this?" asked Henry, holding up a page between thumb and forefinger.

"My book, sir," said Anricks, still equably. "My accounts of the North and my thoughts on the tooth-drawing trade and also my speculations on the nature of toothworms."

"Yours?"

"Ay sir, perhaps I may get it published next time I am in London. If I can come up with a way to prevent holes and rotten teeth, I will be famous and rich."

"What way is that?"

"I think the avoidance of sugar is one thing, for toothworms seem to be attracted to it. In a family where one child loved sugar plums and the other child preferred cheese, it was the sugar plum-eater who had the worms and the holes, although..." Henry grunted and squinted at the writing.

"Why can't I read it?"

"I don't know, it's in English."

Henry flushed and turned it the right way up and started to puzzle out some of the words. "For toothworms, if they exist, must live in the stomach and come into the mouth by way of the throat..."

Elizabeth smiled. Anricks had a strange kind of patience, a watchful intelligent kind that does not allow emotions such as doubt or anger to interfere. Suddenly she found herself wondering about him again. Jesuits were supposed not to lie about being priests, though according to the pamphlets, they could equivocate.

Perhaps she could find out more about Jamie Burn from him.

"Gentlemen," she said, "none of us have had supper and I'm hungry. Shall we eat whatever's left in the larder and be friends?"

There was the end of a hambone, there was more pottage, there were quite a lot of bits of calf, though no one had thought of the perfectly simple operation of putting the bones and some potherbs to a large pot of water and making soup, and there was the remains of the sheep as well.

They served it up in the Burns' dining parlour as one remove with some bread that needed to be toasted to make it edible. They brought in the remains of the beer and the ale, which was just on the turn and would be spoiled by the morrow. Elizabeth invited Mrs Trotter to join them and the Widdrington cousins as well, although they were on watch, strictly speaking, since Henry wasn't about to allow another incident like the last. But they agreed to take it in turns, and she reserved plates for the two on watch first who were Humphrey and Daniel. Hector and Sim were understandably nervous of eating at her table but she reckoned honour was satisfied and served them some of everything and some of the ale they had nearly allowed to be reived as well.

She sat at the other end with Young Henry and Cuddy's mam, Mrs Trotter, and Mr Anricks as well and as the eldest man there Young Henry gave place to him. Mr Anricks said grace. It was slightly unusual. "Blessed be you, Lord God of the World, of your goodness we have this meat and drink to our dinner, which Earth has given and human hands have made." But it wasn't Catholic, not being in Latin.

"Amen," she answered to it firmly and took some of the veal which was excellent even cold; she'd boil it up into a soup tomorrow just on general principles.

They talked of neutral things until Elizabeth thought that you can but ask again and said to Hector, "By the way, were you working for anybody the other night or was it just a bit of foolishness?"

"Foolishness," said Hector who had come at her with a knife.

"Jock Tait," said Sim with a lowering look at Hector. "It were Jock that tellt us he had some buyers for the beer and what would we say to a shilling?"

Young Henry put down his knife and glared at Sim and Hector. Elizabeth managed a repressive glance and smiled at the two lads, neither of them over nineteen, she thought.

"Och," said Hector.

"Did he say who the buyers were?"

Both of them shook their heads. Sim too had a splendid crop of spots though he wasn't as big and broad as Young Henry.

"Did you get your shilling?" Two heads shook sadly. "I thought not. Have you ever ridden with Jock Tait?"

"Ay, o' course," said Hector and Young Henry was now staring busily at his food and stirring the pottage.

"Ay, well, ma'am," said Young Henry. "It's when we're hitting the Routledges and the Carletons that we...eh...well we ride wi' the Taits and the Burns."

"And the Elliots?"

"Wee Colin? No, he's an unchancy bastard though him and Geordie Burn are thick as porridge together."

"So Jock Tait's a good man, is he?"

"Ay," said Sim, "he's no' extra special wi' anything like Young Henry can shoot wi' a gun, but he's a good solid all round man, good wi' a lance and a sword if he had one, and he's good at scouting too."

"I heard tell it was the Elliots who wanted the beer?"

"Nay, ma'am," said Henry, "they like the Burns."

"So who wanted the beer?"

"Perhaps it was Jock Tait himself," said Simon Anricks thoughtfully. "To spoil the funeral, since you say he doesn't like...didn't like the minister."

"Perhaps," she said, "and I heard that Jamie Burn was out last month, reiving. Surely that's not true?"

How very interesting the faces were. Young Henry was surprised, and then thoughtful as if it wasn't such a surprise after all. Hector and Sim were not surprised. Simon Anricks, just for a second had an extraordinary look on his face, of understanding and regret and worry, which closed up at once into conventional shock.

"Ah dinna ken, missus," said Hector with a warning look at

Sim that should have molten his helmet which was sitting beside him on the table.

"Well, never mind, I expect it was just gossip," agreed Elizabeth brightly. "You two can go and relieve Humphrey and Daniel now."

They clattered off while Elizabeth served some more of the mutton to Young Henry and Simon Anricks, then helped herself to half of what was left.

"Jock Tait's the hero of another tale I heard, too," she said while Humphrey and Daniel shovelled food into their mouths. They weren't brothers like Ekie and Sim, sons of one of Sir Henry's younger half-brothers, but cousins. Sir Henry had many sisters and brothers and half-brothers and they all lived round about Widdrington. As a surname it was numerous and had a name for being fierce for the Middle March, where the village actually was. She told how she had found out the horses were looked after by young Jimmy Tait and the scrap of dialogue the boys had given her, how someone called Spiny could wait.

Young Henry put down his eating knife and looked appalled.

"The Earl of Spynie?" he asked.

"I don't know," she answered regretfully. "It could just be a reiver with very wiry hair."

"Good God, if it's him…"

"It doesn't actually help us find the murderers," she told him, "but Jock Tait could. If we could persuade him to give us the men's names and be a witness."

"I suppose going to him with the cousins, grabbing him and hitting him until he told us wouldn't be a plan you'd like?" said Young Henry, good humouredly.

"No, Henry," she said, "it's like all short-cuts—gets very long in the end. If we did that do you think he would stick around to be a witness at the trial? If there is one? He might not tell you anyway, he looks a tough nut to crack. And besides," she added, "you have no jurisdiction of any kind here, this is Scotland."

"I have the right to follow the trod," said Young Henry, "same as anyone else."

"You aren't here on a trod, you're here for a funeral."

He didn't answer and looked mulish. Simon Anricks was looking very thoughtful and she thought she'd do some more stirring, again on general principles. It sometimes made her very tired the way menfolk tried to keep their reiving and other dubious behaviour secret, as if women could be fooled so easily.

"Mr Anricks," she said, "you were friends with the minister. You don't think he really was out last month?"

Anricks answered slowly. "I knew he wanted some money quickly because he asked me about it, but I said I couldn't help him. And he said something then that worried me but I put it out of my mind. I shouldn't have done, I regret it greatly."

"What was it he said?"

"When I said I couldn't help him, he said, no matter, he already knew another way to get the money and he'd look into that."

"Did he say what the other way was?"

"He said he'd talk to the Kerrs, that's all."

"The Kerrs?" The Kings and Princes of the Middle March, in other words. Some of the worst reivers on the Border, north or south. "Cessford? Ferniehurst?"

Anricks shrugged. "That's all he said, I wish I'd asked him but I didn't. I just told him to be careful."

In the end they could come to no conclusion about Jock Tait except to see if they could bribe him. And also Elizabeth had a worry that Tait would know who had told Elizabeth about the horses and young Jimmy might be badly beaten, or even killed. It had to be done with great care, as with everything else on the frontier. The only person she knew who really rejoiced at such complexities and loved working them out was Robin, whom she was duty bound not to contact. Where was he now? Was he well? She'd have heard if he was married because her husband would tell her, immediately, but had he met anyone else? It was right for him to marry someone else, God knew he needed the money, but...

Anricks went to his little guest chamber and Elizabeth recruited Humphrey and Daniel to take the trenchers and dishes into the scullery. They put them in to soak in the bucket of water Anricks had used and left them.

In the bedroom, Elizabeth invited Mrs Trotter to share the big bed rather than the truckle with the hole in it and listened drowsily to a very interesting account of young Cuddy Trotter and how he loved his lessons and how he could read all manner of things like a Bible in the church and a ballad sheet too, read it right off as if he had just heard it and how excited he'd been the month before. The minister had been full of excitement as well; they were talking of all making a journey to Carlisle, all the boys in the school in October and...

"All the boys in the school?" she asked, wide awake again.

"Ay, my lady," said Cuddy's mam, "they wis all to walk tae Carlisle together, him and them and they'd go the long way about it fra here down the Great North Road tae Berwick and they hadnae decided whether to go across the tops of the Cheviots or take the long way round from Newcastle by the old Faery Road behind the Faery Wall, tae Carlisle. He thought it would take a week but..."

"Why not go to Newcastle? It's much nearer?"

"Ay well, it's the choir at Carlisle. He wanted tae see if any o' the boys could be 'prenticed singers there."

"Would you like Cuddy to do that?"

"Ay, I would, for Cuddy could be a clerk or even a minister like Minister Burn hisself but Cuddy canna sing at all so I doot they'd take him. Still, it's an adventure and the boys wis all for it and maist o' the parents. Maist."

"Not Jock Tait."

"Ay and one o' the ithers, but the minister said it was a' or none and he'd see tae it. He was planning to take Lord Hughie as well."

"Why was he doing all this? He didn't have to."

"Ah, that's the Reverend Gilpin for ye."

"I've heard that name before."

"It wis a priest and then a reverend a while back, in England. He had a living somewhere in the South and soft and plenty o' money and instead of sitting on it and getting fat he came oot here to the Borders and made schools for the boys, taught them hisself, he did, and the best he sent tae the university. All in England, though, but Jamie Burn heard him preach once and went tae him and lied and said he was an English Burn. He wis at the Reverend Gilpin's school in the South when the fighting over Queen Mary and the Earl of Bothwell wis on and came North again when his dad sent for him and wis a bonny reiver. But he could ha' gone to St Andrews and when he'd made enough as a reiver, that's where he went, tae the university, to learn him Latin and Greek and Divinity for to be a minister like Gilpin."

"Oh. I never knew. What happened to Gilpin?"

"He wis killt by being run over by a bull, I know that, it got loose in the market and trampled him and he died a month later and all his boys came from far and wide to sing at his funeral, Jamie Burn too. It was in the early eighties, I think, before the Armada, and that's when the minister made up his mind to gae to university and so he did."

"I see."

"Gilpin used to preach wonderful sermons, he'd tell all about Hell and how there wis no Purgatory and how tae stay oot of Hell and get into Heaven—which he said wis easier nor anybody thought, because ye could just clap hands wi' God and He'd see ye right."

"Did you hear him preach?"

"Nay, but in church the minister told us some of his old sermons, which was good ones, when he hadnae the time to think of one of his ain."

"Hmm."

"There's another one where Gilpin says every reiver ye teach to read is peradventure one reiver the less for if a clever man sees no fair way to make his living, why then he'll use foul ways and cause a lot more trouble than a stupid man."

"Very true."

"Ye should read them, they're good and comforting. Like the minister's ain sermons but not one o' his was more than an hour, ye ken."

"So I heard."

"It's a pity they willna make their journey tae Carlisle now," said Mrs Trotter wistfully. "It's a real pity."

As Elizabeth dropped off to sleep, her jaw was set and the expression on her face fierce.

WEDNESDAY MORNING 18TH OCTOBER 1592

She knelt to her prayers with a will the next morning, knelt and practically shouted at God that He should help her with what she thought of as the minister's legacy or she would want to know the reason why. An extraordinary thing happened then: She got the feeling of a vast and intimate smile, a warmth in her chest as if she had understood something important and lovely, except she didn't know what it was.

She stood up and went out, told Young Henry who was practising gunnery in the orchard that the noise was giving her a headache and she would ride over and see if Lady Hume was well. He sent one of the cousins, young Hector since nobody else was around, which she accepted with reservations. Hector was all smiles and "my lady" so perhaps he had learned his lesson. She took a satchel with her, with pens and ink for she had contacts at the Scottish Court, and in particular Lord Chancellor Maitland who had begun as a friend of her husband's and become a friend of hers.

She had already packed up all Poppy's shifts and caps and stockings with her spare kirtles and aprons in a tight bundle inside her cloak which had been loaded onto a pack pony at the alehouse. Right in the middle of the bundles were the three goblets and the dish with cherubs on it that were Poppy's dowry. She had Jamie's will in her petticoat pocket and she couldn't think of anything else apart from the books which would need a string of pack ponies.

On the ride she thought so hard about the letter she was thinking of sending that she didn't notice at first that a man on horseback was paralleling them. She looked about for Hector and saw him, a way away, riding hell for leather in the opposite direction. Her stomach twisted and turned to stone and she looked about, rising as high as she could and peering. Two more riders were just out of sight, popping up every so often.

That was enough. She took a deep and careful breath and thought about it. The track up to the Hume castle was muddy but it went into a wooded area about a mile ahead and since nobody was doing anything yet, she was willing to bet that there was somebody waiting for her in the wood. Three out there, three more in the wood, perhaps.

They knew she must have seen them and they knew she had no man with her to guard her. They were still about two miles from the castle which was a longish run.

Her heart was beating hard and heavy in her chest and her mouth was dry. What could she do? What should she do? If she had been a man her best bet might have been to turn her horse about and ride for the nearest one. Or go into the wood and fight them there. Stupid to think like that, she was not a man.

She really did not fancy the wood; it looked muddy as well as autumn dark. No, so she wouldn't go there. The castle wasn't big, it had a moat and a curtain wall and a gatehouse as well once you were past the wood, of course. It was a scrubby little wood, a copse really, that had been allowed to grow up since the Rough Wooing. Why? The Humes weren't fools, and nor was Lady Hume, away with the faeries half the time though she was. You didn't let stuff like that grow up on the main route into the castle—unless it wasn't the main route. Unless it had been allowed to grow to give a good ambush place for people who didn't know what the right route was?

She hadn't been to the castle but she felt a rightness to that. Why else would they do that? And forbye, they would want the main entrance to the north, toward Edinburgh, not the south.

All right. She put her hand up to her hat and pinned it on tight to her cap, which hid the sore place on her skull and the cut hair. She set herself down into the sidesaddle, gripped with her leg around the hook and put the heel of her other leg into the horse's side so the animal leaped forward and started to run.

She rode at the gallop under the eaves of the wood, bent low to avoid the branches, dodged round a couple of trees and bushes, and then burst out again and rode around the wood and round the edge of the moat. She didn't bother to check the riders to see what they were doing, but kicked the horse again to get some more speed and rode like a madwoman around the curve of the old mound and there it was, a moat and working drawbridge.

The drawbridge was up. She hauled back on the reins and managed not to go into the moat.

There was a shout behind her, there were five of them now. She gave them a fig with her right hand while she rode out her horse's bucking, speaking softly to him, poor soul.

There was a man on the wall, not Cousin William, looking down at her and the men.

"Let me in," she shouted, "they're after me."

"They are?" said the man. "They're no', are they?"

"Ay, they are."

"Why?"

"I dinna ken," she shrieked in broad Scots. "Will ye shoot one for me so Ah kin ax?"

To her fury, the man turned away, bent, picked up a loaded crossbow and aimed it at her. She knew the men behind her were coming up closer.

"Her ladyship says she's sorry, but ye canna come in. She canna help ye."

Her horse was turning and crowhopping still. She only had seconds. She took off her mother's handfasting ring and threaded it onto a bare autumn twig of a hazel bush. Then somebody's strong fist caught the bridle and somebody else came up close to her with a scarf. She looked round at them, hard faces under helmets, wearing jacks that marked them as Burns, though she didn't recognise anybody. She was still buoyed by rage.

"How dare you!" she hissed in English now. "How *dare* you? You will regret this."

"Ay, mebbe, missus. Meantime, ye come wi' us."

WEDNESDAY 18TH OCTOBER 1592

Dodd reached Wendron by mid-morning and found his bird flown again.

"Och," he said when he found he had to ride another ten miles to Norwood Castle where Lady Widdrington had gone to pay her respects to Lady Hume. "I need another horse."

Young Henry Widdrington gave him a little hobby with the warning that the beast had a nasty temper and would bite. He remembered to give the letter to the small man who came out of the house to see him and introduced himself as Simon Anricks. He was trotting up the road half an hour later with his belly growling. Since Lady Widdrington would keep, since she was no doubt blethering on to her friends and had forgotten the time as women did, he stopped by some trees and rocks and ate up the first of the packages that Mrs Burn had given him, which contained a hearty wedge of the pie, bread, cheese, a couple of pickled onions wrapped in waxed paper, and an apple. This was the nicest food he could think of and he ate all of it, especially the apple. Lady Widdrington must have an apple tree or know someone who did and he found he wanted one too. Not a sapling, mind, but a full tree, less for the apples than for what it meant, which was that nobody had burnt the country for at least twenty years.

Well, you never knew. When he had finished the apple which was quite sweet, he looked around to make sure no one was watching and then dug a hole and buried it in the Earth.

He rode on to the Hume castle and found the place open as he expected, though he wondered what had been going on nearby since there were hoofprints of a horse galloping and others overlaying it before heading off across country.

When he rode in there was a sprightly old lady in a hat and velvet gown and her stout middle-aged woman standing behind her.

"Och, yes," said Lady Hume with a sweet smile. "She came to say good-bye and then turned about and went home tae England again."

"Ay," said Dodd, annoyed. How had he missed her then? Maybe when he was having his breakfast? "When was that?"

"A couple of hours ago," said the woman, also smiling. "It wis nice tae see her."

"Ay, thank 'ee kindly," said Dodd and turned the hobby's head and aimed south.

He went quicker on the way back, despite the hobby's tricks, which kept trying to turn his head west instead of south, but Dodd prevailed after a couple of tussles. He didn't want to miss Lady Widdrington again.

He saw Anricks again to the north of the village, riding a hobby and leading a pack pony, looking worried—though from the lines on his face that expression was a habit. He tipped his hat to the man. Then he took another look at the pack which was currently stowed on the pack pony behind him. It was brightly painted with lurid pictures: one showed a man with a swollen face and a scarf wrapped round it. The middle one showed a set of pincers and a bloody tooth, and the third picture showed the same man without a swollen face, happily tucking into a dinner consisting of venison and pork ribs and pot herbs.

"Ye're never a tooth-drawer?" he asked, unable to believe his luck.

"Yes, I am, sir. Do you have the toothache?"

"Nay sir, but I know a man who does, something terrible. What d'ye say to coming tae Carlisle wi' me and drawing his tooth?" He was quite willing to kidnap the tooth-drawer if it was necessary, but he hoped it wouldn't be.

The man's face lit up. "I would be delighted, since I've been planning to go to the West March, but I must confess I was nervous of the notorious robbers and reivers there."

"Ay," said Dodd, not bothering to explain that they were no worse in the West March than the Middle and certainly better than here in Scotland. The man wasn't very large and didn't look at all dangerous with his balding pate and modest black wool suit. "Come wi' me whiles I find Lady Widdrington and give her my respects and then we'll be off." Dodd wasn't that interested in the ordinary-looking woman who had so bewitched the Courtier, but he knew her and must at least greet her while he was in the area.

Back at Wendron, Young Henry was looking impatient. "Where is she?" he asked. "We've forty miles back to Widdrington and it's late."

"They said she'd come back here," said Dodd, also annoyed. Wasn't that just like a woman, gallivanting off on some notion when people wanted to get home.

"And I canna find Ekie nor Sim," said Young Henry darkly. "I sent Ekie Widdrington with her to look after her."

"Maybe she's fallen off her horse somewhere," said Dodd, since he had heard that this was something that did happen to people occasionally. "She can't have gone more than five miles, mebbe less, let's circle the castle at about five miles out."

They did that, heading in opposite directions to get it done quicker, and found nothing. Anricks came with them. When there was no trace of her, Dodd started to get worried as well. Kidnapping of women wasn't unknown in the Borders, although as he understood it, the Widdringtons were a mite tasty for that kind of behaviour.

Then he minded him of the marks near the castle of the galloping horse, overlaid by other hooves, and he cantered back to them, dismounted, and started using his eyes properly. He saw a shod horse, not a hobby, riding toward the castle, saw it slow and then change direction and yes, go into the wood a little, saw broken branches where someone had broken through them at the gallop, saw the swerve at the edge of the moat where the drawbridge was now down, saw the other horses, all of them unshod hobbies surrounding and overlaying the shod hoofprints. It couldn't have been clearer if somebody had set up a little play to show it to him.

"Och, Jesus Christ," he swore disgustedly to the hobby who gave him a horsy leer and shook his head.

He hadn't a hunting horn to call the others so he had to ride around the castle again, now watched by a man on the walls, found Anricks first and told him to go and guard the traces, then Young Henry, who was already scowling. At least the ugly hobby was now cooperating.

"Come and see this," he said without preamble and Young Henry followed him at once.

Anricks was looking at something on a hazel bush when they got there. He pulled it off and brought it over to them as they cantered up and Dodd saw it was a woman's ring, a gold handfasting circle.

"I found this," he said. "It was on the bush over there. Is it Lady Widdrington's?"

"Ay, it is." Young Henry's wonderfully spotty face darkened as they both dismounted and Dodd explained what he could see. Once it was pointed out to him, Young Henry could see it well enough himself.

He loosened his sword and pulled out his horn, winded it and then stood fingering the spot on the end of his nose.

"Four or five of them," he said, "the traces are clear enough, heading southwest. But."

"Ay, but." Dodd shook his head. "Could be. How many men ha' ye?"

"Ekie and Sim are gone, so only two as well as myself, Mr Anricks if he'll come, and you."

"Five, one not a fighter. It's no' enough to fight off an ambush."

"It's a trod now. I could likely call on the Humes...?"

"Could you?" Dodd asked, "There's a boy, a few men, and two women in the castle and I dinna see nae more. And forebye, they could have seen what happened here, why did they not help?"

Why did the old lady in fact lie to him, eh? That was something he'd like the answer to.

"Are any of these tracks from Ekie or Sim?" he asked, casting about for more hoofprints.

"No," Young Henry said after he'd taken another look, "I had Ekie on Butter which is a fat hobby and the tracks would be heavier."

"Ay, so they sold her to the reivers and went off. At least it means they aren't seven."

Young Henry was breathing hard through his nose.

"How long to get some men here?" Dodd asked, though he knew he wouldn't like the answer.

"Most of the Widdringtons are in the Middle March, a forty-mile ride at least. Say half a day to ride back for them and another half day to ride here again."

He had been right. He didn't like the answer.

Anricks had been sitting on his pony, staring hard into space as if he was reading something there.

"I happen to know," he said judiciously, "that Sir Henry Widdrington and my Lord Spynie are meeting near Jedburgh, which isn't nearly as far from here as Widdrington itself. And he'll have taken at least twenty men with him."

Young Henry stared suspiciously at the man while Dodd asked curiously, "So are ye a Jesuit or not then?"

A strange almost fey smile curved the man's mouth under his skimpy beard. "No sirs, I am not," he explained slowly and coldly. "I am unalterably opposed to his Catholic Majesty of Spain and at the moment I am by way of being a pursuivant in the service of Sir Robert Cecil."

Dodd whistled. "Are ye now?" he said. "I've met the man, see ye."

"Have you?" Anricks gave Dodd a look he was beginning to recognise as a reappraisal. "A very interesting personage—tall and handsome."

Dodd laughed shortly. "Well ye havenae met him if ye think that. He's a hunchback, though I'd say he wis handsome, ay, and interesting."

Anricks smiled again. He took a packet of paper out of his doublet pocket and unfolded a letter from it which he passed to Young Henry. "I am well aware of the fact that the last tooth-drawer in these parts, bar one that was a drunk, was in fact a Papist spy, but I am not and I took the precaution of obtaining this."

Young Henry passed the paper without comment to Dodd who turned it the right way up and read it carefully.

"A' right," he said, "let's see yer hands."

Anricks showed his hands palms up. There was a dark scar across the middle of each hand as if he had clutched a bar of red hot iron once and been burnt.

Young Henry and Dodd looked in silence for a while. "What was it did that?" asked Dodd. "I havenae seen the like on naebody else."

"The same thing which gave me the grip I need to pull teeth. Forgive me, gentlemen, but I prefer not to speak of it nor remember it. However the scars prove I have not stolen the commission from another man and I am in fact the Simon Anricks of whom he speaks."

The commission had Sir Robert Cecil's seal on it and was written in a fine italic hand which might even have been his. It spoke of his confidence in Mr Anricks, described the scars on his hands, and asked whoever saw the paper and the scars to help him in all his enterprises.

"Please be so kind as not to mention this to anyone at all, especially not Sir Henry," added Anricks. "I am truly a tooth-drawer as well."

"How will we explain to Sir Henry how we found him?" asked Young Henry.

"I saw him riding west with his men when I was on the road from Edinburgh so I think there will be little difficulty. In any case, no doubt Sir Henry will be anxious to find and ransom his wife, if necessary."

Dodd had listened to Carey ranting on about how he hated the man and how he mistreated his wife and wondered if he would be that eager. It didn't matter, because his wife being kidnapped put a brave on him that he could only ignore if he wanted to lose every scrap of credit or reputation that he had.

Young Henry nodded once. Dodd sighed. He supposed he should stick with the tooth-drawer so he couldn't get out of drawing Carey's tooth. Though now he thought about it, he supposed Carey wouldn't approve of him not taking an interest in Lady Widdrington's kidnapping.

He tried to imagine Carey's reaction to that and found his imagination failed him. Carey would be very upset, to put it mildly, and might take it into his head to do something even crazier than his normal notions, which was where Dodd's imagination gave up. It was hard to beat spying out Netherby tower dressed as a peddler, selling faulty guns to the Irish and causing a riot in a London jail—all things Carey had regarded as excellent ideas in the past.

Without further ado they headed west and south to Jedburgh. At least it was in the right direction, Dodd thought philosophically.

They found Jedburgh full of Widdringtons who greeted Young Henry respectfully, considering his youth, and told him his father wasn't there. He was hunting with Lord Spynie at a small hunting lodge northwards which was sometimes used by the king on his way to a justice raid in the Scots West March. They would be back later in the day, and meantime Young Henry and his men could wait for them. Some of Spynie's men were hanging around in the town as well, the same combination of popinjay vicious courtiers and hard nuts that Dodd had thoroughly disliked in the summer.

They came and insisted on searching Anricks' pack and two of them even dared to question Young Henry until his uncle Thomas Widdrington snarled that he'd vouch for the boy. One asked Dodd his business.

"Ay," he said, "I'm a Dodd, sir."

He was looking as wooden and stupid as he could, helped by his buff coat and lack of helmet and for good measure he tipped his statute cap to the lad in a magnificent purple and tawny padded doublet.

"That's well enough," said the other one, glorious in bright green and yellow. "We ha' tae ask, goodman, for somebody took a potshot at my lord Spynie ainly last month."

"Ay," said Dodd, not bothering to look interested, "what with?"

"A crossbow. He got away too and then he tried again in the night and killed a bolt of linen Spynie had in his bed and then he got away again, so Spynie's no' pleased wi' us."

"Ay, bad luck tae him."

"Ay."

Dodd was more interested in what Anricks was up to and wandered after him. He found him in the courtyard of the biggest inn at Jedburgh, the Spread Eagle, with his pack already taken off the packhorse and both horses in a loosebox.

Anricks took off his doublet and rolled his sleeves up, put on his blood-stained apron and unrolled his instruments in their canvas. The innkeeper brought a sturdy armchair out to the yard and then two more on further instructions and lined them up.

"Teeth drawn," shouted Anricks. "Get your teeth drawn for one English shilling or four Scots shillings. Teeth drawn." He had a weak voice that didn't shout very well, so Dodd offered his services and was soon strolling round the town with the innkeeper's youngest and his drum, bellowing "Teeth drawn! Get yer teeth drawn!" in broad Scots.

By the time he got back a queue had formed that was already out of the stableyard. He watched for a while, ready for drama and screams, but it was boring. The patients sat down in the chairs and told Anricks which tooth was giving them trouble. He poked about in their mouths, sometimes producing gasps and moans. Then he made them drink a great deal of brandy, supplied at double prices by the inn, and gave them a cloth in their hands to sniff. He was pouring out drops of something oily from a brown glass bottle onto it every so often. After a bit they fell asleep and then Anricks was onto them, opening their snoring mouths, reaching in with a steel instrument, placing it carefully round the bad tooth and then clenching his fist and drawing it out. And then he moved on to the next patient.

Dodd had a go at pulling a tooth himself and found it much harder than he expected for the grip was awkward and you needed all your strength to pull. Anricks did two more with crunching sounds and a lot of blood and pus while he was fumbling.

Then the patients would wake up, look around dizzily as if hungover, feel their mouths in wonder and then wander off with their friends, shaking their heads. A few people started scowling at Anricks and muttering about witchcraft, but the ones who had had their teeth drawn shushed them.

"Is it witchcraft, sir?" Dodd asked curiously as they waited for a stout woman to go to sleep. "Is it a secret?"

Anricks shook his head. "No, it's an alchemical miracle. No secret at all. Paracelsus first noticed its effect on chickens and I tried it on myself once I had made some. They are sniffing sweet oil of vitriol, distilled from aqua vitae and vitriol." He gripped, clenched, the instrument slipping. "Hold her mouth more open, please. Thank you." Not a sound from the patient. Again the hands tightened on the instrument and the cracking crunch told Dodd the tooth was out. Anricks produced a large long-rooted tooth that was black all along one side and had two holes in it. The root was full of pus. He dropped the tooth in the bucket and swabbed at the space with a cloth wet with aqua vitae while the woman slept on.

Dodd looked in the bucket, with all the other eaten-away teeth and suddenly felt sick. That was an ill sight to see, to be sure, how your actual teeth could be eaten away. Horrible. What did that for God's sake?

Anricks didn't need him anymore; he had a queue going down the hill now. Dodd wandered out to the yard and found a boy there asking for him, who told him to come and meet Sir Henry.

Young Henry was looking grim and Sir Henry was loudly raging. "Do you believe this about my wife, Mr Dodd, that she went off with persons unknown?" he demanded.

Dodd was about to correct him about what he was and then left it. "She didnae go voluntarily and she tried to escape, the signs were clearer than the nose on yer face," he said stolidly. "And she left her mother's ring on a twig near the place where they caught her."

Sir Henry swung about on his son. "So why didn't ye follow the tracks and catch them?"

"Perhaps because I had no desire to ride into an ambush, sir," said Young Henry, with admirable calm. "Or not until I had enough of my men to back me."

"My men, puppy, I'm the headman."

"Yes, father."

"How did you know where I was?"

Young Henry looked blank. "We thought it was worth trying

Jedburgh because this is where you come to meet with Lord Spynie and we'd heard you were riding west."

Suddenly Sir Henry slapped his son across the face and followed up with a nasty rabbit punch to the short ribs. Young Henry took the slap and only grunted a little with pain at the rib punch.

"Don't think ye can outguess me, boy," hissed Sir Henry.

Young Henry said nothing. His face was a mask under the reddening print of his father's hand. Sir Henry was standing, scowling up at him and chewing his moustache.

"What would you like me to do, sir?" Young Henry asked steadily.

Suddenly Dodd saw fear in the man's face, and couldn't think why. Young Henry towered over him and yet was as respectful as a man should be to his father, no matter how unreasonable. Was that what he was afraid of? That his son was a better man than him?

"Weel weel, wha' ha' we here?" came broad Scotch tones. Dodd turned to see the handsome young man with gold hair that was still the King's lover come striding over to them. Lord Spynie was wearing a smart black satin doublet with diamond buttons and a very nice cutwork leather hunting jerkin over it. He wasn't very tall, a couple of inches shorter than Dodd himself and four inches shorter than Young Henry, but he swaggered and swung a whip in his hand.

Young Henry and his father both bowed to him and Dodd did the same, quietly stepping backwards out of the way. Sir Henry explained that his fool of a wife had got herself captured by reivers while fossicking about in Scotland where she had no business to be.

"I'm sorry you didn't get my message by Roger," Young Henry said, "about the killing of Minister Jamie Burn?"

"I got it," growled Sir Henry. "She had no business in Scotland. She should have minded my business in England."

"Wives," said Spynie, with an indulgent smile, "allus poking about in what doesnae concern them."

Sir Henry stood irresolute, although what he had to do was obvious. He should gather his men, ride out with them and find out who had his wife. And then he should ransom her and follow up with some reprisal raids unless the kidnappers were too powerful, in which case he should wait and take reprisals later and more carefully. That's what Dodd would have done if anyone had been stupid enough to kidnap Janet. Although unfortunately he loved his wife, which would make everything much more complicated. He decided to go back to the inn and the tooth-drawing.

When he got there he found Anricks in an argument with a bunch of sour-looking men in black or brown clothes and white collars.

"Ye say it isn't witchcraft, Mr Anricks," said one of them, "but ye canna deny that ye make them sleep and so they get out of the pain o' the tooth-drawing."

"I do not deny it, that's why I do it. It makes my work easier for they are not fighting nor screaming."

A heavy-looking man shook his head. "The Scripture says, man is born tae sorrow…"

"Ay," said a skinny man with hot eyes, "and it's wrong to try to evade Scripture, so it is."

Anricks shut his eyes for a moment and then smiled brightly. "You are ordering me to stop using sweet oil of vitriol?"

"We are ordering ye to stop using the evil spells that make people sleep."

"Your name, sir?"

"I am Elder Tobermory, he is Elder Stanehouse. That is Minister Birkin."

"Very well, sirs. I will stop using the oil of vitriol and explain to each of my patients why. Thank you."

Nonplussed, the sour men moved away in a body and then stood watching to see there was no witchcraft. Each tooth took longer now because they had to tell the patients why they couldn't sniff the magic cloth: Anricks explained that Elders Tobermory and Stanehouse and Minister Birkin had ordered him to stop using the sweet oil of vitriol, and the elders and the minister had to explain that they had stopped him from using witchcraft and imperilling their immortal souls. The people who still wanted their teeth drawn screamed and cried as he pulled their teeth, which was a lot noisier and the results were not nearly as good and everything took longer.

The elders and the minister were shouting themselves hoarse at some of Anricks' patients by the end of it and the queue had disappeared. When the second to the last one went, Dodd reached out and stopped a boy making off with the box that was now full of shillings. When the tooth was pulled from the last woman who cried steadily throughout but didn't scream, Anricks went and dumped all his instruments into a bucket of water and then used another just to wash his arms and hands, which was a bit dainty, Dodd thought. The woman was weepily thanking Anricks and telling him it didn't hurt nearly as much as having a baby and insisted on paying him an extra shilling for she already felt much better.

They moved to the commonroom of the inn to count the money which amounted to about one hundred shillings Scots and ten shillings English, which was very respectable. Then Anricks went to the market and bought three pack ponies' loads of oats which was good cheap, along with the pack ponies and led them all into the innyard where he paid the innkeeper, also in Scots shillings. The remaining Scots money he used to pay for the ordinary—a haggis and bashed neeps and some ale, which he shared with Dodd.

Anricks was tired and quiet. Dodd was wondering how quickly he could get him to Carlisle. It was too late in the day to make for Carlisle now.

"It's a puzzle," said Anricks, suddenly, apropos of nothing, "why and by whom was the Minister Burn killed."

"He wisnae against yer witchcraft?"

"It isn't witchcraft. It's as natural as a man falling asleep when he's drunk. Just quicker and easier…"

"Whatever. He wisna agin it?"

"He was at first, until I drew one of his teeth for him and then he admitted it might be a good idea. They usually do."

"Has this happened before?"

"Oh yes, especially in Scotland. The elders get very outraged at the thought of people sleeping through something that will hurt. Also the resident barber surgeons usually stir them up. And usually by then my hands are tired anyway and so it works out well enough. They get the blame for the fact that I can't possibly treat all the people who want it."

Anricks took a pull of beer and sighed, cut into the haggis and piled a lot on a silver spoon he took out of his pocket and polished. He ate it with his eyes shut, slowly munching until it was all gone.

"Mm," he said, "it's good."

Dodd tried some and it was good. Not as good as Janet's, but good enough—too much lung and oats and not enough liver in it probably.

Anricks concentrated on the food for a while and then leaned back and drank more ale. He called for some uisghe beagh as well, the northern firewater. Dodd tried a little and wasn't impressed; it tasted very smoky in his opinion.

"So. Minister Burn. Perhaps if I talk through what I know about it, you can find a pattern there."

"I'm no' the man ye want for that. He's got a terrible toothache in Carlisle."

"Even so."

Anricks went through the tale of Minister Burn as he knew it and added that Lady Widdrington probably knew a lot more.

"Ay?" Dodd thought about it and had to agree that it was odd.

"And last month he went out on a raid of some kind," Anricks added with a sigh. "I wish I knew where he went."

"Did he gang oot wi' his family, they're right reivers?" Dodd asked.

"I don't think so, he'd fallen out with his father."

"Who did he go with?"

"He went alone with one remount," said Anricks. "That's what his wife says in her letter to me. Of course he could have met friends later. But he went wearing his best suit and carrying a crossbow and his sword, which was why she wasn't too concerned. It would have been a different matter if he'd worn harness and helmet of course."

Dodd nodded. "Mebbe he had his jack and helmet somewhere else…"

Anricks shook his head. "They're still at Wendron, in a press in his study."

Dodd was silent. "Was he going to kill someone?" he asked at last. "Mebbe my lord Spynie? Someone took a shot at him last month?"

Anricks frowned. "Why would he do that? Why take such a risk?"

Dodd shrugged. "Somebody wis paying him, perhaps?"

Anricks nodded wearily. His mouth was turned down at the ends, as if he had a bad taste in it. "I'm not sure why he suddenly needed money, but he did. I wish I'd…Well, I didn't. And there's a rumour he went to see Kerr of Cessford a week before he went out as well."

Dodd let out a humourless bark of laughter. "Ay," he said, "they're all murdering bastards too. And the Burns. I've tangled wi' them mesen. And Kerrs sometimes ally with Elliots."

The commonroom suddenly started filling up with Widdringtons, followed by Sir Henry and his son who seemed upset about something.

"Sir," he was saying, "will ye not give the man an answer?"

"I'll answer when I please, boy. If my fool of a wife hadn't taken it into her empty head to ride intae Scotland she wouldna be costing me a hundred pounds English now, would she? She can sit it out for a while."

Sir Henry marched to the bar and ordered aqua vitae and pointedly got none for his son. Young Henry's face was swelling a little and his brows were down. He got his own ale and Dodd went up to him immediately.

"Sir," he said, "have ye had a ransom demand?"

Young Henry looked weary as well. "One of the Burns' boys came in with it. We'll swap at the Reidswire meeting stone, each side just five men and the woman on her horse, and a hundred pounds English in exchange."

"Ay. Does her husband have the money?" It wasn't excessive for the wife of a headman, but it was still a lot of money.

"No, of course not," muttered Young Henry. "Who does? Spynie does, of course, and has offered my father a loan at twenty percent interest a week, secured on one of his sheilings and the pasture."

"Ay," said Dodd noncommittally.

"I suppose Father will roar a bit and then take the loan, to pay them off."

"So it's the Burns that have her?"

"Yes. Jock Burn must have come up with the idea at the funeral and bought Ekie and Sim so he could do it."

"Ay," Dodd was uneasy. He had found aristocrats had less ready cash than headmen. How come my lord Spynie was so flush he could lend a hundred pounds cash to Sir Henry? Unless…"Sir, do ye not think it's a bit odd, Spynie having the ready cash?"

Young Henry took a drink of his ale and looked at his hands. His nails were bitten. "Now you mention it, Sergeant, that is odd."

"What if the Burns are doing Spynie's bidding?" Because now he came to think of it, Spynie would want revenge for how Lady Widdrington had outmanouevred him in the summer and lost him some of the King's favour and this was a splendid way to take it. And if something went wrong at the exchange and the woman wound up dead, well, who would care? Not Sir Henry, although there was a man with a bad tooth in Carlisle who would surely take it very hard. Dodd's eyes narrowed and his mouth turned down.

"Which boy was it?" he asked.

"Geordie Burn's eldest son, Young Geordie."

"Is it possible Sir Henry could have known about Lady Widdrington getting kidnapped? Before it happened?" he asked very softly. Because once you thought about the loan and Spynie being around and the clear fact that Sir Henry didn't like his wifey, you also had to ask if this was Sir Henry's revenge as well. Didn't you?

Young Henry stared at the fire and said nothing. His mouth had turned down as well and his eyes were hot.

"Do you think…?" he began, and then fell silent again.

"Well it's possible," Dodd said gently, "isn't it?"

"And the Burns would get the blame which they wouldn't care about." Young Henry's voice was very soft but there was a hard undertone. "Nor my father. The King probably wouldn't care enough to do anything."

"Ay," said Dodd. "It's a problem solved, that it is."

Another long silence. "She came to us when she was just seventeen and I was ten," Young Henry said, "Ten years ago. And she has tried, lord God she has tried to be a good wife to Sir Henry, no matter how he treats her. She was wonderful to us, to me and Roger. She never beat us, she...she...used to...even hug me when I was sad for my mother, though I wisnae her wean and she...she looked after me when I got the measles and my eyes hurt and I was scared I'd go blind and..."

Dodd tactfully went to the bar to get more ale, though frankly the stuff they were drinking in Scotland was dire. Sir Henry was shouting at some of his older men who were gathered round him, laughing. On a thought, he also bought some uisge beagh that was cheaper than brandy and brought it over.

Young Henry took the horn cup, lifted it in his father's direction and drank it off.

"The only thing is, how do we find out where she is exactly?"

"Find her horse, it's a nice jennet called Mouse and shod."

Anricks came by then and they made room for him at the table. He bought a round and sat down, his anxious face quite unreadable. Purely on instinct, and in the hope of there being more than two on the raid, Dodd told him what they thought about the ransom demand.

He, too, was silent for a while and then he nodded. "Yes," was all he said.

He felt for something on his belt and then realised that it was in his pack. A minute later he had paper on the table and was writing at high speed in a neat italic that said he was a good clerk as well as a barber surgeon.

"What are ye doing?"

"I am writing to my lord Maitland, his castle's not far away and I can send it by a town messenger. Maitland's the Lord Chancellor."

"That's a good idea," said Young Henry. "She knows him and she looked after his son for him a few years ago when things were a mite tickle in Scotland. We taught him to shoot and he taught us to tickle trout."

Anricks just nodded and continued to write, which gave Dodd the feeling he had already known that about Lady Widdrington, which was interesting. But then if he was working as a pursuivant for Sir Robert Cecil, you'd expect him to be well-informed.

"When is the exchange to be?"

"Day after tomorrow," said Young Henry, "to give Sir Henry time to get the money."

"So she's likely safe enough till then," said Dodd. "They'll be on their guard, but if it's a put up job, they willna expect much."

"We aren't much," said Young Henry, with a nervous laugh.

"Ay, we are," said Dodd.

"Gentlemen, there is almost certainly at least one Widdrington in Geordie Burn's pay to act as his spy, so shall we leave the subject?"

"Tonight," said Dodd. Young Henry looked up at him and then nodded once, Anricks opened his mouth to argue and then shut it again. He nodded as well.

WEDNESDAY 18TH OCTOBER 1592

Elizabeth had lice, probably from Jimmy Tait, and was already tired of the smell of her only shift. She wasn't exactly sure where she was since she had been brought to the peel tower with a scarf over her eyes and her horse on a leading rein. It was Geordie Burn that brought her in, a big man with black hair and a loud hectoring way with him. He was frightening because he seemed always to be laughing at some private joke at her expense and because he came up too close to her and grinned in her face. However she had long experience at thinking when she was frightened and also at acting a lot stupider than she was.

So she made sure she asked plenty of silly questions about where were they taking her and why were they doing it and her husband would be angry and what were they thinking of and so on and so forth until Geordie shouted at her to be silent. She immediately went silent in what she hoped was a cowed way. It wasn't hard to do, she was frightened of Geordie Burn quite viscerally, and her hands were cold.

When they took the scarf off and helped her down from her horse, she wanted to protest because Mouse was a friend and she had no others. She said nothing while Geordie Burn gestured for her to go into the barnekin and into the peel tower and the horse was taken off, protesting, to the winter pasture on the other side of the valley.

They were quite polite really. Ralph o' the Coates wasn't there, being busy selling horses in Edinburgh. A boy called Young Geordie was sent off with the message about the ransom to Jedburgh where Geordie said the Widdringtons were. There were a lot of Burns there, some of them she even recognised from the funeral. Jemmy and Archie Burn had been to it, she realised, and several others. Archie Burn was friendly to her and showed her his sword which was different from the general run of northern broadswords. His was a thinner blade with a basket hilt, almost a rapier, though very sharp.

"It's beautiful," she said, trying to sound admiring, "but it doesn't look English or Scots."

"Nor it isnae," laughed Archie, "that's Cordoba steel and I got it off a Spaniard when I wis fighting in the Netherlands. The Spaniard had nae further use for it." He laughed again and showed with a slicing flourish of the blade what had happened to the Spaniard.

Elizabeth looked at him carefully. Yes, he and his father fitted the description of the men that had killed Jamie Burn and yes, he had a blade that could have done it, she thought, though she was no expert. Jemmy had a long narrow poignard, too—but then so did several others of the men. And why would the Burns kill one of their own? Even if they had fallen out, you didn't kill the men of your own family, you just didn't.

There was a whole collection of louring toughs with many Burns among them and some Taits and Pringles and Kerrs as well. She got an acknowledgement from Jamie Burn's Uncle Jock who rode in with three stolen cows at midday, taking off his hat to her as he rode by.

At least they had a woman there for propriety. In fact, it was Geordie and Jamie Burn's mother, a faded woman called Maud with grey blond hair under her grubby cap, and wearing a homespun kirtle but a tailor-made woollen gown that was Edinburgh work. The peel tower was an old one, clearly not the main Burn tower, and smelled of mildew and mice. Still she and Maud tried their best to make it habitable with blankets that Maud had brought, which they hung up by the fire that smoked terribly until a crow's nest fell down the chimney in flames.

Then she sat with Maud in the upper chamber of the peel tower and sewed some shirts with her which was soothing and gave her something to do with her hands. One of the louring toughs came up the ladder to the upper chamber with some partly cooked lumps of cow and some oatmeal but she had no stomach to any of it and gave it to Maud.

She listened and said "mm" and "fancy that" and "tut tut" while Maud Burn, who had been a Pringle and had had a hard but successful life with only two babies dead and four sons and a daughter raised, chatted about kine and their diseases, and horses and their many and various diseases and how disastrous the harvest had been.

As the Sun went low in the afternoon, Elizabeth heard hoof-beats and went to the arrowslit to see Geordie Burn setting off with about fifteen men, heading north and east. There goes the ambush in case Sir Henry tries a rescue, she thought and wondered if he would. She didn't know. He might, though for pride not love of course, or perhaps he wouldn't. He would pay up, though, surely? Everyone in the East March would laugh at him if he didn't do something.

She went and sat down next to Maud by the smoky fire, on

an old and uncomfortable stool and heard that Geordie wouldn't be back until morning, the young scamp, but that Ralph was due back any day now with the money from the horses which they needed to buy horse fodder since the harvest had been so terrible, rained on to ruination.

"Ours was bad too," Elizabeth commiserated. There was still some light to see by and she kept stitching the long seam down the side. They talked about harvests and weather.

At last Elizabeth got to say she was sorry about Minister Jamie, Maud's second son, and what a mystery his death was. Maud went silent for a long time and Elizabeth pretended not to see the tears brimming in her eyes.

"Ay," whispered Maud, "but it was like he wis dead seven years ago, when he went tae the university at St Andrew's. His father was gey angry wi' him. And he was such a bonny young man, such a bonny fighter."

"Mm."

"They had a fight over it and Jamie won. His father couldna forgive him for that, though I said tae him, whit de ye expect, he's young and ye're old."

"Did he disinherit him?"

"No, Jamie still has his rights…had his rights to his share o' the land. And his child too, if it's a boy."

"Oh." That was normal. North and South on the Border, the farms were divided and divided as the families bred so you couldn't live on them. The system further south, where the eldest son got all of it, was unfair to the younger sons like Robin himself, but you could see how it kept the estates together. It was better for the families.

"And then last month, well, Geordie was fit to be tied about it, so he was."

"Why? What about?"

"I'm not sure, but…ay, I'm worried."

"Mrs Burn, what was it Geordie was so angry about?"

Maud hung her head over the shirt of coarse homespun linen. At last she said, "I'm no' sure, see ye, but I think Jamie tried to kill somebody important. A courtier."

"Why?"

Maud shook her head. "Ah dinna ken. Somebody important. Very important. And he failed, did Jamie, didnae kill the man at all. And then the man came to see Geordie, came himself with men at his back, all shining wi' silver and gold, and they went off and talked for a long while and then…three weeks later, my Jamie war deid."

All Elizabeth could think of to say was "Ah."

Maud was weeping silently into the shirt on her knee. Elizabeth was still for a moment and then she put down her shirt because anyway it was too dark to sew, and leaned across and put her arms around Maud who shuddered and wept into her shoulder while her hands and her heart got colder and colder.

***

At last the storm was done for the moment. "It's worse when they've grown," Maud said, wiping her eyes with the shirt. "Ye see them grow and they change and they become men and then… they die. O' course we all die, I ken that, but I wish I could hae died instead of Jamie, he was such a fine man and I heard he did well as a minister, preached some fine sermons and had his ain little school."

"Yes, he did, Mrs Burn, and all the boys loved him. They sang at his funeral."

"Och, I wish I could ha gone and seen him put in the ground. Ralph wouldnae have it, he wis still sore at the beating up he took fra Jamie seven year go. But I wish I could ha' gone and maybe heard them sing. Did they sing well?"

"Ay, they did," said Elizabeth, her Scotch well in now, "They did like birds or angels. There's a lad there, only young, perhaps seven or eight and he has the finest voice I've heard in a while, perhaps ever." Perhaps Robin, when he was a boy, might have had a voice as good? Though that didn't necessarily follow, sometimes quite ordinary singers turned wonderful when their voices broke and sometimes the other way round.

"Ay, that'll be a Tait," said Maud. "They allus have good voices."

"I think that's what he wanted the money for, to take all the boys to the Carlisle cathedral and prentice them singers, to get them out of the Borders, you know? Especially little Jimmy Tait. His father wanted ten pounds for him."

"Is that right?" said Maud, in a voice of wonder. "Was he going tae do that?"

"I think so. And I think I know who offered him the money to kill my Lord Spynie as well, the courtier he took a shot at."

"Bad cess to 'em," said Maud, scowling. "Who was it?"

"The Dowager Lady Hume. Lord Spynie's been sniffing about her ten-year-old grandson whose wardship he's just bought and he wants him at Court and she's...she does not."

"Och." Very noticeably, Maud did not ask why going to the Scottish King's Court as Lord Spynie's ward might be a bad thing for a ten-year-old boy. She went silent again. By the time she spoke once more it was too dark to see and the turf fire gave some warmth but not much light. "It's Geordie that wanted ye taken. Ye were asking too many questions. Jemmy and Archie were worried too; ye could see it. And then another message came from...from the King's Court and he laughed his head off at it and rode out before dawn this morning to take ye."

Who could the message have come from? Lord Spynie? Her husband? Why had Geordie found it so funny? And why had Jemmy and Archie been worried? Well, that was easy to answer and it was shocking, that's what it was. To kill their own kinsman, Jemmy's nephew, Archie's cousin, on the say-so of a courtier?

"Will they kill me, d'ye think?"

Silence. What Elizabeth could see of Maud's face was creased with worry. "He's a terrible man, he'll end in hell," she burst out. "He's allus been wicked, he used tae take the kittens the cats had and he took 'em off somewhere and I followed him once and he'd...he'd crucified them. Alive."

"Who?"

"Geordie. My son Geordie!"

"Jesus."

"I killed the poor little things so I did and tellt him not to dae it again and he laughed at me."

Elizabeth felt sick. People had to drown kittens because with most she-cats kindling twice a year, you'd be knee-deep in cats if you didn't. If only there was some way you could geld a quean cat like you could a tom. But you did it as fast as you could, not...not crucifying them.

"He wis eight then. I've never liked him since, though he's my eldest. It was Jamie I loved and I let him run off tae the Reverend Gilpin and I hoped...I hoped..." She sighed and wiped her eyes with the half-made shirt again.

"If he's laughing at me, is he planning to kill me?" asked Elizabeth again, her mouth dry but her heart beating hard under her stays. "Is he?"

Maud shook her head and then she said, very very quietly, "Maybe."

And Elizabeth thought, *I will not go to my death like a cow or a kitten, I will kick and fight, by God I will.*

Maud had lifted her face and was staring at Elizabeth. Her lips were parted and her eyes fixed on something in the distance. "Jamie did it for money to get the boys to Carlisle?"

"I think so, Mrs Burn."

Wednesday Night 18th October

to Thursday 19th October 1592

Although the night was long, it was as difficult as Dodd had expected to find Lady Widdrington's horse. He knew where most of the infield horse pastures were, of course; he had raided all across this country in his teens. But there were a lot of them because you didn't want too many horses in one place. And in the dark it was hard to avoid the men on guard and hard to make out the horses. And then, of course, you had to ride to the next place.

Well, they'd have the next day as well. After the first couple of tries they established a routine. Dodd and Young Henry found the pasture, then they sent Anricks round to distract the guards by pretending to be lost and asking the way. At one place they had checked the horses and found nothing but hobbies and they stood and waited, sweating, for Anricks. They would have gone to his rescue but then they heard a cracking crunching sound of a patient losing a tooth and despite the tension and the impossibility of the job, Young Henry smiled.

A little later Anricks turned up, looking smug. "I used the sweet oil of vitriol," he explained. "It loosens men's tongues like booze does. He told me where they've taken the woman."

And so they rode a few miles across country to the infield of a tower that was once owned by Pringles and now languished in the ownership of two sisters who hated each other and would not be reconciled. Dodd would never have thought of looking there. And there they found Lady Widdrington's jennet, minus her expensive side-saddle of course, looking a little offended at being asked to pasture with such very low-bred hobbies.

"So she's in the tower," said Dodd, trying to see it against the night sky. There was a quarter Moon but it was ducking in and out behind clouds. "Ay, well, of course she is." Nobody was going to make their job easier for them, after all. And it would be nice if they could nip her out quick and if nobody shot her while they did it, of course.

They had moved down the valley and into a little shelter for the sheep in the corner of the worst of the three infields.

"I'll ride for Jedburgh, get my men, and come back here…"

"Ay, yer father will let ye, will he?"

Silence. "I could perhaps gain entrance as a stranger, lost in the hills and then open the barnekin," said Anricks slowly.

"Mebbe," allowed Dodd, "but they'll have her in the tower itself, second floor and the ladder taken away to be sure she disnae take it intae her head to run for it herself. They might chain her, but I think not, she's a lady and they willna think she's dangerous."

There was a dispirited silence. Annoyingly, Dodd found himself thinking that this was where the Courtier would have been useful because he was the one who could think of ingenious unlikely plans.

"On the other hand, Geordie Burn himself is out with his men at the pass into this valley, waiting for Sir Henry," offered Anricks.

"Ay, o' course he is."

Come on, Dodd thought to himself, there's a way of doing it. I'm a better man than the Courtier any day, come on.

Inspiration failed to strike. From where the Moon was, it was now two or three in the morning and dawn only three hours away. If they were going to do anything, they had better do it soon.

Anricks yawned jaw-crackingly. "Gentlemen," he said, "I'm in need of sleep. How about we get a couple of hours each, and think about it again in the morning?"

Young Henry caught the yawn from him. "But she's there and we're here…" he protested.

"Ay, ye're right," Dodd said, "and if ye have a way to get past the barnekin and intae the tower and out again and away wi' out getting her killed, I'm yer man." He waited. "Do ye?"

"No," came a reluctant growl.

They put their horses in amongst the others, on the grounds that hobbies looked alike from a distance and probably nobody had counted them. Then they drew lots for the middle watch which fell to Dodd, and he settled himself in the corner next to Anricks and went to sleep instantly.

He woke instantly as well, knowing he had slept three hours and not one. Anricks was squatting there, hollow-eyed. "I took the middle watch as well," he said. "I couldn't sleep at all."

Strange. Dodd felt rested and refreshed as he often did when he slept out and not frowsty and bad-tempered as he normally did after a night in a proper bed. Young Henry was still fast asleep, looking touchingly young under his spots. There was a strong smell of farts in the little wooden sheep shelter and Henry shifted and trumpeted again. Dodd found himself sniggering.

"I'm afraid I think we need to send Widdrington back for men and conduct a full assault…" said Anricks with a sigh.

"Nay, they'd ainly kill her." He felt glass-headed but he had an answer to the quandary, produced somewhere while he was asleep. "What de ye think tae this?" he said as Anricks took another apple from his pack and gave it to Dodd who started eating it. "It's mad enough for the Courtier, but mebbe it could work."

He explained his idea and then explained it again when Young Henry woke up. It was nerve-wracking and could easily go horribly wrong, but at the worst, it would just give the Burns one more prisoner. At best it could solve everything.

They needed to move fast while Geordie Burn was still out lying in wait for the Widdringtons; it wouldn't work if he was there. At least the weather was cooperating. It was horrible, dark, foggy with a continuous bone-chilling mizzle that was only a slightly lighter grey as the Sun came up somewhere behind the clouds.

Wednesday Night 18th October
to Thursday 19th October 1592

Elizabeth and Maud shared the ancient bed that smelled of mildew and mice just as much as the rest of the place. Elizabeth took her stays and kirtle off but put her gown back on again, glad of Sir Henry's vanity that liked his woman to have a black velvet gown lined in silk and edged in fur, though only coney.

Maud was quiet while Elizabeth knelt to say her prayers and even said an amen to them, then they put the curfew over the glowing turves and climbed into bed. The curtains were too rotted to draw, the wind came through the arrow slits but Maud had brought blankets of her own weaving which were good and dense and still oily from the sheep and once they had three of them over them, they started to warm up.

Archie came at night and brought a cleanish jordan to replace the other one and took the ladder away. The wind was howling at first but then died down and there was the quiet whisper of rain falling. They could hear the hobbies moving about in the ground-floor chamber, the men talking quietly or snoring in the first-floor chamber. They were alone in the upper chamber, under the rafters.

Elizabeth had said her prayers mechanically. She was beginning to wonder why she said them at all, though she remembered the sensation that had filled her when she shouted at God about the boys. Was He punishing her for that? It depended on what you thought God was like, really. Was He a spiteful old man like her husband as He often showed Himself in the depths of the Old Testament? Or was He a strong young man with a charming way to Himself, a man who had much more to Him than that, who was also God? She remembered how gripped she had been when she first read the Gospels, how the personality of Jesus had come through to her in the beautiful muscular language of Tyndale's translation, how it had become a pleasure not a duty to converse with such a person. And then Carey and then...all this. And she was tired of it. She would have spoken to Our Lady in the old way if she could, but if you read the Gospels and the Acts you could see that Jesus' mother was hardly mentioned at all and wasn't so very important. So it was all about Jesus Himself, and the trouble was that He was a man as well as God, and you couldn't expect a man to care about who a woman loved. Could you?

She dreamed a long confusing dream in which she was arguing with a small brown-faced middle-aged Jewish woman, a long complicated argument she couldn't remember, and then the Jewess hugged her and kissed her and told her not to cry, that she would see to it.

She woke up still crying, which was annoying. She managed to stop and dry her face before Maud woke, got up and knelt again to pray and found herself thinking about Robin Carey again, in that sad dragging way from her heart which was probably what had made her cry. So she stopped and got up, dressed, got the fire sharpened up with some kindling and logs. That pig was probably gone off now, she thought with annoyance; how long have I been away? A week? And maybe Poppy has had her bairn by now?

Maud was awake, got up and pulled up her laces, put up her hair and pinned on her cap and then went grimly to the door and opened it onto empty space.

"Archie and Jemmy," she shrieked, "come here."

It was still half dark outside, foggy, raining, cold. There was something going on at the gate to the barnekin. "Archie!" she shouted again. "Bring me the ladder."

After a little while, someone else brought it and she climbed down, paused when she saw by the light of two torches what was happening at the gate and then grinned. "Come on, my lady," she shouted up at Elizabeth. "Come ben and look at this."

Elizabeth emerged and climbed carefully down the ladder which was old and not very sound. She was fully dressed now, her gown on, she even had her low crowned best hat on over her cap, the one she had put on for Jamie Burn's funeral, oh a hundred years ago.

Young Henry Widdrington was at the gate on a tired hobby, looking tired himself.

"The exchange has been done," he explained patiently to Jemmy Burn who was staring up at him suspiciously. "Sir Henry paid the ransom last night and I've come to take Lady Widdrington home."

Elizabeth was shocked. Sir Henry had paid it? Really?

"How did he get so much money at one time?"

"I told you," said Young Henry. "He's friends with Lord Spynie who's a rich lord and gave him the money straight off so I've come to collect my lady. Geordie's rich as Croesus and Ralph o' the Coates will be back any day now from selling horses and, unless you're thinking of killing her…"

Only Archie and Jemmy exchanged glances at that, in a way that made Elizabeth certain. The other Burns were indignant at the idea they might kidnap a woman and then fail to take the ransom when it was offered.

"What about where they were supposed to make the exchange?" asked Archie. "At the river and all…"

"I don't know about that," said Young Henry in a bored tone of voice. "I just know the thing's been done and she's to come home with me."

"Well, we'd best wait for Geordie, any road, he'll know the right of…"

"For God's sake," said Maud, stepping forward with all her maternal authority. "It's obvious, they've made another deal and for more money. Let Lady Widdrington go, I'll smooth it with my husband as soon as he's back from Edinburgh."

"Well but…"

"And I'm tired of her anyway, she can go back to her husband."

Young Henry had her horse, Mouse, behind him as if it were the most natural thing in the world. Elizabeth took the horse's bridle, gave her a quick stroke and a nuzzle and then looked at her back where there was a man's saddle. It didn't matter, she'd ridden astride when she was a lass and even if it was uncomfortable, she could do it. She mounted using the block, sitting sideways on the horse and then bringing her right leg up and over so her skirts and petticoats were under her and gave her some protection.

"Good-bye, Lady Widdrington, I'll mind what ye said to me," Maud said very deliberately. Elizabeth managed a bright smile and a wave to Maud before she turned her horse away.

"Good-bye Missus Burn, thank ye for yer hospitality," she called in answer. Maud actually snorted at that.

Elizabeth's heart was beating hard again as she followed Young Henry slowly down the muddy old path from the tower and down across the infield to the lane that led up to the moors by way of a small hill where there was something of a sheep shelter.

Two men came out to greet her then. One she knew at once as Simon Anricks; the other, she realised, was the bad-tempered saturnine Sergeant Dodd who was looking, as always, as if he had lost a shilling and found a penny.

She stared from one to the other and suddenly laughed. "You were lying?" she said.

Young Henry was looking absurdly pleased with himself. "I was. Now we have to ride back to Jedburgh..."

"All of us?"

"We'll protect you."

She didn't like it, a long chase across country. "Why don't I take one of the hobbies and ride the wrong way with Young Henry, south and west, and why don't you, Sergeant Dodd, take my jennet, Mouse, and go to Jedburgh with Mr Anricks?"

There was a short silence and then, wonder of wonders, Sergeant Dodd cracked a smile. "Ay," he said, "why don't I? Though Mr Anricks should ride the jennet because I'd be heavier and they might see that."

She smiled at him. "Me and Henry will go along the tops of the Cheviots and then come back to Jedburgh from the south. Maybe we'll call at Ferniehurst on the way."

She was hungry, hadn't had any breakfast, but she was suddenly happy and excited. She had given them the slip and even if they caught her, she had tried. By God, it wouldn't be her fault if they did catch her, either. And she thought Young Henry would have something to say about that.

She changed to Dodd's hobby because he was a better horse than Anricks' pony, with a warning from Dodd that he bit. Dodd rode Anricks' horse with only a blanket because they were one saddle short and Anricks rode the shod jennet, who wasn't happy about it.

Dodd and Anricks cantered off on the way up the valley to Jedburgh but Young Henry took her to the deep, dead bracken on the side of the hill where there were some outcrops to break the curve. They got the hobbies to lie down in it and then she lay down on her stomach behind him and found that she was well hidden, especially with the wet and the mist.

It was hard to stay still there as the damp slowly and steadily worked its way inward. But it was worth it. She heard the hoofbeats of Geordie Burn and his men as he rode back to the tower. Though she couldn't see them for the mist and the rain, she heard the shouting when he got the news and then she had the pleasure of hearing them ride like the devil after Mouse's shod hoofprints to Jedburgh.

She got up stiffly with Young Henry, mounted the hobby who stayed true to form and tried to bite her, and then rode south and west with him along the tops of the hills, where the wind blew the rain in folds like blankets and you couldn't see a hand in front of your face sometimes. Young Henry was a quiet clever guide, he took her along windswept hilltops and down wet slithering paths but avoided the worst places and the skree slopes. She was cold, she was wet, and she was hungry, but she felt happy.

***

Dodd rode into Jedburgh, up the Newcastle road, past the old abbey on the hill, with Anricks behind him and headed straight for the Spread Eagle. By the time Geordie and his bruisers arrived, they had had time to give the horses a brush down and get themselves some dinner. Dodd left the jennet in the yard so Geordie could see it when he came in, leaned back in a chair to make room for his stomach full of haggis, and put his boots on the table.

"Where's the woman?" Geordie demanded as he came into the commonroom. "Where's Lady Widdrington?"

"Och, I'm sorry," drawled Dodd, "she isna here, she's gone off wi' her husband already."

"She hasnae and ye know it, I met Sir Henry on the way in and he hasnae got her."

"Och, has he not?" said Dodd, who was enjoying himself immensely. "Where can she be?"

"You know, ye bastard, and ye'll tell me now."

Dodd took his boots off the table, one two, and stood up. "Will I?" he said, "I dinna think so. And forbye I don't know."

Anricks had quietly moved himself to another table where he was busy delving into his pack again.

There was a moment of silence. It was a silence full of calculation while Geordie thought of the number of men he had with him and tried to work out what advantage Dodd thought he had. Dodd wasn't thinking of that; he was thinking of where he was going to hit Geordie first, but another man, an older Pringle, pulled Geordie's elbow and whispered to him, with a lot of nervous gesturing.

"Yer name's Henry Dodd," said Geordie, with his head on one side and his eyes narrowed.

"Sergeant Henry Dodd," he corrected.

"You're *that* Henry Dodd? The one who…?"

"Ay," said Dodd gently, "What of it?"

Geordie hesitated a moment, then walked out of the commonroom. In a minute they heard him mounting up and riding out with all his men, heading south and east for the Burns' lands again.

Anricks was looking at him with his eyebrows up in a way that reminded him of Carey. He had, Dodd noticed, loaded both the dags inside his pack.

"That," said Anricks, "was impressive."

"Ay," said Dodd somberly, "it's nice they still remember me hereabouts."

***

They came to Reidswire where the hills were at their coldest and wettest, just north of the English Middle March, and looking from the tops of the hills with their empty shielings and summer pasture, Elizabeth saw a man riding a horse across country like wildfire, as if the king of Elfland were after him. It was odd. She stopped and looked at him and saw that he wore a jack and morion, polished silver steel, chased with elaborate gold patterns, and two dogs running behind him and she looked again and knew him.

Wednesday Night 18th October

and Thursday 19th October 1592

Word had come to Carlisle the night before of Elizabeth's kidnapping, word that came by winding ways through the Widdringtons and Burns and Fenwicks, until it ended with Thomas the Merchant. He took the trouble to write a letter reporting it to the man he knew as Mr Philpotts and then he went up to the castle as the Sun went down behind rain clouds and asked to speak to the acting Deputy Warden.

Carey was looking very unwell and had a swollen jaw, and deep bags under his eyes. He had been trying to find a tooth-drawer in Carlisle, but the only one in the area was a Johnstone who was busy in Dumfries.

"How may I help you, Mr Hetherington?" he asked coldly as Thomas the Merchant came into his office in the Queen Mary tower. He also had a teetering pile of complaints and was dictating letters to his new clerk, Mr Tovey, a spotty pale youth that Thomas the Merchant instantly ignored.

"I heard something you may be interested in," he said. "I won't even charge for it."

Carey did not return his sly smile. "Well?"

"I heard that Lady Widdrington is taken by Geordie Burn."

"What?" The tone of voice had gone from merely cold to distinctly wintry, with a howling gale and a blizzard.

"I heard tell that Lady Widdrington has been taken prisoner by Geordie Burn while she was at a funeral in Scotland. Her husband's in Jedburgh and they're talking about the ransom."

It was very interesting, thought Thomas the Merchant. Carey could be very noisy when he was in a temper but now he was quite silent for a long time. His colour had gone an unhealthy greyish white.

"Are you sure?"

"I had it from a good source." Why exactly he had it, was of course another matter.

More silence. Then, "Thank you Mr Hetherington."

Carey started on another letter of complaint about the recent raids from the Kerrs of Cessford well out of their usual area and into the West March. Thomas was surprised.

"Well…" he said, "aren't you going to do something about it?"

"What can I do, Mr Hetherington? Lady Widdrington's husband is doing what he can, I'm sure, and as I am not her husband I don't see exactly how I can help unless Sir Henry asks me to turn out the guard for him."

Damn. It hadn't worked. He had got too canny for them.

"Oh. Well. I'll be going then."

"Thank you for the information, Mr Hetherington."

As soon as he was well gone and out of the castleyard, Carey was on his feet and going down the stairs and up the ones to the Warden's Lodging where he found Scrope noodling his way on his virginals through some complicated Italian music that Carey had brought him from the South.

"What is this I hear about Lady Widdrington?" asked Carey very quietly. Scrope gave him an extraordinary look, up quickly from under his brows, then back to the music.

"I heard the same from Sir John Forster, today," Scrope admitted. "Geordie Burn's allegedly got her but I'm sure it's not true, that's why I didn't bother you with it because…"

But Carey had already gone.

Red Sandy did his best, wishing his older brother was there to talk some sense into the Courtier. "Ay sir, I heard it but I didnae believe it and forebye…"

"You think it's a trap laid for me, that I'll go roaring out looking for her and Geordie or Sir Henry can put a spear in me while I do it."

Red Sandy was relieved. "Ay sir, that's exactly what it is, whether it's true or no'…"

"Do you think it's true?"

"Ah, no sir. I think it's a rumour…"

"Then why did Thomas the Merchant bring it to me and my lord Scrope get it from Sir John Forster?"

Och, that's torn it, Red Sandy thought but didn't say. "Ah dinna ken, sir," was what he said.

Carey went back to his paperwork. At last the worst of it was done, helped by John Tovey's speed at penwork, which was impressive.

"Is that the last letter, Mr Tovey?"

"There's a couple more about the horse fodder…"

"They can wait, I think. Get to bed, Mr Tovey. I'll see you in the morning."

John Tovey had a straw pallet bed that he kept rolled up in the office while the large and ugly Scot that Carey had employed in Oxford was already asleep on the truckle bed in Carey's chamber. Tovey took himself to bed while Carey went into his bedroom and brought out a cup of aqua vitae.

"Is your tooth still bad, sir?"

"It's awful, John. I want to bang my head against a wall to stop it throbbing but that won't help. I'll drink this and take a turn outside and then I'll try and get some sleep."

"Cloves help, sir. Oil of cloves is best but if you can just get some cloves and chew them, they really do help—until you can get it drawn, of course."

"Thank you, I'll go down to the kitchen and see if I can find any cloves."

John Tovey was soon snoring and Carey did go down to the kitchen and found that the spices were locked in the spice cupboard. He woke one of the kitchen boys, learned that his sister had the key, and went up to the Warden's Lodging to find her sewing next to the fire in the bedroom.

"Cloves? Yes, I've heard that too." Bless her, she put her sewing by and they went downstairs to the strains of Italian music and she produced the key to the cupboard on the large bunch of keys on her belt and opened it up. Carey tried one clove gingerly, but when he found it genuinely did help, he took a handful and put them in his doublet pocket.

"When are you going back to the Queen?" he asked his sister and she flushed and looked down.

"I'm sorry, Robin," she said, "I just can't stand it in Carlisle anymore. And Young Thomas is in trouble again..."

As far as Robin could tell, Young Thomas was doing exactly what you expected wealthy young aristocrats to do at Oxford and he hoped the boy hadn't managed to pox himself.

He nodded. "Before Christmas?"

She locked up the spice cupboard again and nodded. "Scrope's estates need him to look at them, we've had to dismiss the steward for a ridiculous amount of cheating and padding of bills."

Robin said nothing to that, kissed her quite formally at the door of her bedchamber and went down the stairs again.

An hour later the whole castle was snoring and Carey was still sitting by the embers of the fire in the great hall. He looked around at the place, stood up and went purposefully across to the Queen Mary tower and up to his dressing room where his jack stood on its stand. He changed his clothes for the old woolen doublet he wore under his jack, transferred the cloves carefully, put the jack on and said "Uff" very quietly as the weight went onto his shoulders and his hips. He put his morion helmet on, loosened the straps so they wouldn't hurt his right jaw and strapped on his swordbelt again.

He went quietly down the stairs and out into the stableyard, where he woke two of the strongest hobbies, one of them his own beast, Sorrel, and put bridles on both of them, a saddle on one. They weren't happy, although they ought to have been used to doings in the middle of the night. Perhaps they didn't like it that the bell wasn't tolling.

He left them tied up in the yard and went to the dog kennels where he shushed the excited yelps and wuffs and took Scrope's best lymer, Teazle, on a long leash.

It took time and a bit of doing but he led the horses and the dog down the covered path to the gate and along the wall to the postern gate where he took the horses through one at a time and then gave Solomon Musgrave a substantial tip. He was preoccupied or perhaps he would have noticed who was following him.

He walked the horses down through the town, had another expensive conversation with the guard on the Scotch gate and then was out into the drizzling night. He mounted Sorrel, who he had saddled, put his heels in and went to a steady canter to warm up the horses and the dog before he speeded up to a hand gallop. He assumed Geordie Burn was in cahoots with Sir Henry. He already knew that Sir Henry and Lord Spynie were bosom pals. It was simply obvious what was going on and Carey planned to disrupt it as best he could. It was a pity he didn't have Sergeant Dodd swinging rangily along behind him and moaning about how it would be better to bring all the men, but he didn't. Dodd had taken himself off into the East March in search of a tooth-drawer he'd heard of and Carey didn't expect to see him again until he'd found one, given how Dodd generally was.

And he knew perfectly well that this was probably all an elaborate trap specially for him; he knew perfectly well that Elizabeth Lady Widdrington was perhaps tucked up in her bed... No. The rumour had come from too many directions. Chances were that she had been kidnapped and by Geordie Burn, one of the cruelest and worst raiders in the Middle March after Kerr of Cessford himself. Still, it was probably also a trap.

He didn't care. So it was a trap. Fine. He'd spring it by himself and maybe God would help him get away with Lady Widdrington and maybe he would end cold and staring on somebody's spear. Anything was better than hanging around Carlisle while his bad tooth tried to drill itself through his skull. And he would not have gotten any sleep even if he had stayed tucked up safe in Carlisle castle.

The cloves were helping, though, he thought as he chewed carefully on the pungent spice in his mouth; he was definitely able to think now.

He crossed the Bewcastle waste carefully because it was horribly tricky ground, rocky and treacherous and full of sudden marshy spots, changing horses frequently so they wouldn't get tired. The sliver of Moon dodged in and out of the clouds but by a couple of hours before dawn, the rain had clamped down properly, his jack was wet on the outside, though not on the inside yet, thanks to a lot of beeswax rubbed into it, and he was having to lead the horses over an even more tricky bit. He planned to stay south of the Border until he had to cross into the Burns' lands and he had brought a kerchief of Elizabeth's he had quietly purloined when she came to Carlisle for the funeral of the old Lord Scrope. He'd forgotten he'd done it too, and then found it a few days before in the drawer of his desk.

That was when he heard a snuffling whimpering noise and stopped still. It came again and then a little yelp. It couldn't be?

"Jack?" he said and heard a wuff in the night.

He followed the sound and found the half-grown lymer pup completely covered in mud and stuck in a marsh. He wagged his tail wearily at Carey and gave another yelp.

"Good God, did you follow me all the way here?"

It was a stupid question, obviously he had because here he was. Carey sighed deeply, went and found a long sapling, cut it and prodded it toward Jack who barked at it, and finally held the sapling in his mouth so Carey could pull him out of the marsh. He took the dog to a slightly cleaner pool and washed the worst off and then squatted beside him and hugged his shoulders where they weren't too wet.

The pup was utterly exhausted, could hardly move his paws, but still licked Carey painfully exactly where his jaw was hurting worst.

"I appreciate the faithfulness," Carey said, "but what am I going to do with you?"

The half-grown pup wriggled with joy and panted open-mouthed at Carey. "You can't ride a horse, so you'll have to do the best you can and run," he said. "I'll rest a bit and then we'll take the last part as quick as we can and get to them on a surprise."

It wasn't a very good plan, he knew that, but it was the best he'd been able to come up with. Sometimes simple plans were good because they caught your enemies unawares. He hoped. He arranged the two hobbies on either side of himself and got them to lie down so he could prop himself against one of them and get some kind of rest. Jack came and plopped himself down next to him, and Teazle, the older lymer, took a dignified place on the other side.

At first Carey couldn't sleep although the pain from his tooth had gone down to a sinister drone. He was too wrought up thinking about Elizabeth, wondering if she was sleeping, wondering how she was, wondering what else he could do. Was this how she had felt when he got into trouble in Dumfries in the summer? Perhaps. It hadn't occurred to him how bad she might have felt.

He dozed off and dreamed of being roundly scolded by an elderly Jewish woman he didn't know at all, only she looked a bit like his mother.

He woke at dawn, stiff and aching with the nervous feeling he was late for something, he should get moving. The lymer pup was curled against him and looking up at him adoringly. One of the hobbies had wandered off while he was asleep. He cursed himself for not hobbling them, but he didn't have time to go looking for the animal and he would be perfectly all right for the moment, since he had a clear Carlisle brand. Whoever found him would keep him for a while and then bring him into Carlisle for the reward.

So he mounted up on Sorrel and rode on his way, followed by the dogs loping behind him, and he couldn't help himself, he rode faster and faster, until he was galloping dangerously along the high Cheviots, along the treacherous paths there that wound in and out among the rocks with the dogs strung out, Teazle before and Jack behind and he was late, he knew he was and...

There were two more horses there, one behind the other, over on the other side of summer pasture belonging to the Kerrs, or so they claimed, or the Collingwoods, or so they claimed, bitten down short and rank now from the rain. The leader was a broad tall man in an English jack and a morion helmet, the follower was...

Was a woman. Clearly a woman though riding astride, she had a black velvet gown on, her hat was pinned to her head and she was riding like the devil down toward him, riding like the Queen of Elfland though on a hobby not a milkwhite mare, taking ditches and low drystone walls as if the hobby was Pegasus and...

She lifted her face and the Sun poked a spear out from under the rocky piles of cloud and lit her for a second and then he had his own horse round and he was riding toward her while his heart beat itself out of his chest with joy and relief and joy.

They met by a pile of rocks, Carey stopped his horse on a sixpence and flung himself down from the saddle, ran over to her and helped her down from the saddle and held her, crushed her against him because he had to do it, he had to hold her and feel her body against his, even through the metal plates and leather padding of his jack he had to feel her and he was afraid he was hurting her, crushing her against him but she had her arms around him and was gripping him as tight. He instinctively put his mouth down to hers and she kissed him back for a second, only a second, and then pulled away. The lymer caught up and stood there barking stupidly while the pup flopped on his side and went to sleep.

"Robin," she said.

His happiness could not be stopped by something so trivial, it was flowing through him like a mountain stream, washing away his tiredness and bad temper.

"I know, Elizabeth, I'm sorry..."

She laughed and gripped him tighter. "I escaped, Robin!" she crowed, like a boy after an escapade. "Young Henry came and told them the ransom was paid and Maud Burn backed me up and we just rode away."

Young Henry was of course the man in the jack who was riding at a tactfully slow pace down toward them.

"He did? Wonderful!" It was too. By God, Geordie Burn would be angry. And how the Borderers would laugh. "And you came south and west because they'd assume you'd make for Jedburgh."

"Yes."

"Now then, Sir Robert," said Young Henry as he came near, formally tipping his helmet to Carey. Carey tipped his helmet back and grinned at him.

"Now then, Mr Widdrington, what's this I hear about ye putting a brave on Geordie Burn?"

Young Henry flushed a little, pity about that big yellow spot on his nose, it looked ready to burst. "I suppose, I did," he admitted. "I'm thinking it might be better to make for Carlisle now, though. Sergeant Dodd and Mr Anricks went back to Jedburgh with my lady's horse and Geordie will have found them by now and he'll not be pleased."

"Maybe he'll tangle with Sergeant Dodd and get dead suddenly?" said Carey, with a hopeful grin.

"I don't think so, sir," said Young Henry. "He's a clever man and not a brawler."

Elizabeth had very properly moved away from Carey now and straightened her hat. "I'm not going to Carlisle," she announced. "I'm going to Jedburgh to give my husband a piece of my mind."

The two men exchanged glances and Young Henry coughed hard. Carey was thinking. "I can't go with you in any case, my lady," he said, "although I want to. I don't want to get you into trouble with him."

"I am already in trouble with him," said Elizabeth haughtily. "What he has failed to realise is that he is in trouble with me. How dare he connive with a reiver to have me kidnapped to get me out of the way? How dare he?" She had her fists bunched and the look on her face was frightening even if you weren't Sir Henry.

"I don't want to take you directly into Jedburgh. I could take you to the abbey," said Young Henry. "I think there are a couple of the old monks there and the townsfolk use the church for services but you could likely stay there while I find out if the coast is clear. I wouldna like you to go riding into the town until we know who's there and who isn't."

"Pshaw!"

"Yes," said Carey thoughtfully, "she can hide there while you go into town and roust out Sergeant Dodd and anyone else you think will be useful and then bring her husband to her rather than the other way about."

"If he'll come."

"If he doesn't, that's an admission in itself and perhaps we can start proceedings for divorce," said Carey.

"Divorce?" said Elizabeth, "But that needs an act of parliament?"

"It does," said Carey, "but it's been done before." And nearly, he almost added, it was done for the Queen. Nearly.

"Whom God has joined together let no man put asunder," said Elizabeth in an old-fashioned sort of voice.

"My lady," said Carey, his voice full of compressed impatience, love and fury, "if your husband treated you decently and had given you children, I wouldn't be here. He doesn't and he hasn't."

"I promised to be a good wife to him," said Elizabeth, "in the sight of God."

"Certainly," said Young Henry unexpectedly, "and he promised to be a good husband to you, in the sight of God. I remember, I was there. Has he kept that promise?"

Elizabeth said nothing, looked down at the ground.

"Don't take her by the road," said Carey to Young Henry, "Go across country and carefully. Geordie may put watchers on the road. I'm hoping he's assumed she's heading for Carlisle and is on his way there now."

"Yes, and two murderers with him," said Elizabeth. "Robin, I must talk to you about the killing of Minister Jamie Burn."

She did, quietly, and at length and told him what she thought. "Jock Tait is the man who can act as a witness at the trial, if anyone can persuade him. But Archie and Jemmy Burn did it, as far as I can tell, they did it and raped his wife as well."

"Why?"

"Why? Because she was there and she's a pretty woman and they like to. They nearly raped me when they came back to the manse..."

"WHAT?"

There was the authentic Carey roar, thought Young Henry philosophically; they probably heard that in Jedburgh itself. Elizabeth explained the part about getting hit on the head when the two came back to the manse for some reason, and how if it hadn't been for Mr Anricks and his dag she might have been raped herself.

Young Henry was still furious about it, but he thought Carey was even more angry. He wasn't sure because the man was pale anyway. Carey sat on a rock with Elizabeth beside him and very seriously took her through every incident at Wendron again, including the ones with the boys. Of course, neither of them noticed that they were holding hands like children. And then he said quietly, "If those two come into the West March of England, they will never come out again."

Easy to say, thought Young Henry, less easy to do given the number of people who would be willing to hide them, even if you could get up some kind of hue and cry for them. Maybe he would have the chance to hang Archie and Jemmy Burn himself. That would be good.

They arranged that Carey would wait for Dodd and Anricks at Reidswire, which was only a summer shieling but had quite a good shelter. Young Henry would take Elizabeth to the old abbey and leave her there with the few monks still clinging on in the half-burnt ruins, speak to Dodd and Anricks, assuming they were still in Jedburgh and tell them where to find Carey. The fact of Henry coming into Jedburgh alone might encourage Geordie to think she'd gone to Carlisle which would be very helpful. Henry would then bring all the Widdringtons as well as Sir Henry to her ladyship. With luck Geordie would be chasing her rumour across the Middle March by then.

THURSDAY 19TH OCTOBER 1592

There were five of the friars left of a full complement of twenty, and none of them were as young as they had been. In 1560 the Reformation had come to Scotland with a great ringing of bells and destroying of churches, though it hadn't been nearly as greedy and as violent a reformation as Henry VIII's stripping of the altars in England. The monks lost their jobs but not their lives, many of them left the cloisters with relief to try what men could do who could read and write. Some were allowed to stay in their monasteries and abbeys, cultivating the kitchen garden, looking after the sheep, just as they had before while their numbers ran down in the way of all life. No new novices came to them, until the one novice who had stayed was a man of forty-eight and they elected him abbot pro tem because Brother Constantine was now a little bit forgetful and silly and shook all the time like an aspen leaf, Brother Ignatius was crippled by rheumatism though he still tried to act as infirmerar to the townspeople when they came to him, Brother Justinian was skinny and obsessed by prayer and always in the church at odd times of day and night, and Brother Aurelius was trying to do everything else, including cook which was unfortunate because he was terrible at it.

"Ye have tae be the abbot," he'd insisted to Brother Ninian. "We have tae have one and it's you. Are ye sure ye wouldna like to go and marry some woman or other now ye're grown?"

Abbot Ninian had smiled and answered that he was very happy where he was. Which was true, he liked things to be just so and he liked them always to be the same as the day before which was lucky because that's how things go in an abbey.

And so it was Lord Abbot Ninian and Brother Aurelius who received the young woman and the young man at the ruined guest house of the abbey by the main road.

"This is Lady Widdrington," said the man. "I am her stepson, Henry Widdrington."

Brother Aurelius' round brown face grew watchful, with something else there as well. That was no surprise, thought Young Henry, the Widdringtons were well-known reivers of the East and Middle Marches, and had helped the Earl of Surrey burn the abbey a few decades before. Not all of it, luckily. Abbot Ninian also looked worried.

"What about the...?" he asked Brother Aurelius who smiled.

"They'll be very well where they are. How can we help you, Mr Widdrington?"

"My lady has had a difficult few days and would like to rest for a while here until her husband comes to collect her. No more than that."

Brother Aurelius squinted at the lady. She was wearing a muddy but fine velvet gown and her woollen kirtle was good as well, though old, while her boots though muddy were excellent, and her hat a little fashionable. She looked tired, though. "Well our guest house is, as you see, unusable, but she can come up tae the abbey church and sit there a while if she likes."

"Will that be all right, my lady?"

"Of course, Henry, I'm not made of glass. I'd like to sit down on something that isn't a horse for a while, though. And is there anything to eat?"

Brother Aurelius beamed at the lady. This was what the Austin friars were for, after all, providing sustenance and shelter to weary travellers. He had a kind of kitchen built out of the ruins of the old one and he was sure there was a bit of stew in the pot there and some bread perhaps, though his latest batch had come out a little bit solid—unless their other guests had finished them.

"I'll go and see what we've got," he said. "My Lord Abbot, perhaps you could show my lady tae the church and sit her down there."

The Lord Abbot ducked his head and smiled nervously. "All right, Brother Aurelius," he said. "You won't be too long will you?"

"I'll be making something delicious, ye'll see. There might be a chicken I can catch too." He doubted it. Their other guests had eaten the last chicken, he was sure.

The lady went gravely with the Lord Abbot, who was wearing exactly the same worn black robes as everyone else, and listened as he told her about the cabbages and the roses and how the fishpond was full of fish as if she had been there before and already knew all about it, and then about how they did reformed services in the church so it would look a little strange, but not to worry about it because God was still there.

"There are some other guests I mustn't tell you about," he explained carefully as they went into the huge abbey church, with its rows of round arches disappearing into darkness above. Some of them looked scorched but the roof still seemed to be on. "Brother Aurelius said I mustn't."

"Oh," said Lady Widdrington and gave him an odd look. "Are they reivers or a man like Geordie Burn?"

The Lord Abbot shivered and shook his head; he had heard of Geordie Burn and was terrified of him or anyone like him. "No, no, my lady," he said in his slow deliberate way. "They are friends and they are not even men and they help us with the chanting."

"Angels, perhaps?" she asked, with a smile.

"A bit like angels," he said, worried again, "but they eat a lot."

He showed her to the choir where there were still nice wooden choirstalls to sit in and the altar was quiet with no sanctuary lamp lit. All the saints had been beheaded by enthusiastic Protestants and the paintings on the walls had been sploshed with whitewash. The reformed altar was down in the nave, a communion table, and the old altar had the usual chunk taken out of it where they had removed the superstitious old relics.

She looked around for the candles and Bible, found the new Bible chained to its lectern but the candles were too valuable to leave out when it wasn't a Sunday, she thought. So there was no fire there and it was bone-chillingly cold. And she was still damp from the hillside. She sighed. She would really like to sit by a fire and get completely warm.

"Who's that?" she asked as her eyes adjusted and saw a dark figure in a corner of the church, by the vandalised Lady chapel.

"Oh that's only Brother Justinian," explained the Lord Abbot, "praying as usual."

"Is he?"

"He gets the offices mixed up. We do still sing them, you know, not all of them but some of them. We always sing Vespers. Maybe ye'll hear us."

"I'd like that."

"Brother Aurelius doesn't want you to meet our other guests, so maybe not."

"Hm."

Then the Lord Abbot went away, with an awkward bob of a bow as he went to ask Brother Aurelius what to do next.

Elizabeth sat for a while in the huge old church, resting her back and bum, which were awakening from numbness and protesting about the treatment they'd been getting. But then it just got too cold in there, and too dark with the old friar muttering Latin in the corner, with his eyes tight shut, rocking to and fro and ignoring her completely. She got up and went through the choir and reredos, mainly in splinters though once it had been pretty with gold and paint, she thought, through the sacristy where they had a large locked chest for the candlesticks and candles and altar things, and then out into the afternoon as it turned down toward evening.

She saw something then, just a flicker at the corner of her eye. Firmly ramming down a superstitious thrill she chased after the person, and after a sprint through a neat garden and some dodging round an apple tree, she caught a bony little boy and knew him at once.

"Jimmy Tait," she exclaimed, "good God, what are you doing here?"

"Och, it's ma Lady Widdrington, och!"

"Why are you here?"

Jimmy scratched and then smiled shyly. "I'm singing in the choir, just like ye said, missus, though it's a bit small wi' only the old men and us and…"

"You think this is Carlisle Cathedral?"

Jimmy frowned. "Whit else could it be? We walked for days, an awf'y long way. It's a big town and a huge great church and there's auld monks here though Ah think they're Papists, but no matter, the songs is the same, only the words is different."

"We?"

"Ay, missus, me and Andy and Cuddy and my lord, we walked here, starting in the night and naebody the wiser. Cuddy Trotter cannae sing better nor a corbie, but he come too to make sure Ah wis all right and maybe see if they want a kitchen boy or summat so he can finish learning Latin and be a clerk."

"But…but your parents?"

Jimmy's face clouded. "Ah told my ma I wis off tae the big church but I dinna think she believed me and me dad's off guarding the village sheep in the third infield."

"Andy and Cuddy?"

"Cuddy's got two brothers and two sisters so his parents will be glad he's 'prenticed and Andy...well, Andy said his father'd likely beat him but it was worth it to get to sing every day again and learn more letters and stuff. He wants tae learn French too."

Elizabeth shook her head and then laughed a little. "What did the old monk say?"

"Ay well, the one called Brother Aurelius said we could stay and help the singing and he asked the Lord Abbot, who's a wee bit slow in the heid, and the Lord Abbot said, 'Whitever ye want, Brother,' and so it's sorted."

"Where are the other boys?"

"They're in whit's left o' the dorter, Ah'll show ye."

She followed him to what looked like a mere pile of stones and rubble at the further corner of the burned cloister, but turned out to be one end of a dormitory that still had beds in it, though old and rotten. Cuddy and Andy were playing dice for pebbles and they jumped up and looked about for an escape as she came climbing carefully up the pile of stones. There was a fair-haired boy behind them she recognised from the funeral who stood up and waited warily for her.

They relaxed a little when they recognised her, and Cuddy said, "Whit are ye doing in Carlisle, ma'am?"

"I might ask you the same thing, Cuddy," she replied. "And you, Andy?"

The boy she thought was Lord Hugh confirmed it by bowing to her so she curtseyed. He was in a cutdown brocade doublet from something wide from the reign of King Henry but his boots were from Edinburgh and he had a boy's sword at his belt.

"My Lord Hugh," she said to him gravely, "what on earth are you doing here?"

He flushed and put his old velvet cap back on. "I'm going to 'prentice to the cathedral as well."

"But you can't," she said, wishing it were not so, "you're the heir."

The boy shrugged bitterly. "Then I've come for the adventure if they won't have me," he said, "I can sing, though." And he lifted his voice and sang something Latin, his voice a warm gold against the diamond silver of Jimmy Tait's. "There. I can sing. I don't want to be a laird, I want to be a clerk that sings."

She looked at him with real pity. He couldn't use his gift, only show it off for Court scraps.

"My dear," she said, "you have no choice. You have to be a laird."

"And go to Court?"

"Well it's not so bad," she began. "You learn to be a page…"

"With my guardian, Lord Spynie?"

She said nothing.

"I knew one of his pages, he was a cousin on my mother's side. He couldnae sit down for a week after Lord Spynie picked him out, for all the pretty fat padded breeches he got," said Lord Hughie. "Do ye think I know nothing, ma'am? D'ye think I'm an innocent like Jimmy Tait here?"

Elizabeth could think of nothing to say and Lord Hughie turned away from her. So she sat carefully on one of the other beds and said, "Tell me."

The stories tallied. There had been a council of war after the funeral, with all the boys attending. A council of war was what Andy called it, in fact. Most of the boys were sad about the minister but willing to go back to being crow-scarers and shepherds all the time. Piers Dixon had a sick mum, with a cough that wouldn't go away and she was terrible thin, so he'd stick by her and if she died, then he'd come on his own; the rest of his family wouldn't mind for there were too many mouths to feed anyway. Young Jimmy had spoken up.

"He did, missus," said Cuddy. "It was wonderful." Jimmy Tait blushed and hid his face in his hands, then looked up again. "He said that the minister said that God had given him his voice, for it wisnae something he had learned or made, it was purely a gift, and God gave it to him for a reason and he needed to find out what the reason was and so he'd go tae Carlisle on his own if he had to. And he knew where to get the 'prentice money too."

"The 'prentice money?"

"Ay, it were the down payment on whatever it was the minister was at and Jimmy got intae the manse after the funeral on the quiet and he knew where the minister hid stuff cos he'd been poking around and found it and so…"

"Where's that?"

"Och, in his study, there's a brick in the wall that comes loose but ye canna see it if ye dinna ken it's there and he mostly kept papers in it but when Jimmy looked again he found half of a wonderful necklace all in gold and jewels, so he did. But then he couldnae get out again for the two murderers come in and while ye was fighting them he run upstairs and hid under the bed and stayed there for he was affeared with Mr Anricks and everything and Young Henry and all and then ye found him in the morning and wis nice tae him. And we went that night."

"Show me the 'prentice fee, Jimmy?"

"Ye willna take it, it's ourn, the minister said he wad gi' it to us to get us 'prenticed and to free Jimmy fra his father and…"

"I will not take it."

Jimmy delved into the noxious depths of his breeches and pulled out a bag which he tipped out to show half of a beautiful gold woman's necklace with sapphires and emeralds in it, in the style of seventy years before, at least ten pounds worth, probably much more. There was your explanation for why the men came back for it, if they found out about it after they had got away. She knew it at once. Perhaps Lady Hume had let slip about it when they told her the minister was dead. She heard Lord Hughie sucking in a long breath when he saw it. Then another. And another. He had gone white.

"Thank you, Jimmy. Put it away again."

He put it back, tied the straps round himself again. There was no reason to think such a dirty little boy with bare hard feet would have such a treasure.

Elizabeth sat in thought for a moment. "All right," she said, "I'm going to talk to Brother Aurelius. You stay here."

"Well we need tae go tae the church soon for Vespers, will ye hear us? It's no' very good yet, but it's shaping," said Andy.

"Of course I'll hear you. First I must speak to the brothers."

***

Lord Hughie followed her down the rocks that had been the stairs and made a great production about helping her, which she allowed. "Ma'am, my lady," he said with his voice trembling, "May I speak to you?"

They sat on a bench in the herb garden.

"I know that collar."

"Yes, it's your grandmother's."

"How do you know?"

"She told me about it."

"She...how did the minister come by it?"

Elizabeth was silent a moment. He must have some idea. "I think your grandam offered it to him if he would try and kill Lord Spynie for her."

He nodded. "But she's daft in the heid with her faery forts and all."

"She may be less daft than she seems. And she's also a determined woman and she doesn't want you to go to Court with Lord Spynie either."

"She knows?"

"Of course she knows. I know. Everybody knows."

"Well, why doesn't anybody stop him?"

"He's rich and powerful and he has the favour of the King."

Hughie went silent a while. "So my grandam gave that to the minister so he'd go and kill Spynie, half before, half after. And he tried and he failed?"

"Yes." The boy deserved honesty, appalling though it was.

"And Spynie found out who it was, somehow, and sent two men that had been in the Netherlands so they wouldn't be known, to kill him?"

She nodded. Though now she came to think about it, how

exactly did Spynie find out precisely who had made the attempt against him if they hadn't caught him to torture him?

"And they did it."

"Yes."

"So I caused the minister's death?"

"No, my lord, he caused his own death. He should have told your grandam no, despite her being his great aunt. What was he doing, trying to kill Lord Spynie in cold blood and him a man of the cloth? He should have said, 'No' and trusted in God."

"At least he tried!" shouted the boy. "At least he tried something!"

"You can think it's all your fault if you like, my lord," she said to him brutally. "It wasn't. It was Jamie Burn's pride and anger. It's very hard for a man to leave the fighting trade if he's good at it and I honour him for trying. But in the end, he decided to kill a man, he failed, and he was killed in revenge. Those who live by the sword shall die by it. All he had to do was delay things for two or three years and Spynie wouldn't be interested."

"Ma'am, you're wrong. If it wasn't me; it would be some other boy. Killing Spynie is the right thing to do."

And he turned away and left her.

She found Brother Aurelius happily stirring food in a large iron pot and humming a part of a Magnificat, while three large heavy-looking loaves waited on the bit of board he was using for a table.

"I've spoken to your other guests—Jimmy, Cuddy, Andy and Lord Hugh," she said without preamble.

Brother Aurelius stopped stirring, then started again in the other direction. "Ah," he said.

"Did you tell them this was Carlisle Cathedral or did they…?"

"So that's where they thought they were. No, ma'am, we didnae lie tae them. They arrived at night and asked could they 'prentice to the church here and we couldnae turn them away, could we? Four young boys like that? So we took them in and fed them and at Matins this morning after breakfast, they showed us what they could do, though it was reformed psalms. Brother Justinian taught them some Latin psalms after, and the *Salve*

Regina, the first time he's been interested in anything but prayer for years. We had a kind of sung Mass, too, with English psalms and I officiated which was, strictly speaking, illegal—but you could say it was reformed too with the English…It was beautiful, you know."

"I'm sure it was. I'm looking forward to Vespers."

"I suppose you'll be taking them back to their families now."

"One of them, yes. I'd rather take the others to Carlisle, where they originally wanted to go."

"Ah," said Brother Aurelius, stirring the stew with nameless lumps of gristle floating in it. "Well it was lovely to have them here, even if it was for such a short time." He smiled at her. "Would you help me lay the table in the refectory? Our supper is quite simple, as you see."

Elizabeth found the wooden bowls and spoons and also the refectory which had burned quite badly but still had half a roof. She even found a couple of candles which might help as the Sun went down.

All the monks came, even Brother Constantine came, smiling, and all of him trembling as if he were in an invisible wind. "God bless us," he said, "and especially the new novices." He smiled on the four boys at the end of the table, three of whom smiled shyly back. Lord Hughie was staring into space. Brother Justinian was reading an old worn prayer book; Brother Ignatius was a spry old man with terrible red knuckles like walnuts and a hobble that looked painful. The Lord Abbot Ninian intoned a very long grace in Latin, and Brother Aurelius served everybody except Justinian with stew, and Justinian with a double helping of bread. Brother Ignatius started talking to Elizabeth about the diseases he found were coming to him, as if he already knew her.

Elizabeth was starving but found the stew surprisingly inedible and the bread so solid and rocklike it was all she could do to chew it. She copied the other brothers and dipped it into the watery stew and got enough down to stop her belly protesting. The boys put their heads down and ate every scrap of stew and bread, so she gave Jimmy her remains, saying she wasn't very hungry after all.

They went to the church then, led by Lord Abbot Ninian, and Brother Aurelius brought a sanctuary lamp from somewhere and they lit the two candles from it. Then they sang Vespers.

It was like no Vespers or Evensong she had ever heard. The Latin chants came out in plainsong, sung expertly by all five of the brothers, and around and above them wound the singing of the boys, mainly alleluias. Then the boys sang two psalms and the monks intoned the closing prayer. Was it heretical?

Elizabeth suddenly had a picture in her mind of the young strong Jesus with the older Jewish woman behind Him with her arms folded, both of them smiling at her. She understood something then, although she wasn't sure how. That whenever Jesus spoke to a woman, it was, in a way, His mother He was speaking to, as happens with most young men, and so Mary was far more important than she had thought. For one of the things that had thrilled her about the Gospels was the respect with which Our Lord spoke to women, as if they were full people, not foolish half-men who needed ruling. Not always, and He was positively rude to His mother at the Marriage Feast at Cana— unless He was joking. Also nowhere in the Gospels did it say that Jesus laughed, although He wept twice. And yet Elizabeth was sure she could hear laughter in some of what He said. And it stood to reason He must have laughed sometimes, perhaps when He got drunk at the marriage feast on the wine He had made from water? Perhaps that was blasphemy to think that Jesus Christ could have got drunk at a party, but why shouldn't He? And on His own wine too? Why should He always have been serious or sorrowful or angry—if He was a man as well as God, He laughed too. And what kind of music did He like, she wondered; was His voice good? Surely it was? You didn't hear anything about that either, though surely Jews had ballads and worksongs like everybody else?

Jimmy was singing a Latin hymn from before she was born. *Salve Regina* it began and his voice went up effortlessly into the darkness of the burnt roof and lit it up with sound. She sat there, bathing in the boy's glorious voice, until it ended and everyone gave a little sigh.

They came out to find the cloisters and main courtyard full of men in jacks and helmets.

The boys fled back into the church immediately, but the brothers came forward slowly in a body, led, she noticed, by Brother Aurelius not the Lord Abbot Ninian, who was well back.

It didn't matter. She knew this particular collection of toughs and walked forward calmly to where Young Henry and his Uncle Thomas were dismounting. Henry had her jennet on a leading rein, though the saddle was still a man's. She sighed a little; a side saddle was so comfortable and her bum was bruised from all the riding she had done that morning.

"Now then, Mr Widdrington," she said formally to her husband's eldest son. "Where is Sir Henry?"

"Ay, well," said Young Henry, "he's in Jedburgh right enough but he willna see ye right away."

Elizabeth considered this. It was one of Sir Henry's nasty tricks, to make you wait for your punishment so your imagination could work and you would get nervous. Quite obvious and quite contemptible.

"I don't know that I can ride anymore since you helped me escape from the Burns," she said in a voice pitched to reach everyone in the crowd of men. "Perhaps I'll stay here with the monks."

There was a stir in the crowd of men and hobbies and one man came shoving forward. She recognised Jock Tait, in an old worn jack that may have been his grandfather's from the pattern and a leather cap on his head. You could see he needed a new helmet.

"Missus, d'ye ken where my son Jimmy has gone?"

She didn't answer that. "Why?"

"He's missing fra home. He went wi' three other boys."

"Maybe they were making for Carlisle Cathedral," she said carefully. "You know Minister Burn had a plan to take them there and 'prentice them as singers at the cathedral."

He dismounted and came toward her and she could smell that he had been drinking. "Ay, and I asked ten pounds English from him, ma wife told ye."

"Yes," she said coldly, "how is your wife?"

His eyes slid from hers and he answered in a baffled angry voice, "Ah didna ken he meant it, I wis joking."

"Were you?"

"Well I wisna. But…"

"Mr Tait, your second son is a skinny dirty little boy that has probably never eaten enough in his life. Why do you care what he does? Surely if he goes to Carlisle Cathedral as a singer, he'll be fed and it'll cost you nothing."

Were those actual tears in the man's eyes or the effect of Henry's torch? "I'll miss his singing, so I will. I didna ken how good he was."

"Why not? Did you never listen to him until the minister's funeral?"

"Nay, I didna ken. But Carlisle's a long way…"

Good God, did the man love his son in some way? Really?

"Mr Tait, a voice like Jimmy's only comes occasionally. Carlisle is the best place for him, they'll teach him to use it and they'll teach him to read music and Latin and…why don't you want him to go?"

"I want him to go but not alone on the road to Carlisle, it's a long way."

"I beg your pardon?"

"I want tae go with him to Carlisle and make sure he gets there, missus, naething mair, I swear to ye. Did ye think I'd stop him? Ay, I've given him a thick ear now and again but this…he's ainly seven but he's taken a man's step here and I wish he would ha' asked me…"

"Would you have said yes?"

"Ay, o' course." Perhaps he was lying, but did that matter? Perhaps he was looking ahead now. "Ah wanted to go to Carlisle Cathedral maself when I wis a wean but wi' my grandfather and uncle hangit before I wis born and my father allus riding to fetch us in food, I had to stay at hame and watch the sheep and the goats and the little 'uns."

Elizabeth looked at the man, he wasn't drunk so much as he had taken a drink and it had loosened his tongue. Was it possible he was telling the truth?

She didn't have to decide what to do because a small bony creature came running across the courtyard and flung himself at his father, who fumbled in shock, nearly dropped him and then lifted him up.

"Whit are ye doing here, Jimmy?"

"Ah," said Brother Aurelius with a bland smile, "the boys arrived here last night, very weary and we have given them shelter although unfortunately we are not Carlisle Cathedral."

Jock Tait looked at him and then at Elizabeth and then at Jimmy. "Is that right, Jimmy?"

"Ay, we thought it wis, but it isn't?"

Jock laughed. "Nay, it's Jeddart Abbey!"

"Oh. Is Carlisle further, for we walked an awf'y long way."

"Ay, nay doubt ye did for yer tracks went round on yourself twice."

"Oh. Will ye take me to Carlisle then, Dad? Wi' my lord and Andy and Cuddy?"

"Ay, Ah will."

Jimmy had screwed his face up with a very cynical expression on it. "Ay, and ye willnae fool me and take me back hame and gi' me the leathering o'my life?"

There was a pause and then Jock answered, "No, I willna." Then he swallowed.

"And will ye tell who wis the men that killt the minister so he couldna take us hisself?"

"Now?"

"Ay," said Jimmy, still with that old man's expression on his face. Jock looked at his son as if he was seeing him for the first time. Then he nodded slowly.

"Mr Widdrington…"

"Ay?"

"I've a mind to lay a complaint as a witness agin Archie and Jemmy Burn, for the killing of Minister James Burn, their cousin."

"If we can find a procurator fiscal at this hour, will ye make a witness statement?"

"Ay, that I will. I had Jimmy looking after their horses while they did the murder and then he took two of their horses down to the Border to trade with a merchant I know, to put ye off the track. I know them well from riding wi' them, Burns and Taits is usually friends. I didna ken they were after the minister. I thought it was some ither man o' the village. I never thought they'd be after killing their ain cousin like that—not even Kerrs would do it."

Elizabeth did her best not to be cynical. Possibly that was true, though she doubted it. Never mind, Jock Tait had come round with no persuasion at all.

Young Henry nodded once. "We'll have a hue and cry for them the minute your statement's done," he said, "I think they're with Geordie Burn at the moment. Who now says he never intended to ransom you, my lady, he just gave you shelter."

"Hmf," said Elizabeth, "you expect liars to lie. Well?"

"Well, my lady, will I go back to my father and tell him you're tired."

"No, because he'll hit you again." The combined Widdringtons who were probably the twenty best riders of that numerous and ferocious surname started looking about at each other for someone who would be mad enough to go and tell the old man his wife was disinclined to meet him.

Brother Aurelius stepped forward with a smile on his round face. "I'll do it," he said. "My lady Widdrington is tired and needs her rest although I have to admit we don't really have anywhere here at the abbey that's suitable for a lady."

"What did he tell you, Mr Widdrington?" she asked.

"He told me to take some men and fetch you to him."

Elizabeth's lips compressed together until all the blood left them. "I wish I knew why he treats me like a blood enemy, not his wife," she said. Nobody answered her.

Brother Aurelius came close to her and said kindly, "Perhaps ye'll come and bear me company whiles I clean up the kitchen," he said. There was no guile in his voice but Elizabeth almost said no. Then she thought again, shrugged and went with him.

There wasn't a lot to do in the kitchen as the stew and the bread were finished and there was no more food anywhere. Elizabeth brought back the wooden bowls and spoons, scoured them out with silver sand and polished them, while Brother Aurelius gave a quick wipe to the inside of the great cauldron he had clearly used daily for the last thirty years with no more than a wipe each time. It was a surprise the stew didn't taste better, really. He asked her how she had come to Sir Henry and what he had done and how she had tried to be a good wife to him. She found herself pouring out her heart to him, while he sat by the remains of the fire with his head oddly tilted a little to the side, propped on his hand so she didn't have to look him in the eyes.

"And has he always beaten ye?"

She sighed. "Yes. Sometimes he hits me, sometimes he knocks me down. Sometimes he uses his belt. I'm used to it now but I wish he would tell me what he wants of me so I can do it if I can."

Brother Aurelius took a deep breath in and let it out again.

"It seems he wants me dead now," she added, "if Henry's right that he arranged with Geordie Burn to take me captive."

"Are ye sure of that?"

"No, I'm not. But my stepson is quite convinced."

"And he sent your stepson with men to bring you back."

"He's showing off. Showing me he has men at his back and I don't."

"Hmm. Lady Widdrington, I'll ask ye to do a hard thing. Come with me into the toon to meet your husband, on your own. Will ye do it?"

Her heart was dull and grey that had been lit up with joy that morning. After the fire, the embers. She had to go back to him, it was her duty and besides she had nowhere else to go. But she wished and wished she were a man...Actually a man had little choice as well. Robin was as bound by ties of family and duty as she was.

She sighed. "Yes, Brother Aurelius, I will."

She followed him back to where the Widdringtons had made themselves comfortable with a small fire from some of the beams of wood they'd uncovered. The four monks were sitting in a row near it, Brother Constantine still trembling like a leaf but smiling benignly, Brother Justinian reading his prayer book, Brother Ignatius chatting to one of the men, the Lord Abbot Ninian sitting with his mouth a little open watching the proceedings with amazement and suspicion.

The hobbies were lined up and tethered, most of the men had their helmets and jacks off and the boys were singing one of the psalms. It was a domestic scene. There was a pause and then two voices lifted, singing Tam Lin between them, one Jimmy Tait's in its silver perfection, the other a man's bass voice, a little gruff and out of practice but with a power and force in it that made the eldritch parts with the faery folk more frightening as Tam Lin turned to fire and water in the Queen of Elfland's spell.

She stood just outside of the fire circle, listening to the sound, listening as Jimmy and Jock Tait sang together for the first time.

Brother Aurelius went forward and spoke to Young Henry who nodded and gestured at everyone. The old monk then went quietly to each man and got some kind of answer, while three of the Widdringtons sang the rude song about Lusty Jean and the Fine Young Knight. And then he came back to her.

"I have talked to every one of the men," said Brother Aurelius. "I and they are *ad idem* about certain things and they too believe that your kidnapping was really an attempt upon your life. Let us go down to the town now. I believe your husband is at the Spread Eagle inn."

It wasn't really so late, it was just it got dark early. Elizabeth was aching and still quite hungry after the stew and bread, but mostly she was tired. At least she didn't have to ride tonight since Brother Aurelius was striding down the road from the abbey. Since the townsmen used the church for reformed services on Sundays, it wasn't too bad and had stones laid on the muddiest bits.

She didn't want to go, she wanted to run in the opposite direction, to Reidswire where Robin was waiting for Sergeant Dodd and the tooth-drawer. And yet her feet kept following the sandals of Brother Aurelius.

Thursday Night 19th October

to Friday 20th October 1592

Mr Anricks insisted on hurrying to meet Carey at Reidswire, a place often used for Middle March Warden meetings and as summer pasture. Now the wind swept across it and the rain was horizontal, though by the time they got there, perhaps there was an hour of daylight left and for a wonder the rain had stopped temporarily. The Sun pretended to be fighting to shine through the cloud, but was really sulking.

Carey came out of the sheepshelter where he had lit a fire from the supplies left there by the men who used it. Two dogs were with him who first barked and then fawned on Dodd and Anricks, probably in hopes of food. He tried to smile but couldn't because of the way his face had ballooned, and also he was afraid of having his tooth drawn because the last time he had to have it done, on the left side, it had hurt so much.

There wasn't a chair so Carey sat on a rock with his back to the dry stone wall shelter, and Mr Anricks tipped his head back and took a look.

"Hm," said Mr Anricks. He poked about with shining steel instruments while Dodd stood and stared across the hills where nobody was pasturing cattle and Carey made occasional squawks as Anricks probed a sensitive spot. The dogs lay nearby watching with interest.

"Two teeth have to come out, Sir Robert," said Anricks, "though that may save the third which is a wisdom tooth."

"Get on with it," growled Carey, his hands in fists.

"All in good time," said Anricks, delving about in his pack and bringing out a brown glass bottle and a cloth. "Would you hold him up, please, Sergeant. Now, I want you to breathe in the fumes from this sweet oil of vitriol, keep doing it. I know it's an acrid smell and you'll feel drunk and dizzy and then you'll fall asleep. When you wake up, your teeth will be out." The dogs got up and retired some distance from the smell and the younger one started barking again.

"Are you sure...?"

"Ay, he's telling the truth, sir, I've seen him dae it in Jedburgh."

Suspiciously Carey started sniffing the cloth, he got chatty, talking a lot of nonsense about being executed and a little later he slumped sideways, despite the barking. Immediately Anricks tipped him back, put his pliers in and pulled, then he did it again and then he mopped up some ugly-looking pus that came spilling out of the hole until it was all good red blood. Dodd took a look at the teeth—one was practically gone with two holes right through it and the other had a long tunnel going right down, both were black. Horrible. Teeth weren't meant to be black or brown, they were meant to be yellow. Dodd's teeth were a good ivory colour and not a hole in them either. He had let Anricks check earlier.

It took a little while before Carey came to again, and in that time Anricks explained how he wanted to do an empirical investigation into toothworms which would involve checking Dodd and Carey's stools for worms. Dodd was happy enough to say yes, wondering what Carey would say.

Carey was obviously in a lot of pain when he came round but he shook Anricks' hand and promised him at least a gold angel for taking out the teeth; he felt better already. His jaw swelling was already going down, certainly. The dogs came back cautiously but stayed away from Anricks' pack. Dodd recognised them and said hello—it was a good notion of the Courtier's to bring them, mind.

Dodd was pleased with himself. He had found a tooth-drawer and gotten Carey's bad teeth drawn, now they could go back to Carlisle.

But no they couldn't. "Why not?" Dodd wanted to know. "Why d'ye want tae stay in this Godforsaken place...Ach, it's Lady Widdrington."

"I have to know if she's all right or if her bastard of a husband has...hurt her again."

"Why? Why d'ye have to know? What can ye do about it if he has? Eh?"

"I have to know," said Carey, muffled by the cloth soaked with aqua vitae he was stopping the bleeding with.

"Jesu, ye're…"

"Gentlemen," said Anricks, who was carefully repacking his pack. He had used clean cloths to wipe the instruments he had used and was closing the top. There was another picture there of a fearsome looking worm with large teeth itself coming out of a black tooth with a hole in it, which had made Dodd quite queasy to look at.

"…never going tae pit yer heid in a noose again. Sir Henry's a bad man tae cross as ye found in the summer…"

"I have to make sure…"

"Gentlemen!"

"Ay and ye'll do her harm as well…"

"Shut up, Sergeant, you don't have to come with me if ye're affeared…"

"By God, I'm no' affeared o' any man but it's stupid tae…"

"GENTLEMEN!"

Mr Anricks had produced quite a shout though he coughed afterwards. Carey turned his head to him from glaring at Dodd. "What?" The younger dog said "Wuff?" in exactly the same tone.

"I will ride back into Jedburgh and I will find out what is happening to Lady Widdrington. When I have found out I will take whatever action I consider is appropriate."

"With respect, Mr Anricks, I don't think a tooth-drawer can really…"

"Nay sir, he's a pursuivant for Sir Robert Cecil. He showed me his commission."

Carey put out his hand for it imperiously. A minute later he had sat back down on the rock and leaned his head back.

"What's going on?" he asked. "Why are you here, Mr Anricks?"

"I don't know what's going on, but I am certain that the Maxwell is embroiled in it somewhere, which is why I desire to go to the West March. But first I will ride back to Jedburgh and find out what is happening to Lady Widdrington."

"Why?"

"Because I like the woman, Sir Robert, and for good and sufficient reasons to do with her husband and his activities with Lord Spynie."

"Will you tell me what they are?"

"No. Or not now. I have no evidence. Is there any chance you will keep my identity secret or is it gone the way of all flesh now, seeing I've told three men?"

"I won't tell anyone except my lord Burleigh,"

Anricks smiled gently. "His son is my very good lord so I am quite happy for you to do so. In the meantime I want to get back to the Newcastle road before full dark and so I'll be going."

Dodd bore him company on the way there to make sure he didn't miss the path in the dusk, leaving Carey to take a nap in the little shelter by the fire. By the time he came back, Carey was snoring away with the dogs on either side of him and would not be woken. The old lymer lifted his lip to Dodd and warned him off. And moreover the Moon was behind more clouds making the night pitch-black. Dodd sighed, brought the hobbies into the shelter so no one would ask why they were there, and rolled himself up in his cloak across the door opening. He hoped no one would wake him because burying people took time and was a lot of effort.

Thursday Night 19th October

to Friday 20th October 1592

The Spread Eagle inn was still full of men and lights, torches and candles, a game of ninepins causing uproarious betting, with Sir Henry and Lord Spynie standing in the centre of a knot of hangers-on, holding pewter tankards of the double-double beer, shouting at each other about whether a ram would beat a billy goat in a fight and whether a shod hobby went better than an unshod one in a race in the woods.

Into this hurdy-gurdy came a small modest figure who sat in the corner, drank mild ale, and watched. When he wished, Simon Anricks could be almost invisible. He wasn't sure what he could do about Lady Widdrington and her husband, and he wished he hadn't said that he would do anything nor let out that he was Sir Robert Cecil's man. But what was done was done and if too many people knew what he was, well, he would have to go back south to Bristol and his wife and children. And to be truthful, he would prefer that. Rebecca came to him in his dreams sometimes and told him off for crimes like getting wet or not eating regularly and he always took her in his arms when she did because she was his wife and he loved her. He woke up cold and lonely, so if his cover was blown, he wouldn't mind that much.

Yet he was here because Sir Robert Cecil had been seeing the edges, the outlines, the flippers, and tail of a monstrous plot. Something was going on in Scotland, something that might perhaps give the King of Scotland the throne of England a little earlier than necessary, if you were suspicious, if you thought the King of Scotland might be the kind of man who would do that. The Queen was certainly old, fifty-nine this year, but, unfortunately for James, in excellent health. Was His Majesty of Scotland getting impatient, was he wanting something more than his pension? Were the Spaniards, in particular the ever-patient Spanish king, influencing him? Or was it all imagination, dreams, and fantasy—the way suspicious minds sometimes come up with plots that don't exist? He had agreed to come out of his pleasant retirement yet again to try and find out, agreed because there were important people in London town, particularly Dr Hector Nunez, who wanted to find out something about the Scottish king as well.

He sighed and ordered the ordinary, which turned out to be haggis again. In London it was all steak and kidney pie and liver and onions, here in the North, haggis—thrifty huswifery using up the unpreservable offal first.

He watched Sir Henry, a short, squat man, with a good greying moustache and corrugated ears which spoke of gout and quite possibly stones in his bladder. He was shouting at Lord Spynie still, who was enjoying himself with his hard-cases at his back, still a good-looking young man though his jawline was blurred with too much booze and his eyes were puffy. Anricks wondered why he wasn't with the King and who was with the King now. That was very interesting. Why wasn't he with the King?

Spynie had been in trouble in August, something to do with the Earl of Bothwell and goings on in Dumfries, a series of events involving Sir Robert Carey and Lady Widdrington, which Anricks still wasn't clear about. He had read all the papers reporting what had happened, including a copy of Sir Robert's own private report to his father, and he was damned if he could make out what had been going on. Had King James somehow managed to buy Carey, turn him against his Queen? That was possible, given the length of the two interviews with the Scottish monarch that Carey had been granted.

Somebody had come into the commonroom, and Anricks recognised the round-headed Austin friar. Brother Aurelius was a kindly faced old man with a natural tonsure and not very much white hair, his face oddly familiar-looking. The barman served him with mild ale and no money changed hands; Brother Aurelius went and stood near Sir Henry and Spynie and waited to be noticed.

It took a while. Sir Henry's broad face was red, and his voice had been getting steadily louder. He was laying a bet with Lord Spynie on a fight to be held at the Carlisle race course of three rams against three billy goats to settle the matter.

At last Spynie asked Brother Aurelius' opinion on the matter, in a way that showed he didn't expect anything.

"Ay," Brother Aurelius agreed, "it's a tickle question. And more interesting than whether a shod horse or an unshod horse goes better because that was all settled before the Queen went tae England. I mind me that the Earl of Bothwell ran the race twice with the same four horses, two shod and two unshod, and then again with the shod horses unshod and the unshod shod."

"What happened?" asked Sir Henry, "a dead heat?"

The monk's face beamed at him. "The unshod horses won both races. It was quite definitive."

Away in his corner, listening for all he was worth, Simon Anricks smiled as well. It was too pat; he didn't believe it. Not without running the race again.

"That was the one before this Lord Bothwell, his uncle. Queen Mary's lover."

Spynie smiled at him. "It's said he was a warlock, like his nephew. Perhaps he enchanted the race?"

"Ay, perhaps. In which case why run it? And in any case, my Lord Bothwell backed the shod horses."

"Why are ye here?" asked Sir Henry. "I've never known one of you monks come into the inn."

"No, there's nae reason to," agreed Brother Aurelius. "We make our own aqua vitae and sell it tae the landlord here because it's so good, eh?" The barman smiled and nodded. "I've naething to do with that, it's Brother Ignatius and Lord Abbot Ninian that make it, I anely bring it into town. In the spring. Nay, Sir Henry, I'm here because I accompanied your lady wife here. She's sitting in the parlour now, putting herself around some haggis and mild ale."

"Where are my men?"

"Och, Ah dinna ken. Back at the abbey perhaps, they wis making theirselves comfortable."

Sir Henry paused at that. If he could but see it, there was a message to him in that from his men.

"Well I'm not paying for my wife to get fat on the haggis here. She can wait for me without guzzling…"

"Nay need," said Aurelius benignly, "it's off the abbey's tab which is *well* in credit. The thing is, Sir Henry, she's come back tae ye because it's her duty to dae it not because she wants to, which is a thing I find admirable but sad."

Sir Henry drank theatrically and finished his quart. "Are you going to tell me how to manage my wife? You? You've never been married—unless it's tae a choirboy." Some of the men laughed at that; Lord Spynie smiled.

Brother Aurelius was smiling too though the smile was a little strained and his face was redder. "Ay, perhaps it's a mite silly in me, that I should want tae speak up for a woman that's done her best to be a guid and obedient wife tae ye. She's made mistakes, ay, and she says now she shouldnae have come into Scotland wi'out your permission, but she thought since ye were here yerself it wouldnae matter if she came to organise the funeral of Minister Jamie Burn."

Sir Henry snorted and put the pewter tankard down. "All I ask of her is that she stay at home and do as she's told. That's all."

"Nay Sir Henry, that isnae. You ask of her that she have no gossips nor friends, that she has nae part o' the marriage bed wi' ye and that she take your ill-treatment of her. That is not what God meant marriage to be..."

"It's none of your business, brother—my wife, my business."

"Ay, it is my business, Sir Henry, because I was once a Widdrington and I willna see ye bring shame on my surname with your goings on. The way ye treat your wife is only one of them, ye hear? My name was once Roger Widdrington and I'm yer uncle, in fact, d'ye mind? Yer father's younger brother? Yer memory's got worse if ye dinna remember me for I let ye fish in the abbey's fishponds when ye came to see me when ye were a wean, before the change. I've lived a long while and I still live at the abbey because I choose to and, thank God, the Jeddart folk are kind enough to let us stay until all of us go to God. But ye, Sir Henry, are an embarrassment and a shame tae the Widdrington name and, by God, it *is* my place to tell ye so."

Sir Henry had an ugly expression on his face.

"You can't tell me off about my wife. She's mine."

"Nay, she isna. She's a creature belonging to God and the way ye treat isnae designed to show her the error of her ways and bring her to better ones. It's designed tae hurt her and make her despair, Sir Henry. It's designed to bring her down. It's a shame and a scandal to your surname, so it is, there's not a one of your men that I spoke to that hasnae respect for your wife—more respect than for ye, though of course they fear ye."

Sir Henry roared and grabbed Brother Aurelius by the throat of his robe, shoved him backwards to the bar and leaned him over.

"Shut yer face, old man…"

Brother Aurelius' face was as red as Sir Henry's and he had the same full-throated roar despite being bent backwards.

"Old man, is it? Ye're auld yerself, Henry. Ye're the headman of the Widdringtons, and ye bring shame on all of us by treating her the way ye do. There's no kinsman of yourn older than ye are, save me, and so I'll do it, I'll put the shame and the disgrace of it back on your own heid, Sir Henry. If ye do not treat your wife better and kindlier than ye have, may ye be cursed, may all your doings miscarry and may yer life be short."

Sir Henry seemed to be turned to stone by this. Lord Spynie backed away from him and space opened up around him in the crowded commonroom.

Brother Aurelius flicked away the hand still holding him, stood upright and breathed deep. "See if that'll change your ways," he said. "But I doot it." He shook himself and walked to the door of the commonroom. "Ye're not long for this life, Sir Henry. I willna see ye again, I think. Good night to ye."

When he came into the warm little parlour where Elizabeth was starting to doze off after an excellent meal, she saw at once he was still annoyed.

"Never mind," she said to him. "I never thought you talking to him would help."

"Nay missus, I mishandled it and let him sting me. I'm sorry—that, I am." The old man looked so rueful she could have kissed him. Instead she brushed as much of the mud from her gown as she could and repinned her hat and cap to her head. Then she settled back.

"He knows I'm here. He can come and get me when he chooses and he'll want to keep me waiting so I'll be more affeared of him," she said. "So I shall get some sleep."

In the commonroom the shouting was louder yet, though Sir Henry's face had lost the bonhomie it had. Simon Anricks was watching him carefully, the way he looked at Lord Spynie, the way Lord Spynie looked at him. He was also casting ugly glances at Anricks, although Simon could think of no way in which he could have offended the man.

At last Sir Henry came over and sat down heavily in the chair next to Anricks. "Is it true ye use witchcraft to take out teeth?"

"No," sighed Anricks, "I use sweet oil of vitriol which makes men sleepy so they pass out. It works on chickens as well. I can take out teeth without it but it's very much easier for me to use it."

"Are you lying to me?"

"No, I'm not," said Anricks. His voice had become very level.

"Well it's a pity because I could find a use for a witch or a warlock now."

Anricks nodded. "The friar's curse. Yes."

Sir Henry drank, aqua vitae this time, and wiped his moustache. "I'll treat me wife as I choose."

"Why?"

"What d'ye mean, why?"

"She's only a woman. If you're...ah...worried by the curse, you've only to treat her better and kindlier. That's what he said, isn't it? 'If ye do not treat your wife better and kindlier than ye have, may ye be cursed, may all your doings miscarry and may yer life be short.' To avoid the curse, treat your wife better and kindlier than you have."

Anricks met the man's eyes full on and Sir Henry found he had a cold acute look to them which chilled him. Anricks went on with the same deadly quiet in him.

"It isn't her fault that you're in debt to Lord Spynie and you can't pay it back. It isn't her fault that you haven't made anything like as much money as you thought you would from the Deputy Wardenship of the East March. And it isn't her fault that you've the gout and stones in your bladder and that causes you pain. But something about her is important to you, Sir Henry, and I'm surprised you've forgotten it."

"What?" Sir Henry's moustache was jutting and his brows were right down. Anricks' voice was quite weak and whispery and it went softer still.

"Remember whose niece she is, Sir Henry. She is the beloved niece of my Lady Hunsdon and she is thus the niece of Henry Carey, Baron Hunsdon, who is the actual Warden of the East March, not you. He gave her to you in marriage as a part of the governance of the East March, not for your own satisfaction, nor in fact, hers. His wife is very unhappy at the way you treat her and so, naturally enough, is he. Because it embarrasses him too. Being a kindly man, he is angry at your cruelty."

Sir Henry was staring at Anricks as though at a cockatrice. "How do you know...?"

The smile became colder and the weak voice softer. "If Hunsdon chose to come north to Berwick, he would find out a lot about the Deputy Wardenship you would prefer him not to know. If he were to kick you out of the Deputy Wardenship, which he might, you wouldn't be naked, no, you'd still have your surname. But your life would be considerably harder."

"Are ye threatening me?"

"No, Sir Henry, I am telling you the facts of life. But you might consider kindness as a better policy all round. I've been married for years, and I like it. I have five children and another on the way and I love my wife. But you do not have to love your wife to have a perfectly pleasant life with her, if you treat her with some respect."

Sir Henry had a baffled ugly look in his eyes which did not bode well for Elizabeth but Anricks had done his best. He had given Sir Henry a very quotidian reason for treating his wife better and his Uncle Roger or Brother Aurelius had given him a superstitious reason. If it didn't work, then Anricks thought Sir Henry's life would indeed be short, if only because of the fire-eating youngest son of Baron Hunsdon, if nothing else.

The next morning, when the sky was grey though the Sun was fully up, Dodd felt someone step stealthily over him and go out onto the flat area leading down to the river. He came to his feet with his sword in his hand only to find Carey standing there, while he pissed, staring to the north.

Considering the probable time, Carey must have slept for twelve hours straight through, maybe more. His face was pale but the swelling was almost gone and he looked better, though his expression was unhappy.

"She's there, at Jedburgh," said the Courtier, more to himself than to Dodd. "She's there with her bastard husband who arranged for her to be kidnapped and I'm here and..."

"Ay," said Dodd, doing the same as the Courtier against a stone and then going into the second part of the little shelter where the hobbies were and bringing them both out, stamping and snorting and sulking because they were hungry and didn't have any food. He hobbled both of them and let them go onto the turf by the river where there was some sour tough grass and a few thistles. He didn't have any food either so he wasn't inclined to sympathise with them. He couldn't eat grass, could he, though he'd tried once. The dogs came out and marked the corners of the shelter again, then came hopefully to him. They found he had no food either and started sniffing around for rabbits, though probably all the game in the area was hidden in its burrows.

"She wisnae intended to be ransomed either. It was all a scheme of Sir Henry and Lord Spynie's."

"Do you think I'll ever have her?" asked the Courtier in a self-pitying voice, "or will I have to wait even longer, until I'm an old man of forty or fifty?"

"Och, God," said Dodd. "Ah've tellt ye and tellt ye. Ye've enough credit in the West March to call out fifty men who'd follow ye and I'll bring the Dodds and the English Armstrongs, ay and mebbe Jock o' the Peartree Graham would come oot for ye for the mischief and then we'll run the rode of all time to

Widdrington and take her from him and ye can kill him yerself, personally."

"Yes, but then she wouldn't marry me."

"She would. She'd come round in the end. They allus do."

"I just…I can't think straight without her. Seeing her, holding her yesterday…"

It's given it to ye bad again, thought Dodd, but didn't say. The dogs had wandered off in their quest for food.

He started to look around for firewood to replace the stuff they had burned and let Carey blether on about the woman.

"And she's so beautiful and I don't know how she takes the knocking around she gets from her husband and…What the devil is that?"

Dodd was very glad to have a break from Carey's perpetual mooning over the woman. "What?" He realised the dogs had suddenly started galloping across the valley, barking.

They squinted against the rain on the other side of the valley and saw first the dogs, especially the yellow pup, and then the riders, five of them, surrounding one man who had three laden pack ponies behind him. Dodd recognised the horses more than the man himself who was small and unprepossessing and growled,

"They're stealing Mr Anricks' pack ponies from him."

"So they are. Well, we can't have that."

The two of them sprinted to where their hobbies were cropping the grass and unlooped the hobbles. The dogs were in among the horses now, doing as they'd been trained, leaping up and down, biting at the hobbies' bellies and dodging sword blows. Dodd jumped up to the biting hobby's back and Carey jumped onto Sorrel and they charged straight across the valley and into the five men. There was a quick exchange of blows and then the five Elliots thought they didn't want the pack ponies that much anyway and turned their horses about and ran away, with Carey singing "*T'il y est haut!*" after them as if he was in the hunting field and the dogs giving chase ahead of him, barking their heads off. A dag fired behind them and clipped one of the horses who stood on his head and galloped off at an angle up the hill with his rider clinging to his back like a monkey.

That had put a bit of colour in Carey's cheeks. He cantered back to Anricks who had his dag in one hand and the leading rein for the pack ponies in his other hand. The pack ponies were heavy laden and swinging about and neighing in protest and one of the packs was about to come loose and fall off. Carey dismounted quickly to secure it while Dodd chased after the lymers who were already coming back, wagging their tails joyfully. The pup was triumphantly holding a man's riding boot in his teeth which he proceeded to worry to death.

"What's in the packs, Mr Anricks?" asked Carey with a smile. "Gold dust?"

"Oats that I bought in Jedburgh with my earnings from drawing their teeth."

"Ah, gold dust, indeed. I might be interested in them if we can get them to Carlisle. We need to get a move on, for the Elliots will go and fetch their friend Geordie Burn and all of his friends to come at us again."

Ay, thought Dodd, with the Bewcastle waste to get through and all. Lovely.

They went back to the shelter and packed up as quickly as they could. Anricks had been shopping in Jedburgh, for one of the ponies had a good faggot of hazel withies to replace the wood they had burned, and some penny loaves and cheese and a pottle of beer for them as well as some scraps from the inn for the dogs who fell on it ferociously and had finished it all in four seconds.

They ate as they rode and Carey took Anricks' gun and cleaned it for him since he was curious about why it hadn't needed a match. It had an improved kind of lock on it, Anricks explained, the latest technology, much better than the wheel locks with their complicated winding up clockwork arrangements. He had two pistols, the other one was a normal matchlock. His new one came from Germany and Anricks had bought it from an armourer in London and this was the first time he had actually fired it in anger, what with the rain. Dodd took a look at it too as they rode south and west and the rain came down and made everything smell of wet leather and wet steel and wet human. Oh, and of pungently wet dog. He didn't like guns, thought a longbow was better because you could loose thirty shafts a minute once you had the way of it, and longbows didn't explode in your hand either. But even he had to admit the German gunsmithing was impressive. And the dag hadn't misfired, the way Carey's normally did, even if Anricks only hit a horse's rump. He insisted that was what he had been aiming at. It was obvious that Carey was now on fire to get a German gun like that as well and was cross-examining Anricks about where and how much, when Dodd caught a glimpse of helmets behind a veil of rain.

"Och," he said, giving the dag back to Anricks to reload, and drew his sword again, wishing and wishing he was wearing his comfy jack, not the buffcoat and statute cap. Carey was of course in a jack and morion, but at least Anricks had no armour at all. That made him feel a little better. The dogs had noticed and were growling with their hackles up, though wisely not running forward.

Carey had seen them as well, there were fifteen of them now, though at a good distance so he couldn't be sure if they were Burns or some other bunch of reivers who fancied getting themselves sorted for horse fodder for the winter. Someone in Jedburgh would have told them all about it.

"I suppose it was stupid of me to try and bring the ponies across the Border by myself," said Anricks in an abstracted tone of voice as if it was someone else he was talking about.

"Ay it was," said Dodd, "but ye werenae to know. Shall we give 'em one of the ponies as blackrent and try and take the rest on to Carlisle?"

Carey was standing up in his stirrups trying to see the other riders better; they were coming closer in a bunch now.

"One of them's got a morion," he said in a thoughtful tone of voice and then laughed and put his heels in, urging his horse up to a gallop in the direction of the riders.

Was it Geordie? No, Geordie didn't have a fancy helmet, his helmet was a plain metal cap like most men wore. Kerr of Cessford? Could be, God forbid, or Ferniehurst or...

Swearing under his breath, Dodd got his hobby to run in an ugly lumpish way behind Carey who was clearly driven woodwild by thinking about his woman and was tired of life. At least Anricks was sensible, as he was continuing south with the ponies at a reluctant trot. The dogs stayed with Anricks, growling menacingly but clearly not fancying their chances against that many.

Halfway to the riders, Dodd saw what Carey had seen and put his sword away again. Good Lord, hadn't the spot on Young Henry's nose burst yet? It was like a beacon.

Carey was already leaning over to shake young Widdrington's hand. "I'm delighted to see you, Mr Widdrington, I thought ye were some of Geordie Burn's ugly crew."

Young Henry nodded. "Ay, we're on a trod, sir," he said. "We've a witness statement in the killing of Minister Burn fra Jock Tait and there's hue and cry for Archie and Jemmy Burn."

"Same surname?"

"Ay sir, and it's not even as if they're at feud like the Kerrs of Cessford and Ferniehurst. They wis paid tae kill him by a courtier, Lord Spynie." Young Henry's expression was one of disgust. There was nothing wrong with killing somebody for money, of course, but killing one of your own surname for an outsider? That was disgraceful.

"Well I don't like to hold you up, but we have a small packtrain with horsefodder over there and the man who drew my bloody tooth is trying to get it to Carlisle unpillaged so…er…"

"Of course we'll ride with ye over the Bewcastle waste, sir, we heard they've gone to Carlisle in any case."

"Where are they headed after, do you think?"

"Bound to be the Low Countries or Ireland, sir, nowhere else for them to go. And they've been there before. That's why nobody knew them hereabouts. They were exiled eight years ago for something about a girl and a man gelded."

Carey nodded as he swung in with the men, and Dodd took up his usual place behind him and to the left to watch his back. The dogs were wagging their tails again and stuck close to Anricks since he had the food.

Anricks had recognised Young Henry as well and shook hands with him, eyeing the flamboyant spot on his nose as if professionally interested. There were plenty of other spots on the man's face, but that was definitely the worst. Dodd remembered getting a few spots when he was a lad but Young Henry's crop was something special. And as a youth, Dodd had had more important things to worry about—like killing Elliots and not dying.

They skirted the Bewcastle waste in the wind and the rain but nothing worse than that. Though this was the wind that left your skin feeling like it had been scoured with wire wool and rain that found its way down your neck and into your boots and made all the leather you were wearing weigh four times as much as it should.

The horses were tired by then, especially Anricks' ponies and his hobby which had done an extra twenty miles to and from Jedburgh, so they called in at Thirlwall Castle. Carleton welcomed them and even gave them some food, pig's liver and onions of course, though he explained that his wife made a kind of meat paste with liver with fat on top which made it keep longer. The younger dog had sore pads and was exhausted and the older lymer was tired too, so they left the dogs there along with Anricks and the pack ponies and ten men to guard him.

Carey was impatient to get to Carlisle and so Carleton lent them horses and they rode the final sixteen miles almost in silence, Carey, Dodd, Young Henry, and the five remaining Widdringtons, along the Giant's Road which was a little bit safer than the Waste.

They went into the castle where the Scropes were clearly packing up to leave, Philadelphia standing imperiously in the castleyard where her own trunks were being packed with a remarkable number of velvet kirtles and black bodices and white damask aprons that had never once seen the light of Carlisle. It was evening by then and the trunks were being shut. Philadelphia instantly stopped what she was doing to scold her brother for going off like that again. She had been so worried, all sorts of rumours were coming from the Middle March, had they heard that a churchman had been done to death in Scotland, in his own home as well?

Over a gigantic meat pie of Philadelphia's own raising and sundry potherbs and bread, Young Henry told the full tale of what had happened to the churchman, dabbing away at the end of his nose with a handkerchief where his spot had messily burst at the most humiliating moment for him. Carey had already heard it from him on the way over and he excused himself toward the end of the meal so he could avoid eating any of Philadelphia's legendary kissing comfits. Dodd followed after him nosily and found Carey in the stables talking to the boys, chief among them Young Hutchin Graham, who was starting to grow seriously now, had big hands and feet and was wearing clogs because his feet had got too big for his boots.

"There's two men, Archie and Jemmy Burn," Carey was saying gravely to them. "They took money from my enemy Lord Spynie—remember him, Young Hutchin?—to go into Scotland, find a man that was a minister and kept a school for boys like you and kill him. Their own cousin."

There was some shocked tutting but these boys were practical. "And?"

"I will give a gold angel to any of you that brings me a true word on where they're hiding. They've come to Carlisle and they might be in the town, or they might be at someone's tower. I want them."

"What'll ye do to them?"

"I'll hang them."

"Can we come and see it?" asked Young Hutchin Graham.

"I don't know. If I can, I'll give them their long necks at Carlisle Castle but if I'm in a hurry, I'll hang 'em wherever I catch them."

The boys scattered, talking about the angel excitedly and arguing over who it was on the coin, was it a man with wings or was it an angel and if so, which one. Young Hutchin waited until Carey was out of the way and then trotted purposefully down into the town where one of his respectable cousins had two guests in need of hiding.

Scrope went out with Sir Richard Lowther the next day on a tour of the West March, checking the defensibility of the fortresses and the state of the paths and roads. Carey stayed in Carlisle, and bought Anricks' oats when they came plodding in late in the afternoon. Anricks had paid out a hundred shillings Scots for them, which were only worth a quarter of an English shilling, thanks to debasements by the Scottish king and rampant forgery on the Borders. So he paid one pound, five shillings English. Carey was perfectly happy to pay three pounds English for the oats, which were good, and Anricks kept the pack ponies. Dodd found this very impressive.

"How did ye know he would pay that for them?" he asked Anricks, over a pint at Bessie's.

"I didn't. I also took the risk that my oats would be reived from me on the way and that they wouldn't be as good as I thought. I could have ended up with no oats at all—for instance, if you and the dogs hadn't driven off the raiders who tried to take them from me—but luckily I didn't. So I owe both you and Sir Robert something for that."

"Ye do?"

"Yes. Will seven shillings and sixpence be enough for you?"

"What?"

"For helping with the pack ponies, specifically driving off the Elliots."

"Och...er...ay, that's...er...thanks."

And Anricks counted out seven silver shillings and six pennies just like that, onto the board. After a moment, Dodd took them. Extraordinary. He rather thought he had just earned the money with not a hint of larceny about it. He couldn't wait to tell Janet; she'd split her sides.

"Whit about the Courtier? He might not want the money, though he allus needs it, ye follow?"

"Oh yes, Sergeant, I do. I'll recompense him in other ways, more fitting to his station."

"Ay."

They finished their quarts companionably while Dodd wondered why such an odd person was really in the West March of England and what he was really doing. He knew a pursuivant was just a term for a spy or a man that did other men's dirty work. While there was dirty work in plenty in the West March, he didn't think the tooth-drawer would be interested in the Johnstones and the Maxwells or the way the Carletons were playing off Lowther or how the Grahams added to the chaos. Maybe he was indeed interested in the Maxwell, who was a Catholic, after all. He mentioned how Carey had been betrayed by the man in the summer and found himself telling the tooth-drawer a couple of stories himself, until he noticed and shut his mouth grimly. Anricks listened well, in a way which drew stories out of you.

"And now I need to find a man called Thomas the Merchant Hetherington and lend him some of my money."

Well, Dodd knew where that one did business so they headed down to English street and halfway there they saw a big ugly man in a leather cap with three tired-looking boys, the smallest of them carrying his newly whittled clogs and his feet covered in mud.

Anricks stopped dead and stared. "By the Almighty," he said, "it's Cuddy Trotter, Andy Hume, and Jimmy Tait. How did you get here?"

"Och, look Dad, it's the tooth-drawer, Mr Anricks, the minister's friend," said the smallest of them, tired but shining with pride. "We're here tae 'prentice tae the cathedral, Mr Anricks. We walked all the way and stayed at a place we thocht was it but it wasn't and me dad came and he said, ye've done a man's work, Jimmy, Ah'll take ye there maself and we walked and walked and he only carried me a bit and so we're here now."

"Well, that's wonderful, Jimmy. You must be Mr Tait?"

"Ay sir, d'ye ken where the cathedral is, for we're all tired and I'm fair famished as well."

Anricks seemed relieved and pleased to see them. "Mr Tait, I'm going to take you to the best inn in Carlisle so you and the boys can rest and then the boys can test for the cathedral in the morning."

"Ay, but we havenae cash…"

"I've just made some with my tooth-drawing in Jedburgh and so it'll be my treat. Where's the young Lord Hughie?"

"He stayed behind at Jedburgh, said he had something to do before he came," said Jock Tait.

"Then, please, allow me."

And he bore them along to Bessie's inn, hard by the castle gate, illegal but tolerated and bought them all the ordinary and pints of mild ale for the boys and a quart of Bessie's incomparable double-double for Jock Tait. And there he got the rest of the tale from them. They were all too tired to do the running around that boys usually do but when they'd finished every scrap of the haggis and bashed neeps and a bag pudding too with a sherry and sugar and butter sauce for a treat, Jimmy Tait turned to Andy and hummed a note. Andy grinned and hummed one back and there they were, singing like birds in a tree, the new ballad of Scarborough Fair with an old tune to it.

"Why aren't you singing, Cuddy?"

"Canna sing, that's why, sir, but I can read and write and mebbe I could learn to play an instrument cos I can read the music well enough just not sing it."

"Do you want to 'prentice at the cathedral?"

"Ay sir, that's why we've all come."

Anricks nodded and after a while he slipped away from the commonroom, with Dodd following him, and stood looking down at the cathedral.

"Are you there, Sergeant?"

"Ay, Mr Anricks."

"Perhaps you could tell me the best way to the cathedral?"

"I'll show ye," said Dodd who was nearly dying of curiosity.

They went to the gate into the cathedral precincts where Mr Anricks spoke quietly to the doorkeeper who eyed him fishily but brought him the Bursar, as he asked.

"There are three boys that want to join the choir," he

explained. "Two of them have fine voices but the third...you'll want him paid for, yes?"

The Bursar allowed as how that was possible. "I am related to a wealthy merchant in London," said Anricks. "He gave me a banker's draft for a large sum of money, more than sufficient to cover the cost of the boys' education. I am willing to sign it over to you to ease the boys' path and also that of a lad called Piers Dixon, if he should come too."

Well the Bursar couldn't possibly say whether the boys would be good enough to...The Choirmaster? He was rehearsing with the boys now. Could he come now? It was very irregular, sir, and I don't...

Anricks took out a piece of paper and spread it on the table. There was complete silence.

Half an hour later the Choirmaster, Bursar, and Bishop were walking down the road to Bessie's, along with Anricks and Dodd who was wondering exactly how much the banker's draft was for. He also wanted to know how it came about that Anricks had it. There was no gold anywhere to be seen, but the Bursar, the Choirmaster and the Bishop were all acting as if a large quantity of it was somewhere close, but was shy and might run away if they were rude or made sudden movements.

At Bessie's they found a singsong in progress, being conducted by Cuddy, with Jock Tait's bass mixing with the boys' voices as they sang, his old jack off and steaming by the fire. The Choirmaster listened carefully with his eyes squinting and then went to Jock and asked if he could hear the boys sing solo. Andy sang the *Twa Corbies*, which was a little grim but you couldn't mistake his alto. Then Jimmy Tait stood on the table, didn't wait, didn't pause to get some hush, just launched into the old song of *Greensleeves*, high up the register, bang on the note, and with a world of longing in the old song that seemed to come from somewhere far older than he was.

The Bursar's and the Bishop's mouths fell open and the Choirmaster seemed to hold his breath for the entirety of the song. When Jimmy finished, the whole of Bessie's stayed quiet for a moment and then there was clapping and a lot of roaring and shouting. Someone was passing a hat round. Meanwhile the Choirmaster came to Anricks and said,

"Thank you sir, for bringing him to my attention. How old is he?"

"I think he's about seven years old."

"God be thanked that he came here now. The older boy will only give us a couple of years and there's no telling after that, but he will give us five, maybe six. We will not need your banker's draft, sir…"

The Bursar started to protest at that but was quelled by a glare from the Choirmaster. The Bishop nodded gravely in acquiescence.

Jimmy Tait was unconcernedly picking his nose, sitting on the table while Andy chatted to a man near the front of the crowd about where they came from.

It happened so quickly, nobody had time to react. Two men in cloaks, one by the door, the other further in. The one further in moved toward Jock Tait purposefully.

Jimmy Tait looked up as he fished carefully for an elusive lump of snot in his nose and then he froze. Seconds later he was standing on the table screaming and pointing.

"It's them, it's them, they killt the minister."

The man in the cloak moved up close to Jock Tait, while he was reaching for his knife, grabbed his shoulder and made the short forceful motion with his right arm that said he was stabbing Jock, stabbed him again.

'Dodd swept his sword out and bellowed, "Castle to me!" But he couldn't get past all the people in the way. The screaming and the shock gave both of the men the time to slide out the door while Jock Tait looked down at himself, puzzled and brought up his hand bright red with blood and Jimmy Tait screamed and screamed.

Dodd raced out into the night, found that two of the guard, Red Sandy and Bangtail, were at his back and chased the two men down Scotch Street to the Scotchgate where the postern was open and two hobbies waiting. The men jumped onto the horses and rode like the devil up the road.

Bangtail came trotting past him. "Ye go git the deputy," he said. "We'll follow 'em, eh, Red Sandy?"

Dodd turned and sprinted back through the town and up to the castle, too many bloody stairs, up to the Queen Mary tower where he found the deputy's Scotch servant snoring already, down again and up to the Warden's Lodgings where some warbling was sounding through the grim old stones.

Carey was singing with his sister. Dodd appeared at the door and spoiled the party by still having his sword out. Carey actually finished the verse and then came out to him, listened as he explained what had happened, scowled and went back to Philadelphia whom he kissed and then left still holding the music.

They went down into the town where Anricks had Jock Tait laid out on a table at Bessie's with a crowd of folk breathing down his neck. Jimmy Tait was squatting next to his father, gripping his hand, and Andy and Cuddy were standing at the head and foot of the table with their eating knives out and their teeth showing.

"They've run, lads," Dodd told them. "They had hobbies waiting at the Scotchgate." There was a growl from some of the townsfolk at this, which was right because that postern should have been locked shut at this time of night. Andy and Cuddy put up their knives but Jimmy stayed where he was.

Carey greeted the Bishop and the Choirmaster who were sitting nearby, the Bishop with his hands folded while the Choirmaster was watching the proceedings intently.

Jock Tait was still conscious, his jerkin open and his shirt up round his armpits. Anricks had his doublet off and his shirtsleeves rolled up and his gory apron on again. There was blood all over the place, bright red some of it. The woman known as Bessie's wife was holding up a candle behind him and Anricks was holding a pair of his dental pliers in the flame.

"Hold still, Jock, if you can," said Anricks as he reached into the larger of the two stab wounds with the pliers and squeezed. There was a hissing sound and a smell of pork and some of the red blood seemed to stop. Jock shut his eyes and grunted. Anricks paused for a moment, mopping blood with a cloth and then he heated the pliers again and did it again and then again. Jimmy put his other hand on his father's fist and held tight, while drops of blood rolled from the side of Jock's mouth. But the blood from the wounds almost stopped.

"There now," said Anricks, "I'm not an expert at stab wounds but I think I've stopped the worst of the bleeding." He took a bottle of Bessie's best aqua vitae and sprinkled it round the wounds and then he took a needle and thread and sewed up the holes as if he was a tailor mending a coat. Then he poured on more aqua vitae and bandaged Jock up.

"I've done the best I can," he said to Jock, "it all now depends on whether he got anything vital in there, but I don't think he did, not your liver and not your gut either. So you might live, Jock, that's all I can say."

Jock made a creaking sound that might have been a laugh. "Ay, an honest barber," he said. "It'll take more'n this to kill me."

They kept Jock on the board and six of the men brought him up the stairs to one of the guest rooms, with Jimmy still holding his hand. But by that time Jock had passed out.

Anricks was washing his hands and arms in a bucket of water out the back and, surprisingly, washing the pliers he had used as well when Dodd came downstairs again. Carey was standing there, talking to him calmly as if he hadn't just been delving about in a man's guts.

"I got the idea of using heated pliers from people who don't stop bleeding when I draw their teeth," Anricks was saying. "I have no idea if it will work since this is the first time I've tried it. Most likely he'll die from a fever in the belly, that's what kills people who have been stabbed if they don't bleed to death. Usually they bleed to death, so perhaps the pliers will work."

Andy and Cuddy came up to him. "Thank you for trying to save Jimmy's dad," they said in chorus, then looked at each other uncertainly. "We know who they are, sir," they said to Carey, who was by far the most fancily dressed man there and therefore must be in charge. "They're the men that came to kill the minister. We'd know them again anywhere. They're Archie and Jemmy Burn and they killed him and they tried to kill Lady

Widdrington and now they've tried tae kill Jimmy's dad when they were just made friends for the first time because he's the witness."

Carey nodded seriously at them. "We'll do our best to catch them and hang them," he said. "That's a promise."

"When ye catch them, ye willna compose with them?" asked Andy anxiously, "not even if their friend the courtier asks ye?"

"Especially not if Lord Spynie asks me," said Carey.

**

Bangtail came back an hour and a half later to say that the two of them had gone to ground at a small tower owned by the Grahams, a mere five miles out of town. He didn't think they had noticed that they were being followed for he and Red Sandy had kept well back and well apart. Red Sandy had stayed by the tower in case they moved or went anywhere else.

Carey smiled at that and said, "Well then, let's try and catch them unawares."

They called out the guard quietly, all of them, not just the ones that were supposed to go out on patrol who happened to be Thomas Carleton's lot, but all of them, even the ones in bed at the castle. Thomas Carleton roused himself out as well, jack on his back and his tarnished morion helmet on his head, chuckling quietly at something.

At two in the morning, the Courtier inspected the men lined up in the castle courtyard. Scrope and Sir Richard Lowther were at Gretna, last he heard, before they went into the Debateable Land and met with some of the Grahams and Armstrongs there. Perhaps they would also meet the Maxwell, the current Scottish West March Warden who was being elusive about a Warden's Day, although it had been years since the last one. And so, as acting Deputy Warden, he had the authority to call on all of them and he did.

They didn't bother with remounts because the tower was so close to Carlisle and rode out with muffled hooves and harness, with a turf carried in Carey's saddlebag ready to light if necessary.

None of the slow matches on the guns were lit, but Dodd and Carleton had firepots for them when the time came.

Thursday Night 19th October

to Friday 20th October 1592

The Jedburgh inn's parlour door opened and young Lord Hughie came in, walked and sat opposite Elizabeth while she dozed in the blessed warmth of the fire. She opened her eyes and saw him but sat there quietly. His young and beautiful face looked peaceful again.

"I just came to say good-bye," he told her. "I'm going back to my grandam in the morning."

"How did you get here?"

"I have feet, ma'am, though they're sore. I followed you and Brother Aurelius down from the abbey."

She looked at him carefully. "You aren't going to 'prentice to the Cathedral?"

Slowly he shook his head. "You're right," he said, "they won't have me. I was going to lie about who I was but with Jimmy Tait's father there, that won't work. And they'll be afraid of my Lord Spynie. I'll go home tomorrow."

She sat up. There was something wrong here, he seemed too calm.

"How will you find the way?"

"I'm sure one of your men can see me right back to Wendron. Perhaps I could borrow a hobby from Mr Widdrington since I've blisters on my feet."

"Are you sure?"

"Oh yes. I'll wait until Cuddy, Archie, and Jimmy are away— they're leaving before dawn tomorrow with Jock Tait—and then I'll go. It's for the best."

She couldn't put her finger on what was wrong but she nodded and smiled.

"The King of Elfland's collar was payment from an English archer for services rendered by my grandam, I realise that now."

Elizabeth nodded. She didn't see any point in arguing otherwise.

"You know Cousin William?" asked Lord Hughie. "You know how old he is?" Elizabeth shook her head. "Well he was born in 1545," said the boy quietly, "because he's forty-seven now. I only just worked it out. My Lord my grandfather claimed him as a byblow, said his mother died giving birth. Of course my grandfather loved my grandmother dearly, always did."

Elizabeth took a deep breath. "He was your grandmother's?"

"Yes. Everything was confused in those years with the destruction and the burning, and I know she stayed at a convent for a while. We still had them in Scotland then. Humes are blond not brown."

"Ah." Elizabeth felt somehow satisfied, as if she had suspected this without knowing.

"The other half of the necklace is probably still in Norwood Castle," he added, "since my Lord Spynie isn't dead, unfortunately."

"He's here, you know," she said anxiously, in case it was a surprise to him.

"I know that, ma'am," he told her gently. "I've met him now and I'll be going to Court as his page next month."

"No, you can't."

"Why not, ma'am, who's going to stop him?"

"I will."

The boy shook his head, still gently, bowed to her and left the parlour.

She sat up and gripped her hands together until the knuckles went white, put her chin on her fists and thought harder than she ever had before. Then she ordered paper and pens, since she had left her satchel with the Burns, and wrote a letter to Chancellor Maitland of Lethington the like of which he had probably never received before nor would receive again. Then she went in search of the landlord and found Lord Hugh already had a bedroom and had locked the door. She found a young man from the Widdrington surname and sent him off to Maitland with the letter.

Saturday Night 21st October

to Sunday 22nd October 1592

They didn't ride fast, with Bangtail showing the way and when Red Sandy rose up from the bank of bracken where he'd been keeping an eye on things, they were within half a mile of the castle and everything was quiet.

"Are they still there?"

"Ay, they're in the farmhouse but there's a tower there and it's all open," whispered Red Sandy, "If we can…"

Somebody's gun went off, the boom from it cracked around the valley. Carey's head whipped round.

"Who the hell…?"

Somebody was on watch at the farmhouse. There were torches and lights; they could make out men running into the tower and a boy on a fast pony galloping away northwards.

"Ay," said Carleton blandly, "there he goes. They're Grahams in there and if ye dinna prevent it we'll all be taken prisoner."

"Why?" asked Carey with interest as if they were talking about a horse race.

"The lad's gone tae the Debateable Land to fetch out the Elliots. So now."

And Carleton leaned on his saddlebow and watched him.

Dodd was expecting fireworks; he got none. "Andy Nixon," said Carey evenly, "I want you to go back to Carlisle, rouse out Mayor Aglionby and ask him to lend me all the Trained Bands of men immediately. Bring them out here to me as fast as ye can."

"Ay sir," said Nixon, turning his horse and riding back down the road.

"Ridley, Little, Hodgson."

"Ay sir."

"Rouse out your surnames, gentlemen, bring them here to me, Warden's quarters on it." The three men headed down the road at a gallop while Carey looked oddly at Carleton who had his brows raised.

"I'd ask you to fetch your surname, Captain Carleton," he said, "But I'm thinking they might be busy, eh? Come with me."

He drew his sword, turned his horse and smiled at the twenty men remaining. "Come on," he said, "let's see if there's any insight left at the farmhouse."

Whatever the men in the tower expected, with their door locked and men on the roof with long bows, crossbows, and a couple of guns as well, they did not expect the twenty men of the guard to come close to the tower. The men took turns ducking and firing until Carey sprinted to the farmhouse, kicked through the door, ran inside and found, as he expected, no women and practically no furniture.

"It's a trap!" said Dodd furiously, behind him. "The Elliots will be here in an hour…"

"Yes," said Carey, "it's a trap. What did you think? And bloody Carleton's in it up to his neck as well."

"Goddamn it…"

"Do you want to go back to Carlisle?"

Dodd stared at him in puzzlement. "No, why?"

Carey grinned at him and actually laughed. "So let's see what a bit of modern siegework can do, eh?"

Carey hurried outside, and wandered near the tower. A gun fired and two crossbows loosed, missing him and he retreated. He had all the men off their hobbies, with the animals kept to the back. The men in the tower were shouting insults at them and one showed his arse to Carey.

"Tut tut," said Carey mildly. "Such language."

He had the men ring the tower just out of range with

instructions to try and draw their fire but do their best not to get hit.

Then he spent a while drawing patterns in the mud and counting under his breath. Dodd took a squint at them: a triangle with square boxes on each of the sides, that was all.

"We need two beams, twenty-five feet long," Carey said after a moment, "or fruitpicking ladders. Nothing less than twenty-five feet long."

"Why?"asked a bewildered Dodd, "The tower's only twenty feet high, it's a short one."

"Ladders are always too short, aren't they?"

"Ay sir."

"No, they're not. Not when I'm doing the besieging."

They looked about for anything long enough but there was nothing. So Carey sent another man all the way back to Carlisle to bring back one of the ladders to the castle walls which he thought might be right. Also ropes, picks, and axes, as quickly as he could, don't wait for the Trained Bands. At least he told the man to hurry. By that time the bells were tolling from the farms and pele towers in the area, and Carleton and a couple of his cronies had found firewood and started a fire.

The Ridleys were the first to come in, fifteen men and another twenty-seven on their way from farms further south. Carey thanked them all for coming out for him, promised that if anything came of it they would get first chance at the loot because they were there first, and placed them around the tower and some in the farmhouse itself with arquebuses to point through the windows. When the Littles and a lot of Hodgsons came in later, he did the same. There were two rings around the tower, one facing inward, the other facing outward.

If Carey was worried about the Elliots, he didn't show it. He sat down by Carleton's fire and talked affably about various sieges he had been at in France and asked courteously about Carleton's experience with seigework. Carleton admitted he hadn't much, and he wondered what Carey was doing. The Elliots would be here soon, did he know that?

Then Carey took a spade from the farmhouse and started digging a ditch parallel to the tower while the men inside jeered at him and threw lumps of shit.

"It shouldn't be very needful this time," he explained to the fascinated men whilst ducking flying turds, "but this is the right way to dig a ditch so the men you're besieging can't shoot you."

At that point the man Carey had sent to Carlisle for the ladder turned up with four men on horseback, carrying two ladders between them. Carey stopped digging, laid them on the ground, and measured them by pacing along them and then grinned again.

Dodd found his relaxed attitude alarming. What insanity was he planning now? He soon found out. Carey started anyone with a bow or gun shooting as steadily as they could—the clear superiority of longbows over guns showing now, in Dodd's opinion. He explained to Dodd exactly what he wanted him to do, which Dodd found first appalling and then funny. But he could do it. He knew he could.

Friday 20th October 1592

Elizabeth was offered a bed in one of the better guest rooms by the innkeeper, with his own daughter to keep her company. He refused her money, said that the abbey would see to it. She even had a nice fresh linen shift from the innkeeper's wife for a shilling, which she thought was money well spent. While she was undressing she found the book of "The Schoolmaster" still in her petticoat pocket where she had put it and forgotten it. The small book was well-thumbed—she looked at it and then put it back. She'd give it to Poppy when she got home.

She slept well in the big bed with the polite innkeeper's daughter. And then, in the early morning she heard a scraping and then a bellowing and a shouting, dull thuds, and then someone light came running along the corridor full pelt, jumped out of the window.

She got the innkeeper's daughter to stop clutching her and got dressed in record time. When she came out of the room she found the place was a bedlam with Lord Spynie's young men stamping around and shouting.

She looked out of the window, saw a dung heap with a deep imprint in it and tracks in the mud running away, uphill toward the abbey. She trotted downstairs and asked the landlord what was going on.

"That boy, Lord Hugh, he tried to stab my Lord Spynie and got away."

"Ah," said Elizabeth, "I see."

"Bide there ma'am and dinna be afraid. Your husband has gone out with my lord to take the young murtherer."

"He succeeded?"

"No, he couldna get past my Lord Spynie's men, but he could have…"

"A pity," she said coldly. "Thank you."

With all the stamping about and shouting, nobody was interested in a woman. She needed a horse and she took one with a Widdrington brand, sighed at the man's saddle and mounted carefully.

She put her heels in and drove the animal up the path to the abbey where she could already hear her husband having a good loud argument with Brother Aurelius about where Lord Hugh might be. Lord Spynie and his men and some of the Widdringtons were searching the abbey, the Widdringtons notably unenthusiastic about it.

She knew where he was because she knew he had a plan. She went straight for the church, leaving the hobby to mill about with the others. At the back of the church she found the little door that led up to the tower and it was shut but not locked. She went through it and barred the door on the inside. She went up the narrow spiral stair, round and round and up and up in the dark, moving by feel except when part of a huge window let some light in.

The last part was all in darkness and she was breathless. Maybe she was wrong…?

She opened the door at the top which led to the tower's roof and the fine view north and south across all the Border country. Lord Hugh was looking at her anxiously from where he was perched in his breeches and shirt, sitting on the battlements, kicking his bare heels above a drop of hundreds of feet. He was smeared with dung from the dung heap.

Elizabeth came through the door and bolted it behind her. Parts of the tower were blackened with smoke and in one corner the leading had melted and was letting rain in to do damage to the timbers.

She came and stood by Lord Hughie and looked all the hundreds of feet down. It gave her a sick and dizzy feeling in her stomach but also a tempting thought. She could sit on a battlement like Hughie, swing her legs over the drop and then…Oops. And all her troubles would be over. Wouldn't they?

It was a terrible sin, the sin of despair which denied the goodness of God. Yet she felt it would be a relief to end the constant sadness, the constant pulling of her heart toward someone she couldn't have. And what if God wasn't good, what if He really was a vicious old man like the Bible showed Him in the parts every fire-eating minister quoted?

She looked at Lord Hughie.

"Lord Hugh Hume," he said thoughtfully. "What a stupid name. Typical of my grandam. I'd rather be an Ian."

Elizabeth nodded. "Trying to get the tombstone right?"

Lord Hughie looked sideways at her and smiled.

"I like it up here, it's just like climbing a tree," he said.

"No, a tree's much safer. Look how smooth the stone is."

"He was planning something, I knew he was, from how nice he was. I slept in my breeches and when I woke at dawn and heard the scratching at the lock, I drew my dagger, and got behind the door."

Elizabeth nodded. Son and grandson of reivers, what did Spynie expect?

"When they came in I tried to stab him but I couldn't get through the padding and his men stopped me so I left the dagger and ran. It doesn't matter. At least I tried."

"You planned to come up here, anyway."

"Yes ma'am, I did. But how did you know? I even made sure the window above the dung heap was open."

Elizabeth smiled and didn't answer.

"Yes, I planned to come up here, high up where it's clear... well, a little bit clear..." The weather was closing in after a bright sunrise, it would be raining soon. "I'd sing a song and then I'd jump."

"And your grandam?"

"She won't know," said Lord Hughie gently. "And she'll see me dancing with her other dead at the faery fort."

"I think she'd know. In fact I think it will kill her."

Hughie shrugged. "She's old. I'm sorry for it, but I willna be Spynie's bumboy."

Play for time, she thought, even while a part of her longed for the simplicity of it. Only you couldn't do that. You would end in Hell for sure.

"Aren't you letting him off lightly?" she asked. "Just jumping off? Why not tell all of them why you're doing it? Why not tell him?"

"He'd just laugh. Or lie. Or both." Still Hughie was looking thoughtful.

"I tell you what," she said, impulsively. "I've a mind to come with ye."

"What?"

"Yes, when you jump, perhaps I'll jump too."

"But...why?"

"My husband beats me. I can't have the man I love," she told him recklessly, not even feeling the shame of it that she couldn't make Sir Henry happy, that she had fallen in love with another man. "I try and try to do what God wants, and nothing changes. And I'm tired of it. So maybe I'll jump too."

"No, my lady, you can't do that, they'll bury you at the crossroads with a stake through you..."

"I'll be dead, I won't feel it." She leaned forward and looked down, half to frighten the boy, half in earnest. "That's how they'll bury you too, my lord."

"No, I'll make it look like an accident."

"God will know."

"My lady, do you think God cares? I thought maybe He did but when the minister was killed…He doesna give a fig for you or me. If He did, my dad wouldna be dead and I wouldna be in this fix. I don't want to die but I canna see an alternative. Sooner or later Lord Spynie and his friends will get me where they want me. That's why I tried to stab him before I ran."

"How do you know so much, Lord Hughie?"

"I've watched the dogs doing it though they dinna seem to mind. And my cousin Christie tellt me about it a lot when I was younger, how Christie would try and hide but it did no good."

"Where's Christie now?"

"Oh, he drowned in the summer in a river. It was an accident. He was drunk, they say." Lord Hughie's voice was bleak.

Elizabeth couldn't think of any answer to that.

"If God cared, my mam wouldnae be dead," said Hughie. "If God cared, my grandam wouldna be away with the faeries either. And my father wouldna be dead forebye. That's the one that matters."

Elizabeth said nothing. What was there to say? It was true. After a little she asked, "What about Cuddy and Archie and Jimmy?"

"Yes, they'll do what they want, go to the cathedral school and be clerks. I can't do that. I have to be a laird because I'm the heir."

"Do you think they'll be sad about you?"

"Ay, a little, but not for long. They'll be too busy learning music and singing and learning Latin."

"What do you want, my lord?"

"I don't want to be a laird. I want to go to school and learn Latin and then I want to study all the poems and the stories. I want to read Virgil. I want to read Juvenal and Catullus. I don't want to go hunting, it's boring, though Cousin William keeps taking me with him and explaining it to me again. I want tae study."

"Have you told your grandam?"

"Ay, of course, but she disnae understand, she cannae even read or write."

There were shouts and far below a banging on the door, people were looking up at them from the ground and pointing.

Hughie stood on the battlement, balancing easily.

"I'll jump," he shouted. "I'll jump because of Lord Spynie. I dinna want to be his bumboy nor anyone's bumboy, d'ye hear? Not his, not Sir Henry's, nor anybody's bumboy! I willna do it!"

Elizabeth stood still, turned to stone like one of the gargoyles. The blood roared in her ears. Was that why she couldn't please her husband? Was that it? Dear God, she had never thought of it. It hadn't crossed her mind. And yet she had no part of the marriage bed with him after he consummated their marriage. And was that why he was so close to Lord Spynie?

She felt sick.

"What are you saying?" she heard herself gasp.

Hughie looked down with damning pity on his face. "Och missus, did ye not know? He's in love with Lord Spynie, allus has been and Lord Spynie uses it. Christie told me about it, even said he felt sorry for the old man. Everyone knows except his family."

Her head was spinning. She put her hand on the battlement to steady herself.

"Are ye all right, my lady?" he asked, bending down to her. "Are ye well?"

"Yes, I am," she said firmly, taking a breath and holding it. Well that made sense of everything. If her husband was a lover of men...like the King? She understood now why he had hated her so from the start, especially if he had lost his heart to someone vicious like Lord Spynie. Robin was worthy of her love; Spynie was not worthy of anything. To have your heart dragging after someone like that...It was horrible and against the law of God, but it made sense. It made sense and suddenly she could feel compassion for the old man whose heart yearned after a spoiled Royal minion.

"Good my lord," she said formally to the boy, "please don't jump. Please."

"I canna see another way out."

"Yes, but I can. I will take you into my fosterage—I don't think my husband will want you for...for a catamite..."

"Nay," agreed Hughie, "he's not like Spynie that way. But he allus does what Spynie wants."

"And I will send you to school in Carlisle, to the cathedral."

"What about the wardship?"

"I've already written to Chancellor Maitland, who is in charge of the Scottish Court of Wards..."

There was a sudden crashing and the door popped open as the bolts broke. Lord Spynie stepped through delicately, holding a dag with a fancy lock and no slow match, followed by three of his bully boys and three of the five Widdringtons that Young Henry had left behind when he went after Archie and Jemmy Burn. At least the Widdringtons were looking very unhappy.

She stepped between Lord Spynie and the boy. Spynie scowled and tried to sight past her but she moved. Hughie was poised for flight like a bird on the battlements, a wingless bird who wouldn't soar but would drop.

"Get out of my way," sneered the King's favourite.

"No," she said brightly, "let's discuss this. You are going to return my Lord Hugh's wardship to Chancellor Maitland for what you paid for it. He will hold it until my lord is of age. My Lord Hugh will not go to Court and will not be your catamite, sir, do you understand?"

"Out of my way, ye stupid bitch."

She walked forward feeling light as a feather and quite happy. She walked right up to the gun and put her left forefinger over the hole that the bullet came out of.

"Now," she said, "I'm not at all sure what happens if you fire your gun. I expect I'll lose my left hand. But maybe you'll lose your right hand. Maybe the gun will explode. I don't know. Shall we find out?"

And she smiled long and slow at him.

One of the men on the roof of the Grahams' tower was finally hit and while the other three dragged him down, the men of the castle guard ran with the two long ladders, up to the corners of the tower, placed them and started climbing as fast as they could. Dodd was first over the top and took out one of the men there with one sweep of his sword, and the other defenders ran to the trapdoor and scurried down it, locked it on them.

They had the roof. Dodd gave the thumbs-up to Carey down below who stopped the firing. Then he looked about on the slate roof and found a corner where the slates were loose. They started taking the slates off with the picks and mattocks and found they could look straight down into the tower's upper room where nine Grahams and two Burns were standing about arguing and shouting at each other. Dodd got off as many slates as he could by kicking them, threaded a rope around the roof beam, sat on the beam and swung down, dropping straight on top of Archie Burn—as he later found out—who broke his fall nicely. He punched the man in the head just to make sure, though. Red Sandy followed him through and then Bangtail and the rest of the men, and after a couple of blows and one man gone with a sword through his leg and a fountain of bright red blood, the Grahams in the tower started laying their swords down and asking for quarter. Dodd insisted they be given it. He didn't want a feud with the Grahams.

He went down the ladder into the bottom half of the tower to make sure, found only frightened hobbies there, and so he opened the first floor iron gate and put the ladder down again.

Carey was first up it at speed.

"The Elliots are on the horizon," he said. "We're moving into the tower."

The ten men and one corpse who had been in the tower were now tied up and dropped temporarily in with the hobbies while all the twenty-two men of the castle guard scurried into the tower and the several hundred Ridleys, Hodgsons, and

Littles came in close, surrounding it and facing out.

"There," said Carey in a pleased voice when all the rushing around was done, "that's the nicest turnabout I've seen in a while. Well done, gentlemen, that went like clockwork."

There was a shout from outside and Carey went to see through the open iron gate. "The Trained Bands are on their way, too," he said with a stupidly happy grin. "Look there!"

Dodd squinted into the distance, annoyed that Carey had seen them first and saw Blennerhasset's Troop, Denham's Troop, and Beverly's Troop jog-trotting along the road from Carlisle with their jacks and helmets on, one with pikes, one with arquebuses, and one with mixed weapons. You could always tell the pikes; it looked so sinister, a block of sharp long spears all moving as one, rippling with the pace of the men.

"Oh yes, my beauties!" Carey crowed and even Dodd had to swallow down a grin at the sight of the four hundred and fifty reinforcements coming at a very nice pace along the road with Andy Nixon jogging at their head along with the captain of the Trained Bands. Behind them was Nick Smithson, the de facto leader of Essex's deserters, and all seven of his men behind him, which was nice to see.

Over on the Border hills a troop of cavalry was coming at a much faster pace because they had further to go and somehow hadn't spotted the Trained Bands yet. The Trained Bands saw them and picked up the pace from a jog to a run, and ran that last half mile to where the Ridleys, Littles, and Hodgsons were cheering them on.

"Thank you for coming out to me, gentlemen," sang Carey in an effortless bellow. "In your troops now, pikes to the fore, arquebuses back, FORM SQUARES!"

Dodd knew that Carey had been training the city bands since the summer, but was impressed when the men of the city of Carlisle sorted themselves out into two neat pike squares, backed by arquebuses facing in the direction of the Elliots. Meanwhile the men from the nearest surnames had collected their hobbies and mounted and grouped themselves loosely in families at the back and sides.

And there was a wagon coming down the road with Anricks sitting on it. He was too far away to see, and yet Dodd knew it was him from the set of his hat. He decided he preferred to meet his blood enemies on a horse and so he followed Carey as he slid down the ladder, boots either side of it and went for his own hobby.

Carey was mounted on Sorrel. Andy Nixon came over to him.

"The men of the Trained Bands of Carell City are ready, sir," he said and tipped his helmet to both Carey and Dodd.

Carey sent some of the youngest of the surnames out into the countryside to scout for any more Elliots on their way. Carleton came out of the farmhouse at that moment and blinked at the battle lines with men running to and fro into place by their mates and the arquebusiers all busy with their weapons, loading them, and lighting slow matches.

Then he looked at Carey and stated the obvious. "So we'll have a battle?"

Carey smiled at him. "No need to worry, Captain," he said affably, "ye can get back to yer fire if ye like."

Carleton's smile almost slipped and he paused.

"So is this how ye do things in France and the Low Countries?"

"Ay," said Carey, the Berwick man showing, "sometimes. Wait till ye see what guid foot troops can do to light cavalry, given pikes and guns."

Carleton didn't answer. Dodd felt a warm and savage smile across his face as he sat on his restive hobby and waited for the Elliots to arrive. There were five hundred of them he thought, squinting into the rain on its way, at a rough guess, maybe seven hundred, more than enough to take the twenty-five men of the guard but now quite evenly matched. And this way of running a battle was new to him but he was seeing the implications of the pikes and guns already. Every man with an arquebus had it loaded now and a slow match lit and they had done the loading with that precise sequence of motions that Carey had used when he loaded a caliver in the summer. They had done it quickly, too. There was every chance that with the pikes to fend off the horses, they could reload two or three times in the battle. What could that do to a bunch of lightly armoured horsemen? There was no armour could keep off an arquebus ball, that he knew.

The Elliots rode closer, down to the trot now, they could see in the dawnlight what was waiting for them. He saw Wee Colin Elliot at their head and his smile got broader and he started to laugh. Och, God, this was wonderful; this was worth all the riding about and going down to London and being up all night again, even bathing. This was worth it. He wasn't even going against the agreement between the Dodds and the Elliots, brokered by Gilpin and Lord Hunsdon that had sent him to Carlisle because the Elliots were coming into the West March of England armed and arrayed for battle. Just not expecting the battle they would get, of course.

The men of the guard had seen him laughing and looked at each other in wonder, then they started to laugh, too. Carey glanced once at Dodd, raised his brows and then settled himself on his horse, a little to the fore, in his plain English jack and his fancy gold-chased morion helmet, his beard showing strongly now since he hadn't been able to bear a razor on his face with his toothache. No sign of swelling now, he looked quite impressive and dangerous, what was more, with that light devil-may-care smile on his face. Och, God, yes! Dodd almost found himself liking the Courtier.

Dodd allowed himself to think of his father for the first time in years, dead on the end of an Elliot spear in a nasty little mess of an ambush, just after telling Dodd a joke so the remains of the laugh were still in his throat as he saw his father shudder and stare and his eyes roll up. The end of Dodd's boyhood right there in that second as he got the rest of his uncles and cousins to run, as they ran away from the Elliots who came after them on horseback and cut them down, as they hid on the hill in the bracken and the Elliots came by on foot to finish them off and he lay still and marked them, every one in his memory. For this. This glorious moment when he would kill Wee Colin and his brothers and uncles and cousins, all of them. Maybe he would leave the girls alive, he wasn't as bloodthirsty now as he'd been in his teens. Maybe.

The Elliots had come to a stop and were looking uncertainly at the pikes and the arquebuses. Carey watched them with interest. Nothing happened. Horses stamped and jingled bridles, the men breathed. Nothing happened.

FRIDAY 20TH OCTOBER 1592

She stood there so long that her arm got tired and then a man came up behind Lord Spynie. It was Cousin William.

"My lord," he said, "the King is here."

Spynie turned, his gun wavered and then Cousin William punched him on the point of his jaw and knocked him down. Two men behind him took Spynie's gun and picked him up, hanging.

"Is the King really here?" asked Elizabeth, after a deep shaky breath. "Because if he is, I have something to say to him."

"Ay, he is."

"He is?"

"Ay, ma'am, and my lord Chancellor Maitland as well."

Elizabeth turned to Lord Hughie in delight just in time to see him sway dangerously where he stood on the battlement wall. How she moved so fast she never knew but one moment she saw him sway, the next she had hold of his shirt and the moment after that, Cousin William had caught his arms and was lifting him up and over onto the stone flags.

Lord Hughie was pale but he rallied. "Jesu," he said, "as soon as I didn't want to, I nearly did."

Elizabeth almost laughed. She turned to one of the men, Humphrey Fenwick it was. "Where is my husband?" she asked.

"He wouldna come up with Lord Spynie," he said with utter contempt. "He was affeared."

Lord Spynie was shaking off his helpers and rubbing his jaw. Then he found that somebody had taken his sword. "I want to see the King?" he said desperately to some more men coming up to the tower roof.

"All in good time," said one wearing Maitland of Lethington's livery. "My lady's first tae see the King."

She went slowly down the stairs, her legs wobbling inconveniently with reaction so she had to keep stopping to steady herself. The constant turning made her feel giddy as well and she stopped at the bottom for a while. Then she went out into the green that had once been cloisters and was still a garden, if winter-blasted. There, in his padded black and tawny doublet, high hat and grubby linen was the canny twenty-eight-year old who was still, somehow, ruling Scotland—and had been since he was two years old. She stepped forward, breathing through her mouth so she wouldn't smell him, and went to both knees in front of him.

"Lady Widdrington?" he asked.

"Your Majesty," she said, purely out of habit, though the Scottish custom was to call him "Your Highness." She saw that it was just like calling a goodman 'Mister'—he liked it. So she stayed where she was and said it again.

He smiled at her. "Lady Widdrington," he said, "I'm fair delighted to see you again. I suppose your friend Sir Robert Carey is…"

"In Carlisle, sire," she said, carefully not thinking about how it felt to hold Robin tight against her, "as far as I know."

He looked disappointed. "Weel, weel, off yer puir knees, come ben and tell me all about it. The Humes are well stirred up and we canna have that, can we?"

Ah. That was good. She looked for Cousin William who being Scottish was standing behind her with his neck bent and saw what had happened. It was one thing for Lord Spynie to collect bumboys from among the unimportant, but Lord Hughie was a laird in his own right, or would be. So it was quite a different matter for one of the family that ruled the Scottish East March, even a cadet branch. That was why Cousin William hadn't come after Lord Hughie as Jock Tait had come after Jimmy; he must have been talking to Earl Hume.

So she stood and took the King's arm when he offered it to her. As the rain came down in spots and sheets, they walked to the part of the abbey that was most watertight and warm, the old warming room where there were three rough bunkbeds for the monks and all their clutter as well. Every single sock in the place had holes in it.

She told the King almost all of the tale of the killing of Jamie Burn as they walked, and he clucked and tutted like an old Edinburgh wifey. Brother Aurelius came in proudly with a big bowl of some horrible stew which the King took one spoonful of and then ignored. He kept on listening.

And at the end of it all he gave her a kiss on the forehead. "My, you're clever for a woman," he said. "Sir Henry is lucky to have ye and I shall tell him so. My lord Earl Hume is taking over Laird Hughie's wardship so the land will not be wasted."

No, she wouldn't be patted on the head and dismissed like a good dog. She wondered how she could say what she needed to say, and then she decided to just say it and hope for the best.

"Your Majesty…" she started, changed her mind then changed it back. "Your Majesty is an honourable prince. Why do you allow my Lord Spynie to behave so dishonourably with his pages?"

There was a long silence, too long. She sank to her knees again and waited for the blow, the arrest. At least she had tried.

There was a long liquid sniff. The King was wiping his eyes with a disgustingly dirty handkerchief. "I think it no harm if a man loves another man, as King David loved Jonathan," said the King softly. "No harm at all."

She shook her head. "That's not what I mean," she said. "Men, yes, if they must. But children? Surely it's a black dishonour to a man that lies with a boy or girl that is too young, that is only nine or ten."

The King half shrugged. "Yer arse heals up," he said. "My old tutor George Buchanan would have laughed at ye. He'd say it was none of your business."

Elizabeth could hardly believe what she was hearing. "It's no dishonour to the children," she said carefully, "only to the strong men who force them."

"Ay," said the King after another long silence that made Elizabeth nervous again. "Ay, mebbe I'm too soft with those I've loved."

He looked into the excellent fire in the warming room's hearth and sighed. "Ay," he said very quietly, "ay, ye're right. He willna like it, but ye're right."

Surprisingly strong hands lifted her off her knees. "Now my Lady Widdrington, I heard tell of a wonder the ither day, of a barber surgeon that pulls teeth by magic, Simon Anricks by name. Eh?"

"Well I don't know how he pulls teeth, sire, but..."

"D'ye think he's a Jesuit?"

She paused. "I don't think so. I don't know for sure but I don't think so because he was a friend of Jamie Burn, who was a minister in the Kirk and very firm for the new religion. He's a clever man, though. He did tell me something quite horrible. He thinks the Earth goes around the Sun not the other way about."

"Does he now?" laughed the King with delight, "Och, God, I must meet him and dispute with him. Whit a mad idea!"

And she laughed with the King at the craziness of the notion.

SUNDAY 22ND OCTOBER 1592

Dodd couldn't stand it anymore. He rode over to Carey, followed by Andy Nixon and Bessie's Andrew Storey. He was first to speak.

"Sir, will ye not order the onset?"

"No," said Carey.

"Why not? Sir?"

"I don't want a battle."

"What?" Dodd's eyes were nearly popping out of his head with fury. "Ye dinna want a...Sir, give us leave to set upon them now!"

"No."

"Sir…" Dodd fought for control, breathed deep. "Sir, these men killed my father and my brothers and my uncles and my cousins and they've come thinking to surprise ye upon weak grass nags such as they could get on a sudden…"

"No."

Dodd leaned forward, trying to get him to understand. "And God has put them into our hands. Into our hands so that we should take our revenge of them for much blood they have spilt of ours."

"Ay," came Andy Nixon's bass rumble, "and ours."

"And ours, sir," said Storey. The Ridleys and the Hodgsons nodded and grumbled. In a moment Dodd thought, perhaps he could lead the onset himself.

"Gentlemen," said Carey in a carrying voice, "I'm only asking you to be patient for five minutes. That's all. If I were not here and ye were, ye could do as ye please, but being as I am here present wi'ye, if I give ye leave to kill all these men, then the blood ye spill will lie very heavy upon my conscience. So I pray ye gentlemen, forbear for five minutes. I'll send a messenger tae the Scots to bid them be off, and if they do not go before the messenger turns back, then ye may have at 'em and me with ye."

"I'll be yer messenger, sir," said Dodd, thinking that there's more than one way a message can be delivered. Carey eyed him coldly.

"That's Wee Colin Elliot, isn't it?" and Dodd's face must have given him the answer because he nodded once. "Andrew Storey, will ye take the message?"

"Ay, sir…"

"Sir Robert," said Anricks who had finally arrived with his cart, "may I be your messenger since I have no family interests here?"

Carey looked at him sharply too and nodded. "Thank you, Mr Anricks. Please be good enough to tell Wee Colin that I can hold back my men for as long as you are there with them and not longer."

Anricks swung himself down from his cart, took out his handkerchief to wave and walked across the intervening land.

There was a rise to the tower so most of his way was downhill. He stopped, reconsidered, and took a hobby from one of the Ridleys. Then he continued uphill to where the Elliots and some loose Grahams were milling about Wee Colin and his brothers and uncles and cousins.

He spoke for a while, Dodd straining to hear, although he couldn't of course. Once Anricks flung out his hand in a gesture at the wagon. He turned his horse to go back and Dodd tensed, ready for the charge.

There was confusion and then he saw that the bastard Elliots were galloping away, almost tripping over each other in their haste to get back over the Border. Minutes later they were all gone and Dodd had a pain in the pit of his stomach and a sick feeling. They were gone.

Carey gestured for the men to wait in case it was a feint. Dodd watched hopefully but there was no feint. The Elliots were well away.

The ranks of pikes broke up and the men with the arquebuses grounded their slow matches and started the painstaking dangerous process of fishing out the wadding and balls and emptying the barrels of powder since they couldn't afford to waste it.

There was laughter and joking, men shaking each others' hands and saying it was worth it to see Wee Colin Elliot on the run, and they'd make sure the Courtier wasn't around next time, boasting of what they would have done, could have done but highly delighted to have got out of a battle and actually having to do it.

Dodd sat there with the ball of rage still in the pit of his stomach as Carey led out the men that had been in the tower and found out which of them were Archie and Jemmy Burn. The Grahams were already talking philosophically about ransom.

"We'll take ye back to Carlisle," he said as Dodd rode up, his face long and sour.

"Ay," said Archie with a grin. "If ye send to my Lord Spynie ye'll find he'll buy us out, so he will."

"I think we're worth ane hundert pounds English to him," added Jemmy, his hands also bound behind him. "Each eh? Ye heard right. Ye'd like that, would ye not? I've a letter in my doublet that says so."

Andy Nixon felt in Jemmy's doublet, found paper and brought it to Carey. He read it to himself.

Carey paused. "One question," he said. "Which of you two is it that likes women?"

"Och both of us, sir, they're allus hot for it," said Jemmy with a sly grin. "Are they no', Archie?"

"Ay, the bitches like it strong. The minister's wifey was fun, the way she cried and squealed and that woman in the manse at Wendron, she'd have been good, too, only a man wi' a gun turned up."

"Ah," said Carey. He beckoned Carleton with the firepot, dipped the corner of Spynie's letter into the hot coals, waited as it caught, let the fire climb the paper and dropped it onto the turf when it was well alight before stamping it out. Archie and Jemmy watched as if they didn't understand what they were seeing.

Carey turned formally to Andy Nixon and Dodd. "As acting Deputy Warden, I can say of my own knowing that these men have committed March Treason, in that they brought in the Scots in their behalf to wit Wee Colin Elliot and his surname. Do you agree?"

Andy Nixon nodded seriously. Dodd thought for a moment. "Ay," he said eventually, "even apart fra the murder of the churchman, it's March Treason, right enough."

Carey's face was cold. He paused a moment longer. Then he said, very clearly, "Hang them."

"What...?" spluttered Jemmy. "Ye canna..."

"Lord Spynie..." began Archie.

Andy Nixon knocked Archie down and lifted his large fist to Jemmy who subsided.

There weren't any good trees so close to Carlisle but they set up the ladder against the side of the tower again and wrapped ropes around two of the battlements. They took Archie up first, who was crying and begging, making wild claims about Lord Spynie. They put the noose around his neck, asked if he had anything to say and when it was just more of the same, Dodd kicked him off the ladder. Damn it, the rope broke his neck so he didn't even dance. Jemmy went in silence, white as a sheet and his eyes rolling. Andy Nixon kicked him off and he hardly danced either.

From below, Carey watched with a bleak expression on his face, waited for twenty minutes to be sure they were dead. Waited another twenty minutes, still and cold, and then allowed them to be lowered to the ground and their corpses put on Anricks' wagon. In the wagon was hidden one of Carlisle Castle's smaller cannon under piles of arrows and sacks of arquebus balls and a couple of barrels of gunpowder and a tarpaulin over the top. God, what a chance they had missed.

They headed back for Carlisle, harnessing two more hobbies to the cart to help with the extra weight. You would have thought it was a wedding party, everyone was so happy.

Dodd went too, no longer nearly weeping with frustration and rage, but with the ugly sour anger settled back in his stomach for good. They could have had them. They could have wiped out every Elliot, been done with the bloodfeud the right way, the way it should be. Right then Wee Colin and his bastard Elliots could have been staring at the sky and the undersides of crows. But they weren't. They were over the Border and still alive, an offence every one of them, personally, to Henry Dodd.

He would never ever forgive Carey for letting the Elliots get away.

HISTORICAL NOTE

With this book we finally come into the purview of Carey's own memoirs—the incident at the end is pretty much as I describe it...The reason for it, according to Carey, was that a churchman had been murdered in Scotland. That's all he says, which I found irresistible. Well, yes, I use some artistic licence but not that much. I quote directly from the memoirs as well. Annoyingly, I remember finding a reference to the incident in a letter from Lord Scrope but I haven't been able to find it again. No doubt it will turn up after this book is published.

The Reverend Gilpin is also a real historical person who seems to have taken on his mission to the Borderers for no better reason than that he knew they needed it and he believed God wanted him to do it.

Cast of Characters

Tim, barman at Wendron
Simon Anricks, barber surgeon who might be a Jesuit
Clem, alehouse boy
Lady Elizabeth Widdrington, Carey's love
Mr Tully, horse trader
Blackie (a grey), murderers' horse
Pinkie (a chestnut), ditto
Milky (black), Tully's horse
Mouse (dark chestnut), Elizabeth's horse
Mary Trevannion, Elizabeth's cousin, learning huswifery
Mr Heron, Widdrington reeve
Poppy (Proserpina) Burn, Minister Jamie Burn's wife
Minister Jamie Burn, the dead churchman
Dandelion, cow with good milk
Mrs Stirling, midwife
Young Henry Widdrington, Sir Henry's eldest son
Jane, Kat, Elizabeth's dairymaids
Prince, Jamie Burn's horse (hobby)
Rat, Elizabeth's horse (half-hobby)
Sir Robert Carey, Elizabeth's love
Johnny Forster, eldest son of Sir John, Marshall of Bamburgh
John Carey, Sir Robert's elder brother, Marshall of Berwick
Lady Agnes Hume, dowager lady
Jock Burn, Jamie's uncle
Ralph o' the Coates Burn, headman of the Burns, Jamie's father
Laird Hughie Hume, heir to cadet Hume estate
Maitland of Lethington, Scottish Chancellor
Maria, village girl
Jemmy Burn, Ralph o' the Coates' younger brother
Archie Burn, his son

Humphrey Fenwick, Widdrington cousin
Sergeant Henry Dodd, Land-Sergeant of Gilsland
Patch, Dodd's horse (hobby)
Sorrel, Carey's horse (hobby)
Twice, Blackie, other horses (hobbies)
Young Hutchin, young scoundrel
Andy Nixon, member of Carlisle castle guard
Sim's Will Croser, ditto
Bessie's Andrew Storey, ditto
Red Sandy, Dodd's younger brother
Bangtail Graham, member of Carlisle castle guard
Janet Dodd (née Armstrong), Dodd's wife
Kat Ridley, Lady Hume's tiring woman
Jack Crosby, Sim Routledge, Wendron villagers
Cousin William, Hume byblow
Jimmy, Hume groom
Hector (Ekie) Widdrington, Widdrington cousin
Sim Widdrington, ditto
Daniel Widdrington, ditto
Piers Dixon, schoolboy
Andy Hume, schoolboy
Cuddy Trotter, schoolboy
Jimmy Tait, schoolboy
Jock Tait, Jimmy Tait's father
Goodwife Tait, Jimmy Tait's mother
Goodwife Trotter, Cuddy's mother
Clemmie Pringle, Wendron baker
Sandy, Eric, dogboys at Carlisle
Butter, Ekie's horse (hobby)
Geordie Burn, Ralph o' the Coates' eldest son, Jamie's eldest
    brother
Young Geordie, Geordie Burn's son
Nick Smithson, leader of Essex's soldiers
Denham, leader of one of the Carlisle trained bands
Blennerhasset, ditto
Beverly, ditto
Jack, young lymer dog

Teazle, older lymer dog
Lady Philadelphia Scrope, Carey's younger sister
Lord Scrope, Warden of the English West March
John Tovey, Carey's secretary
Brother Aurelius, Austin friar at Jedburgh abbey
Brother Constantine, ditto
Brother Justinian, ditto
Brother Ignatius, ditto
Lord Abbot Ninian, Lord Abbot of Jedburgh
Lord Spynie, Royal favourite
James VI, King of Scotland

A CLASH OF SPHERES

Letter from Sir Robert Cecil

to the King of Denmark.

Draft.

To His Royal Highness, Christian IV of that name, King of Denmark and Norway, etc etc. [His Highness is but 16 years and still under regency, be very sure we have all his titles here]

Your most Royal Highness, [check correct address]
 You have asked me to make some description and account of Sir Robert Carey and his henchman Sergeant Henry Dodd, of whom you have heard little but rumours and the varied accounts of your spies at the Court of Scotland, which it is my pleasure to supply, being hopeful of your Royal Highness' favour and regard, and being also certain that when once you have been apprised of Sir Robert's character and circumstance, you will view him with as much favour as I do, no less and perhaps no more. *[be sure the Danish translation is accurate here]*
 You say that your royal sister, Anne, Queen Consort of King James of Scotland, has written to you of the man, wherefore I will unburden myself perhaps a little less discreetly than I might otherwise have done.
 Sir Robert is the seventh surviving son of my Lord Chamberlain, Henry Carey, Baron Hunsdon. It is worth making some explanation of Baron Hunsdon's antecedents since they are material to the character of Sir Robert.
 To be blunt, Your Highness, it is more than likely that Baron Hunsdon is in fact Henry VIII's natural son, by his erstwhile mistress, Mary Boleyn, older sister of the more famous Anne. *[a little touch of scandal may entertain His Highness]* Thus

Baron Hunsdon is both cousin and half-brother to our most revered Sovereign Liege, Elizabeth of England, Wales, Ireland and France.

The royal bastardy means that Baron Hunsdon has no claim whatsoever to the throne and nor do his numerous children. Happily, My Lord Baron is not in any way ambitious but serves his mistress the Queen a great deal more faithfully and effectively than most people realise, who think him but a Knight of the Carpet. *[perhaps excise, not relevant]* Most of his children are or have been at Court and often high in favour.

Sir Robert first served Sir Francis Walsingham as a youth in embassies to Scotland and France. During the Scottish embassy he received great favour from the young King, your brother in law, James of Scotland. During the French embassy, he seems to have disgraced himself through his carnal appetites with some of the most puissant ladies of the French Court, which ended in a debtors' prison from which he was extricated with some difficulty and more expense by his esteemed father. I am aware of at least two probable bastards and there may be more. *[more to entertain His Highness! Nb. One possible bastard may be a Guise instead.]*

He returned to England and served the Queen at Court, although not without incident. There was a fistfight with Sir Walter Raleigh over a tennis match before either of them had become knights, and several duels. He became an MP and gave satisfaction therein.

Against the Armada, he served with his friend, the Earl of Cumberland, on the *Elizabeth Bonaventure*, where he was able to render incidental but important service to the Queen before succumbing (although not fatally) to a jailfever on board ship. He had also served the Queen in an unusual manner, during the final days of the Queen of Scots, but I am not at liberty to disclose details. *[excise?]*

He has been to war several more times and acquitted himself well, most notably under the Earl of Essex in France in 1591. There he was knighted by Essex for help in turning aside the Queen's just wrath with her unworthy favourite.

Last summer in 1592, he decided to become his brother-in-law Lord Scrope's Deputy Warden in the English West March, despite there already being an incumbent called Sir Richard Lowther. Certes, he was restless at Court and in need of knightly exercise, since he has proved to be an able soldier and a very much better captain than *[deleted]* many. He also owed considerable sums of money, in particular to his tailor, and there was an entanglement in London from which he urgently needed to flee. However there is also the matter of his extraordinary affection for his cousin, Lady Elizabeth Widdrington, née Trevannion, who lives in the north with her elderly husband, Sir Henry Widdrington, Deputy Warden of the East March.

I am not entirely clear about the progress of this love affair, but as Lady Widdrington is, by all accounts, a woman of principle and determination, it is yet possible that he has not breached her citadel and intends to marry her as soon as her husband is dead. This would be a very foolish mistake on his part because the lady only has a jointure of five hundred pounds and he currently owes three thousand pounds at least. It goes without saying that Sir Henry Widdrington regards him with considerable suspicion, jealousy, and loathing.

On arriving on the Borders, Sir Robert was immediately embroiled in an incident with the Graham surname, the upshot of which was that he somehow prevented the kidnapping of the King of Scots from Falkland palace by the 2nd Earl of Bothwell. Unfortunately, the precise circumstances are murky. Later that summer, after showing his capacities at coroner's inquest in Carlisle, he journeyed to Dumfries to meet with the King of Scots while His Highness was on his Justice Raid against the Grahams.

Precisely what transpired at the Scottish Court, I have not been able reliably to make out, except that Sir Robert became involved with an Italian spy and had an affair with her; somehow earned the enmity of the King's favourite and Minion, Lord Spynie, and also Lord Maxwell, current Warden of the Scottish West March; took extremely foolhardy and potentially treasonous action in the matter of some firearms; and emerged with quite severe injuries to his hands but the renewed favour of the King.

In the autumn, he was ordered to London by his father. There he became involved in a riot at the Fleet Prison during which Sir Thomas Heneage, Vice Chamberlain, had his nose broken *[by Sir Robert]*. During the ensuing lawsuits, he decided to leave London and head for Oxford, which was then expecting the Queen on her Progress, leaving his mother Ann Carey, Lady Hunsdon, and his henchman, Sergeant Henry Dodd, to deal with the consequences of his dispute with Sir Thos. Heneage, which they did ably and with dispatch. In the course of these events, I was able to be of some service to Lady Hunsdon, a matter of great satisfaction to me.

At this point it is worth mentioning his henchman, Henry Dodd, Land-Sergeant of Gilsland who is serving as one of the sergeants of the Carlisle Castle guard.

I have had the pleasure and interest of meeting Sergeant Dodd in his own person and he is considerably more than the simple dour Border reiver he appears to be. It seems he should be the headman of the Tynedale Dodds but is not for reasons that are obscure but connected with a feud between the Dodds and the Elliots in the 1570s. *[too much admission of ignorance?]*

While he was in Oxford, Sir Robert was commissioned by the Queen to investigate a very delicate matter. During the Queen's Entrance in State into the City of Oxford, Sergeant Dodd saved the Queen's life, for which he was well-rewarded.

Shortly after his return to the Borders, with some ex-soldiers of My Lord Essex's, Sir Robert was involved in an incident at a tower known as Dick of Dryhope's, in which he called out the Carlisle trained bands, but honourably and skillfully avoided the bloody pitched battle that seemed inevitable.

This has made his name on the Borders and the Queen has now been pleased to grant him his official warrant as Deputy Warden.

He is close to the Queen, who sometimes calls him "her Scalliwag": to be given a nickname by Her Majesty is a signal of highest favour, so that I am proud to be known by her name for me, slighting though it is. However he has not yet successfully turned her favour into offices nor a pension nor a monopoly, from which I conclude he is either remarkably inept, unlucky, or else as unambitious as his sire. He seems mainly concerned with his affair with Lady Widdrington and with bringing peace to the Borders, rather than profiting personally by his office, a very remarkable and unusual circumstance. *[can you think of another instance?]*

I am now extremely concerned at the state of politics at the Scottish Court, particularly with regard to the Catholic earls. I beg of you, Your Highness, if you have any information at all on the King of Spain's intentions in Scotland, I pray you will tell me it. I have already dispatched a particularly effective and able pursuivant to the Borders and I am considering a journey north, which is not a matter I undertake lightly, owing to the infirmity in my bones from which I suffer. But I believe Spain is plotting against Scotland and England and would give my right arm to know more.

It goes without saying, all of this information is strictly private and not to be shared with anyone.

I remain Your Highness' most assiduous and secret *[?]* servant,

Sir Rbt Cecil, Privy Councillor.
[not sent]

LATE AUGUST 1592

Their dalliance had progressed in a stately fashion from whispers and stolen kisses in corridors, to dancing while the musicians played for them alone in crowded sweaty halls and banqueting tents full of unimportant other dancers, to light-fingered explorations of stocking tops and codpiece and stays, to this. Marguerite was heavy-eyed and languorous and, thank the Mother of God, not inclined to talk too much. Meanwhile the man who said his name was Jonathan Hepburn and that he sometimes worked for the Earl of Bothwell, was lying flat on his back, utterly spent, letting the sweat dry on his skin.

She yawned, stretched like a cat, got up and went to the door of the little servant's chamber, where the man whose chamber it actually was, waited patiently and counted his cash.

"Do you have any wine?" she asked in a voice that was tinged with a foreign language. For a wonder, it turned out that he did, and for a paltry English shilling would give them some. She brought in two pewter goblets of white wine. Hepburn sat up on his elbow and took the goblet, toasted her, and drank.

It was dreadful, acidic with a suspicious fishy aftertaste, but he got it down.

Of course, Marguerite was a married woman and it showed in the stretchmarks on her stomach and the dark aureoles of her very nibblesome nipples. She had given her lord at least one or probably more children. But her hair was blond and so was her crotch and she had a luxuriousness to her that Hepburn associated more with Southerners. It was business, all business, but, by the God of the World, sometimes you could mix business with pleasure. The fact that she was married to a very dull conscientious man by the name of Sir David Graham of Fintry was what was important. He was not a Border Graham, not one of the notorious clan of five brothers who had gone south in the 1520s, kicked the Storeys off their lands, and helped turn Liddesdale into the complete thieves' kitchen it now was. He was from the northerly respectable Grahams. There were interesting rumours about him but the most interesting thing about him was a stone-cold fact. He was a Groom of the King's Bedchamber, by hereditary custom.

"My dear," Hepburn said in the caressing voice he used for all women, "what if your husband catches us?"

She frowned and plumped down next to him on the narrow servant's bed with the sour sheets. "He would be very angry," she said with a sigh, chewing her bottom lip, "He might kill you and hurt me. Or kill me as well."

"Surely not, so old-fashioned?"

She shrugged and her voice took on a tinge of bitterness. "He killed a young man I looked at—only looked at, honest to God—and he was very cruel to me. The King hushed it up. He locked me in a storeroom where it was very cold and dark and there were many spiders."

Hepburn nodded. That was what he had heard. Now, was the other rumour true?

"Perhaps we should not see each other for a while," he said sadly, "so he doesn't get too suspicious."

She shrugged, quite French although she wasn't French, started billowing linen over her head. "If you are already tired of me..." she said, her voice muffled.

Hepburn jumped up from the bed and embraced her. "How could I be tired of you?" he whispered and she tweaked him where he was demonstrating that he was not tired of her at all, which made him gasp and her giggle. No help for it, he had to take the risk. This last detail was simply too important to go on mere hearsay. "I'll have to go to a priest this afternoon, but I don't care..."

"What will he give you for penance? Fasting?"

"Perhaps," said Hepburn who had fasted for religious reasons but not on any priest's say-so. "Will you too have to find a priest? Or are you a Protestant...?"

"What? And now be utterly damned forever? I would never

be so silly. I am a Catholic." She grinned impudently at him. "I have found a very nice tame priest called Father Crichton who never gives more than a decade of Aves, a Paternoster, and a Gloria."

Just for a moment, Hepburn had to hold his breath. Was Crichton actually here, in Scotland? He had had no idea, thinking the man was still in northern Spain. "Is he a Jesuit?"

"Yes, but he is nice," she giggled and wriggled at the way he was stroking her breasts through the fine linen of her smock, "Not as nice as you, but nice."

"He isn't supposed to be as nice as me…" He was busy nuzzling her neck. "When did he arrive?"

"He came with my Lord Maxwell and his Italians in April or May, I think, to help with the new Armada but stayed at Caerlaverock. Now he is at Court and everyone who is not a stupid Lutheran or Calvinist goes to him."

That Armada, too, if it existed, had been wrecked by storms.

"My priest is old-fashioned and strict. Perhaps I could confess to your nice Father Crichton?"

She giggled again. There was something so relaxing about a feather-headed woman with stunning blond curls down her back. "Why not?"

Emilia had been dramatic and very sexy and had been completely resistant to his plan, which she thought stupidly risky. And then she had suddenly gone off with the Deputy Warden of the West March, Sir Robert Carey, so she could buy his guns and take them to Ireland, as if that was less risky.

"Wherever did he find you, Sir David Graham?" he wondered to himself in the Deutsch of his childhood and she answered him in Low Dutch. "In the Spanish Netherlands, of course, where I was living in a very boring village full of very boring Protestants."

"But you are from Antwerp," he guessed shrewdly and was rewarded by a kiss on the mouth which he enjoyed immensely. "Originally."

Her face suddenly crumpled like a child's. "I don't want to think about poor Antwerp," she whispered, her mood changing like a cloud crossing the sun, "I never want to think about it."

Hepburn looked at her carefully. She must have been a child at the time of the Spanish Fury in Antwerp. Had she been there?

"My dear..." he began.

"Never! I never want to think about it!" she shouted in Low Dutch and hit him in the chest with her fist, as if he were another man entirely. Hepburn put his arms around her to quiet her and found she was kissing him greedily, desperately, scratching his back. After one second of hesitation—what had brought this on?—he went with it and took her again, like an animal, while she moaned and tears pushed their way out under her eyelids and finally she screamed so he had to put a hand over her mouth. He took it away when she bit him and she then looked at him with old eyes and said, "Never say that name to me again."

"All right," he said, managed a light smile and she smiled back at last. Jesu, who could fathom women? It was beyond him.

There was an anxious knock at the door.

"Sir, my lady, I must go serve the Queen in half an hour," came a voice.

"Give us ten minutes," said Hepburn, picking his hose up from where he had folded them and laid them down carefully. Marguerite was already at her petticoat forepart, buttoning and pinning with a will.

They came out separately, went in different directions. Marguerite hurried to the Queen's chambers where she sat on a corner cushion and gossiped with one of the Queen's plump Danish women. Jonathan Hepburn went down to the buttery to get himself a quart of ale to help him recover and with thinking out the next stage in his very elaborate plot that would end with James VI of Scotland dead, and Scotland and England in murderous chaos.

The Grahams took up position under the Eden Bridge at about four o'clock in the morning, as near as anyone could guess, with the sky perpetually leaking rain. The water was freezing cold and high as well and the horses all protested about it as they splashed in and stood there sulkily, huffing and puffing.

"He'll be back before five, I guarantee it," said Wattie. "Naebody'll want to be oot in this any longer than they have to."

The bridge itself would not keep you dry, because it had been raining long enough for the stones themselves all to be leaking in the places where they had worn and there were potholes going right through. It was an old bridge. Some said the builders of the Giant's Wall had made it for a sort of warm-up for the Wall itself.

Archie Fire the Braes pushed another man called Sooks Graham out of the one remaining dry spot there. Well dryish. His pony was wet obviously and so were his legs and boots. There was a whispered sequence of snarls, and then Sooks shoved another man out of a slightly drier spot and so on down the line to the youngest one there who philosophically stayed under the last bit of parapet which gave no shelter at all but did conceal him from anyone crossing the bridge at night.

"And ye're sure *he'll* not be there?" said another man.

Wattie grinned and scratched under his helmet rim. "Ay, certain sure. He took offence at the doings last month and he'll no' come in wi' us, but he willna help the Courtier, see ye."

The youngest had a rough iron cap over his golden hair which was lent him by his cousin Sooks, since the colour was such a liability at night despite being dirty. He lifted it and scratched like Wattie at a place where it rubbed.

"He'll have the other men of the guard, though."

"Ay," said Wattie cheerfully, "It's Sergeant Dodd I worry about."

Young Hutchin nodded and wondered what it was about Sergeant Dodd that made everybody so careful of him and wondered how he could get some of that stuff himself.

"What about the new men from the South he's brung in?" he asked.

"Och," laughed Wattie, "who's worried about a bunch o' soft Southerners? Not me."

Everybody sniggered a little. They stood in silence for a while, as the dripping eased off.

Wattie put a hand out. "Damn, it's stopped raining," he said thoughtfully.

Young Hutchin moved his hobby out a couple of feet and back in again. "Ay, it has." It was still raining under the bridge, as the puddles on the bridge dripped through slowly, but outside it had eased off to basic miserable dampness.

Wattie sighed. It would have been a lot better if the rain had carried on but you could never rely on the weather, except to be as thrawn and contrary as it could. They would have preferred rain, so it had stopped raining. Well, the night was still as black as pitch and that would have to do. The men they were waiting for did not usually carry torches.

***

Carey was wet and uncomfortable but in good spirits. He had brought the four southerners who had learnt to ride well enough, and started teaching them the finer points of Border life. For a wonder, nothing very much was happening on either side of the Border, and just on the off chance and on impulse he had forayed into Liddesdale a way and found a remarkable number of cattle and horses penned up in a narrow little valley. He had taken a close look at them on foot by the light of his only dark lantern and found three different brands in four animals, grinned wolfishly, and given his orders.

Dodd was not there, being safely at home with his wife in Gilsland. To be honest, Carey was quite glad to be rid of him because from being a naturally dour and taciturn man, since the incident at Dick of Dryhope's tower, Dodd had become... well, sulky was too weak and nebbish a word, really. If Carey got more than four words out of him in an evening, he was doing well. He had not expected Dodd to like what he had done but it was now more than a month in the past and he was getting tired of the whole thing.

Still, this would be good practice for the new men and the other Borderers would enjoy teaching them the arcane art of cattle-driving with the four-legged treasure they had found.

It being so dark and raining, of course the herds had protested loudly at being moved and gone in dozens of different ways, while the loose horses trotted about uneasily. A couple of calves got free and went exploring, and Perkins fell off his horse when he went after one of them, which entertained Bangtail, Red Sandy, and Sim's Will no end. Bessie's Andrew, no longer the youngest and least important man, started shouting, and then someone else's horse stood on his hind legs while his rider cursed and beat about with the ends of the reins until he calmed down again.

"We should have brought the dogs," said Carey, making a mental note to bring Jack and Teazle next time and see if Jack might make a better herding dog than he did a hunter. The men of the guard were now circling the cattle, making little yips and yarks until they finally got the cattle moving out of the valley and into the main run of Liddesdale, southwards. The horses went with the cattle, not liking to be alone and shying at everything.

Yes, it would take at least an hour longer to bring the stolen cattle in, but it would be well worth it and Carey felt he needed something to cheer him up. He was probably going to lose his place when Lord Scrope finally went south to his estates, and he could turn his share of the booty into much-needed cash.

He spotted two cows and a heifer making a break for it northwards and went after them with a high *yip yip*, galloped his pony round them and turned them about so they were running back to the main herd. He whacked the lead cow with the butt end of his lance and found Bessie's Andrew there on the other side to encourage them a bit more.

The herd heaved itself together again and started moving west at a dignified lollop with a lot of question and response in the lowing. Most of them were English kine from the brands and it stood to reason they would prefer to go south to more familiar fields, so it was sheer obstinacy that was sending them west. Bangtail and Red Sandy galloped their ponies into the path and turned them with more shouted yips and yarks. All the cattle stood and bumped each other, lowing questioningly.

There was a bony old screw up the front, with a crumpled horn, tossing her head and barging other cows when they went the wrong way. He could almost hear her, "Ay, this way, ye lummocks," and just for a moment tried to imagine the cow politics that had made her the leader but his usually vivid phantasy could not cope with this and he found himself laughing quietly at himself. Still, what was it Dodd had said about even goats having degree in their herds and refusing to follow an underling?

"Sim's Will," he said, "get that animal with the crumpled horn and bring her to the front. No, not that one, the bony one."

It took a moment for Sim's Will to get a rope round her neck and then Carey took the rope's end and forged his way through the pungent beasts and the mud until he and the old lady were at the front. She bellowed loudly and set out for the south with decision, sniffing the air and mooing and, for a wonder, the others followed her at last in mostly the right direction.

An hour later, as they came over the last hill, he could just make out Eden Bridge and the Sauceries beyond and relaxed because they were nearly home.

***

Wattie cocked his head, accidentally tipping a helmet's brim of water down his neck.

"What's that?" he asked uneasily, "There's a herd of cows there…"

"Bringing them in for market?" said Fire the Braes, who knew less than most about such things, as he had been at the horn since he was in his teens.

"At this time? The gate's aye shut and will be for another two hours, whit's the point of it?"

They hushed as the mixed lowing and sound of hooves

came closer and closer. Suddenly the noises went up a notch with anxiety and the sound of hooves became confused, the drumming stopped just before the bridge. Wattie signalled the other Grahams to stay still and quiet.

"What the devil's got into them?" demanded a Court voice just above them, "They were moving very nicely a moment ago, why won't they go onto the bridge?"

A single horse's footsteps rang above them, and Wattie was sitting on his mount like a stone fountain, with the puddle water still running down, his head tilted and his mouth open.

That was when Hutchin's mount, which had been bad-tempered all night, straddled his legs and let fly with a long stream of pungent shit, right into the water.

Dinna let him notice, Wattie prayed to his nameless god of reivers, *go on yer flash Court sprig, ye dinna ken*...He glowered at Hutchin who couldn't really be blamed.

There was a scuffle as Carey turned his horse on a sixpence and galloped back to the herd, while his voice bellowed, "Bring them on!" They stood still while the hooves went around to the back of the herd and then came the boom of a dag being fired into the air.

The lowing went up to near panic levels. The kine had heard gunfire before and didn't like it. They tried to go back, found men with lances and ropes in the way, turned about and found the bridge was clear, but more frightening men on horses with lances and swords and bows were coming up the river banks on either side as Wattie's relatives decided to take a crack at the valuable Deputy anyway, seeing they had come so far and spent two hours standing in the wet in the river. And seeing the Deputy was worth fifteen pounds on the hoof, dead or alive. Fire the Braes was shouting something incomprehensible about the kine, Wattie was bellowing purple-faced at them to stop and there was Carey in a panicking sea of cattle, finishing reloading his dag, putting it in its case and drawing his sword, whacking the arse of the cow with the crumpled horn with the flat of it and charging forwards.

She let out a moo that was more a battle cry and lurched forwards, tossing her head and looking for something to gore in revenge, found a pony in front of her and stuck the crumpled horn in, found a space clear of men and horses and barged into it, followed by all her sisters, nieces, cousins, and second cousins plus the strange cows and the strange horses, all following her in a chaotic bunch because she was in front and moving.

The press of them running onto the bridge barged the next horseman backwards, so the hobby lost his feet and the rider fell off, the third was ridden by Fire the Braes, who was laying about him with his lance, so they went round him and then took him with them. Another boom from behind confirmed their feeling that they did not like loud bangs and they wanted to get away from them, so they went up to a speedy trot and then a run and bowled over another horse as they stampeded over the bridge, their eyes rolling and their horns tossing.

And there was the blasted Deputy in the middle of it, plastered with dung from a nervous heifer, swapping blows with the still-shouting Wattie Graham and another cousin who came up from the other side, until Carey bent with a wicked look and tipped the man out of his saddle, then turned to deal with Wattie again. He found the kine had shoved him in the opposite direction and took a shot at him with his other dag, missed but hit somebody else.

Somehow he still had hold of the old cow's rope, so he kicked his horse to keep up, and went with her while yet another Graham tried to go the other way to Liddesdale and got shoved off the bridge into the river while his horse did the sensible thing and scrambled to stay with the herd.

Just as the other Grahams turned to run, Carey caught sight of golden hair and bellowed, "Hutchin Graham, I want to talk to you!" but couldn't go after him because he, too, was being carried along in the flood of animals. He kept his seat, caught up with the old lady again, as the cows came off the bridge and galloped down and into the Sauceries and trampled down the fences...And then they stopped because there was lovely soft rich grass there, nurtured by some of the town's nightsoil, the meadows being kept for the garrison's horses. And so they fanned out and started to enjoy the feast while the sun notionally came up behind the clouds.

Carey's legs were a bit bruised from the crushing, but for a wonder, nobody had stuck him with a horn. He rode up to the old cow, took the rope from round her neck and gave her a slap on the shoulder in thanks. He got a glare that reminded him of his mother, which made him want to laugh.

All eight of his men came trotting up, some of them with prisoners who would ransome very nicely. None of the prisoners was Wattie Graham, but Fire the Braes was furious.

"They're ma ain cattle ye've reived from me, ye bastard!" he shouted and Carey looked mildly offended.

"They've got a wonderful range of brands," he said, "Pringle, Storey, Ridley, I think that one is an English Armstrong."

"They're mine, damn ye!"

"No, I think you reived them, Archie."

"Ay," bellowed Archie, his hands tied behind his back in fists, "Ay, Ah worked hard to reive them and they're all mine, stolen fair and square!"

He realised that Carey was laughing at him and so were some of the men, especially Andy Nixon, the square Carlisler who often now was second in command. "Och, piss off, ye lang streak o' puke."

Nixon lifted his fist but Carey shook his head. "Well now," he said conversationally, as Perkins and Garron and East, commanded by Nick Smithson, tried to do something about the fences so the cows wouldn't wander off again. "What were you doing waiting in ambush under Eden Bridge like a bunch of god-damned trolls, only not so pretty. How many of you were there?"

"At least forty...Ah'll tell ye nothing."

"Well, you will after I've put you in the Licking Stone cell for a bit," said Carey, his voice oozing sympathy which made Red Sandy and Bangtail start snickering again. "It's not much fun, I'm told. It'll be much harder for you to talk to me once your tongue has swollen to twice its size with licking a few drops of water off the rough stone wall." Although from the way it had been raining recently, Carey rather thought Fire the Braes' real problem would be not drowning. However Fire the Braes was not to know that.

"Och," Fire the Braes said as Nixon attached him to the other two prisoners by a rope and jerked on it. "Ay, it was all Grahams, for the brave ye put on us last month, taking and hanging our cousins and guests…"

"For murder. And mentioning Lord Spynie."

Archie shrugged, "So what? And Ritchie of Brackenhill put the price up on ye, tae fifteens pounds and a helmet, so we'll no' be the ainly ones…"

"Forty men?"

"Mebbe thirty."

"That's what I thought. And someone had a try at me last week in Bessie's, only Bessie's wife saw him and cracked his skull with a jug."

"Ah dinna ken," said Fire the Braes sulkily.

"They say your tongue bleeds as well and then clots and so it cracks open…"

"Jesus, will ye stop? I came in wi' Wattie for the money and the fun of it, and now ye're threatening me wi' the Licking Stone cell and I'll no' have it, any of it."

"It's been busy all month and then in the last week it's gone silent as the grave, what's that about?"

"Ah dinna ken!" shouted Archie and tried to lunge at Carey who backed his horse a couple of paces while Andy Nixon and Bangtail hit the reiver a couple of times to quieten him and teach him manners.

"So, let's see, we've got Fire the Braes, Sim's Jock Graham…"

Bessie's Andrew Storey hurried up to him, "There's one shot dead, three of them got trampled by the kine, one's still alive and the other two died, four ran intae the town, the rest forded the river upstream and ran for Liddesdale, Wattie Graham with them."

"Where's young Hutchin Graham? I swear I saw his hair."

"Dinna ken sir, probably ran intae the toon as well."

"They'll be at the postern gate arguing with Solomon Musgrave by now. Separate out the horses, we can always find a use for them and some of them have no brands on them."

He trotted to the northern town gate, the Scotch gate, where he found it shut, the postern gate shut tight and the gate guards denying stoutly that they had seen any Grahams, that there had been any Grahams anywhere—that Grahams existed, that there was a postern gate at all, and if there was that it had ever been opened all night and certainly that there had ever been five people who might have gone through on payment of an irregular toll and certainly weren't Grahams...

Carey sighed, trotted back, brought in the three reivers on their feet and one slung over a pony's back, along with the eight men who were all looking very pleased with themselves, as well they might, except for Perkins who was protesting at being nicknamed Falls off his Horse Perkins.

AUGUST 1592

The Maxwell castle of Caerlaverock was tucked away in a part of Scotland almost nobody ever went to, except the people who lived there, near Dumfries. It was beautiful, certainly, in the opinion of the owner, the current eighth Lord Maxwell, ably backed by the Maxwell surname and their Herries cousins. When they weren't nose-to-nose with the Johnstones for the leadership of the Scottish West March, Maxwells had been known to make quite good West March Wardens, for a given and small value of "good." Now the old feud had broken out yet again and nothing mattered, save killing all the bloody Johnstones in whatever way seemed most expedient to the Maxwell.

He had had a splendid idea and was in the process of selling it to George Gordon, Earl of Huntly, the Earl of Erroll, and the Earl of Angus.

They were at a private supper in his private parlour where the silver loot from his and his ancestors' raids going back to before Flodden, shone softly in the candlelight. Father William Crichton squinted at the plate sometimes, recognising the chalices and patens robbed from monasteries during the Reformation, and some that looked to be English work, too.

He said nothing about any of it. He was a Jesuit and they always took the long, the educated view.

He was also the Maxwells' house priest, because Maxwell, like most of the northern earls, held to the old Faith, not the new ridiculous religion that had swept the country in 1560 when Crichton had been a pious young lad.

"*Benedicat vos omnipotens Deus...*" he intoned, letting the beautiful Latin carry him along. The polished table was spread with the first remove, and the lords had their heads bent. There was haggis though it was really a peasant dish, a vast salmon from Maxwell's river, a haunch of beef, quite possibly from the Maxwells' own herds, venison from a hunt a week and a half ago, hung to perfection, quails and some potherbs like turnips and neeps. Oh, and a sallet dressed with vinegar. Maxwell had an Edinburgh cook who had once worked in the Royal kitchens.

Unusually, once the venison had been broken, the lords served each other and the servants filed out. One large young man with freckles pulled the door firmly shut behind him. Father Crichton heard him draw his sword and his two feet stamping down on the floor as he took up position.

For the first ten minutes there was silence apart from the sound of knives and spoons scraping the occasional silverplate, napkins thrown over shoulders being applied to fingers, more manchet bread being asked for, silver spoons being used to sup the gravy made with red wine and a piquant sauce made of capers and lemon.

For the next half hour everyone talked about hunting, with occasional diversions into fishing and golf, Edinburgh tailors, fishing, hunting, golf, and the feud with the Johnstones which the Maxwell claimed was going exactly as he wanted it to, despite the setback caused by the stupid interference of the Deputy Warden.

The first remove was cleared by the servants filing in, and the second remove brought in with spitted chickens, blankmanger, more pathetic lettuce, quince cheese and sheep and cow cheese with a magnificent cartwheel tart with twelve flavours of jam in it like a clock. They drank to Maxwell's wife in thanks, although of course she was not present, having tactfully gone to visit her mother.

"Well," said Father Crichton, who was very full, "perhaps we could begin?"

"Ay," said the Maxwell, rubbing the continuous eyebrow that went from one side of his face to the other, "Ye all ken why ye're here…?"

"Och," said Huntly, leaning back and loosening his belt, "Ye're thinking of bringing the Spanish in again, are ye not?"

The Maxwell was a little taken aback. "Well, I am, but…"

"Ffft," said Erroll, pulled out his purse and gave Huntly a handful of debased Scotch shillings. "I thocht sure it's the French."

"The French are busy," said the Maxwell primly, "it has to be the Spanish King."

"Ay," said Erroll sceptically, "he's sending troops, is he?"

"He will," said the Maxwell positively. "He will because…"

"He willna," said Angus. "He disnae know nor care where Caerlaverock is, nor Lochmaben and…"

"He sent another Armada aginst the English again this summer…"

"Where is it?"

"Well it met some bad storms in the Bay of Biscay and they're refitting in the Groyne…"

"Ay, like the last one," said Erroll, drinking wine gloomily. "I swear the Queen of England's a witch."

There was a chorus of agreement about the unnaturalness of storms in Biscay in summer and they drank confusion to the old bat who had England in her grip and seemed to have a personal hold on the stormy weather as well.

"He might send another Armada next year, but…"

"Willna do nae good, she'll scatter that one too…"

"Will ye listen?" shouted the Maxwell and they quieted. "Father Crichton here has a canny scheme that will help the King of Spain to win England and incidentally wipe out the Johnstones by the way."

Everybody laughed except Maxwell.

"Ay, I thocht that would be in there somewhere..." said Huntly cynically.

"Ay, and why not, ye've some feuds yerself, Huntly..."

"Hush," said Erroll who had noticed Father Crichton stand up.

He stood there for a moment, plain and unassuming, in a good plain suit of brown wool. "Ye recall the paper written by the King a few years back on the pros and cons of the Spanish having England?" It was obvious nobody did but this did not matter. "His Majesty of Spain has now seen a copy and finds it interesting."

"Ay, but King James isnae a Papist, is he?" asked a shocked-sounding Huntly, who was a Papist himself, "He's a sodomite, sure, but..."

"He isnae reformed neither," sniffed Angus, which produced a laugh. "He's neither one nor the other." More sniggers.

"My lords," said Father Crichton with a small proud smile, "I think the one thing that we can be sure of is that the King is a...Jamesist."

There was a pause and then a lot of laughter at this dangerous witticism. Father Crichton waited it out.

"The proposition is this, My Lords," said Father Crichton, "that we take the usual assurances and bonds of manrent from our tenants and families while the King of Spain sends men quietly over the winter months, in hundreds here and there, some via Ireland, until there are at least four thousand *terceiros* based around Dumfries."

"How will we feed them?" somebody asked.

"The King of Spain will send food and money as well. While they are waiting they will need martial exercise and so my Lord Maxwell will lead them out..."

"To wipe out the Johnstones?"

"To deal with any disaffected elements in the area. Then when the spring storms have abated, the King of Spain will send a small Armada up through the Irish sea, using Irish and Cornish pilots, to meet us here. And in the summer of 1593 we march on England, down through the Western marches of Wales to Gloucester and Oxford. So the English willna ken they've been invaded until we're at Oxford perhaps, and London is open to us."

Father Crichton had been thinking about this plan for many years. It had some features he did not plan to share just yet, but as a peaceful man who had never been in a battle and dealt amongst the high abstractions of maps and orders, he was modestly proud of it. He thought of it as invading the soft underbelly of England and he rather thought the English would surrender and do a deal, once they realised how rotten their land soldiers were. Their frighteningly able sailors would not be able to do anything once the *terceiros* were ashore. There were hints that some of the men at the Queen's Court would be happy to do deals with the King of Spain and return to the arms of Mother Church. It was also said there was nothing an Englishman would not do for money.

"Hm," said Huntly, "what about King James, he's allus looked forward to getting the throne of England."

"He may not be disappointed," said Crichton carefully, because King James was indeed a problem, not least because nobody knew which way he would jump when it came to it—Catholic or Calvinist? "The King of Spain may prefer to rule through a vassal King, although he is the true heir through John of Gaunt and also his late wife, Queen Mary, not the bastard Elizabeth Tudor." Father Crichton didn't mention that Scotland could be swallowed later and converted back to the True Religion. "After he takes London, he will be King because everything flows from that, but there is more than one way to rule a conquest."

"It's a long way to go, Dumfries tae London."

"The Armada will resupply from the Irish sea," said Father Crichton, who had never seen Wales except in maps and assumed it was basically flat with some rolling hills.

They discussed the plan and Father Crichton brought out some specially drawn maps that showed as clear as day that it would be easy because nobody English would expect to be attacked from the northwest. The Queen would be guarding the south coast and the Cinque Ports as usual, not the approaches from the north. She trusted James and knew that he was considerably less martial than she was herself.

"Ye know," said Maxwell, "Queen James might even give his permission, seeing as the Spaniards would be only on the west coast and well away from Edinburgh and he disnae like a fight."

"Why should he give permission?" asked Huntly.

"Well the King of Spain's awfy rich, is he not? Why not bribe King James? I know he's annoyed with the Queen of England because she's cut his subsidy this year."

They all nodded thoughtfully.

The Maxwell spoke up again. "And besides," he said with a grin, "think of the plunder."

Father Crichton sat down again and listened with satisfaction as they talked about the rich pickings from the fat and easy lands of England. In a little while he would bring up the idea of assurances that they could give the King of Spain to convince him that they would do what he wanted, because the King of Spain had made a point about that. Philip II didn't trust the Scottish nobles as far as he could notionally throw them, which wasn't far since they were all fit young men and he was old and spent his days sitting at a desk.

Father Crichton made a quick prayer that the Lord Jesus Christ would bring the holy work to a satisfactory conclusion, with the Mass once more being said all across the sad, spiritually thirsty lands of England and Scotland, and of course, himself as Lord Chancellor.

AUTUMN 1592

Sir David Graham of Fintry was feeling tired and sad. His back hurt from standing too much, his knees hurt from kneeling, his ears hurt from the howls of drunken laughter coming from the King's privy parlour where the King was entertaining some of his favourite nobles with a late supper—the pheasant and partridge were in pieces and a custard had been thrown for no very good reason that Sir David could discern although everybody found it very funny and the King was saying "Splatt!" at intervals, with tears of laughter rolling down his dingy face.

Lord Spynie was now prancing about with a tapestry wrapped around himself, imitating one of the Queen's fatter ladies in waiting. The Queen wasn't there of course, but in her own apartments with her ladies. Now Spynie had the tapestry as a cloak and was guying the Earl of Bothwell who had once been a friend of the King's, and was now at the horn. Sir David had to admit that Lord Spynie was a very good mimic, if you liked that sort of thing. Personally he didn't.

He sighed and shifted from one foot to the other. As one of the King's Grooms of the Bedchamber, he was waiting to help His Highness to bed when he finally finished his hilarity and since the King was in the room, he couldn't sit down like Lord Spynie and put his feet up on the table. Or, no, to be fair, Spynie was still pretending to be Bothwell, flirting with an invisible witch with his feet up.

He shifted again. He had a lot to think about, some of it connected with a highly intelligent and ingenious engineer who was also properly respectful of Sir David, unlike a lot of the young men at Court. He hadn't really noticed the man until he had some particularly bad news about the thirty years a-building of his castle near Dundee. He had been upset and was telling one of his few friends at Court about it in an antechamber. Sir George Kerr hadn't been able to do more than sympathise but a curly haired gentleman with pale grey eyes had stopped leaning against a wall and asked with nice courtly respect, what the problem was.

"Part of the curtain wall is falling down again," said Sir David, mournfully. "I've turned off the masons but that didna stop it falling down again."

"Have you surveyed for running water?" asked the man.

"Eh?"

It turned out that the man's name was Jonathan Hepburn, he had been the Earl of Bothwell's man until the recent problems and he was, among other things, a mining engineer. And so, the following week when Sir David was off-duty again, Hepburn had ridden to Dundee with Sir David and spotted that there was a small stream under the wall where it kept falling down. He had spent a few days organising the cutting of a small culvert to take the water away and all was immediately well. The rebuilt wall stopped falling down.

Sir David couldn't help liking Jonathan Hepburn, he was so respectful, so interested. All the other Grooms of the Chamber, even Sir George Kerr, thought he was mad building a fortress with a tower at Fintry, when fortified houses were now all the fashion.

"Ay," he told Hepburn over dinner in his parlour, with his pretty young wife, Marguerite, mercifully silent with her eyes modestly cast down, though her pale skin was looking oddly pink. "See ye, I'm old enough to mind the sights I saw in the Rough Wooing of Henry VIII, when we looked out from our old wooden tower and saw all the land speckled and pecked with fire from the English men at arms."

"They didn't come to Dundee, did they?"

"No, though they burned Edinburgh, so they did."

Hepburn shook his head disapprovingly. Sir David waved his silver spoon.

"And they might have burned us, they verra well might have and that was when I swore to do anything in my power to make Fintry strong. I was only a wee lad but I remember it as if it were yesterday, I swore to rebuild Fintry of stone so it could keep out the English."

Hepburn nodded. "A noble aim," he said. "What can be more important than a strong castle where a man can put his feet down and know that it is his, and everything within it."

Marguerite suddenly made a coughing noise into her hanky, coughed quite a lot and went quite red, then stood, curtseyed to her husband and retired to the hall to finish her coughing fit. Hepburn didn't even follow her with his eyes, as most men did.

"Ay," said Sir David, his heart swelling. "Ay."

Young Hepburn had had many excellent ideas for strengthening what had already been built and improving what was planned.

They rode out and checked for more streams undermining the walls and found another unexpected place that needed dealing with, this time by diverting the stream so it fed into the moat.

Sir David had never known his young wife to be so well-behaved—there were no quarrels, no incomprehensible shouting matches. She was often impertinent and frankly too lively for his nearly sixty-year-old body and she had even protested when he dismissed two of her women when he felt they were plotting against him. But on this occasion she had behaved herself perfectly, almost as if she wasn't regrettably Flemish and a merchant's daughter.

It turned out that young Hepburn was also a Catholic, since his family came from a part of the Holy Roman Empire that had a Catholic prince and so was Catholic. Sir David approved of that: he couldn't bear the way starveling peasants in homespun and clogs would start haranguing their betters, even the King, on the wickedness of vestments and the importance of salvation through Grace alone. That kind of thing was simply none of their business.

Sir David had built a little chapel in the main Keep at Fintry, of course, and it gave him immense pleasure to bring young Hepburn proudly to Mass there, where he promptly availed himself of the opportunity to go to confession. Sir David's priest was elderly, but Hepburn even knew of a Jesuit that was new come over from Spain and introduced Sir David to him.

And now Hepburn had confided to him that he was worried about Sir David's wife, the pretty and feather-headed Marguerite. She was certainly quieter, a welcome change.

Well Sir David knew that Hepburn had no opportunity for dalliance—he was very careful to keep his wife by his side all evening and at night, at Fintry, of course, she was his bedmate. She had much to do with the household during the day and occasionally she couldn't be found anywhere, but then she would reappear in the dairy or the wet larder while Hepburn might be on quite the other side of the castle, checking the mortressing. And of course she was often with their children, who had two nurses and a tutor for the eldest son who would inherit, in another part of the castle so they wouldn't disturb Sir David nor get entangled in the building works. He visited them occasionally.

The new corner tower was nearing completion—young Hepburn had been interested in how Sir David could afford to spend so much on masonry.

"It's nae secret," said Sir David, as they sat on ponies at a couple of miles distance from the castle so they could assess the whole of it. "I'm Groom of the Bedchamber to His Highness and offer him his nightshirt or his wine—not the cap, just his nightshirt—and help him dress in the morning. There's rarely fewer than ten petitioners at any levée and they all want to pay me."

"So there are compensations for having to stay up so late…"

"Oh ay, all the other grooms do the same, more than me in fact, it's quite traditional, ye ken."

"Of course. We must have traditions."

Sir David was glad Hepburn thought that. He had hated the disruption caused by the silly girl who had been briefly Queen and had been very happy to see a male Stuart on the throne again, even if he was under two years old and nominally a Protestant.

Hepburn smiled a little. "Does the King actually take the nightshirt?"

"Eh no," said Sir David, "we generally can only get him to change it when he's been sick on his old shirt."

"Ah," said Hepburn, looking away and studying an unremarkable bush very fixedly.

At last Sir David had asked his wife if she was well, not ill with anything female, perhaps? He knew she wasn't pregnant again; he would have known at once because she was infallibly sick and cross. She said she was perfectly well but still looked worried.

And that was when he had started to wonder. Was it happening again? Did this wife too have a lover? He had of course dealt with the young man-at-arms who had looked at her, dealt with him very satisfactorily with a knife in the kidneys. But this was different; he knew no blame had attached to her with the man-at-arms, despite her blond hair. Had she taken another man into her bed, was she unhonest? It was a horrible thing to think of, it made his whole body shiver and go cold; he couldn't bear to be fooled again.

Young Hepburn had spotted him looking pensive, boiling internally with fear and rage, and asked him respectfully if he was well—just the same question Sir David had asked her. Sir David had passed it off—a little dyspepsia after a big post-hunting dinner for the Earl of Huntly, that big red-headed man with the bright blue eyes and the slow canny smile, whom the King seemed to like so well, he could do no wrong. Not even knifing the Earl of Moray to death was wrong when done by the Earl of Huntly, it seemed. Hepburn had been all solicitude and recommended a powder to ease the acid stomach, which had been bitter but had worked.

Sir David thought it was a tragedy that women were such fickle, flighty, unreliable creatures. You couldn't talk to them about anything interesting like architecture or hunting or even golf. And what if she was untrue?

"Maybe I could send Marguerite to Fintry," Sir David wondered. "Perhaps the Court is too wild for her, encourages unsuitable...er...thoughts."

Hepburn thought that would be a bad idea—she would be bored at Fintry, and everyone knew where idle hands led. And Sir David had to admit, though not to Hepburn, that there was another problem with that: What if she did in fact have a lover and invited him to Fintry? He didn't think he could bear that, just the thought made him tremble: his beautiful safe, beloved castle, violated by the violator of his wife. If she did have a lover. He had no evidence, only a feeling.

So he watched her covertly, paid one of the Queen's chamberers to keep an eye on her and suffered silently, wondering. Sometimes he thought she did have a lover, sometimes he was sure she didn't. Sometimes the tension of not knowing made him sweat as if he had a fever.

It didn't help that Hepburn was now not so available, he was deep in plans with the King for a masque—one of the newfangled Court entertainments that encouraged such deeply unsuitable behaviour in the Queen's women. This one was a masque of the Seasons with the ladies of the Court risking lungfever in the draperies that almost but not quite hid their nipples. He liked seeing a bit of nipple, did the King, and had been known to take a suck on them when very drunk.

Being an engineer meant you could design scenery and toys for masques as well. It was wonderful what the young man could do— he was even designing fireworks, with the help of the Frenchmen with their mysterious slitty-eyed demonic-looking assistants.

But did Marguerite have a lover? Did she? Why would she need one? Sir David tupped her every Friday night, regular as clockwork, whether he felt like it or not because he knew she was prone to attacks of the mother—and the King's own physician, no less, had advised him that regularly swiving her would help. So why would she take a lover? If she had? Why?

He had a new Court suit made for himself, green brocade trimmed with gold velvet. It had been a while since he did that and he thought he looked very elegant and manly in it, and young Hepburn had thought so too. Sir David was quite proud that he had kept his figure and only had a little potbelly; he wasn't going bald at all though his hair was grey; he had the long lantern jaw of the Grahams which always aged well; he was wealthy though most of his money went on building his castle, of course. All in all, he was as suitable a husband as you could find anywhere in Edinburgh. So why..?

Hepburn had listened to him friendlywise in the same antechamber where they had met, waiting for the King to finish playing cards with his nobles. Perhaps Sir David had rambled on a bit, for Hepburn had then coughed and asked the extraordinary question "Sir, have you considered buying your wife some new gowns?" Sir David just blinked at him. "Only both her Court dresses are five years old and have been remade twice and relined three times and I couldn't help overhearing…"

"Why would I do that?" asked Sir David, genuinely baffled. "They are not worn out yet."

Hepburn went into such a paroxysm of coughing that Sir David was quite concerned for him and told him to help himself to the wine.

"Some firework fumes must have caught in my throat," wheezed Hepburn. "Of course, it's a matter for you, but I have found most women are happier for a new gown."

Sir David thought about that for a long while because he now valued Hepburn's opinion and normally took his advice—but in this case, he decided, Hepburn was wrong. Why should he waste money on Court gowns for his wife when she had two perfectly good ones, plus everyday kirtles for when she was not on show? There was nothing at all wrong with the old gowns, except they were not designed in the foolish style with the Spanish farthingale that made women look as if they were standing in a barrel. In any case he had the corner tower to complete which was taking all his ready cash but would last for generations.

And then something very odd happened. The King suddenly caught sight of Marguerite in her oldest gown and gave her a twelve-yard dresslength of rose coloured velvet, with six yards of white damask to make her a new gown that would also do for the Masque of the Seasons as Spring. Marguerite was ecstatic.

"Oh, the King, he is so kind," she bubbled to her husband, while she was brushing her beautiful golden hair that evening, something he normally enjoyed watching. "He saw I have nossing to wear…"

"Well, my dear, you do have your perfectly respectable cramoisie damask…"

"…and Pow! Just like that, he gives me beautiful velvet and say, I must be sure and show him when the Queen's tailor has finished it. I will have it trimmed with freshwater pearls which are not at all expensive, Sir David, and perhaps some mother of pearl…" And so she went happily into a long explanation of styles which Sir David found painful in the extreme although he said "Yes dear" every so often.

It was painful because he had a thought about a possibility so outrageous he couldn't quite believe he was thinking it at all…And yet Henry VIII of England had scattered his seed with abandon, and hadn't Maria, James' foolish mother, been touched with scandal? The disgusting English Queen had been tupped by everybody at her Court, including her horsemaster and a hunchback. It was a fault of royal personages: they could, so they did. Yet surely James...preferred men.

Sir David had witnessed many horrible and disgusting things while serving the King as Groom, like the times when the painfully young and spotty King and the corrupt French Duc D'Aubigny had gone to bed together like a married couple. Sir David did his best never to think about it, just as he did his best never to think about Lord Spynie's young pages, who often had red eyes and a reluctance to sit after a party.

But then the King seemed to have grown out of it and had a Queen now and as far as anyone could tell had consummated the marriage. And surely a girl as beautiful as Marguerite might tempt even a God-rotted sodomite.

When Sir David consulted Hepburn on the matter, all he would say was that he was sure Marguerite was honest, that he had never seen the King make any improper suggestions to her and he was sure that the matter of the dresslength of rose velvet and the six yards of white damask was just the well-known and foolish generosity of His Highness.

Yet the thought came between Sir David and his food, between Sir David and his sleep. When he closed his eyes, he saw the King kissing Marguerite, fondling her breasts with his greasy dirty hands, sweating between her legs...It turned his stomach to lead and made him feel desperate because even if he sent her home to Fintry, who knew what she might get up to, and if he kept her here at Court...Well he couldn't watch her all the time. The chamberer hadn't reported anything but perhaps she had been rebought by someone with longer pockets than his...

He asked Hepburn again and saw Hepburn's eyes become opaque.

"Sir," he said, "I can but do my best, but if a woman of the Court is being pursued by the King, there is not a lot she can do about it."

And that was even worse. It had honestly not occurred to him that she might not be willing (though she had been happy about the gown, women were flighty), that James might be using his Kingship in so ugly a way. To be honest, he wouldn't put anything past the man since he was so deep-dyed in the sin of sodomy and, worse still, a Protestant.

It was only when he went home to Fintry on his weeks off and could see the tower and the walls that he felt a little better.

And then James began one of his fits of economising and started talking about reducing the number of his Grooms from eight to six.

It was obvious. The King would send Sir David home to Fintry, where he would not be able to do any more building without the daily influx of shillings and crowns from hopeful petitioners. And Marguerite would be defenceless in the King's power.

DECEMBER 1592

Carey took off his jack with the help of his servant, Hughie Tyndale, who made faces at what the jack was plastered with. "Don't clean it yourself," Carey said. "Get Young Hutchin to do it if you can find him." Underneath was a worn old hunting green doublet trimmed with velvet that was just about respectable enough for Bessie's. He also left his fighting boots with Hughie, who was getting quite good at cleaning off horrible things.

He didn't have another pair of long boots, but he had a pair of shoes which could cope with the mud, pulled them on, put a new tall-crowned hat on his head and walked quickly down the covered way to Bessie's. He was starving, and Bessie and her wife had set up their usual glorious breakfast for the men of the guard.

And at least he could eat the bacon now. He felt the healed gap in his back teeth with his tongue and shuddered. God, he had felt so ill.

He was having an argument with Sim's Will about which would win in a fight, two rats or a badger, when Bessie's wife, Nancy, sat herself down next to him in the common room and refilled his leather jack for him. In London he would have had his own pewter tankard behind the bar but Bessie didn't allow any such things in her house on account of the fact that they got damaged when you hit people with them—unlike leather jacks which weren't quite so bendable or expensive. Carey felt that reflected the irrationality of women.

He tipped his hat to her since she had curtseyed first before she sat down and raised a quizzical eyebrow.

"There's something I heard about ye, Deputy Warden," she said, "that there's been two letters come fra the Queen for ye. Have ye seen either one?"

He sat up at once. "No, I haven't."

"Ay well, one came wi' the regular postbag from Newcastle the day before yesterday."

"Did it now?"

"Ay, and there's another package for ye at Thomas the Merchant, but he'll tell ye about that as he wants the shilling."

"And the other letter? Who's got it?"

"Ay well, all the post is supposed to go to the Warden, but it often gets stopped by Lowther."

Carey smiled at her and lifted his ale in toast.

Once his belly was full of bacon, sausage, egg, black pudding, mushrooms, fried apple, and some interesting fried roots from New Spain via Newcastle, he felt quite sleepy but knew better than to take a nap yet. So he called Nixon to back him and strode on down into the town to the more respectable English Street, where Thomas the Merchant had his quite impressive three storey house with carved beam-ends and smart saffron yellow paint.

Thomas the Merchant was in front of the house talking to the Carlisle steward.

"I'll take the kine without brands that ye dinna want to slaughter, of course, and what about the horses?"

"We're keeping those. We always need more horses."

"Ay well, I'll come up and look at the beasts later..." That was when Thomas the Merchant spotted Carey and his face took on its normal wary expression.

"Ay, Deputy Warden, can I help ye?"

"You can," said Carey, doing his best not to beam at Thomas. "I heard tell you had a letter for me."

Thomas nodded and led Carey inside to his hall, where the plate was locked tight into two large cupboards chained to the wall. There he gave Carey a large official-looking packet stitched into double thickness canvas and addressed in old-fashioned Secretary hand "to the Deputy Warden of the West March, Sr Rbt Carey, Carlisle Castle."

He stared at it for a few seconds, wondering where it could have come from since most official correspondence (and there was a lot) was addressed to him as plain Sr Rbt Carey, Carlisle.

He flipped the packet over and saw the red portcullis stamp on the back and sudden joy lifted him up and he nearly gave a little jig of triumph right there in front of Thomas the Merchant. He didn't of course. He caught himself, bestowed an alarmingly sunny smile on the suspicious-faced old miser, and strode out into English Street which was crowded with people going out to work in the fields while the weather held.

All the way back up to the castle, with Nixon at his back, he had to stop his feet from breaking into a volta and also stop himself sprinting up the covered passageway. Once he had left Nixon behind and gone into the keep, nobody was watching and so he ran laughing up the stairs of the Queen Mary tower and did his jig on a landing where there was nobody to see except a tabby cat, watching sparrows from the windowsill, who didn't care. At the top of the narrow spiral staircase to his chambers he found his secretary, John Tovey, was still snoring and wasn't at all offended. He was on the palliasse—the two of them, Hughie and John, had come to an agreement where each alternated between the truckle bed and the floor.

He was still at a jog when he went through into his study and sat at the table that did duty as his desk, piled high as it always was with papers. Tovey's clerk's desk was in the corner with a candlestand next to it.

He turned the packet over and over in his long fingers, excitement still rising in him. Was it? At last? The Tower mark and the address. Could it be? Had the old bat finally...?

He pulled out his poinard from the scabbard at his back and slit the red stitching at one end, took out the inner packet and slit that stitching as well, which was yellow—which meant the Cecils. Inside were several sheets of paper.

The first he saw was odd—a passport to go into Scotland, dated from a week ago and no expiry date. But the second...

It was his warrant as Deputy Warden of Carlisle. It made him as official as illegibly small Secretary script and impressive seals could achieve and it was also signed and sealed with her Privy Seal by the Queen.

With it there was a private letter from the Queen, written by a secretary in Italic but signed by herself as his affectionate and loving cousin and aunt. He skimmed the letter, which was short and only filled half the paper—she had heard of his standoff with the Elliots and thoroughly approved of the way he had resolved it, and that there had been no effusion of blood between her aggressive Border subjects.

"Yes!" he shouted, punching his fist into the air and kissing the letter. John Tovey woke up, groaned and turned over, then sat up looking embarrassed.

"Sorry, sir..." he began.

"Run and fetch me some wine if you can find any. Scrope may have some," Carey said and punched the air again. Then he sat back down in his uncomfortable chair and shut his eyes. He suddenly realised that a knot of tension that had been in his stomach for a month or more had magically dissolved away. The Queen was a woman, you could never be sure how she would react to anything and there had been a part of him that thought exactly the same as Sergeant Dodd. Another part had insisted that if you wanted to make any headway with the Borderers, you had to get away from blood repaying blood through the years.

It had been very hard to sit there and let more than five hundred Elliot reivers escape but he knew it was right. It was not just a clever or politic or Queen-pleasing thing to do, but the right thing. Dodd had violently disagreed and made his displeasure known, so now Carey felt he had lost the man. It was a pity. Andy Nixon was loyal and almost hero-worshipped him, he knew, while Nixon's new wife was always bringing him pastries and pots of jam. Perhaps Nixon was as good a fighter as Dodd, and a better wrestler, but he didn't have half the brains.

He read the Queen's letter again, more carefully, which was enough to delight any courtier, although typically it said nothing about the Deputy Warden's fee. And it said nothing about the passport into Scotland either, which was a little odd. Perhaps the letter she had sent to Scrope confirming the choice of Carey for Deputy Warden would explain it. Carey did not plan to go into Scotland at all if he could help it, although he had recovered completely from the last time.

Tovey came back with wine and Carey poured him some, explained why and they toasted the Queen. Tovey was pleased once he understood the importance of the warrant. It was official. Nobody could turn him out without the Queen's permission. God, it would be fun to watch Lowther's face when he showed the warrant to Scrope. Maybe Lowther would fall into a conniption fit with rage and die and save Carey a lot of trouble. He hoped so.

He read the letter again, folded the whole packet back up and put it in his doublet pocket where it warmed him like a hand-warmer full of coals.

AUTUMN 1592

Sir David Graham was in a terrible state, a state he had been in before with his first wife, and he knew of only one way to feel better. And yet he felt utterly horrified by the idea and at the same time grimly vengeful, because hadn't the King betrayed him first?

He was sure that Marguerite had a lover now, he had found lovebites on her shoulder and he never gave her lovebites. He had said nothing. She seemed to have no idea she had them and continued prattling away about the beauty of her new kirtle with its Spanish farthingale and the pink velvet and the white damask until he could have screamed. But that was not his way. He had always been a quiet man, not given to displays of temper. That did not mean he had no feelings, only that he chose not to wave them around in public.

Finally he got Hepburn to himself on the links opposite the port of Leith. The weather was bad, blustery and raining, but he had needed to get out of the Court and blow the cobwebs out of his ears and Hepburn had agreed to come with him and play a little golf. Not a proper game, only practising.

He teed off and struck the ball well, it flew away avoiding the trees and landed in some long grass. Hepburn had hit his ball well too, but shorter.

They ended closer together on the green and while Hepburn lined up his putt, Sir David struggled with himself and finally burst out,

"If he were not the King, he would already be dead."

Hepburn stopped for a moment. "Sir David?"

"The man who debauched my Marguerite. If he were just a man, even an earl, I would have killed him by now."

Hepburn looked straight up at him. "How? In a duel?"

Sir David snorted. "No, why should I honour him by fighting him? He's scum. He laughed at me yesterday morning, asked me if I was well, and all the time…All the time…"

Hepburn sighed. Then he straightened up and leaned on his golf club, the wind blowing his falling band sideways. There was no one else on the links and they hadn't brought a boy to find the balls.

"You believe it truly is the King?"

"Yes," ground out Sir David. "He can go to the Queen's apartments any time he chooses and swive anyone he likes. And Marguerite has a lover's bite and the kirtle…I'm sure it's the King."

"It could be some other man. It could even be me."

Sir David laughed indulgently at that. "No, no, Jonathan," he said. "You're not a God-rotted sodomite, but you are more interested in your alchemy and engineering than you are in women. I can tell."

"Ah," said Hepburn. "Well then, perhaps it is the King. But what can you do about it? I have said this before, he may be a coward but he is clever. You can't carry so much as an eating knife in his private apartments where being a Groom of the Bedchamber might help you, there are always at least five other people with you..."

"Poison, in his first cup of wine in the morning. He's always thirsty in the morning, knocks it straight back."

"They will know who gave him the cup."

Sir David smiled wolfishly. "Not if I don't give it to him. I serve it out, taste it, and sometimes he takes it from me, sometimes a chamberer gives it to him, sometimes the Groom of the Stool gives it to him..."

"Who is that at the moment?"

"Sir George Kerr does the office at the moment, but I don't want him to give the cup because he is also one of our Catholic association."

"Yes," said Hepburn. "The association with Huntly and Erroll?"

"Of course. It's a very good idea from your Jesuit, Crichton, about bringing in Spanish troops to the west coast."

"I had heard something about it."

"Well, I'm not supposed to tell anyone. Anyway, sometimes, if a petitioner pays a lot of money, sometimes he can give the King his cup of morning wine. So we find someone who wants something big and he can come into the King's levée and as he will give the cup, everyone will blame him."

Hepburn looked at Sir David with real respect. "That's ingenious, Sir David. Brilliant."

Sir David twirled his golf club roguishly. "I think so. Of course it's not just any levée that petitioners can actually take part in. Usually they stand and watch at the other end of the bedchamber and come forward after His Highness is dressed. The next is the New Year's morning, but I can wait for my satisfaction if I have to."

"Yes," said Hepburn, chipping his putt and missing the hole by a mile. "We will need to choose the man to do it very carefully."

They talked for a while about who could do it, came to no conclusion. Hepburn rode back to Edinburgh with Sir David Graham who was now somehow happy, as if making the decision had helped settle his uneasy soul.

Hepburn was awed at how well his plan was going: he had hardly had a plan when he started, only he had heard something about Sir David and his first wife, how jealous he was, how the lover and the wife had both died quite suspiciously, how there had been a man-at-arms that had fallen for Marguerite and who had died also in mysterious circumstances in which he had somehow stabbed himself in the kidneys.

Hepburn knew he himself was a killer, although generally he didn't do the actual killing, he...facilitated it. He could see through people so easily, their jealousies and their ugliness, he felt he was providing a vermin-killing service. Sir David did not know what he was, which made him easy to control. Spynie was another one like Hepburn, they got on well and Hepburn facilitated him as well. He was even making friends with the King he had come to kill on behalf of the Spanish Most Catholic Majesty, and he could do it while still looking for the best way to end him. It was exciting and satisfying, it excited him to fool everybody into thinking he was a helpful respectful man with engineering skills and good address, when in fact he was so much more. He felt he was looking at the Court from a great height and laughing as the ants below him ran around excitedly while he pushed them one way and another with twigs and bits of paper and carefully killed some here and some there. Out of policy he normally liked to have two different and separate attempts running at the same time, one a little earlier. Then, if the proposed victim discovered or fought off one, he would relax and be easy meat for the second attempt.

It had taken so little to get the King to give Marguerite the pink velvet and the white damask; a mention of how mean her husband was, a wink, the idea planted in the King's mind that he could somehow shame Sir David into treating his wife better through royal largesse. The King was always clumsily trying to get the courtiers around him to treat each other better, as if they were not there through greed and ambition, as if they were all friends really. It was ridiculous but very useful. Then a couple of careful lovebites on Marguerite during one of their trysts in the storerooms at the back of the court and the thing was done.

Hepburn shook his head. He had made his peace with the demiurge of this World, with the Aeon who ruled everything. You had to choose: either the Demiurge, the Power of the World, or the Christ who had foolishly tried to oppose him and been crushed. Some called the Demiurge, the Devil. He called him God and felt the power run through him when he called on him. Fools called them Anabaptists: he had taken the trouble to read some of the difficult sacred texts in Latin and his conclusions had been rational, not emotional. He had no interest in the Sophia, the female expression of God. Women could worship her under the guise of Mary the Mother of God, the Theotokos, if they wanted. He thought they were fools of a different kind, but they were women and inferior. Sure, the Albigensians had tried to bring the Christ into the World by what they did and they had been crushed as well, by Saint Dominic, the Demiurge's servant. He chose not to be crushed. He would follow the Power of the World and when He died, he would go to His side to serve Him more.

In the meantime he would obediently go to Mass and confess what he chose because as far as he was concerned, the Catholic Church was clearly the main tool of the Demiurge, not at all His enemy. He had travelled through the Netherlands, making himself useful wherever and whenever he could, and he had been recommended at last to San Lorenzo where he had actually met the Spanish King and talked to him of his ideas. He had the precious copy of the paper outlining his ideas with Philip's *Fiat* written on it and he thought that when Scotland descended into chaos with the death of the King, he would certainly become a lord at least, possibly a King. The Spanish King didn't know about that part of it, but thought Hepburn was another Catholic fanatic as he was himself. Another fool.

He was careful and he was clever. He would survive and conquer and perhaps in a year or two, he would be running Scotland.

LATE AUTUMN 1592

Janet Dodd née Armstrong was wondering if it would really be such a sin to murder her husband. It would be a sin, obviously, and petty treason moreover, but surely she had justification?

Henry Dodd had never been the happiest of men but there was something solid and dependable about him. Yet since the Deputy Warden had let the Elliots escape from Dick of Dry-hope's tower without a battle, he had gone from taciturn but essentially friendly to a stone-faced silent man she did not know. Even love-making didn't help which it always had before; he seemed somehow abstracted as if his thoughts were far away and nowhere pleasant, until their tussling under the bedclothes while Bridget snored in the truckle bed became more like a fight. Not once since the Elliots had he asked to count her freckles, not once had she shucked her shift so he could admire her and love her breasts and hips, not once had she felt that blessed sensation halfway between a sneeze and utter joy that made her feel warm and happy all the next day. Not once. It was as if a stranger got into bed with her wearing Henry's shirt and Henry's face and tupped her as if she was a ewe.

She was seeing to the vegetable garden and she dug angrily. She had got a couple of her English Armstrong cousins to come and dig in two ponyloads of manure which she had obtained for nothing from the Carlisle stables. Henry was off on his precious big horse Whitesock, checking the northern boundaries of Gilsland for moving marker stones. Gilsland was now theirs but she couldn't feel happy about it any more. She felt lonely, despite being surrounded by people, most of them some sort of cousin and one, Bridget, her half sister.

Suddenly one of the women holding poles for the men fixing the fencing over by the infield, clapped her hand to her side and doubled up. Janet dropped her spade and ran over.

"What is it?" she asked, "When is the baby due?"

It was Goody Ellen, a cousin, married for five years to Willie's Simon and proudly pregnant, but not fully gone yet. Was it six months?

"Not till Candlemas," gasped Ellen, tears of fright in her eyes, "Och it's bad."

Ellen hadn't had a baby before. Maybe these were ghost pains and she was just making a fuss...

"Oh...Oh, God, I canna hold it..." gasped Ellen, trying to grab her crotch round her belly. Janet lifted her wool kirtle and saw her petticoat was suddenly wet and stained, mainly water but blood and brown stuff there as well.

"Ekie!" she shrieked to one of the boys tidying beanvines, "ride for Mrs Hogg, off ye go now. Say Ellen's gey early and her waters have broken."

Ekie was quite a young boy, maybe eight, but had a good head on him. He stood and stared for only a second before he sprinted for the tower and the stables.

"Take Angel," she shouted after him. "He's a good galloper and ye've ten miles to go."

Mrs Hogg lived near Carlisle and was the best midwife hereabouts, a tough flinty woman who had faced down drunken husbands and, it was rumoured, raiding Grahams.

"Och, God!" shrieked Ellen again, "Oh God!" Janet got Ellen's arm over her shoulder and helped her over the ruts in the field, onto the path, waiting for another set of shrieks to quiet, urged her along. "Willie's Simon, fetch me my aqua vitae, quick as ye can, lad." Ellen's husband had been running towards them from the wall at the far end of the infield but Janet had never heard good of husbands at a birthing and in any case he knew where she hid the stillroom key.

Janet found Rowan Leaholm on the other side of Ellen and they helped her along until they saw Big Clem the blacksmith come running up the path from his forge. He caught Ellen up and held her in his arms like a baby while she twisted and clutched her belly and cried out. His face was sad: his own wife had lost a wean in the upset of a raid that summer.

Janet saw young Ekie come trotting out of the courtyard and good lad, he had tacked up Angel properly and was giving the horse a chance to warm up before his gallop, that was good sense and nice to see. The lad was cantering as he went over the hill in the direction of Carlisle.

They got Ellen up into the tower and into the little room Janet used as an infirmary and still-room, laid her on the bed where she sat up and shrieked again. Willie's Simon was there with a horn cup of brandy which she gulped and then gasped again. Clem thundered downstairs in silence with his broad kindly face troubled and sad.

More brandy went into her and then some more. Sometimes you could stop a miscarriage with brandy, Janet had heard, and at least it helped with the pain. Bridget was there as well. "Will ye go ben and tidy away any tools and such," Janet said, thinking of the valuable sickles and spades getting ruined by the rain. "I'll stay with Ellen."

Janet sat and waited as patiently as she could, trying not to think of all the things that went wrong with having a babby. She liked Ellen and didn't want her to die. Although in ten years of marriage she had been barren, there had not even been a missed mense, yet she had seen plenty of her women go through birthing. Once the baby had stuck in a girl's narrow hips and although Mrs Hogg had killed the baby, which was already blue and spent, and taken it out in bloody pieces, the girl had been too exhausted to live after three days of struggle. What was her name, that poor blonde slip of a thing, she couldn't remember, it was back when she was new to being the mistress. The curse of Eve the pastors called it, and it was a curse, but if it all went well and the woman was successfully churched, it didn't seem to matter about the pain or the mess, the baby paid for everything. Providing it didn't die, of course.

Ellen shrieked more quietly and turned restlessly. Ah, the mess. There were plenty of women who went down to the stables to have their weans so they wouldn't have the trouble of washing the sheets after. Also it was considered lucky, since hadn't Jesus Christ Himself been born in a stable? With the ox and the ass kneeling to Him?

Janet fetched the coarse hemp sheets from the back of the linen press that were already a little stained with other people's blood since you often couldn't get it all out once it had set. She sat Ellen up to take the other sheets off and took her kirtle off as well. It didn't seem to have taken much harm, her under-petticoats were slimy and horrible but it hadn't soaked through. She and Bridget undressed Ellen down to her smock and Bridget took the kirtle and the sheets off to soak the sheets in water and try and see if she could sponge the stains off the kirtle.

Then she uncovered the birthing chair and brought it out from its corner, wiped the dust off it. Ellen saw it and started to cry again.

"The baby's coming too early."

"Ay, it is," Janet said.

"Do ye think it might live?"

"Do ye know when ye quickened?"

"It was May…No, July, late July when he quickened but I'd been feeling awfy sick before that, couldnae eat nor drink."

"He's just in his seventh month." Janet found she was shaking her head.

"D'ye think Mrs Hogg could put it back in and sew me up, do ye think? Oh God."

Janet waited. "I think once the waters have broken the babe's got to come out, will he or nill he."

Ellen cried harder and Janet shouted for someone, found Willie's Simon at the door and ordered him to fetch the brazier to keep Ellen warm and some ale for her to mull. It was going to be a long day. At least the wean hadna decided to come in the middle of the night, that was something.

Mrs Hogg arrived riding pillion with Ekie on Angel and clattered up the stairs in her hobnailed boots. Janet leaned out of the staircase window and told Ekie to walk Angel and rub him down and give him a bran mash and Ekie said "yes, missus" politely, despite the fact that he clearly knew all that. Mrs Hogg was a plump comfortable-looking person until you got on the wrong side of her, and then watch out. Janet found herself wondering if the midwife knew any good spells or potions to help with her barrenness, but she would ask later.

The midwife had her big leather bag and took her sleeves off and rolled the sleeves of her shift up to her shoulders, tied them there with a tape, put on a wide hemp apron. Then she smeared her hands with tallow and put her hands up Ellen's smock and felt about for what seemed a long time. She stood up and came to Janet saying, "Can I get a pottle of ale, missus, my throat's fair dry fra the ride."

Janet poured her a cup of ale over in the corner.

"It's breech and very early," she said. "When's it due?"

"Candlemas."

"Ah." Mrs Hogg's chin went down on her chest. "Ay, a May baby. Well she'll need to go a-maying again."

There was another loud shriek from the bed and Mrs Hogg went over to her, took her hand. "Now then," she said, "save yer shrieking, hen, it'll get worse before it gets better."

A new thunder of feet on the stairs and there were the nearest two of Ellen's gossips at last, her sister Mary and Katherine from the dairy in a bustle of kirtles and aprons. They sat down next to Ellen on the bed and hugged her and then held her hands while she twisted and tried not to shout.

Katherine had a good voice and she started singing a spinning worksong, all about spindles and pockets and in very poor taste if you listened the right way.

Janet trotted down the stairs to see that things were going along. She and Dodd had decided to hold a pig killing for the last survivor of the boar piglets, since he was showing signs of temper and he was racketing about in his pen, trying to dig his way out. Pigs always seemed to know what was in the wind but she wouldn't be sorry to see this one die, he was a nasty piece of work, too much of the wild boar in him.

She made her rounds, looked in on the horses as always, Penny, Shilling, Angel and Samuel the donkey, she considered where she could put a goat pen if she decided to keep goats which were a new-fangled idea for the Borders though she liked the sound of an animal that could eat anything, she checked the stores of grain and hay and straw and found as she always did this year that there wasn't enough.

Her mind started circling and worrying on the problem. She thought she would have to sell or kill one of the horses and Dodd wouldn't like that. Really she should have sent old Shilling to the knackers last year, but she was fond of the old gentleman and couldn't bring herself to do it. But she had to do something.

The cattle were all in the well-guarded infield, eating the stubble, the sheep were in the nearest outfield, away on the hill crossed by the Giant's Wall, which was horribly muddy from the rain. The soil was so waterlogged she wasn't expecting much from the winter cabbages. All the men were tired and cranky from having to keep a guard, and starting to come in for their dinner.

She delegated serving the men and the boys to Bridget who was already stirring the large cauldron of pottage and slicing the bread to go with it. She hadn't eaten since breakfast but wasn't hungry.

Back in her little infirmary, Mrs Hogg had just finished another rummage under Ellen's smock and was drinking the last of the ale. Ellen was hiccupping badly and her gossips were getting drunk. There wasn't really room for her but Mary budged up on the bed to let her sit down. Then Willie's Simon appeared at the door, his face like a cow in calf himself.

"Is she gaunae be all right?" he asked Mrs Hogg desperately, "Is she?"

"It's in the hands of Our Lady," said Mrs Hogg.

"What can I do?"

"Naething, this is women's work."

"Can I rub her back for her, she likes it..."

"Her gossips can do that, out ye go, get yer pottage."

"I dinnae want it, I'm a good stockman, I've helped cows and sheep give light to their weans, I can..."

"Men fight, women birth, so get oot," said Mrs Hogg who had a brisk way with husbands. Ellen stopped panting and reached her hands out to her husband. "It's best ye go," she said kindly, "The babby's too soon and the wrong way up, so mebbe he'll die, but we can try again once I'm churched, hinny."

Willie's Simon looked confused. "Too soon?"

"Ay, he's not...he's not properly cooked yet, see ye..."

"But..."

"It's all right," said Ellen softly, "We'll make another baby, eh?"

Willie's Simon's face cleared a little. "Oh, but..."

"And this one might live...Ooorgh...ooorrgh...Ah shit, I need tae shit..."

Janet shoved the young man bodily out the door and slammed it, while Mary and Kat jumped off the bed. The last thing she needed was somebody fainting.

"Ayaaergh!" howled Ellen and Mrs Hobb felt her quickly and then nodded. So they moved her between them to the birthing chair where she sat with her legs apart and her smock up and Mrs Hogg knelt like a priest at an altar in front of her with her hands slick with tallow.

Mary and Kat helped keep Ellen steady from either side while Janet put her back against Ellen's back and her feet on the wall and supported her while she bore down.

"Ay," said Mrs Hogg coolly, as something that looked oddly like a plum appeared between Ellen's legs. "Go with it, hinny, wait for the wave to come and then go with it. Aright, get yer breath. Can ye say an Avvy?"

"Dinna ken..." panted Ellen, tears and sweat pouring down her face. Janet wiped it with her apron.

"Well say it wi' me, Avvy Maria, grass a plenty, dominoes take em, benedictus two in mules and arybus..."

Ellen screamed and her face turned purple, the plum between her legs got bigger, then smaller, then much bigger and turned into a very small baby's bottom. Mrs Hogg took hold of it and pulled, pulled out one little foot and then another and they dangled, looking strange. Mrs Hogg was tutting.

"Aright, hinny, yer doing fine, let's have another Avvy Maria..."

Janet turned and braced her feet against the wall again while Mary and Kat held Ellen's shoulders.

"et benny dictus fruit venter twee…" sang out Mrs Hogg, "Come on hinny, ye're a good strong lass, give it all ye've got, let's get the head out." Ellen went a darker purple, her neck corded as she bore down and slowly Mrs Hobb pulled and there were shoulders and pulled and pulled and finally, there was a tiny baby with a big head, dark blue, very tiny and skinny with something funny on its back.

Mrs Hogg held it to one side, christened it with water from the bucket beside her, muttering the words as fast as she could as the little chest fluttered. Yes, there was something red and ugly on his back, in his back, was that bone…?

Janet craned her neck to see and as the water touched his forehead he struggled and fought but couldn't get his breath, it was as if the air was made of steel for him, and he gave a little sigh and went limp. Mrs Hogg was already bundling him up in a cloth, hiding the strange wound on his back and she glared at Janet to stay silent.

"He's not…he's not supposed to be blue…"

"No, hinny, he's not. He couldna breathe. He lived till I christened him, but he's just too little and he's deid."

Ellen clutched the baby and howled like a dog while her gossips wrapped their arms around her and cried. Mrs Hogg left the cord and just patted Ellen's back. Janet said quietly through the noise, "What was that on his back?"

"I'll tell ye later, it'll do her nae good to know."

Janet went and opened the horn-paned window wide and then they waited for the afterbirth which came plopping out a little while later. Mrs Hogg caught it in a bowl and cut the cord and there was no blood. She took the bowl to the light of the sunset and moved the liverlike thing about, checking it closely.

"Ay," she said in a pleased voice, "that's all there. Ye'll be well enough in time."

Ellen's face was covered in snot and tears as she held the tiny bundle to her chest and sobbed deep wrenching sobs that came from her belly.

"Ay," said Mrs Hogg, not a tear on her face, "Ye cry, hinny, cry away the sadness." She mopped Ellen's legs and quim and belly with cloths from the bucket. "Now let's get ye back on the bed."

Janet, Mary and Kat carried Ellen bodily to the bed, where they pulled her dirty smock off over her head, one arm then the other arm, so she could still hold the baby and she shivered suddenly. One of Janet's own smocks went on over her head and a pair of breeches to hold the cloths. Everything went immediately into a bucket of cold water to soak for the night. And all the time she cried and cried for the tiny unbreathing baby, that was paling now.

Mrs Hogg put a knitted shawl from Kat around Ellen's heaving shoulders and then sat beside her and waited for the worst of the storm to pass. Eventually she asked gently, "Will ye let me lay the little one out for ye?"

"Why did he die? Why didn't he stay inside me? Why did he come too soon?"

Mrs Hogg shook her head. "Naebody knows why anybody lives or dies, ainly God and His Mother. But I'll tell thee, child, he was baptised whilst his little heart was still beating and he'll go straight to God, so he will, straight to heaven he'll fly and he'll be an angel there."

Ellen's tears were thick and slow now. "But why did God want him?"

"Ah dinnae ken, hinny, but perhaps He wis short of they smaller angels ye see in books, ye ken, the fat babies wi' the little wings. And maybe the baby was helping ye, so he came too soon while he was little so ye wouldna have too bad a time of it. So he wouldna hurt ye too bad."

There was a disbelieving giggle in Ellen's throat between the tears. "It can be worse?"

"Oh ay, it can be worse and longer. A breech is allus bad but ye only took a couple of hours. Next time it'll be much easier, I promise ye."

Ellen was no longer clutching the little bundle, she was holding it as if her baby had gone to sleep. "What did you christen him?"

"I christened him John, I allus do. John or Mary. That's why there's so many Johns and Marys hereabouts because sometimes the water of baptism wakes them up and they live."

Ellen nodded.

"Will I lay out your wee Jock for ye now?"

Ellen looked down at the baby's grey face with the open grey eyes. "Ay," she said, "He's deid, isn't he?" She gave the baby into Mrs Hogg's arms and she took him away.

Janet went and got an old sheet to do as a shroud and helped hold the floppy little thing while Mrs Hogg washed him down quickly and swaddled him tight and then laid him on the windowsill. The wound in his back was shocking, laid open down to the backbone.

"How does that thing happen? With the back?" whispered Janet.

Mrs Hogg shrugged. "Naebody knows. I think the Devil gets his lance and stabs the baby in the back and sometimes the heid too, cos the Devil's a coward of course. Isnae a thing anyone can do about it although the midwife I 'prenticed with, old Mother Maxwell, she said that if the mother likes beer that makes the babby strong enough to turn the spear aside. And if she sleeps with a horseshoe in the bed, that keeps the Devil and the faeries away anyway."

Janet nodded. She would pass the medical advice on to Ellen later. "Have you eaten, Mrs Hogg? Can I get you anything?"

"Ay, I'm tired, I could take a sup to eat."

They passed Willie's Simon squatting against the wall in the passage, crying into his hands. Mrs Hogg bent down to him and touched his shoulder. "Ye can go to her now, if ye've a mind to," she said.

"Is the babby...?"

"Ay, son, the babby's dead, it was too little to breathe. Ye go and comfort your woman, she's a brave strong lass."

Willie's Simon shut his eyes and breathed out hard, then stood up. "Will we have more..."

Mrs Hogg laughed. "Well that's up tae ye and the lassie, eh? But yes, ye will and they willna come too soon."

Willie's Simon braced his shoulders and went into the infirmary and Kat and Mary came out, complaining that they were hungry. They all went down the spiral stairs to the warm hall where Janet had pestered and pestered until they had a modern range in the corner for charcoal as well as the great fireplace for lumps of cow, that always had a stockpot hanging over the fire and bubbling away.

Janet sent the girls for bowls and decanted platefuls though it was very late for dinner and served Mrs Hogg herself with the best maslin bread. Mrs Hogg ate with a will and so did Janet and she sent a lurking boy up to the infirmary with bowlfuls for Willie's Simon and Ellen.

The girls went off to tell what happened to the other girls and Janet fixed Mrs Hogg with a gimlet eye. "What was that ye were saying about May babies and maying?" Mrs Hogg had a peculiar expression on her face, a mixture of regret and determination.

After a while she spoke softly, "It's the mumps."

"Mumps?"

"Ay. If he's nobbut a child when he gets it, he just looks funny for a while and has a sore throat. But if a young man gets it badly his…"

"Balls swell up."

"Ay they do. Now they sometimes turn black and then he usually dies but more often they'll swell up and hurt and then go down again and he thinks he's none the worse. And he isna, except his woman will never get with child."

"*What?*"

"It was Mother Maxwell noticed that too and she told me." Mrs Hogg was avoiding looking at Janet. "All I can think is that the stuff that's in his balls gets soured somehow so the little mannikins he plants in his woman are dead or hurt or something."

A lot of young men had got the mumps in 1582 before the execution of the Scottish Queen, for it had been a while since there had been mumps on the Border. Including one Henry Dodd who had been in the castle guard at Carlisle for good and sufficient reasons connected with the Elliots.

Janet remembered it, how she had gone to visit him at the castle barracks and found him in his little bunkbed, his feet hanging off the end and he had been in terrible pain and terribly frightened and finally told her why in a whisper and she had fetched cold water and cloths and a raw steak and made him more comfortable.

She had loved him already, already chosen him to be hers and putting wet cloths on his poor hot swollen balls had been like the most natural thing in the world: it was only later that she had been astonished at herself. And that was why he was so terrified of illness, of course.

She stared at Mrs Hogg. "Henry..."

"Ay," said Mrs Hogg, "so I heard."

After a moment Janet let out a kind of cross between a laugh and a sob. "So that's why none of the potions nor the Lady's springs nor anything has worked and there's never been a babe."

"Ay."

"Jesus!"

Mrs Hogg leaned forward over her clean and polished bowl. "That's a fine pottage, missus. May Ah have some more?"

Janet moved like someone who had been hit on the head, got the soup, brought the bowl back. There was a large lump of rabbit in it. She didn't bring any for herself.

"So...?"

"So," said Mrs Hogg, scooping up beans, "Ye've a problem, for a man that's nobbut a tenant may want to keep his tenancy and pass it to his son, ay, but he canna know if his lord will say yes. But the man that has the freehold of a place must have a son to inherit."

Janet swallowed. Was that why Henry had turned so sour? Was he wanting to get rid of her because he thought she was barren?

No, surely not. Not Henry. They hadn't talked about it...but no. She thought of the wicker basket wrapped in linen under her bed, that she took out carefully every Sunday to wear the green velvet London hat to church. She knew that word was spreading of Henry's stroke of luck in the south, when he had somehow persuaded the Queen to give him Gilsland's freehold, and none of the stories about it were half as wild as the truth.

"Mrs Aglionby told me about the freehold," enlarged Mrs Hogg, "She was quite amazed at it. And the Carletons are fit to be tied, so I've heard."

Janet grunted. She didn't care about the Carletons.

"There's no chance of him making a babe in me? Or anyone else?"

"None. Willie's Simon got the mumps too and he's made no babes."

"But…"

"Ellen came to me for a potion last year."

"I was wondering did ye have anything…"

"…and I told her to go a-maying," said Mrs Hogg, dipping her spoon. "Go a-maying, jump the fire on St John's night, light Lammas torches, scare off the Devil on All Soul's night, dance on Christmas night and light the candles on Candlemas. Do ye follow, missus?"

Janet didn't know how pale she had gone, her freckles were stark on her milk white skin. She only felt the wild whirling in her stomach.

She didn't want to go with another man. She hadn't even looked at another man since she clapped eyes on Henry, for all his dourness, for all his silences and the ridiculous way he would never let himself laugh at anything and the strange shy sweetness of his smile when he let it happen…She didn't want anyone else.

Yet if Dodd couldn't plant a babe in her, that was a disaster. A disaster for them both.

"That's what I said to Ellen," said Mrs Hogg, "and she greeted for she's an honest woman and she didna want to, but I told her it didnae count when the man couldn't make a baby. It seems she saw the sense."

"Ay, and lost the baby. Is that not a punishment from God?"

Mrs Hogg paused thoughtfully. "It may be," she allowed, "but God also said go forth and multiply to us and if your right husband canna make a baby in ye, what are ye to do? Eh?"

Janet said nothing. It depended how much you believed of what the pastors said God was like. "Besides, ye could say that Our Lady herself played St Joseph false when she went with the Holy Ghost, eh?"

Janet had never heard it put like that, was that some kind of heresy? Yet it made sense. You could say Jesus Himself had been God's bastard. She was shocked at herself for thinking such a thing but...

"I know plenty of women who have gone a-Maying to find a babe, and plenty of them have their babes safe and well, ay, and growed up too," said Mrs Hogg. "I say, think on it and do what seems to you to be right."

Janet wasn't aware she was nodding.

"Well that's a very nice pottage, missus," said Mrs Hogg in the same tone of voice, "Thank ee kindly for it."

"Your fee is five shillings?"

Mrs Hogg shook her head. "Nay, missus, I only take half for a dead baby. 2/6 is fine."

"Five shillings," said Janet firmly.

***

Carey was whistling a little ditty that explained how autumn was mellow and fruitful as he went to find his brother-in-law, Lord Scrope.

As usual, the overbred ninny was in the stables. Today he was preparing to take Buttercup's litter out in couples on a hunting expedition and there was Jack with his yellow coat and enormous clumsy paws and floppy ears, shoving past his brothers and sisters to get patted by Carey.

"Good morning, My Lord, and what a very pleasant morning it is, too...And Sir Richard, I'm delighted to see you too," breezed Carey loudly. He smiled at everyone. This was joyous because Sir Richard Lowther was scowling at him suspiciously from over by the kennels. Carey favoured him with an especially bright smile and let him stew for a while.

He looked over the dogs, agreed that they needed exercise, opined that perhaps it was too blowy and damp to fly the hawks and then allowed himself to be persuaded to take one of the merlins. That was really a woman's bird, but Philadelphia had gone south to serve at the Queen's Court again. She hadn't been happy in Carlisle but her hawks still needed exercise. Would it be possible to send her favourite hawks south to London so she could fly them in Finsbury Fields? He would need to find a good cadger for the journey; it was a long way.

"You seem very happy, Robin," said Scrope pettishly.

"Oh I like it here in the north, My Lord," Carey told him. "And of course there's the letter from the Queen that I received today." Oh it was fun, the way Lowther glowered and started to move away. "I'm sure you've seen it, My Lord, there is always a copy that goes to the Lord Warden, isn't there, Sir Richard?"

Habet, thought Carey, I've got you. Scrope stood there, his scrubby little goatee not improving his face by adding chin at all. The hawk on his fist looked twice the lord he was. "Oh," he wittered, "And what did she write?"

Carey could not help himself, he practically crowed. But he kept his voice casual as he explained, "She's pleased with me, My Lord. She thoroughly approves of the way I dealt with the Elliots and she has kindly sent me my warrant as Deputy Warden of the English West March." He paused theatrically. "Surely you have your copy of it, My Lord, I'm sure Mr Secretary Cecil is very careful about such things."

Scrope stood like a halfwit with his mouth open for at least a heartbeat and then he frowned at Lowther, who seemed to be trying to find an exit from the stableyard where there wasn't one by the kennels.

"How peculiar, I should have got it by now. I'll ask Richard Bell about it."

"No need, My Lord," said Carey, very helpfully, "Here's my copy and the Queen's letter as well."

Scrope scanned the letter, checked the warrant and said, "Er...yes, I wrote a report about the incident at Dick of Dryhope's tower to Her Majesty, saying that you not only prevented what could have been a very nasty battle but you made Wee Colin Elliot look like a fool and a coward which has done his reputation no end of harm. I heard from the King's Court that two of his cousins have come in and composed with His Highness and given hostages. I was both surprised and pleased, Robin."

Despite his instant irritation at being called Robin by Scrope, Carey bowed to him. "My Lord, I am exceedingly obliged and grateful to you."

A long liquid snort was Lowther's only comment on this as he finally found his way round by the door and stalked away from the stableyard.

In the end because the western sky was looking ominous with rain, they only went out to Eden meadows to fly the hawks at the lure and they brought the young dogs to run alongside the cow-shattered fence which was still being mended. The herd of kine was penned in the upper half of the racecourse because there were a couple of hundred of them and no wonder Archie Fire the Braes Graham had been upset. The real owners would have to come in and identify their animals and pay the Warden's fee for the finding of them and were slowly doing so as word spread.

Carey flew the little merlin at the lure and laughed to see how fiercely she flew and how much she looked like his sister. She even had the same way of cocking her head impertinently. He would write to her about the birds with the next dispatch bag.

He also took the time to tell Scrope what he thought had been going on with the ambush under the Eden Bridge. His theory was that the Grahams had been intending to ambush and kill him before he could receive his warrant so he would still be unofficial, which begged the interesting question of how they knew about the warrant before he did.

Scrope looked shocked and worried. "I'm sure you don't mean that Lowther purloined the warrant and then set the Grahams on to kill you? I'm sure he wouldn't do a thing like that, Robin."

Carey, who had been about to suggest that Lowther was doing exactly that and worse, stopped and stared at his brother-in-law. Surely nobody could be that obtuse, could they? He absentmindedly fed bits of meat to the merlin and nearly got his finger bitten. Jack was staring at a distant figure on a pony with a packpony following. Suddenly the dog gave a joyful bark and galloped off, pulling along the older dog he was coupled with to teach him hunting, busted through a part of the fence that had just been mended and ran across the Eden Bridge. "Anyway," said Scrope, his reedy voice taking on an admonitory note, "you simply have to get along with Sir Richard while I'm away at my estates because both of you will be in charge."

"Surely Lowther can't still be Deputy Warden…?"

"Of course he can, his warrant is during pleasure, as yours is, and Her Majesty has said nothing about him quitting the office."

"Well I am sure the question slipped her mind when she…"

"It's not like the Wardenry itself, where there is only one warden at a time. Theoretically I can have as many Deputy Wardens as I like."

Carey was furious and frustrated and trying to think of something he could say to squash the ridiculous idea, when Jack came galloping back, wagging his tail like a flail and still pulling the older dog along who was looking martyred.

Carey gave the merlin to the falconer, took his hawking glove off and dismounted to uncouple Jack who barked happily, ran off for a couple of yards, came back, barked, looked at the slowly approaching horseman, barked again, galloped away, came back and barked. "Seems very excited about something," commented Scrope.

"Yes, My Lord," said Carey and to get away from the idiot before he said something unwise, jumped back on his horse and sent it uphill to the road where he let the horse go to a full gallop after Jack.

He soon recognised the smallish plain-looking, balding man and while he wasn't quite as delighted as Jack, he was pleased to see him. "Mr Anricks!"

"Sir Robert," said Anricks, taking off his hat and making a shallow bow in the saddle, which Carey acknowledged with a tip of his hat. "I am very pleased to see you, sir."

Carey grinned at the expectant Jack who was looking up at Anricks with an expression of such hopeful pleading on his face. "Jack never forgets any man who feeds him. You are forever his best friend."

Anricks shook his head at the dog. "I'm sorry," he said to the dog, "I have no food left."

Jack continued to look hopeful and Anricks sighed, produced half of a small pasty from his doublet front and threw it to Jack who caught it with a single snap and gulp and went on looking hopeful.

"Come and meet my brother-in-law," said Carey. "I don't think you have yet, have you?"

Anricks shook his head and so Carey accompanied him to where Scrope was flying a tiercel falcon at the lure and introduced him as a scholar and sometime tooth-drawer and by way of being a merchant as well. Anricks made a very competent bow, though it also said to anyone with an eye for such nuances that he had been a royal clerk as well. He added with a cough, "Sir Robert, how is your tooth and jaw?"

"Very well, Mr Anricks, nearly healed up completely."

"I should like to inspect it later, I prefer to do that if the tooth was very bad..."

"Oh don't worry, I..." Anricks gave Carey a hard stare and Carey thought of the warrant the man carried from Sir Robert Cecil. "Of course."

Anricks included both of them in another tidy bow and then kicked his pony and continued into Carlisle, with the packpony sighing and plodding along behind and Jack running up and down a couple of times and looking surprised.

Scrope's huntsman caught the dog and coupled him up with a different and sturdier hound and they went after hidden rags and jumped stiles until the short morning had already turned itself around the low noon and become afternoon. Carey was suddenly beset with tiredness. He yawned for the fourth time and remembered that he hadn't had dinner, breakfast was hours in the past, and he hadn't slept since the night before last.

He made his excuses and went back to the keep, came into the Queen Mary tower whistling again because at last he had his warrant and the fees from the herd of kine and all was right with the world, trotted up the stairs and went into his chambers.

John Tovey was in his study at his desk, coping with the routine correspondence that Carey hated so well whilst Hughie Tyndale had gone down into the town to work with the trained bands. He was a good pikeman, was Hughie, which was no surprise when you considered his size and the breadth of his shoulders. There was something else about Hughie, something oddly off about him, as if he was a lutestring not tuned aright, but Carey hadn't worked out what it was yet. Hughie gave satisfaction as a tailor and was big enough to back Carey when he needed a henchman. Carey was sure he was being paid by somebody to give news reports of his doings, which was no problem at all—he was the son of Lord Hunsdon and used to being spied on by servants. Was there anything more than normal bribery? He wasn't sure.

Carey shucked off his nearly respectable arming doublet at last, took off his shoes, canions, and stockings—the stockings needed darning again—and got into bed with a sigh. "Will you draw the curtains for me," he called out to John, and his secretary came and did that, pulling cautiously for the curtains were at least fifty years old. According to legend that spectacularly silly woman, Mary Queen of Scots, had slept in that very bed, probably under the very blanket, when she came south on the run from her own subjects.

Carey always wondered where her ghost was and then fell asleep at once.

***

Hughie Tyndale was coming back from the muster feeling happy. He had tripped that bastard Hetherington and then blamed it on someone else, he had drunk a lot of beer afterwards. He had called in on Thomas the Merchant Hetherington to give in his usual letter and receive his shilling. The letter went to the mysterious hunchback in the south called Mr Philpotts.

When was he going to kill Carey? It was a good question, complicated by the fact that Carey seemed to have a lot of people queuing up to kill him and didn't care. Of course, if somebody else succeeded in doing it, Hughie could always claim it was him really, but he wondered if Mr Philpotts would know the truth.

There was another complicating factor which he had not seen fit to tell anyone since it was his business. Henry Dodd, the most evil man in the world. That wasn't business like Carey was; Hughie had no feelings one way or the other for Carey. He would get thirty pounds in his hand for killing the Deputy Warden according to the man who said he worked for the Earl of Bothwell. Mr Philpotts' money made him pause, but in the end he would kill his man and get his money. He liked killing and the fact that he could tailor often made people forget that he was not weedy or round-shouldered the way his late uncle had been. And hadn't that been a satisfying life to take, his uncle choking on the garotte and never knowing who it was killed him.

But Dodd? Hughie knew that Dodd was the man he had been put on this earth to kill. That was personal, that was family, that was vengeance sweet and late.

So should he do Dodd before or after Carey? Either of them was hard enough for they were both right fighting men. Together they would probably be impossible unless he could get Wee Colin to attack them.

So it had to be separately. Poison for Carey? Since Oxford, Hughie had more respect for poisoners—it was ticklish to get the right dose into the right man—hadn't the dose intended for Carey gotten into him and nearly killed him? Although white arsenic was always good, odourless, tasteless, slow acting. Yes, he would have to investigate where he could get arsenic from. He thought he could buy it from an apothecary to kill rats. Not in Carlisle though. Too much risk of a busybody finding out. And Carey didn't have any routine food for himself: he generally ate in Bessie's or even in the castle if he was short of money. So maybe not arsenic either.

Hughie shook his head with all the thinking which was giving him a headache. He wanted to kill somebody soon. It was more than a month since he had last seen the pretty sight of the red on the white.

And Dodd? Well, Dodd would be a big swordblade through the head or crossbow bolt in the back or better yet a knife in the guts so he would die slow and screaming to pay him back for what he did, or all of them, or torture. Hughie made pretty patterns of red and white on the defenceless chained white body of Henry Dodd in his imagination with Dodd naked in a dungeon somewhere, or even just one of the Elliot towers in Tynedale, chained, hurt, weeping. Maybe Hughie would chop his fingers off one by one and his toes or better yet use the Boot on him and the pinniwinks and then chop his mashed fingers off...

It made Hughie feel warm and happy but he knew it was unlikely and risky and he would probably have to settle for a knife in the guts, but that would do. That would do perfectly well.

He was sitting in a boozing ken by then, its red lattices quite newly painted and he asked for double ale because he was feeling rich. Not as rich as he would feel after he got the thirty pounds but quite enough to afford double. Like most lords, Carey paid well in theory but barely at all in practice.

He hadn't noticed the little man when he came in, but he noticed when the man came up to his table, bold as brass and asked if he was Sir Robert Carey's valet? "Ay, I am," he answered breezily. "Would ye like to buy me a drink, Ah'm fearful thirsty." It was a bit cheeky, but nobody asked something like that right out if they weren't after something.

The balding man smiled and went sliding his way to the bar and back again with a quart jack for Hughie and a pint for himself, being so short and weedy.

"Cheers tae ye!" said Hughie and then grinned. "Whit can Sir Robert Carey's man do for ye?"

"Nothing hard," said the man who had a fearful southern accent, "I just want you to stay here for an hour or so."

"Stay in this boozing ken for an hour," said Hughie. "Nay, I cannae do that, I'm due to go and help him with his..."

Sixpence appeared in the man's scarred palm and twinkled there.

Hughie beamed at it. "Now ye wouldna be after thinking of killing the man, eh? For if ye do, I'd need tae hunt ye down and kill ye yerself for spoiling everything, see ye? And that'd be annoying for baith of us."

"It would," agreed the man. "How would it be if I swear not to kill the man nor rob him."

Hughie looked at the man with his weak squinting eyes and round clerk's shoulders and laughed. Some chance there. "Ay, that's fine," he pronounced indulgently, picking up the sixpence. "Now awa' wi' ye, ye're interfering wi' my drinking."

And just like that the man was gone and Hughie supped his second quart and leaned back and looked about. With sixpence extra on top of the shilling he felt rich enough to go to Mme Hetherington's and wap one of her whores. That was a luxury he hadn't been able to afford since he had done the job for Hepburn in the spring, certainly not while he was chasing Carey in London and while in Oxford he hadn't felt well enough anyway. He sighed happily. Life was good.

CARLISLE, DECEMBER 1592

Carey slept for two hours and then came to feeling much better and also uneasily aware that there was an unknown man in the room. He slipped his hand stealthily under the pillow, waited a couple of seconds, grunted, turned over on his belly and then erupted out of the bed with the knife in his hand and his teeth bared.

Simon Anricks blinked at him with interest from where he was sitting on one of the three clothes chests cluttering up the room.

"Yes," he said, "the situation with the Grahams is worrying, isn't it?"

Carey's heart was galloping and he went to pour some wine for himself and his guest.

"How may I help you, Mr Anricks?"

Anricks was staring at the wall with the expression of someone who was thinking of how to explain something to a half-witted nobleman. Carey had seen Anricks' warrant but still didn't like it that the man had come into his bedchamber while he was sleeping. Where the devil were Tovey and Tyndale? He wondered where the key to the bedchamber was, since he should probably start locking it.

"Of course, if I had had a pistol or a crossbow—a crossbow for preference—then I could have just shot you where you lay and you none the wiser until Judgement Day," said Anricks coldly, "which would ill repay your parents' care of you, nor Mr Secretary Cecil's concern, nor indeed the Queen's manifest affection for her cousin and nephew."

Carey stared at him. "There is," continued Anricks quietly, "a certain dash and fire about you that makes you so careless of your safety—and indeed a very gentlemanlike courage—yet, I put it to you, Sir Robert, that sooner or later the dice will come down snake eyes and you will die."

For a moment Carey was too astonished at being told off by a mere tooth-drawer to do more than stare open-mouthed at the man. Then he got angry.

"Well sir, I do not know why it concerns you nor why you believe you can rate me for going to sleep…"

Anricks stood up. His voice became metallic. "I do not rate you for going to sleep, sir, I rate you for going to sleep in an unlocked room."

"My servants should be…"

"They should but they are not. It took me two minutes and sixpence to persuade your valet to delay coming to your chamber for an hour—although he did at least have me swear I would not kill nor rob you since he had never seen me before in his life—and Tovey went down ten minutes ago to get bread and cheese and beer at the buttery, since he can no longer see to write, which anyone could guess. I watched you snore for those ten minutes and no one has come in nor asked why I am here. It will not do, Sir Robert."

Anricks crossed his arms and stared at Carey. He had cold pale brown eyes which seemed to amount to more than he was, because in appearance he was unimpressive in his worn brown wool suit, the fashion ten years past, and a stuff gown with velvet trim and his bald head shining under his ancient cap.

"In fact I came to discuss the Queen's letter and proposal with you, but I am now wondering if you have even read it yet?"

Carey scowled and took out the packet. "If you mean this, I most certainly have read it and am very happy that she thinks so well of me as to send me my warrant..."

"Then you have not in fact read the secret section." Anricks looked as if not rolling his eyes was costing him considerable effort.

Carey blinked at the packet, pulled out the Queen's letter and sniffed it. His eyebrows went up and he sniffed again, went to the watch candle, lit two further candles in the stand on his table and held the letter carefully close to the flames until the paper warmed up and the brown letters showed on the blank back of the letter.

Anricks twitched slightly at the shout of laughter that came from Carey.

"Good Lord, Mr Anricks," he said affably, "you must think me a fearful dullard as well as foolhardy. Now does this stay or will it fade?"

"It will fade."

"Then excuse me while I note down Her Majesty's words to me." He dipped a pen and scribbled on the back of a bill for horsefeed. Anricks managed not to sigh at this further carelessness and sat back down on the clothes chest. He ached all over from the ride to Carlisle.

"Well," said Carey as he finished and the lemon juice words faded. "Her blessed Majesty is full of surprises."

"Yes," said Anricks, "May I read it?"

Carey hesitated only a second before handing over the horsefeed bill and starting to pull on his stockings and canions again.

Anricks scanned Carey's scrawl, then handed it back. "It is important you find an excuse to go to Scotland and talk to the

King about the lords Huntly, Errol, and Angus who, it appears, are plotting treason."

"Again?" shrugged Carey. "They're always doing it. They're Catholics. Luckily they are also rotten at it."

"The Queen and Mr Secretary Cecil are concerned that this time it's serious. There have been various oddities going on in Spain this year, activity in the Irish sea. They have been concerned for some time, in fact, which is why I am here."

"You in particular?"

"Unfortunately, yes. The Queen has an exaggerated idea of my abilities due to some adventures I had in 1588…"

"1588? During the Armada? Anriques?"

"Er…yes sir…"

"Mr Anricks, I believe I may once have met your…your extraordinarily courageous and beautiful lady wife, Mrs Anriques. It was while I was serving under my Lord Howard of Effingham and Sir Francis Drake. In fact I may even have been a small part of bringing her to an interview with My Lord Howard in which she explained the Armada's true purpose and which inspired Sir Francis Drake to the stratagem of the fireships."

Anricks came to his feet. "You! You were the Court sprig who got her to the Admiral?"

Carey bowed. "I was, sir, and I heard more about it later from Sir Francis Walsingham."

"If you had not got my wife to the Admiral, sir, I believe we would now be fighting the Spaniards in England, or dead."

"Dead certainly, or I would be. Well…I believe this calls for something better to drink than the usual Carlisle rotgut." With a courtierly flourish he unlocked a small cupboard and brought out an unassuming bottle and two small Venetian glasses, poured, and gave Anricks one. "Sir, if you will permit, a toast to your brave lady wife and to yourself, sir, since Walsingham told me that without what you did, we would have lost the Battle of the Calais Roads."

Anricks flushed, tapped glasses and drank, paused, looked quizzically at the booze and then drank some more. "Did he tell you any of the details?"

"Not many. I would delight in hearing the tale from your own lips, if it please you to speak about it. Sir Francis was eloquent in his praise of you and your family and he was not a man who praised easily or at all. I think I myself earned two or three grudging words in several years' service to him."

"Sir Robert, is this…is this drink made of bacon?"

Carey chuckled. "No, it comes from the Highlands of Scotland and they call it in their barbaric tongue 'whishke bee,' which means exactly the same as aqua vitae. It is smoked in some way, but it's made from barley and distilled like a brandy."

"It's good," said Anricks, smelling the liquor and sipping again. "Very good." He shut his eyes and rolled it round his mouth and seemed to put his whole being into tasting the stuff, as if it was holy.

Carey watched with interest and when Anricks had swallowed, he opened his eyes and smiled a little. "On the occasion we were speaking about, for various reasons, I was captured by the Spanish and sentenced to the galleys, in fact to a galleas in the Armada itself. Up until then, I often didn't pay attention to my food, but just before my arrest, I had eaten some particularly fine membrillo paste—quince cheese you call it here—with goat's cheese which was so good I *had* noticed. The remembered taste of the cheese and the membrillo somehow sustained me while I was a slave. So when I was free again, I swore that I would always notice the food I ate for not to notice is in fact ingratitude and insult to the Almighty, maker of the Universe, who gives us all that we eat and drink."

Carey bowed a little. "Amen, sir," he said.

They drank more whisky.

"So," said Carey, "Walsingham said that you had retired to be a merchant in Bristol. If they have winkled you out of retirement, what's the reason?"

"What do you think?"

"Yet another Armada?"

"Precisely."

"Aimed at Scotland?"

"Perhaps."

"There was a rumour of one last summer but it was scattered by storms."

"As I remarked earlier, sooner or later the dice will come down against us and I am concerned lest 1593 be the year when that happens."

"Surely even the King of Spain can't afford another Armada so soon after…"

"That Armada wasn't destroyed. They lost some ships, sure, and others were damaged but more put into La Corunna—the Groyne—and are being refitted as we speak."

"So why Scotland?"

"Well, Sir Robert, the west coast of Scotland is wild and empty and the people there are Catholics insofar as they are anything. In fact the same is true all the way down through Cheshire and the marches of Wales, Gloucester, even Bristol… Well, Bristol is Protestant like most ports, but still there are a lot of Catholics. The Jesuits have been running missions into the West Country for ten years and it's starting to show."

"My mother says most of Cornwall is still heathen with a lacquering of Rome. I was born in the Marches of Wales and I don't recall much religion there at all. Most of them only went to church at Christmas and Easter, if they went at all."

"And sir, how many of your neighbours were enthusiastic Protestants? Any? Most of the nobility in the area is Catholic from sheer inertia, with the exception of My Lord Earl of Essex and he is a courtier."

"Would they truly fight for the King of Spain against the Queen?"

"Perhaps not. Perhaps they would revert to the noble English instinct to hate the foreigner. But who knows? Put an army of thirty-thousand in the field, led by the *terceiros*, the best troops in Christendom, offer the young men the choice of being killed or marching with them…"

Carey nodded slowly.

"Nobody understands how close a call it was in 1588," said Anricks. "We were so lucky. If Medina Sidonia had been less seasick, if Drake had hesitated to use the fireships when he did, if…Well. I think it true that the Almighty, for reasons best known to Himself, thwarted the Spanish for I can scarcely think of any other reason for our luck. But how long will He favour the English? The Scots of the West Coast and the Highlands are fine soldiers, if undisciplined, and the kerns and gallowglasses are from Ireland of course and they can run for days barefoot through the forests and bogs…"

"Carlisle?"

"I could take Carlisle in three days."

"Treachery?"

"Of course." Anricks gulped the rest of his Scottish drink. "Then you have the castle cannon to knock at the doors of Chester, Gloucester, Bristol, and then you take Oxford and the Thames valley lies before you. London would fall a week later."

"It couldn't be that simple," protested Carey. "How do you feed your men?"

"Personally I would put a force into Bristol early on a surprise and send supplies up the Avon."

"Thank God you aren't King Philip's admiral."

"He has cleverer men than me to do his bidding, believe me. But thank the Almighty by all means, Sir Robert. In England we think ourselves very fine soldiers but we are woefully untrained, underequipped, and inexperienced. Our sailors are the best in the world but our soldiers…" Anricks shook his head.

Carey, who had seen some shocking things while fighting in France with Henry of Navarre, made no answer to this.

"In a way of course," muttered Anricks, "the Spanish have been battering at the locked front door of the Cinque Ports when all the while the yard gate has been banging in the wind and the kitchen door kept by a little girl."

"But King James would never allow…"

Anricks had taken his old fashioned velvet cap off and was kneading it between his hands. His bald head had a little island tuft of hair in the middle.

"If he was offered a lot of money, gold, to look the other way whilst Caerlaverock and Lochmaben and Dumfries filled up with Spanish soldiers?"

Carey scowled as he considered the point. "Well, His Highness of Scotland is of course as easy to buy as any man, possibly easier, but...no. I think not. His Highness has spent most of his life dreaming of how easy that life will be when he succeeds, as he surely will if he is spared, to the throne of England. Would he take the risk of allowing thousands of foreign soldiers to build up in the west, waiting to march south? No."

"What if he didn't know?"

"Don't be ridiculous. It's fifty miles east to west and the comings and goings from so many men, the supplies, the food... no. Maybe you could keep the secret for a week or two but sooner or later His Highness would know."

Anricks nodded unhappily. "Or they go east first, take Holy-rood House and kill the King, then go south down through the rich plunder of the Merse. Once they have a good handgrip on any part of this island, they can go anywhere they want."

Carey said nothing, his strategic imagination working. That was the key, of course. Once the...the virginity of the blessed land of England was breached, troops such as the *terceiros* would be unbeatable at first, simply because none of the trained bands from the cities and the counties would have the faintest idea of what to do. By the time they had learned it would probably be too late. It was true what Anricks said, unpleasant but true. The Borderers would be better at the fighting as light mounted troops, but even they were used to the dance of reivers, not a disciplined killing machine like the Spanish King's 3rd legion.

As it had in 1588, the thought made Carey feel cold and hot at the same time, hot with rage, cold with fear. The fear was colder now because he had served in France and seen war at close quarters.

"Mr Anricks," he said, "I agree with every word you say, sir. But what do you want me to do? I know the Maxwell unfortunately. Huntly, Erroll, and Angus I have only met briefly, years ago, at Court. I would love to give the Maxwell a set down, I admit."

"Mr Secretary Cecil feels that to begin with, if we know which way King James is likely to jump, we will be in very much better case. If he is for the King of Spain, we will need one kind of action."

"What?"

"A Warden Raid from the English West March into Dumfriesshire early next year to find out if any Spanish troops are there or preparations being made for them."

Carey nodded. "And if His Highness is against the King of Spain?"

"Well then, King James can run his own Justice Raid into the area, find the troops if they are there and deal with them himself."

"He will need help," said Carey. "He's a very peaceable prince is His Highness."

"I don't suppose anyone has the least idea what the King thinks?" Carey laughed and Anricks smiled. "No, he is verbose and liable to go into print at any moment, but somehow it all adds up to rather less than nothing."

"What about the Earl of Bothwell?"

"Has anybody seen him recently? I know he is at the horn but where is he?"

"Last heard of," Carey said, "he was playing football in Liddesdale. He is now rumoured to have gone to the Highlands."

"I'm not surprised, this Scottish drink is very fine. I would go to its source if I were him."

Carey poured again from the bottle and toasted Anricks.

"There's one good thing about the bloody man," said Carey.

"What's that?"

"He's a Protestant. He says he was not engaging in witchcraft a couple of years ago which may or may not be true, but at least he is not a bloody Catholic."

For some reason Anricks smiled at that while Carey paced up and down the room.

"Well, but, Mr Anricks, this is all speculation, isn't it? Are you sure it isn't all some phantasy that we are frightening ourselves into fits with?"

Anricks sighed. "No, I am not sure," he said. "It could indeed be all moonbeams and mist. Mr Secretary is doing his best to find out from Spain, there are little straws in the wind...A very interesting recent letter from your lady mother, for instance, saying that the Spanish had kidnapped three Irish pilots whom she freed in her ship..."

"Oh, God," said Carey hollowly, "what's she up to now?"

"She says she visited Mrs O'Malley to lay in some Irish aqua vitae and heard that four more had gone to Spain voluntarily for a lot of gold and the promise of land."

"Where?"

Anricks shook his head and spread his hands. "Nobody knows. New Spain perhaps? There is so little to go on. Conclusive proof that this is all a phantasy and the Spaniards are not planning to put troops ashore at Dumfries would be most welcome to me for then I could go home to my wife and children and enjoy the blessed tedium of life as a middling merchant in Bristol. But."

"Yes," said Carey, "but..."

He came over and sat on one of the other clothes chests, facing Anricks. He still had the Scotch drink in his hand, so he split the remnants between them.

"Well, Mr Anricks, I put myself at your disposal as the Queen asks. What would you like me to do?"

Anricks inspected the floor which had some very elderly rushes on it since Goody Biltock had gone south with Philadelphia Scrope and there was nobody to terrorise the castle servants.

"I want you to come with me to Scotland, to Edinburgh and the King's Court."

Carey's eyebrows danced upwards. "Good Lord, has His Highness invited you?"

"He has indeed." Anricks felt in his doublet pocket and produced a very official letter asking him to come to philosophise for the King at Court as soon as he could.

"Latin not Scots, eh? Very philosophical."

Anricks gave a small smile. "It appears that Lady Widdrington told him of something I had mentioned to her and now he is all afire to have a proper dispute about it."

"Oh? What about? Nothing theological, I hope."

"Why?"

"Because His Highness considers himself a first class theological brain and I don't think I could stay awake long enough to cheer his victory at the end."

"He is that good a theologian, is he?"

Carey smiled. "He is the King."

Anricks smiled back. "I don't think it is a theological matter, precisely. It is the question of the heavenly bodies like the Moon, the Sun, and the stars, and so forth. Do they move and if so, how?"

Carey squinted as he dredged his memory. "Something to do with crystal spheres? And they move around the Earth like a complicated onion. I'm afraid I was usually absent playing football when I should have been studying the globes."

"Quite so. My opinion of it comes from Thomas Digges, his preface, where he refers to the theoretical suggestion of a Polish priest called Copernicus, oh, about fifty years ago."

"Oh yes?" said Carey politely.

Anricks leaned forward with the enthusiasm he could never hide for the beautiful simplicity and rightness of the new thinking, which blew away all the ugly epicycles and epi-epicycles of Ptolemy and Aristotle's system.

"You see if we place the planets around the Earth in the traditional er...complicated onion arrangements, some of their movements are crazy and make no sense. Why, for example, do Venus and Mercury reverse themselves every so often, what is called by astrologers, movement retrograde."

"They are dancing? There is a very complicated Court dance which claims to follow the movements of the planets..."

"Er...no." Anricks couldn't understand why nobody seemed to care about the sheer untidiness and ugliness of the old system. "Well," he said, "perhaps I am a little crazy myself for setting such store by it. Briefly, Copernicus, his idea is that all the heavenly bodies move around the Sun—with one exception—which produces a scheme of exquisite order and righteousness." The glass cups became planets along with a penknife and a couple of stones, the bottle the Sun. "Here is the Sun, at the centre of everything, very befitting. First around him goes Mercury, which removes his retrograde quite, then Venus which removes hers. Then comes the Earth and around her flies the Moon. Then Mars, then Jupiter and Saturn and then we are at the fixed stars."

Carey was staring fixedly at the cups, frowning. "The retrogrades?"

"Well sir, see, if this glass is the Earth and this Venus and all spins around the Sun thus, for some of the year Venus moves to the other side of the great circle and from our perspective, she is moving backwards. But all is as it was, it is just a trick of perspective."

Carey was still staring.

"Do you see, sir? Do you see how the Earth moving and the Sun being fixed answers?" Anricks' voice was timid. It was normally at this stage that people started to laugh at him.

Carey blinked owlishly. "Yes!" he said. "Yes, I do."

Anricks was astonished. "You do?"

"Yes. But Mr Anricks, what holds them up? The crystal spheres?"

"Certainly. We can keep our onion, it just has the Sun in the middle and the Earth moving…"

"Clean contrary to how it looks."

"Of course. I sometimes wonder if the Almighty is having a little fun with us."

"What about in the Bible where it says that Earth is flat like a shield and the sky a tent?"

"That cannot be true for didn't Magellan sail all the way round and now Sir Francis Drake himself? Again it is a trick of perspective."

"God is fooling us?"

"I prefer rather to think," said Anricks quietly, "that the Almighty is gently testing us, giving us riddles to solve to entertain us."

Carey laughed a delighted boy's laugh that said he had gone looking for a beetle and found a frog. "Doesn't it make you queasy to think that the Sun is still whilst the Earth moves?"

"No, I rejoice in it…"

Suddenly Carey clapped his hand to his head. "Good God," he said, "you're the madman."

"I beg your pardon?"

"A long time ago, nearly ten years now, I had a swordmaster who complained of a friend of his who had a crazy notion about the Earth going round the Sun and how it made him feel seasick."

"Was he a big heavy man with black ringlets, who yet could move lightly and featly?"

"Yes, and he made me lose my temper and knocked me on my arse for a demonstration of how temper could undo me. How is he? Is his name Mr Tucket?"

"No sir," said Anricks quietly, "his name was David Becket and a truer friend did never live, I think. Alas, he died fighting in 1588."

"I am sorry to hear it." They had a couple of drops left of the Scottish drink.

Anricks raised his Venetian cup. "Then I give you, David Becket."

"David Becket!" answered Carey, tipping his glass to get the last drop. "But it's clear then, you are the madman."

"I am. And here I am planning to go to Edinburgh to dispute with a King about whether the Earth goes round the Sun. Quite quite insane."

"Maybe not," said Carey judiciously. "I think the King of Scotland will love the idea if you put it to him right. We'll be there over Christmas."

"I hope not."

"We will. How many followers are you planning to take to Court?"

"I don't know…Maybe one for me and one for you?"

"Quite quite woodwild, Mr Anricks. I will need both my servants and at least four men-at-arms if we are not to look very paltry. And also we will be crossing the Middle March at the height of the raiding season. Unless you prefer to take the Giant's Road east and then go up the Great Northern Road through Berwick to Edinburgh."

"Although I have begun to build quite a practice at tooth-drawing in the West March, I would prefer not to dare the Middle March again at this season," said Anricks primly.

"So would I. So the Giant's Road and the Great North Road it is then."

"When should we leave?"

"It depends. Do you have any better clothes?"

"Better clothes?"

"Yes, Mr Anricks. The Scots King may be a barbarian who has never to my knowledge washed his body, nor shifted his shirt more than once a month and barely wipes his face and hands, but you are an English philosopher and must at least appear civilized."

"Well…I…have some brocade doublets and hose and a velvet gown or two that my wife had made for me, but they are in Bristol and with the best will in the world, I doubt they could be here in less than a week."

"Hm. We must see what the Carlisle tailor can do for you—we may catch him before he shuts up shop if we go now."

And Carey swept Anricks off down the stairs, pausing only to lock his chamber door with newly rediscovered con-scientiousness.

CARLISLE, DECEMBER 1592

It turned out that Anricks had plenty of money and could afford a brocade far too rich for a philosopher, especially one who was also a part-time tooth-drawer. He had no idea of fashion at all, so Carey chose a nice fine wool in a dark cramoisie since black and green accentuated his yellow complexion and made him look liverish. He put his foot down firmly on Anricks' diffident hopes for tawny taffeta trimming and lining and settled on a narrow black brocade trim that only the expert eye would be able to discern as coming straight from the Low Countries. It was quite a surprise to find it in the Carlisle mercer's shop.

At the tailor's, he ordered a shell made and the suit cut out by the master tailor himself, found a perfectly respectable shirt with blackwork on the cuffs in the depths of Anrick's pack and had it and a couple more wrinkled grey horrors laundered. Hughie agreed to do some of the sewing of the doublet and the journeymen did the rest.

In return Carey agreed to read Thomas Digges' preface at least, which Anricks lent to him. He came back to Anricks with some questions. Anricks had been to visit the son of his patient Jock Tait, who had nearly survived a knife in the guts, but had finally died, a week after the stabbing, of fever and pus in his intestines, to the extent that they swelled up until Tait looked pregnant. Strangely the external wounds had already healed. It had been a painful death and Anricks had been glad when the man had mercifully died. He had not had the chance to talk to Jimmy Tait since then and found him a little sad and thoughtful but also delighted with the metrical psalms he was learning and beginning to play the lute. Anricks got the impression that Jock Tait had not been an ideal father and would not be greatly missed, although the boy was anxious about his mother and determined to bring her and his sister and brother to Carlisle. But Anricks needed cheering up and so Carey did his best.

"Did you know that cannon don't shoot straight?" Carey asked.

"They don't?"

"No. Everyone thinks they do, but they don't, nor bullets. When you are laying a cannon to fire at a distance, you must always allow for some curve. Just like with an arrow, but much less. Why is that?"

Anricks stared at him. "I don't know."

"But why don't cannonballs go in a straight line until they run out of wind from the gunpowder and then drop?"

"I have no idea. What has that to do with the Earth going round the Sun?"

Carey smiled a little boy's rueful smile. "Nothing. I was just wondering about it, all those circles. How about looking at the planets through spectacles? Could we see what they are made of?"

"Certes, there are people who are studying to grind the glasses fine enough though at the moment there is a problem with rainbows and clarity."

"What about the Sun? Is it a planet?"

"No, it seems it really is a huge great fiery ball in the sky."

"What is it made of?"

"I don't know. Sulphur perhaps since it is yellow."

Carey nodded. "This is all part of your speech."

"Why does it matter?"

"Because you have to make the truth sound good to the King, otherwise he will turn it into a joke and get drunk. Or drunker."

"And is the naked truth not good enough?"

"No, Mr Anricks, it isn't. This is a public dispute, a species of theatre, and he may have some good scholars ranged against you to make you look foolish."

"Is that so bad? Then he can defeat me and feel reassured at how clever he is."

Carey laughed. "Yes, a good point. But you must give him a good show. If you do, he might make you his pet philosopher and keep you at his Court and that will give you the chance to find out what is going on with the Catholic earls."

Anricks smiled. "I see."

"Yes. You are the dancing bear and I am the bearmaster and whenever this dispute happens, whether at Christmas or New Year, you will give such a dance that King James will want more of it."

"I do not want to be at Court for Christmas."

"Who asked you, Mr Anricks? Nor do I, but I suspect we must."

"You don't want to spend Christmas at…"

"The key word is 'spend'. Christmas at the Queen's Court means at least one new suit and possibly some outrageous costume for a masque although she is not as addicted to them as His Highness. Plus I will certainly have to get His Highness a gift for New Year's Day which will cost a fortune and completely wreck my finances..."

Anricks leaned over and touched him. "As my bearmaster, I believe I can finance you to a limited extent..."

Joy struck Carey's face. "You mean I could have a new Court suit?"

"Well..."

"My old one is with my father in London and really it's growing a little out of fashion now it's more than a year old—I haven't completely paid for it yet—but perhaps I could have something in the Scottish style with the padding King James likes..."

"Well..."

"Now the question is whether damask, brocade, satin..."

Anricks had the feeling he had somehow carelessly unleashed a monster, but thought Carey deserved something for the way he had instantly backed him—and, although he didn't admit this to himself, for being one of the very few people who didn't laugh at the new Cosmology. Considering the dangers and the difficulty of the Scottish Court, it was praiseworthy how quickly he had agreed...Was that suspicious? Sir Robert Cecil had been concerned that Carey might have done some kind of deal with King James on his own account. That could be one interpretation of the mysterious doings at the King's Court while James had been on his abortive Justice Raid to Dumfries in the summer, although there were plenty of others.

Carey himself was happily burbling on about the different kinds of brocade that might be available and Anricks watched him, sitting at his ease in Bessy's common room, with the remains of his pie on the pewter plate beside him. Chestnut-headed of the dark red not the carrotty kind like Her fiery Majesty, Anricks thought the portrait of him he had had painted for his knighthood had done him no favours. It showed the tense cautious courtier with the fashionable shaved forehead in honour of the Queen, not the expansive, very slightly drunk Deputy Warden in front of him.

Sir Robert Cecil had spoken about Carey when he came personally to Bristol to ask...perhaps better the word "beseech"… Simon to come out of retirement and find out what was happening in Scotland, if anything. He had spoken of Carey with surprising respect, that he was no more a Knight of the Carpet than his father, that he was a remarkably able soldier and also had the ability that Walsingham had, of being able to winkle the truth out of complicated and opaque circumstances.

Cecil's hunched back always pained him when he rode long distances, something he had never allowed to stop him. A jolting carriage was no better. He had sat uncomfortably on a pile of cushions in Simon's parlour, eating the wonderful crisp wafers that Rebecca could prepare and drinking the rich dark sweet red wine of Oporto. Cecil tilted his head so it was straight, even if his body wasn't. Every so often he would stand and pace about, full of nervous energy.

"I have read all the secret reports on you, Mr Anricks, and I think there is not a man in England as well fitted to the work as you."

"But I do not want to come out of retirement. I like being bored."

Cecil closed his eyes a moment and smiled his remarkably sweet smile, then moved again, easing his back.

"I suppose money…"

Simon spread his hands, palms down. "I have plenty of money, far more than I need and if I were ever in want, my respected father, Mr Dunstan Ames, Deputy Comptroller of Her Majesty's Poultry, would help me and if he failed, why then my uncle Dr Hector Nuñez would step into the breach."

"Is that the Dr Hector Nuñez who is importing boatloads of tobacco from New Spain to London?"

"Yes."

"And you would not be interested in a knighthood which you certainly deserve for your actions during the Armada…"

"No. I am a Jew."

Cecil smiled again. "I know no legal nor chivalric reason why you may not be knighted, but admit that a Herald might correct me on that point. But there is always a first time for anything."

"No, it would be ridiculous."

"If money and honour don't move you, what might?" Cecil asked almost playfully. "Safety? The safety of your people? It moved you before?"

Simon narrowed his eyes and looked at Cecil in silence for a long moment. Cecil at last moved uneasily.

"Sir," said Cecil, "I could tell you that your people's continued quietness rests on your continued service to Her Majesty, but you would know it for a black lie. Her Majesty has told me that you are all of you forever her own Jews, and yours and your wife's service to her at the time of the Armada was of such an order that she will not again blackmail you."

Anricks tilted his head in acknowledgement. "That is good to know," he said, his pale brown eyes still cold.

Cecil sighed. "However, the Queen will not, no matter how we pray that she may, live forever and after her comes, we hope, King James, VIth of Scotland, Ist of England. God willing and if his luck holds."

"Yes," said Anricks. "Or the King of Spain, of course, which I would prefer not to see."

"Amen," said Cecil. "There is at least no Inquisition in Scotland."

"Are there Jews?"

"I don't know. Nor does anyone know what the King thinks of Jews."

"Hm." Anricks was thoughtful. "Well Mr Secretary, you appear to have found the key that will unlock my retirement."

"It does you honour that you will do for your tribe what you will not do for money or honour."

Anricks made no answer to this. He seemed depressed and poured a large glass of Oporto wine and drank half of it.

"Ah...would you care to see some of the documents I have had copied or would you..."

"Tomorrow," said Anricks firmly, "Today I am going to get drunk on this excellent booze and mourn my shattered peace."

"Would you prefer me to leave, sir?"

"No, Sir Robert, my wife has had the guestroom cleaned, swept, piled high with pillows and new candles arrayed everywhere. She is at this minute in camera with the cook, devising a dinner of spectacular opulence in your honour. She would kill me if you went to an inn."

"That sounds delightful...Er...the dinner, I mean..."

"And besides, I don't hold it against you, for I am sure you are at the orders of that red-haired..."

"Termagent? Amazon?"

"Careful, Sir Robert, we are skirting treason here."

"Witch, perhaps. I would give a great deal to know how she is always one step ahead of me in intelligence-gathering?"

"She has her own intelligence service, mostly of women, commanded by her *muliercula*, Mrs Thomasina de Paris."

"Good God!"

"I thought you knew."

Cecil laughed. "No, I was blind."

Anricks refilled his glass and Cecil's with Oporto wine, lifted it. "Then to the red-head, long may she reign!"

"To the red-head, Mr Anricks! Hear hear!"

Anricks knocked back the wine, then paused. "Oh all right, Mr Secretary, let's see these documents."

It had been worth it although as with most raw intelligence there were a lot of documents and very little pattern. A couple of reports on the activities of a Jesuit called Father William Crichton who seemed the dangerous kind, since there was nothing suspicious about him except that he had been in northern Spain and was now in Scotland. An incoherent tale told by a Herries cousin who had guarded a private supper for the Maxwell, the Earls of Huntly, Erroll, and Angus at which Crichton had said grace and then talked for a long time. Some accounts in Spanish, copied by someone Simon suspected might be one of his brothers, detailing the kind of refitting going on at La Corunna. An account from a mad Irish chieftain that his two best pilots, expert in the Irish sea and its wildly treacherous currents, had disappeared from Ireland and reappeared in Spain where someone had stuck a knife in one and knocked the other on the head so hard that he could remember nothing any more, and thus had returned. Anricks smiled: that was definitely one of his brothers, probably Joshua.

"Not much to go on," said Anricks, putting his spectacles down and refilling the glasses again. He wondered what sort of hangover you got from Oporto wine.

"Straws show which way the wind blows," said Cecil owlishly. "Or they don't."

It had been a very bad hangover and Anricks had resolved never again to get drunk on Portuguese sweet red wines.

In the name of the Almighty, thought Anricks coming back to the bacon-smelling fug of Bessie's common room, Carey is still burbling about his Court suit...Anricks stared in honest amazement and was caught.

Carey laughed and clapped him on the shoulder.

"Ah well, Mr Anricks, we all must have our enthusiasms. Mine for fashion and making good clothes, yours for the new gospel of the heavens according to Capricorn..."

"Copernicus, as explained by Thomas Digges."

"Yes, quite so."

"Have you come to a conclusion about your new Court suit?"

"Indeed I have." There followed a tirade of quite extraordinary detail and dullness, in which it became clear that while the Carlisle tailor was good enough for a mere philosopher, and indeed for Carey's ordinary clothes, he was not at all adequate for Carey's outfit to wear at Court at Christmas and so they would take Carey's best black silk velvet doublet and hose with a few trifling alterations, but that when they arrived in Edinburgh, Carey would have the Edinburgh tailors make a proper Court suit for him in the very highest fashion and all that remained to be settled was the fabric, linings, trim, and buttons, particularly the buttons.

Anricks wondered aloud how much high Edinburgh fashion might cost, heard the sum of eight hundred pounds mentioned which nearly made him faint until he realised Carey was speaking in pounds Scots which were only worth a quarter of an English pound because the Scottish King debased his money, while the English Queen was very particular about her money and its fineness.

Two hundred pounds English was still a substantial sum and Anricks darkly suspected that Carey might be very good at telling good clothes, but might not be very good at knowing what they cost on account of not wanting to know.

However the clothes certainly had given Carey enthusiasm for going to Scotland and he had the excuse that it was politic for the new official English Deputy Warden of the West March to introduce himself as such to the Scottish King and councillors and ask for a Warden's Day after sixteen years without one.

At any rate that was what he said to Lord Scrope when the ninny got querulous about not being able to go to his estates just yet.

"What am I supposed to do while you're away? The Grahams are riding and the Armstrongs and Elliots and the Maxwells are hitting the Johnstones…They all seem to have gone mad."

"Yes, My Lord," said Carey, "It is because of the harvest."

"What? Why would the harvest make the surnames raid?"

Was it possible he didn't know, Carey wondered. "The harvest was very bad and so they haven't much barley or oats and so they're raiding to get the animals to sell so they can buy some. The trouble is, prices everywhere in the north are high because nobody in Scotland has much barley either."

"Oh. Well why don't they ship some in?"

Have you looked at a map recently or ever, Carey wanted to ask. It's hard to get ships here from anywhere. Ireland is in as bad case or worse than Scotland. That means you have to bring it in from the Hansa or even further south. Anricks had said something about writing to his family about the dearth, but the seas were closed for winter and it would take a week for a ship to travel all the way up the Irish Sea from Bristol, even if the weather stayed calm, which it wouldn't.

"Yes My Lord," he said because he couldn't be bothered to explain it to his idiot brother-in-law. He added an outright lie. "I hope I'll be back before Christmas."

Sergeant Dodd was comfy in his old jack, with the padding worked in the Dodd pattern, though he had been thinking that maybe now Janet had a new hat, he could buy a new helmet, maybe even a morion, with some of the money from London. He would talk to his wife about it when he got back...

Then he remembered their quarrel and his long face soured. It hadn't been so very much, all things considered, it was just...

She had asked him why he was so silent and miserable, and he had finally told her, venting his fury at Carey for letting Wee Colin Elliot and all the bastard Elliots get away. He could not understand why the man had done it, could not, when he had them so nicely in a trap. He had tried to put it down to madness, plain and simple, since the Courtier did many things that were crazy, but in fact Carey had not been acting as crazy as usual and had in fact run the whole encounter beautifully, right up to the moment when he had casually swept the world from under Dodd's feet, and let them go.

Dodd still felt sick every time he thought about it. And then, what had his wife said about it, when he told her why he was upset? She had said that sure, it was annoying, but wasn't it grand that Wee Colin Elliot had taken such a blow to his credit with no one having to die, especially Dodd. And he had stared at her and stared at her, thinking, where's the woman who kicked Bangtail in the balls last summer for betraying them to the Grahams?

"Whit does it matter about dying," he had managed to say, despite the shock, "so long as the Elliots do too?"

"Matter?" Janet had said. "Weren't ye telling me about how fat the south is where they have nae feuds? It's over ten years since the Dodds and the Elliots were at each other's throats, ye beat 'em fair and square then, let's leave them be so long as they leave us be."

Dodd had sat by the fire with his mouth too full of what the Elliots had done to his dad and his mum and his uncles and his cousins, too full to say a word and she knew the story anyway.

Wasn't she an Armstrong, English branch, but still, they had plenty of feuds. And what you did in a deadly feud was you wiped out the other side, if you could, first chance you got.

She had kissed him lightly on the head, not noticing his stillness and gone out to make sure everything was locked up tight and the girls upstairs, and Ellen still recovering in the stillroom and the men downstairs on the first floor of the tower or out guarding the outfield and the boys in the stables and each animal where it should be.

She came back, went up the narrow spiral stair and still he sat, howling winds flying through him and the black ball of rage filling his chest. His wife agreed with Carey, the arch traitor. Why?

At last he had gone upstairs and lain down next to his wife in their proud half-testered marriage bed, and then when she turned to him and snuggled up, he had turned away silently, turned his shoulder to her again, shutting her out completely.

He hadn't slept much that night and rose in the morning early, feeling even worse than usual. God, he wished there was a potion that could wake you up.

Janet was already up of course, and that was when he had decided to ride out on Whitesock again and continue inspecting the boundaries of Gilsland, making sure no boundary stones had gone wandering and checking were the ditches clear and the fences strong around the coppices to stop the deer eating all the new shoots. He would also take a look at the large sections of the Giant's Wall that ran right through Gilsland, and think whether they were ready to be mined for more stone. He had meant to do it weeks before but had been busy.

Whitesock was a friend at least, a horse with a steady commonsense most unusual in any beast. Dodd had not found anything yet that could make Whitesock shy or bolt and he let the big brown head nuzzle his chest and fed him some carrots. All horses were mad for carrots and they also liked apples.

Out on the bare hills, he felt a little better again with the wind blowing and no actual rain for a change. The land was as dour and ugly in winter as he felt himself to be and even pushing

Whitesock up to a gallop on the top of the wall and jumping the broken parts didn't make him feel happy for more than a minute or two.

He had not taken any men with him, although now he thought of it, Willie's Simon needed distraction because of the dead baby after years of trying to make one. At least Willie's wife wasn't barren like Janet, though. Dodd had his sword and his lance but that was normal, he wouldn't have felt dressed without them.

So he loosened his sword and took his lance in his right hand and had Whitesock jump down to the Road from the Wall when he saw two men riding towards him in the direction of his tower.

They were wearing cloaks which in Dodd's opinion was a waste of time in the wind and there was one in the front with a clever canny face and loose brown curls, while the other man was clearly a bodyguard of some kind, with the battered face and lance to prove it. His jack looked Scottish, East March, perhaps he was a Dixon or a Trotter.

He slowed Whitesock to a walk and then stopped where the Wall would give him some shelter to his back if it came to a fight and Whitesock nickered and stood silent, all four hooves planted, also staring hard at the strangers.

They picked their way down from the higher bit of road by the Wall and also slowed down. Finally they came close enough to be heard.

"We are looking for a man called Sergeant Henry Dodd," the foremost one said loudly, "Land Sergeant of this place." That one was wearing a hat and no helmet, whereas his bodyguard had an iron cap. The hat had a small brim and was tied to his head with a scarf.

"Ay," said Dodd after a moment's thought. "Ye've found him."

The first man untied the scarf, nearly lost his hat immediately, took it off and bowed in the saddle and then tied it back on again.

"My name is Jonathan Hepburn and I work for the Earl of Bothwell. I'm pleased to make your acquaintance, sir."

Dodd leaned slightly, not feeling in the mood for courtliness. "Ay," he said.

"Well," said the man brightly after another moment of silence, "This is lucky. I was expecting to have to go all the way to Gilsland to find you, sir. I would like to talk to you if I may, if we can find a place to get out of the wind and perhaps get a bite to eat and something to drink…"

Dodd sighed; he didn't want to talk to anyone. And why was the man calling him "sir", when it should have been "Sergeant." For a moment Dodd thought of taking both of them back to Gilsland tower but then thought better of it. "Well," he said reluctantly, "there's a Widow Ridley keeps a little alehouse not far from here. We could go there."

Half an hour later they were at a cottage in a little knot of cottages a little way into the Middle March, only different from the others because it had the statutory red lattices, last painted ten years before and almost invisible in the grey dusk. An old woman with white hair like a dandelion clock exploding out from under her cap was sitting just inside the door, out of the wind, knitting a stocking at a startling rate. She came out as they dismounted.

Dodd she knew, of course, and she bobbed a curtsey to him which always made him feel uneasy, so he tilted his neck in return.

"Widow Ridley," he began but the stranger interrupted him.

"We were hoping for something to drink, Goodwife Ridley," said Hepburn with a charming smile. "And would ye have aught to eat for we've not eaten since this morning."

Widow Ridley's eyes travelled up and down both of the strangers and then she bobbed a tiny curtsey and led them into the small front room where the Thirlwall drunk was asleep in a corner, and sat them down on the other side of the fire from him. The curfew was taken off, the peat turves brightened up though they put out more heat than light, and Widow Ridley went to tap three quarts from a barrel into leather jacks.

"Is this double beer?" grunted the bodyguard.

"It's ale and it's good," said Widow Ridley snippily. "Ye can have water out the well if ye want."

"Not beer? Ale upsets ma stomach."

Widow Ridley looked outraged. "This wilnae do ye anything but good, ye great lummock, d'ye want it or no'?"

"You want it, Dixon," said Hepburn, looking amused. "Do you have any stew or pottage, goodwife?"

"Hmf. It's no'got saffron in it, wilna be good enough for the likes of him."

"Please mistress, I'm very hungry," said Hepburn.

She went into the little kitchen and brought back three bowls of what was probably her own supper, a thick bean pottage. Dodd accepted his which had a lot of bacon in it, Hepburn said thank you and Dixon got the bowl without any bacon and what looked like a big gob of spit on it. He started eating it anyway. She disappeared again and they heard her clogs in the mud. A moment later she was back with two hunks of bread and a burned bit of crust, all probably borrowed from a neighbour, and of course Dixon got the crust.

"Will there be anything else, sirs?" said Widow Ridley haughtily.

"No thank you, mistress," said Hepburn obsequiously and was rewarded by a complex sniff. She went and sat down in the kitchen again and they could hear the furious clicking of her needles.

"Well," said Hepburn with a smile, "I expect you would like to know what this is all about, Sergeant Dodd."

Dodd didn't answer. He would, but why admit it?

"I am under the orders of My Lord Earl of Bothwell to make you a certain offer." Another inviting pause which Dodd didn't bother to fill. He liked silence.

"We understand you work for Sir Robert Carey?"

"I'm Sergeant of the guard at Carlisle, ay."

"And we know you've fallen out with him over the very foolish way he let the Elliots go in October. Anyone would really. My Lord Earl is also annoyed with him over the way he spoiled the raid on Falkland palace last summer."

Dodd said nothing. Then "No," he said.

"No?" asked Hepburn, looking puzzled. "You haven't fallen out with him?"

"I have, ay. But I willna kill him and there's the end of it."

Hepburn smiled yet again. God, he was greasy. "No, no, we wouldn't ask anything like that. Just a certain absence."

That was different. The Grahams had asked him not to be there a few nights before when he was due to go on patrol and had been willing to pay him ten shillings which he had taken. He hadn't yet heard how that had played out, but judging from the deafening silence from Carlisle, not too well for the Grahams. One of the lads would have ridden out to tell him if Carey was dead, if only to bid him to the funeral.

"Ay?"

"We think Carey will soon be going into Scotland."

Dodd shrugged. "I doot it. And if he does, he may not ask me, he kens I'm mithered with him unless he's a stupider man than I tek him for."

"If he asks you, we want you to say yes."

Dodd sighed deeply. More travelling into foreign parts, more sleeping who knew where. At least he would understand the people, his Scots was quite good.

"Ay well, if he asks. And then what?"

Hepburn handed over four crowns, a pound, not Scots but sterling.

"At some point I will ask you not to accompany him and that is all."

"Ay?"

"That's all."

Dodd stared hard at the man. He was wearing a plain wool suit, some dark colour hard to tell in the firelight, with the indefinable look of having been tailored. His plain white falling band was clean and his cloak was a thick prickly grey wool with the oil left in it, you could see the way the damp dewed on it and didn't soak, from hill sheep clearly. It was a nice cloak, densely woven, perhaps from the herds near the lakes to the south west. His face was square and the beard neatly trimmed, somehow neutral. If it wasn't for his unruly curly hair, it would be hard to remember him.

"Ay," he said, wanting to hand back the pound but somehow

the money stuck to his hand. It was enough for a plain morion helmet. "We'll see."

"Oh Sergeant Dodd," said the man softly, "not a word to Carey and don't play me false, d'ye understand. We ken where yer wife lives."

Dodd said nothing. Of course he did, if he knew Dodd's name. He didn't like being threatened, although you had to expect it when you took money. He wasn't worried. God help the man who took on Janet Armstrong in a fight. Perhaps Hepburn caught this for he smiled again.

"It's only a little thing we're asking ye to do," he said, "We're not going to kill him. Just teach him a lesson and send him back to London."

Dodd said "Ay," again and that seemed to satisfy Hepburn because he settled back on the bench and started asking questions about horses and the harvest like a normal man and Dodd didn't feel like answering. The conversation petered out as Hepburn got tired of trying to hold up both ends of it. They finished their pottage and Hepburn paid a ridiculous amount in sterling because Widow Ridley had quadrupled her prices just for him.

And that was all wrong because Dodd knew that the Earl of Bothwell was at the horn and he would have heard about it if the Earl had robbed a town or raided Lord Maxwell's cows and insight which was the only way he could have laid his hands on so much cash.

Gimlet-eyed, Widow Ridley watched from the door as Hepburn and Dixon mounted up and rode on the way they had come if they came from Edinburgh. Anyway, their horses were Edinburgh animals from the brands. Her knitting became louder as she spat after them.

"I wouldnae trust them further nor I could throw them," she snapped and Dodd nodded slowly.

"Missus Ridley, can I sleep on yer bench here like your ither guest…" The Thirlwall drunk hadn't moved all the time he had been there. "Only it's dark and the rain…"

"Ay, ye can, Sergeant," said Widow Ridley. "Mebbe ye'd like to bring in yer great tall horse if he'll fit, since it's the raiding season."

Dodd looked at her in astonishment. "I take that verra kindly, missus," he said. "Ah'm fond of the beast and he'd make a good raid of a poor one."

Widow Ridley smiled a little for the first time, so her face wore the ghost of the way she looked forty years gone, before her teeth fell out and her wild hair went white.

She did more than allow the horse in the house, she brought in some straw to lay in the corner and Dodd carefully walked Whitesock in through the door—he had to put his head down to get through though there was space under the rafters once he was in. Not even that spooked him, he just neighed curiously and then stood still to be untacked and whisped down and then she brought in a bucket of mash for him. He nickered his lips in thanks and she patted his strong brown neck.

"Once upon a time, I'd ha' got on my pony and ridden out into the rain to tell my father of such a horse," she said. "Come quick, Da, I'd say, it's a good one."

"Not now though," said Dodd, suddenly worried.

"Nay, not now," she laughed at him. "They're a' deid."

It made Dodd feel unaccountably better to know that the great London horse was in the same room with him, as the Thirlwall drunk snored and Whitesock blew and whickered in his sleep and eventually Dodd slept on the bench with an old homespun blanket over his shoulder and his saddle under his head.

Ten miles away by then and following the wall carefully to Haltwhistle, the men were walking their horses and wishing they had stayed as the weather closed in.

"God, he's a dour one," said Hepburn. Dixon grunted.

"Do ye think he'll do it?" Hepburn asked a mile later when they had realised they had overshot Haltwhistle and would do better heading for Hexham. Dixon shrugged.

"What does it matter?" he asked. "When do we kill him?"

"Probably after Carey's been arrested," said Hepburn thoughtfully. "Once the King is dead. Then we do Dodd."

Dixon grunted again. "I'm bringing my brothers in for that job," he said. "I dinna like the looks of him."

SOMETIME IN AUTUMN 1592

Father William Crichton looked at the pieces of paper that had cost him such a lot of time and work. They were blank and at the bottom were the careless signatures of the Earls of Erroll, and Angus, also lesser fry like Auchinlech and even two Grooms of the Bedchamber. Not one of them was a forgery. Huntly had promised to sign a blank piece of paper too. Above the signatures, Crichton or anybody else could write anything he chose. As a guarantee for the Spanish King and a test of good faith, they were a triumph.

He had met all the men when he was at Court, at Falkland, very secretly. One of his reasons to be there was that he had been meeting the King and doing his best to persuade him to join the scheme. His Highness had even invited him to a small hunting lodge in the park and then seen him alone except for a page, in the evening after the hunting was finished and the King was at his ease eating a light supper of partridges and venison.

"Your Highness," he said while the King drank wine by the pint. "My liege the King of Spain…"

"Mr Crichton, ye are a Scot, are ye not?"

"Yes, Your Highness."

"Then I am your liege, not the King of Spain."

Crichton had coloured up at that, embarrassed. "Your Highness," he said humbly, dropping to one knee off the little stool he had been given, "I apologise, of course you are temporally. But I see the King of Spain as my spiritual liege because he is a Catholic."

"Surely then that's the Pope?"

"And the Pope, Your Highness."

"A man should have one, perhaps as many as two lieges. I canna tolerate three."

Crichton did not know what to say.

King James smiled and beckoned a red-headed lad with a crumpled ear to pour some more wine for him. "Och, dinna fret. I'm no' Her Majesty of England to have your bollocks off and burned and your guts intae the light of day and yer body cut in four parts so the angels will be at their wits end to put ye back together on Judgement Day."

Crichton, who had nightmares sometimes about being hanged, drawn, and quartered, made a little noise in his throat which had gone dry. "I'm very glad, Your Highness," he managed sincerely.

"Nay, the Boot and the pinniwinks will do for me," grinned the King buttering some manchet bread, "And then a nice rope."

"Ah…"

"So get off yer poor aching knee and tell me about yer idea," said the King. "Ye'd have the King of Spain land his troops at Dumfries and such like western ports and stay here over winter, then in the spring they march south and take England. Yes?"

Damn it, thought Crichton, they weren't supposed to spill the whole plan, Huntly was just to feel him out…

"Well…"

"Or is that no' the plan?"

"Not quite. For instance, problems with supplying the troops means they will likely bring them in the New Year to shorten the time of them being idle."

"Tell me all about it," said the King with an expansive gesture. "That ye know, anyway."

"Well that is the plan, I don't know all the bureaucratic details but the King gave me his *fiat* at the beginning of this year. He has read your paper about the possible benefits of Spanish rule which you wrote at the time of the Armada and liked it and asked that you be apprised of his…er plans. You see, I thought, and the King of Spain agrees with me, that perhaps it would cause less effusion of blood all round if the landing were not contested nor the troops troubled while they were in Scotland and perhaps we could buy some supplies from you at good prices and arms as well and…er…so on…"

"I've got an idea to prevent the effusion of blood," said the King, waving a partridge leg. "How about the King of Spain doesnae land troops anywhere in Scotland, doesnae keep sending Armadas for the storms to scuttle, and we all settle down and start trading and making money out of each other. Eh?"

Crichton looked at him in bewilderment. Had he really just implied that trade was better than war? "But Mother Church…"

"Ay, the Church," said the King. "Now I've allus longed to be a Catholic."

"You have?"

"Oh ay, it wis the religion of my dear martyred mother so it was, and I feel a great spiritual longing to be part of the great Universal Church again."

Crichton was nearly trembling with excitement. "Your Highness, this is wonderful news! I can…"

"I've often thought of getting baptised into the Catholic Church and leading my poor benighted subjects back to their spiritual Mother," said James, turning his eyes up to heaven. "The trouble is, at the moment if I did any such thing I would be in battle the following week and at the horn a week later. Which wouldna suit me, ye understand."

"You truly believe your subjects would revolt…"

"Ay, they would. Some would not," said the King, splitting another partridge with his black-nailed fingers, "but Edinburgh, Aberdeen, Fife, even little Leith, the cities would be up in arms. Ye recall what happened to my poor mother."

"But John Knox is dead and in Hell now."

"Ay, but Chancellor Melville of Aberdeen University isnae and he's a strong puritan, he thinks of only one thing which is the advancement of Calvinism. I've just had tae sign a dreadful law that removes bishops in favour of presbyteries. Presbyteries! God save us, wi' the poor silly creatures having tae decide for theirselves what's right which they mostly dinna want to nor cannot."

"Shocking!" said Crichton sincerely.

"Ay. So any clue to anyone that I'd like to make a change in religion and I'd be oot, ye follow?"

"Of course," said Crichton, wondering if the King was actually talking treason. But no, he was the King. If he said it, it could not be treason.

"So ye see, Father—I can call ye that?" Crichton nodded faintly. "Let's take all this a little softly, a little quietly. And in any case, how can I possibly agree to troops building up fifty miles from Edinburgh? Even if I'm all for this plan to take England and cast down the auld bitch who's docked ma subsidy this year, and if I'd be willing to form an alliance wi' the King of Spain—which would be in the nature of a minnow forming an alliance wi'a perch, d'ye not think?—but even if I were... Thousands of soldiers and not mine running around the West March, I dinna like it."

"I can talk this over with Huntly and Angus. Perhaps we can find another place to land the soldiers, perhaps in the Highlands?" said Crichton, who loved maps but had never seen an accurate one.

"Good idea," beamed James, who had stalked deer all over the Highlands.

Crichton dipped his head. His mind was racing. If the Scottish King would declare himself a Catholic that would change everything. *Cuius regio eius religio* was the maxim all over Christendom because it worked: as the King, so the religion.

And of course a large number of Spanish troops in the West would certainly encourage the King to declare himself a Catholic, would give him a perfect excuse in fact. And then perhaps the King of Spain's general, yet to be decided, could indeed join forces with James and then both of them could invade England from the north. The strategic possibilities were breathtaking.

"Just tell 'em their old dad disnae want Spanish troops bothering him, eh?"

"Yes, Your Highness," said Crichton. "I am very honoured that Your Highness has seen fit to explain so much to this poor priest." I'll be a Cardinal, some part of him was singing, for a coup like this, a Cardinal's hat at least!

"Ay, ye should be. They'll credit ye with ma conversion and make ye a saint, I shouldn't wonder."

"Oh, I doubt that," said Crichton with smug modesty while all the time the back of his mind was singing, Cardinal's hat! Cardinal's hat!

"And not a word to anybody, eh?"

"Of course not."

"Besides, I don't want war with Spain. Why not wait until I inherit England so I'm King there by right and then make the change? Surprise 'em all one morning? What's all the hurry?"

Having been in Spain, Father Crichton could answer this. "His Catholic Majesty is not a well man and I think he reasonably fears to go to Judgement with his great failure to take England back into the fold on his conscience."

"Ah," said the King, nodding wisely, "I see. I see. So tell my naughty northern earls, Huntly and Maxwell especially, no Spanish troops in Caerlaverock, not even to wipe out the Johnstones, or I'll run the Justice Raid of all time into the west and burn it down."

"Yes, Your Highness."

"We'll meet again, Father Crichton, I've enjoyed talking tae ye."

Father Crichton bowed himself out, with a couple of partridges wrapped messily in a handkerchief to keep him going on the road back to Edinburgh. In fact, as soon as he was out of sight he had headed west again. He knew Huntly and Maxwell would instantly reject the idea of putting troops ashore anywhere other than Dumfries, no matter what the King thought, but he thought he could sell the rest to them.

At the hunting lodge, the King, who was mentally drafting a very careful ciphered letter to Sir Robert Cecil in England, spotted that his young page was looking troubled.

"Whit's the matter, Rob?" asked the King.

"Well, Your Highness, when ye met Chancellor Melville here last week, you told him how much ye love the precious word of God and that you would always protect and save the church of Calvin and Knox in Scotland and that the Catholic earls are a thorn in your side..."

James laughed, wiping his fingers on the napkin over his shoulder and dabbling them in the waterdish, wiping them sketchily again. "I'm caught," he said. "Yes, I did."

"And then today you said to that priest that ye'd like to be a Papist?"

"Ay, that's true."

"Well, which is it, sir?"

"What?"

"Which one were ye lying to?"

The King stopped laughing and looked grave. He beckoned the boy to him and the boy came and stood there with a frown of puzzlement on his face.

"Now, Rob, ye know what a King is?"

Rob opened his mouth and left it open. "He wears a crown."

"On special occasions, ay, I do."

"And he goes hunting and signs papers."

"Yes," James laughed. "Anything else?"

Rob scowled in thought which James had already discovered didn't come easily to him.

"People do what you tell them to, usually."

"Sometimes," said James, with a touch of bitterness.

"And that's it," said Rob looking triumphant.

"Well there's an important bit about being a King that ye've left out."

"Och, and ye've a Queen…"

"Ay, though that's not it. The thing is, Rob my dear, God chose me to be King. God protected me all through my childhood when many ill-affected men kidnapped me and might have killt me. God made me King. Now when ye meet God on Judgement Day, He'll say tae ye, Rob, were ye a good boy and did ye allus tell the truth and did ye allus do whit yer elders and betters tellt ye to?"

Rob thought carefully, his handsome brows bulging with the effort. "Yes," he said at last.

"Well that's verra good, lad, I'm pleased tae hear it. Whit do ye think He'll ask me at Judgement?"

"James, were ye a good man?"

James shook his head. "Nay Rob, me dear, that's whit he'd ask if I wis just another man. But I'm no' a man, I'm a King. So I get another question. James, He'll say to me, James me lad, were ye a good King? Were ye a King like David or Solomon or Hezekiah, did ye do yer best for every one of yer subjects, Catholic or Protestant? Did ye keep the peace as far as ye could?

Were ye a good King?"

Rob was staring at him. "Oh."

"And I hope I'll be able to answer tae Him and say, like ye, 'Yes, I was good.' But to be a King is a position that comes to ye fra God and is sacred. And sometimes you have to do things that would be bad if you weren't a King. Which is why when I spoke to both Melville and Crichton, I told them what they wanted tae hear."

The poor lad was standing with a napkin between his rawboned hands and was frowning again. "But which one did ye lie tae?"

James ruffled his hair. "Both, me dear, I was lying to baith of them."

DECEMBER 1592

They rode out of Carlisle on a cold morning. The blustery weather had stopped and after that it had turned suddenly cold, so cold Carey wondered if it might snow. The winds were all from the northeast and cut to the bone like a knife.

At Carey's suggestion, Anricks had written back to the Scottish King, also in Latin, thanking him for the invitation, accepting the challenge to a game of planets, a battle of the spheres, a duel of philosophers, and explaining that Sir Robert Carey would provide him with an escort because the Deputy Warden had business with His Highness as well. The note that came back with the same messenger said that Sir Robert would be very welcome and King James added a scrawl in Latin which welcomed his good cousin and hoped they would get in some hunting if the weather permitted.

With them went Red Sandy Dodd and Bangtail Graham, Tovey and Tyndale, Leamus the Irishman from the Earl of Essex's deserters, and the sixth man was Dodd. Carey had written to Dodd in Gilsland, a letter politely allowing the possibility of a refusal, but Dodd had written back on the back of the letter saying he would meet them at the Wall in Gilsland around nine o'clock. There were also two lads from the castle guard to act as messengers and grooms which made ten, enough for respectability. Everyone was rationed to one remount maximum and there were five packponies, two of which were for Carey and Anricks. It bore out the saying that if you wanted to send one man from A to B, then you needed one man. If you wanted to send two men, then you needed four men and so on.

Dodd was there at Gilsland, sitting on Whitesock with another pony on a leading rein, his lance pointing to the sky, his new morion polished and his face slightly harder than the stones of the Giant's Wall behind him. He lifted his fingers to his helmet to Sir Robert and Sir Robert responded with a nod, and then Dodd joined their party at the back. Nobody said anything.

They made good time along the Giant's Road and reached Newcastle by evening, stayed the night in the great carting inn there, and then went up the Great North Road and by a strange coincidence found themselves in the little post village of Widdrington as the quick evening came down.

Carey had sent one of the lads ahead to warn Sir Henry Widdrington. As they rode into the courtyard there, they saw Roger Widdrington come to meet them, whom Carey hadn't seen since the last time he went to Scotland. Roger Widdrington had some trouble meeting Carey's eyes and took refuge in pomposity as only a seventeen-year-old can.

"Yes, we have space for your horses, Deputy Warden, though the hobbies will have to double or triple up and for your men as well, though some might have to sleep in the stables. Mrs Burn is still here and she has taken her chamber which is why we are one room short. Her baby is due any day now. Perhaps you would care to be introduced to her, Sir Robert. I know Mr Anricks and Sergeant Dodd have already met her."

"If the lady is well enough to receive me," said Carey with

a slight bow. "I heard something of her sad tale from...Well... er...I heard it."

"Where are Sir Henry, his wife, and your elder brother?" asked Anricks as he let himself carefully down from the horse and staggered slightly.

"Sir Henry and his lady wife and Young Henry were invited to Scotland by the King a few days ago," said Roger. "It's most inconvenient, what with the raiding season. I was out on the trod last night but one, though we didn't catch anyone."

"Did any of that big herd of cattle we brought into Carlisle last week have East March brands?" Carey asked Red Sandy, speaking a little loud because Dodd hadn't been there and so would get none of the fees.

"No," said Red Sandy stolidly, "West or Middle March only."

There was the usual flurry as the horses were bedded down for the night and the men sorted out where they would sleep, mostly by tossing coins. Meanwhile Roger Widdrington bore Carey and Anricks off to introduce Carey to Poppy Burn.

Elizabeth had done her best to make her small guest chamber suitable for a lying in, with the walls hung with cloths and the window carefully sealed to stop bad airs coming in.

Poppy was even bigger than before and moved very awkwardly with her legs apart. She had on an old let-out English gown of Elizabeth's and was reading a book when Roger knocked and opened the door. She was a bookish woman; there was a pile of other books on the little table, including a couple of books of chivalric tales, and Ascham's *The Schoolmaster*, an old and worn copy lying separately from the others.

Mr Anricks went in first and she greeted him with delight, struggling up from her chair. "Why Mr Anricks, what are you doing here? I think you've drawn all the loose teeth in the village. Are you going back to Scotland?"

"Yes, Mrs Burn, I am now officially a philosopher. May I introduce Sir Robert Carey to you, ma'am. Sir Robert, Mrs Proserpina Burn, Mrs Burn—Sir Robert."

"Well," said Poppy holding out her hand with a smile, "I have heard so much about you from Elizabeth. I am delighted to meet you at last."

Carey bowed over her hand with every Court flourish available to him, because she was a pretty woman even if she was nine months gone. She managed an adequate curtsey.

"I am sorry for your loss, ma'am," said Carey, "However I am very happy to be able to tell you that I hanged your husband's murderers personally last month, from Dick of Dryhope's tower, both of them, father and son."

She clasped his hand. "Thank you, sir, I heard that you had, but thank you so much for coming to tell me personally. Now I have had my revenge, I can think of the babe." Carey bowed again. "I heard there was nearly a terrible battle but that you convinced the Elliots to withdraw with no loss of life."

"Almost none, yes," said Carey. "Although we would have won the battle, it is the way of these things that good men's lives will be lost. Much better the Elliots ran away which has made a laughing stock of the whole surname. And I had what I had come for, the murderers."

"You risked a pitched battle just for my husband's killers?"

"Say rather that I risked it for the sake of justice, ma'am," said Carey very courtlywise. "Justice for him and for you."

There was a pause and then Poppy Burn said something odd. "It is a dark and terrible world I have come to. Thank you, Sir Robert, from the bottom of my heart."

Carey bowed again and then Poppy looked sideways at Anricks.

"Sir, although Mr Anricks is not a man-midwife, he is by way of being a medical man. I wonder if you would leave him with me so I can consult with him?"

"Of course," said Carey, and went out, thought about sticking around just in case, but then caught the smell of roasting pork from the kitchen and went down to investigate.

"Mr Anricks, you know how I am placed," Poppy said to him familiarly as he brought up a stool to sit on. "I have decided that the minute I am delivered and if spared, churched, I desire to go home to my family in Keswick."

Anricks nodded.

"A very suitable place to go, since the manse is no longer yours," he said. "Although I haven't heard yet that a new minister has been appointed to Wendron."

Poppy bowed her head and then looked up at him. "Please Mr Anricks, I have no right to ask this, but would you accompany me?"

"I'm sure," said Anricks judiciously, "that if you want him to, Mr Roger Widdrington will accompany you to the mouth of Hell itself."

"Ah." Poppy smiled a secret smile. "Well. But will you do it if I need an escort?"

"If I can. I may of course be dead."

"Why? Are you going into danger?"

"I am going to King James' Court to dispute with him or possibly his wise champions as to whether the Earth goes round the Sun or vice versa as popular superstition will have it."

"Earth goes round the Sun...Oh no, Mr Anricks, I am sure you are mistaken."

Anricks sighed and resisted the temptation to explain why it made such better sense. She was a woman and very close to her time. He didn't want to do or say anything that might upset her.

"Perhaps I am," he said peaceably. "However, His Highness wants a proper academic dispute about the matter."

"Well I hope it goes well for you. Can I ask if you would take a packet to Edinburgh for me?"

Anricks bowed. "Certainly," he said, and she brought out one of her usual packets, double sewn in canvas and sealed. He took it, felt it, and smiled.

"Not so thick as usual."

"Yes, although it was hard to write," she said, her eyes quite feverish. "I hoped you would come back or perhaps I would have given it to the carter in the end."

"Sometimes the more prosaic messenger is the safest."

"Do the usual thing with the packet, leave it in the jakes, behind a brick, at the Maker's Mark in Edinburgh."

"Of course," said Anricks, took the package and put it into the breast of his old woollen doublet. "Can I help you in anything else?"

"It was Lord Spynie who ordered the death of my husband, wasn't it?"

"Please ma'am, I beg you will not trouble your mind with…"

"It was." Tears were glittering on her eyelashes.

"Yes, it was. Though you know the circumstances. For that crime, I do not entirely blame Lord Spynie."

She nodded and for a moment she shuddered as if she was doing something that needed huge effort. "You are saying I should not think of pursuing him."

"Yes," said Anricks baldly. "God knows, the man is evil but in the rough and tumble of Scottish Court life, it was fair enough. Also, vengeance is mine, saith the Lord, I will repay."

"Indeed," said Poppy, "Though Mrs Sterling the midwife says sometimes the good Lord needs a bit of prodding, being infected with His Son's notions about forgiveness."

Anricks inclined his head. He could say nothing to Christianity with its very laudible and peaceable scriptures on the matter and its total ignoring of them. Also his opinion on vengeance had changed over the years.

"Now, serious matters are done," said Poppy, clasping her hands round her belly and giving a big smile. "Tell me about your wonderful wife and children, Mr Anricks."

So Anricks smiled and spoke about Rebecca and how the latest child had been born while he was away which he found both a relief and a worry: a relief since he didn't have to hear the cries and shouts of his wife in labour, but also a worry since he couldn't know until several days after if his wife had survived and if she was well, which thank the Almighty, she was as of her last letter. The eldest boy was nearly nine now and a clever lad who already spoke Portuguese, Spanish, and English and…

He left her dozing and passed her woman coming up with supper on a tray for her, recognised the smell of pig and sighed.

In the parlour where the family ate, he saw the first remove laid out. Politely they had waited for him, which did him no good at all, so he claimed stomach trouble and picked at the pot herbs and the remains of a chicken and also had to turn down a liver sausage that smelled good even to him.

Carey was probing Roger Widdrington for more information on why Sir Henry, his wife, and eldest son had also gone to Court.

"Well I think His Highness took a great liking to Lady Widdrington last time they met and it's quite normal for Sir Henry to spend a lot of time in Scotland," said Roger.

"Oh. Is he getting a pension from the Scots King?"

Roger again took refuge in pomposity, his downy chin scraping his small ruff. "I'm sure my father's loyalty to Her Majesty the Queen is absolutely unimpeachable..." he began, looking worried.

"Of course it is," said Carey, waving away the tempting quince sweetmeats in the second remove. "I asked because I know Sir John Forster in the Middle March certainly gets something from His Highness and has for decades. And James of course has his 3000 pound subsidy from the Queen to keep him on the straight and narrow."

Anricks thought he would rescue poor young Roger and also he was genuinely curious. "Are you looking for something similar, Sir Robert?"

Carey smiled sunnily. "Who knows? Of course, I wouldn't turn His Highness down if he offered me a pension, that would be rude. And I wouldn't like to break tradition now I have my warrant. I can always use the money to pay my men."

"Ahum," said Roger, "Well. Tradition."

"Really, I'm more curious as to whether Sir Henry will be seeing Lord Spynie again."

"I'm afraid I have no idea..." said Roger, looking panicky.

"Ah," said Carey, "I thought so. How is his gout?"

"A little better," said Roger, grasping at this safer subject. "He has started taking an empiric dose made of crocus bulbs which does seem to help."

"The same as My Lord Burghley," said Carey. "He was suffering badly when I saw him at the Queen's Court in Oxford.

I'm sure the crocus bulbs will do the job. And how is my esteemed elder brother John?"

"He is still having trouble with the Berwick town council…"

"Of course he is, he's a pompous ass and so are they…"

The gossip about the doings in the East March went on and on and eventually Anricks could not stomach any more candied eringo root nor quince cheese and took his leave to go to his bed in the other guest bedroom. It was a familiar room, with a couple of palliasses on the floor, a truckle, and a testered four-poster, so he modestly took the truckle. He got ready for bed, carefully used his silver toothpick and toothcloth, said his prayers and then looked at the packet Poppy had given him.

He looked too long for he soon heard Carey's step on the stairs and had to put it away half unpicked.

Carey nodded at him, undressed, knelt to say his prayers, and rolled into the bed with his shirt on and his long legs poking out under the blankets. Five minutes later his firm snoring started echoing through the night and Anricks understood why neither Sergeant Dodd nor Red Sandy were using the palliasses and were probably happily asleep in the stables with the horses.

Anricks sighed and looked up at the handsome coffered ceiling, sighed again, turned over, sighed once more and turned over again. His body was aching from the two days' brisk ride with only changing of your horse to break the monotony and from the lumpiness of the bed at the inn at Newcastle. He was very tired and while he tried not to think of the time when he had slept like the dead, lying naked on naked boards with a hundred other men's snores rumbling around him, he seemed to have lost the trick of it now.

***

Dodd had almost enjoyed the various kinds of pork they had been given in the hall, along with a savoury bag pudding full of herbs to soak up the gravy, and excellent beer. He had listened to Red Sandy and Bangtail arguing the old question about whether Scotsmen had tails. Leamus the Irishman had said in his soft foreign accent that he had been quite sure that Englishmen had tails until quite recently and Bangtail ended the matter by saying that he didn't know about the Scots men but the Scots women definitely didn't have tails the last time he banged one which caused everyone to howl with laughter.

The two lads were both called Archie so they had some fun with that and hit upon calling the one who was as tall as Carey with wider shoulders and much bigger feet, Little Archie, and the one who was a bantam with thick black hair standing straight up and generally took messages, Big Archie. That would do for the moment, until they had done something that would make a better byename.

"Is it true that the Deputy is still sweet for Lady Widdrington?" asked Red Sandy, munching the chewy bread.

"Ay, it is," said Dodd and his mouth turned down at the thought of it. Was that why he had let the Elliots go? Because he was sweet over a woman? And she wasn't even an Elliot, she came from Cornwall with one of those weird names.

Red Sandy tried again. "D'ye think he'll get her or no'?"

Dodd shrugged. He really didn't care one way or the other. Red Sandy poured him some beer which he hadn't asked for and exchanged looks with Bangtail.

"So," said Red Sandy, "are ye still sorrowing over the way we let the Elliots go or is there aught else bothering ye, brother?"

"What?" staid Dodd, looking at him as if he had gone wood.

Red Sandy repeated the question word for word.

"Are ye having me on?" Dodd replied and the black anger expanding again until it felt like all his body was tight with it.

"The Elliots, right," said Bangtail, looking anxious and was ignored by the Dodd brothers. Leamus swung his lanky legs over the bench and wandered off.

"Only ye've bin a right sour streak of shite for the last month," said Red Sandy loudly and slowly, "And we're a' getting tired of it so I wondered had something else happened?"

"What more d'ye need?" hissed Dodd and found he had hold of Red Sandy's shirt collar. "He let them go!"

"Right, fine," said Red Sandy, not even trying to take Dodd's hand away. "Tell ye what, brother. I dinna care how sour and thrawn ye are wi' the Deputy, but will ye not treat us the same, eh?"

And Red Sandy stared Dodd in the face until he let go of the collar. Dodd didn't know what to do or say, but in the end he stood up and walked to the stables where he dossed down next to Whitesock who nickered welcomingly to him and then laid his great head down in the straw next to Dodd's.

Dodd's chest felt full as if it was going to explode and for a moment he almost put his arm around Whitesock's neck. But then he stopped himself and forced his eyes shut against the burning in them and somehow went to sleep.

In the morning he found that his own arm had betrayed him by creeping around the horse's neck in the middle of the night when he hadn't noticed, which made everything worse, not better.

EDINBURGH, DECEMBER 1592

For the first time ever, Lady Widdrington found she was enjoying herself in Edinburgh. She made sure Sir Henry had plenty of time to chase Lord Spynie by making herself scarce and she did that by following the King's suggestion and meeting the ladies of the Queen's Court, and sitting with them or walking in the gardens of Holyrood Abbey with them or sitting sewing with them or going out on a hawking expedition with them on days when it wasn't raining.

She had now met Queen Anne and usually found her with her Danish ladies, playing card games and singing songs in Danish that sounded rude and certainly made them giggle. Queen Anne was a plump fair-haired girl who seemed quite sad and worried about something. She had been Queen of Scotland for two years, but there was no baby yet and of course tongues had already started to wag about it so that was probably the trouble.

She was a friendly woman, quite informal, with her attractive Danish accent and after Lady Widdrington had made sure she lost to the Queen a few times at Gleek, she was looked for by her and often called to Her Highness' apartments in the older part of the palace that still looked very much like an abbey, and had beautiful carvings on the walls and in the window niches and Gothic arches. After a little, she was invited to share a bed, sometimes with one of the fatter Danish ladies and sometimes with a pretty empty-headed wife of one of the King's Grooms, Marguerite Graham. She was more than happy to be in the world of women and save Sir Henry the trouble of thinking up excuses for why he didn't want to sleep with his lady wife. And it even pleased him a tiny bit, because her being associated with the Queen gave him more status. What could be more unexceptionable than a Danish lady-in-waiting or a Flemish chamberer?

Often she couldn't sleep as she lay in bed next to the great pink snoring pillow of a woman, and then of course her thoughts wandered to Carey, which she tried to stop because that hurt her, and then her thoughts usually wandered back to the ugly interview with her husband at Jedburgh.

They had been in the remains of the once mighty and beautiful Jedburgh Abbey, and the King had not at first been present in the room. Nosy though the King was, he respected proprieties usually.

Lady Widdrington had been all across the March, into Scotland, back down to Jedburgh and she was still shaking from the encounter with the young Lord Hume on the church tower.

Her husband had not come up to the tower because he was afraid of heights. The King had arrived in the middle of it all and pronounced that Lady Widdrington must come to Edinburgh and meet his Queen. Of course she had agreed and then gone, her heart pounding, to meet her husband in the old abbey warming room.

He had been angry with his usual smouldering rage which she had spent such effort and pains when she was younger to understand and find something rational in it.

"Well, wife," he had sneered, "What have ye to say for yerself?"

Elizabeth considered this as an opening gambit. She was long experienced in this kind of discussion. Whatever she said would be wrong, she knew that. If she apologised for going into Scotland without his permission, that would be wrong. If she told him her reasons why she had gone, which she felt were perfectly rational, and excused herself, that would be wrong. Whatever she did or said would be wrong because she herself was irredeemably wrong because she was a woman.

She also knew that whatever she did or said, at the end of all the words and the shouting, she would be beaten because beating her made him feel better about everything else. She didn't understand why, but it did. Temporarily.

So she said nothing. She knew he hated her silence too, but that wasn't why she did it. Nor was it because there was after all nothing to say. She simply couldn't be bothered to fight him because not only was he an old man always in pain from his gout, but he was also a man in love with somebody he couldn't ever have and she felt sorry for him. She probably couldn't ever have Robin Carey either, so she knew exactly what her husband went through every day of his life, poor man.

She was careful not to smile at him, though strangely she wanted to. There back in the old abbey warming room with its pungent smell of socks and rarely washed old men, she took off her damp velvet gown, unlaced her kirtle unfashionably down the front and heaved it off over her head, left her petticoat and bumroll, undid the top of her smock and let it fall down so her shoulders and upper back were exposed above her stays and then went and knelt at his feet, so he could beat her and get it over with.

She shut her eyes and waited for the belt to come whistling down on her shoulders, crushing the internal child that always wailed and wanted to know why. She thought that the last set of welts had healed up but there were scars on her shoulders that often opened up again when Sir Henry felt particularly poisonous.

He was taking his time and she sighed. She crossed her arms over her chest to protect her breasts and waited for the onslaught.

Come on, she thought, you've given me time to get nervous, get it done and then I can go home and sleep.

A draught caught her and a different sweaty smell and she realised that the door was open behind Sir Henry. She looked expecting to see one of the Widdringtons and what she saw astonished her.

The King was standing there, in all his soft-edged glory, staring with a very peculiar expression on his face. Not lustful, as she might have expected, seeing her smock was down over the top of her stays, but extraordinarily compassionate. She was steadied by that. She stayed on her knees where she was, since she might as well.

At last Sir Henry turned to see the King, his unused belt dangling from his thick knotted fingers. He bent his neck and said thickly in Scots, "Can I no' be private with my wife?"

"I came to say farewell, Sir Henry," said King James in a reasonable voice, "and this is what I find?"

He brushed past Sir Henry and raised Elizabeth. "Madam," he said, "put yer clothes on." So she pulled up her smock and tied the laces, fought her way into the damp and muddy kirtle and then put the gown round her shoulders. Her hat she had taken off when she dozed and her cap was firmly pinned to her head with a dozen long pins as usual. She sighed because now it was all to do again so Sir Henry could satisfy whatever it was in him that thirsted for her pain. Her skin was shrinking again from the remembered pain of blows, leaking into the future.

She sighed again and turned to go, found King James there again.

"Lady Widdrington," he said very softly, "d'ye mind what I tellt ye of George Buchanan, my tutor?" Yes, she did. She had been shocked. She nodded. "Buchanan liked to beat me too, said it would make a better King of me if all the sin fra my mother had been beaten out of me. My scars are on ma bum, see ye, and it was only when my dear friend D'Aubigny wept over them that it occurred to me there might be any objection to them. I will see what I can do again."

"Thank you, Your Majesty, but I'm afraid there isn't much you can do," she told him, "I just wish…"

Sir Henry was still standing there like a post, only his eyes flickering between the King and his wife.

"Ay, what d'ye wish?" whispered the King.

She found her eyes suddenly full of tears and tried to push them back. "I just wish he could have Lord Spynie and be happy," she said in a rush, not knowing until she heard the words what she was going to say.

Oh God, Sir Henry was right there in the room. What would he do to her now?

Suddenly the King embraced her, which nearly knocked her out with the smell. "Och Lady Widdrington, ye're the kindest woman I've ever met. Will ye go ben whiles I speak to your husband?"

She found her hat with shaking hands and put it on, then went out to the remnants of what had once been a fine set of cloisters and got her shaking knees to walk about until she stopped quivering like a hunted deer and could think straight. She was wrung out. Now what would happen to her? She wondered exactly how angry Sir Henry would be with her at what she had said. Had he heard it? Had he been listening? Would the King be angry with her? Maybe not, since he had said she was kind.

She was a little surprised about George Buchanan, that leading light of the Reformation in Scotland, that stern beacon of righteousness, though not very. She was old enough to know that the more righteous a man seems the more ugly his private life tends to be.

So she walked until Young Henry came and found her and walked with her, his head bent and his spotty face grim and strained.

"If he ever beats you again, ye're to tell His Highness," said Young Henry. "By letter or messenger or whatever. Sir Henry isna a Scot and he is the Deputy Warden of the East March but King James says he willna have it."

"Young Henry," she said to him, "I know Sir Henry hates me and blames me for all his ills. So what happens if he can't vent his spleen on me? Do you think he'll start to like me?"

Young Henry stared at the ground for a while. "You should go home to your mother and father," he said.

"In Caerhays castle?" she said, "In Cornwall? At the other end of the country, hundreds and hundreds of miles away? Don't be ridiculous."

Even now she still thought it ridiculous, though deep inside her she longed to see her mother again. She had stopped writing to her because Sir Henry read the letters which meant she could not tell the truth. Sir Henry had not the wit nor the acting ability to hide his feelings as she did, he was a constant boiling presence beside her, even when he wasn't there, of rage and dull fury and somehow she couldn't help feeling compassion for him in her heart, for how sad and unhappy he must be. She knew this could only annoy him and it did. Yet there it was: she was still very afraid of him, although he hadn't actually beaten her since Jedburgh. She was afraid of his ire and yet she couldn't keep the compassion out of her voice whenever she answered him which made him all the more furious. So generally, as much as she could, she avoided talking at all, or just said gently and humbly, "Yes, My Lord," or "No, My Lord," which he hated even more. If only he could just divorce her. Unfortunately that was impossible short of a private Act of Parliament and they were not peasants just to part and not see each other again. Poor man, he didn't even know what he wanted from her.

So at the King's winter Court in Edinburgh she was more than happy to sleep next to big pillowy Danish girls or silly sweet Marguerite, who was often not in her bed when she should have been. She started learning Danish to pass the time which made the poor Queen cheer up and giggle at her terrible pronunciation.

CAERLAVEROCK, DECEMBER 1592

William Crichton was sitting in a stuffy little wooden box with a grill to one side on a very uncomfortable seat with a thin cushion on it, his breviary open in his lap although he didn't really need it. There was a lot of noise of someone arriving and then the other door opened and shut and a man knelt down in front of him on the other side of the grill. Despite the darkness, Crichton knew exactly who it was since he was the lord and the lord goes first. As far as Crichton could make out, Maxwell was wearing a black damask doublet with black satin trim and a small ruff and that made his permanent scowl from having eyebrows that met in the middle even more forbidding. He cleared his throat and coughed, which was understandable since the little confession booth was left over from the days before the Reformation when Holy Mother Church had held them all in her hand. Which was to say, it was old, full of woodworm and, as far as Crichton could judge, had been frequently used as a jakes by desperate serving men and probably dogs.

"Bless me, Father, for I have sinned..." intoned the Maxwell and then went into a baroque recital of sins of the flesh, including many instances of fornication, impurity, impure thoughts and actions. Maxwell did not mention killing in battle or on a raid, since to his mind only a fool would call them murders, though he grudgingly included plenty of assaults and two actual murders, if you could call them that since one had been of a Johnstone found alone on the hills and the other had been when he was drunk. When the regrettable tale finally wound itself to the end, Father Crichton wondered what would happen if he refused the Maxwell absolution for the continued habitual feast of sin which no doubt was the same as last year and doubtless would be the same next year. Nothing good, he suspected, and he would shortly be sold to the English authorities.

He gave a rosary as penance, to be prayed at the Maxwell's convenience. Then "Ego te absolvo..." he intoned in the sacred washing of the black soul of the Maxwell and tried not to dwell on the more outrageous bits of the confession. Was it really possible to do that to two women or had the man just been boasting?

After the Maxwell had gabbled through his prayers, crossed himself, and risen from the kneeler, let himself out again, his household came in with the same grubby stories, although his lordship had made a better tale of it. His wife came in last with a prosaic tale of anger and envious thoughts and one beating of a servant girl she suspected, correctly, of bedding her husband.

George Gordon, the Earl of Huntly, was due to come to Caerlaverock soon and then the two of them would travel to Edinburgh with at least half of their households for Christmas.

Crichton would rather have stayed at Caerlaverock to receive the first *terceiros* once the seas calmed down in the spring. But Maxwell wanted him in Edinburgh and as he was Maxwell's house-priest, that was that.

The night before they set off they were sitting by the fire in Caerlaverock hall and roasting chestnuts and Huntly said apropos of nothing else, "Well, what if we kill the King?"

It's the sort of thing you just don't say, thought Crichton, unless you're lord of thousands of acres and an entire clan and regard yourself as a prince in your own right. "I think it would be a bad idea," he said.

Huntly laughed at him, said that the King was a pervert and a sodomite as well as being a goddamned Protestant and surely he deserved to die.

Yes but he's the King, thought Crichton anxiously. *And he might become a Catholic.* Aloud he said to Huntly, "Well, My Lord, he showed good favour to ye after ye murdered the Earl of Moray..."

"Ah didnae murder him, I killt him and he deserved it."

"Then killed him."

"Ay, the King fancies mah bum, allus has," explained Huntly, throwing a chestnut in the fire to watch it explode, "And I'm married to one of his precious D'Aubigny's daughters and he's aye sentimental..."

"Ye got away wi' it," said Maxwell. "I wish I could do the like to that bloody man, John Johnstone, the bastard."

Crichton thought about telling the two lords some of the things Jesus Christ had said on the subject of enemies, vengeance, and forgiveness and he knew he would never do it. It was just as well that neither Huntly nor Maxwell could read since they had spent their teens learning more useful things like swordplay and the names for different groups of animals. It was also just as well that neither knew any Latin except for rote learned prayers.

The Protestants were so set on everyone knowing scripture, everyone reading and hearing the Bible in their own language at church, insisting that everyone should know the Word of God. It was foolishness and irresponsibility—the Word of God was like gunpowder, apt to blow up people's lives if not treated with due care and in particular, kept away from peasants.

The lords were still sitting by the fire, surrounded by a hairy carpet of wolfhounds and currently discussing the best way to murder the Johnstone without getting caught for it.

"Ye could do it," said Maxwell to Huntly, "Ye'd get away with it again, ye know ye would…"

"Why should I?" asked Huntly as a chestnut cracked like a pistol. "Johnstone's no' my blood enemy, he's yours. Ye do it."

"Ay but the King disnae fancy mah bum and I'd get warded somewhere cold wi' no women…"

"Ah cannae help that," said Huntly. "And forebye it wad be a sin for me to kill a man I had nae blood feud with, would it no', Father?"

Crichton hesitated and said, "It certainly would be a sin for ye to murder the Johnstone…"

"There ye go, ye're trying to get me to commit a sin, Maxwell, so shut yer trap about it, eh?"

"For God's sake, killing the King is a wee bittie of a sin," protested the Maxwell. "Why are ye so fussy?"

"I'm not gonnae commit the sin of killing the King," said Huntly. "Somebody else is, isn't that right, Father?"

"Well…er…"

"And forebye somebody else will get the blame," added Huntly, laughing a lot. "That should make ye happy, Maxwell. That's funny, is that..."

Maxwell was struggling to look as if he knew all about this. "Ay," he said also laughing, "that's hilarious. Will he greet, d'ye think?"

Crichton desperately wanted to ask who was planning the outrage but didn't dare because then they would know he didn't know. Instead he kept his countenance and blinked down at his hands. Who could it be? Not Spynie, the man was gimcrack, totally dependent on the King and he knew it. The Ruthvens weren't allowed close enough to the monarch and he couldn't think of anyone else who would dare? Was it one of the other lords in the association, perhaps? Huntly? Maybe?

Suddenly Crichton had to get out of there. He had the awful feeling he was going to weep because something he had set up with loving care was suddenly twisting out of his hands. Did the King of Spain know about this plot, whatever it was? Had he given it his *fiat* as well? Couldn't he see that for all his faults, King James was more useful alive than dead?

He stood up, bowed to the company who ignored him, went out of the hall and found the narrow staircase that led up to the battlements. Up he went and up, getting breathless and finding his fear and horror burning out of him, until he could look out into the long cold night and the stars above him. It was freezing and he had brought no cloak, but he stood there and stared up at Orion marching across the starfield with his little dog behind him.

He wanted to pray and so he prayed for King James' continued health and he also prayed for the souls of the lords who were trying to bring in Spanish troops. If King James had been excommunicated like his appalling and scandalous cousin of England, of course, he would have had no qualms. Well not very many. But James had not been excommunicated, he had been very careful about that—and had he not said in so many words that he wanted to be baptised a Catholic? Hadn't he? Directly to Crichton himself? That would make it doubly a sin to kill him since he would have had no chance to purge his sins and would thus go to Hell for being a Protestant.

And there was the paper he had written in the 1580s before the Armada sailed the first time, looking at the pros and cons of the Spanish invasion from the south. How that paper had got into the King of Spain's hands, Crichton didn't know, but it had. Was it all just coneycatching? Had King James himself arranged for the paper to end up in Spain, to keep the Spanish off his back while they got on and conquered England?

Crichton sighed. He had to find out more about this plot, if it existed. Maybe King James is a Protestant through and through and would never turn to Rome, but he's a man and it's a sin to kill anyone, even in Scotland where life is so cheap.

He said the *Pater Noster*, three *Aves* and a *Gloria*, and went down the stairs to see if there was anything left for his supper.

EDINBURGH, DECEMBER 1592

Their little procession was now within five miles of Edinburgh, coming up the last bit of the Great North Road which wasn't in as scandalous a condition as the parts further south, with the big green and brown mound of King Arthur's Seat on their right. Carey had sent Little Archie ahead to warn the King's majordomo of their arrival. He and Anricks were wearing their best available clothes, him in the black velvet doublet and hose, Anricks in his new suit and a gown borrowed from Scrope without asking, looking very self-conscious. The cut was good and Carey was particularly pleased with the way the doublet pulled Anricks' shoulders back since he had a tendency, like many clerkly men, to round shoulders.

He looked critically at everyone else, riding politely in twos, all reasonably smart and wearing newly cleaned jacks and polished helmets.

Now that was interesting. Dodd had a brand new helmet, a nice plain morion with the curves and peaks that kept the rain out and made it hard to knock off. Carey had seen it but had not noticed it which was embarrassing.

Carey had himself and Anricks riding after Bangtail and Red Sandy, then behind him Tovey and Tynedale, then Dodd and Leamus who ignored each other, and then the final lad, Big Archie, the small man with a shock of black hair, leading all five of the packponies on his own hobby. Now that was also odd. Big Archie looked different.

Other than that, they were looking good. Carey let his favourite hobby, Sorrel, drop back until he was next to Dodd and smiled across at him.

"I like your new helmet, Sergeant, where did you get it?"

Oddly Dodd's neck flushed red at that and he said in a strangled voice, "Aglionby in English Street."

"Oh, is that the mayor's brother?"

"Ay."

"Well it's a good one then." Carey wasn't wearing his helmet, it was packed with his jack on the last pony, ready for the journey back. He didn't need it this close to Edinburgh, even in barbaric Scotland. Instead he had a high crowned hat that he hadn't been able to resist in Oxford and Mr Anricks had his old hat since Anricks' usual hat was an ancient soft bonnet, twenty years out of fashion, that a London beggar would have disdained to wear, a little too horrible even for a tooth-drawer, let alone a philosopher.

Dodd was staring woodenly to the front now and so Carey contented himself with dropping back once more to take a look at Big Archie, the groom who was leading the packponies. The ponies all looked fine, being unshod. None had lost a shoe or gone lame for a wonder, their packs were carefully stowed and nothing was on the point of falling off. Even the groom was wearing a respectable black doublet and a bonnet pulled down on his head and...

Carey slowly took another look at the groom. He would have sworn that the sprig of the Carletons now known as Big Archie was smaller and didn't have the length of jaw or those piercing blue eyes though his hair was in tufts and sooty black...

"God damn it," he said wearily, "it's bloody Young Hutchin Graham again."

"Nay sir, I've the look of him, sir, but I'm a Carleton..."

Carey swiped the bonnet off the lad's head and found that the sooty black hair was in fact plastered with some combination of soot and grease, underneath which was Hutchin's golden hair, unmistakeably.

He swiped sideways with the revolting bonnet, back and forth, whacking Young Hutchin with it so the young devil had to lean over to the other side of his pony and cling like a monkey, all the while protesting that he was a Carleton, sir. The others were staring and trying to hide their grins, except Dodd, still looking grimly ahead.

"Do I have to strip you and put you under the pump to get that disgusting stuff out of your hair..." bellowed Carey, and Young Hutchin finally put his hands up and shouted, "A'right, sir, a'right, I came with ye to make sure ye was all right..."

This so astonished Carey that he stopped hitting the boy with the bonnet and said, "What?"

"To mek sure ye was a'right..."

"Ballocks, Young Hutchin, you came with us either to sell your arse in the best market..."

"Nay sir," said Young Hutchin indignantly, "I'm no' that way..."

"Or to get your revenge for last time."

There was a pause. "Ay sir," said Young Hutchin, with a crooked grin, "Ye've the right of it."

"Dear God! This is Edinburgh, you blithering nitwit, King James is King here, do you understand and..."

"Ay sir, but I'm not here to dae it, see ye, I'm spying oot the lay of the land and seeing what's here and what the strengths are. Do ye like mah hair, Ah did it masen..."

"Your hair is simply disgusting, Young Hutchin, but it might put Lord Spynie off for long enough so you can run crying to your mother...

"Nay sir, I canna do that, she died birthing me," said Young Hutchin with some dignity. "And I've growed a lot since last summer, see ye, all me breeks is too short and I've gone through two pair o' clogs…"

It was true that puberty had clearly hit the beautiful boy that Young Hutchin had been with unusual force. His legs and arms were four inches longer than they had been while his feet were in a man's pair of boots, very old ones, and his hands were rawboned and large. On the logic of dogs with big paws, he had a considerable amount of growing to do yet.

"And you've come to scout out the King's Court, no more?"

"Nae more, sir," said Young Hutchin glibly.

"What about that ambush you were in with your wretched uncle a few days ago?"

"Och that was in the way of business, sir—poor Uncle Wattie, he's fit to be tied again and ye got maist of the kine he reived in the autumn and Archie Fire the Braes is gaunae be expensive."

Carey nearly cracked a smile at that. "When did you make the swap with Archie Carleton?"

"Ay, I sold me funeral suit cos it's too small for me and I got the new doublet and breeks cheap…"

"You mean you stole them?"

"Nay sir, and then I had enough money to bribe Big Archie, and I shadowed ye all across the moors and we swapped last night while ye were in the inn at Berwick. That bit wis fun."

Grudgingly Carey nodded. "Well, that was very good work shadowing us," he admitted, "I had no idea."

"Thankye sir. So I can come wi' ye sir."

Carey sighed heavily. "I could send you back…"

"Ay, and ye ken very well, I willna go…"

"…in irons with an escort…"

"Och sir!"

"But very well, Young Hutchin, you may accompany us. Maybe my Lord Spynie won't remember you."

"Nay, he willna wi' me hair like this."

"God almighty."

Carey returned to the front of their little column where

Anricks was waiting expectantly. Carey explained some of what had happened in Dumfries in July and Anricks nodded.

"So that was what was at the root of your trouble with Lord Spynie, I did wonder. And he's an ill man to cross."

"Mr Anricks," said Carey heavily, "in all my life, I have never crossed a man that wasn't an ill man to cross."

For some reason Anricks started to laugh at that, a creaking kind of laugh and eventually Carey started to laugh as well.

Soon the walls of Edinburgh were frowning on them from their left, but they didn't need to enter the towngates at all since Holyrood House was a converted abbey a little way outside the Netherbow Port. They met the Vice Chamberlain at the end of the Cowgate and were directed through the old Gothic gatehouse into the abbey grounds.

Of course the King's palace in Edinburgh wasn't anything like as enormous as Whitehall nor as much of a labyrinth. Carey had spent nearly a year there in his late teens in the train of Sir Francis Walsingham's embassy. They found themselves lodged in the oldest part of the palace, on the back wall, in the monks' old storehouses and infirmary. Sir John Maitland of Thirlstane, the Lord Chancellor, had come away from his beloved Thirlstane for Christmas and the New Year and he bore Carey and Anricks off to feed them venison pasties for supper.

They ate privately in a parlour and since Maitland was rich, the food was very elaborate and often unidentifiable, so Anricks simply said a prayer and tucked in. Carey was being updated on some very complicated politics to do with the northern earls, Huntly, Erroll and Angus, and Anricks found himself sitting beside a large fleshy man with a big nose, a few years older than him.

"Ah, yes," said Maitland, waving a hand at the two of them, "Mr Simon Anricks, Mr John Napier, pray be introduced to each other since ye are both by way of being philosophers and ye baith have opinions on Thomas Digges."

Almost unable to believe his luck, Anricks turned with interest to Mr Napier and within five minutes was deep in conversation with him about an astonishing addition to the *Ars Mathematica* which he had invented. They switched to Latin and went at it hammer and tongs, with bits of paper being produced and scrawled on and Anricks looking more and more delighted and impressed. It took quite a lot of work to separate him from Napier when the supper and the music finished.

***

Alexander Lyndsay, Lord Spynie, was sitting at a late supper in his own private parlour at Holyrood House. There were four young men with him and two boys, all dressed in elegant livery with a nice variation in the styles, the same damask handled differently for each boy by Spynie's own tailor.

Spynie was drinking excellent French wine and eating some delicious goose liver sausage with toasted manchet bread. But mostly he was just enjoying watching his youngsters argue and brag and wrestle with each other, vying for the honour of being his bedmate that night. Occasionally Spynie thought sentimentally about young Christie Hume who had died in the summer, drowned while drunk in a river. He also thought wistfully about the beautiful young Lord Hume. He always wanted the next thing, the new thing, someone fresh.

It was clear to him that she had thwarted him again, that bloody woman the old man was married to, Lady Elizabeth Widdrington. She had thwarted him in the summer when he had wanted revenge on the new English Deputy Warden who had dared to come after him with a sword when all he was doing was offering that remarkably handsome Graham boy the chance of bettering himself. She had now thwarted him again at the top of Jedburgh tower and that was not to be borne. That needed action. He didn't know or care whether the bitch had let Carey into her hellmouth, though he assumed that she had, but he did know that they were sweet on each other which made them both nicely vulnerable.

He was trying to bring the threads of his plots together and his high forehead wrinkled as he looked into the fireplace. Like many blond men with fine clear skin, he was ageing rapidly, not helped by the white lead he used to hide his occasional pimples.

The oldest young man, a doddering greybeard of nineteen, noticed and glanced across at the two fifteen-year-olds, matched twins, bought from the slums of Edinburgh. They moved into the corner, picked up two lutes and started to play softly.

Spynie liked music and he liked being catered to, but what he was about was taking some serious thinking.

First, of course, there was Hughie Elliot, or Tyndale as he called himself. So far he was the best of the lot. That eminently useful and helpful man called Jonathan Hepburn had found him and used him for a couple of little jobs and found he was good at both his trades, the tailoring and the killing. Hepburn got him to London where Carey had been embroiled in some family problem, but had failed to insert him into Carey's service. However when he sent Hughie to Oxford, Carey had snapped up a tailor who could also fight like a trout a fly.

The brow wrinkled again. According to Hughie, somebody had nearly succeeded in killing Carey at Oxford, which Hughie had regarded as a personal insult. Spynie wondered about that: he didn't mind who killed the man or how, he wasn't fussy that way, he just wanted him dead. Now Hughie had gone a bit quiet despite being quite close in Carlisle and in Carey's sevice, which gave him multiple opportunities. Perhaps a visit was due? Or no need, because Carey was bringing his servants to Edinburgh with him, according to rumour. That was for the very fine opportunity of the Disputation. The King had thought that up for himself, but when Spynie learned that Carey had invited himself along, he was overjoyed.

So he could be sure to twist the knife in Lady Widdrington, he had enthusiastically backed the King's desire to invite Sir Henry and his wife to Edinburgh as well as the enormous spotty lump of Sir Henry's eldest son. And now Hepburn had reported by letter that he had just suborned Sergeant Dodd, Carey's best henchman, so it was looking even better for Spynie.

There was a loud knock on the door and Sir Henry came in when one of the younger boys opened it for him.

Sir Henry was becoming a bore in Spynie's opinion, though he still found it tickled him to get such doggy looks from the old man. He came into the parlour wearing his Court suit of black brocade with a ruff, his corrugated ears and bulbous nose making him look troll-like.

"My Lord Spynie!" said Sir Henry delightedly, as if there could be any surprise at finding him taking his ease in his own parlour. "D'ye want to go hunting with the King tomorrow?"

Spynie brightened up. The weather had been terrible, so bad you couldn't even play golf.

"Yes," he said, "is he asking for me?"

"No," said Sir Henry, "he just said anyone who fancied some sport could come with him."

Spynie did his best not to look disappointed. Gone were the days when His Highness would tickle his ear and invite him by name and then they would sneak off from the usual disorderly throng and go and disport themselves in the coverts.

"Ah, well," he said, trying to be philosophical.

Sir Henry came and sat down near Spynie and took the cup of wine from the littlest boy, drained it, held out the silver cup for more.

"I'll go," he said. "He's hunting *par force de chiens* and I love that though it plays merry hell with my gout."

Spynie really didn't care about Sir Henry's gout but smiled at him anyway. "It's certain Carey is on his way with this tooth-drawing philosopher His Highness is so excited about?"

"Ay, he's just arrived. Reason for the hunt, in fact."

Suppressing his annoyance at not being told this first, Spynie said, "Good. Then I'll come."

Sir Henry grinned wolfishly. "When are you going to kill him?"

"I'm not sure yet, I want to make sure of him," lied Spynie because he never told anyone that kind of thing.

"Poison?"

"Possibly. I haven't decided yet."

"I want my bitch of a wife to be watching."

"Sir Henry," said Spynie, quite annoyed, "do ye want the man dead or do you not? So long as he dies, I dinna care how it happens and if he falls off his horse and breaks his neck tomorrow I will be just as happy as if I had put white arsenic in his wine myself. Happier because no one will think to blame me."

Though now he came to think of it, that might make a good end for Carey, even better than having Hughie do it. He tapped his teeth and stared vaguely into space while he thought how you might achieve a tragic fall while riding to hounds for one particular man and no one else. There were ways and means. Which would be best?

Sir Henry's fond smile at him annoyed him though he didn't show it. "Ay, ye're right," said Sir Henry with a sigh. "It's a good thing ye've got the brains."

"Yes," said Spynie, slightly mollified. "Where is she, your wife I mean?"

"Buttering up the Queen, so I heard," said Sir Henry with the scowl his face always wore when he thought of his wife. "And learning Danish, God save us. I've not missed her."

"Just so long as she doesn't interfere again," said Spynie, also scowling. The stupid bitch's interference in the summer was a large part of the reason why Spynie was not now drinking the King's wine in the King's Privy Parlour and kissing the King long and lingering on the mouth. For some inexplicable reason the King had not liked their proceedings at all. You would think the disgusting Englishman was some kind of relative. Worse, it had somehow turned the King personally against Spynie as though it was all Spynie's fault. He still hoped to get back in the King's good graces and in his bed, but the old delightful intimacy was not there any more and nor did the King laugh at Spynie's jokes, which annoyed him because he worked hard at them.

Just for a moment Spynie toyed with the idea of seducing Sir Henry. Probably he would have to get him drunk first because Spynie suspected the old man was still a virgin that way and then...But his stomach always rebelled because Sir Henry was such an ugly old man. Useful but old and gouty and might well turn squeamish too. No, tonight it would be Jeremy, who was in the full flower of his so-temporary masculine beauty and was not at all a virgin, nor squeamish.

Also recently Sir Henry had started smelling of old piss which Spynie didn't approve of at all. The King smelled terrible too but there was something exciting in that, an animal smell like a boar.

Still Sir Henry was useful, remember that, and while Spynie was not the King's Minion any more he needed useful people totally devoted to him and his interests. He wondered again who was the King's latest—or did he have one? Spynie hadn't noticed anyone new at Court who was pretty enough despite the way powerful nobles brought likely boys and lads in their family to Court to see if they could catch the King's eye, just as they would with their daughters if he had been interested in women. They were wasting their time with the boys, James was not interested in children either.

Spynie smiled at Jeremy, beckoned him over and kissed him on the mouth, a sign that the choice of the evening was made.

Some naughty spirit made him say to Sir Henry, "Would you like to take one of my boys as your bedfellow, Sir Henry?"

And bless the old man, he looked puzzled and said, "No, I prefer to sleep alone because of my gout. Thank you." Was that a look of panic under the puzzlement?

The twins were still assiduously playing the lute but the two new boys, one only eight, looked at each other and the eight-year-old shuddered. Poor ugly old man, no one wanted him.

Spynie beckoned the youngest two boys over and told them to clear away the food but leave the wine.

He had the beginnings of a plan now and he decided to ask young Matthew, one of his henchmen, to fetch him Jonathan Hepburn. He thought the plan quite a good one and felt a tickle of excitement at the base of his stomach, the feeling he got when he was removing someone who stood in his way. Carey would be dead in a couple of days.

***

Early next morning, Carey took Anricks off with him to the best mercer in town where he dallied for what seemed to Anricks like several hours over different kinds of damask and taffeta and velvet. Then he went to the best tailor in town, as recommended by Maitland where Anricks made good on his promise to buy Carey a new Court suit in the latest Scottish fashion, despite the eye-watering price of nine hundred-ninety pounds Scots, including the cloth.

Carey then was very completely measured and since he hadn't used that tailor before, Mr Arbroath the Master tailor, promised him a shell in coarse linen by the following day, before they even spoke about the fabric or the trim which Carey hadn't been able to decide on at the mercer's.

And it was on the way back from the tailor with Carey still burbling on about some damask from the Low Countries which had taken his eye and was even more wonderful than some other damask and leafing through about twenty swatches that all seemed very similar, when it happened.

The first thing that Anricks noticed was that the tailoring related burble had stopped and the next thing he noticed was that Carey had also stopped in the middle of the Linenmarket.

In fact he was standing stock still so the Edinburgh crowds had to part for him, his face shining with happiness.

Anricks followed where he was looking and found a little group of richly dressed ladies, who had just come out of the milliners' street and were talking in a mixture of a Germanic-sounding language Anricks didn't know, and broken Scotch as they walked along.

In the middle of them was Lady Widdrington, gravely repeating something like a verse, her face relaxed and remarkably pretty, in her usual severe doublet style bodice and kirtle and with a fur trimmed black velvet gown over the top, her cap covering her hair and a not quite fashionable hat on top.

She felt someone's eyes upon her, looked round and saw Carey.

First she stared back and her face too lit up so it was as though two invisible sunbeams were spearing down from the grey sky to light their faces alone. One of the maidens with loose fair hair elbowed another blonde in a married woman's cap and hat and the whole gaggle of them also stopped.

Carey was the first to recover the use of his wits and he bowed low and elegantly to all of the ladies, who of course curtseyed back in a group, except for Lady Widdrington who was two seconds behind the others.

Then Carey strode over and asked Lady Widdrington to introduce him to so many beautiful ladies, and were they the Danish Queen's ladies and how wonderful it was that they were and how did they like Scotland?

It was well done, thought Anricks, for he did not really speak to Lady Widdrington at all once the introductions were made. Yet he found out that Lady Widdrington was currently staying with the Queen's household, and where that was and regretted that the Queen wasn't a good rider and so would not ride to hounds in the hunt the day after, and finally dragged Anricks into introductions as the philosopher who would be disputing on the movements of the heavenly spheres. Most of the girls shuddered at the idea of the Earth moving instead of the Sun, except for one who remarked that she knew of an astrologer living on an island who was studying that very thing.

And then Carey made his bows again and the girls all curt-seyed, the maidens all made eyes at Carey, and off they went. The minute they turned the corner, Carey scowled and led the way to a boozing ken where he sat and called for double double ale for both of them.

Anricks was agreeable and took a pull of his ale which he found quite strange tasting now he was used to hopped Bristol beer. Carey stared into space, then turned to him.

"You know of course that Lady Elizabeth Widdrington is the woman I am going to marry?"

"Yes, I know, Sir Robert. If I didn't know before, which I did, I would have known at once from your faces."

Carey smiled briefly. "However," he said, "the fact that Lady Widdrington is here in Edinburgh means that her foul husband, Sir Henry, is also infallibly here which is very bad news for me and quite a problem for you."

"How so?"

"Sir Henry and Lord Spynie are normally in cahoots as the Scots say and they want…"

"To kill you. Yes, I had surmised something of the sort."

"Do you not see that as a problem?"

"Sir Robert, I don't. If they succeed in killing you, I shall be sorry but I will continue with my disputation as a means of getting close enough to King James to find out his thoughts on the Catholic plan against Scotland, if it exists." Carey smiled. "And if they do not succeed in killing you, why then I shall continue with my disputation with your help. I don't see your putative murder as affecting me greatly, one way or the other."

Carey chuckled. "Philosophy?"

Anricks smiled too. "And if I should unfortunately get killed in mistake for you, or die of plague or in a bear attack or some such, then I expect Sir Robert Cecil will find some other poor fool to dig into the matter. I doubt we are as important as we think we are."

Carey raised his jack to Anricks and they both drank.

"However it is also philosophical to take precautions and this puts a different complexion on tomorrow's hunt."

Carey raised his brows. "You think Sir Henry and Lord Spynie will try something?"

"Of course they will, it is a golden opportunity. Men such as you, Sir Robert, break their necks while hunting every day of the week and I would imagine, Lord Spynie's men are prospecting for a convenient place as we speak."

"Yes."

"We should sit and draw up a list of likely ways they might try to kill you at the hunt—I would also advise a gorget under your doublet."

"It'll be infernally uncomfortable."

"Not as uncomfortable as a wire snare pulling tight on your bare neck, which I regard as second only to a rope between two trees in likelihood."

"True."

Anricks finished his drink and smacked his lips judiciously. "I see this not as the kind of murder where they come after you mobhanded—or not yet. More a sneak attack."

"Well neither of my servants can ride well enough so it will have to be Sergeant Dodd at my back, despite the fact that someone has bought him."

"Perhaps I could do something to the purpose as well," said Anricks, "although I am not sure what."

"Will you come hunting, Mr Anricks?"

"Certainly not, sir. I am a philosopher and it is a well known fact that philosophers do not hunt... Mr Napier does not either."

"Why is that?"

"Chase after a pack of hounds, all day, on horseback, risking your neck although no one is trying to kill you—most unphilosophical. And besides philosophy is in itself a kind of hunt as we follow the tracks of the vagrant thought and search the coverts for the scent of the white hart of truth."

Carey applauded. "Nicely put," he said. "Will you use that in your speech?"

"I might," said Anricks, "but I was going to start with a disquisition mathematical on the differences between the Ptolemaic and the Copernican systems. Mr Napier was helping me with it yesterday evening."

"Mathematical?"

"Yes, you know, if there is a language of the universe, a language of the angels as Dr Dee calls it, I am certain it is mathematics. Sure, that's the language the Almighty speaks, as Maimonides says."

"And there I was praying in English. Or should it be Latin?"

"There is an argument for speaking Latin or Greek or even Hebrew to the Almighty so we remember He is unlike us, being eternal and all powerful whereas we are short-lived as mayflies in comparison, and puny. Normally I think English is as good a language as any to speak to the Almighty in and comes as easily to my tongue as the Portuguese."

Carey nodded. "Personally," he said cautiously, because philosophers are notoriously sensitive, "I would keep the *Art Mathematica* to an absolute minimum since His Highness understands nothing of it, and use words."

"Oh," Anricks looked crestfallen, "are you sure? They say he's very clever. I wrote something of my disputation late last night, inspired by Mr Napier's wonderful new numbers, with the mathematics laid out very simply and clearly...though indeed there is something odd about..."

"May I see it?"

Anricks pulled some crumpled sheets of paper out of his sleeve pocket and handed them to Carey, who squinted, frowned, tried the sheets the other way up and focussed on them for a while.

"I'm sorry," he said at last, "my arithmetic is good enough for siegework and artillery and playing cards, but I can't make out any of this."

"Really?" said Anricks in a huffy tone of voice, "I thought it was all a bit easy."

Carey coughed. "Well maybe for you, but I am certain that His Highness will make even less of it than I did and if you try to win your dispute with mathematics, you are doomed."

"But Sir Robert, as Dr Dee says, the world is written in mathematics..."

"Yes, but His Highness doesn't speak Mathematics. You would be better saying it in Dutch."

"But that is the point, number is a universal language that needs no translation, once you understand the concepts..."

"Mr Anricks," said Carey gently and firmly, "since I may have my neck broken for me tomorrow, take heed of me today. Trust me, His Highness will be at best bewildered and at worst bored. Find a way to translate it into good Scots at least."

"But...Oh very well!" And pettishly Anricks went out and threw the sheets of paper into the kennel running down the middle of the lane.

They stood and walked down through the town to Holyrood House—nobody but a fool would try to get a horse through the streets of Edinburgh just before Christmas. It was like London.

Back in the street they had just left, the boy who had been shadowing Carey and Anricks, carefully picked the sheets of paper out of the kennel, wiped the worst of it off on his breeks and trotted after them into the palace and gave them to one of Lord Spynie's men.

"I'm certain sure it's in cipher, sir," said the boy excitedly, completely forgetting Carey and Anricks' prior conversation, "like the Pastor was telling us, or maybe alchemy or astrology cos it isnae normal, is it?"

Lord Spynie's man gave the boy a Scotch shilling and put the sheets away in his wallet. It looked like witchcraft to him. He didn't think Carey was anything except a good Protestant, but you never knew with philosophers.

**

Dodd was in an old storeroom that still smelled faintly of cheese and was made cramped by multiple shelves, but already had a bed and truckle in it. He gave Bangtail and Sandy the bed and took the truckle for himself, because he didn't want to sleep next to his brother who was a notorious kicker and roller-over and besides, he was still annoyed with him. Leamus, the Irish deserter, looked around, clearly decided against asking to sleep with Dodd, wandered out in his loose-limbed way and wandered back with a palliasse, a pair of sheets and a blanket. He cleared a bit of floor of rushes, inspected the wall and floor minutely, put the rushes back and placed the palliasse equally carefully on top, tucked in the pair of sheets and blankets and then wandered out again. Dodd put his doublet and hose from Oxford on a shelf, hoping it wouldn't get too cheesifyed, got into the truckle and turned away from the bed so he could sleep.

But he couldn't. Bangtail and Sandy talked for a while and then went to sleep. Leamus came back with a loaf of bread and a pottle of ale which he put on another shelf, undressed quietly, folded his jerkin for a pillow, muttered to himself for a while and then got into his bed and fell asleep. Had he been praying? Dodd shrugged. He didn't care if the man was Catholic or Protestant or both, so long as he did what he was told, which so far Leamus always had.

However he had a problem because Carey had bidden him to the hunt tomorrow and Hepburn had stopped him around the back of the stable block and said he could go but must drop back once the silver trumpets began to blow. It added more bad feelings to the brawl inside him because it went against his grain to betray a man like that. It was as if the dependable black ball of rage was still familiarly there but on top of it sat something green and growing like grass that said he shouldn't do it, despite Carey being the man who let the Elliots get away, despite all that, he shouldn't do it.

Next morning, Leamus was up first and brought in a bowl of water for them to wash in. He carved the bread into four hunks, produced a round cheese from Bessie from his pack, and poured out ale into their horn cups. Everyone was astonished at this and said thank you to him, at which he smiled a little and said, "My da' always said that any fool can be uncomfortable. It takes a clever man to be comfortable." That was the longest sentence anyone had heard him say since the silly comment about Englishmen having tails, and then he went silent again.

Dodd took the largest hunk of bread and cheese and drank the ale but said nothing, feeling ill. It wasn't just the morning being morning, he had slept badly. So he was even more wooden and silent when it came time to go and meet Carey, found both of them had been given one of King James' Arab crosses each to ride in the hunt, and almost forgot himself to talk about the beautiful bay animal, which annoyed him again.

She was beautiful, though, and he patted the arched neck and blew into the nostrils which horses liked, and admired the compact shape of her body and her delicate hooves. Would she be nimble enough in the forest—the shape of her and her short back promised speed, but how would she do with loose footing?

Carey was inspecting his chestnut gelding too, passing his hands down the legs, lifting the hooves, feeling the hindquarters and getting nudged a couple of times for carrots, which he hadn't got. "Oh you *are* beautiful," said Carey to the horse, patting his neck and grinned delightedly across at Dodd. "These will go like the wind, Sergeant, you'll see."

He couldn't help a small smile in return, because this was a horse of a completely different nature to a hobby; even

White-sock would look awkward next to her. So it was true that the King had a wonderful stud at Falkland palace with Arab stallions and the Grahams hadn't got the best of the herd.

At the meet, there was a milling confusion of men and horses and servants and mounted attendants like Dodd, a cart full of musicians and a train of packhorses with the vittles. Spynie was there in his smart intricately cutworked black leather jerkin worn over a red doublet to show off the cutwork to advantage. There was a looming red-headed man in a feathered bonnet and a velvet doublet on a large handsome horse with some charger in him, whom Carey pointed out as George Gordon, the Earl of Huntly. Dodd knew the Lord Maxwell with his monobrow of course, and three more Maxwells at his back who were arguing loudly about whether a buck could be got to fight a horse and which would win.

Typically Carey, who was wearing his second-best suit, the hunting green, rode straight into the middle of them, bowed all around and asked after Lord Maxwell's beautiful Irish wolfhounds.

"Och, they're somewhere about," said Lord Maxwell, looking for them, "They're the best deerhounds in the country, of course I'd bring them. There they are!" He whistled and a boy ran over holding the four leashes with the wolfhounds trotting gravely behind him. They smelled Carey and let him lean right down from the saddle to pull their ears, smelled Dodd and left him alone. Lord Maxwell's smile changed from honest pride in his dogs to a courtier's smile and Carey smiled back so all was as dishonest as could be.

"How's the West March of England?" asked Maxwell.

"Remarkably peaceful for the time of year," said Carey with a knowing grin, "which is to say not peaceful at all since it's the raiding season. I found a lot of cattle in Liddesdale on patrol last week and also saw off a Graham ambush."

"Ay, I heard," said the Maxwell dismissively. "Any of them mine?"

"We found no Maxwell or Herries brands," said Carey blandly, since he knew that Maxwell was careless about branding his beasts, "So, no. I am surprised to see you here at all, My Lord."

"Oh? Why? The King likes me again."

"Of course, My Lord," said Carey very smoothly, "but didn't the Johnstones just raid a lot of your horses from near Lochmaben?"

Lord Maxwell scowled. "Ah hadnae heard that," he growled.

"Oh my mistake, probably just a rumour. Could I trouble you to arrange a Warden's Day, My Lord? It's now sixteen years since we had one in the West March and well past time for one."

The Maxwell, who had only agreed to be the Warden so he could use the office against the Johnstones, nodded vaguely, "Ay, we should, o'course."

Trumpets sounded at the King's approach with his own attendants and Carey turned his horse to face in that direction.

"How's the Deputy Warden, Sir Richard Lowther?" asked the Maxwell, with heavy meaning.

"Well, I know he has gout, poor man," said Carey with false sympathy, "which never improves any man's temper, and of course for some reason he is not at all pleased that I have just received my warrant from the Queen as Deputy Warden and so we have to work together." Carey favoured the Maxwell with a particularly happy smile and trotted away, glancing back once to see the Maxwell impatiently beckon another Herries cousin and send him off with a verbal message.

Dodd knew it wasn't true about the Johnstone raiding the Maxwell's horses and thought Carey had said that purely to spoil the man's sport for him. He trotted after Carey and set himself behind him to the left, glad he hadn't worn his jack or helmet as no one else had one.

The King rode into the clearing and everyone took his hat off and at least bent the neck to him. The King was in a dark purple doublet and hose and high leather boots which disguised the fact that he had had rickets as a child—quite mildly compared with Sir Robert Cecil—it just meant he was shaped like a tadpole with broad shoulders and puny legs.

"Och, what a goodly show!" he said to the assembled company. "We'll have some sport today." His sweaty grubby face with traces of breakfast egg in his beard beamed upon them because King James was never so happy as when he was pursuing deer across country at a gallop.

If he had been inclined to talk to anyone, Dodd would nevertheless have been struck dumb at the beauty of James' horse, a wonderful grey with a high arching neck and a high pace, a pure Arab and perhaps the father of Dodd's own mount, since he was a stallion.

"Och," he said, struck to the heart at it. It was too much, he almost had tears in his eyes as he watched the beautiful beast prance and sidestep while the King spoke to each of his nobles in turn.

"I think His Highness calls his horse Whitey," said Carey quietly in his ear. "Something about not letting him get too big-headed."

Dodd almost cracked a smile, but remembered and just said "Ay," and carried on staring hungrily at the animal. Carey shook his head in amusement and moved away.

To start with it was all milling about as the dogs cast around for the scent and the younger ones became excited about rabbits and snapped at other dogs they didn't like and the Master of Hounds used his whip to break up a dogfight that broke out over by the musicians' cart.

Carey sat his horse and watched patiently. If he had been riding Sorrel he would have let the reins loose so the horse could cast around in case there was anything a hobby could eat in the bare winter forest. However he was riding a horse he didn't know, so he kept them tight and discouraged any messing about by the horse. He didn't really need to: the horse had been beautifully schooled. Dodd was nearby on his own part-Arab and Carey had to admire the way his body went with the horse and controlled her without even thinking about it. He didn't even know what a centaur he was.

Yet Dodd's face was stony and dour, and not from its natural set. Silence and rage breathed out of Dodd like a smell—maybe it was a smell, since the wolfhounds hadn't done more than greet him. It looked like he wasn't going to forgive Carey any time soon.

Suddenly the hounds all moved together and gave tongue, and they were off across country, streaming out in a long comet's tail around the King, a couple of trumpets calling. It was a short run, they caught some young rascals with just a couple of points against a deerfence, and the forward hounds pulled them down and killed them and then the whole pack gave tongue again and went after something new.

Carey was keeping up with the King, a few ranks back as was suitable, with Dodd sticking to his back like an ugly limpet. He was watching all the people around the King, had seen Spynie quite a long way from the centre and found a shifting population of tough Border earls, there went Kerr of Cessford, and Earl Hume, and one or two handsome young men, but no one figure staying close to the King.

So the King hadn't found a new minion yet, eh? Carey thought back to his own youth without regret—Lord, what an innocent he had been. He looked around behind him, saw Dodd as usual behind him, saw the beaters running behind the horses and thought he glimpsed Bangtail running among them but then lost him again behind some trees covered with ivy.

There was a knot of nobles all shouting at each other and the Earl of Huntly burst out of the middle of them, his face alight, and galloped hell for leather after the King whose white horse was floating ahead like a speedy cloud, ripping through undergrowth and leaping brooks as if his hooves didn't quite touch the ground. It was easy to forget, but in fact the King was a superb horseman and not at all shy when in the saddle hunting, although he was notoriously frightened of knives and guns, which his aggressive subjects thought very strange. As a result of this eccentricity, none of the nobles were armed with anything more than hunting knives, nobody had any kind of gun, swords were absent, of course, even crossbows were only in the hands of a few men-at-arms to finish off anything more dangerous than a deer.

Huntly had caught up with the King and shouted something at him and the King turned his mount on a sixpence and came back to the stand of trees where everybody was waiting for the hounds to find the scent again. He happened to be near Carey and brought his horse prancing alongside and beamed at him.

"Sir Robert Carey, what a pleasure to see ye again, cousin, how is Carlisle?"

"Still there," said Carey drily which made His Highness laugh.

"Ye've brought yer tooth-drawing philosopher, have ye not?" Carey bowed. "Ma Court's in need of a philosopher. Lord knows, we hae a sufficiency of dominies and ministers but not a whiff of a philosopher, apart from a couple of mathematicians. How's he shaping?"

As if Anricks was a hunting dog, thought Carey, highly amused. "Well, Your Majesty," he said, "he is working on the first part of his dissertation."

"Ah, excellent. He's no' here, is he?"

"No, Your Majesty, he says it's a well known fact that philosophers do not ride to hounds but spend their time hunting in mental coverts, pursuing the white hart of truth wheresoever he may flee."

King James laughed again, he loved flights of rhetoric which was why Carey had unblushingly stolen Anricks' trope. "Och that's pretty. I havenae got a proper philosopher to dispute wi' him so I'm thinking I may take the job maself."

"Your Majesty is an extraordinary prince," said Carey, his heart sinking. "Is there another ruler in Chistendom that could be able to do such a thing?"

"Mebbe, mebbe not," said King James complacently, "but I dearly love a good intellectual argument so...Och my Lord Huntly, are ye back, what did ye catch?"

"Only a few does, Your Highness," said Huntly, some twigs in his hair and his hat over his ear. "I let them go. There's a full crop of staggards and rascals in this forest and no need for killing the women." He turned and winked at Carey for some reason and laughed.

"Ay, ye're right."

They were waiting for the hounds to take the scent again and Carey imagined the frenetic activity behind the copses and deerfences as previously captured deer were released from cages and driven towards the King and his party.

And then the King spotted something himself and they were off again, a little group of stags running before them, flashing their rumps in and out of the trees. There went the King, Huntly, shouting and singing, the Maxwell, Spynie…Spynie was looking over his shoulder at something and Carey looked over his own shoulder to see what it was. Nothing there was more interesting than holly bushes. He kicked his horse to a gallop and followed the leaders, heard the clear cold tones of silver trumpets in the distance, felt rather than saw that Dodd had suddenly fallen back. There were two attendants on either side of him, keeping pace with him, forcing him slightly off course. He was headed for a copse that was clear of undergrowth. Spynie was still breaking his neck to look back at Carey and now Huntly was as well. Suddenly Carey went icy.

The wonderful horse was galloping too fast to stop quickly so as he passed between the first two trees, he hunkered right down to the horse's neck, felt something swipe his hat off, tried to slow the horse, took his feet out of the stirrups, felt rather than saw something else and felt the horse lift in a desperate effort to get over whatever it was but wrongfooted and the back legs tangled in something. With a panicky scream the horse went over sideways and Carey just managed to jump clear out of the saddle and roll into a hollybush.

As he lay there winded and surrounded by prickles, Carey saw Bangtail run past followed by Red Sandy, straight into the holly patch and into a fight, which bashed to and fro until Bangtail's head and shoulders suddenly appeared between the bushes dealing a wonderful headbutt on his opponent's face which produced a fountain of blood from a mashed nose. Red Sandy emerged from the prickles on the other side and caught the man nicely behind the ear with a cosh that he then politely put away in his jerkin. The two of them dragged the man out between them with holly leaves in their hair.

"The other one ran," said Red Sandy breathlessly as he passed.

Somehow the King was there, looking thoughtfully down at him from his grey.

"Sir Robert, ye've lost your hat."

Then he looked at the crashing in the brambles where the horse was trying to get up and a strange look of terror crossed his face. "*T'il est haut!*" he shouted and galloped off immediately to the group of nobles, including Huntly, trotting up behind him, galloped between them and rode on ahead as they turned their horses and whipped them to a gallop behind him. If he hadn't been the King, Carey would almost have thought he was fleeing from something terrible, fleeing for his life. But no, surely not. Kings don't do that.

Carey was still crowing for breath but started picking his way out of the hollybush which seemed determined to hang onto him like something out of a ballad about the Faeries, and made half a dozen holes in him every time he moved.

Wheezing, he fought clear of it and staggered over to where his horse was flailing about in the winter brambles, both his hind legs caught in some kind of thick wire. One leg was at an ugly angle and another of the attendants was standing there, staring but not doing anything.

Carey caught the panicking great head and put his weight onto the forequarters which weren't injured although the hooves were kicking. He held the head, muttering sweet nothings until the animal had calmed a little and then looked along the beautiful ruined body to where one of the foresters had come up and was examining his hindquarters carefully. Scored in two places by what had tripped him, both his back legs were still tangled in the wire and one of his legs was clearly broken. The forester looked up and shook his head slowly, reached in his pack and pulled out a crossbow.

Carey had only met the horse an hour before, but still his heart hurt for the stupid destruction of such a lovely animal. He didn't even know his name. So he held the horse's head tightly, whispered more endearments in his ears and put a hand over his eyes as the forester came up, aimed the crossbow at the centre of the chestnut forehead and loosed the bolt. After that there was only a shudder and the usual smell of shit and the glorious horse was knacker's meat.

Carey's heart was still thumping and so he waited a minute

before he let go and stood up and found Dodd standing nearby with his statute cap off in respect.

His hands were shaking too, more for rage than for fear because he knew exactly who had caused the fall and how. He went over to the man Red Sandy had coshed who was still unconscious and kicked him to check, then went back to where the rope had been and finally discovered his wounded hat. He also found the rope still there, tied at neck height between two trees and looked very carefully at it before he untied it and took it down.

"Och," said Dodd a little way away, his face stricken for a moment. He still had his mount, who was tethered to a tree a little way off and neighing anxiously in the direction of the knacker's meat. Mother and son, perhaps?

"Here we are," he said, the rope under his arm, as he untangled the wire from the horse's legs. He chucked the rope at Red Sandy. "Nice little trap, rope first which I ducked under and then a double wire at the horse's chest height. He tried to jump it, but..." His voice suddenly seized up and he stopped, had to breathe carefully in and out a couple of times. "Not possible," he finished bleakly, staring straight at Dodd who was examining the ground in front of him.

"All right, ye!" said Red Sandy to the man he had caught, whose hands he was roping behind him. The man was coming to but was still googly eyed. "Who paid ye?"

"S...Spynie is m...my good lord..." came the mutter which only confirmed what Carey already knew. Who else had been craning his neck, looking to see him fall? No one. Apart from the Earl of Huntly whom Spynie could have told.

More attendants were coming up with a cart, and a slide. They roped up the dead horse's back legs and dragged the body onto the cart and then closed the back, touched up the carthorse and trotted off in the direction of Holyrood House and the kennels most probably. It wasn't so unusual for a horse or even a man to be killed in the hunt, what was unusual was the means.

"Sir, are ye hurt bad?" asked a gruff voice, and there was another attendant, an elderly man with a bag full of bandages.

"No, no, I'm not," admitted Carey, after a look all over himself. Holly scratches aplenty and bruising on his shoulder and back where he had hit the ground when he rolled, but nothing worse. "Do you have another mount for me?"

"Ay sir," said the man, beckoning up a young groom with a fresh horse for Carey. Not an Arab this time, but a perfectly respectable hunter. What Carey wanted to do was have a drink but that seemed out of the question. Or maybe not.

"Do ye have any brandy?" he asked the man who seemed to be some kind of surgeon. A shy smile lit the man's face.

"Ay sir, would ye prefer aqua vitae or whishke bee?"

"I'll have the whishke bee, if I may, goodman."

There was a look of approval and a small flask was produced which Carey drank from and nodded because it was very good, though not as smoky as the stuff he had drunk in Carlisle. More of an earthy taste.

"All right," he said to the young groom, checked the bit, the girth and then swung himself up and adjusted the stirrups. "Sergeant!"

Dodd was already mounted again and his face returned to its usual granite.

"We'll see if we can catch the King again," said Carey. "Bangtail and Red Sandy, thank you very much for catching that bastard… Was it Mr Anricks that suggested you come along as beaters."

"Ay," said Red Sandy, "and he paid us forebye, he's a nice man and sensible. Said we wis tae try tae stop ye breaking yer neck."

"Well take the man back to Holyrood House and put him in a storeroom for the moment. I don't think my Lord Spynie is likely to try anything more against me now."

Bangtail knuckled his statute cap and they started trotting the man back to the palace. "Och, ye can run or we'll set light tae yer breeks," Carey heard one of them say at the man's protests as they disappeared between the trees.

Carey looked long and hard at Dodd who said nothing. And so he put his heels in and galloped off after the King and his nobles who had left a trail behind them.

The man who said his name was Jonathan Hepburn was extremely angry. As far as he could tell from a couple of foresters he had paid, the idiot Lord Spynie had made an attempt on Carey's life, botched it, and then left the English Deputy Warden with a prisoner who could say who had arranged for a rope and two wires to be stretched across the man's path. Worse still, Spynie had asked Hepburn to tell Sergeant Dodd to hang back at the silver trumpets but had not explained why. As he had done as he had been asked, that meant that Dodd could say Hepburn had been part of the plot against Carey, which in fact he hadn't, since he had come up with a new use for the mad Courtier and needed him alive for the moment.

He was tired of working for Spynie in any case since the man was often stingy and ungrateful. He didn't need the ex-minion any more, since he was now working directly for his Catholic Majesty, and had two bills of exchange from the King of Spain, one of which he had turned into a tidy sum of money at the Steelyard, where they gave him a better rate. He had got rid of Dixon as well, since the man was stupid as well as aggressive.

Spynie came back from the hunt early and found him and begged him to do something about the man Carey's men-at-arms had just captured. Hepburn was tempted to tell Spynie to do it himself, but didn't on the grounds that information was like gold and you didn't give it away. Instead he looked through the maze of old abbey store rooms, disturbed a clerk at a standing desk who said Hughie would most likely be in Sir Robert Carey's rooms working on his clothes. So he went to find Hughie Tyndale who was sitting crosslegged on a table in the old infirmary, sewing away with a will on Carey's new court suit. Hughie lifted his head and smiled as Hepburn came in.

"Och," he said, "It's nice tae see ye again, sir, though I've not killt Carey yet…"

"No, that's fine," Hepburn answered, "I don't want you to kill him at the minute, I've got another job for you."

"What's that, sir? Will I kill anybody else for ye?"

"Yes," said Hepburn and saw Hughie grin and smack his lips. "I need something tidied up."

They talked for a while about how best to do it and after a while, Hughie came back from a poke around and said he'd found the locked storeroom but didn't have the key. He picked up a leather bag from the corner as he went. Hepburn took a quiet look around the place, found no key, but had some skeleton keys he had found useful in the past. Hughie was curious and interested and so they both went to the storeroom. Hepburn banged on the door, heard a doleful, "Yes, sir."

"We've come fra Lord Spynie to help you," said Hughie, grinning.

"Good," said the man in relief.

Hepburn went through a few of the keys, found one that worked. Hughie Tyndale unlaced his sleeves and rolled his shirtsleeves up, opened his bag, put on a voluminous blue butcher's apron over his clothes, went in with his favourite thin wire with wooden handles, there was a brief struggle and a glottal sound and then Hughie came out again, showing thumbs up. Hepburn took a glance and saw the man's head almost off and blood everywhere, didn't see the need to check any further, and locked the place up again. Hughie carefully took his butcher's apron off and wiped his garotte with a clean corner. Then he left the apron stuffed into a hole in the wall they passed where there was an airbrick. There was not a speck of blood on Hughie's clothes anywhere which was quite impressive and so Hepburn paid him and Hughie put his wire back in his pocket and sauntered off whistling tunelessly, to the tiny suburb around the northern corner of the Edinburgh walls which was apparently where the tarts could be found.

And then Hepburn went to the main hall of Holyrood House, slipped in at the back and drank some wine, watching as some of the servants rolled around completely drunk, just like the King of an evening, and some of the henchmen got in a dagger-stabbing game that they were all very good at, stabbing between their fingers faster and faster. Idiots.

Most of the Court was off hunting with the King, but the Queen didn't hunt. And killing excited him, made him feel the power of the Demiurge flowing through him, made him want a woman.

He went into the gardens where Marguerite often walked in the afternoons. Usually they met late at night when everybody was asleep, but he needed her now. So he walked in the gardens, taking a tiny risk, passed Marguerite as she walked with some of the Queen's women, laughing and giggling, paused to wink at her once and then passed on, pretending not to know her.

Twenty minutes later she was trotting through the storerooms right at the back of the palace, where there were stables for visitors filled with ugly hobbies and a couple of good horses. Hepburn had spent the time waiting for her in checking his precious leaden tanks for leaks and found nothing, which relieved a worry. When he heard Marguerite's quick footsteps, he hid behind a door, then stepped out and caught her and she squeaked once, then melted into him and said things to him in Flemish which made him more excited.

He half-carried her into the unimportant looking storeroom where he had put the leaden tanks and the lead half globes when he had brought them a few weeks before. Then he unlaced himself with suddenly clumsy fingers, lifted her skirts and impaled her like a fish on a hook, set her back against the wall whilst she wrapped her stockinged legs around his kidneys and bucked and threshed until he bit her again and she cried out behind his careful hand over her mouth.

Hepburn and Marguerite stood like that for a few minutes while Hepburn got his breath back and Marguerite felt the glorious happiness washing through her that cleaned away Antwerp and made every risk worthwhile. Then Hepburn set her down and kissed her again with that smile of his that she loved, that said he was cleverer than anybody.

They were too experienced to speak. Hepburn picked up his hat which had fallen off in the heat of the moment, laced himself again, gave her one more kiss and walked out of the storeroom. Marguerite counted conscientiously to one hundred, made sure that she was tidy and had no telltale smears on her, and also walked away.

Behind them both, high up in the rafters and lying full length along one of the main beams was Young Hutchin, in a state of some excitement himself. He had to wait and deal with it before he could climb down from the place he had scrambled into when he had heard Hepburn coming. He jumped down onto one of the lead tanks which had given him a useful leg up to the rafters, straightened his clothes and went out, looking extremely smug. She was a pretty one, the blond woman, a bit old maybe, but juicy and she was wearing pretty clothes of brocade and velvet which meant she was important. He had been impressed with the whole thing. Could he hold a woman up like that and swive her? Not yet maybe, but he would one day. He let his imagination work on this for a while and had to visit the jakes on the way. God, the courtiers were a randy bunch—Carey had been at the women too, the Italian lady, when he had been at Court in Dumfries. One day, Young Hutchin promised himself, he would do it too and sooner rather than later because he honestly thought he might explode if he didn't.

**

Anricks was still standing at his clerk's desk a couple of hours later with papers spread out in front of him. He had carefully unpicked the sewing on his packet from Poppy Burn, and then tried a number of different decoding methods on the carefully ciphered pieces of paper. Anricks still wasn't sure whether the text came from Poppy herself or somebody else but couldn't think who that somebody else could be or how they could meet with a woman who had taken her chamber. He had remembered to ask Roger Widdrington about Poppy's gossips and found she had no gossips in Widdrington and had only the girls in the house to look after her. No man had come near her since Sir Henry Widdrington had left.

So the text came from Poppy. Who had taught her to cipher and why? There was a dull itching of frustration under his breastbone because so far her cipher had utterly defeated him.

With the previous packets he had copied out the whole ciphered text very carefully and then delivered them where Poppy asked, sending the copy south to London to try if Sir Robert Cecil or Mr Phelippes could get any more from them than he could. As far as he knew, they hadn't.

He sat back and stretched his fingers. What was the index book? He shut his eyes and tried to imagine the shelves of books in Minister Burn's study, but no, that was the wrong place to look. Poppy Burn would need the book to hand, would need it now, in fact. He thought back to her chamber at Widdrington, thought of the book in her hand...No, that had been a book of sermons and quite new. The book she used would be older and well-worn...There was something. He pictured the little table with the pile of books, the one book lying off to the side, open...What was the frontispiece? A man with a bush over his shoulder...No, it was a schoolmaster holding a birch which was quite funny because Ascham argued eloquently that to get the best out of the pupils, the schoolmaster should not birch his charges too often.

His heart was thumping with excitement as he delved into his pack and found the book. Ascham's *The Schoolmaster*. A different copy and he hadn't read it yet, but he thought it was the same edition since it had the same picture at the front. His hands shaking slightly, he settled down to try what that would do.

Half an hour later he paced around the room stretching his fingers. He was sure it was the right one even though it still didn't make sense because it didn't make sense in a way that wasn't random letters, there were repeated words—"und" for instance. She had used the book to give letters, not just words, page number, paragraph, word then the individual letters. Sometimes she used the same sequence of numbers for the same word which was bad practice but understandable if you were in a hurry.

At the end of the letter where you usually found the words that gave you your start was no name but a short word "liebe". He knew Latin, French, Italian, Spanish, Portuguese but no Allemayne and that was what he suspected the letter was in. Deutsch. Or perhaps a Scandinavian language since the Queen was Danish. Why Allemayne? He didn't speak it even badly which now annoyed him. He scowled at his careful copying, then sighed and packed up all the sheets of paper, put them back into the packet and sewed it up again with the same thread in the same holes, reattaching the seals with a knife heated in a candle. He would take it to the place Poppy had said, the Maker's Mark, Edinburgh and see if he could catch a glimpse of the man who picked it up. He hadn't yet, because the man didn't come at a regular time.

Now he had to find someone who could translate the Deutsch for him, someone he could trust. That would have been simple in London or Bristol, but were there Deutschers in Scotland? And how was it Poppy Burn came to be using Deutsch? Surely the letter came from someone else? On one point he felt he could relax—most Allemaynes were Lutherans so apart from the question of why packets of ciphered letters were going to and from the Scots Court at all, surely there wouldn't be anything too deadly in it?

So when Carey came back from his day's hunting, muddy and carrying his half bent hat rather than wearing it, Anricks was eager to tell him the whole tale of the secret packets.

Carey was looking tired and sad which was odd after a day spent hunting and had eaten in hall with the King so Anricks sent Hughie Tyndale down to the buttery to get him some ale and bread. Hughie was by contrast very happy and smelled of drink, but did the errand willingly enough.

"Yes," said Carey as Anricks cut the bread, said grace and thanks to the Almighty for it, and tucked into a slice of liver sausage he hoped wasn't pork and some pale winter butter. He didn't think the liver was pork, it was too strong flavoured, more venison. "Spynie had exactly the attempt at me you predicted, but two traps, a rope at head height for me and two wires at chest height for the horse who had done Spynie no harm that I can think of."

Anricks tutted. "But you survived?"

Carey smiled faintly. "Clearly. The horse didn't, though. Broke his damned leg."

"Oh." Was that why Carey was subdued? Remarkable.

Then Carey brightened. "Oh but Bangtail and Red Sandy were there as you arranged and caught one of the men who pulled the wires tight at the right time. Shall we go and interrogate him?"

They went down to the storeroom as soon as Anricks had finished, Carey produced a key and flourished it open, marched in and stopped immediately. His boots were sticky soled with blood and there was a strong stench of shit.

Anricks brought a candle and examined the corpse carefully. He had been garrotted and there had not been a fight because his hands were still roped together.

"Damn it," said Carey, "Damn it to hell."

"The door was locked…"

Carey examined it and tried a couple of other keys in the lock. Two worked. "It's the old abbey, I suspect that the monks weren't too particular about locks except for food, drink, and money. Anybody could have come in and done it."

They locked up the corpse again and left him there until they could decide what to do about him since there was no way of finding out who had garrotted him. Clearly Lord Spynie was the man who had given the order, but there was no way of proving it and Carey didn't want to take the blame. There was always the Lough in the north of the city, if necessary.

It was already getting dark but the gates to the city weren't shut yet, since it was close to Christmas and, more importantly, New Year when everyone always gave presents. Carey was down in the dumps again, so they took a walk through the crowds and after Anricks had checked carefully for followers, he broke the matter of the Deutsch letter with Carey. Carey listened carefully, his head cocked, his old hat pulled down on his head and the wounded hat in a sack in case they could find a milliner who could cure it. The torches on the walls and shops along the main street leading up to the castle flared and caught in the wind and the shop windows were bright with lanterns.

Anricks didn't say where the letter had come from and Carey didn't ask, which showed as nothing else did that Walsingham had had the training of him. Anricks finished by saying he was not now so concerned, since most Allemaynes were Lutherans after all.

"Not all of them," said Carey, surprised. "The southern Allemaynes are Catholic and under King Philip's cousin, the Holy Roman Emperor."

Anricks was embarrassed. "I should have remembered that," he admitted, "although it's out of my field. So we are back at the beginning. Do you speak any Deutsch?"

"No, only French. But there must be some Hansa merchants here. Shall I take your copy of the letter for you, Mr Anricks, so you can work on your dissertation?"

Anricks coloured. He had not worked on it since Carey had told him not to use mathematics. All the fun had gone out of the project now—how could he say anything to the purpose without using mathematics, the language of the angels?

Carey smiled at him and wagged a finger. "Mr Anricks, if you want the King to adopt you as his pet philosopher, then you can be eccentric, your hair can stand on end…"

"I wish I had that much hair."

"You can quote Greek and Latin to your hearts content but…"

"Yes I know…"

"Translate it into Scotch. I can help with that, my Scotch is reasonable but you must write it first."

Andricks sighed. "But…"

"Find a way. Or no pet philosopher you. Ah, this is a good place."

They were in the milliner's lane, in front of a shop with glorious highcrowned beaver hats lined up on its shelves, the torches at the front flaring backwards from the wind and the lanterns making ominous shadows.

Carey dived into the shop, having to duck his head once he was inside. Anricks waited outside, anxiously thinking of beginnings for his dissertation, watching the little puppet play in the shop. Carey brought the wounded hat out of the sack, the hatter took it sadly in his hands, turned it round, examined the ropeburn mark across the front and slowly shook his head. Carey looked unhappy and came out.

"He says it can't be mended," Carey said, and stood there with the hat in his hands, turning it.

"I never thought it could."

"Well but…" And Carey fell silent and looked at the ground.

Suddenly Anricks understood. "You need a new one, don't you?"

Carey smiled the smile of a boy who has dropped his sweetmeat in the mud and is now offered the possibility of a new one by his nurse. "Yes, I do, Mr Anricks, but what with the new Court suit…"

Anricks was married to a wonderful woman of character who combined intelligent economy with judicious spending on important items. He rarely had to think about money at all, except when he bought another large load of books, or occasionally an entire library that had been sitting in someone's barn since it was robbed from a monastery. And Rebecca was usually good-humoured about those purchases. Books were sacred to her too, as to all Jews. As he had said to Cecil, he had plenty of money, although he thought Carey could beggar him in a year. Never mind, he thought, it's an investment.

"I don't see how you can wear Court duds and not get the right hat to go with it," he said, reverting to the London speech of his childhood. Together they went back into the hatshop.

***

Janet was counting bushels of grain again while spinning with a dropspindle. She found it soothing, the spread and twist of the oily wool between her fingers, the twirl of the spindle as it went down, pulling and twisting the fibres behind it, and then winding up the wool onto the spindle and repeat. It was one of those handcrafts, like knitting, that you could do with your hands without troubling your mind, once you got the way of it. But she was still worried. She couldn't make the bushels add up to any more than they were, which was not enough. Was it poor old Shilling's death sentence?

At least the weather wasn't as wet and muddy as it had been. It had turned cold in the last few days and there had been a frost the night before which meant they could start harvesting the Brussels sprouts, strange newfangled things they were but they were tasty and a welcome change from cabbage. She left the grain in its wickerlined pits and went out of the store shed and up the ladder to the barnekin wall, where she could walk all along the creaking fighting platform with her thick shawl over her shoulders, her cap pinned on tight against the wind and think.

She tried not to think of Henry who was off in Edinburgh with the Courtier. She couldn't help thinking of him and his soulsickness but really she needed to work out what to do about the Widow Ridley who had come to Gilsland the night before with her grandson and was sleeping in Janet's trucklebed.

The Widow Ridley said she had two tales to tell but had only told one of them. It was confused but it was about Henry and how he had brought in two mysterious bad-mannered strangers, man and master, eaten and drunk, talked for a long while and then gone. Money had changed hands, from the strangers to Henry. Henry had spent the night in her commonroom, along with his great tall horse. There was more but Widow Ridley had been tired and nodding off and so Janet sent her to bed.

"I cam to tell ye, missus, because I thocht ye'd want tae know what yer husband was at and that they were apothecaries or wizards or both and because I'm short of grain maself and could do with some money and I know ye're a fair woman."

Janet considered. Widow Ridley had walked all day to come and tell her and she didn't like the story at all. Who were the men and what were they doing and where were they going and did the money that changed hands have anything to do with the new helmet Dodd had bought a day later. He said he had found the extra money in his doublet pocket after London, which she knew was a lie because she had checked the doublet for money before she brushed it and hung it up filled with sprigs of rosemary and wormwood to clean it out.

She could give Widow Ridley a shilling and she would, but she didn't know what to do. There was nobody to ask. The Courtier was in Edinburgh with her husband, she couldn't ask Lord Scrope because he would patronise her and then forget about it, she couldn't bother Sir Richard Lowther who would probably refuse even to talk to her, Lady Scrope was now with the Queen in London and Lady Widdrington with her odious husband, and Janet knew that most of her gossips like Ellen or Bridget or Rowan or Kate Nixon or even Mrs Hogg would know no better than herself what to do, while the other women around were mostly young and daft or old and set in their ways.

She felt very lonely. Surely Henry was doing something dangerously stupid, quite possibly he was betraying the Courtier, possibly the Grahams had bought him completely to kill Carey. Possibly it was something utterly different to do with the Border.

If Dodd had been bought to kill the Courtier, what should she do? Henry was her husband. If the Courtier was her husband's enemy now, then he was her enemy as well, surely. Except she liked the Courtier and it wasn't just that he always called her Mrs Dodd, rather than Goodwife, or always bowed to her curtsey, and had helped all those months ago with her haying and had looked uncommonly pleasant in his shirt and breeks on her haycart. Well, not entirely.

She paced up and down the fighting platform with her spindle and suddenly realised she had filled it completely with a good thin tight thread and needed to go down the ladder to get a new one and another couple of baskets of lambs-tails too.

She sighed and stared to the north and east. She could say she had come to Edinburgh to buy grain with some of the London money, because the prices in Carlisle were outrageous, and she could go to Richie Graham of Brackenhill and buy well-forged Scotch shillings at eight to the pound sterling, not four, which would help a lot even if the prices in Edinburgh were daft as well, which she suspected they would be. And she could be with Henry over New Year and maybe he wouldn't be as grim and silent as he had been and maybe she could find out what he was up to.

She sighed. It was a serious matter to go to Edinburgh because she had to take the Widow Ridley, which meant a cart, which meant at least four men and herself which wasn't enough for the Middle March, the state it was in. But she felt she must do it: inside her was something that was set like flint and said, "Go to Edinburgh with the Widow Ridley." She hoped it was an angel and not a demon, and then laughed at herself for her phantasy and stepped quickly down the ladder to fetch another spindle.

***

Carey, or rather Anricks, had bought a high-crowned marvel of a beaver hat which he was now wearing and, Anricks had to admit, looked good in. This morning he had tried on the shell at the tailor's, asked detailed questions, suggested a different way of working the armholes to allow easier movement. The tailor promised the new doublet shell by the next day and Carey had narrowed the swatches down to ten, including two possible taffetas for the lining.

Dodd was nowhere to be found which meant Carey was very watchful, was wearing his swordbelt and poinard since he was not in the presence of the King. He and Anricks sauntered along, enjoying the rare watery sunshine although it was cold, and the crowds—not nearly as close-packed as London which was a proper city and Westminster as well, but still respectable. Carey was looking at the way the people were dressed and finding it fascinating. The style was subtly different, especially among the richer merchants, a more Allemayne look. Carey saw many men wearing the peculiar multiply-split cannion breeches called something like plunder-hosen which you now only saw on beggars in London.

On which thought he turned aside to ask something of a storekeeper in such braid Scots, Anricks had to ask what he'd said.

"I'm trying to find a Deutscher for you," said Carey, "but I think they're all at Leith."

As that was the seaport for Edinburgh, it made sense.

Eventually they hired a couple of spavined nags at a branch of Hobson's livery stables, and rode out through the New Port, along the northward road for about three miles, past the golf-course. Leith was pretty much all port and soon they found the Hansa Steelyard with its stockade and small wooden tower and its waterfront and cranes and little church. They had some argument at the gate but were let in and led to a comfortable house where sat a grave-looking solid man with greying short blond hair and a beard behind a desk. He took the letter, refused payment, and gave it to his clerk who hurried off to translate and presumably copy it.

Carey and Anricks sat peacefully on the bench while Carey wondered what form the next attack would take. Man with a knife? Gun? Crossbow? He didn't like the feeling that he had a large white target painted invisibly on his chest, accustomed though he was to the Grahams' antics. For most of that family, it was simply business, perhaps with the exception of Wattie Graham. Spynie seemed more malevolent.

Through the open door he looked at the businesslike people all busy bringing in cargo from the round-hulled ships, packing it onto carts and sending it south on the main road, to Edinburgh. There was only one ship that was taking on cargo, hides, unfinished cloth, some barrels. That was the trouble with Scotland. They didn't make a lot that anybody wanted to buy. Everyone looked very respectable and serious and they clearly didn't let any poorly dressed people inside the gate which Carey approved of. Even the men operating the walking wheels for the cranes were decently clad in good hemp shirts, jerkins, hose and usually boots.

Anricks was scribbling something on some paper with a piece of graphite. Carey took a squint at it from the side and was disappointed. More mathematics, damn it!

"Why is it taking so long?" Carey asked, wondering if they could find any tobacco to drink the smoke of.

Anricks looked up and blinked. "So that they can get it copied to send to their masters in Augsberg or Frankfurt."

"Oh. You don't mind?"

Anricks shook his head. "What can I do about it, I need it translated." He paused and looked out the door. "Maybe I should learn Deutsch."

After a while a younger man in very splendid split plunder-hosen in yellow and blue came and bowed to them both and invited them into another office to discuss their document.

That was a larger office, lined with handsome oak panel-ling that glowed yellow with the sun coming through a glazed window. They were brought wafers and wine while a blond heavyset middle-aged man in a magnificent dark brocade and fur-lined gown sat and read both documents and the young man stood near the door.

"I am Herr Kauffmann Hochstetter, from Augsberg. Vere did you get this?"

For answer, Anricks produced his warrant from Sir Robert Cecil and Hochstetter took it and read it carefully. He gave it back. Carey was starting to feel uneasy. Anricks seemed placid enough but there was something wrong. He started looking for avenues of escape. The prospects weren't good: the little office building was in a fenced-off enclosure around the docks, with one heavy gate, the fence was high and sturdy. He concentrated on looking as elegantly empty-headed as he could.

"Yes," Anricks was saying, "I am a pursuivant for Mr Secretary Cecil."

"And the document?"

"Is from somebody I believe to be a spy but I don't know who for."

"And vat is your interest in this, Mr...ah..." Hochstetter said to Carey.

"Sir Robert Carey, cousin to Her Majesty of England," said Carey languidly, although in fact his ears were working hard. That had set the Allemayne back a little.

"Ja?" he said.

"I am accompanying my friend, Mr Anricks," added Carey blandly, "who is the real expert in these matters..."

"But vere did you find this?" asked Hochstetter with a frown.

"Herr Kauffmann," said Anricks, still patiently, "you already

435

have a copy of it. May I have my own copy of the text back if you prefer not to translate it for me?"

Carey stood up. He had finally identified the sound that had been worrying him.

"Well well," he said beaming fatuously. "This is all very pleasant, but I'm afraid I must be going along now, you'll let us know about it when you've finished the translation, I'm sure, lovely meeting you Herr Kauffmann Hochstetter, very sorry but I must get back to Holyrood House where the King is waiting to play backgammon with me."

Anricks opened his mouth to argue and then stood and bowed to the Herr Kauffmann and let Carey sweep him out into the smaller office, whisking past the young man at the door, across the yard, towards the gate, gently talking all the time while Hochstetter followed them but seemed at a loss to know what to do.

"Don't look back," said Carey in French while he sauntered to the gate, which was open to let some more carts in, and slipped through behind the horses with Anricks in front of him. There was a sound of multiple running footsteps behind them and Carey speeded up to a run, propelled Anricks to his horse, gave him a leg up without asking him, leaped onto his own nag's back and whacked the reins across the animal's withers to wake him up. Moments later they were galloping back down the road from Leith, not very fast admittedly, but at least a bit faster than the running pikemen behind them who soon gave up. Carey laughed uproariously at them and gave them two fingers and a fig over his shoulder, before whacking Anricks' horse across the backside and speeding up. Anricks concentrated on hanging onto the saddle and trying to find the stirrups.

They got back to Edinburgh, returned the sweating animals to Hobson's, and went straight to Holyrood House and to the rooms Carey was using. At least Carey's room was locked although seeing what had happened to Spynie's man, Anricks didn't place too much confidence in that.

He was still breathing hard and sweating as Carey unlocked the door, threw his brand new hat onto a chest and poured himself some Italian red wine. "What made you…?"

"Marching footsteps in the distance, coming towards me," Carey replied, downing his wine in one. Anricks did the same. "I've never liked that sound."

"Me neither," said Anricks, paling further. His fingers on his wine glass were gripping too tight and shaking.

"Next time there's a riot against the Hansa, I'm going to be in it," said Carey. "How dare they try to arrest us?"

"It's urgent to find out what the letter says," said Anricks. "At least I had Tovey make another copy of it…"

"Of course you did, you're not stupid," said Carey. "Come on, let's find the King and break the matter with him."

That was easier said than done—the King was hunting again, but only with his favourite lords and had given strict instructions that he was not to be bothered. Anricks had painstakingly copied out the letter again twice and they stood in an empty antechamber where there was a wealthy-looking man, staring grimly into space and drinking. Carey thought he was one of the Grooms of the Bedchamber.

"Well," said Carey thoughtfully, "we go to the Queen."

"But she's a woman…"

"She's the Queen and she's Danish which is almost Allemayne. Come on!"

Carey led the way with long impatient strides to the other wing of the palace, on the other side of the garden that had been the cloisters, where the Queen's apartments were. He asked humbly at the guarded doors if he could speak to Lady Widdrington very urgently. After a lot of argument, the man-at-arms agreed to ask the lady and after about half an hour, Lady Widdrington appeared at the door with a young Danish girl they hadn't seen before by her side, wearing an informal pink English kirtle, who kept giggling.

Carey, of course, flourished a beautiful bow and Anricks did his best. Lady Widdrington curtseyed but the girl didn't which Anricks thought was rather rude of her.

"I am very sorry to disturb you, my lady, but I have a very serious matter to put to you."

"Oh?"

Carey explained about the packet, the Deutsch text and the way the Allemaynes of the Steelyard in Leith had reacted. Lady Widdrington nodded and smiled. "Well, your...your Deutsch is good, isn't it?" she said to the girl who was staring straight at Carey with great curiosity.

"Not so fery gut, but I vill look," said the girl and took the paper from Anricks with a big smile. Anricks started looking anxious again.

The girl scanned the text, raised her nicely plucked eyebrows and read, "My dear bruder, quickly this is for say your...your plan, your idea of killing Solomon cannot verk and iss wrong and you must instantly stop. I know you my husband betrayed, which I do not forgive, but still my bruder you are and I must try. Do not kill Solomon. My love."

Lady Widdrington blinked at the page. "What does that mean?" she asked.

Carey was looking thunderstruck and also pale. "Solomon?" said Anricks, "Who is Solomon?"

"It could mean the King," he said slowly, "Also of course, any wise man, but it could..."

"Solomon?"

"Well, the King is very wise of course..."

"It iss zee old rudeness," said the girl, looking haughty, "Zat my Royal husband is truly the son of David Riccio, Queen Maria's secretary."

"Your..." began Anricks and then found Carey's hand on his shoulder, pressing him inexorably down to the rushes as Carey himself knelt on one knee.

"Your Highness," said Carey, with his head bowed, "please forgive my intrusion and my stupidity..."

"Stuff ond silliness," said the girl, looking highly delighted, "I made Lady Viddrington bring me with her for she should haf a woman and I vont see the man vat steal her heart and make her sad for she cannot haf you."

Both Carey and Lady Widdrington had gone bright red.

"Now ve should talk, yes? I vil go back, put on a robe and

come out viss my dear Lady Schevengen wot speak Deutsch gut."

She grinned at both of them and slipped through the door.

"We were playing cards," said Lady Widdrington, a little helplessly. "Unfortunately, I got a bit drunk on flower-water last week and…"

Carey was smoothly on his feet again. Anricks stood up and then turned aside as Carey stepped across the space between himself and Lady Widdrington and took her shoulders gently in his hands. "Please…" he breathed. "Please…" The man-at-arms was tactfully staring into space.

Lady Widdrington put her hands up to Carey's neck and pulled his head fiercely down to hers. Anricks didn't know what happened next because he made sure he didn't see and stood staring at a painting of some Greek gods in the Italian style and thought longingly of his Rebecca with her plump belly and stretch marks and wonderful soft dark hair.

"Well," said Lady Widdrington half laughing, "that tastes much better than last time…mmmm…"

Carey hadn't spoken and they were busy again until Anricks heard some loud thumps on the other side of the door and coughed loudly.

By the time the Queen came through the door in a magnificent purple velvet gown with her hair up and her cap arranged to show some of her smooth blond hair, followed by a stout matron in cramoisie who seemed to be complaining at length in Danish, Carey and Lady Widdrington were again at a decorous distance. There was only a distinct nibblemark on Carey's lower lip to show that anything had happened at all.

"Now zen," said the Queen, looking even more pleased with herself, "ve go in ze parlour."

They went to a panelled room nearby, filled with chairs and cushions and some little tables and some of the Queen's women were there, disposed gracefully. Carey smiled at all of them and bowed, told them not to bother getting up to curtsey because he was only paying tribute to their combined beauty and virtue. Some of them giggled at that.

The Queen called for sweetmeats and some Danish drink, as

well as candles as the sky darkened, and sat herself down in the chair with arms that had the Scottish cloth of estate with the Danish royal arms impaled.

Carey and Anricks went back on one knee but the Queen told them rather irritably to stop all that English nonsense. They sat on padded stools instead and a girl brought round a tray with little Venetian glasses on it, filled with a clear liquid. Everyone took a glass, including Carey and Anricks, and then stood and clinked the glasses together, the Queen shouted "To My Lord and King and husband!" and tipped it back in one.

Everybody else shouted "Prost!" and also tipped the liquid back, so Carey did the same as did Anricks. Simon found his throat gripped by a fiery hand. When he managed to breathe out again, he found there was a delightful scent of peaches that came with the fumes, as if he had become a dragon breathing a summer day.

"Mm," said Carey appreciatively, "what is that wonderful drink, Your Highness?"

"Schnapps," said the Queen happily, and leaned forward with a black bottle. "You like?"

"Yes, yes, I do," said Carey and got another little glassful.

"Zo. Lady Schevengen is much better at Deutsch than I and she says viss me on the meaning. Zo. If Solomon is my Royal husband, zen he is in danger. How did you catch ze letter?"

Anricks explained carefully that he had left the original packet in a jakes at a Scottish alehouse, drunk a pint of good beer there and left. The alehouse was dark and crowded and he had watched but no one came to pick it up while he was there.

"You are a spy. Do you hef a varrant?"

Anricks handed over the letter from Cecil and again opened his hands to show the scars across his palms.

"Ah," said the Queen, "I know vot zet is, you ver in ze galleys."

Anricks bowed. "Your Highness is very perceptive."

The Queen looked at him beadily. "Ven?"

"1588."

"Ssank you Mr Anricks, I vil not trobble you about it again. Now, Sir Robert, do you haf a plan. Lady Viddrington says you alvays haf a plan."

440

"Not yet, Your Highness."

"You vill—zo Lady Viddrington says sometimes you plans go wrong, eh?"

"That's certainly true, Your Highness," said Carey with a scoundrel's smile, "for instance, last summer a plan of mine to scout out Netherby tower to find out why the Grahams were stealing so many horses went very badly wrong indeed."

The Queen put her head on one side and half closed her eyes.

"Go on!" she said imperiously.

So Carey told the story of how he had treed himself on the top of Netherby tower with the nefarious reiver Jock o' the Peartree Graham as his prisoner—and how that meant he found out that Bothwell and the Grahams were planning to raid Falkland palace and kidnap the King and that he had spiked Bothwell's guns by telling Jock all about the wonderful horses kept around Falkland palace.

He told it well, with becoming modesty and an eye for the ridiculous, even telling how Jock had tricked him. The Queen first giggled and then shouted with laughter. "I vundered how so few men ve had could beat off so many raiders. How fonny. Zey stole ze horses and not the King."

"Yes Your Highness. But my plans don't usually go quite that wrong."

Lady Widdrington stared at him severely when he said that and he reddened again.

"Not usually!" he protested.

"It's a fery fonny story," said the Queen judiciously as she poured herself more schnapps. "Now vot can ve do about zis maybe plot against my husband."

"There are two things we must do," said Carey with decision. "Firstly, we must make His Highness of Scotland aware..."

"But he vill be so frightened," protested the Queen.

"Er...Your Highness?" said Carey, honestly nonplussed.

"He gets fery frightened about sings like ziss," said the Queen, "And he...vell, it iss not gut for him to be so frightened."

Carey was staring at her, his brows knitting. Anricks realised that he really could not understand the idea of an adult male and a King being frightened of anything, much less admitting it, so before he said something disastrous, Anricks put in, "Also, we don't actually know that Solomon means the King. But I feel you should increase the number of guards around him, double up the tasters in the kitchen and so on."

The Queen nodded firmly. "Yes, ziss I can do. I vill write to him and say I haf had a bad dream and he must be fery careful."

Anricks wondered if she had been listening.

"Well perhaps…"

"Und I vill summon my Lord Maitland of Thirlstane, the Lord Chancellor, and put zis in his hands," said the Queen. "Ziss too I can do. Perhaps I vill ask my scryer as vell. Whose is the plot?"

"Oh, I think that's obvious, Your Highness," said Carey. "Ultimately."

"Yes?"

"The King of Spain is at his tricks again and this is also a plot against England."

"Go on."

"Her Majesty of England is now…ahem…over fifty years old…"

"Fifty-nine, I sink."

"Er…yes. She will not have a child of her body. Forgive me for my tactlessness, but the King does not have an heir of his body yet either."

The Queen looked down, coloured and nodded sadly. "Iss true," she whispered.

"No matter," said Carey with a shining smile, "By the grace of God I am certain you will soon have a lovely little prince— but there's the weakness. At the moment nobody in England is too worried about the Queen's age because they have got used to her childlessness. They know that no matter what she says, His Highness of Scotland will eventually inherit the throne of England."

The Queen nodded, her lips firming. "He iss looking forward to it fery much."

I'll bet he is, thought Carey but didn't say it. "Now imagine what would happen in England if His blessed Highness were to be assassinated?"

The Queen nodded. "No heir. Only Philip of Spain."

"And Arbella, God help us, and a few others. Here in Scotland it would be the most terrible, the most tragic blow, from which God preserve us, but in England…? Civil war. And then Spain comes in, perhaps from the north, and we are too busy fighting each other to fight the Spanish."

Suddenly Anricks realised something: the traces Cecil had seen *had* been a plot, the thing was true; the sea monster was sticking his head out of the water to show he was not a mere phantasy. In fact it was a bigger monster than they had realised, a shrewder and more dangerous secret blow against England and Scotland both. At least he was not wasting his time.

"Vould the English be so stupid?" the Queen was asking.

"Yes, Your Highness, we would," said Carey positively, "so we must assume that the person to be assassinated is His Royal Majesty and find out how the deed is to be done and who the immediate plotters are."

"Off course. Do you know how to do zat?"

"No, Your Highness, I don't. But I'm sure something will come to me. It usually does."

"Mm. Ass long as ve can, ve do not tell the King, understand? You do not know how he is, he gets so frightened and he remembers his fosterfazher assassinated and his beloved D'Aubigny poisoned, and all the people who haf been killed around him and zen he cannot be Kingly. He iss a merciful and gentle prince, but not a fighting man, understand?" Carey bowed to her from his stool. "Understand, Sir Robert?"

"Your Highness, I…yes."

"Ass long ass ve can, ve keep ziss quiet. Also it is better if the assassins do not know that we know."

"True. You will consult my Lord Maitland?"

"Off course. I vill do it now." She sent one of the younger girls off to fetch a clerk and dictated a letter to Lord Maitland, telling him of the problem.

"Will the letter be ciphered?" asked Anricks.

"Off course. Grigory is a good cipher clerk, he takes dictation straight to code."

Anricks looked at the finished letter and found a simple substitution code that he thought he could break in under an hour, but said nothing.

They drank confusion to the Spanish in more schnapps and then the Queen announced that she was tired and so there was a gathering up of embroidery and a piling up of cushions as the procession formed to go back to the Queen's Privy Chambers.

Carey escorted them to the double doors, bowed elaborately to all the women, even the fat ones, so he could bow as elaborately to Lady Widdrington. He went on one knee to kiss the Queen's hand and she blushed and giggled. She was eight years younger than the King and sometimes it showed.

At last it was all finished and Carey came over to Anricks and blew his lips out like a horse. Then he grinned like a schoolboy.

"I've just had an idea."

Anricks had not yet learned to be cautious when Carey said that and so he smiled back. "What is it?"

"Come with me, we can soon find out if it will fly."

And Carey started striding away on his long legs like a heron so Anricks was forced to trot to keep up.

"Don't you think it's a bit late..." he puffed.

"No, this is the perfect time," said Carey blandly, increasing speed.

***

They came to a new set of apartments, this time made out of the monks' old dorter, but quite a long way from the magnificently decorated apartments of the King. Carey sauntered up to the handsome lad on guard at the door and said to him breezily, "I want to see my Lord Spynie right now, in a matter of national importance. Go get him, there's a good fellow."

The lad scuttled off, his eyes big and Carey leaned against the wall where there was a tapestry. "He will keep us waiting," he said. "Do you want to go to your bed, Mr Anricks?"

Anricks would have slept on the floor to see this. He shook his head. "Do you think this is wise?" he asked and got the same look Lady Widdrington had got when she had asked him if scouting Netherby tower dressed as a peddler was wise.

"No, I don't think this is wise," said Carey, "if by wise you mean never doing anything out of the ordinary. However I don't want to try and protect the King while also having to look over my shoulder for more fancy attempts on my life. So this is expedient. Who knows what will happen?"

They waited. Carey started wandering around the ante-chamber looking at the paintings and sculptures, some of which were scandalous.

"How long will he keep us waiting?"

"Could be an hour if he needs to get dressed again."

Anricks wondered if he had made the right decision or if he would have to sleep on the floor after all. It was already past ten o'clock.

"Is his wife or mistress there?" Anricks asked naively and Carey laughed.

"He's probably sending the younger boys to bed."

"Boys?" asked Anricks and sighed heavily.

"Ay," said Carey, making a grimace of distaste.

They waited a while longer and then Carey found a back-gammon set on a windowsill and they sat down to play.

After five minutes, Carey offered Anricks a penny a point which Anricks insisted should be notional pennies only, for honour alone. This was just as well because Carey started losing heavily and by the time Spynie's guard finally came back, he owed Anricks several purely notional pounds.

The young guard cleared his throat and said that Sir Robert and his man might enter the parlour where Lord Spynie would meet him.

"One moment," said Carey and hopped his men along to what he was sure was a devastating triumph, only to find that he had been neatly trapped.

"Mr Anricks," he said, "who taught you backgammon?"

"An African prince named Snake. I taught him chess. He usually beat me at both games."

"You play chess? We must play some games."

"I prefer the game with no dice and the puissant queen…"

"So do I, especially as it is in compliment to Her Majesty…"

"No, it isn't. It compliments Queen Isabella of Castile on the occasion when she marched her men across country to rescue King Ferdinand of Aragon…"

Spynie's man gave an offended cough and Carey looked up. "Oh, yes," he said, "My Lord is ready? How splendid." He unhurriedly put away the men, closed the box up and put it back on the windowsill. "By the way, Mr Anricks is not my man, he is a philosopher of independent means and he is here to take part in a learned dispute."

Spynie was waiting in the parlour, wearing a blindingly flashy suit of red and tawny velvet, slashed with yellow satin and around him were six youths in his livery, in varying attitudes of toughness, one actually paring his nails with a long poinard.

Carey took the scene in and smiled indulgently, while favouring Spynie with the barest shadow of a bow. "Dear me," he said softly, "were you worried I was going to come and take revenge for your ridiculously incompetent attempt at killing me during the hunt yesterday? Which did me no harm but killed one of the King's best horses?"

Spynie looked uncomfortable. "You aren't?"

"No, no, my dear fellow," said Carey with his eyebrows up, "it's all part of the game, isn't it? And you've tidied up the man we caught in the forest with a garrott, so there are no potential witnesses that can speak against you." The young tough who was using his poinard to pare his fingernails slipped and blood burst from his thumb. He rushed out of the room, sucking furiously at the wound.

"Such a palaver over one blond boy. Have you seen him recently? He's done some growing."

Interestingly Spynie flushed.

"No need for all your roaring boys," said Carey, waving

his fingers negligently in their direction, "this is much more important."

"Sir Henry Widdrington..."

"I know, it's very sweet how you treat your elderly lover, poor old man. I'll deal with Sir Henry in my own time and at a place of my choosing. Now would yould lke to hear something interesting that may be about your sometime lover, the King?"

Spynie shrugged.

"This is from a packet of papers uncovered by a friend of mine after all sorts of adventures," lied Carey. "We don't know who it is from or who it is addressed to, but the meat of it is as follows." He gestured at Anricks who started reading the translated letter. At the mention of killing Solomon, Spynie stopped looking deliberately bored and sat up.

"Is that about the King?" he asked.

"I don't know," said Carey, with interest. "Is it?"

"What do you mean...?"

"Well it could be your own plot to kill the King, couldn't it?"

"Don't be stupid, of course Ah wouldna kill the King..."

"You're no longer his minion, are you? Maybe you are resentful. Maybe the King of Spain has bought you..."

Spynie drew his poinard and advanced on Carey who drew his sword and stood *en garde*. "Careful," he said very quietly, "I'm not manacled in a cellar this time."

Spynie stopped, breathing hard. "I would never..." he began, "Never. I love him. Do you understand? I love him. If he doesna love me, that's hard, but I still love him."

"Really?"

"Ay," said Lord Spynie bleakly, "really." He sheathed his poinard and took a cup of wine. "Ah would die for him." It was not said with any bluster, but quite matter of factly.

Carey paused and then put up his own weapon. "Then help me find the plotters and kill them," he said.

Spynie swallowed some wine and nodded once. "Read it again," he ordered Anricks who did so without complaint.

"The letter was written in Deutsch and was sent to Edinburgh," said Carey. "I can't tell you any more about it because it was collected from a jakes in an alehouse called the Maker's Mark and I don't know who collected it."

"Have ye told the King?" asked Spynie, biting his thumbnail.

"The King has been hunting all day. We have told the Queen who has written to Maitland. She asked us not to tell the King yet."

Spynie nodded. "Ay," he said, "that's better, much better."

Carey's eyebrows were almost at his hairline but he said nothing.

"Ye've nae idea who?"

"Of course not," said Carey, "or he would already be dead. Oh, speaking of that, we put the unfortunate servant you ordered to try and kill me, into the Lough. He was already dead from being garrotted, I assume by somebody you hired."

Spynie was abstracted and just nodded absently at this.

"I assume that's all right?" said Carey, not looking at any of the henchmen.

Spynie shrugged. "And it's not just another kidnapping, he's tae die. If Solomon is the King."

"Who else could he be?"

"I dinna ken another man named Solomon."

"Perhaps you could use your resources to find who is to do the deed?" suggested Carey in a thin voice. "After all, My Lord, you know the Scottish Court much better than I do. Perhaps ask around?"

"Ay," said Spynie, "Ah can dae that."

"And tell me what you find. It's important to share information in these cases."

Spynie shrugged again. He was deep in thought or what passed for thought in his case. Carey turned his back on the man and went to the door.

"Sir Robert," said Spynie in an oddly strangled voice, "Ah…"

"Yes, My Lord?"

"Ah…thankye for telling me."

For answer Carey bowed shallowly to the company and left, followed at a trot by Anricks.

They hurried back through the sleeping palace to Carey's

rooms. Carey needed help with the points of his doublet, gave up trying to wake Hughie so Anricks untied them and then undressed himself without help since he had never bothered with a valet in his life, apart from when he was at home and wearing something complicated and civic. Then he spent some time using a toothpick and polishing his teeth with a toothcloth and salt.

"Is that a good defence against toothworms?" Carey wanted to know.

"Yes, I believe it is the only defence because it removes their invisible eggs," said Anricks who had worked up a very satisfactory theory about toothworms and desperately wanted to tell someone. And so Anricks must instruct him in the use of the silver toothpick and rough cloth while explaining his theory and he continued explaining while Carey got into the main bed, complained that his teeth felt peculiar, rolled over and fell asleep.

***

Lord Spynie was lying awake in bed. His tussle with Jeremy had not been a success and the young man had finally given up trying, turned on his side and gone to sleep. Spynie was staring up at the tester while the voices ran round his head. Could it be? It couldn't be. But the Maker's Mark? No, surely not. But that was Hepburn's usual alehouse. Lots of people went there, Spynie did himself, it had good beer, and a very good ordinary, mainly pies with flaky pastry. Hepburn was so helpful, so respectful, so convenient. Look at the way he had dealt with Spynie's abortive attempt at killing that bloody man, Carey. Just because whoever received the letter must be a regular at the Maker's Mark, didn't mean...

But what if it did? What if Spynie was closely associated with a man who needed to be told not to kill Solomon? What then?

Spynie turned over for the fourth time and tried to think. What could he do? Maybe ask Hepburn, forbid him...No, don't be ridiculous. If he truly was trying to kill the King, why would he listen to Spynie? In fact, if Spynie had realised what he was

449

trying to do, might he not kill Spynie himself? He was good at that, after all.

Spynie actually put his fist in his mouth to stop himself from crying out. He wanted to protect the King, but suddenly, now it came to it, his bowels had gone to water and his head was spinning. This wasn't what he had meant when he had said he would die for the King. He wasn't sure what he had meant, but whatever it was, it wasn't this.

And maybe Hepburn was innocent. Maybe he really was just a mining engineer from Keswick where a lot of them spoke Deutsch...

Oh God.

Spynie turned over again. I'm ill, he thought frantically, I'm sick, I'm not well. I'll keep my chamber. I'm feeling sick and I need to shit, I'm ill.

Deep inside him was a better part which said he should get up, collect his henchmen and arrest Hepburn tonight. He ignored it, as he always did, and soon the little voice quietened.

He couldn't sleep, though.

***

Young Hutchin Graham had found a dairymaid at Court who would let him suck her tits and was very happily doing that in the back of the palace dairy while doing his best to sneak his other hand up under her kirtle. She spotted him, smacked it down and slapped his face. "I told ye, only above the waist!" she said, popping the tit out of Hutchin's mouth and stuffing it back into her stays. "No more fun and games for ye today, young fellerme lad."

"Whit about tomorrow?" asked Young Hutchin pathetically, and got another slap.

"Ah'm no' gaunae spoil myself for a reiver and that's that, so ye can tek what I gi' ye or go sell yer bum tae Spynie."

"I wouldnae do that," protested Hutchin. "Whit dae I want wi' a man, it's girls I like, two of them fer choice, in the one bed and then Ah could suck the tits of one and the other..."

The third slap resounded and Hutchin's head bounced lightly off the wall while Mary, if that was her name, flounced off. Hutchin sighed because Mary had very nice plump white breasts and enjoyed him sucking them.

He got up and limped out of the dairy towards the stables where he checked on the horses and found Dodd there as well, seeing after Whitesock for the night. Dodd grunted at him and kept on brushing the horse down, though his coat was already like satin.

"Whit's wrong wi' ye, Sergeant," Young Hutchin asked cheekily, knowing he was risking a serious buffet and getting ready to dodge. "Ye've not said mair than four words all the time we've been here and none o' them wis thanks, yer face is like the rainy day they'll hang ye on and ye punched Red Sandy yestereven for nothing mair than asking ye how ye were."

Dodd grunted again and didn't answer, so Hutchin took the precaution of climbing up onto one of the hayracks and added, "Are ye still sulking over they Elliots, eh?"

Dodd's face tightened and became even darker. "I am not sulking."

"Well at least I've doubled yer count of words. And by the way, ye are sulking, my Aunt Netty used tae sulk jest like that, drove my Uncle Jim wild it did, for ye couldnae get anything oot o' her of why, jest grunts and a shoulder and sour looks, ay, like that one yer giving me now, though I ken verra well it's just the Elliots."

Dodd grunted and went to Whitesock's other side.

"And ye willna drink wi' anybody and when yer eating ye willna say anything and…"

The tail was taking Dodd's attention now. Whitesock snorted and tipped a hoof. Unusually among horses, he liked having his tail seen to and never kicked out over it.

"Ye shouldnae ha' punched Red Sandy," pronounced Young Hutchin from the very top of the hayrack. "It disnae matter if ye sulk at the Courtier, but Red Sandy's yer blood and he means well. And I know two more families of the Elliots came in to compose as they dinna like the Courtier's fancy ways wi' besieging and they don't want it tae happen to them and he's got his warrant oot of it."

Dodd gave Whitesock a carrot. "Finished?" he asked.

"Nine," said Young Hutchin triumphantly. "I dinna wonder at ye petting yer horse so, he's the only friend ye'll have left, ye fool, how the devil will ye get yer surname to back ye if ye've punched every one o' them?"

Dodd paused and then started fiddling with Whitesock's mane. The hobbies doubled up in the two nearest stalls were watching cynically, you could almost hear them tutting.

"Ye dinna understand," Dodd managed to say.

"Ye're telling me I've nae feuds? I'm a Graham, ye're telling me I dinna ken about feuds and battle and killing? I'm a Graham."

"Have ye killed yer man yet, Young Hutchin?"

"Not sure," said Hutchin, his eyes like slits. "Mebbe. I stuck him wi' me dagger, mebbe he lived, mebbe not, the bastard."

"Ah wis younger nor ye the first time I killed a man, I knowed he was deid because he bent over and all red shining blood cam oot of his mouth and ma friend got the ither one right in the back and so we got away."

"Ay?"

"We were happy, laughing and then later Daniel said, d'ye think he wis married and I said I didna know nor care and then later…well, I thought about it."

"What was it started the old feud up again."

Dodd sighed. "Three sheep and a cow that went missing fra the Elliots' herds and so they raided us for our cattle and my dad killed Wee Colin Elliot's dad wi' his lance."

"Good work," said Young Hutchin. "And then it was a blood-feud, o' course."

"Ay."

"But ye won, did ye no'? They had to come in and compose?"

"Ay."

"So what's changed since then?"

Dodd wouldn't answer that and walked out of the stable, wishing he hadn't said so much to Young Hutchin. It was true. The Elliots had come into the West March of England as part of a trap to catch the Courtier, but so far as he knew, they had not raided the Dodds since the peace.

But they were Elliots. That was the trouble right there, they were Elliots and he hated every one of them, severally and collectively. They were Elliots and he could still hear them laughing as they cut the throats of his uncles and his cousins.

He would have given a lot for a pipeful of Moroccan incense and tobacco which made him feel so peaceful, as he stood by the door of the stables and listened to Young Hutchin trotting briskly about, talking nonsense to the horses, bringing them their nighttime buckets of water.

Good God, he had forgotten to give Whitesock his bucket. He went in and found Hutchin had watered the horse along with the others, and so he walked out again. The ball of black rage was still sitting there in his stomach making his meat taste of nothing, dust and ashes in his mouth, and for the first time in his life he wondered if he was the only one who had it. Did other men not have it? For example, the Courtier, did he have such a thing?

Well, I'm damned, he thought bleakly, I know that, why wouldn't I have a black ball of rage in my gut? God, I wish I could have a pipe of tobacco.

Hutchin wandered out and nodded at him. "Now then, Sergeant," he said, as if they hadn't had a conversation, which Dodd appreciated. He got his tongue and voicebox to work. "Good night, Young Hutchin," he said gruffly.

"I'm no' sure," said Young Hutchin, "but I think that makes fifty words." And he disappeared into the night.

***

Janet watched Widow Ridley with her fluffy white hair around her grubby cap like a starburst as she put herself on the outside of a meat and onion pie with vigour, despite having only two teeth, one on each side of her mouth, to bite with. She managed with a great deal of mumbling and sucking.

"Now," she said, "I've minded me of the other tale I came to tell ye."

453

"Ay," said Janet absent-mindedly. She was thinking that this particular batch of meat pies wasn't one of her best and was wondering why.

"These men that spoke to Sergeant Dodd and gave him money, Ah'd seen them before, so I had."

"Oh?" Across the hall table, Janet caught the two girls' eyes and reminded them with her eyebrows that they were to clear the trenchers that hadn't been eaten, and the piecrusts, and clear the jacks and wipe the tables and take the leavings to the chickens. They sighed in unison and got up to do it.

"Ay," said Widow Ridley, taking another sup of her ale. She had a powerful taste for ale, did the Widow Ridley for this was her third jackful. She didn't look at all drunk though. "They passed along the Giant's Road, west to east, a couple of weeks ago, with a cart and three more men and in the cart were strange magical things. There were strange leaden tanks that sloshed and slopped and there were things ye use for distilling like pelicans and tubes and heavy leather gloves wi' chainmail on them, all wrapped in sacks."

"How do you know?"

Widow Ridley chucked. "I wis curious, so I looked," she said. "Now one o' the tanks had sprung a leak at a corner and fra the hole dripped oily stuff that had a magic spell upon it for it made steam and smoke arise fra the cart bottom where it dropped. I just happened to dip my finger in it, by accident, ye ken, and then my finger was on fire wi' invisible flames so Ah had to wash it off wi' water and it wis covered in blisters for a week and more and it's no' right yet." She waved a red finger at Janet. "The men carefully poured this oily stuff into two round bowls they had with them, propped them on the cart and then set up a fire and mended the leaden tank and tested it wi' water from ma well and then poured off the water and it had taken the magic for didn't it burn the weeds around my jakes so they havenae come back yet. And then they poured the oily stuff back in the tank and fixed the leaden lid upon it again."

"How long did all this take?"

"Two days and they paid me for it, five shillings I got,

English, and then they went on eastwards and they didna tell me where they wis going but I heard one o' them say, Edinburgh. So now."

And she sat back and held out her jack for more ale.

"That's a very interesting tale," said Janet. "Are ye saying the men were up to mischief in Edinburgh?"

"Why else were they so close-mouthed about where they wis going. I asked 'em four times and they told me lies each time, until I wis sitting in the jakes and heard them by accident. What's they men that try to make gold?"

"Miners?"

"No," said Widow Ridley, her voice far away, "though…"

"Alchemists."

"Ay, that's it. Alchemisty things they were and now I think of it, I've heard they furriners down in Keswick speak like that cos they wis all speaking furrin with coughs and gasps, but then he spoke to me in English, quite Christianlike."

"He?"

"The man that gave Sergeant Dodd money."

Janet waited for the inevitable. "And they had funny hose on and they had tails."

"Did they?"

"Ay, and then off they went along the Giant's Road, talking furrin again."

"And the alchemist…"

"Bought yer man, Mrs Dodd, ay."

"Are ye sure?"

Widow Ridley bent over with laughter. "Ay, o'course, I know the look of a man being bought."

It struck Janet that placed where she was, the Widow Ridley may have had more custom than you might think and might also know a lot of smugglers.

Janet smiled very kindly at her and brought her a jug of her best ale. "Mrs Ridley," she said, promoting her from Goodwife, "I should have talked to you long ago."

"Ay. Cheers."

"Can ye think of anything else about this alchemist?"

"Ay," said Widow Ridley thoughtfully, "everything smelled nasty, kind of metal and sour. He was a nice-looking lad wi' curly brown hair and grey eyes, quite square of the face, calls hisself Hepburn."

What on earth did they have in the tanks? "And they were going to Edinburgh?"

"Unless I heard wrong. Which I might of, see ye, ma hearing's not what it was."

"Had you ever seen such things before?"

"Nay."

"Thank you for telling me all this, Mrs Ridley, though I'm not sure what to do with it."

"Yer man's mixed up wi' a witch and an alchemist. Ye should fare tae Edinburgh and fetch him back home before he gets in trouble. They're fools, men are, allus going after the latest bauble. Go after him and fetch him back, like Janet did in Tam Lin."

Janet smiled.

"Will you come with me, Mrs Ridley?"

For answer, Widow Ridley stretched out her hand. Janet put two shillings English into it. Widow Ridley examined the money carefully, then put it in her stays.

"Ay," she said, "Ah'd like tae know what they witches is at."

***

Carey faced with a mystery and nothing to get hold of, concentrated on the only thing he could.

He started by looking for Allemaynes. Apart from the ones at the Steelyard whom he didn't want to tangle with again without a squad of pikemen at his back, there weren't many. He had just come from the Tollbooth where they had the records of foreigners, mostly reputable merchants like Herr Kauffmann Hochstetter, or gunsmiths. He had followed up one lead and found a small house full of blond young men who invited him to join them for a beer and then gave him some extraordinary light-coloured beer which was weak as to flavour and quite weak as to the booze as well. It tasted…interesting. They were trying to start a brewery to make more but admitted they hadn't got very far.

"Ve haf gut beer but not enuf," said one of them seriously, and Carey agreed that it was a serious problem and went in search of more Allemaynes. For completeness he looked for Frenchmen as well and found a few and talked to them happily in French, enjoying the beautiful music of the language and the memories of the beautiful women who had taught him so much, some of it French.

He went back to the Court, found the King was hunting again and Anricks was talking to John Napier incomprehensibly about mathematics. He decided that Edinburgh was boring and he was bored and furthermore at a stand with the problem of who might want to kill the King and how, so he went out again to the best inn in town and decided to get as drunk as he could on the basis that this might make something happen.

He got into a game of cards with some men from the King's troop, they were gunners and talking about cannonball weights and mortars and the terribleness of the serpentine powder they were supposed to use. When he put the question to them of how do you kill someone specific with gunpowder, they loved it.

"Ay, it's easy to kill a lot of anybody," said one of the gunners called Peter, "but killing one somebody is harder."

"Nay, it's no'," snorted another gunner called Mick, "ye just use a lot and mek sure the gunpowder is under the floor of his bedroom."

"Didna work wi' Darnley, did it?"

"No, but they had it under the wrong room."

"What about the fuse?" asked Carey. "It might go out."

"Use several," said a gunner called Harry. "Ye'd need to anyway."

"So maybe your man is suspicious and they search the cellars."

Peter shrugged. "Naething better than a fireworks display— all the gunpowder there. People are strange. If it's labelled fireworks, naebody thinks it's gunpowder."

Now that was interesting. "Does the King like fireworks?"

"Ay he does, though he disna like guns, ye ken. There's allus a fireworks display at Court at Christmas or New Year's," said Mick. "The Queen loves 'em. Every Christmas if it's no' pouring wi' rain, or New Years' if it was, there's rockets and all sorts let off fra the gardens of the palace. The people come to watch fra outside though they can't see everything so good as the King."

"And he's not worried about the bangs?" asked Carey, betting on a chorus and losing to a better chorus.

"Och he's nowhere near 'em, he's at the front looking over the courtyard and there's all mermaids and centaurs doing dances and the fireworks are just a part of it."

Changing his mind about getting drunk, Carey went and talked to the firework makers who were in the process of setting up the racks and cages at the other end of the garden, well away from anything that could burn. He watched the strange yellow family with slits for eyes filling tubes with gunpowder and paper and mysterious glittery powders, and watched some men measuring out the lawns and hammering in stakes where the benches would be.

He talked to everybody, trying to get a picture of how you could kill a nervous King who wouldn't have any kind of blade or weapon in his presence. It was surprisingly hard now he thought of it, but it must be possible.

He even spoke to the Lord Chamberlain, and was thoroughly patronised. "Any man in the room, ay, and some of the women too would give their lives for His Highness..."

"Yes, of course, but..."

"That letter, which Maitland told me about, says dinna kill Solomon."

"Who else could Solomon be?"

"It is a foul calumny on the honour of Queen Mary..."

"Of course, but..."

"We've men doing naething but guarding him. We've asked at the Steelyard and Herr Kauffman Hochstetter has nae idea who it could be—they don't want the King dead either."

"Of course not. There would be chaos..."

"Ah dinna see what else we can do," concluded the Lord Chamberlain, with a superior little smile. "The King is safe."

You could try and use your imagination, Carey thought, considering what his own father, Lord Chamberlain Hunsdon, would be doing down in London if he had a warning like that. *Oh sorry, you don't have an imagination.* Based on something that had happened once at Kenilworth a long time ago when he was a lad, Carey went back and asked the firework makers if you could aim a rocket for the King.

"Well, ye could, if ye knew in advance where he was gaunae be, but the King likes to move around and so likely as not ye'd end up killing somebody else and ye wouldnae get a second chance."

"Could you not bring a gun into the Court and fire it under cover of the explosions from the fireworks?"

"Ay, ye could, if ye can get one in range, but he doesnae like anyone near him he doesnae ken and certainly naebody with a gun, he really doesnae like that and I heard tell he has armour under his clothes which is why he willna shift his shirt."

"Really?"

"Ay, it's ainly chainmail they say, but it's good and fine and it'll keep knives and spears off. Not bullets though unless they're from a distance. And guns are terrible for accuracy. A pistol maybe, but ye'd need to be up close and it's verra hard for anybody he doesnae know to get sae close."

Carey was thinking of King James with new respect—he had clearly put some careful thought into not getting murdered like so many of his ancestors.

***

Dodd found that Young Hutchin Graham had seemingly attached himself to him and so Dodd, who was bored at Court and really only needed to attend Carey when he went hunting, paced around Holyrood with the boy, who was interested in Lord Spynie's rooms and while following Dodd was less noticeable and less vulnerable.

He found them, like most Royal apartments, to be a series of rooms leading into each other with an antechamber and a single set of double doors giving entrance at one end and a small spiral staircase for the servants at the other. He haunted the servants' end of the rooms and was kicked out twice and then came to Dodd who was waiting in the courtyard for him, shaking his head.

"Ay, it's too hard to get to him in his bed."

"Unless ye sell yer arse."

"I've been talking to Crispin, the youngest of his henchmen, down in the buttery, and they all have to sit around in his parlour of an evening, playing lute or cards or some such, and then he picks one of them tae gae to bed with, and it's usually different, though half the time it's Jeremy, the biggest one."

"Ay," said Dodd, considering, "are ye thinking of killing him or warning him?"

"Killing him," said Young Hutchin, "o' course."

"Well he didna kill you. Nor any of yourn."

"So what?"

"So mebbe ye could try warning him, or frightening him."

"Why?"

"If ye kill him, ye'll likely hang for it. D'ye want that?"

"Ah will no', I'll get away wi' it…"

"Ye might, sure. But this is Edinburgh and ye've a powerful long way back to the Graham lands and if ye kill Lord Spynie, I'm thinking the King will be a tad mithered wi' ye."

"I'm mithered wi' Spynie."

"Ay," said Dodd drily, "but it'll take ye longer tae die when they hang ye. Think about it."

"Well what else can I do? I've come all this way and spent a ton of money on this."

"Ay, and boasted about it."

Hutchin didn't answer that. "Well? Are ye saying I shouldna kill him nor knife him nor beat him up…"

Dodd sighed. "I'm saying ye canna. Ye're nobbut a reiver and ye havenae the men nor the way of getting at him. He's got henchmen, ye havenae. He's rich, ye're not. He's the King's Minion and ye're the son of Hutchin Graham, that got caught and hanged two years ago for reiving the Fenwicks' cattle and killing two of their men."

Young Hutchin's face got longer and sourer. "Ye're saying I canna…"

"I am. Let it be. Come back when ye're older and…"

"Would ye say that about the Elliots?"

"It's different."

"I may not get the chance again. Mebbe I'll be dead by next year like me dad?"

"Ay," said Dodd, staring into space, "that's likely."

"Ye're useless," snarled Young Hutchin. "I willna. I'll get him somehow."

He marched off with his head held high and Dodd shrugged and started whittling a piece of firewood with his knife.

***

Nobody could just up and go a hundred miles to Edinburgh from Carlisle, unless you were a young man riding post. It took complicated organisation and a lot of people. First Janet called on her younger brother, Geordie, at a loose end at her father's tower, to come and run Gilsland for her in her absence. She gave him a long list of things he must do or not do: what if she wasn't back in a month, what if they got raided although he protested he knew all about that—and made him repeat the list three times. Then she got hold of her sister-in-law, another Eliza, and gave her a longer list of things she needed to cope with, including getting the flax retted when it was ready because that was the only crop not ruined by the wet weather and she was very glad she had planted so much of it. Eliza was young but steady and seemed to have good sense whereas her brother Geordie was as flighty as a maid, like all men.

If she had been a man she might have ridden over to Keswick where the Allemayne miners were and asked some questions, but Keswick was sixty miles in the wrong direction entirely and she didn't have the time.

Widow Ridley was charmed at the idea of going on a trip to Edinburgh for the first time in her life and sent her grandson ten miles there and back to her inn to lock it up properly and get her best kirtle and hat and some other things. She couldn't ride any more, of course, but Janet knew they would need a cart anyway and she could sit on that. At least the weather was frosty and looked set to stay that way which had hardened up the mud. They would go on the drovers roads, winding through the hills until they got to Hawick and then they would continue over the main road from the south to Edinburgh.

Janet couldn't empty Gilsland in the raiding season, but she took as many of the men as she dared, six of them, all in their Armstrong jacks and helmets, one Ridley, and a boy to run messages. Widow Ridley was chatting nineteen to the dozen in the cart and Janet had managed some kind of horse for each of the men, and old Shilling for herself.

They needed at least half a stone of food a day for all those people and thriftily Janet took the oldest sausages still hanging on from last year's pigkilling, not the new ones that weren't properly smoked yet. That was one reason why she needed the cart and also for last year's linen as well.

She thought it might take as long as ten days to get to Edinburgh, considering the cart, and she quailed at the dangerous country they would be travelling through, and how much the whole expedition would cost. Or rather her head quailed; her heart was telling her that this was no impulse, she needed to be in Edinburgh. She needed to rescue Henry from himself.

On the cart, under all the linen and uninteresting loaves of bread, was also a carefully calculated three small barrels of her own flower-water, distilled in the summer, of elderflower, of raspberry, of blackberry, when it had been too wet to go out. Around Janet's waist, under her stays, was Dodd's moneybelt with half of Dodd's money from London in it.

And so she set off, her face set, her hat pinned to her cap, her second best kirtle on her back and a shawl over her shoulders that her mother had knitted, for luck, her best kirtle and spare shift and her London hat stowed in the cart as well. She had two ponies pulling it but she soon decided to put two more in the traces, for it was heavy.

It was dark, long before dawn, the winter stars across the sky like silver dust and Widow Ridley stepping out instead of sitting in the cart on the beautifully made and fulled linen. Janet was proud of that, it wasn't easy to find places to stretch the linen where it wouldn't get muddy but she had done it and she was proud of the bolts of cloth she and her gossips had spun and woven last winter. Maybe it wasn't fine enough to pass through a gold wedding ring, like in the ballads, but fine enough.

She had changed her mind about buying Scots shillings from Ritchie Graham of Brackenhill since Brackenhill was in the Debateable Land. Better not on the whole to alert the March to her existence. She would use the little smuggler's road through Newcastleton, to avoid the Debateable land and Liddesdale, join the road that led through Hawick and so to Edinburgh. She hoped. Once she was past Hawick she should be well enough. It was seventy-five miles, she thought, or thereabouts, all the way to Edinburgh, nobody really knew for sure and she hoped the weather would stay frosty and that they made the fifteen miles or more to Newcastleton before nightfall.

As the hours passed she moved back and forth on Shilling, seeing the tidied winter gardens, seeing the infield where they had plowed in the barley and the wheat since it had gone bad in the wet, seeing some outfield that had been abandoned to marsh grasses, seeing horses and cattle penned up away from the road. They got past Bewcastle and she thought of stopping there but they had made good time so she tried for Newcastleton. She knew there were eyes on the hills that were watching her little party and it was only a matter of time before…

It was almost a relief when a patch of hillside moved and became twenty men in jacks and helmets as the sun westered behind them and shot rays of copper and gold under the grey clouds. Who were they? Were they Elliots or Grahams or Armstrongs…

Widow Ridley woke up from her snooze on the cart and began knitting again and the two men who were helping to push, mounted up.

Janet drove her heels into Shilling who had been stumbling along like the most exhausted horse in the world and the old hobby caught the scent of the other horses and sidestepped then drove forward. He even lifted his mane and whinneyed and she patted him to calm him.

Thanks be to God and Our Lady, she knew the man at the head of the troop. In fact he was her second cousin.

"Now then, Skinabake Armstrong," she said to him as he came towards her and he tipped his steel cap to her.

"Now then Missus Armstrong," he said, using her family name not her married name. But still he knew who she was married to.

"Och," said Janet with a big smile, "I'm glad to see ye, Skinabake, there's terrible thieves and reivers hereabouts."

"Ay," said Skinabake, since in fact his troop of twenty were some of the worst of them.

He fell in on her left and his men paced on either side of the road, hemming them in. Under strict instructions, the men didn't look to right or left but kept on going, except for Widow Ridley's grandson who peered nervously from one reiver to the other.

"Sergeant Dodd ordered me tae Edinburgh," she lied, "he wants tae buy some feed and so we've got the linen to sell o' course. He's busy off somewhere at the moment."

"Ay, where is he?" asked Skinabake, his brow creasing. Sergeant Dodd in a known location was one thing, Sergeant Dodd roaming around anywhere was another.

"Ah dinna ken, Skinabake, d'ye think he tells me everything," she laughed and the frown deepened. "Now I wis just thinking, it would be great to see some of my ain family for this part of the March is allus tickle and worse at the moment and I could do with some right fighters to protect maself and Widow Ridley here."

"Ay," said Skinabake, looking back at the cart and seeing Widow Ridley waving cheerily from the top where she was driving.

Janet skewered Skinabake with another smile.

"How's yer mother, Mariam Ridley?" she asked, then over her shoulder to the cart, "Is that a cousin of yours, Widow Ridley?"

"Ay, mebbe."

"Well enough," said Skinabake, not liking to admit he often hid out with his mother when Sir John Forster was on the trod. "Going on for sixty now."

"Is she, by God? I wouldnae have thought of her as fifty yet," said Janet. "So, Skinabake, could ye see yer way to protecting me and Widow Ridley and my people until we get to Edinburgh. Ye'll come well oot of it, I promise, I'll sell the linen and pay ye."

It was notorious that reivers didn't like cloth, although they took it, of course. It couldn't run.

The six young men in their English Armstrong jacks continued stolidly, as instructed and young Andy Ridley, Widow Ridley's grandson, was well back and almost out of sight on a fast pony so he could ride for help if need be.

"Ay," said Skinabake, his brow frowning ever more deeply.

"Come on," said Janet, "Ye can do it—or are ye out on the trod yerselves?"

She knew that they weren't, nobody had a lump of burning turf on his lance and they had been heading towards England at sunset. That meant they were on a raid, she knew it and so did they, but she had some hope they wouldn't know that she knew it.

"Nay," said Skinabake, "Ainly…ah…visiting."

Visiting Carletons and Tailors and Musgraves, I'll be bound, Janet thought but didn't say.

Skinabake licked his lips. She moved Shilling to block his sight of the cart and smiled. "Will ye dae it, Skinabake?" she said winningly, "I'd feel much safer wi' you and yer men guarding us."

Of course he could easily tell his men to take the cart and the horses and leave them to walk home. He could but she was his second cousin. If he did rob her he would have to kill all of them, especially Janet herself, and word might still get back to Will the Tod, Janet's father, which would be bad for him, and also to Sergeant Dodd which would probably be fatal. Janet had just offered him a way to get money with much less risk.

His brow suddenly cleared and straightened and he smiled his gap-toothed grin at Janet.

"Ay, o' course missus, we'd be pleased tae."

"Ye will?" gushed Janet, "Och, that makes me feel so much safer, I heard there wis Elliots round about."

"Ay," said Skinabake wisely, "Ah heard Wee Colin's trying to rescue his reputation after Dick o' Dryhope's tower, did ye ever hear the like."

"Nay, I didnae."

Skinabake sent half his men off with instructions she didn't hear but could guess at perfectly well. They were to wait until whoever they were raiding had heard that Skinabake's troop was guarding Janet Dodd's expedition to Edinburgh and then they were to hit them hard and fast and drive off the prime stock.

Oh well, thought Janet, *at least he's guarding us*. He put five men ahead and five behind and rode alongside Janet until she took pity on Shilling's theatrical stumbles and dismounted to walk for a bit as the sun disappeared and the evening came on and it got colder. She really hoped she hadn't missed the drover's road and that Newcastleton was close and then she saw the little red lights of the village over a brow of the hill and put two of the men at the front of the cart to stop it going too fast down the hill. Widow Ridley hopped off the cart and walked next to her, making eyes at Skinabake who pretended not to see. With luck there would be a packtrain she could add herself to and say goodbye to Skinabake who could not be trusted.

At the tiny inn she found that the regular packtrain from Carlisle was a day ahead of her which was a pity but couldn't be helped.

She and Widow Ridley doubled up in one bed and half the men went in the other bed and the other half of her Armstrongs kept watch in the stables to see nothing surprising happened to the horses. Skinabake and his lot refused her offer of a room for them, on the grounds that the village was full of Liddles, and disappeared to somewhere on the dark hills, probably stealing chickens. And they were halfway through the most difficult part of the journey and the linen and the booze and herself and Widow Ridley were still intact and the weather was still frosty so the mud was hard as iron. Perhaps only four more days to go, thought Janet, as she dozed off with Widow Ridley snorting in her ear.

CHRISTMAS WEEK 1592

Carey was checking the kitchens as Christmas loomed and the Court filled up with holly and ivy. He was painstakingly wandering into and poking around each of the four different kitchens at Holyrood, talking charmingly to the cooks and finding out what manner of men were working there and who they were. He found that, as with the Queen's kitchens in Whitehall, their fathers and grandfathers had served the Kings and Queens of Scotland for generations and also none of them knew when or if the King would eat the food they produced. There were no new cooks except a boy of eight newly apprenticed and all of them were Protestants. Peculation there was in plenty, so that King James was probably paying for three times as much food as the Court actually ate, but that was traditional.

He talked to the gardeners, he talked to the huntsmen, he made a foray with Lady Schevengen into the Queen's apartments and talked to her servants, and he found nothing. He checked among the holly and ivy hanging around the carvings and found no knives or crossbows there, he searched carefully through all the public rooms and found no weapons, he interviewed each member of the guard with Maitland beside him, and found again, no Catholics, only Protestants.

The King went hunting almost every day and when he could he went too, and found that the beaters and attendants were sometimes Catholics, coming as they sometimes did from the Highlands, but that the King was happy with this and that the kind of Catholics they were had barely heard of the Pope and generally gave their allegiance to some abbot or other.

Christmas was a worry to him so he went to the handsome St Giles' cathedral in Edinburgh and checked every inch. He was still looking for gunpowder and so he also checked the crypt; he drew a blank there as well. Carey thought that the King's constant hunting was paradoxically a good thing, so long as he didn't break his neck by accident, since a moving target is always hard to hit.

On Christmas Eve all the young men of the Court went out to the woods and found a magnificent oak tree to be the Yule Log, a large and heavy tree the foresters had already selected and cut down and trimmed. They sang songs around it and tied a ribbon round it and then roped it up and hauled it slowly but steadily to Holyrood house, across the empty winter fields, drinking very large quantities of lambswool and ale as they went. It took them several hours so everyone was magnificently drunk by the time they hauled it past the walls of Edinburgh.

Edinburgh's gates were closed because Edinburgh and especially Edinburgh's ministers did not approve of Christmas which they held to be a Papist feast. You could see the heads of children peering over the wall as the gentlemen of the Court sweated the Yule Log the last half mile and a few gave cheers before they were hushed by their mothers. Carey was with them, hauling on a rope with the best of them, in his hunting doublet and drinking slightly less than everybody else. It took a lot of trouble to get the tree through the old Abbey gate and across the courtyard, partly because nobody could pull steadily in one direction any more. Some of the watching woodsmen and servants had to help at that point, smiling broadly.

Once they got the tree into the great Hall, the women were waiting to decorate the Yule Log with more ribbons and little cakes and nuts glued to string and they cheered as the sweating men hauled it in. Everybody danced then, except Carey who said he didn't know the measures. While the young men handed the women round and spun on the spot, he stayed by the tree and examined it minutely, tapping it all over to be sure there were no hidden compartments full of gunpowder. The King was there, next to the Earl of Huntly, clapping and cheering with the rest of them, but Lord Spynie was nowhere to be seen: he had caught a mysterious fever after Carey visited his apartments and was seeing nobody at all except Jeremy and the boys. None of the lads looked worried though and he was eating plenty. Carey had tried to get in several times but had been turned away each time, which irritated him immensely because it stood to reason Spynie knew something he wasn't telling.

Once they had the fire sharpened enough, they rolled the Yule Log into the fireplace with the tactful help of the woodsmen, and the enormous tree lay there, filling it nearly completely, and gradually its lower parts started to burn. The wood was dense and hard: it would take at least a week for the whole of it to burn through.

They all toasted the Yule log in whishke bee and then they sang it another song, very ancient and with nonsense words in the chorus and a haunting tune, before some began leaving to go into the audience chamber with the King for a very late supper. Carey stood in the hall with the woodsmen for a while, looking at the tree and sipping his whishke bee. Would it be worth seeing the Queen's scryer to track down whatever was being plotted against the King? Carey didn't approve of that kind of thing, apart from astrology of course, which was perfectly scientific. Although with the new picture of the Heavens he was still trying to get used to, he couldn't think how astrologers would deal with the fact that retrogrades were just a trick of perspective. Did it mean that when your life went wrong, that too was just a matter of perspective? Surely not.

Huntly was still there and seemed to be in an uproarious mood, a large pink faced, red-haired man in his early thirties, whose track record was lamentable: in only February of that year he had knifed the Earl of Moray and set fire to his house. He had been caught in active treason times without number but the King let him go...

Carey almost stopped breathing. Did he speak Deutsch? Surely he could employ a clerk if he didn't since he certainly couldn't read?

Quietly, Carey moved through the people until he was close enough to the Earl of Huntly to hear him guffawing at something the Maxwell had said. The King had already gone to the audience chamber for supper.

"Och, that's funny is that," Huntly was saying and then he saw Carey and deigned to notice him. "How now Sir Robert, how's yer bum?"

Carey's eyebrows lifted slightly. "Well enough, My Lord," he answered, "Why?"

"Only I wis thinking of when ye took that fall in the hunt, did ye hurt yerself?"

"Oh no, only I got spiked by the jealous holly. The poor horse had to be killed for his leg was broken by my Lord Spynie's wire."

"Spynie's wire?" Huntly roared with laughter, "There's an excuse for yer falling off."

Carey smiled thinly.

"Why were ye tapping the Yule Log, were ye looking for sweetmeats?"

"Not exactly, My Lord, I was looking for hidden compartments holding gunpowder."

"What?" More loud laughter. "To kill ye?"

"No, My Lord, the King."

"What makes ye think that, eh, Sir Robert? We're no' at the Queen's Court here."

"Nonetheless, I have evidence that His Highness' life may be in danger and I would be exceedingly grateful to you, My Lord, if you could tell me of any suspicious men at Court."

Huntly looked thoughtful and nodded, his eyes twinkling. "Ay, I can think of one man, right now, keeps creeping aboot the Court, asking questions in the kitchens and the Queen's rooms and he wis tapping the Yule Log not five minutes ago, looking for a secret compartment for to hide gunpowder in."

Carey sighed.

"Ay," said Huntly, with a fatuous grin, "He's English too, Ah wouldna put naething past him!"

Carey was annoyed but didn't show it. "I'm afraid I have no idea whom you mean," he said coldly, "Apart from yourself, being such an excellent candidate."

"Och no," said Huntly, leaning over Carey, breathing alcohol. "I dinna need to kill the King, cos he fancies ma bum."

"Ah," said Carey, moving away, "How fortunate for your lordship." He had reached the other side of the hall by the time the earl had worked out the double meaning, which got him an ugly scowl to which he smiled blandly.

At least one thing was clear. The murderer, the man who was giving the orders, was clearly the Earl of Huntly. Who was working for him was not clear—perhaps he would do the deed himself, since he seemed to have a taste for murder. But Carey relaxed slightly. It's always good to know who your enemy is, and the Catholic Earl was certainly in it up to his neck, probably along with his usual friends, the Earls of Erroll and Angus.

He noticed Young Hutchin standing near, also gazing at the Yule Log and clearly thinking of something else, his horn cup of whishke bee empty. He hadn't seen him recently so smiled and nodded at the lad.

"How are you liking Edinburgh, Young Hutchin?"

"Ay," said the lad, now no longer a boy but not yet even a youth. "It's…interesting."

"Have you scouted out Lord Spynie yet?"

"Ay." The line of Hutchin's jaw hardened. "He's no' easy to get to and being ill means he's impossible."

Carey nodded sympathetically. "He didn't even come out to bring in the Yule Log."

"Sergeant Dodd said I shouldna kill him because he didnae kill nor hurt me, just insulted me. I should let it be or some such. I canna understand it."

"Ah," said Carey, "I can see why you're confused."

"And I've thought and thocht of a way to get intae his rooms and there isna," Young Hutchin said with frustration. "They're even on the second floor so ye canna get in by a window, if they were open, which they arenae, or big enough, which they are, just."

Carey considered this. He had seen Jeremy on the end of another rope, around the tree, with two of Spynie's henchmen and he knew all of them would be in the audience chamber tucking into venison pasties.

"What would you do if you did get in?"

Young Hutchin stared at him in mystification. "Whit?"

"All right. Just as an exercise, how would you get in?"

"Ay, the jakes is an old one wi' a hole that just lets out onto the wall and there's a nice bit of ivy…"

"It's a garderobe…"

"…I could climb but somebody might see me before I got ma head out the seat of the jakes, if ye follow."

"I do. May I suggest doing the climb in a shirt only so you can wash yourself off afterwards?"

"Whit?"

"And if you got into Spynie's apartments, what would ye do?"

Young Hutchin obviously hadn't thought about this. He frowned heavily. "Ah…mebbe I wouldna knife him, sir? Cos Sergeant Dodd said I'd hang for it and it'd take me a long while tae die?"

"A very good point."

"So…ah…mebbe I'd tell him what a bastard he is?"

Carey looked at Hutchin with grave disapproval. "I'm disappointed in you, Young Hutchin Graham, surely you can think of something better than that?"

Hutchin stared back at him for a moment and then a slow evil smile lit his features. "Mebbe I could take him a little present, eh?"

"Hm."

"Like a knife stuck in an apple, ye ken, tae mean his heart or…"

Carey too had an evil smile on his face. "I have a much better idea."

***

Spynie hated being cooped up in his apartments, he was drinking too much and the King hadn't asked after him once, which broke his heart. He had a few books but wasn't good at reading and anyway, he preferred hunting in one form or another. His henchmen did their best to keep him entertained but the boys had run through their repertoire of lute music three times and he was tired of it. He heard the celebrations in the hall and the audience chamber and longed to join them, but...he was frightened. He had let Jeremy and Paul and Peter go because if he hadn't, he knew they would just have gone anyway, so he had the two littlest boys with him and one guard.

So when there was a firm knocking on the door, it was almost a relief. Perhaps the King had come to visit, as he always used to do when Spynie took sick, even when Spynie had a dose of the clap after visiting the tarts to the north of Edinburgh, His Highness had come to see him and suggested all sorts of doses and arcane medicines. Not now though and Spynie missed him.

So when the door was opened by the youngest boy—was that Eric? Spynie wasn't sure—he was very disappointed when that bastard Sir Robert Carey strolled in, carrying a jug of lambswool and two silver cups. Carey set the tray down and served them both with the mixture of hot cider and egg, lifted his cup and gave the toast of "His Highness' good health and confusion to the Spanish" which meant Spynie had to drink. He only sipped, being cautious about poison in drinks he hadn't seen made or that had been made by someone other than his own servants.

"I was sorry to hear that you were ill," lied the Deputy Warden.

"A flux, that's all," lied Lord Spynie who in fact felt he was going mad with boredom.

"Do you have any ideas about who the Deutsch speaker might be, the one who received the letter about Solomon?"

"None at all," lied Lord Spynie. Carey watched him gravely for a minute.

"Who was the man who arranged the killing of the person who tried to kill me on my first hunt with the King?"

"Ah...I don't know what you mean."

"The plot was yours, and a remarkably clumsy one. The unfortunate servant whom we had locked up was dispatched efficiently and without leaving any clues, from which I conclude that the man who did it was not yourself, My Lord, but a...a consultant."

"Sorry, canna help ye."

"And quite possibly the man who is planning to assassinate the King. Of whom you said, My Lord, and I quote, I would die for him. At the least I would like to talk to your...consultant."

Spynie fixed a ghastly grin to his face.

"No idea."

Carey thought about drawing his poinard and using it on the ex-favourite until he bloody opened up, but decided that Spynie would just scream for help and he would end up arrested again. In any case, he was not going to kill an eight-year-old and a ten-year-old boy to cover his tracks.

"So what are your plans after the King is dead?"

Spynie didn't answer that.

Carey started wandering around the room, looking at the paintings and the statues and Spynie watched him, hating him, wishing he could come up with some clever answer and deep inside him the panic was growing again, along with the paralysis.

"Of course, My Lord, I know you're a good Protestant, so much less likely to be plotting against His Highness," said Carey, after contemplating a picture of Leda and the swan in which the swan seemed more enthusiastic than strictly necessary.

"I am," said Spynie, "I would never..."

"Then perhaps you could help me with the man I think is the most likely plotter of them all. He's a Catholic, first and foremost, he has done it before, many times and he..."

"The Earl of Huntly?"

"Exactly."

"Ah." Spynie thought hard and fast. Anything to keep Carey from thinking of Hepburn—and in fact there had been rumours of something in the wind, and the Earl of Huntly was in very high spirits this Christmas, which he normally was when plotting. "Ay, now ye mention it, I've heard rumours mesen."

"What kind?"

"Och, the usual, he's in with the Jesuits, he's in with the King of Spain, he's planning to bring Spanish troops to the West Coast...Nothing hard and fast, ye ken, just servants' talk."

Carey nodded and came and sat on a chair by the bed where Jeremy sometimes sat. "Is he staying at Court this Christmas or in Edinburgh?"

Spynie shook his head. "He hates Edinburgh and the ministers hate him back, so no. He's at Court with a few of his henchmen and the rest are at Falkland."

"Where?"

"Where what?"

"Where at Court is he staying, My Lord?"

"Why do you want to know?"

Carey simply regarded Spynie gravely, like a schoolmaster wondering how stupid a boy could be. Spynie coloured up.

"He's on the other side of the courtyard, in the Queen's old rooms, before they refurbished the abbey for her."

Carey nodded. "And how many of his men will be there this evening?"

Spynie shrugged. "Most of them will be attending him at Court, he likes to make a good show."

Carey smiled at him, an alarming smile, all teeth and sparkling blue eyes. "Now, My Lord," he said quietly, "I wonder if you could help me? Nothing hard. Just invite the Earl of Huntly to play cards with you tonight."

Spynie looked mutinous. "Ay, but then he might guess and he's awfy big and loud, is Huntly…"

"I'm asking very little of you, My Lord," said Carey, "considering that I'm wondering if the Earl of Huntly is planning to kill the King somehow. Yes, I want to search his rooms while he's not there and you can make that easier. You don't even have to die for the King, just bloody play cards."

Spynie contemplated the floor with its smart white rushmats. Perhaps he could do that, perhaps that wouldn't be too difficult. And perhaps it was Huntly at that…Although…No, he wouldn't think about it. But he could play cards with Huntly.

"Ay," he said, "I'll do it. Tonight. I'll send Eric to him now to ask him, say I'm feeling better but I'm bored." And he beckoned Eric who came trotting over, looking nervous, told him the message, listened to him repeat it back and then watched him struggle to open the big door and trot off down through the interconnecting rooms. He was a pretty boy, though a little easily scared.

"Thank you, My Lord," said Carey, "I expect I will see you tomorrow, since you seem so well recovered. His Highness was saying he would like to see you when he goes to church on Christmas morning."

"He would?" said Spynie and then calmed his beating heart because, probably the Englishman was lying again.

"He would," lied Carey. "He wanted me to tell you particularly. If he has to live through an interminable sermon by Chancellor Melville on the sins of the flesh and the sinfulness of Christmas, you can suffer too."

Spynie grunted. He had to admit that sounded like the King.

"So," said Carey, gathering the cup from the table at Spynie's elbow, putting all on the tray and picking it up, "Merry Christmas to you, My Lord. And to you, young henchman as well."

Sandy, the ten-year-old who was showing regrettable signs of acne, opened the double doors for him and he tipped the lad a Scotch sixpence, paced out. Spynie scowled moodily at the fire. You had to admit, you could see what the King had seen in him. Thank God, he hadn't replaced D'Aubigny for whatever reason, or Spynie would have remained forever just another impoverished minor Scottish nobleman.

Half an hour later, the Earl of Huntly came bounding into the rooms, followed by a number of ruffianly Gordons. He made Spynie's elegant chambers suddenly look quite small, and stood with his fists on his hips demanding to know what game Spynie wanted to lose at, Gleek or Primero, and bellowing with laughter.

It was only when Spynie went to bed several pounds poorer at about three o'clock that he found the dead rat lying in its lifeblood between the sheets on his four poster bed. It made his heart thud and was very upsetting, because what was a rat doing in his bed and did it have plague? He slept in the uncomfortable truckle bed and had the two boys with him but didn't even feel like doing anything because he was so frightened of the plague.

Carey found Young Hutchin out the back of the horse yard, using the pump to get rid of some of the ancient shit covering him. He was naked and shivering but looked very pleased with himself.

"I have another job for you, Young Hutchin," said Carey, handing him a horse blanket to use for a towel. "Why didn't you keep your shirt on?"

"Ah've only g-g-got the one," said Hutchin, wrapping the blanket around himself. "Whit d'ye want me tae do?"

"I want you to break into another set of rooms for me," said Carey, pouring out the remains of the lukewarm lambswool and handing the silver cup to Young Hutchin, "Get that down ye and I'll give you one of my shirts so you can use your own when you climb up another garderobe."

"Ye will? Whit d'ye want me tae steal?"

"Er...nothing, thank you. I want you to find the key and open the main door, so I can come in and search the chambers."

"Whose?"

"The Earl of Huntly."

"Why?"

"For good and sufficient reasons, Young Hutchin."

"Ay, but I've never met him and he hasnae given me any insult..."

Carey handed Hutchin a shilling. "Half now, half when we're back here and everything has gone perfectly."

"Ay sir, I'm up for it."

"I've taken a look and I think the garderobe is in the same position but there isn't any ivy, so I'll boost you up..."

Young Hutchin's heart was beating hard and slow when he went out into the courtyard again with Carey, carrying horse-blankets. The sounds of music were coming from the audience chamber and they had to stop several times and he had to hide in bushes when drunken nobles and their henchmen went past. Carey did a very good impression of somebody too drunk to see and pissed into a flowerbed on one occasion.

At last they found the place in a smaller back courtyard where the garderobe hung over the back of the wall. It was a tricky climb, sure enough, and Hutchin felt scared. Carey was wearing his arming doublet which was just as well because he still had a bit of the shit on him as the water had been so cold. Carey had said, if you see or hear anything that frightens you, just run and get out of the place and he left the horse blankets under the garderobe just in case. Which was nice of him, Hutchin thought. He stole a look at Carey as he looked carefully around the little courtyard and saw the man had a smile on his face again. Hutchin smiled back. It was exciting to be doing something so mad, as if the Courtier was an uncle and they were raiding someone dangerous for his favourite horse, to put a brave on him.

Carey half-squatted and Hutchin put his bare foot onto his thigh, got up to his shoulders and hunched there as Carey straightened with a quiet "oof " noise, and held the wall to steady himself. Hutchin had seen acrobats at Bessie's in Carlisle doing something similar, and he stood on Carey's shoulders and wobbled, holding onto his hair, put one hand up, then another one, found a ledge, found a hole with one toe, went up a little way, found another hole for his other toe, another ledge for one hand, slippery, broken, a staggering smell of fresh shit, got both hands up, muscles bulging, got one toe on the ledge, found a big stone to hold onto, it pulled out and fell while Hutchin gasped, but Carey wasn't there any more, he had gone to find his way round to the chambers by the normal route.

Somehow that gave Hutchin strength, that Carey trusted him. He got his hand into the hole left by the stone, boosted up again, found another slippery ledge and the round hole of the seat above him, shoved at it one handed, found it was nailed down, pushed, tried again, then lost his temper and punched it, breaking it, nearly slipped right back down again, braced his back against the front wall of the garderobe, punched again, it gave with a cracking sound that sounded like the trump of doom, got both hands up to the hole and pulled himself up, through it, thanking the god of reivers that his shoulders hadn't grown yet, and squirmed through the shit, piss and a crusting of old sick and out into the garderobe.

Very carefully he opened the door and stepped out. Two men were asleep on palliasses, and a third on a truckle bed. They all sounded drunk. Were there any dogs? Most people kept their dogs in kennels but sometimes womenfolk liked to have little dogs in bed with them…Well, nothing was barking, so he padded through the Earl's bedchamber with its four poster bed, through the inner chamber, through the parlour and found the double door which was locked. Where was the key?

Hutchin looked for hooks, looked in pockets, found nothing, felt under the bed, nothing. He was beginning to panic and his right knuckles were sore and bleeding. He went to the door, tapped on it, heard Carey's voice on the other side breathe, "I'm here."

"Sir, Ah canna find the key…"

"Look in the keyhole," whispered Carey and Hutchin looked, found the key, unlocked the door.

The doorhandle turned, the door opened. Carey came sliding through the door in his socks. "God, you stink," he said with a grin and Hutchin wanted to giggle. "Anyone there?"

For answer Hutchin held up three fingers and mimed sleep. Carey nodded. He crept through into the parlour, checked drawers very quietly, checked clothespresses, filled with velvets and brocades, went on into the bedchamber and checked under the mattress and the bed. At last he checked a clothes chest in the corner and found some sheets of paper.

Carey took them out, squinted at them in the light of the stars. "Hm," he said.

One of the servants on the palliasses turned over and snored loudly and Carey and Hutchin went still as statues. The servant got up, went blearily into the garderobe and took a long luxuriant piss.

While he was in there, Carey shoved the papers back in the clothes chest, grabbed Hutchin's shoulder, propelled him through to the parlour and out of the door, shutting it quietly. He picked up his shoes and hat in his other hand, crossed the floor and ran down the stairs to one side, two at a time. Carey paused at the service door, saw no one, and they sprinted across the small courtyard, then Carey stopped, turned, sauntered back, picked up the horseblankets under the garderobe, sprinted again. They took a back route to the stableyard and stopped at the pump and finally both of them laughed.

"You've left shitty bare footprints all over Huntly's chambers, he'll be upset tomorrow. Let's get ye clean and get rid of that shirt too."

"Och, sir, I like it."

"You'll have to launder it yourself then…"

"Och."

Carey had left soap there which he handed to Hutchin and manned the pump so the boy could wash in freezing cold water for the second time that night.

"My mam would say I'll get me death of lungfever…"

"Good thing she's not here then…" said Carey callously, pumping away, paused and then added, "God rest her."

"Ay," said Hutchin, with a grin, "It's a pity I didnae steal nothing, I'd like a souvenir."

"Too dangerous. When Huntly sees the shitty footprints he'll know you were there and I'm thinking he'll be furious. So better have nothing to hide, he'll probably get the King to search the whole palace."

"Ay," said Hutchin. "Did ye get what ye wanted, sir?"

Carey paused. "I think so. I found sheets of paper, some with numbers on them, though it was too dark to see them, one I think might have been a money draft on a bank in Antwerp and there was one with nothing on it and Huntly's signature across the bottom of the blank page. It's all very interesting."

"So his lordship is a traitor, eh?"

"That's already clear. I think he's plotting to kill the King too."

"So will ye blackmail him or kill him or what?" Carey didn't answer.

The boy was now much cleaner than he had been before he started climbing up garderobes and Carey went into his bedchamber where Tyndale and Tovey were both snoring, but the truckle bed was unoccupied because Anricks was staying with Napier in Edinburgh. He picked his oldest shirt, brought it out and Hutchin put it on with a cheeky grin.

"I'll smell like a lord in this."

"Not for long, and try and keep it under your jerkin until it gets a bit grey." Carey took Hutchin's old hemp shirt, rolled it up and then thought better of it, sighed, took his sleeves off and rolled his own shirtsleeves up and then went and rinsed it out under the pump.

Hutchin thought this was very funny. "Ye'll not get rid of it?"

"No, if I was Huntly, I'd be looking for a shitty shirt tomorrow too. If I could, I'd burn it. I should have let you stay naked to get up into his chambers."

"Och, hemp disnae burn well, and the smoke stinks. Leave it wi' me, I've an idea though I'll wear your lord's shirt tonight, it's nice and soft, so it is."

Carey was unrolling his shirtsleeves, and lacing his sleeves back on just at the upper tabs. Ceremonially he handed Hutchin his shirt, a second English shilling and a Scotch sixpence. "That's for beer tomorrow," Carey explained. "I'm buying your silence as well, Young Hutchin."

"Ay, o' course. See ye tomorrow, sir."

Carey nodded. "Thank you, Young Hutchin. And Merry Christmas."

Hutchin knuckled his forehead to the Courtier, and trotted out to the stables where he usually slept in one of the horse's stalls where it was warm and smelled comfortable. Carey could hear him chuckling to himself as he went.

He prayed and got into his bed, thinking hard about the Earl of Huntly. In London, in Whitehall, it would have been so simple. If Carey had found anything like as incriminating in the chambers of an English lord, he could have taken the documents to his father and shortly after the man would have been in the Tower. But in Scotland…The King liked the Earl of Huntly and also felt grateful to him for helping him get free of the Ruthven raiders all those years ago. Nothing was simple in Scotland.

Carey would have to catch Huntly red-handed, but before he actually killed the King. God, that would be ticklish.

***

As the Armstrongs plodded on northwards the next morning, the day before Christmas, heading for Hawick which was about twenty miles away, Skinabake and his men kept close. The road was much worse and all uphill so Widow Ridley was off the cart and walking along, knitting at a stocking with one needle in a case on her belt, her right hand clicking away with the other needle and her left hand holding the cart's side to help her along. The horses were blowing and complaining and every so often one of them would stumble on the icy mud. Janet took a look at the cart's axles which seemed firm enough, but she hoped the road wouldn't get any rougher.

"Ay," said Widow Ridley breathlessly, "ye'll need tae be rid o' Skinabake soon and I'm thinking he willna go easy."

Janet snorted and was answered by Shilling behind her as if they were having a conversation.

"O' course ye've got the barrels of brandy under the linen. That might help."

"Skinabake?" Janet laughed shortly. "He's got a head like a rock."

"Ay, how is he wi' valerian and wild lettuce?"

Janet smiled at her. "Have you got some?"

"Ay, 'appen I have," said Widow Ridley and chuckled. "I brung maist of my stillroom cupboard, allus do when I go to Carlisle, the herbs are wrapped in my best kirtle. Ye never know what you might need."

"Could you put some in the top barrel without Skinabake seeing you?"

"Ay," Widow Ridley giggled like a girl, "I use it to quiet the lads when they come in excited after a raid, don't want 'em busting my place up, do I?"

Janet couldn't laugh. She was afraid she had made a terrible mistake. Maybe she should have stayed safe in Gilsland and sent a message to Dodd—but in his current mood he would probably have ignored it. And she thought the linens would sell well in Edinburgh, especially if she could get there before New Year's day when people looked for presents. And she wanted to see the Courtier and tell him about the alchemist and his magic water. She shook her head and sighed. She had gone too far to go back now, she had to see it through. Please God, the weather stayed frosty.

Widow Ridley elbowed her in the ribs. "Dinna be sae sad and sorry for yersen," she said. "Skinabake's no' the worst of them by a long road."

"Ye're enjoying yerself, Mrs Ridley, are ye not?"

"Ay, Ah am that. Never been tae Edinburgh afore."

"Me neither."

"Och, ye don't say."

"Carlisle, o'course, and Berwick once, but never Edinburgh." Janet paused. "So I'm relying on you tae keep me out of trouble."

Widow Ridley looked sideways at her, Janet managed to keep deadpan as the old woman started to heave and laugh until she began coughing and Janet cracked a smile.

In the end they made it to Saughtree at the top of Liddesdale, and were given a barn to camp in which was kindly of the Elliots there since the frost was a hard one that night. They had a little fire and didn't use the aqua vitae since Skinabake and his men seemed quite well-behaved, helped get the packs off the ponies and one of them even sang some of the old songs for them, and some new ones as well that Janet hadn't heard.

They took the night in two watches. Janet couldn't sleep, she sat up watching the fire for a long time, wrapped in her best cloak that she had woven and fulled herself, of black sheep's wool so it was dark brown and quite prickly for it was new. She dozed off at last and woke up in the blackest part of the night, knowing that something was very wrong. She listened and heard nothing. No snores. Or just a few.

She stood up, listened. There were sounds in the night, foxes barking, badgers snuffling through the gorse but...

She walked quickly to the large double doors of the barn and found no one there, not Skinabake nor any of his men. Her

Armstrongs were still sleeping, and the two lads supposed to be doing the guarding, fast asleep with the barrel of Janet's aqua vitae between them. She stood there for a moment, honestly wanting to scream and go and kick both of them in the balls. But the situation was too serious for that.

She went back to the door, opened it a little and looked out. Her nightsight was well in since the fire had gone down to coals in its little bed of rocks—the barn was only half full of hay anyway. She looked and listened and smelled the cold air. Nobody. Skinabake and his ten tough young men had disappeared as if the faery folk had happened by and kidnapped all of them.

She ran back to the fire, kicked earth onto it, kicked Cuddy her bastard half-brother awake, bent down to hiss in his ear, "Cuddy, wake up!"

His eyes blinked open, focussed and then he was awake. "Whit?" he whispered.

"Skinabake's gone and all his men," she hissed, "sometime while I wis asleep and Jock and Archie sleeping too."

"Och. Fuck," said Cuddy, sat up on his elbow, saw Archie and Jock with the barrel, scowled and laid down again on his side. She was about to rate him for going back to sleep when she realised he was listening to the sounds in the ground. She held her breath.

"Ah can hear horses," he whispered, lifting his head, "A lot. More than twenty. They're coming close quietly, their hooves are muffled."

"Och," said Janet and for a moment she felt murderous fury at herself and at the Borders where they would not, could not let a married woman and an old carlin take a trip anywhere, much less Edinburgh.

Cuddy was sitting up, putting on his helmet.

"A'right," she said, "Get the other lads up and ye're to ride for my father…"

"No, Janet, we'll fight for ye," he said, pale with fright. "They willna take ye without a fight…"

"Happen they might be on a raid…" said Jock's Jock Armstrong on Cuddy's other side, his own head pressed to the ground.

"They might, but this village is full of Elliots."

Cuddy and Jock's Jock looked at each other. "Well but…"

"I think they're Elliots and they're after me," she said coldly. "That would put a good brave on Sergeant Dodd, d'ye not think, his wife taken by Elliots?"

"Och, fuck," said Cuddy again. "I hadna thought of that."

"Please dinna use Scottish obscenities," said Janet primly, "Nor had I, to be honest, which I should have. We should ha' gone by the Giant's Road."

She stood awhile in thought while the young men got themselves together—they were all sleeping in their jacks so only needed to get their helmets and sometimes their boots on.

"All ye lads, leave the cart ponies and Shilling wi' me, take all the ither horses and ride for me dad's tower. He'll know what tae do."

"But ye'll be all alone…"

"I willna, I'll have Widow Ridley with me for propriety and whoever it is coming willna ken where ye are and that might make him cautious. Ye can have the Ridley lad hang back on the fastest pony to see what happens if ye like, and if they are on a raid, ye can come back to me."

"Ay," said Cuddy unhappily, "Ah dinna like it, Janet."

"Nor do I. Now do as I bid ye."

They were already up and tacking up the horses, and a few minutes later they opened the double doors and broke southwards down Liddesdale, galloping for the English Armstrong lands and Will the Tod's tower. Janet went and sat by Widow Ridley and listened to the beat of their hobby's hooves fading. She thought of something, went and collected the brandy barrel, put it back on the cart under all the linens wrapped in their hemp.

Widow Ridley was putting her cap on, grabbing handfuls of startling white hair and shoving it under the linen, while more escaped from the other side and then she drove a pin into the middle of it and grunted.

Out of the night materialised fifty more riders, the hooves muffled with rags, with the square quilting of Scotland on their jacks, Liddesdale helmets, their lances and Jeddart axes, led by a small nippy dark-haired man carrying a dark lantern, that she had never met but still knew at once.

Janet stood up. "Wee Colin Elliot," she said with magnificent contempt and curtseyed. "Welcome."

CHRISTMAS DAY 1592

Anricks spent Christmas at John Napier's house happily playing with the wonderful toys mathematical he called his Bones. After the Earl of Huntly had caused a fuss looking for someone who had trailed smelly footprints all over his chamber and failed to find anyone, the Court got itself together to process to St Giles. The King and all his Court and his Queen and all her ladies attended the Christmas Morning service at St Giles where Chancellor Melville excelled himself in the length, complexity, and tedium of his sermon, and gained the admiration of every minister who heard it. Since church-going was always compulsory on Christmas morning, Simon Anricks and John Napier were there as well, giggling like a couple of schoolboys while they wrote notes to each other in mathematics. Spynie was nursing a hangover while the Maxwell, Huntly, Erroll and Angus were all at a Catholic Mass said by Father Crichton in a private chapel at Holyrood, once used by the sainted martyr, Queen Maria. The King blandly insisted to the ministers that he had no idea where the Catholic earls went on Christmas Morning, silly boys that they were, because he was busy listening to the minister's sermons in Edinburgh town.

Afterwards His Highness returned to Holyrood House and ate an immense dinner which included a swan stuffed with a peacock, stuffed with a goose, stuffed with a duck, stuffed with a chicken, stuffed with a pigeon, stuffed with a blackbird, stuffed with a wren, which everyone admired.

Jonathan Hepburn was getting worried, he had to admit. He had two plans in play, one covering the other, either one could work. He had Marguerite to keep happy although she was becoming terrifyingly adventurous, he had the complicated and dangerous alchemical plot in hand, though not active yet, everything was in a delicate balance and here came the Deputy Warden, in long boots, trampling through, asking questions.

How the bloody man had laid hands on Hepburn's sister's stupid and dangerous letter, he didn't know, but he had. The worrying message from his cousin in the Steelyard had made that clear—it was a real pity they had muffed the opportunity to arrest Carey and his odd little hanger-on and clap both of them in irons until it was all over. There might have been a bit of fuss from the King, but it could always be smoothed over by nice thalers, after all. However, his cousin had failed to act firmly enough.

But the family firm of Haug and Company now knew something was in play and Hepburn had received another letter from his brother in Keswick, asking querulously if it was true that he was planning to kill the Scottish King—and in a simple cipher as well, as if it being in Deutsch was enough to keep it secret. He had responded immediately that he was not, that it was a lie, that his sister must be mad and that nobody should pay attention to the vapourings of a widow about to have a baby. Until he could get to Keswick, that was all he could do.

He had to assume that the Scottish *domus providenciae* was alerted, but that they had kept it from the King as they normally did because of his cowardice, so the *domus magnificenciae* would be racketing on as usual. It was inconvenient and annoying but he thought he had proceeded cautiously enough that his original plans could continue.

He worried about it though, he couldn't help it. And yet, logic told him that the best thing to do was nothing. He avoided Carey as much as he could, until the man somehow caught him in the hall after the Christmas dinner and asked him if it was true that he was originally a mining engineer from Keswick.

"Ay, it is," he answered with his best boyish grin, "only I got bored with digging and went to seek my fortune in the Netherlands."

"Did you find it?" asked Carey lazily, "I mean your fortune?"

"Ah no," said Hepburn ruefully, "Not yet. I was young and stupid."

Carey smiled. "I've often thought of taking ship to Flushing and selling my sword to the highest bidder. Whenever I get tired of being told what to do by idiots."

"Hah!" Hepburn laughed. "Do you think that stops in the Netherlands? It doesn't."

Carey laughed, poured them both some wine from the nearest jug, took a drink immediately. Hepburn did too and made a face. As usual in Scotland, it was terrible.

"So how did Allemaynes come to be digging holes in the hills around the Cumberland lakes?" Carey asked. "I know Allemaynes are the best miners in the world..."

"No, I'd say the Bohemians are, but anyway. The Queen invited us back in the sixties, and my family's firm decided that there were good signs that there might be metals there, so we came, my father Daniel Hochstetter and one hundred-fifty miners from Augsberg. Have you been to Keswick, Sir Robert?"

"No," said Carey, very friendlywise, "I haven't. It's only sixty miles from Carlisle so I'm afraid I have to make some excuse and my excuse is that all the cattle-raiders, robbers, and murderers are in the opposite direction. Why do you call yourself Hepburn, if your name is really...er...Hocksteader?"

"That's why," said Hepburn. "Who can pronounce Hochstetter? I find it hard to say myself and I've had plenty of practice. My lord Bothwell gave me permission to use his surname when I was working for him."

"Ah." Carey was having some trouble drinking the wine. "And did you ever know a man called Hans Schmidt, the gunsmith?"

Hepburn didn't let his smile become fixed, allowed himself to look puzzled, then reminiscent, as if Schmidt had no importance. "Slightly," he admitted. "Not very well and it turned out he wasn't a gunsmith at all, didn't it. Where is he now? I've not seen him since the summer."

Now that was good. Carey looked away and his face twitched

a little. "Oh, I think he's dead," he said. "He made an enemy of Lord Spynie after all."

That was what Hepburn had heard and it was good news. "He was a coneycatcher and not a very good one," he said callously. "Bold but stupid."

"Yes," said Carey. "Tell me, do you know a woman called Poppy—Proserpina Burn?"

Hepburn paused for just a second, frowning in thought. "No, should I?"

"I don't know."

"She's not at Court, I think."

"No, she's the widow of a Scottish minister of religion who was murdered about two months ago—I hanged his murderers myself."

Hepburn lifted his cup in toast. "Well, I'm delighted that justice was done," he said respectfully, but saw no answering smile.

"Thank you," said Carey gravely. "Is it true that you are arranging the scenery for this year's New Year masque?"

"Yes, I am," Hepburn said, happy to get away from areas where he had to lie, back to areas where the truth was the best concealment. "I can show you my plans, if you like. You see, I want the King to be in the middle with the Earth above him…"

"You don't hold with Copernicus his theory that all goes around the Sun?"

"Of course not," said Hepburn, a little testily. "Mr Anricks has worked up a very pretty theory about it but in fact William of Ockham made it clear two hundred years ago that if we have two answers philosophical, we should always pick the simplest. Not in human affairs, perhaps, but certainly in philosophy. The Sun manifestly rises in the east and obviously sets in the west and appears to go around the Earth which clearly seems to be the centre of all. Why not agree with the simple answer that that is in fact what it does, instead of some Papist flight of fancy that has every planet flying around the Sun and the Earth itself flinging itself through space?"

"Well…"

"Depend upon it, if we were rolling around the Sun, the seas would show it and the winds would show it and why wouldn't we ourselves feel the motion?"

"Well Mr Anricks is very convincing…"

"Madness often is. He may be convinced himself but that doesn't mean it's true."

"No…"

"Are you watching the fireworks this evening?"

"Of course, if they're on…"

"It's looking like snow to be sure, but I think it will hold off until the last rockets have been fired."

"Oh, why? Scottish weather isn't usually so co-operative?"

Hepburn couldn't tell him that the Demiurge would see to it so he laughed instead, looking round at the small knots of gentlemen and ladies talking and some dice games starting up. "In fact I must ask you to excuse me, Sir Robert, because I'm helping with setting some of the fuses and suchlike, although the Han family have most of it in hand."

"The Han family?"

"The Chinese, who are the best firework makers in the world, and their French managers. We are lucky to have them. They are related to the family that makes the Queen's fireworks in England and they even say it was the Chinese who invented gunpowder— when everyone knows it was a Papist monk looking for a cure for constipation." Hepburn paused and grinned. "And he found it."

Carey laughed again at that and so Hepburn hurried out of the hall. He was sweating lightly when he met the French Master Artificer and went to look at the arrangements in the gardens in the deepening dusk. All through the evening he found himself arguing both sides: he should kill Carey, to stop him interfering; he should not kill Carey, because he had fooled him. He set the fuses, advised on more than one for each rocket, checked the metal cages and tubes were firm, while the war went on in his head. From the fireworks platform at the end of the garden, by the storage sheds and lean-tos, he looked out at the Court assembling on the benches in the cold evening to view the fireworks, saw the torches flaring and pages running around with jugs full of mulled wine and beer, saw the musicians gathering in their carts, their Chapel Master coming to make final arrangements, saw the lads from the stables gathering as close as they could get to the fireworks, held back by ropes and scowling men-at-arms. Should he kill Carey or not?

The King and the Queen arrived with the King's favourite nobles, including Lord Spynie for a wonder, and the Queen's ladies in waiting. He had looked into using the fireworks to kill the King, of course. It would be a lot easier to kill Carey.

The music started, a new composition. On the beat, the Master Artificer lit the first fuse and watched as it burned towards the first array of rockets, before stepping back behind the metal shield. Hepburn took cover there too and found Carey standing there, talking to the Master Artificer animatedly in French as the rockets coursed their way into the pitch-black skies and burst into flowers of blue and white and gold and red.

Just for a moment, Hepburn was angry and then he relaxed. Of course Carey would come to watch the fireworks from the Artificer's shield, that was where he could make sure none of the rockets had been misplaced, nor the Roman candles pointed horizontally instead of vertically. That was why Hepburn had not used the fireworks, in the end. There were too many people involved, too many hands, it was not controllable.

So he laughed with Carey, listened with satisfaction to the "oohs" and "aahs" from the crowd, shared some brandy from his flask. Carey now seemed more interested in the Earl of Huntly and even asked Hepburn if he had seen Huntly anywhere near the fireworks. Hepburn was able to answer with complete honesty, that he hadn't and he thought the Earl would be very noticeable.

They stood surrounded by the peppery sharp stink of gunpowder and the smoke as the Scottish Court besieged Heaven with its ordnance of flowers and waterspouts and spinning wheels and a flag of St Andrew in blue and sparkling white at the end, all made of purest fire, all lasting a few seconds and then dying, unlike the mysterious stars hidden behind the sour-smelling clouds.

After the show was over, they shook hands and Carey ambled back to the main crowds of the Court where King James was drunk and shouting and the musicians kept playing until the falling flakes of snow sent everybody back into the hall.

Carey was thoughtful as he stood around in a group of other gentlemen, by a tapestry, watching the Queen's ladies dancing a charming Danish dance together, very like an Allemande in fact. He felt he had drawn a blank with Jonathan Hepburn, the man seemed as honest as anyone at Court could afford to be and friendlier than most. He dismissed the man from his thoughts because he was now certain the man to watch was Huntly and he was trying to think how he could work out what the earl was planning. Sadly, being mainly illiterate except for his signature, Huntly had probably not written notes on how to kill a king.

Then he caught sight of Anricks, deep in conversation with John Napier again, and went after him, brought him to bay just outside the hall.

Napier continued down the corridor, heading for the gate, saying he was for bed and perhaps a little more calculating, as if it were something he did for fun to relax him. However Carey had urgent business with Anricks.

"You know that the Dispute about the Heavens is set for New Year's Eve and His Highness will dispute with you and Napier, as the defender of Ptolemy," Carey said to him.

Anricks had clearly forgotten everything about it and stared back at Carey, going paler and paler.

"His Highness?" repeated Anricks.

"Yes, indeed."

"Oh."

"So how is your own speech progressing, Mr Anricks? May I hear some of it?"

"Ah," said Anricks, reddening a little, "I own I have been studying mathematics and not writing my speech..."

"You only have a week," said Carey, looking very unhappy.

"Yes, but these mathematical Bones are so beautiful..." And Anricks launched into a long abstruse explanation about squares and square roots, during which he accidentally fell into Latin and continued in that language, so that Carey's eyes glazed over in minutes. To save himself from actually falling asleep in the face of Anricks' enthusiasm, he asked if Napier had published a book of his new numbers. Anricks looked annoyed as he reverted to English.

"No, he is much more interested in his book about the Apocalypse," said Anricks sadly, "which is worthy, of course, but still…He is far too modest about his new numbers, says they are only mathematical tricks to make calculating the Number of the Beast easier."

"Well I suppose that makes some sense at least. Will he assist you in the speech?"

"Ah no. We have differing opinions on the celestial spheres and will be on opposing sides."

"Really?"

"Yes, Mr Napier is quite old fashioned in some ways and seeks to keep some of Ptolemy: he avers that all the planets save the Earth do indeed go around the Sun but then the Sun, and all the rest too, goes around the Earth."

"Oh. Is that possible?"

"It is possible if the Almighty were quite insane," said Anricks irritably, "but since the chief virtue of Copernicus is its simplicity and Napier's notion is even more complicated than Ptolemy, I think we can dismiss it."

Carey hid a smile. "Must things philosophical be simple?"

"Yes, Sir Robert, they must. Which is harder to do, complexity or simplicity? Which is more beautiful? Which makes sense? William of Ockham made all this very clear two hundred years ago."

"Ah…"

"Well, Mr Napier's fixed on it so he will speak about it. What happens after His Highness wins the Dispute?"

Carey smiled. At least Anricks was always realistic.

"There is to be a masque of the Planetary Spheres and then all finishes with a dance of the Queen's ladies who will dance whichever pattern the King judges is true."

"Wearing very little?"

"Of course. And either they will circle the Earth, or they will circle the Sun or presumably they will circle Mr Napier's Sun while it circles the Earth. Personally I hope Mr Napier's view prevails."

"What?" Anricks' face was horrified.

"I would delight in seeing the Queen's ladies dancing around the Sun as he dances around the Earth. I think it could be quite funny, with plenty of collisions especially as the ladies will all be very drunk."

Anricks put his hand over his eyes and let out a low moan.

"And you've written your speech, have you?"

"Er...no."

"Nearly finished it?"

"Ah...not exactly."

"But you've started it?"

"Well..."

"Mr Anricks," said Carey, putting his hand on Anricks' arm and looking into his eyes very seriously. "You have six days. Get on with it."

"But..."

"I, your bearmaster, say, Hup, hup, hup! Write your speech, Mr Anricks!"

***

Wee Colin Elliot tipped his helmet back on his head. "Mrs Dodd," he said, "I'm told yer husband is in Edinburgh."

"Ay," she said, proud of herself because her voice was steady and she was talking to Henry's blood-enemy. "Perhaps."

"Where are yer kin?"

"Run away," she said. "Gone home. They're not here now."

"Ay," Wee Colin looked about him. "Skinabake Armstrong's gone as well," he said. "That's lucky, is that."

Janet said nothing. She stood beside the cart next to the silenced Widow Ridley and heard the few winter birds hurting the air with their hope. Would he kill her?

"Well, Mrs Dodd," he said, leaning his arms comfortably on the saddlebow to talk down to her, "ye'll come wi' me."

"Why?" said Janet, "What use are we tae ye, an old woman and the wife of Sergeant Dodd? D'ye think ma husband will pay a ransom for me? He willna."

Wee Colin laughed, showing good teeth and a twinkle in his blue eyes. "Nay Mrs Dodd, I ken that. He'd choke on it so he would. No, I want him to come to me, on his own."

"He willna do it."

"He will. Come on wi' us, missus, we havenae got all day."

Very slowly Janet hitched the unwilling sleepy ponies to the cart and then gave them nosebags as a reward. She hitched Shilling to the cart as well. Even more slowly she tidied up after them, found a glove, a sock and two crossbow bolts left behind, and then went to the head of the lead pony and took off the nosebags. They got the cart out of the barn and started up the hill to get out of Liddesdale, the worst part of the March. Wee Colin and his fifty raiders paced beside and around her.

It was mostly Elliot country, she knew that, but wondered if there might be any Dodds or Armstrongs around—except Skinabake, of course. She wouldn't make that mistake again. If you're willing to sell out your second cousin, what else might you do? She didn't think there would be any Dodds and if there had been once there certainly wouldn't be any now. Besides she was an English Armstrong and she did know that her father would be highly delighted to raid the Elliot herds with a cast-iron excuse.

Wee Colin would not let her be, asking her questions and seeming unoffended at her stony silence. "What d'ye know of our bloodfeud wi' the Dodds?" he asked once and she said, "I know ye lost."

"Ay we did," he said, tapping his teeth with his thumb. He smiled easily, did Colin Elliot. "And what did ye make of the doings at Dick of Dryhope's tower?"

"Ye lost that too," she told him. "Worse, ye were outmaneovred and then ye looked frightened. Were ye?"

"Frightened? Ay, Ah was," said Wee Colin affably and she looked at him sidelong. "Yer Deputy Warden had us lined up for the slaughter between the pikes and the arquebuses. I fought in the Netherlands maself for a few years, I knew what he was at. Never expected to see it on the Border."

Janet made a short "huh" noise.

"Ay," said Wee Colin, "I didna fancy it. I hear Henry Dodd's offended at the Deputy for letting us get away."

She decided to go back into silence and anyway they were going steeply uphill on a very rocky road and poor Shilling was groaning and puffing even though he wasn't pulling anything. Widow Ridley had already got down to walk, her knitting needles clicking away.

"Tugger, Wattie's Watt, Blind Jock and Eckie, come over here and help wi' the cart," ordered Wee Colin and four of the men came over and started helping to push the cart and get it over the worst rocks in the road. They complained about it but not very much which was impressive.

"How far to yer tower?" Widow Ridley asked in a querulous voice.

"We'll see where we are come nightfall, Mrs Ridley, I'm expecting it to snow," said Wee Colin. "Why is the cart so heavy?"

"It's full of linen," said Janet, "We were taking it all to Edinburgh to sell."

"Och," Wee Colin shook his head. "That's a pity. I wis hoping ye had some food there."

"I have, but not enough for all your gang."

"I'd take it very kindly if ye'd share with us."

Janet sighed. It wasn't as if she had a choice and at least he was asking politely. "Bread, cheese, sausage, in the hemp bags. Help yerselves."

"Your kin have gone to fetch Will the Tod."

"Ay, my father," Janet said. "I hope so."

For some reason Wee Colin laughed again. "He'll be out in a day or two, barring snow, mebbe four days if he calls on William of Kinmount. He's got ten days for the hot trod."

Janet didn't dignify that with an answer. She could feel his eyes on her, shrugged. What would happen, would happen and there was very little she could do about it now. The whole expedition had been a daft idea, she had been wood even to think of it, and if both she and Henry got out of it alive, she wouldn't blame Henry if he decided to beat her black and blue.

Wee Colin Elliot was the headman of a large surname and had been for ten years, his tower was the biggest of all their towers but that was not where they went as the skies darkened over their heads to purple. Instead they stopped at a little tower a way from the road to Hawick, no more than a fortified house with a squat keep and a strong fence around it. He didn't explain whose it was and Janet didn't ask.

And yet Mrs Elliot was there to welcome them at the gate, she was a Fenwick and Janet curtseyed to her since it didn't hurt to be polite and Widow Ridley did the best she could with her knees as they were.

They were led up the stairs in the tower, to the third floor where the family lived. Janet caught a glimpse of a woman with a veil around her face, peering at her and another older woman who smiled friendlywise and she and Widow Ridley were led into a little chamber with a truckle bed in it and a jordan and nothing else. On the bed there was a tray of gritty bread, cheese and pickled onions and a pottle of ale which was very welcome for both of them were hungry. Nor did they lock the door on her which surprised her but she was too tired to do more than tiptoe to see out of the arrowslit. Dusk was coming on and the ugly black clouds coming from the northeast with a sour smell on the wind.

She sighed and sat on the bed next to Widow Ridley who was unpinning her hair, taking her cap off, and attempting to plait her hair. Janet watched her struggle for a minute and then tapped her shoulder and took over the job. They ate their supper in silence and Janet put the tray on the floor when they had finished.

She wished she had her Bible to read. She was getting better and better at reading though she still had to read it aloud to herself, as Henry did too, and she was right in the middle of the exciting bits about David. To her surprise, the linen was still in the cart with the barrels and about half of the food. It hadn't been pillaged as she expected and she had seen it pushed into a storage shed. The horses had all been unhitched, given some feed and settled for the night in a stable nearby. Again that was a surprise. She would have expected them to be sent to the paddock to mix with their new stablemates, not given expensive grain.

"I wish…" she started.

"Ye wish I hadnae tellt ye about they witchy things and the man that bribed Sergeant Dodd."

"Yes," said Janet, annoyed at being so easily read.

"Ay well, he may surprise ye, Wee Colin, he's got a steady head on him." She was knitting again, turning the heel.

"If you told him…"

"Nay, how would I do that, d'ye think I'm a witch? But I think mebbe Wee Colin Elliot's been waiting for this day for a long weary while."

Janet nodded. It was a good answer to Dick of Dryhope's tower. Dodd's blood enemy now had her as his prisoner. Nothing good could come of that. All she could hope for was that her father would come for her but now she thought about it, why should he? There was ransom to be demanded and depending on the price, paid or argued over. Henry wouldn't like that. He wouldn't like it that Skinabake had clearly sold her to the Elliots, and he wouldn't like it that she had been taken on her way to Edinburgh. He wouldn't like having to go so far into Elliot territory to rescue her. They had all heard and laughed at the tale of Geordie Burn in the Middle March being fooled when he took Lady Elizabeth Widdrington. She didn't think anything like that would happen to her. Why had Skinabake sold her? It had been going well enough until then.

She shut her eyes and bit down on her bottom lip to stop herself crying. Widow Ridley was already tucked up in bed, still knitting and powering through the foot of the sock.

"Och hinny," she said, "come ben tae bed. What can ye do about it now?"

***

In the morning nothing was any better. It was cold and the clouds were still hanging low and threatening over the little valley with a sprinkling of sugar on the hillsides but it was too cold to snow. There was no fire in the room and so they stayed in bed and Janet dozed while Widow Ridley finished off the sock and cast on another one.

Eventually booted feet came up to the door and a spotty girl came in with a tray of more gritty bread, cheese, and ale for them both, took the old tray away. Janet started pacing, facing the first day of inactivity since last winter but this time she hadn't even any linen to hem. It felt very strange to have her hands doing nothing and she found they got up to peculiar antics, twisting and knitting round themselves.

By an hour later she was enraged that the jordan was full so she tried the door and found it unlocked, since it was distance that imprisoned them, not walls. She took the jordan, fully prepared to throw it in the face of anyone who questioned her.

On the narrow stairs she met Colin Elliot's wife, the serious looking brown haired woman she had curtseyed to the night before. She curtseyed again because it was her tower and said, "Will ye show me where to tip this, Mrs Elliot?"

There was a pause. "I told Annie to empty it in the morning when she brought your breakfast," she said, her eyes narrowing.

"Ay, well, she didna."

"This way," and Mrs Elliot showed her out to the yard where she tipped it onto the dungheap and sluiced it in a buck of rainwater.

She went to go upstairs again and Mrs Elliot hesitated and then said, "I'd like tae speak tae ye, Mrs Dodd, if ye've the leisure?"

Well that was prettily put. Janet nodded. "I'll go and help Mrs Ridley to get dressed," she said, "then we'll both come down."

Widow Ridley was very happy to come down to the second floor hall of the tower where there was a good fire burning in the great fireplace. They sat side by side on a bench while Mrs Elliot took the chair with arms. Girls were running in and out with table linen and there was a large log sitting burning slowly in the fireplace and holly and ivy decorating the walls.

"Mrs Dodd," began Mrs Elliot, "Ah was niver so grateful in my life when my Mr Elliot came home two months ago and said he had escaped a massacre."

Janet nodded gravely. "I heard about it."

"Now I don't know why the Deputy Warden let them get away, but I'm grateful, believe me."

Janet said nothing at first, then said hesitantly, "Sir Robert Carey is a courtier from London wi' strange notions. He wants tae stop feud here on the Borders. Ye cannae do that without some show of goodwill, I think. He had your man and his surname in the hollow of his hand, coming in for their friends the Grahams. And by not crushing him, he said, if ye want peace, I do too."

Mrs Elliot nodded. "That's what Colin thought. What did yer man think tae it?"

Janet paused a long time before she answered. Should she lie? If she told the truth, what should she say about herself? Unwillingly she found herself thinking of what Mrs Hogg the midwife had said and the war it had started in her chest.

"I'll tell ye straight," she said at last, "he's very angry. He still wants tae finish the feud the old way."

It was no secret, after all. Alone of all the men there at Dick of Dryhope's tower, Henry Dodd had wanted slaughter and death.

"Could ye convince him otherwise?"

Janet laughed. "It wad be a waste of time tae try," she said. "It's a new way of thinking and Henry's old fashioned. He still loves bows when everyone else is mad for guns and pistols."

Mrs Elliot nodded slowly again. "Wee Colin has a plan," she said. "He thinks I dinna ken what it is but I've known him long enough and I got his brother to tell me." Janet raised her sandy brows. "He doesnae want ransome for ye. He ainly brought ye to this tower because it's gaunae snow and when it has, he'll take ye on to Edinburgh." Janet did her best not to looking disbelieving. "He's already turned down an offer of ain hundert pounds fra yer father and another of a hundred and fifty pounds fra Kinmont Willie."

"My God," cackled Widow Ridley, "that's a lot o' money for one thrawn ginger cow."

Janet found herself blushing. It *was* a lot of money and her father and uncle had made the offers quickly. That was a high compliment.

"So what's his plan?" asked Widow Ridley, leaning forward.

"He'll help ye both get to Edinburgh and you will carry a challenge to single combat to your husband. Just Wee Colin Elliot and Sergeant Dodd, alone, to try the matter on their ain bodies."

"Och," said Janet and sat back, feeling sick.

"Ay," chirped Widow Ridley, "I see his thinking. It's clever and brave. As long as Sergeant Dodd's alive, the old feud's alive so with him dead, it will die. And if Sergeant Dodd kills Wee Colin, he may accept that as an end. He'll be at the horn in England in any case."

"Brave?" asked Mrs Elliot.

Widow Ridley was enjoying herself. "Och Wee Colin may be a bonny fighter but Henry Dodd has got something special, he's a natural killer like Geordie Burn or Cessford, but halfway sane. Wee Colin's got no chance. Mah money's on the Sergeant."

In the distance, Janet thought that the book on that fight would probably be large.

Mrs Elliot frowned. "I think he could win, but I don't like it, I admit. They could both die of their wounds."

Janet thought but didn't say, that it didn't matter about wounds, Dodd would win. Maybe he would die later, but not before he had killed Elliot. Suddenly her eyes filled with tears which infuriated her. She had always known she was likely to be a widow, but she had always assumed she would have children. Now she knew she wouldn't, or not from Henry, it made her heart sick to think of him dying.

But if he fought and won the duel, perhaps that would ease the anger in him against the Elliots. Perhaps.

"Do you want me to carry the challenge?"

"Ay, that's whit I said. If ye say ye won't, Wee Colin will just use a messenger."

"Ah'll do it," piped up Widow Ridley with unseemly enthusiasm.

"Ay," Janet thought. "If I carry it, and Mr Elliot has helped me tae Edinburgh, Sergeant Dodd will still say yes."

Mrs Elliot sighed. "I ken that. Ay well, I've given ye warning." She laughed a little. "My man's pleased as punch wi' his idea, says it'll finish the feud whatever happens. Can I ask ye to see to that, Mrs Dodd? When they fight, if my Colin is killed, will ye hold yer man to the deal?"

Janet reached forward and caught Mrs Elliot's cold right hand with hers.

"There's ma hand, there's ma heart," she said. "I will, I swear it."

Mrs Elliot smiled. "Ye never know with a fight," she said. "But thank you. Now, I must get back tae my kitchen, see ye, I've a goose to bake."

Wee Colin Elliot spoke to her later as the skies dumped their snow in fat flakes that were soon falling so thick you couldn't see a hand in front of your face. He was standing in front of the fire in his Sunday doublet, not his workaday jack, the white linen of his falling band making a bold sight against his weathered face. He was a nice looking man too, blue eyes, black hair, for all he was so short, about the same height as Janet herself.

She had to remind herself that it was Christmas, which she had all but forgotten with all the botheration. Here in the little lesser tower, they were a long way from any kirk and there was no feasting of the surname, although dinner had been good with a roast goose and breadsauce and some more of those Brussels sprouts, along with the cabbage and bashed neeps and fried sippets and a good smoked and boiled ham. The families round about had come in to receive the hospitality of the headman. They had all gone home early, with nervous looks at the sky.

"D'ye think he'll take my challenge?"

"Ay, o'course. Even though he's not the Dodd headman."

"I know Jamie Dodd, we've allied on a couple of raids and he's a sound man."

Jamie Dodd was about six or seven years younger than Henry, and his youngest brother, but they hadn't met for years. He was young to be headman of a riding surname but that was accounted for by the feud and the way it had taken so many of the fighting men.

"What does Jamie think to yer plan, Mr Elliot?" she asked.

"Ay," said Wee Colin, "he's no' agin it. He thinks I should use a champion."

"Then Henry will not come."

"I ken that. Besides, Mrs Dodd, that's not how I do things."

"A pity."

Wee Colin smiled. "Ye're so sure your man will win?"

"Ay," she said, and shut her mouth with a snap.

"Ye're saying I've no chance?"

"Ay, ye've a chance. It's a fight."

"I wonder what my odds will be in the book?"

Janet didn't answer this for a while. "Mr Elliot, ye're set on this?"

He looked down at his brown square hands. "Ay."

She sighed. "I'll take your message and we'll send a message back to ye. I think we may have to wait a bit though," she added and went to peer out of the upper door, with the ladder below it to the ground. Snow was falling silently on snow that was already settling, a siege of feathers.

***

The morning of St Stephen's Day brought them a new world in Edinburgh, everything made new and beautiful, all the dung-heaps turned into respectable hills, all the roofs and walls and fences draped in white blankets, the young dogs running around barking, the cats touching the snow with disapproving paws and shuddering back to the fires.

Children were soon playing in the snow, throwing snowballs and building snowmen, while the dominies and ministers hurried about telling them it was idolatry and the work of the Devil and to take them down at once. By evening it was snowing again on half swept streets and soon the footprints were blurred again.

King James went hunting the day after and Carey and Dodd went along with the mob of nobles and attendants. It was the most perfect hunt Carey had ever seen, bright and the snow dazzling in the forest where it hadn't been trampled, trees black against it and a long run after a most splendid hart of fourteen points that the dogs finally pulled down on the Leith links as the sunset echoed his blood across the sky.

They all rode home down the road from Leith, with the King talking animatedly in the middle about what he would do with the hart's antlers and then the Earl of Huntly started up an old song in his astonishing bass. Carey knew another version of it in English and answered him and then all the other nobles and attendants and foresters came in on the chorus. The sound of the powerful deep voices singing as they rode back through the snowy fields with the crows starting from their rookeries made the hairs on Dodd's neck stand up.

And the next day it froze hard again, but the day after that it was a little warmer and the icicles were lengthening and by that time the snow had become a nuisance, with great piles of it beside the main streets and all the alleys and wynds turned to deathtraps of ice and slush.

By then, true to his word, Wee Colin Elliot had taken Widow Ridley and Janet Armstrong across the naked hills and onto the main road from Hawick again. They stayed the night in Hawick where the innkeeper wouldn't take her money and then he and twenty of his men accompanied them all the way to Edinburgh, so they could see the walls and the great lump of rock that was Arthur's Seat, still cloaked with nearly virgin snow.

Wee Colin nodded to Janet then and rode back down the way to Hawick, leaving her with Widow Ridley and the cart and all of the horses, including Shilling whom Janet was riding. It took them the rest of the day to get to Hollyrood House since the road was slippery and dangerous and they went at a slow walk, and even when they came to the Abbey gate, there was a long argument to be had with the men there about who they were and where they had come from. They had to send someone to fetch Henry Dodd in the end.

EDINBURGH, NEW YEAR'S EVE 1592

Young Hutchin Graham was talking to one of the hobbies while he got the knots out of the hobby's mane. Partly because he was bored with all the high doings at Court and now bored with the snow in which he had built a snowman secretly because he wasn't a wean any more, but also because he was feeling worried and upset and the stables were warm and dry and smelt nice of horses and hay and a little bit of horseshit. He didn't know where Sergeant Dodd was, which was just as well.

That was the problem. He had been in the small storeroom with the leaden tanks in it, the night before, despite the foul smell because he liked to imagine himself as the man he had seen swiving his woman there. Then he had heard voices in the passageway, and dived behind the tanks to hide, peeked out and seen the same man with the curly hair, but this time with Sergeant Dodd. They stood by the door and talked in low voices, and Dodd's face was sullen and bad-tempered as usual.

He thought he had heard the name Carey mentioned, at which Dodd's face darkened even more, and then, clear as a bell. "Kill him after New Year's Day."

"Not tomorrow?"

"He has a job to do for me on New Year's morning. Kill him if you can in the afternoon."

"Ay, I can."

"It may not be up to you. New Year's Day, in the afternoon? Understand?"

"Ay."

And then the man with the curly hair counted twenty gold angels into Dodd's hand, and the Sergeant tinkled them into a leather purse and put it in the pocket of his jerkin. Then they both went out, leaving Young Hutchin stunned and fearful.

"So, Sorrel," he said, "whit do ye make of that? Should Ah tell the Courtier or no'? Cos Dodd'll get another fifteen pounds from Ritchie Graham intae the bargain and…well, ye see ma trouble?"

The hobby sidestepped and swung his tail.

"Ye know the Courtier best," Hutchin said. "Whit should I do? If I dinna tell him, my family will ay be happy and if I do… there'll be mither wi' Sergeant Dodd and the mood he's in, that could be the end o' me."

Sorrel snorted and shook his head.

"Och…" Hutchin began and then stopped for there was a commotion outside in the yard.

***

Carey stood at the door of the King's audience chamber, an addition to the abbey built by the King's grandfather, James V, and nearly as large as the hall. He was receiving the guests to the Disputation, many of them respectable merchants and ministers, some with their wives. After the Disputation, there would be a Masque by the Queen's Ladies and the King's Gentlemen, and the point of it was to give the Queen's Ladies a chance to wear very pretty diaphonous semi-classical robes and to give the Gentlemen a chance to show off their dancing and leaping and their outlandish and expensive costumes.

Anricks was standing on the other side of the door in his cramoisie brocade suit, looking very philosophical and Carey was happy because his own new suit fitted him well and looked magnificent, being of dark green damask and black velvet in the Scottish style with a peascod stomach and a ruff, trimmed with narrow gold lace, the canions daringly the same fabric as the doublet, with a set of wonderful buttons in gold which Anricks had also paid for without complaint. His new high-crowned beaver hat completed the look and gave him even more height. He thought that he alone of the entire Scottish Court had bothered to bathe early that morning after breaking the ice in the Lough, since there were no baths nor stews that he knew of in Edinburgh, thanks to the ministers closing them all down on the grounds of sin. But he could not contemplate the New Year without washing himself beforehand; that was what ten years of serving at the Court of the very nasally sensitive Queen did to you.

At one end of the audience chamber, on a dais, were the King and Queen's thrones, the King's of gilded wood with arms, the Queen's of whitepainted wood without arms, both of them with a cloth of estate over them, both empty at the moment. The King would take part in the Dispute in the audience chamber but then everyone would process into the hall for a banket and to watch the Masque. The Queen would take part in the Masque with her ladies and then join her husband on the dais in the audience chamber to say goodbye to the guests.

At last everybody was there, including Maitland of Thirlstane, the Lord Chancellor, and the Catholic earls as well who were to play a prominent part in the Masque. The Queen and her women wouldn't come until the Masque so everyone could gasp at their costumes. Women couldn't be expected to take an interest in the planets or even know what they were. They were having a New Year's Eve party in the Queen's chambers.

At last King James, in his purple suit, now with a greasy stain down one side of the doublet, stepped down from his throne and paced into the middle of the audience chamber, smiling and his eyes gleaming.

"Guid evening, My Lords and gentlemen," he said to the crowd. "I am here not merely as a King but in the guise of a Philosopher King as in Plato, to dispute a matter of true and vital importance—what do the Planets or Spheres do? Is it true that they dance around the Sun or is it true that they dance around the Earth, the centre of the Universe and the world created by Almighty God? We shall try this matter a little, important as it is, for do not the Planets affect us and our lives through their influences in astrology?"

Carey leaned over to Anricks and whispered, "I hope you are prepared?"

"No," said Anricks, "I am not. I have struggled to write a speech and find I cannot do it without mathematics and so I have put the whole into the hands of the Almighty and rest content with whatever He decides to inspire me with."

Carey looked at Anricks with his eyebrows up. "Are you joking?"

Anricks smiled. "No. All is in the hands of the Almighty as it always is."

"Jesus Christ." Carey thought for a moment and then shook Anricks by the hand. "Well, you have more balls than I have ever had. Good luck."

King James had been making a few jokes about people who had found the planets thwarting them. Now he lifted his tones. "And to oppose me with his own plan for the Universe, I call upon Mr John Napier and to oppose me with the Copernican plan for the Universe I call upon Mr Simon Anricks."

There was a sprinkle of ironic clapping as Napier stepped forward, clutching a sheaf of papers, wearing a new suit of tawny and a tight ruff. He bowed to the King and the assembled company, looked about and blinked.

Anricks waited for half a minute and then stepped forward himself, bowed to the company and genuflected neatly to the King. His face was looking interested and contented and not at all nervous.

"Now," said the King, "What order shall we follow, gentlemen?"

Napier seemed struck dumb by this, opened his mouth a couple of times and then shut it.

"Mr Anricks?"

"Your Majesty, my opinion is that as the King, the representative of the accepted order and, as it were, the reigning champion..." some people laughed at the pun "...you should begin and state the situation as it currently obtains among the planets. Mr Napier should follow you because he is Scottish and I should come last of all because I am only English and speaking for a revolutionary... yes, gentlefolks, a *revolutionary* theory." There was another light tittering. "And then Your Majesty should sum up all the arguments in the manner of a judge and make your decision."

James smiled gently at him. "You will not become nervous, waiting so long to speak?"

Anricks paused and then smiled back. "Possibly. But then I might gain some inspiration from your speech and Mr Napier's. Perhaps you may even convert me back to Ptolemy again."

Some more people clapped and the King stepped into the centre and began to speak. He spoke well, in his pleasant canny Scotch, describing the world as everyone knew it to be, immoveable and solid, in the centre of the Universe with the Sun and planets whirling round it in their complicated patterns. He quoted many authorities, including Lucretius, he dealt with the unfortunate epicycles and epi-epicycles as examples of the wonderful complexity of God's Mind, and in an hour he brought himself round to the conclusion that all is exactly as Ptolemy and Aristotle before him described, the crystal Spheres in their appointed places and the Earth at the centre as the home of mankind and the Saviour, Jesus Christ.

It was a good speech, little touches of humour here and there, and quite short at only an hour. Everyone cheered and the King knocked back a cup of wine in one.

Napier stepped forward next, shining with sweat, his sheaf of papers visibly trembling in his hand. He began speaking in a mumble, got louder every so often and then softer and Carey soon lost track because Napier was doing exactly what he had warned Anricks against and speaking mathematics to an audience of mathematical virgins. The King drank more wine, stopped pretending to be interested and started gossiping with Lord Huntly and then, when he arrived at the King's elbow, to Lord Spynie.

The incomprehensible mumble continued until Napier turned a page, suddenly looked wildly at it, glanced up bewildered and said, "Alas, I have forgot the rest of my speech which I think I may have left at home..."

"Our thanks to Mr Napier for his very learned explanation of how the Planets all go around the Sun and then the Sun goes around the Earth," said the King and hiccupped. "Now Mr Anricks, what have you to add?"

Anricks stepped forward. "I am not a learned man, unlike the King or Mr Napier, I am only, as they say in France, an amateur of astrology," he began. "I would like to conduct an experiment here in this chamber and for it I will need six men. First, to dismiss Mr Napier's rather ugly Universe?" He brought forward the nobles who would take part in the Masque, some already wearing their costumes, disposed them with Earth at the centre, who happened to be the Maxwell, because he was wearing a lime green doublet and hose, the Moon and the Sun (or Lord Huntly) circling the Earth and then the other planets circling the Sun. He commanded them to begin and within minutes all the planets had bumped into each other and the Earth, to Maxwell's annoyance. Before a fight could begin between Maxwell and Mars, he stopped them, disposed them with Maxwell in the middle and Moon and Sun going around first, and the other planets in orderly pattern after. This began circling quite well and then Anricks spoiled it all by calling out "Mercury, go backwards" and "Venus, go backwards" which caused chaos. Again he stopped the experiment. "I am very sorry, Ptolemy," he shouted, "but your Universe will not answer." Everyone laughed, thoroughly enjoying the whole thing and especially that they weren't listening to a learned disquisition but watching drunken nobles falling over each other.

The King was watching with interest. Anricks, went to him, bent the knee and then spoke quietly to him which made him laugh.

Anricks brought the King into the centre. "Firstly, I should explain something. In this our play of the planets, for the real, the true Universe, we cannot use anyone other than the real, true King, even my Lord Huntly will not do. For the real Sun is much much bigger than the Planets and it is a long way away. The fire of its heat is immense, it flames day and night, it IS day and night for when the Earth turns to it there is day and when the Earth turns away, there is night. The Sun is not really a planet, gentlemen, but it is most clearly a King."

He pointed at the King. "Here, gentlemen, we have the Sun, the King, whose light shines on all of us. We place him in the centre because the centre is the place from which all things flow. Now we put Mercury here, and Venus. The Earth comes next, with her partner, the Moon." He had Maxwell hold hands with the young man in silver tissue which made both of them uncomfortable since neither was a bugger. Then he placed Mars, then Jupiter and Saturn. "Pray begin My Lords, begin your circles. Circle around the King, the Sun, as your lord and master and perceive the beauty and fitness of Copernicus his Universe!"

Despite all of them being drunk, the nobles did a very creditable job of circling the Sun, there were no collisions and even Maxwell and his Moon circled without incident.

"But Mr Anricks," said the King, his fists on his hips, enjoying himself immensely. "This would work just as well around the Earth, and does."

"Yes, Your Majesty, if we forget that the Sun is huge and at a great distance. It is, according to Arab calculation, millions and millions of miles away and millions of miles across. How can so great a celestial body circle something that is smaller and not made of flame? The Earth would be burned to a crisp. Here we have not only the solution to the problem of the retrogrades but also to the fact that the Sun is made of fire and enormous. I say that the Sun is naturally the King of the Planets and that naturally the Planets dance attendance upon him."

He went on one knee to the King again. "My tale is done, Your Majesty."

Very prettily, because they were after all courtiers, the other nobles ceased circling and each knelt on one knee to the King in the centre who clapped his hands and laughed.

Anricks stood and backed, to leave the King to find for tradition and commonsense and say that the Earth was naturally the centre, as the Masque in the hall would shortly display.

Carey clapped him on the shoulder. "Mr Anricks, wonderfully done! If they had not set the whole masque up to circle the Earth, you would be the victor."

Anricks was flushed with exhilaration and triumph. "I know," he said, "I think His Highness wishes he did not have to find perforce for tradition. But never mind. I have done right by dead Copernicus and that is all I ask."

Carey shook his head in wonder. "I have never seen a scholarly argument done in such a way before."

"This is what happens when you put all in the hands of the Almighty, I find," said Anricks, a little complacently. "I am afraid I can't take the credit."

Carey took his hat off and bowed to the philosopher. "Truly marvellous. Now all we need to do is find the assassin, arrest the Earl of Huntly for treason and our triumph will be complete."

Anricks looked concerned. "I suppose we need to leave that too in the hands of the Almighty," he said, "although that is always a risky thing to do. I could have stood mumbling like Napier, after all."

"You're right," said Carey.

In the bedlam of the hall at New Year's Eve, with everyone shouting once the drink had got to them and laying into the first remove of venison, boar, and a forest's offering of creatures harvested by the King's hunting, Carey concentrated on the wine rather than the food. He found himself surrounded by Danish girls who wanted to tell him something and couldn't say it in Scots, possibly because all of them were helplessly drunk.

He was just trying French on the youngest and juiciest of them when his sleeve was pulled from behind and he saw a wild-eyed Young Hutchin Graham, hatless and sweaty.

"Sir, sir," said Young Hutchin, and then Carey couldn't hear the rest because the girl next to him squealed loudly and started play-fighting the girl next to her until they both fell off the bench. He wasn't entirely clear how he had gotten himself surrounded by the girls. Their mistress the Queen was now sitting next to James and pretending not to notice as Lord Spynie sat himself down on His Highness of Scotland's royal knee. "Ye've got to come wi' me," bellowed young Hutchin. "It's important, Sergeant Dodd says ye've got tae come."

Carey was suddenly no longer drunk. Sergeant Dodd had not made himself scarce, he wasn't needed to attend on Carey at a civic banket nor a Masque, but did this mean that Sergeant Dodd was about to earn his cash?

"Tell him to come here," he said, reaching out with his eating knife for the leg of a duck. "Why should I traipse off..."

"Nay sir, it's important and Janet Armstrong wants ye too."

"Oh." Carey had great respect for Janet. "What's she doing here and not in Gilsland?"

"She came to tell ye stuff ye need tae know, will ye come?"

Carey looked across the roaring crowd. The King was lecturing both Anricks and Napier on something, there was the upraised finger.

"Oh all right," he said, turned to bow to the juiciest Danish girl, kissed her hand and was rewarded by a clutch at him and alcohol-fuelled giggling. Disentangling himself from the other girl, he sidled across the floor between the benches full of people, bowed elaborately to the King who waved his finger and moved to the door where Red Sandy was waiting, an utterly alien presence in his plain jack and plainer helmet.

"What is it?" he demanded and found himself almost running across the courtyard and down the covered passage to the stables.

There in one of the small yards he found Sergeant Dodd, Janet, and an old woman waiting for him, next to a sturdy cart.

"I must get back..." he started.

"Sir Robert," said Janet firmly, her ginger eyebrows knotted and the freckles standing out on her nose, "one of the reasons I came all this way to Edinburgh was so you could hear Widow Ridley's story and decide what it means." Carey looked as patiently as he could at the old woman, who curtseyed to him, then turned to Janet.

"Where do I start?"

"With the cart you saw."

Over many minutes, Carey picked out Widow Ridley's story. "Foreigners?" he asked. "What kind?"

"The kind ye get in Keswick," Janet told him, "Deutschers. Though one of them spoke good English."

"Allemaynes? Go on."

In the cart were strange things. Widow Ridley enjoyed herself describing how witchy they were until Janet intervened, asking about the strange oil that burned her finger. She waved it.

"I think you are talking about an alchemist's labor-et-oratorium," Carey said, who had seen the inside of one while he was down in London. "But it's not illegal unlike witchcraft..."

He saw Janet give her husband a look that should be rights have have stuck four inches out of his back. Dodd ducked his head and glowered at his boots.

"The same man, Mr Hepburn, came back and talked to Sergeant Dodd."

"Oh?" said Carey. "Mr Hepburn?"

"Ay," said Widow Ridley, "And what did they talk about, that's the question."

Dodd folded his arms and kept glowering at his boots.

A heavy silence seemed to emanate like treacle from Janet while Widow Ridley watched with the interest of a lizard on a rock.

"Och, for God's sake," Dodd finally snarled, "he wis paying me to get oot of the way when Spynie was having another crack at killing ye."

"Oh, I know about that," said Carey. "I sorted that out with Spynie."

"Do ye know how much Spynie was paying my husband, Courtier?"

"Well no, Mrs Dodd, it's really his business. I object to the fact that he didn't tell me he was getting paid to steer clear of me at certain times, but I can hardly object to his getting the money…"

"I seen the tanks you saw, Missus Ridley," said Hutchin suddenly. "They're in one of the back stalls here, full of stuff…"

"One pound in my alehouse," said Widow Ridley,

"I know, it paid for his new helmet…"

"And ten pounds last night, according to what Young Hutchin Graham told me," said Janet, also folding her arms. "Sterling."

It was an awful lot for a simple bribe. Far too much really. "Well," Carey said, "I don't object to bribery. How can I? The entire governance of the country rests on it."

But his eyes had gone to an intense blue and never left Dodd's long angry face. There was a silence.

Carey spoke first. "Sergeant Henry Dodd," he said, back to the Berwick man, "if ye've been paid to kill me, now's yer chance, ye willna get another like it for I've come straight fra the

King and he doesnae allow even daggers in his presence. As ye ken full well."

He drew his eating knife, useless though it would be against a man like Dodd. Carey stood waiting, trying to relax, trying to watch Dodd all over for his first move. Considering he was wearing a jack and helmet and had his sword, the fight probably wouldn't last very long, even if Carey could get in close and grapple, because Dodd was a far more skilled wrestler than him.

He wondered what his father would do when he got word his youngest son was dead. What would Lady Widdrington do or his mother—he didn't know, couldn't imagine. They were women and thus completely unpredictable. He swallowed.

At last Dodd lifted his brown eyes to Carey's. Carey saw black anger there that chilled him, struggling with something else. Dodd drew his sword slowly, as if for the first time in his life, he wasn't sure.

From the corner of his eye, Carey could see Young Hutchin had his dagger out and was backing. Then there was the sound of another sword being drawn and when he looked for the source of the sound, he saw it was Red Sandy Dodd. Well, that tore it, if he had ever had a chance, he didn't now.

Red Sandy moved fast towards Carey, who backed up quickly to get the wall behind him and prepared for the first blow...

And found himself looking at the back of Red Sandy's jack as the man turned and stood with his sword raised to cover himself and Carey.

"Brother," said Red Sandy thickly, "I let ye do something flat wrong before because I was nobbut a lad and couldn't stop ye. Ah'm bigger now so ye'll have to come through me to get at the Courtier, d'ye hear?"

"What?" Dodd's mouth twisted. "Ye?"

"Ay," said Red Sandy, his voice steadying. "Ah ken ye're much better than me wi' yer sword and yer fists but I reckon ye've gone woodwild so mebbe that'll give me a chance."

Another person moved suddenly and Carey at first couldn't think who it was. Hutchin? But he had climbed up to one of the high mangers and was sitting there with his dagger still out and his legs dangling.

It was Janet Dodd herself, standing on Red Sandy's left side where she wouldn't get in the way of his swordarm.

"Ay," she said, "I think Red Sandy has the right of it, ye're woodwild and dinna ken what ye're doing. How Wee Colin Elliot would laugh at ye, killing the man that beat them all wi'out a battle, ay, they'd raise their glasses to ye for that."

And she folded her arms again and tipped her hip and stared at her husband while Carey tried his best not to find her attractive.

Everything held in the balance for one second more and then just as Carey was trying to think how he could work with Red Sandy to disarm Dodd without getting killed or accidentally killing Janet, Dodd moved. He sheathed his sword impatiently and his face didn't move as he went to the next stall and started tacking up Whitesock, who nickered with interest.

"Ye're in charge of the men, Alexander Dodd," said his brother, "until himself sells the office anyway. I've business with Wee Colin Elliot."

He mounted up, bent right down over the horse's withers as he went out of the stable door and they heard Whitesock's shod hooves on the cobbles of the stableyard.

Carey let his breath out shakily. As always happened when he was ready for a fight but didn't fight, his hands were trembling. It took him four tries to sheath his eating knife and then he turned to Red Sandy and Janet who were looking stunned.

"Thank you Mr Dodd, Mrs Dodd," he said formally, and saw with shock that there were tears in Red Sandy's eyes. Not in Janet's though.

"Ay," she said, "but be careful, he'll kill ye next time he sees ye, certain sure of it."

"Of course," said Carey, "if he's taken the money. Do ye really think he's wood."

"Ay," she said, "he hasnae acted reasonable or hisself since Dick of Dryhope's tower. He's wood."

And then suddenly she crumpled and he had to catch her

before she fell and she wept into the shoulder of his brand new damask doublet, risking watermarks.

Only for a second, thank God she stopped before damage could be done, stepped back and used her apron to wipe her eyes and blow her nose. "I'm sorry, Deputy," she said, "it willna happen again."

Widow Ridley stood up from where she had taken shelter behind a feedbin and held Janet's hand. "Come on, Red Sandy," she ordered, "find us a place to stay in this palace. I'm going sightseeing tomorrow."

***

Carey went back to the hall which seemed to be rocking slightly with the noise, thinking hard. If Hepburn had given Dodd ten pounds to kill him, presumably half the final fee, it was clear he worked for Spynie and Sir Henry. If he was also an alchemist from the Allemaynes in Keswick, that was significant but still didn't meen he was looking to kill the King. Just because someone had written to a Deutscher in Deutsch, saying don't kill Solomon, it didn't necessarily mean Hepburn was also plotting to kill the King. Carey shook his head. He was sure the traitor was Huntly—but perhaps Hepburn was working for him. It might be an idea to find Hepburn and clap him in irons though.

The ladies were giving a preview of their dance in the Masque, trotting about holding *papier maché* globes painted with astrological signs and symbols and with a *papier maché* god or goddess sitting on them. They were quite large but light because they were hollow. There went Mercury, Venus, Mars, Saturn, and Jupiter, very nicely painted. From the feathered wings adorning the pretty bare and powdered shoulders of the Queen's women, it was clear they were playing the angels who carried the globes on their shoulders and thus enabled them to move.

The girls handed the globes to the servants who carried them back to the hall ready for the Masque and everyone followed in a disorderly procession, talking at the tops of their voices and discreetly hurrying so they could be first in the queue for the banket of sweetmeats after the lords and ladies had served themselves.

In the hall the benches had been pushed to the side, a magnificent banket table laid along the other side so the central floor was clear for the dancing and it had even been swept clear of rushes. In the middle of the floor was a chair with arms and a kind of scaffolding over it, elaborately decorated with ribbons and garlands of holly.

There was Hepburn and two others, carefully carrying a magnificent *papier maché* globe, painted with all the latest discoveries of the world. Cathay was there, decorated with curiously snaky dragons, and so was the great southern continent which clearly must exist to counterbalance the northern continent and which someone would discover any day now. The Americas were there, the bulge of New Spain and even some of the coastline of the northwestern part of North America, where only savages lived and also unicorns, griffins and sphinxes.

It looked heavy and they were carrying it with particular care so Carey offered to help and they said they could manage. He watched while they set it on the high frame and sniffed.

"What's that funny smell, a sort of sourness?" he asked.

"The glue," said Hepburn, "unbelievable quantities of glue." He smiled.

Carey smiled back and asked, "The other globes were light enough for the women to carry. Why is the Earth so heavy?"

"It is made of lead to denote its firmness and immovability," said Hepburn. "Because it is at the centre of the Universe, the Earth must counterweigh all the other Spheres so they can revolve around it."

For a second, Carey contemplated trying to arrest Hepburn immediately. Could he do it? He didn't think so. The man was organising the scenery for the Masque, the King would be very annoyed to have that disrupted. Carey would have to wait and take him after the Masque was finished.

Apollo the Sun went past, dazzling in golden armour, a little patched and let out for the Earl of Huntly was wearing His Highness' refurbished costume from years before. With him was

Artemis the Moon, a handsome young man wearing quantities of silver tissue, since women couldn't possibly act with the men.

Across the floor Carey saw Lord Spynie, now very prettily decked out as Aphrodite or Venus and he had a job not to roar with laughter since the breasts were strapped on upside down and Spynie was too drunk to notice. He was used to ridiculous costumes and stories for Masques but this was bidding fair to be something special. Maxwell wandered past, still in his bright green, talking intently to two of the Danish girls.

More Danish girls tottered past in a flock, carrying sugarplate bowls of sweetmeats and jelly and little spoons made of sugarplate too, while the gods, goddesses and other gallant gentlemen went in hot pursuit of them, also carrying ridiculously dainty plates laden with sugar. It made Carey's teeth hurt to think about it.

Carey found himself some green cheese and nibbled that. Anricks was deep in conversation with his rival Napier again. Amazing how they could find so much to talk about concerning numbers.

Lord Spynie was now surrounded by his young henchmen—ah, somebody had spotted the breasts and was helping him to take them off and put them on the right way up. Sir Henry was there too, a cup of brandy in his hand and his face twisted with misery—what in God's name was troubling him now? Oh, his foot was swollen and wrapped in bandages, he had the gout. Automatically Carey scanned the room and found Lady Widdrington among the older women of the Queen's household, not unfortunately scandalously clad in bits of white silk and some straps. She was talking slowly and with many gestures to an old lady. For a moment Carey was lost in thought as he imagined what Elizabeth might look like if she was wearing some scraps of silk and straps instead of the doublet style velvet Court bodice and a brocade kirtle in cramoisie that she was actually wearing. She looked well in it although as usual she had her modest married woman's cap over all her hair, so you couldn't tell what colour it might be except that it certainly wasn't blond unless she coloured her eyebrows, which of course she might…

Somebody was standing on his foot and there was a pungent smell of piss. Carey looked down and found Sir Henry had limped over and put his good foot on Carey's dancing slipper.

Carey looked down at Sir Henry, shifted his weight and then slowly and carefully put his other shoe on Sir Henry's bandaged foot, so they stood ridiculously caught, as if in the middle of some mummer's trick at the theatre.

"Really Sir Henry," he said sweetly, "you should be more careful."

"Puppy!" gasped Sir Henry, beads of sweat appearing on his forehead, "Aaah, get off…"

"Certainly, sir," said Carey, increasing the pressure. "The minute you get off my foot."

Sir Henry moved his good foot and Carey slowly released his bad foot which clearly made the old man want to cry out. Spynie was looking their way and grinning under his fetching blonde wig. Had it been his idea?

"Sir Robert," hissed Sir Henry, "I challenge you to a duel for looking lasciviously at my wife, sir. And for corrupting her."

Carey thought about this, breathing through his mouth so as not to smell the stink coming from the man. The bill was probably foul: Carey unusually had no idea what his face had been doing while he was staring at Elizabeth but judging by the content of his thoughts, it probably had been lascivious enough. To any other man he would have bowed and apologised profusely, but he didn't feel like it with Sir Henry.

"Certainly, sir," he replied. "Name your place and your weapons."

"Pistols," hissed Sir Henry. "We will have to find a place on the Border."

Carey stared at Sir Henry gravely, both eyebrows up. "Lord above, Sir Henry, aren't you going to choose a champion?"

"I will kill you myself," hissed Sir Henry, "you impudent cocksure bastard, so I can have the satisfaction of telling my bitch of a wife that you're dead."

Carey controlled his breathing as the best way of getting a hold on the fury building up in his belly. "Of course, it's more likely it will solve our problem and I will marry your grieving widow."

"Ye willna, because ye'll hang for my murder, so one way or another, I'll get you."

"Dear me," said Carey, "you have forgotten that I am a cousin to the Queen and have a right to ask for an axe. And I think this is a course of desperation, Sir Henry." He moved away in case Sir Henry tried to stick him with his eating knife and also to get away from the smell. "I suppose it's because the gout will kill you soon or perhaps your kidneys, since you stink of piss, Sir Henry, which I'm sure isn't healthy. Is it Spynie's idea for a duel? It's a better means of getting rid of me and you than his pathetic assassination attempt."

Sir Henry's face had such a number of emotions chasing across it that Carey felt like laughing, so he did. "Good God, man, can't you see it? He's bored of you and embarrassed by you. Well, never mind, I take your challenge, ye poor gouty old man, and may God ha' mercy on yer soul."

That was when he looked across the room and saw that Huntly was wearing a sword, against all King James' careful rules, he was armed.

There was dancing while the Masquers were getting ready and the ravaged remains of the banket cleared away, so he flung himself into it and found he was a great favourite with the incredibly drunk and funny Danish girls who weren't masquing, but used the figures of the dance to get across to the King as quickly as possible. The King was standing to one side and singing tunelessly along with the music. As soon as he was close enough, he went on one knee to him.

"Your Highness, the Earl of Huntly…"

"Ay, does he no' look fine in my old Apollo costume, even though he's a little too big for it…"

"He has a sword…"

"Och, Sir Robert, it's made of painted wood, that sword, d'ye think I'm a fool?"

Carey suddenly felt very embarrassed. Of course it was, the King was emphatically not a fool. "Your Highness, I am the fool," he said, "I apologise for troubling you."

The King put his hand on his shoulder. "Up ye get, my dear," he said, "Ah ken ye mean well, but my dear Earl of Huntly wouldna hurt me."

"Well, Your Highness, he hurt the Earl of Moray..."

"Ay, true, but that was a deadly feud. Will ye no' join the dancing, I like to watch ye leap."

All of a sudden Carey had the feeling that he was driving a chariot, hopelessly out of control, heading for a cliff with a white and a black horse fighting each other in the traces in front of him, which he rather thought was an image from Plato.

Obediently he joined another row of dancers and jogged past the astronomical spheres on their stands and the leaden globe of the Earth on its scaffolding above the chair where the King would soon sit. There was something odd about that chair, it had a few little spots of black on it as if someone had shaken a dish of coals over it, but he didn't have time to wonder about that, he was holding hands with a Danish girl and spinning her round as they thundered past.

**

Hughie could hardly believe his luck. He had only gone into the alehouse for a quart on the off chance and there was Henry Dodd himself, sitting by himself, stonily eating the ordinary which was haggis of course with bashed neeps and fried sippets of bread to soak up the fat and drinking the ale while the alehouse racketed around him. He didn't look as if he was enjoying himself but then he never did and had got even gloomier after Dick of Dryhope's tower.

Hughie gave out that his name was Tyndale but it wasn't. He had had to be very careful coming back to Edinburgh and in fact until now he had not been into the town at all but had stayed in Holyrood House out of sight because it was less than a year since he had been banished from Edinburgh for a year and a day for the accidental killing of his uncle. Certainly the murder had looked like an accident, which Hughie had planned carefully to achieve. Since then his life had been transformed what with doing a few killings for the man who called himself Hepburn and a few for himself too.

There was only a month or two to go but he still didn't want the nuisance of being arrested again and certainly not of possibly being hanged. He had been all the way down to London to find and attach himself to Carey and had finally got himself a very cushy job with the man himself, if you didn't mind a fair bit of sewing, which he didn't. He was good at it, after all. In due course, Hughie would kill Carey and earn his thirty pounds sterling. Not yet. Hepburn had told him very clearly that Carey was off-limits until the day after New Year's day, and then he could kill the Courtier any way he liked.

But in the meantime, here was Henry Dodd, sitting in a booth in an alehouse, grimly eating haggis and that was an opportunity not to be passed up because Hughie's right name was Elliot and he was a younger half-brother of Wee Colin himself.

So he elbowed his way through the crowd to the bar, using his size and height, got himself a quart and came and sat down opposite Dodd. The face noted him and got longer and grimmer.

"What d'ye want?" said Dodd. "Did Carey send ye?"

"Nay," said Hughie genially, "Only I wis wondering why are ye here paying for food when ye can get it free at the King's Court?"

Dodd grunted. He was in his jack, his helmet—a nice new morion—on the table next to him where he could get at it easily. He hadn't taken his swordbelt off though. Hughie knew how to use a sword though he was better with a pike because of his size. However he had no plans whatsoever to fight Dodd with a sword, that wasn't his way at all.

No more words from Dodd. Hughie asked, "Where are ye going Sergeant, are ye taking a message."

"In a manner of speaking," said Dodd. "Wee Colin Elliot challenged me to a duel and I'm carrying my own message to say I accept."

"First blood or to the death."

Dodd gave him a contemptuous look. "Death, o' course."

"Ay."

"Wee Colin's."

"Ay."

Dodd finished his ale.

"I hear ye took money to kill the Courtier," said Hughie carefully. "Is that true?"

"Ay."

"So is he dead then?"

"What do ye care?"

I'm due a lot of money for killing him meself, Hughie nearly said but didn't. "He owes me wages," he said, because it was true.

"Well last I saw of him, he wasnae dead," allowed Dodd.

Hughie smiled happily. "Och that's good news, is that. Nor wounded?"

"Nay."

"So where are ye going?"

"Ah told ye, Ah'm gaunae find Wee Colin Elliot, we'll fight and I'll kill him," said Dodd coldly. "And then I'll probably die meself."

"Och," said Hughie, "So ye'd rather kill Wee Colin than the Courtier?"

"Ay," said Dodd, "O' course."

Hughie sat back to think. Was it worth it? Yes, definitely. Could he do it? He thought so. Would Dodd believe him? Only one way to find out.

"I know why ye wantae kill Wee Colin," he said carefully. "And I'm really a Fenwick so I'd not be sorry to see him dead."

Dodd nodded once and waited. In the complex entanglements of the Border, the Fenwicks too had a long-running bloodfeud with the Elliots. It was quiet at the moment and there had been a couple of marriages to try and heal the breach, but nobody forgot a bloodfeud. How could you? A bloodfeud meant men dead.

"So," said Hughie authoritatively, "Ah ken where Wee Colin Elliot is the day, he's spending New Year wi' his sister and doing a spot of raiding in the East March and I know his sister because her man's a Fenwick cousin of mine."

Dodd had sat back, his eyes slitted. "Ay?"

"Ay. I could take ye there in mebbe two days and then ye could do it and naebody to interfere. I cannae help ye get out again after ye do it and ye'll have to talk to the bastard Elliots, but I can take ye to where Colin Elliot is."

"Hmm. I just want the mither done with."

"Well I won't help ye, I'm just a tailor, me, I'll leave the killing to ye."

"I don't need yer help."

"Good."

"What do ye want oot of it?"

"Your horse, the one ye call Whitesock," said Hughie who had cast many covetous looks at the big sturdy beast. "I think ye willna be needing him again."

Dodd nodded. It was a fair price for the work as well. He looked into the distance as if he was talking to someone else and Hughie felt the hairs go up on his neck.

"Ay," said Dodd, with a short sigh. "Ay. It's a good idea. We'll need supplies and some horsefeed since the grass is under the snow, but ay. Is the tower near Jedburgh?"

"Nay," said Hughie. "Stobs." That was in fact where his poor sister lived, though he hadn't seen her for years. Never mind. They wouldn't get that far.

**

At last the Masque had started although nearly everybody was too drunk to walk. His Highness was sitting under the leaden Earth, lolling sideways and laughing while the girls wafted about waving their arms and singing verses about Venus and Mercury and then formed an outer ring of angels, some of them semiconscious and distinctly fallen. The men pranced and kicked and jumped. Huntly was particularly good at this despite his size and large feet. Apollo the Sun had never been known to leap so high or disposedly when King James had been wearing the costume.

Napier and Anricks were deep in conversation like a couple of lovers and Carey looked around for the man organising the props in the Masque. He was nowhere to be seen and nor were his men. Carey poked his head out of the door and asked one of the guards where the four artificers had gone.

"Mr Hepburn went down to get some air, sir," said the man. "And his men with him."

Carey looked back at the Masque. Apollo was on one knee, speechifying in verse to the King and explaining that Apollo was the King's servant and sought only to do him good with his bow and arrows. He hurried over to Anricks, extricated him from his conversation with Napier and said,

"Something is wrong, Mr Anricks. Mr Hepburn, the masque artificer has gone and his men with him."

"An explosion?"

"Maybe. Will you search all the rooms nearby and I'll look in the cellars."

He ran out of the door, down the stairs to the winecellars, searched through each of the arched vaults more by smell than sight since he only had a candle, found nothing apart from barrels of wine and more importantly, no lit fuse. He went to the stables, found Hutchin currycombing the horses, and learned from him where he had seen the tanks. They went to look and found the tanks open and empty, nothing else there and four of the better horses gone from the stables.

He sprinted back up to the hall, where the Maxwell and Huntly were advancing on the giggling King who kept slapping his arms as if he was being bitten by insects. Anricks was arguing with the musicians who were sawing away with a will as everybody circled around the King again, Apollo the Sun, Mercury, Venus, the Moon, Mars, Jupiter, Saturn, all partnered with blond Danish girls with their costumes askew and their nipples popping out.

He used his fist on the open door and produced a loud thumping which made the nearer dancers slow and get bumped into by the next dancers. The whole stately sight tumbled into chaos.

"My lords, ladies, gentlemen, please leave the chamber at once!" He used his battle roar which produced a moment of silence.

King James stood up. "What are ye at?" demanded the monarch angrily. "*You* leave at once."

Carey looked up at the globe above the King, and suddenly got it. The round shape, the deadly liquid that Widow Ridley had dipped her finger in, everything.

He pointed at it. "Step away from the chair, Your Majesty..."

King James goggled at him. "Wha'?"

Carey saw it then, a crack from pole to pole in the leaden globe above the King splitting slowly, something oily leaking. "Ware the globe!" he shouted and started sprinting across the floor as the world went slow. Anricks saw it too and he was nearer, he sprinted for the King before hunching his shoulders and making an excellent football tackle on the King which carried both of them sliding several yards away from the chair and the scaffolding, with the King underneath him.

The painted globe was opening like an egg broken by an expert cook, from the bottom to the top and from it came a quantity of oily liquid which poured onto the chair and the velvet robe the King had left there.

For a moment nothing happened and then smoke began to rise. Before their eyes the velvet robe and the upholstery and the very wood of the chair started to char and blacken as if it was burning in an invisible fire, and a horrible sour smell was growing while the invisible fire caught the rushes and floorboards and blackened them too.

Carey had never seen anything so terrifying as the slow ghostly fire, but he pulled down a tapestry to try to put it out.

"No," shouted Anricks, "This is oil of vitriol, stay back and find some lye quickly, or we'll have a fire."

The smoke was getting thicker. The King picked himself up off the floor, gasping and shaking. Suddenly he ran from the room, crying like a child. Anricks chased after him.

The Queen had already gathered up her ladies and swept them from the room, mostly frightened and not drunk anymore, although some were still giggling in bewilderment. Carey thundered down the stairs again, followed by a couple of bodyguards, across the courtyard, through the stables and into the yard behind where the laundry was and three lyedroppers standing in a row. They emptied them out carefully for the lye was caustic and put the lye into buckets which they carried upstairs into the hall full of smoke and tipped it onto the spreading fire. The first bucket produced a hissing and foaming which made one of the guards run, but the next produced less and the one after that, less again until there was a charred mess in the centre of the hall, bad smelling smoke dissipating and an expensive velvet robe and a chair turned to a charred mess.

**

Anricks chased after the fleeing King of Scotland, up many flights of stairs and into the small rooms under the roof where the palace servants lived if they were important enough. At the end of the corridor the King ran into a room with just a bed in it, stood wailing for a minute and then crawled under the bed. After hesitating because of his new suit, Anricks crammed in under the bed as well.

"Your Highness, I must check your clothes for oil of vitriol…"

The King had his eyes tight shut and his thumb in his mouth and was making little whimpering noises.

"Please, Your Highness…" No response so Anricks found his tinderbox in his sleeve pocket and with shaking hands made fire and lit his candle stub. There were a few black edged holes in the purple brocade but thank the Almighty, the oil of vitriol hadn't gone through the padding. There was a watch light on the window sill and Anricks lit it and brought it under the bed where the King was rolled up tight, eyes still shut but tears pouring down his face.

"*Maman*," he was whispering, "*Ou est maman? Je veux maman, je vous en prie m'sieur, maman…*"

For a second Anricks didn't understand, but then he did. The King was begging for his mother who had been taken from him when he was eighteen months old.

What do I do, he wondered desperately and then he thought of his own children and what he would do for them. He crawled back under the bed and held the King tightly from behind, difficult with a fullgrown man.

"*Je m'excuse*," Simon said, his voice shaking, "*Je suis désolé, votre majesté, mais vostre mére n'est pas ici.*"

The King nodded, sucking his thumb.

"*Je sais*," he said, "*mais ou est-elle?*" Where is she?

"I don't know either," Simon said, still in French, "But you must be brave…"

James opened his eyes, turned over and blinked at Simon. "Brave?"

"Yes, Your Majesty, you must be brave. It's very important because you are the King."

"The King?"

"Yes, Your Majesty."

The whisper was almost too soft to hear and hard to understand with its lisping childish French. "But I am not brave," said the King, "I am a coward. I am always afraid."

"Well," said Simon, "So am I. I am not brave but I pretend to be brave, I do what a brave person would. I act, Your Majesty."

There was silence from the King. "*Ça marche?*" That works?

"*Oui.*"

"Oh."

"*Ça suffit*," said Simon, suddenly hating the cold ambitious men who had taken the King from his mother all those years before. "*Vous etes brave, tres vaillant. Et soyez calme.*"

"*Oui*," said the King, "*Je suis calme.*" And the King smiled suddenly at Anricks and then shut his eyes and went instantly to sleep, lying there on the cold dusty floor, with Anricks holding him.

He lay for what seemed a long time and then heard light footsteps tiptoeing into the room.

Very carefully Anricks wriggled out and climbed stiffly to his feet and saw the Queen, still wearing her artful draperies but stone-cold sober.

"How eez he?"

Anricks crept to the door carrying the watch candle and beckoned her outside.

"He is sleeping, Your Highness."

"Sleeping? He never sleeps after somessing like zis, he cries and wails and says sings I not understand in French…"

Anricks gestured that the Queen should look for herself and held the candle so she could see.

"Good God," she said, "he is sleeping. How did you do it, sir?"

"I…ah…" Anricks hesitated, wondering if he should be tactful or honest. "I…spoke to him in French, which is a language I speak, and it seemed to calm him and so he slept."

The Queen suddenly smiled. "And you held him, no?" she said, "I see it from the marks in the dust. This is vot I should do. Yet he always say he speaks no French and vos late talking."

"I think perhaps when he is upset he remembers…"

"Vat?"

"His mother?"

"The mermaid Queen? Surely not. He vas alvays taught to hate her."

Anricks bowed because one does not contradict a Queen. She contradicted herself. "But yes, I have heard him say 'maman' when he iz like zis. That is French for 'mutter', is not it?"

"Yes, Your Highness."

"Poor poor one." The Queen smiled at Anricks. "I vill hold him now and you may go downstairs and help Sir Robert find the vicked men who tried to kill him viz magic vater."

"Oil of vitriol."

"Vatever it vos. I vill look after him. He vill vake up soon. I vill be here."

Anricks watched as the Queen slid herself under the bed. He bowed, left the watchcandle on the windowsill, went looking in the other bedrooms and finally found a shawl folded up on one of the beds. He brought it in and passed it under the bed to the Queen.

"Sank you," she said, "zo I not feel ze cold usually."

"Still," said Anricks. "When shall I tell your women where you are?"

"Vait at least two hours. In fact tell zem only I am viss the King."

Anricks went slowly down the stairs, feeling exhausted and longing for Rebecca, his own shelter and safe harbour, longing to put his head between her breasts and tell her what had happened.

***

When they had put out the invisible flames with the lye, they gathered everything together using spears and pokers from the fire, and put it all into the Yule log fire which smelled truly terrible but crackled and burned with ugly yellow flames. Carey was checking behind all the old dusty tapestries, in cupboards, nooks, window seats, because he couldn't believe there was no gunpowder. James' worthless father, Lord Darnley, had been blown up with gunpowder and because he had somehow escaped, then been strangled in his garden. Whenever Carey looked at the King of Scots now, mentally he heard the boom of a large explosion, which annoyed him almost as much as his repeated dreams of his own execution.

Huntly and Erroll had ridden into town, ostensibly to stop the Allemaynes getting away, which Carey didn't believe would do any good at all, seeing how they were both Catholics and Huntly was still his prime suspect for the originator of the plot. And so he went to the audience chamber where all the great and good of Scotland were discussing the doings at the tops of their voices, found Maitland of Thirlstane, got him to swear out a general warrant, and at midnight had the satisfaction of battering a door in and finding the Maxwell in bed with two of the Danish girls.

Ignoring a lot of angry shouting from the Maxwell after the girls had fled, Carey searched the room, found some ciphered papers and, joy of joys, hiding in a cupboard with a false back, a very dull-looking man who happened to be reading a Catholic breviary.

Scotland wasn't England but still Carey hauled him out of there by the scruff of his neck, and the Maxwell too in his shirt, hastily put on, and took them down to the cellars and looked them in separate rooms. It was immensely satisfying.

However, knowing the King of Scots' ridiculous softness, he reckoned he only had until morning.

Carey marched into the room where the priest was sitting in irons, looking pale and lost.

"I am Sir Robert Carey, Deputy Warden of the English West March, and acting for my Lord Maitland of Thirlstane." The man said nothing. "Your name?"

"William Crichton."

"Are you a Jesuit priest?"

"Yes. His Highness knows this, I have disputed with him theologically several times."

In England that would be enough to hang, draw and quarter him, but this was Scotland where the King seemed intent on convincing the Catholics that he was a Catholic and the Protestants that he was a Protestant.

Carey showed his teeth in an unpleasant smile. "Jonathan Hepburn just made a hideous attempt against the sacred life of His Majesty, in which he might have been burned to death by oil of vitriol."

"Oh my God."

"What I want from you, William Crichton, is a full account of the whole thing. From start to finish, including all main actors and your part in it."

"In exchange for?"

"I will let you go. This isn't England."

"And if I don't?"

Carey leaned over Crichton and drew his finger across his throat. "I'll do it myself," he said conversationally, "since it is no sin for an Englishman to kill a Jesuit, as they account it no sin to make attempts against the life of Her Majesty of England."

Crichton looked appalled. "I am a man of peace."

"Certainly you are, William," said Carey, still leaning, "and I am not. I know the Maxwell may protest about his house priest getting his throat cut, but probably not very much because of all the things you know about him."

"My Lord Maxwell is a good Catholic..." began Crichton

and then stopped because Carey was laughing at him. "Well he tries to be," he finished lamely. "How is His Highness?"

"I don't know."

"And you will let me go."

"Perhaps."

Crichton swallowed. "But…"

"Do you want me to give you to my Lord Spynie?"

Crichton went ashen. "But…"

"Speak up quickly then. I should think he's very upset. At his masque being spoilt. He'll be here soon, I expect."

Crichton was silent a moment and his lips moved as if he was praying. Then he tried to move his hand to the table but rediscovered the chains on his wrist.

"Hepburn refused to tell us anything of his plans," he said, "he just guaranteed that King James would be dead or very ill…I thought poison…"

Carey said nothing.

"I was never happy about it," Crichton said. "If the King had been excommunicated it would be legitimate although still dubious, but he hasn't. Yet the paper came from the King of Spain saying, '*Fiat!*' And my Lords Maxwell and Huntly said it would be a great blow for Holy Mother Church. Besides he has no right to the throne, since his father was David Riccio…"

Carey looked nonplussed. "He inherits from his mother anyway."

"The Salic law…"

"Is in France, not Scotland."

"Well, anyway. Maxwell thinks that and it's hard to gainsay him. And Huntly."

Carey had his notebook out. "Anyone else?"

"Erroll of course, Angus, Auchinleck."

"Any more?"

"Fintry. I was never sure what he was going to do. Another of Hepburn's plans. And there was Sir James Chisholm of Cromlix, but that would be later when we needed to organise the supplies for the Spanish troops in Dumfries."

"Are there any there now?"

"No, the King of Spain refused to commit any troops until he heard that King James was dead or...or incapacitated."

Carey nodded.

"As soon as he hears that, the troops he has waiting in La Corunna will board fast ships, travel in three squadrons up the Irish Sea to Dumfries. By that time of course there would be civil war in Scotland and England and their landing would be substantially unopposed. Maxwell, Huntly, Erroll, and Angus would then march the troops south to Bristol, Oxford, and take London."

"And the first stage in all this was killing the King?" Crichton looked away. "When he had done nothing against you and indeed treated you with favour and gentleness."

"It was for Holy Mother Church."

"And a cardinal's hat for you." Carey was disgusted and spat deliberately into the corner. Crichton looked fixedly at his hands. "Anything else?"

"Sir George Kerr is waiting in the West near Paisley for the message that the King is dead. He'll take the papers to Spain..."

"What papers?"

Crichton hesitated. Carey leaned towards him and said again, "What papers?"

"There are papers that...that the lords have signed..."

"What's on them?"

"Nothing. No, really, they are blank and the King of Spain can add to them whatever he likes."

Carey smiled. "Which lords apart from Huntly have signed these blank papers?"

"Maxwell, Erroll, Angus..."

"Has anyone sent a man?"

"I don't think so."

"The name of the ship?"

"The Beauty of Lennox."

Carey showed his teeth again. "William," he said, "I think you have just helped me. If the papers get to Spain, that is the signal to send the troops? Yes?" Crichton nodded. "You were a traitor to your King and now you are a traitor to the Catholic church, a much better thing to be. What does Kerr look like?"

"Like most Kerrs, he's red-headed, good-looking, one crumpled ear and corrie handed."

"Left handed, you mean?"

Crichton nodded. "I never thought it was right to kill the King..." he began, but Carey had already left the room and locked the door, leaving him to sit in irons and contemplate his future.

Carey found Lord Spynie was waiting for him, and the ex-favourite immediately went with a troop of men-at-arms to Lennox. There was a good road to the little town of Glasgow and they rode out of the Court at three in the morning with a warrant for Kerr's arrest so there was every chance they would be at Lennox by noon. Carey considered riding with them but after some thought decided he needed to stay at Holyrood House and keep an eye on things there. Besides, he was due at the King's New Years Day levée—Sir David Graham, one of the Grooms of the Bedchamber, had asked him personally if he would like to be there to give His Highness his cup of morning wine and wish him a Happy New Year, and of course he had agreed.

EDINBURGH, NEW YEAR'S DAY 159(3)

Carey rose at dawn to get ready for the levée, after three hours sleep, proud in his new suit and Anricks tagged along because he said he had a petition to ask of the King. He was carrying two packages carefully wrapped in damask. They lined up outside the Kings Great Bedchamber, only to find he was in his privy bedchamber still and not to be disturbed. They waited while in the distance there came a characteristic hammering sound. Carey looked at Anricks and Anricks looked modestly at the ground.

"Is that the King and Queen...?" he asked.

"Maybe," said Anricks and looked prim.

The King eventually moved to the Great Bedchamber and they entered in a line, Carey and Anricks last, to find him sitting up in bed looking very perky although his shirt was revolting. The ceremony began with the Napkin with which the King sketchily wiped his face and hands. Then Sir David beckoned Carey to a table at the side of the room and gave him a goblet of wine after ceremonially tasting it. Carey took the goblet and a napkin for his shoulder, bowed, and walked slowly to the King in his bed, who was smiling at him, went on one knee to him as he would have done to the Queen of England. Just as he would have done at Whitehall, in the sight of the King he took a mouthful of the wine. And froze.

It was poisoned. He knew the taste, hidden by spices and sugar. Belladonna, just as it had been at Oxford, he knew it at once and his stomach twisted in reaction. He nearly spat it straight out, looked at the King, thought of dropping the goblet, thought of many many things, knew that the King had noticed, felt the poison furring the inside of his mouth, so he spat the mouthful carefully onto the napkin on his shoulder and mouthed to the King, "It's poisoned."

The King grinned and said, "Och it's nice to see ye, Sir Robert, gi's the booze then..."

He grabbed the goblet and to Carey's horror, tipped it up. But then he noticed the King's Adam's apple wasn't moving and so he didn't knock it out of the King's hand as his first impulse had been. Carey immediately stood and turned, looking all round the room, while his body hid whatever the King was doing with his goblet of poisoned wine.

Eight other petitioners were waiting patiently at the other end of the chamber, Mr Anricks was nearer the bed. The other Grooms of the Bedchamber were holding a clean shirt for the King, and his waistcoat, hose and doublet, his stockings and his shoes, but one man was walking slowly and ceremonially to the door with the jug of wine.

Carey went after him, through the small door and said, "Sir David, may I check that jug, please?"

Sir David put it on a table, turned and looked at him and the fear in his eyes told Carey all he needed to know. He grabbed the man's hand and found the little phial palmed in his left hand which was shaking.

Sir David brought up a small poinard he had hidden in his sleeve, against all James' careful rules and Carey grabbed his right hand with his left, got a little cut, grappled, trod on his toes, brought his knee up, missed the crotch but hit his thigh, then pulled his head back and butted Sir David on the nose so he went down. Moments later two of the guards came through the door and grabbed both of them. Carey was more concerned to keep the blood from his hand off his brand new duds and insisted on wrapping the napkin round it and holding it up so the bleeding would slow. They waited as the slow process of the levée continued, for all the petitioners had to have their say.

***

Simon felt abandoned. He had counted on Carey to be there when he made his all important approach to the King—but Carey had suddenly chased out of the Great Bedchamber, in pursuit of the elderly nobleman carrying the jug of wine. The King had dribbled a lot of wine onto his already filthy shirt, had put the goblet on a small table by the bed.

Now other nobles, including Huntly, paced forwards to offer the King a clean shirt—which he refused—and then a magnificent Court suit of peach and pale tawny taffeta cannions and a doublet of equally splendid yellow and peach damask studded with diamonds and topazes. They helped him into it, with smooth practised movements, in itself a show of the King's magnificence.

He was feeling afraid, so much was riding on this. He had done his best with the Dispute, with the help of the Almighty, and now it was his job to find out…What?

What the King of Scots thought of Jews.

He waited whilst the other petitioners went forward to speak to the King…Two portly merchants, a Highlander looking uncomfortable in hose and doublet, a scrawny man with a lot of papers, a young blond Allemayne. All had presents for the King, of course, as it was New Year's Day. Thank the Almighty, he had remembered the necessity of gifts and taken the trouble to buy two suitable presents in Edinburgh in the week after Christmas, at a huge premium.

His hands were sweating. He held the damask-wrapped gifts with the tips of his fingers so the damask wouldn't be marked, waited modestly until the last. Carey had been invited, but Anricks had had to pay, rather a lot, in fact, to all the Grooms of the Bedchamber. Never mind. It was worth it.

"Ay, Mr Anricks," said the King affably, sitting in a carved chair and drinking more wine from a Venetian glass he had just been given by a merchant. "I enjoyed yer disputation last night."

"Thank you, Your Majesty."

"Get up off yer knees, mon, this isnae the Queen's Court. Now then. I've decided not tae clap ye in irons for knocking me over since ye had such a verra guid reason for it."

"Yes, Your Majesty."

"Ah dinna recall what happened after but my Queen says ye helped her and so Ah'm verra grateful," said the King with a smile which did not reach his eyes.

"Ah...My memory too is deficient, but I am glad Your Majesty's Queen is pleased with me."

"So. Whit have ye got me for my New Year's gift?"

Anricks presented his gift and the King unwrapped it to find a copy of Thomas Digges. He laughed. "Ye're determined to convert me to Copernicus, then?"

"Your Majesty needs only to read the Preface," said Anricks humbly. "I own the main part of the book is not new and in fact quite dull."

James laughed again at that.

"This is Sir Robert Carey's gift to you, Your Majesty," said Anricks, "It is a book on venerie, hunting, but I am afraid I cannot say how good it is for I have not..."

"Ah...wonderful! *La Vénerie de Twiti*! I've been after this for a long weary while, ye can tell the long-shanked Deputy Warden thank ye very much for it!" And King James opened the book and started reading immediately, but then remembered himself and put it down. "Mr Anricks, have ye a petition for me?"

"Yes, Your Majesty." Anricks took a deep breath. "I would like to petition you to look with favour on my people."

The King tilted his head, suddenly like a falcon. "Oh?"

"Perhaps you do not know, but I am a Jew, of the tribe and lineage of Abraham. I would like to pray you that you look with as much favour upon us as does Her Royal Majesty, your cousin of England."

There was a pause, but Anricks knew his cause was already lost.

"Ay well," said the King coldly. "I will, o' course."

"Thank you, Your Majesty, that is all I ask," said Anricks smoothly, backed three steps and then turned to follow Carey through the unremarkable door he had disappeared through. Inside he had a great yawning emptiness where before he had been afraid. For when Anricks had said he was a Jew, he had been watching King James' face carefully and across it he had seen travel, in the blink of an eye, a look of disgust.

The Ames, Anriques, Nuñez, and Lopez families would be buying land in Constantinople.

***

Carey was checking the new napkin he had wrapped around his left hand where the cut in the web between finger and thumb was still producing blood when the King came through the door looking colder than he ever had in Carey's experience. He was carrying his goblet, still full of wine.

"Sir Robert, ye're wounded!"

"A cut from Sir David's dagger, Your Majesty. You didn't...?"

"Nay, I didna. I pretended. How did ye know...?"

"I was accidentally poisoned while I was serving the Queen on progress in the autumn: I knew the taste immediately."

"Ay? We'll hae this tested o'course but if Sir David had a knife..."

"And a phial to bring the poison in."

"I hate knives, I willna have them in my presence." He bent to Sir David and slapped his face, despite the blood and snot from the broken nose. Carey felt his forehead which felt distinctly sore. Not as sore as a broken nose though: mentally he thanked Bangtail, who had given him lessons in head-butting.

The slapping brought Sir David round more or less. "Sir David," said the King sadly, "ye've served me well all my life, I remember ye when I was a lad. Why? For God's sake why?"

"You…you debauched my wife, you…you…"

"I what? Debauched? Your wife?"

"My poor little Marguerite, you tupped her like…"

"Me? But Sir David, ye were serving me when the Duc D'Aubigny was here, ye know I'm no' a lover of women, or I wisnae until this morning. What made you think that?"

"The dresslength…She had a lover…Lovebites…"

"Ye're wood. I gave a dresslength to the Lady Schevengen as well, d'ye think I'm wapping her?"

Sir David rolled his eyes. "But someone was her lover, she had lovebites and I never give lovebites…"

"Fetch the Queen," the King said to one of the guards and the young man sprinted away.

Anricks had come through the door from the Great Bedchamber, found Carey holding up his hand with a bloody napkin round it and took him through to the antechamber where Anricks poured whishke bee on the cut until it stopped bleeding and then ripped up another napkin with his teeth to bandage Carey's hand properly. No more blood soaked through although hand wounds are often very bloody. Anricks didn't think it would need stanching or cauterising.

By the time they came back, the Queen had arrived and was holding the King tight while he smiled down at her. The Queen had tears in her eyes.

"What's happened now, Your Majesty?" Carey asked.

"Poor little Marguerite," the Queen said. "Poor poor girl. There vos no harm in her."

"It seems Sir David killed his wife last night, throttled her in his bed," said the King distastefully. "Dear God, man…"

"She had a lover, she betrayed me," muttered Sir David.

"Ay," said the King, "And you betrayed me. If it hadnae been for Sir Robert, an Englishman, I wad be suffering and dying by now. And ye thought I had swived yer wife. Dear God, when? I'm never alone."

He turned aside, his mouth wry. "Sir Robert, are ye well aside fra yer hand? Ye didna take hurt fra the poison?"

"No, Your Majesty, I spat it out." That wasn't entirely true since Carey was feeling quite sick and dizzy, but he put that down to reaction.

"A'right then, gentlemen, and my dearest Queen. Nothing has happened. We'll review how the tasting is done, make it more English I think. Sir David, ye'll confess the whole thing and…"

"But she betrayed me," whispered Sir David. "If it wasn't the King, who was it?"

"What d'ye think, my dear?" the King asked the Queen.

The Queen shrugged. "Sir David iss a fool," she said. "Ve all knew she vos haffing an affair with Jonathan Hepburn, it vos obvious."

For some reason Sir David started crying into his hands and would say no more.

***

When Janet Dodd awoke, she found the Court like an animal that has had a fright: confused, uncertain, and taking refuge in the familiar. Then when the King and Queen showed themselves, walking through the snowy garden as if nothing at all had happened, it relaxed and went about its business.

Lady Widdrington came to find Janet and Widow Ridley, and found both of them in their best kirtles, and Janet with a wonderful green hat on her head, preparing to go to market to sell the linen and take a look round the town. She talked to them and heard the tale of the mysterious alchemist and brought them both to the audience chamber to tell the King and Queen.

King James had changed his doublet and hose which was very unusual for him and was magnificent in tawny and peach, although he still hadn't shifted his shirt.

He was affable and friendly and a little abstracted, wiggled his fingers at Janet for her promptness and Widow Ridley for her curiosity, gave the Widow a silver goblet with the King's crest that he had just got from a merchant. He promised Janet a pension.

The Queen came personally to see the linen sheets and aprons and ordered the elderly lady in charge of the Sweet Coffers to buy the lot of them at a very fair price, which Janet added to her moneybelt. She tasted the flower-water and snapped that up too. The money was enough for extra feed this year and even next year if they needed it, which God send they wouldn't.

Janet couldn't go home yet since Henry had disappeared and she didn't want to think about what he was probably doing. So she and Widow Ridley went into Edinburgh and exclaimed at everything, the house where John Knox hadn't lived but a silver merchant had, and the alehouses, and the Tron and the Tollbooth and of course the castle, partly wrecked and in piles from the gunpowder and cannon in the siege twenty years before, with scaffolding and masons getting on with rebuilding it.

***

George Kerr was at Lennox, already aboard the ship that would take him to Spain, through the dangerous winter seas, stowing his chest. He heard the sound of boots on the deck, looked through a hatch hoping to see his friend Sir David Graham and his men and instead saw the minister of Paisley, Andrew Knox, looking grim and behind him was Lord Spynie. He knew he was doomed. He took the two most important pieces of paper, the one from the Spanish King and the one setting out how and where the troops would land and be disposed in Scotland, and he gulped them down in strips with a lot of good wine.

He would have started on the blank sheets with the signatures of the Scottish Catholic lords, but by that time the cabin door was juddering to the kicking and the bolt broke and seconds later he was on his face on the deck, protesting that he was a merchant, until they found the papers and then he shut up. The minister of Paisley looked at him with contempt and then stood carefully on his hand.

"Traitor," he spat. "Traitor tae the Kirk and to the King and the realm."

"I am not a traitor to the true Church," he answered, rather well he thought, and got kicked hard in the ribs.

"Ye admit you are a traitor to the King and the realm," said Spynie, kicking him a couple of times in the crotch. "Good, that saves time."

They couldn't head back to Edinburgh without some rest, for the horses as well as the men, and Andrew Knox put them up in his manse in Paisley. They left Kerr in the town lock up where the ministry of the town came to dispute with him and break his legs in the Boot. They slung him weeping across a horse three hours before the next sunrise, and headed back to Edinburgh.

On the 2nd of January 1592/3 they had acquired the full plan of the Catholic earls along with a complete account of the King of Spain's addendum requiring the murder of the King before he committed any troops, leaving both Scotland and England without an heir and safe for Spain to invade.

***

James listened to Carey as he gave his report verbally—he started on both his knees but James soon had him on a stool with wine at his elbow. The two books that Mr Anricks had given him for New Years' presents lay on the table. One was Thomas Digges, on the revolutions of the planets, as yet unopened. The other book was the magnificent volume on hunting by Twiti which was lying open with a goblet keeping the place.

"D'ye think it could ha' worked?" asked James.

"Yes, Your Majesty," said Carey, "both realms are vulnerable until you have at least one son. With you gone and no issue, I hate to think what would have happened here or in England. It could have triggered the Bond of Association and started a general killing of Catholics, which would, as night follows day, have led to civil war. We have only to look at the state of France to know we want no such thing."

"The Bond of Association was originally against my martyred mother."

"It was, of course, because she would not stop plotting."

"Surely that was her duty, as a sovereign monarch detained illegally in another country."

Carey smiled. "It was, Your Majesty, and I conceived it as my duty if she succeeded to kill her and her fellow Papists."

"You signed it?"

"Of course. Most of the Court did, it swept the country."

James heaved a sigh. "What d'ye think to it now?"

"Perhaps I am less enthused," said Carey carefully, "for since then I have been in France and seen a land riven by civil and religious war."

James nodded. "All I ask, ye know, is that I may be a peace-maker. That's all."

"Her Majesty too wishes she could do away with war—though for her, her chief complaint is the expense of it."

"Ay," said James, "typical woman. So let's see these papers."

Carey handed over the blanks with their flamboyant semi-illiterate noble signatures across the bottom.

"No mair?"

"No Your Majesty, he had disposed of any others. My Lord Spynie is not sure how as there was no fire nor ashes, but he may have eaten them since he looked green about the gills."

"Was he given the Boot?"

"Yes, Your Majesty," said Carey with a quick grimace of disgust, "The ministers insisted. It didn't take long."

"Ay," said the King, "the ministers are awfy keen on it, I find. We'll hang the poor fellow as soon as we can. We'll hang that fool Graham of Fintry as well."

"I think he is at least half mad."

"Ay and he has a verra nice inheritance which will have tae be confiscated for a while, I fear. I'm deporting Father Crichton back tae Spain."

Carey said nothing for a moment and then asked, "And the Catholic earls? Maxwell, Huntly? Angus?"

"Ay well, they've been verra naughty boys and will have tae be warded for a while but then..."

"You will free them."

"Ay," James blinked at the window where it had started to rain an unpleasant mixture of snow and rain, a kind of flying readymade slush. "I know ye think Ah'm wood fer not clapping them all in irons and having their heads off. The ministers think the same—they are having a day of fasting in thanks for my deliverance, God save them."

"At least execute Lord Maxwell and the Earl of Huntly, Your Majesty. When I think of what they tried to do to you with the oil of vitriol..." said Carey, slipping off the stool onto his knees again.

"The engineer, Jonathan Hepburn?"

"I'm not clear how much he did nor who he was working for, but I know he brought the oil of vitriol from Keswick, whatever he was doing with Marguerite on the side. He rode from the Court as soon as it was set up and we don't know where he went."

"Might he have gone back to Keswick?"

"Yes, or he might have taken ship for the Netherlands at Leith."

"Find him," said the King. "Find him and kill him. He's an Englishman and now he's run, I dinna have jurisdiction and my cousin of England might be annoyed. So I leave it to ye, Sir Robert."

"Yes, Your Majesty," said Carey firmly, "I will be honoured to end his life. And Maxwell and Huntly..."

James leaned over and caught Carey's face between his two soft fleshy hands. "I know," he whispered, "If it werenae for the wee Jew philosopher that knocked me over and backwards, I'd likely be dead or burning to death in invisible flames. D'ye think I dinna ken that? D'ye think I dinna ken that they all think I'm soft as shite and silly and they call me Queen James, and worse, d'ye think I dinna ken? Ay, I ken, and still I'll forgive them and keep forgiving them and keep on forgiving them until they understand or someone else kills them. I will have peace, Sir Robert. I will have peace in my lands and with Spain and with France too, I *will* have *peace*, by God."

He let go of Carey's face and drank so the Englishman wouldn't see the tears in his eyes, before he could snort them down, waiting for the cynical smile, the supercilious look.

Carey stayed where he was for a moment, his chestnut head bowed. When he spoke it was in an oddly strangled tone of voice.

"I think Your Majesty is the bravest Prince I have ever heard of."

"Ye do?"

"Yes. It's easy for a Prince to seek war, that's instinctive to men, it's expected of him. But for a Prince to seek peace—that takes true courage."

"Ay?" James thought about it. "Ay, perhaps it does."

"I will help you in any way I can, Your Majesty," said Carey. He sounded sincere. Maybe he was.

"Thank ye," said James, "Now be off wi' ye and take yer wee Maimonides south, too. There's nae more need for him to stay here and spy on me."

Carey rose gracefully to his feet, bowed, backed to the door.

"Ay, tell my cousin of England and her little hunch-backed Secretary, thank you for sending him."

"Yes, Your Majesty."

"And tell Lord Spynie to come in now."

Carey bowed again as he went out the door. James sighed. Such a pity the handsome Englishman was in thrall to the she-devil still, as Buchanan called all women, though his lady love Lady Widdrington was a remarkable woman with almost a man's intelligence. In fact he had recently come to appreciate more the softer plusher charms of women and had enjoyed himself with his young Queen, more than he would ever have expected. Still for companionship and sheer delight, there was nothing to match a young man, such as Spynie had been, or as his darling Esmé Stuart, Duc D'Aubigny had been before the lords had poisoned him. That he could not forgive, try as he might and the Gowrie family would pay for it one day. But Huntly and Angus and Erroll and all their silly conspiracies? They were just naughty boys, after all, Huntly especially whom he couldn't help sighing over.

James stood and looked out of the window. God had given him a mission and he had known what it was since the age of five when he had watched his foster father, the Earl of Mar, bleeding to death from a dozen stab wounds. He had promised himself through tears and gritted teeth that he would be a peaceful monarch and he would have peace. He had never forgotten it.

***

Dodd kicked his tired pony up a small hill and down into the slushy valley. Half an hour before it had started to sleet and they were still six miles from Stobs.

Dodd had said maybe four words the whole way and they had taken it in turns to sleep in a sheepfold. Hughie had thought he could kill the man then but found Dodd watching him every time he got up and so he pretended he had a flux and went out into the snow and wind each time.

Now they had been riding all day, slowed down by the slippery snow and the sleet. On the other hand, Dodd was tired. He was riding the pony because an unshod pony was much nimbler among the rocks and tussocks of the hills. Men guarding the herds in the infields had asked their business and Hughie had explained they were going to his sister at Stobs. Two men, one obviously not a good rider and not a reiver despite his size, were only a threat if they were scouting for a larger party. They were taking a message, they said.

Hughie was tired as well but the hope of seeing the pretty red blood on the snow and the anticipated joy of killing, actually killing Henry Dodd, kept him going. When he brought that head in to Wee Colin's hall, there would be fire and feasting for sure, he'd be the star, maybe Wee Colin would reward him. And then he could go back to Carey when the weather was better and tell him some lie about where he had been and then later on kill him too and get his thirty pounds from Hepburn.

He was trailing behind again but Dodd seemed tranced by the sleet and the difficulty of the ground. Maybe now? Very very quietly he took his favourite weapon out of the bag at his back. It wasn't a full-size crossbow but it had a very powerful bow that he was just able to cock. He stole another glance at Dodd who was negotiating a slippery spot. Quickly he fitted the crossbow stirrup to his toe and pulled upwards. It was hard but he was strong and he managed it with no more than a grunt. Lost in thought, Dodd didn't even look back.

Whitesock noticed and pulled at the leading rein Dodd was holding, tried to pull away, neighed. Dodd glowered at him and pulled the rein sharply. "Will ye get on!" he snarled.

Now was the time. Hughie kicked his pony up the little hillock, putting in the heavy bolt as he went up behind Dodd who was in an argument with his horse, up close to the jack, leaned across, close enough to touch him and his fingers were numb but he levelled the crossbow and pulled the lever and the bolt went straight into Dodd's back, hopefully into a kidney.

"Aah…" he whispered, and that was good to hear, he was in agony. He clapped his hand to the bolt, found it—ay, it was a good way in—tried to draw his sword but couldn't do it, managed to draw his dagger with his other hand.

Hughie had backed off. Whitesock pulled free with the leading rein trailing and whinnied high and deafening, again and again. Slowly, like taffy falling off a stick, Dodd leaned over and over until he was lying alongside the pony's neck and then slower still he fell off into the snow where the sleet fell on him and the bolt sticking out of his back.

Hughie waited a minute and then dismounted from his own pony, drew his sword, went over to where Dodd was lying with his face in the snow, slowly writhing, his lips drawn back in a grimace of pain. Hughie set himself, trying to remember how did the executioner do it. He wanted Dodd's head off neatly, not with all meat and bone dangling, but through the neckbones and gullet where it was soft and easy.

"Ma name is Hughie Elliot," he said loudly, in case his blood enemy could still hear him, "And that's why ye're gaunae die."

He took aim with his sword and one eye half closed against the sleet, lifted it and then screamed and dropped the sword.

The bastard had stabbed him in the calf, Dodd's dagger was sticking out of his leg.

For a minute, Hughie kicked Dodd as hard as he could, then he picked up the sword, set himself again...

And something bit his arm and pulled him over. He staggered on the ice, the blade in his calf hurting, dropped the sword again. Then he saw Whitesock with his eyes white and rolling, his ears right back and his ugly tombstone teeth pulling and biting at him, rearing up, striking with his front hooves, shod they were... Hughie ducked once, and the second hoof caught him neatly on the head so he went down half-stunned. Then Whitesock turned his back, kicked out with both back feet, Hughie went down in the snow on his back.

The last thing he saw was the outraged horse rising up above him and he felt the front hooves come down again and again on his chest, trampling him with iron hooves until his chest was jelly and his heart had stopped.

He didn't hear Dodd making little pants and grunts because the pain was so bad and he didn't see the horse lie down on his belly in the snow beside him.

By that time Hughie Elliot's eyes had set and a crow had already spotted the unexpected meal and was dropping down through the falling snow with joyous caws.

GLOSSARY

"at the horn"—outlawed

"at the lure"—flying a falcon at a piece of meat or a bunch of
    feathers on a string

"attacks of the mother"—original term for hysteria

"hunting *par force de chiens*"—hunting with dogs

"infirmity in my bones"—rickets

"out on the trod"—out in pursuit of reivers

"take her chamber"—a woman would stay in one room for the
    final weeks of pregnancy

Allemaynes, Deutsch—Germans

apothecary—like a modern chemist or druggist

bag pudding—steamed savoury pudding, often made with suet

banket—a buffet of sweets, creams, custards and cheeses, after
    a feast

bedfellow—someone you slept with, not necessarily sexual

birthing stool—a stool designed to help a woman squat in the
    second stage of childbirth

blankmanger—medieval dish made of almonds, cream and
    chicken

bonds of manrent—hiring a man to be a soldier for a fixed
    time, Scottish

boozing ken—small bar or pub

Border reiver—a member of the riding surnames, persistent
    cattle thief, horse rustler, murderer

breeks—breeches, fighting breeches were made of leather

buttery—means buttlery, where the bottles were kept, later you
    could get food there too

Calvinist—variety of Protestant who follows the teachings of
    John Calvin

carlin—old woman

Carlisle trained bands—the men of the city would train together to fight, often as pikemen or arquebusiers

Candlemas—ancient Catholic festival on 2nd February; originally Imbolc

chalice—the cup that holds the wine in a Catholic Mass

chamberer—someone who would do slightly menial tasks like changing the Queen's bedlinen

codpiece—a flap of cloth tied at the top of the hose, to hide the privates. Often stuffed to look larger

conniption fit—epilepsy or a stroke

cramoisie—very popular colour in Elizabethan times, dark purple red

dag—smallest kind of firearm, a large gun firing one shot at a time, with a heavy ball on the bottom of the grip to balance the barrel and hit people with when you missed

Demiurge/Aeon—Gnostic idea—an angel who had set himself up as the Ruler of the World, but wasn't God

dominie—Scottish word for a teacher

domus magnificenciae—the part of the Court that contributed to the King's magnificence, nobles, courtiers

domus providenciae—the part of the Court that kept everybody alive, servants, cooks, men-at-arms, gardeners

dresslength—twelve yards (at least) of fabric, the minimum amount needed to make a kirtle

duds—London slang meaning clothes

dyspepsia—bellyache

fig—rude gesture formed by putting the thumb between forefinger and second finger, making a fist and waving it

first remove, second remove—a meal would be composed of a group of dishes, mainly meat and fish, and then the table would be cleared and a second group of dishes would be brought of poultry, cheese etc.

flower-water—distilled spirits from summer fruits and flowers, eg elderflower water. Not very watery

flux—diarrhoea

galleas—cross between a galleon and a galley, there were four of them in the Armada gallowglass—Irish mercenary, allegedly from Gallway

gossips—a woman's best female friends, her god-siblings

Groom of the Bedchamber—gentlemen who attended the King in his bed

garderobe—indoor toilet in a castle, a small room jutting out from the wall with a clear drop under the seat

haggis—Scottish delicacy consisting of a sheep's pluck (liver, lungs etc) minced up and mixed with onions and oatmeal, very tasty

hart—a mature male deer with at least 12 tines to his antlers, therefore six years old

heifer—cow before she has her first calf

hobby—small sturdy horse or pony, native to the Borders

Hobson's livery stables—a successful chain of livery stables, where you couldn't choose which horse you hired, hence "Hobson's choice"

infield—fields nearest the tower or farmhouse

insight—the contents of a house that were moveable, pots, pans, blankets etc.

jack—two meanings: 1) a leather mug, 2) a padded leather coat with no sleeves and metal plates between the leather to ward off blows

jailfever—typhoid or typhus fever, not really distinguished

jakes—outside toilet

Justice Raid—the King of Scotland would run a raid on his subjects and burn down their towers to teach them better manners

kern—Irish mercenary

kine—old plural of cow

Knight of the Carpet—a knight who had never been to war

Labor-et-oratorium—literally, where you work and pray. Shortened to "laboratory" which means very much the same

lamb's tails—little rolls of carded wool for spinning

lambswool—a drink made of hot cider and beaten egg

levée—the King's official getting out of bed in the morning

liege—a feudal lord

lungfever—pneumonia

lute—instrument like a guitar but with 12 strings and a round soundbox

Lutheran—variety of Protestant who follows the teachings of Martin Luther

lye—alkali formed by dripping water through woodash, used for cleaning and to make soap

manchet bread—best white bread, made of sieved flour

marker stones—notorious for going wandering, they marked boundaries

maslin bread—second best bread, with the wheatgerm and some bran left in. Very nutritious

milliner—hatmaker

minion—male favourite of a King (or Queen)

minister—Protestant priest in Scotland

mithered—annoyed, cross

monopoly or patent—awarded to favoured courtiers by the Queen, they allowed the courtiers to make money by being the only person allowed to sell a particular item—like sweet wines (Dudley, Essex) or playing cards (Sir Walter Raleigh)

morion—curved helmet of the period

muliercula—tiny woman, midget

nebbish—incomprehensible Northern insult

New Spain—the Americas

outfield—rough pasture, further away from the tower or farmhouse

palliasse—straw mattress for sleeping on the floor if necessary

paten—the plate to hold the Host during a Catholic Mass

pelican—alchemical device

petticoat forepart—the pretty triangular part of a petticoat that was deliberately displayed

pinniwinks—Scottish word for thumbscrews

poinard—long thin dagger with a very sharp point

postern gate—small gate in a bigger one to let in one person at a time

pottage—thick soup made with beans, vegetables and bacon, standard peasant food

Ptolomaic system—the Sun goes around the Earth which is at the centre of the Universe

puissant—powerful

pursuivant—someone who pursues, heraldic term but also meant a secret agent

quince cheese—what the Spanish call membrillo

Rough Wooing of Henry VIII—the war he fought against the Scots in the 1540s to persuade them to marry the infant Mary Queen of Scots to the infant Prince Edward. Failed

serpentine powder—basic ordinary mixed gunpowder, quite weak

Spanish farthingale—the petticoats shaped and stiffened with hoops like a crinoline to hold the skirts out, first in a bell shape and then in a barrel-shape late in Elizabeth's reign

stays—boned and reinforced bodice or corset

swive—have sex with

terceiros, tercios—the troops of Philip II's 3rd legion, the best and most-feared troops in Europe

the Boot—instrument of torture which broke the legs from the ankles up

the Groyne or La Corunna—major port in Galicia

thrawn—stubborn

tup—have sex with, especially sheep. Male sheep

Warden Raid—the Warden would raid a particular area and burned down towers to teach the reivers better manners

Warden's Day—a meeting between the officials of the Scottish and English march to sort out who had stolen what and try and arrange compensation. Could be quite exciting

Warden's fee—what the Warden got for finding and returning your cattle

wet larder—where you salted meat and made pickles

whishke bee/uisge beatha—whisky

white lead—poisonous face paint

wood—woodwild, mad

CAST OF CHARACTERS

in no particular order

* historical person
in parentheses: mentioned, not met

(Christian IV of Denmark, Norway etc) *
Queen Anne, wife of King James of Scotland *
Sir Robert Carey *
Sorrel, his usual hobby
(Henry Carey, Baron Hunsdon—Carey's father) *
Lord Scrope, Warden of the English West March *
Sir Richard Lowther, Deputy Warden of the English West
    March *
Lady Elizabeth Widdrington, Carey's love *
Sir Henry Widdrington, her husband, Deputy Warden of the
    English East March *
Alexander Lindsay, Lord Spynie, the King's ex-Minion *
Lord Maxwell, Scottish Border lord *
Henry Dodd, Land-Sergeant of Gilsland, Carey's henchman
Whitesock, his favourite horse
Sir Robert Cecil, Privy Councillor *
Margeurite Graham
Jonathan Hepburn or Hochstetter
Sir David Graham of Fintry, Groom of the Bedchamber to
    James *
Wattie Graham of Netherby, Border reiver *
Young Hutchin Graham, nearly a Border reiver *
Archie Fire-the-Braes Graham, Border reiver *
Sooks Graham

Bangtail Graham, man-at-arms, Carlisle castle guard *
Red Sandy Dodd, man-at-arms, Carlisle castle guard
Sim's Will, man-at-arms, Carlisle castle guard
Bessie's Andrew Storey, man-at-arms, Carlisle castle guard
Andie Nixon, man-at-arms, Carlisle castle guard (Kate, his
    wife)
Pringle, Garron, East, Perkins, Leamus—Earl of Essex's
    deserters, now new men-at-arms
Nick Smithson, leader of the Earl of Essex's deserters
(Ritchie Graham of Brackenhill, gangster) *
(Sim's Jock Graham, Border reiver)
(Solomon Musgrave, gate guard)
George Gordon, 6th Earl of Huntly *
Father William Crichton SJ *
Francis Hay, 9th Earl of Erroll *
Sir George Kerr, Groom of the Bedchamber *
Bessie Storey *
Nancy, her wife *
Thomas the Merchant Hetherington, businessman *
Hughie Tyndale or Elliot, Carey's valet
John Tovey, Carey's secretary
James Stuart, King of Scotland, 6th of that name *
Janet Dodd née Armstrong
Bridget, her half-sister
Ellen
Mary, her sister
Katherine, her gossip
Willie's Simon Amstrong, her husband
Ekie, 8 year old boy
Mrs Hogg, midwife
Mary Leaholm
Big Clem Pringle, blacksmith
Geordie and Cuddie Armstrong, Janet's brothers
Wide Mary
Cousin Rowan
Penny, Shilling, Angel, horses
(Samuel the donkey)

Jack, a lymer dog
Teazle, a more experienced hunting dog
(Buttercup, Jack's mother)
Richard Bell, Scrope's secretary
Wee Colin Elliot, headman of the Elliot surname
Simon Anricks or Ames
(Rebecca, his wife)
(2nd Earl of Bothwell) *
(Mme Hetherington)
(William Douglas, 10th Earl of Angus) *
(Lord Howard of Effingham) *
(Sir Francis Drake) *
(Sir Francis Walsingham) *
(Medina Sidonia, Spanish admiral) *
(Mrs Grainne O'Malley) *
(Goody Biltock)
(Thomas Digges) *
Dixon
Roger Widdrington, son of Sir Henry *
Young Henry Widdrington, eldest son of Sir Henry *
(Lord Burghley) *
Big Archie Carleton
Maitland of Thirlstane, Lord Chancellor of Scotland *
(Dr Dee) *
Herr Kauffmann Hochstetter
Peter, Mick, Harry, gunners
(Young Hutchin's Aunt Nettie and Uncle Jim)
Annie
(Jamie Dodd, headman of the Dodd surname)
Widow Ridley
Andy Ridley, her grandson
(Dunstan Ames, Simon Anricks' father) *
(Dr Hector Nuñez, Simon's uncle) *
(Joshua Ames, one of Simon's brothers)
Chancellor Melville *
Mrs Proserpina—Poppy—Burn
(Sir John Forster, Warden of the English Middle March) *

(John Carey, Carey's elder brother) *
Little Archie
Matthew, Eric, Jeremy, Paul, Peter, Sandy—Spynie's henchmen
Skinabake Armstrong, Border reiver *
Mrs Elliot, wife to Wee Colin

1592

Sir Robert Carey, Deputy Warden of the West March, is wrestling with his deep adoration of Lady Elizabeth Widdrington, struggling to check his contempt for her elderly, abusive husband - will the man never die? - and trying to solve the bloody murder of a local minister.

Carey's investigations will lead him north to Edinburgh, the raucous seat of James VI, and a darkly elaborate plot to topple both sides of the border into murderous chaos.

Plunging readers straight into the rowdy world of late-sixteenth century border reivers and unfettered Elizabethan intrigue, *Swords in the East*, the third chronicle of Sir Robert Carey's adventures, collects the novels *A Chorus of Innocents* and *A Clash of Spheres* under one volume.

❧

'I love P.F. Chisholm's mysteries! Robert Carey is irresistible... and best of all, it is all true.'
SHARON PENMAN

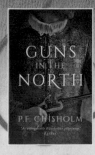

GUNS
IN THE
NORTH

P.F. CHISHOLM

£9.99   Fiction   Historical

9 781786 696151

www.headofzeus.com
ALSO AVAILABLE IN EBOOK

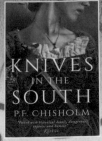

KNIVES
IN THE
SOUTH

P.F. CHISHOLM